ALL

THE

ANGELS

AND

SAINTS

✝

ALL
THE
ANGELS
AND
SAINTS

---

r.r. bryan

HAWK
PUBLISHING
GROUP

TULSA
hawkpub.com

LIBRARY OF CONGRESS CATALOG IN PUBLICATION DATA

All the Angels and Saints / r. r. bryan

[1. bryan, r. r. - Fiction-United States.]

Cover by Müllerhaus Publishing Arts, Inc.
mhpubarts.com

ISBN 1-930709-58-7
Library of Congress Control Number: 2005927833

Published in the United States by HAWK Publishing Group.

HAWK Publishing Group
7107 South Yale Avenue #345
Tulsa, OK 74136
918-492-3677
hawkpub.com

HAWK and colophon are trademarks belonging to the HAWK
Publishing Group. Printed in the United States of America.
9 8 7 6 5 4 3 2 1

for

FR. RANDY P. ROUX

†

PROLOGUE

THE ROBED MAN SAT motionless in the faded light, hoping the wait would end soon. His back ached, a victim of the granite bench crafted centuries earlier by a nameless artisan. He whispered another prayer for strength, and guidance. The grumbling in his lower stomach boomed like rolling thunder as it reverberated off the marble walls and floor. He smiled cautiously at the natural indiscretion, not daring to rise, fearful a crackling vertebrae would resonate into the next week. Quiet was observed at all cost during late hours in the Vatican.

Father Luigi Giuseppe Vincenzo investigated the lives of sainthood candidates. His colleagues called him the saint-maker. The Pontiff had acted favorably on more of Father Luigi's findings than those of any other investigator assigned to the Congregation for the Causes for Saints. Twice the priest had made confession on his vanity; another loomed ominously. But penance for a venial sin was not what had the priest worried. This young nun whose life and untimely death he had chronicled into the manuscript—the *positio*—he held so tightly, this one deserved special treatment.

Saints … the static electricity by which the vestments of faith cling to the souls of the faithful, those special heroes, martyrs, miracle-workers, selfless caretakers of the sickly, deserving of veneration by his faith, his church: the Holy Roman Catholic Church … Father Luigi's *raison d'etre*.

The massive oak door opened wide enough for a rapier of light to pierce its way to his feet. Not a word was spoken. The saint-maker rose, grateful for the relief to his back, thankful for the awaiting audience.

Only the hollow echo of slippered feet gliding across the emptiest of hallways remained when he was gone.

BOOK ONE

I

H E CAUGHT HIMSELF STARING at the reflection in the mirror, first at the age
spots and protruding bluish ridges on the backs of his hands—subtle reminders of his own mortality—then at the sunken eyes, and the dark circles unflatteringly
framing them. The hands trembled slightly as J. Bradley McHenry fought to focus
on the matter at hand, the simple act of tying his necktie, which after three tries was
still not right. Too short again. He exhaled deeply, and concentrated on the fourth
attempt. There was no more time for this trivial effort that had him so tied in knots
of a different kind.

Hold it together, Mac. He admired self-control in others, and loosely counted the
virtue as one of his own. He didn't consider himself particularly virtuous, although
he'd cut way back on the alcohol and profanity. He'd never smoked. And in all their
twenty-seven years together he'd remained steadfastly faithful to his beloved wife
Elizabeth. Not an unimpressive short list, but at the moment self-control and patience were struggling for survival.

Using his breathing thing, as he called the relaxation technique Elizabeth had
schooled him in, the fifty-two year old lawyer coaxed the stubborn necktie into a
nicely done half-Windsor. He wondered why all the fuss, until he remembered the
day's agenda. If it were only an opening statement to the jury, or arguing a motion
before the court, he could count on years of experience for help. He faced the unfamiliar today … this get-together he'd devised … this Celebration. The broth in which
he now simmered was of his own making.

He forced away thoughts of what lay ahead. Right now he needed something positive to regain confidence and purpose. He looked again at the tie that now hung so
splendidly, and allowed a brief, faint smile. Sunlight squeezed through the louvers of
the plantation shutters, suffusing the spacious master bedroom with its brilliance,

suspending a billion motes in mid-pirouette, casting the man in the mirror in a different light. Perhaps it wouldn't be so difficult for him after all.

A quiet tapping broke the silence. Turning to the door, he smiled broadly at his twenty-two year old son, William Christian McHenry. At six feet two, the azure-eyed Chris was calendar material in his navy blazer, tan slacks, and club tie, despite the unpressed shirt and unshined shoes. Mac wouldn't be critical of the shirt and shoes, not today anyway.

"You and Mom wanted Danny and me ready early. We've been waiting downstairs." Chris flashed the devilish grin that had been his trademark since parturition, showcasing the dimples … his way of amping up the charm. "Hey, where's Mom?"

Mac checked the bathroom and walk-in closet. Nothing.

"Well, son, I don't know. She was here a minute ago, while I was engaged in mortal combat with my tie." He paused to consider options. "You and Danny check downstairs, and I'll take upstairs."

Chris gave a thumbs up. "I'll check outside, too. It's azalea time, you know."

"Good idea," he said, putting on his suit coat. He cast a last glance in the full-length antique brass mirror he and Elizabeth had hard-traded a French Quarter dealer out of years ago, when finances were leaner, before their lives had taken on a nice middle-age comfort. He took a quiet, deep breath, held it momentarily, and slowly exhaled—his breathing thing again. He needed all the strength he could manage.

"The tie won," Chris said as he was closing the door.

Mac turned to an empty room. He cocked his head to the side, shrugging as he looked down at what he considered a fair result—there'd be no fifth try—and left to find his wife.

He scaled the stairs two at a time, pausing momentarily at the upstairs landing. He ignored the boys' closed bedroom doors to his left, heading down the hallway in the other direction, passing the gallery of pictures that decorated the hallway wall—the McHenry family's wall of fame. He barely slowed as he walked past the multitude of framed snapshots that memorialized their children's growing years, those reminders of first steps, first birthdays, first Christmases, first days of school, first Holy Communions, first proms. Everything so carefully arranged by Elizabeth. He knew them by heart. But he was on a mission, and resisted the temptation to stall before one or two that this day were a little more meaningful than the others. He continued on past the game room, to where the hallway ended. Where he knew she waited.

Other than the mild case of nerves, and the struggle with his tie, it had been a good morning so far. Opening the door, he hoped it would stay that way.

He would be disappointed.

✝

2

Elizabeth sat on the edge of the bed. The semi-darkness of their daughter's room did not hide her look of despair, or the wetness on her cheeks. She wore a sleeveless taupe linen dress, chosen no doubt more for comfort than fashion. The dress's understated elegance complemented her trim frame. Despite the sadness radiating from his wife, she was as alluring as ever. At forty-eight she still looked like the young coed she was when they first met.

He moved silently close by, allowing her this last moment alone. He groped for the right words.

"Honey," he whispered, "if you're ready, we really do need to go." Seconds ticked off with no reply, no visible reaction.

"It's time, Elizabeth. Please."

Elizabeth Anne Rogers McHenry looked up from her lap, where her gaze had been fixed on a small object around which her hands were delicately cupped. Puffy lids and pinkish eyes said everything. The ache in Mac's heart returned. He suppressed the urge to raise his voice.

"You've changed your mind, haven't you?" Swallowing to clear the rising lump, he continued. "You know this won't mean as much if you're not there."

He brushed her soft hair with his lips, and gently put a hand on her shoulder. "I love you, Elizabeth."

She covered his hand with hers. "I don't want you to worry about me. I'm all right, I really am. Better now than in a long time, in fact. I just can't go with you today. Last night, I thought I could." Her eyes searched his for acceptance, forgiveness. "Maybe if I had more time. But I know it needs to be done now; it can't wait, for all the right reasons. I need you and the boys to go on without me." Her voice trailed off.

There was no fight left in him. Arguing with her would prove useless. He squeezed her shoulder a second time, then turned to leave. He didn't look back and she didn't look up. He stopped in the doorway. "You know where we'll be, if you change your mind." She only nodded. He pulled the door halfway shut behind him.

Head bowed, he trudged back down the hallway, his thoughts on the small, sterling silver frame in his wife's lap. Nicole's first-grade school photo … a favorite of Elizabeth's. His chest tightened and the burning sensation in his throat was back. *No, you can't … you've got to hold up, stay in control.* Blinking at the forming wetness, he swallowed hard, and headed back down the stairs, wondering all the way if it would ever end.

––––––––––

"Where's Danny?" Mac asked Chris as he entered the den. "I thought you were both ready."

"Uh, Pop, did I misunderstand you, or did you just ask me if I found Mom?" Chris followed the glib response with another flash of the captivating grin. "Which, by the way, I didn't," he said, answering his own question matter-of-factly. "And I don't know where my brother is, he wasn't here when I came in a minute ago."

"I'm sorry, I guess I'm not thinking too clearly. Mom's upstairs, in Nicole's room. She's not ready right now, but might come later." Inwardly he chided himself for the white lie.

There was a resonant clarity in his father's voice that told Chris it was time to let up, to stop the foolishness. He nodded, the grin no longer visible. "Actually, I saw Danny heading upstairs a few minutes ago. I think I heard him say he'd left something in his room. I'm surprised you didn't pass him in the hall."

"Well, I didn't see him, and we still need to go," muttered Mac, more from exasperation than irritation. He paced the room, pausing in front of the large picture window to admire Elizabeth's many splendidly-colored azalea bushes, brought to bloom by the early and plentiful spring rains. Mac turned to Chris. "Would you please run upstairs and tell your brother we have to leave. I do not want to hit that festival traffic." Grabbing his keys from the parson's table just outside the kitchen, he headed toward the door to the garage. "I'll be in the Lincoln."

Moments later, the air conditioner on its highest setting, Mac was fuming. *Where are those boys?* As he grabbed for the door handle, Danny—twenty-six year old Lieutenant Daniel Earl McHenry, Marine aviator—stepped out of the back door. Resplendent in his full military dress blues, white belt and gloves, he half walked, half marched the short distance to the waiting car.

My God, what a sight! Forgetting the lateness, Mac allowed himself to relax, and admire what he felt would make any father proud. At a shade over six feet one, weighing in at one hundred eighty-two lean pounds, his older son approached the car with the wide and confident Pepsodent smile that suddenly appeared when the braces came off at fifteen.

He opened the rear door. "Hi, Dad," Danny said, removing his cover—Mac had learned "cover" is Marine for cap—as he glided into the back seat.

Mac answered with a *Hi* of his own, adding, "Son, you've never looked more handsome. It means so much to us you could make it home this weekend." Mac stopped, and took a deep breath. "Mom's not coming with us right now. I think she'll come later, though. After she's had a little more time to sort through a few things." He silently hoped he hadn't just told his second white lie of the day.

Danny hesitated an instant. "It's okay, Dad. She'll be there with us anyway, in spirit. Besides, like you said, she might surprise us. The day's young."

Mac nodded. The unspoken respect flowed both ways as his son nodded in return. Mac impatiently sounded the horn. Before frustration could harden to anger, Chris bolted through the back doorway.

"You can ride shotgun," Danny said as Chris opened the rear door. "I'll take it on the way home."

"You got it, bro," Chris said, closing one door and opening the other.

Breathe, Mac. He resisted the urge to scold his younger son.

Danny spoke. "Did you see Mom?"

Mac's mind was elsewhere, so he didn't hear the question, or see Chris turn to Danny, an index finger held to his lips signaling this was something they could discuss later, outside their father's hearing. Nor did he see Danny's furtive wink.

Steering the Lincoln down the driveway and into the street, Mac thought of how long it had been since his sons had bickered over such boyish things as who'd ride shotgun. They'd stumbled through those early years of uncertainty, of rivalry for their father's attention, and of self-doubt and raging hormones, and everything in between, until they emerged one day as if from cocoons, their three-and-a half-year age difference notwithstanding, as best friends. The bond had strengthened as they'd grown older.

His reminiscing was interrupted by Chris asking how many might be at the Celebration. "Your mother and I sent out about forty announcements. Most everyone said they'd come. Some said they'd mentioned it to others we hadn't thought about, who asked if they could come, too." The conversation ended there.

What a nice gesture. The question was Chris's way of apologizing for holding them up, to break an awkward silence, calm his father. Mac's nerves were calming now, no thanks to the tie, the encounter with Elizabeth, the loss of patience with his sons.

He drove down scenic Pinehollow Lane, passing the fairways littered with electric carts whose occupants took such delight in hacking and cursing their way to lower handicaps and greater meaning in their lives. He eased through the guarded entrance of the gated estates that had been their home for eighteen years, heading down the narrow straightaway bordered by a palisade of pines and oaks, their leaf-burdened limbs and branches forming a majestic, if slightly moth-eaten canopy. Splotches of sky peeked through, forming a Rorschach-like mosaic. The splendor ended as the car reached the intersection of Highway 21, thankfully ahead of the festival traffic.

His earlier thoughts returned to this crazy notion he'd conceived of holding a Celebration for his daughter, to tie up loose ends so they could all move on. This would be Mac's deliverance day.

He realized his thoughts were robbing him of time with his sons. "Boys, I'm glad you're with me. I didn't want to make this drive alone."

Neither son spoke. The only recognition Mac got for his words of thanks was a firm pat on his shoulder from Danny. There was more than one person in the car with a crowded mind.

The drive continued, into and through the sleepy, quaint village of Madisonville, past the stately live oaks and sycamores, reinforced by the battalion of tall pines that proliferated in this picturesque south Louisiana nook, past the library and the small cemetery with its headstones dating back two hundred years and more, past the family's church and the already bustling restaurants along the waterfront. The drawbridge closed, they hurried across the Tchefuncte River, already swollen with the first of many watercraft there for the festival. Mac imagined himself mingled with them, at the helm of *Nepenthe*, his sailboat. Today would have been a good day for a sail … if it weren't for this other business at hand.

Mac didn't know the theme of this festival. Not that he should, but since so much of the commerce of this quiet little river town depended on the numerous festivals it sponsored throughout the year, he reasoned he should pay more attention to such things. He owed at least that much in the name of community spirit. The thought got filed away as something to work on later.

The fifteen-minute drive ended as he turned off the highway and into the Marina entrance to the neighboring subdivision. The security guard signaled her well wishes with hands clasped in prayer position after she waved him through.

Mac wound slowly down the familiar streets, past the stately homes with their *Southern Living* landscaping, finally passing the grand old mansion. He brought the car to a stop under the mammoth live oak that stood vigilantly near the water's edge.

Mac and the boys parted ways. His sons headed over to the Tchefuncte. All three McHenry children and their many friends had boated, fished and played since their earliest years in this river.

"Boys, don't wander off, and don't get carried away with the moment and take one last swing for old times' sake," Mac bellowed across the greenbelt. He smiled as he caught them rolling their eyes in the same way they had all their lives. His gaze stayed fixed as Chris and Danny started toward the big tree, with its ropes dangling from the gnarled limbs that ideally reached farthest out over the water, until he turned and headed in the opposite direction toward an old, dear friend.

Mac checked his watch. It was slightly more than an hour before the Celebration would begin.

———————

While the carefree Chris went ahead without him, a pensive Danny turned and watched as his father's deliberate gait took him toward the kindly man who had given first Holy Communion to all three McHenry children, who had stood by through the past year and a half of turmoil with a steady presence, never pushing, now ready to lay healing hands and words on this still open wound. While Danny was not a prayerful man yet, he nonetheless allowed himself a wish, an intention, for this day to be the rendering his father needed. The rendering they all needed.

———————

"Hello, Father," Mac said as he neared his friend and pastor of over fifteen years. "I thought I'd find you here when I didn't see your car at the church."

Father Paul Robichaux—Father Paul, or even just Paul to many of his less respect-ful parishioners, but always, and only, "Father" to Mac and Elizabeth—was the rector at St. Joseph Catholic Church in Madisonville. The rural parish was usually a four-year rotating assignment the New Orleans Archdiocese used for younger priests who needed to commune with the less gentrified than New Orleans had to offer, and for the older priests headed out to pasture. This particular parish held together in gradual decline over the years almost in spite of itself. That is, until Father Paul arrived.

Taken at once with the charm and scenic beauty of Madisonville, not to mention its two thousand or so colorful and mostly Catholic citizens, Robichaux zealously set about to restore the aging church while expanding the parish infrastructure. From the first, he'd relied heavily on certain parish leaders. Mac McHenry was one such leader. The priest had cultivated his relationship with the lawyer as much as any other congregation member. Elizabeth and Mac donated generously with time and money. It did not take long for the two men to develop a healthy respect for one another, then a deep and abiding friendship. Mac admired the man's religious spirit, his passion for the salvation of his fellow man, and above all else his humility. In a more secular sense, he also respected the priest's ability to run the parish business with the precision, thrift and drive of an entrepreneur, which in a sense he was. Mac had long since accepted that St. Joseph parish was richer and more spiritual by his presence. The rift over his daughter was now settled. Familiar feelings had returned.

The smiling priest shook Mac's hand warmly and firmly. "I'm surprised, actually, that I got here before you. I came early to take care of the details, you know, those things nobody seems to think about until it's too late." The two men averted eye contact to take in the normally pristine greenbelt, now crowded with rows of folding chairs facing a small stage. "But I was wrong," Robichaux said, swinging his arm in an arc over the panorama. "Someone has obviously gotten here first, and been quite busy."

Nodding agreeably, Mac released his grip and turned his eyes toward the rows of chairs. "The stage is set, yes, but will all be ready and fine when the show starts?"

Not answering, the priest said simply, "Come now, Mac, walk toward the river with me. Let's talk for a while. We have some time."

Robichaux stopped abruptly. "Where's Elizabeth?"

Once again Mac chose his words carefully. "She's still considering whether or not this is right for her. I'm betting she comes later." White lie number three, and counting.

Robichaux frowned, and muttered *I see* as he took Mac's arm, heading them in the direction of the bulkhead, to a measure of solitude. They made small talk until the first guests arrived. Mac frowned in their direction.

Robichaux spoke. "Mac, I know you're not ready to play host. I'll leave you here with your thoughts 'til it's time. I'm good at this, remember?"

"You know me too well, Father." Mac surged with gratitude.

Alone with the better part of an hour to reflect on what had brought this day into being, to prepare for the most difficult delivery of his life, Mac closed his eyes in silent prayer and let his thoughts wander to a time when all had seemed right, and warm, and safe. To a time eighteen months earlier, when no part of him had died inside. To a time when his daughter was still alive.

†

3

HE AWOKE ABRUPTLY, STARTLED by the movement beside him. The moon's glow cast the room in a hazy monochrome, the color of the daguerreotypes in his law office. His wife resembled an antique bronze statuette. "Elizabeth, are you all right?"

"Something is wrong. I feel it. Oh, God, Bradley, I am really scared." Since their first meeting she'd called him Bradley, not Mac like everyone else. He'd never argued against it.

She was trembling.

Mac smoothed an assuring hand along his wife's forearm. "How long have you been sitting up like this?" The radio alarm by their bed registered four-fifteen.

"I don't know … an hour or two maybe. I didn't want to wake you." She smiled weakly. "I can't have you thinking I'm a neurotic old wimp."

Mac rubbed his eyes, gaining ground on his torpor. "Would you like some tea?"

"That might help. I'll get it."

He stopped her. "No, you stay in bed. I'll get it." He rose, and put on his robe. "The Chamomile, right?" He took her silence as yes.

Headed for the kitchen, Mac's thoughts were on his wife. He instinctively knew her fright came from concern for her children. Her babies grown and scattered—one son in the military and another struggling with college, a daughter in a foreign land teeming with danger—there were reasons enough to be worried. Fear was something else … something new altogether.

He flipped on the light, then pulled the box of tea from the pantry. He filled the copper teakettle, lit the fire and waited for the telltale whistle. It was too early for the *Times-Picayune*, so to kill the wait he rested his head in his hands, elbows on the countertop, and cleared his thoughts for the day ahead. There were a couple of timber sales contracts to prepare, a will to draw for Arthur and Effie Hebert, and a host of other transactional matters. His bread-and-butter stuff that gave him a break from the constant pressure of trial work. He loved the courtroom, but getting older had slowed him down a bit. He was glad to have the office work as a diversion.

His thoughts returned to Elizabeth. Uncharacteristically, he'd not questioned her obvious fear. In matters affecting family, he and Elizabeth always had engaged in what Mac thought of as spirited debate—their way of fleshing out true feelings. Much of the foundational strength of their marriage was built on this concept. It rarely meant they did not share the same feelings and emotions; it was simply a matter of promoting tempered restraint for the common good, a way of staying in control. In that way they remained a collective clear head.

This was different. Something fierce, something quite powerful had a grip on his wife, and he wasn't sure how to handle that. His first instinct was to resort to playing the traditional calming role. Truth was, the sheer power of his wife's fear also had affected him. He could not shake the image of Elizabeth sitting upright in their bed, knees buckled under her chin, hands clasped at her ankles, rocking, gently rocking, murmuring in whispered prayer.

In the darkness outside, approaching the end of the circle drive to the two-story Acadian, the van pulled to a stop, its lights out. The driver, a tall young man in his early twenties, switched off the ignition, and turned to the passenger.

"I don't feel right about this, Elise. This is low even by your standards." The driver was thinking beyond the outright lie his passenger had told the security guard to enter the exclusive, private subdivision without the requisite advance call.

She ignored the slur. "It might as well be us," she retorted, the emphasis on *us*. "In a few hours, the whole world will be knocking on this door, and no one will care about who was here second. This could be just the break we've needed." This time her emphasis was on *we*.

The driver shook his head side to side, stopping once the woman seated next to him caught his eye. "Oh, Ken, stop it with that pathetic, droopy-eyed Cocker Spaniel look. You're breaking my heart. You forget, we're not in a cheery business most of the time. Sometimes tragedy is involved." Not one to quit even when she thought she was ahead, she added, "Do you think if we don't go up to the door what has happened will somehow not have happened? Or the next group would hesitate to knock on their door?"

She bore down harder. "Come on, Ken, get over yourself. Daylight will be here soon, and any one of our cutthroat competitors will be able to grab the story off the same wire we did. Think how much better it will be for News Nine when we break the story first."

The driver exited slowly. Walking around to the side of the van, he noticed a downstairs light was on. A surge of hope filled him. *Just this once, please, let's be too late.* He opened the side door to the van bearing the oversized "9" on its side, encircled by the words "Live" and "News," and pulled out his equipment. The cameraman was ready.

His passenger was thirty-year-old Elise Miller. The consummate newshound, and frequent object of disdain, she nevertheless enjoyed a sizable following for her probing, investigative and usually intrusive style of telejournalistic reporting. She knew the enormity of the story she would break locally, ahead of the rest of the country. A story large enough to catapult her to one of the national news networks. Any pang of conscience she might share with her cameraman partner of three years would be as quickly forgotten as yesterday's stale news and bad fast food eaten on the run. Elise would not be thrown off track by the naiveté of her younger and less driven partner.

"Well, Ken, are we ready?"

He mumbled something resembling *yes.*

"Then let's start the show."

They covered the two dozen paces to the front door quickly. Poised to ring the doorbell, Elise heard the unmistakable whistle of a teakettle. Sharing no more than a quizzical expression with her associate, she did not hesitate to push on the lighted button that would ring a chime throughout the house at Number 46 Empress Drive, in Tammany West Estates, home to Mr. and Mrs. Mac McHenry.

———————

The whistle jarred Mac from thoughts of his wife and the day he faced at the office. Before he could pull the kettle from the stove the equally familiar sound of the door chime caught his attention. *Must be a neighbor.* There had been no call from the guard station. He turned off the burner; the tea could wait.

Flipping on the porch light as he opened the door, Mac reflexively jerked his arm upward as a shield. The blinding light came from the direction of a tall man standing behind a woman whose face he vaguely recognized but could not immediately place. Using his hand as a visor, his eyes straining to adjust to the glare, he squinted at the woman. She spoke into a microphone.

"Mr. McHenry, I'm Elise Miller, News Nine, and we are here to talk to you about reports of the death of your daughter Nicole—Sister Nicole—reportedly killed in a rebel uprising last night in her Guatemalan village of Refugio." Pausing only to draw another breath, she continued before her stunned greeter could respond.

"We know from the wire service reports there were a number of deaths, that she is listed among them. Have you been informed yet by any church officials, or anyone else, of any details surrounding this most devastating tragedy?"

The same icy fear that grabbed Elizabeth now strangled Mac. His lips quivered, his cheeks twitched. He groped for words, but all he could think of was how badly he wanted this woman to disappear, to never have appeared. Ten minutes earlier he'd been soundly asleep. How could so much have gone so wrong so quickly?

"What—What are you talking about? This is crazy. I don't have anything to say to you. I need you to leave." The lady started to speak, but Mac cut her off.

"I mean *now!* Get out of here! How dare you come to my house like this!" Mac felt the crimson begin to color his cheeks and ears. He pushed the door.

"Mr. McHenry," she persisted, her free hand pushing back against the door, "we know this must come as a shock to you, but your daughter was internationally prominent. Her miracle last year reached a global audience. We are asking for words to comfort those who will be as saddened by her death as we know you are. Please share with us, so we may in turn share with them." She shoved the microphone within an inch of his lips.

Without another word Mac shut the door in her face. He stayed in the same spot, feet riveted to the floor, trembling uncontrollably, wondering what to do next. He heard the woman's voice, fading as she berated her associate for cutting off the minicam before she could capture the expression on his face. *What kind of person would do this?*

He wondered if Elizabeth had heard, and what to tell her if she hadn't. He had finally placed the newswoman, however, and began to fear what she'd said might have some truth to it. And to pray it didn't. He walked past the kettle, steam still rising from its spout. Elizabeth's tea was no longer on his mind as he entered their bedroom.

"Who was at the door?"

Mac knew before he answered his expression had betrayed him. There was no time to prepare for the worst.

"Bradley, what is it? Tell me what is going on." She rushed to him, her fingers were vises on his forearms. "Oh my God, it's one of the kids. I knew it. I just knew it. Tell me, now."

"There was a news crew at the door ... Elizabeth, I—I—" He averted her stare.

"What aren't you telling me?" Not a question, it was a demand for an answer.

"Nicole. It's about Nicole," was all he could manage. Mac felt like a beggar as he looked into his wife's eyes for something—anything—to make a clinking sound in his empty tin cup.

Elizabeth was frozen. He felt her grip on his arms turn clammy. Her mouth barely opened, but no words uttered. Her pleading eyes moved, first to his left eye, then to his right, rapidly back and forth, time and again. He wanted to tell her this was all a horrible mistake. All he could do was lower his head and pull her to him. Her grip relaxed, and she fell slowly into his arms, sucking in air as she simultaneously forced it out, crying out her daughter's name. He swept the tousled graying hair from her eyes as she softly wept, praying, "Oh, God, please no, oh please no, please don't let this be ... "

"Elizabeth, we don't know anything for sure. If there were a problem, the Church would have been here first, to tell us about it. She's a nun, for God's sake, one of *them*."

An idea came to him. "I'll call Father Robichaux. He'll know what we should do." Elizabeth was regaining some control, able to speak through the staccato sobbing and silent prayers. It was not the full cup he'd have liked, but it was a start.

Mac helped her to the sitting area. When she let go, he reached for the phone to call their pastor. The private line to the rectory rang only once.

"Father, this is Mac." He didn't wait for a reply. "Have you heard anything this morning about Nicole? Is she in any danger? A newswoman was just here with an unconfirmed report that, that—" He could not complete the thought as he fought to continue. "I know it's early, and I'm sorry for the intrusion. We need you to make a call, wherever you have to. Call and let us know our Nicole is safe. Please. And hurry."

"Mac, I've heard nothing of this," a steady voice responded. "But let me come over. I can be there in a few minutes, then I can call from your home. Whatever it is, I'll be there to help."

"I'll let the guard know you're coming."

Mac and Elizabeth waited the eternity it took for their priest to drive the three and a half miles down Highway 21 from the parish rectory to their home. The Community coffee was brewing when he arrived, the aroma of chicory heavy in the air.

15

✝

4

E
LIZABETH," THE PRIEST BEGAN, "Mac's told me what's happened, the unfortunate business with your uninvited guests. I've heard nothing of such news, I assure you. Let's see if we can learn something official, what do you say? Something to ease your—" He paused, searching for the right word, the politically correct expression. "—your concerns."

Mac sat next to his wife at the kitchen table, and watched as she went through the motions of dipping her teabag into the cup of hot water he'd finally poured her. Mac invited the priest to sit with them.

Seated, coffee steaming from the cup in front of him, Robichaux made his call. The stillness ended soon enough. "This is Father Paul Robichaux for Monsignor Everett, please."

A short wait later, a terse conversation ended with the priest reminding the more senior official, in an urgent tone, to call as soon as something was known. It was now a few minutes after five, less than an hour before the morning sun would break Lake Pontchartrain's eastern horizon. The day promised to be another hot, humid one.

"Monsignor Everett did not know anything, but will make the calls to find out about Nicole. He's a seminary classmate, not a particularly close friend, but dependable. He'll be able to tell us something shortly." Robichaux's glance alternated between Mac and Elizabeth. The silence seemed endless.

Elizabeth finally spoke. "Oh, Father, are you sure there isn't something we can do?"

"Nothing except wait for the monsignor's call. I know how difficult this is, but sometimes waiting is all we can do." He lightly patted her clasped hands.

While Elizabeth and Father Paul struggled to make conversation, Mac left the room, unnoticed, fresh with a thought, surprised the idea had not already occurred to him. He headed for the den and the television set they rarely watched. The cable service subscribed to many years earlier was of little use since their children left home, except for the local news, and the frequent hurricane watches this part of the world mandated.

Mac did not notice Elizabeth and the priest entering the den. Their eyes followed his stunned and horrified gaze, fixed on the screen lighting the darkened room. Nicole's familiar face showed as an inset in the upper corner of the screen, superimposed on a crudely-configured map of Guatemala. The unseen announcer was telling the viewing audience, in typically unemotional newsvoice, "Again, for those of you who may have just tuned in to this special broadcast, we have a confirmed report of the death of Sister Nicole Michelle McHenry. She was killed last night at the hand of rebel insurrectionists in the tiny village of Refugio, located in the north central mountain region of Guatemala. Sister Nicole recently captured the attention of the world with her miracle healing of a young village girl who had fallen victim to a vicious fever. We have few details at this time, other than there are other deaths. The Guatemalan government is claiming the uprising has been quelled. Please stay tuned during the day for more, as we now return to our regular programming."

As the photograph of the slain daughter of Mac and Elizabeth enlarged from its smaller, insert size to cover the full screen, the anonymous announcer concluded, "Sister Nicole, twenty-three, Catholic nun, has been confirmed dead." Beneath her image, in tombstone, were the years of her birth and death: 1971 – 1994. A second later the screen was filled with the image of a man in a plaid sport jacket pointing at a new automobile offering the quietest ride ever.

Elizabeth raised her hands to her mouth, then collapsed before either man could react. Mac watched helplessly as his wife's head struck the corner of an end table, ricocheting onto the wood floor with a resounding thud. He sprang to her side, instantly fearful at the sight of the broken skin above her left temple, the trickle of blood puddling on the glossy parquet tiles.

"Help me, Father," Mac ordered, and the two men lifted her to the couch. Her breathing was shallow, but her pulse was strong. Viscous redness seeped into the throw pillow Mac placed under her head.

A minute later, despite Mac's efforts to revive her, Elizabeth was still unconscious. The bleeding had been slowed by the crude bandana Mac formed from a floursack towel he found in the kitchen. Now was not the time to dwell on the tragic news. His wife needed attention. He lifted her limp body and headed for the front door, again ordering his friend. "The Emergency Room at Covington General is closest. Let's go in your car." They were loaded and gone in one minute.

Mac stroked his wife's face, brushing the hair back from her ears and eyes. He spoke hushed words of solace and comfort, words imploring her to know everything would be all right, it was all a mistake, Nicole couldn't be gone, just couldn't be ….

If he'd looked up, Mac would have seen the driver's lips barely moving, silently praying the same thing.

An hour later, Elizabeth was resting comfortably in a private room, hooked to an electronic monitor. The machine coldly beeped out red numbers in silent cadence, heart rate first, then blood pressure, systolic over diastolic. Mac stared hypnotically at the medical metronome.

The torture of waiting took its toll. Needing solace, Mac left Elizabeth's side to stroll the empty corridor of the emergency wing. He met his concerned parish priest in the outer hallway and quickly forgot his craving for solitude. "She's in shock. They're giving her something intravenously to calm her. It's a concussion, but the good news is it's very mild."

Robichaux put his hand on Mac's shoulder. "When might she come around?"

"We don't know. It could be any minute, or … perhaps much longer. I've called our friend Barrett Dupuis, over at the Tulane Clinic. He'll be here in an hour, and will watch over her until she's ready to go home. However long it takes."

The mixed expression of hope and desperation on Robichaux's face left Mac hoping for more. The friends parted in different directions without speaking further.

Mac walked on, slowly, windlessly adrift, trying not to succumb to the same fear and grief his wife had. As he had for so many clients in times like this, he must take charge, help facilitate the recovery process.

Years of doing so for others had not prepared him for this test. He was in uncharted water. Worse, he was teetering on the brink of his own physical and emotional collapse. He was certain of the horrible truth from the news bulletin. Further denial was useless. All that remained was official confirmation. Then the details. He would need total clarity of mind, reasoned and measured control. For Mac McHenry, grief would have to wait.

––––––––––

"Mac, I've heard from Monsignor Everett." The priest's expression said everything.

"What can you tell me, Father?" Mac sat in the nearest chair, burying his head in his hands, nervously smoothing back his hair. *Why? Oh, dear God, why?* His heart pounded. He thought the veins in his neck might explode from the pulsing pressure.

"There aren't many details yet, I'm afraid. There was an uprising in Refugio, and Nicole was somehow caught in the middle of it. The village priest you met when you and Elizabeth visited Nicole last year, Father Art Hurkinen, suffered a bullet wound and a mild heart attack, but he is alive and it looks as if he will recover."

Robichaux sat down beside his friend. "Do you want me to go on?"

"Did she suffer? Was she …?"

"Mac, I honestly don't know. I've been told only that one of the rebels is responsible. It's possible he also lived in the village."

"How can that be? Those people in her village revered her. It's just not possible."

"The Church has sent investigators to Refugio. I've told Monsignor Everett to get word to me as soon as he learns anything more. He won't hold back, Mac. Whatever the Church learns, you will learn also. I promise you that."

"Where is she now? What's being done with my daughter?" He could not bear to say *with my daughter's body.*

"I don't know that either. There are still no phones. All we have is a report from Reuters, and it is sketchy at best."

"I don't care what it takes, but you get word to the Church, down there or wherever, that I am coming for my daughter. I don't want her touched. Do you understand? Not by anyone. I'm going for my daughter."

Robichaux squinted. "Mac, this is something the Church is prepared to handle. Why not let us take charge?"

"Father, as soon as Elizabeth is out of danger, I am flying to Guatemala to bring my daughter home. Now, do you get the word out, or do I?" Mac squared his jaw resolutely. He had a point to make, friend or no friend, priest or not.

"I'll take care of it."

"Thank you." Mac started to walk off, when Robichaux stopped him.

"Mac, I just want to say," the priest began, eyes glistening, "I would trade my own life at this instant if it would bring Nicole back, you know I would. I've never felt so helpless as a priest."

Shouldering yet another burden Mac left to go call his sons.

———————

Elizabeth came to, restlessly. Mac was at her side. Before she could say anything, Mac had placed his forefinger upon her lips, hushing any excitement. Groggy from the pale yellow liquid dripping into her forearm and rendering her senseless, still in shock, still frightened, she did not quickly calm. But calm she gradually did, as the chemicals continued their slow work on her. Before speaking they reached for each other. Mac and Elizabeth embraced, their separate feelings of panic and disbelief, of acceptance of the inevitable, flowed one to the other and back again in a negative current that drained rather than energized. Mac held his wife tightly, strongly, and did not let up until he felt her relax, and her breathing slow to normal. Then, in the way a parent releases the tenuous grip at a toddler's first step, Mac relaxed his hold, and allowed Elizabeth to slowly settle back into the fold of her bed, where they might look at each other in this new light, where they could gather their thoughts and feelings before speaking.

"Why our Nicole?" Elizabeth's tears returned. "Did they hurt her? Did they hurt my baby? You can tell me. Please, I want to know."

Mac dabbed his wife's tears away with a tissue. He waited before speaking.

"We don't know what happened yet, only that she's gone. I'm sorry, Elizabeth. I can't bear telling you this. I have the same questions you do."

"The boys … our boys. We must—"

"They've heard. They'll be home tomorrow."

She closed her eyes, and pulled his head to her bosom. "What are we going to do? How will this nightmare ever end for us?" He did not answer … there was no answer.

Even as they quietly spoke, alone in this darkened, unfamiliar, sterile place, wondering if their daughter suffered in death, or was tortured or brutalized, wondering even more how this had all come to pass, Mac felt a stranger's presence. It took him awhile to realize it, a little longer to define it. For the only time in his life he could remember, Mac felt guilt. In the days to come this marauder would appear randomly, as if it were the fish on the end of his line, tugging, making Mac feel like the cork at the surface, buoying and bobbing, a constant reminder of the man's failing: *You should have saved her. This was all your fault.*

The struggle with this new demon lasted until dawn, when out of sheer exhaustion Mac's chin fell to his chest, and restless sleep overtook him.

———————

Elizabeth was released after a day and a half in the hospital. Mac was there to take her home to grieve. Mac, too, was going home, in a sense. He had remained at Elizabeth's bedside all he could, leaving only to clean up and nibble on the run. His appetite had all but disappeared. The food friends and neighbors had delivered to their home, in the Southern tradition of showing sympathy, had gone largely untouched.

Mac's one-man law office had been kept running in his absence by Paulette Sonnier, his secretary of seventeen years. A widow with grown children, she was as devoted to Mac and Elizabeth as they were to her. Through the years the two women's relationship had grown to a friendship without barrier. Thus it came as no surprise to Elizabeth when Paulette greeted her at the door of her own home. In typically bold fashion Paulette announced she would stay in the downstairs guestroom until Elizabeth was able to cope again. There was no argument.

Mac was thankful his sons were home. Both had demanded information he couldn't provide. They were all in a vacuum when it came to details of Nicole's death. Tension mounted within Mac over the elusive explanation the Church had yet to provide. He also noticed tension in his sons, especially in Chris. The usually jovial youngest child appeared to be harboring more than grief. His older brother, schooled in warfare, understandably might have malice on his mind; Mac could handle that in time. Dealing with a problem once it had been defined came easy to the lawyer. This thing with Chris, however, might need some work.

The two clerics were only priests, not ranking members of the archdiocesan hierarchy as Mac would have expected. Arriving unannounced moments after Elizabeth's return home, they were there to help, if they could, with Nicole's return. The meeting was brief, and Mac surprisingly and uneasily found himself orchestrating most of it.

"Mr. McHenry," the older of the two began, a bit too tactfully, "the archdiocese is prepared to bury Sister Nicole in either the cathedral's private cemetery in Guatemala City, or in one of the archdiocesan cemeteries in New Orleans." He added, "We do this for our own."

Mac was mildly offended—who *did these interlopers think her family was, anyway?*—but let it pass. Feigning politeness while he thanked them for the offer, Mac rejected both alternatives. He told them the family had other plans.

"Mr. McHenry, are you certain we cannot be of more help to you?" the other priest asked. "Those whose lives are lost while in the service of the Church usually provide in their final declarations their wish for the Church to care for them in death. We know your daughter did not leave such a declaration, but have you considered this might have been her wish?"

"Gentlemen, thank you for dropping by, but the matter has been decided. I thought the Church knew my plans, and frankly believed you'd come here today with details of my daughter's death. Since you've told me you have no details, we really have nothing more to discuss. I am leaving tomorrow morning for Guatemala, and will return with my daughter. She will be buried a few miles from here. You may take some comfort it will be in a largely Catholic cemetery, but it will not be in either of the places you have suggested. Now, that being settled, is there anything else I can do for you? Perhaps some ice water before your trip back?"

As he watched them drive off, Mac wondered why they'd come. He'd wanted information, but got none. Two low-ranking priests, and a message of sympathy on his recorder from the archbishop over in New Orleans, that was all. One way or another, with or without the Church's help, he would learn why his daughter was dead.

✝

Mac McHenry's arduous journey would begin early the next day. It would continue for a year and a half. Rarely would he travel further than within himself, a distance infinitely beyond the miles separating the borders of America and Guatemala.

5

As she watched her husband prepare for his trip, Elizabeth allowed herself to take note of the detachment in their lives in the past forty-eight hours. Twenty-seven years together was proof enough she was right about this. She needed, no, craved, the uncompromising strength her husband had never before failed to demonstrate, yet now did not.

She kept this to herself. The unselfishness that was her strong suit did not yield to the losses she now felt, real and imagined, first at the unbearable news of her daughter's death, next that her husband might be drifting away as well. Lying in their bed, watching him pack, she reached deep for strength. To question him now was ill-advised; the timing was all wrong. It could wait, if still necessary, until his return.

She prayed he wouldn't be gone long. Something, some inner voice, whispered time was becoming precious to her.

———————

While he packed, Mac made light conversation with his wife. It turned serious when she suggested he take the boys. "Elizabeth," he'd explained, "the boys asked to come, but I said no. They need to be here, with you. I don't know what to expect when I get down there. The last thing I want to worry about is losing another child."

The horrified look on Elizabeth's face made Mac instantly regret what he'd just said. The only comfort he took was it brought an end to any argument on the issue of their sons going with him.

After the packing was done, Mac went over his itinerary with Elizabeth again, exhausting her in the process. They embraced, and said their good-byes then; he would not awaken her in the darkness. They agreed it was better that way.

Elizabeth was asleep in a few moments. Mac made sure the alarm was set before he settled in next to her. Thoughts swirled feverishly within his head. Sleep, if it came this night, would be far from peaceful. Resigned to a restless night, Mac turned his thoughts once again to the woman beside him and how it had begun for them twenty-seven years earlier.

§

It was the fall of nineteen sixty-eight, his final year at Saint Louis University Law School. Mac's parents were able to send him a little money now and then, but for his first two years the young man from Des Moines had gotten by largely on grants and scholarships, and working night watchman jobs where he could study long into the night without interruption.

He'd gotten lucky his third year when a job in the student bookstore opened up. It gave Mac the freedom to work around his class schedule. More importantly than a return to a normal sleep pattern, it put Mac in the mainstream of campus life. The day job also resolved to his great personal relief an issue that had worried him all those nights he'd been alone at his watchman's jobs: he had not become antisocial, as he'd feared. Life had picked up for Mac McHenry, SLU 3L.

He caught himself noticing the female students as they checked out through his counter, his gaze no longer shyly fixed downward. He spoke only cautiously; fear of rejection held him back. Hardly, he mused, a quality for an aspiring trial lawyer to possess. He looked up from the register one day to see a certain tall, pretty brunette. Possessed of porcelain skin, a captivating smile, and the most incredible emerald eyes, he caught himself staring at her. Buoyed by the sparkling eyes and smile that together seemed to crush him with the force of a tidal wave, he gambled.

"Didn't I sell you two pencils just yesterday?"

"Yes, you did." Her reply rang boldly. "And two the day before that. And two more the day before as well." Mac's puzzled stare and the awkward silence prompted the coed to continue. "I was prepared to buy two pencils a day as long as it took for you to notice me."

She held out her hand. "I'm Elizabeth Anne Rogers, from Louisville, Kentucky. I'm a junior. Education major."

Mac somehow managed to say his name. "I'm Mac, Mac McHenry. Joseph Bradley McHenry, 3L … third year law." The touch of her hand sent a wave of warmth through him. Her skin was luxurious. His eyelids felt heavy. *What was happening here?*

She jerked her hand back. "Mac doesn't suit you," she said, her smile vanishing as she headed toward the glass door. "You should insist on Bradley." She was out the door before he could say another word.

Immensely attracted to this pretty girl who apparently had thought she'd seen something in him, something that had brought her back under the pretense of needing pencils, of all things, but whose reaction at his only words had been one of aversion, Mac made an impulsive decision. One he would forever be grateful he'd made. He closed his counter twenty minutes early.

She hadn't gotten far, and seemed genuinely surprised when, short of breath from his sprint, he came up beside her.

"Hey, I'm sorry if I—"

She cut him off abruptly. "You don't need to apologize. It's nothing of your doing."

"Then why'd you bolt away from me? I don't understand."

"Look, you're very nice. I was attracted to you the first time I went through your counter. You're shy, but most of all polite and respectful. Not many here are. That impressed me."

"And?"

"Okay, it's like this. My father is a lawyer. All our family friends are lawyers. Let's just say lawyers aren't my favorite people and leave it. Nothing personal against you, but I've seen what being a lawyer does to a man. I'm sorry if this offends you … I can see by your expression it does."

Surrounded by students demonstrating against the war in Southeast Asia, or casually tossing footballs and Frisbees or hovered around someone playing a guitar and singing a peace song, a lot said already and much more waiting to be said, not wanting to jeopardize any further the already fragile bond between them, Mac stood frozen in their defining moment. He was ill prepared for this, but did what he'd been brought up to do: he spoke from his heart.

"Listen to me, Miss Elizabeth Anne Rogers from Louisville, Kentucky. I don't know anything about what kind of man or lawyer your father is, or all of the other lawyers you know, and at the moment I don't much care. I'm more interested in the man's daughter. But if she thinks less of me because I am about to become a lawyer, well, that speaks of pure ignorance, and I am better off without ignorance in my life." This time it was Mac who turned to leave.

She'd grabbed his arm. "Wait. Don't go. Please."

His courage bolstered by the unrejected headfirst lunge, Mac invited Elizabeth to a stage production put on by the drama department, which neither of them enjoyed.

There were too many feelings surfacing as anxious fingers intertwined while nervous hearts pounded.

On the walk back to Elizabeth's dorm Mac asked her out again. "When?" she'd asked. "When you don't have a date with someone else."

"That's easy enough," she'd told him. "How about forever?" Mac nearly choked. Sensing in her the same longing he felt, he kissed her. The walk back to his room seemed both endless and instantaneous.

Six months of courtship followed. In the spring, two months before his graduation, Elizabeth said *yes* to Mac's proposal. They would marry in two years, when Elizabeth graduated. In the meantime, Mac would scour the St. Louis area for work. Everything had been so set in place. Then, in the midst of their planning, came the unexpected.

More as a favor to his only uncle, a vice president in the accounting group for a major oil company, Mac scheduled a job interview with the vice president of the company's legal department in New Orleans. Elizabeth had been less than thrilled, but did not stand in his way.

Time and solitude toyed with Mac on the unending bus ride. He knew nothing about oil law. He shivered at the thought of leaving Elizabeth behind. He just knew his nerves would expose a lack of conviction … that he'd failed the interview even before it had begun.

He shouldn't have worried. The company offered Mac considerably more than the starting salaries his classmates were getting. Sensing any hesitation would send the wrong message, Mac quickly accepted. He had not been prepared for such decisiveness when he'd left Saint Louis; this was a contingency he and Elizabeth had not considered. Mac would just have to work out things with her later. He hoped she would like being married to a lawyer who worked for an oil company. In exotic, entrancing New Orleans, no less.

The idea, in all its simplicity, came to him on a particularly long stretch of highway somewhere near Shreveport: they would get married immediately, and move to New Orleans together. She could transfer to a good school there. How could she reject such logic? Then he remembered his no-nonsense fiancée, the woman who would most certainly be astonished he could make such a decision without even discussing it with her.

As she would do again many times in the years to come, Elizabeth surprised him.

"Bradley, this is wonderful news!" she'd jubilantly exclaimed. "This is something you've worked hard for, something you deserve. New Orleans will be wonderful for you."

"I was hoping you'd think of it in terms of us." He was getting nervous.

"Please don't take this the wrong way. I want to be in your life. I want to be your life. But if I am to be either, it can't be only part-time, or occasionally on your terms. It has to be unconditional." Elizabeth's message was clear. Without hesitation he promised her in matters of family he never again would fail to consult her, that every decision impacting their lives first would be discussed with his wife.

It was settled. In a matter of days Elizabeth made arrangements to transfer to the H. Sophie Newcomb Memorial College of Tulane University, as Mrs. Joseph Bradley McHenry. Then came the hurried wedding, and Mac's introduction to Jed and Regina Rogers. Elizabeth's father was every bit the arrogant tyrant Mac had imagined from her descriptions. Mac took an instant dislike to the man, knowing the feeling was mutual. The warmth from his future mother-in-law more than made up for the void left in Mac by her husband.

It was not the grand wedding everyone had hoped for, but there hadn't been time. Mac smiled as he recalled the stunned expression on his new father-in-law's face. It was as if he'd kidnapped the man's daughter. Mac forced himself not to gloat. The honeymoon was a drive to New Orleans and a frantic search for an apartment.

It had been years since Mac had dwelled on their beginning. *His present and future so uncharitably taken from him, what else was there now except the past?* he wondered, as he drifted off into a short, restless sleep.

———————

Mac's trip to Guatemala City started badly, then got worse.

At Moissant Field in New Orleans Mac was overwhelmed by the news coverage of his daughter's death. Her photograph, indeed photographs of the entire McHenry family, ubiquitously appeared on the pages of magazines and newspapers. The public held onto its fascination with the life and death of the slain nun. Mac's wish for privacy was irreverently denied.

There was no escaping the attention. People stared, like the curious do, and whispered behind cupped hands and sideways glances as he walked to his departure gate. Others were bold enough to approach him as strangers, to offer their expressions of condolence and support. Trying not to offend these well-intentioned souls, Mac simply endured the interruptions the best he could.

He was pushed to the limit after taking his seat on the connecting flight to Guatemala City. First-class had been sold out, so Mac was forced to the coach section. Comfort and free drinks weren't what mattered; once again he was denied privacy he desperately craved. Seated across from an obnoxious yokel from Oklahoma, who already had had entirely too much to drink and was oblivious to the drama surrounding him as he bore down with inane conversation, Mac had finally, as politely as he could, excused himself and made his escape to the first-class cabin. A worried attendant asked if she could help. Numbly Mac could only mumble he just needed a moment away from his seat.

After a quick glance back to the coach cabin the attendant was looking knowingly into Mac's eyes. She offered to silence the boor, but Mac stopped her. He would manage, he told her.

Mac did not see the Hispanic couple seated in the row to his right quietly summon the attendant and whisper something to her.

The attendant caught Mac just as he was headed back to more abuse from the cowboy. "The couple in 2A and 2B would gladly exchange their seats for yours and the empty one beside it," she told Mac. "They told me not to take no for an answer."

Mac was ready for the kindness. He graciously accepted the couple's offer.

Grabbing his carry-on bag from the overhead compartment, as the drunk stared wide-eyed at him, Mac headed for the first-class section. Passing the elderly couple in the aisle, Mac stopped to thank them.

The man, much shorter than Mac, looked up at the lawyer and offered his and his wife's respects, expressing to Mac in broken but understandable English their sorrow for his personal tragedy. Maybe it was the softness in his voice, or the simple relief of escaping the rude passenger, but Mac found himself genuinely touched by the man's expressions, and offered his hand in thanks. The little man and his wife both grabbed at Mac's outstretched hand, held it briefly, then nodded in unison as they silently moved on toward Mac's vacated seat.

Buried alive in thought, Mac was unaware the flight attendant was talking to him. "I'm sorry," he said, "my mind was on something else. What did you say?"

She crouched next to him, her voice audible only to Mac. "I hated to barge in like this. I was just taking food and drink orders and checking on my other passengers. I don't suppose I could interest you in either the prime rib or the orange roughy could I?"

Mac shook his head *no*.

"Look, Mr. McHenry, and I apologize if I'm out of line here, really I do, but my guess is you'd like all the privacy you can get right now. So, if you need me, just punch the overhead button right there, okay? Otherwise, I won't disturb you. Will that work for you?" Then a friendly smile.

Relief surged through Mac as he looked into her imploring eyes.

"Remember, I'm only a punch of the button away if you need anything."

Mac murmured *Thank you* over her shoulder as 1A and 1B ordered the California burgundy with their prime rib dinners.

†

6

Left alone at last, a long flight ahead, Mac's thoughts turned to the trip he and Elizabeth had made to Guatemala little more than half a year earlier. Their first real vacation in five years, to the country their daughter had chosen for her field mission.

It was a time of mixed emotion for him, but of pure elation for his wife. Mac had yet to understand why his daughter, who he had just *known* would enter his law practice one day, had walked away from her perfect life to pursue the calling of a nun. Staunchly Catholic, Mac felt torn by this harshest of ironies. His angst was not shared, however, by his wife, who accepted Nicole's decision and delighted in the thought of visiting her in a strange land, and in the opportunity to share whatever part of her daughter's new life she could.

Mac's unease got the better of him during their flight. He lost control, and snapped at Elizabeth over something trivial. She gave him the rebuke he deserved.

"Bradley, it's time you got over this problem you have with Nicole's choice. I've seen in her letters the serenity we worried so long was missing in her life, and you should, too." She didn't stop there.

"Life may not always work out the way Bradley McHenry wants it to. Okay, you lost a future law partner, but I've lost my first real chance at grandchildren. Nicole's marriage to Tommy we'd thought would happen won't, which leaves our sons as the only chance we'll have to be grandparents. And I don't need to tell you what unlikely candidates they are for the altar any time soon." Mac groused; Elizabeth had made her point.

To keep his mind off the hurt he still felt, Mac had tried to picture life in Guatemala. Try as he might, he could not have been more unprepared for what greeted them. Soldiers were everywhere, sporting automatic weapons and menacingly gesturing at those who appeared to do nothing more than stray off some invisible chalk line. Fear showed on the faces of those on whom oppression had grabbed ahold and would not let loose. The festive spirit typically associated with Central America simply did not portray itself in this place. Had they been ordinary tourists, their stay would have been measured in terms of how quickly the next flight out left. For sarcastic effect, as he traded dollars for *quetzals*, Mac questioned what kind of nation would name its currency after the national bird … or was it vice versa?

Elizabeth had gone on to meet Nicole outside the terminal, while Mac got their luggage. The two women were still embracing when he emerged half an hour later. Mac could tell quickly Nicole had lost weight, but otherwise hadn't changed since the send-off a year earlier. He was also relieved she hadn't wrinkled like an old prairie woman, as Elizabeth had feared.

"Daddy! Daddy!" she'd shrieked, running toward him at full speed, her habit lifting off the ground. Mac dropped the bags just in time to catch her in full stride, and every unkind, tormented thought vanished. He hugged his daughter ferociously, his tears unstoppable.

"Oh, Daddy, you old softie," she said, wiping his eyes dry with her sleeve. "Mom's been telling me to beware the grouch. What does she know anyway?" She hugged him again. Mac watched Elizabeth wipe her own eyes.

"C'mon, let's load up," Nicole said with a last squeeze on her father's hand. She grabbed a small bag at Mac's feet. "We've got to leave soon to make the halfway point before it gets too dark. It's maybe six hours from here." That was all the warning Mac needed to hear.

"What is this?" Mac asked incredulously, staring at what could once possibly have passed as a pickup truck. "Does it run?"

"This is our transportation the archdiocese has graciously loaned us for a few days. Don't knock it."

"Couldn't we just get a car?" Mac begged. "I saw a rental counter in the terminal."

"If you were truthful with the clerk, she would tell you rentals can't be driven where we're headed. It's too risky."

Mac stared open-mouthed at his daughter, who gave him a mock grin as she climbed into the driver's seat of what appeared to be a demolition derby casualty.

There were only dirt roads after civilization faded from the rear view mirror. The only air conditioning was the dusty breeze blowing through the open windows. The road dust blended with the sweat from Mac's face, and the mixture found its way into his mouth. As he spat the salty mud onto the Guatemalan soil the thought crossed his mind it was, for the moment, a physiological necessity, but given time in this place it could just as easily become a display of contempt.

In less than two hours on Guatemalan soil, he already loathed the place. How would he ever accept his daughter's decision to call this land her own?

§

They spent an uneventful night in another small village at the halfway point, rose early and were in Refugio early afternoon on the second day. Nicole explained to her parents they were being put up in a very small house normally occupied by a fellow employed by the Reuters news service. "His name is Evan Montgomery," she told them, "and he's fifty-five years old. He's assigned to all of Central America, but spends more time in Guatemala than the rest of the area combined."

Apparently a thirty-year civil war is newsworthy to the world, Nicole explained further, and this older fellow, who had gained some level of prominence reporting the Vietnam conflict as a much younger man, could do no better than Guatemala at the present. Mac sensed that there was a vague respect for this fellow their daughter spoke of so sadly, but he kept it to himself.

Mac unloaded their bags into what he called the guest bungalow, while Nicole and Elizabeth went exploring. If anyone truly lived in the small cottage, Mac saw no sign of it. There were no photographs, no clothes in the crude dresser, no basic toiletries a man would need. Mac stretched out on the bed, worn from the two-day trip. He awoke with a startled jerk.

"I didn't want to wake you, but there's someone we have to go meet," Elizabeth was saying.

"I must have dozed off," Mac mumbled through a wide yawn. In moments, still groggy, he followed Elizabeth through the twilight into the heart of Refugio, straight to the quaint wood and adobe church. Nicole was waiting beside a short man in a black shirt and trousers, and the telltale white collar.

"Dad, Mom, this is Father Art Hurkinen, our priest." Mac could see the pride in his daughter's eyes. He shook the padre's hand, and accepted his invitation into a small courtyard where a table had been set. There were four chairs, and food piled high. Mac realized then how hungry he was.

"I'm from Gwinn, Michigan, which is way up there, in the Upper Peninsula," the priest began. "One day I decided the cold was no longer tolerable. At my advancing age, my joints were getting too stiff at twenty below, you understand. So I asked for a warmer climate, which of course meant a transfer. I had hoped the archdiocese in Marquette would arrange for a move to Arizona, New Mexico, or possibly Southern California. I would not have been unhappy with Texas, as long as there was some warmth to break seven months of freeze."

Mac helped himself to more of the delicious fish and corn stew Father Art handed him. "But, as I soon learned, the Church had points much farther south in mind for me." Mac smiled as the priest glanced all around the table. He saw Elizabeth smile at Nicole at the same time. The glow in his wife's expression spoke of the great warmth around the table.

"You must be careful what you pray for," Father Art wistfully concluded, pulling Mac back to the conversation, "as your prayers may well be answered." Mac laughed aloud.

They ate and talked without concern as the happy time passed. When he saw his wife's eyelids begin to droop Mac spoke up. "I think we're all tired. Why don't we call it a day."

"You'll get no argument from me," Elizabeth said. "Take me away, *Señor* Bradley," she swooned playfully. Good nights and thanks were exchanged quickly with the priest, who left the McHenry family under the church's archway, only a faint moon-glow distinguishing them from the shadows.

"Good night, Nicole," he said to his daughter as they hugged again. "Thank you for such a wonderful day. How will we ever top this tomorrow?"

Mac saw her wink at Elizabeth as she said, "Oh, we'll find something to interest you. Now go get some sleep. And take this beautiful woman with you." Mac watched as his wife and daughter held each other tightly.

"I'll be there at six in the morning for you. Be ready," Nicole called into the darkness.

§

The day's final adventure began shortly after Mac said good night to his wife, when something crawly and ornery scratched at their door, and scampered off at Mac's shout—more out of fear than bravado. The windows had to stay open, to keep them from suffocating in the heat. Long before dawn Mac heard Elizabeth mutter she was ready for such a merciful end. But the windows stayed open, and the quiet sounds outside were deafening. The slightest rustle of the leaves conjured images of slithery, scaly creatures moving bloodthirstily along. Even the robust Mac prayed hard for dawn to hurry.

When first light did come, it brought with it Nicole, clearly fresh from a night's rest. She laughed at the dark circles under her father's eyes. "It might take one or two more nights before the sounds become familiar," she said.

All Mac could manage was his usual grumble.

§

After morning Mass and a light breakfast the trio set out promptly at eight, Nicole at the helm of the battered loaner. Mac asked why Refugio's clergy did not have their own full-time transportation.

"We don't need it," Nicole replied. "The archdiocese sends a truck up here twice a week, which is how we get supplies, and mail. Our needs are met."

"What about emergencies?" Elizabeth asked, squeezing Mac's hand fiercely, as if the second the truck was gone they all would be stranded in crisis.

"As illogical as it may seem, Mother, we are entirely self-sufficient in Refugio," Nicole calmly answered. "Besides, there is no gas station within a hundred kilometers. That's why you saw those gas cans beside the church. We serve such a small area, it's easier to walk or, when we need to, catch a ride on the archdiocese's truck.

"Oh," she added, "and we have Evan's Range Rover when he's around. See, we're not so helpless as you might think."

Mac returned the squeeze, letting Elizabeth know to drop it. He could tell from her wrinkled forehead she was biting her tongue. Mac, too, was concerned, but did not want their first day together to turn into an inquisition on safety and danger. He'd have plenty of time later to visit with Father Art on just how wise it was to be in Refugio without a vehicle. Meantime, he had another thought on his mind.

"Wasn't the Church going to send two nuns here?" Mac asked. "Where's the other?"

"Daddy, I wrote you about that. The one who was supposed to join me here changed her mind about mission work. The Church is still looking for a replacement."

"Well, it just doesn't seem right you being here alone ... the only nun in this place." Mac caught Elizabeth's squinty glance and did not pursue the matter.

"Aren't you curious where I'm taking you?" Nicole asked through a Cheshire smile.

Mac bit first. "Let me guess. We're headed toward some of those ruins you wrote us about."

"Remind me not to tell you so much in my next letter. I have ruined my own surprise."

"I swear, Bradley," Elizabeth interjected, "must you always know everything?"

Mac, the scolded antihero, didn't respond, and kept quiet while Nicole salvaged his gaffe with a brief lesson on Guatemala as she maneuvered the group along more bad roads bordered by stunningly scenic countryside. She explained how the country was divided into twenty-two departments, which are similar to states but more like regions. Refugio lay in the largest one, El Petén, usually just referred to as Petén, bordered by Mexico to its north. Petén comprised a large percentage of the northernmost part of the country and contained the largest and most impressive Mayan ruins. Other, smaller departments, such as Chimaltenango, Quiche, Huehuetenango, Izabal, Retalhuleu, Escuintla, and Guatemala, also containing ruins, were to the south. Guatemala, she lectured on, was roughly the size of Pennsylvania. With a population of just over eleven million, half of which were of Mayan descent and the remainder of mixed Spanish and Mayan blood, Guatemala was the most densely populated Central American country. Most inhabitants spoke Spanish, she told them, but many still communicate only through tribal dialects.

She impressively detailed the country's historical evolution, explaining that until it had declared its independence in 1821 Guatemala was ruled by Spain since the early part of the sixteenth century. Under military rule since the early 1980s, the government consisted of a single figurehead political party. The rule had been harsh, she continued, as much on people situated at the sub-poverty level like those in her village of Refugio as it was on the dreaded rebel bandits who roamed and marauded in the outer departments. She spoke with despondency at this political news, the only low point in their day together.

"How does this strife affect life in Refugio?" Mac asked. "Or the rest of Petén?" he added. "I saw the soldiers everywhere yesterday, the airport, all along the roads. They didn't look too friendly to me."

Nicole's face tightened as she cemented her lips around words that remained choked inside. Mac nudged Elizabeth before the worried mother could say anything. They didn't talk politics, geography or soldiers again as they continued on toward their destination. Mac's thoughts by then had turned to what he'd come here to confront, but couldn't. *Why had his daughter come here? What had been so oppressive in her life she had to run here to escape? What could he do to make her reconsider?* Mac stayed silent, wrapped in his thoughts as his wife and daughter carried the weight of conversation. He was still lost in his thoughts when the truck came to an abrupt stop, and his daughter's voice rang loud.

"This is Tikal," Nicole said proudly, letting the spectacle speak for itself. "It was a major Mayan city, existing for centuries upon centuries. It covers over twenty-five square miles, and there are more than three thousand separate constructions. Five of them are more than a hundred and twenty-five feet tall. Tikal was home to perhaps as many as one hundred thousand Mayans during the Late Classic period."

Mac let go of his doubts and hard curiosity. He glanced at his wife, who like him was ogling the massive temples, palaces and shrines their daughter had just unveiled.

"We have time to climb only one structure," Nicole said ruefully. "Pick it, Mom."

Like a child choosing from a plate of freshly-baked cookies Elizabeth pointed at the tallest of the temple-like structures. "That one."

"My favorite," Nicole concurred, smiling grandly again. "It's Temple I, in the Great Plaza. We need to hurry, it's a monstrous climb."

Mac and Elizabeth, fit from years of casual jogging and healthy diet, were no match for their daughter, who climbed the hundreds of steps effortlessly. Mac stopped near the midway point, not so much to rest but to pause and savor all he could: the magnificent view around him, the beautiful day, the warmth radiating from their daughter, who, despite his own misgivings of the life she'd chosen, had become a mature, confident, poised woman. Seeing her in the nun's habit was still unfamiliar and discomfiting to him, but, he reflected, in time it surely would pass. This moment, right then, was for him another step in the direction he needed to be heading, toward acceptance. He vowed not to let his reluctance to accept his daughter's decision interfere with this day, or those to come.

Forty steps above him his wife and daughter were in hushed conversation. "Dad's still not happy with me being a nun, is he?" Nicole asked, looking straight into her mother's eyes for the truth.

"Give him time," Elizabeth counseled. "No matter what else he might be thinking, or wanting, your father wishes more than anything else for your happiness. Believe that."

Mac was still dwelling on his vow to himself when the shouts of the two women rained down on him from above, urging him onward. Unhesitatingly he broke from his reflection to resume the climb, mentally preparing himself for a witty retort to the playful jabs awaiting the straggler.

The descent was as strenuous as the climb. While they rested before starting back to Refugio, Nicole tied up the historical loose ends as she explained how the ancestors of her villagers had fled when the conquering Spanish arrived. Besides Petén, they had scattered as far as Mexico to the north, and to the more arid places to the southwest, where they grew corn and a few other vegetables, notably the prized peppers that served as a major export crop. The descendants of those immigrants to the south were today housed on the large *fincas*, or plantations, owned by the wealthy Spanish. The government kept no records of their births or deaths; they had no civil rights whatsoever. The Catholic Church was trying to change that, to teach them to fend for themselves, often at great risk.

"The Church," Nicole began, "believes it's better to educate them than to keep them wards of their own poverty and illiteracy. Give them a fish, and they eat for a day, but teach them to fish, and they eat for a lifetime."

Mac saw the pride in his daughter's face. He felt ashamed, and foolish. He looked at Elizabeth, who was reading his thoughts, and smiling at him as she wrapped herself in his arms.

"Dad," Nicole said, interrupting her parents' moment, "you asked about the soldiers earlier. I wasn't sure what to say. I think I'm ready to try now." Drinking from the canteen, she wiped her brow with the sleeve of her habit and spoke solemnly.

"The natives have no friends. There is no lesser of two evils. The soldiers have been suspected of butchering the Indians … in the southern part of the country, not this far north. The government doesn't intervene because it is also rid of what it perceives as a blight. Then there are the insurrectionists … rebels, bandits, outlaws, whatever you want to call them. The Indians pose them no threat, but the rebels have also been known to kill them mercilessly. So far the rebels also have stayed away from this northernmost frontier. But we hear they may be moving in this direction. That is probably why we now see soldiers. They weren't here, at least in this part of Petén, when I arrived a year ago."

"I don't understand," Mac blurted. "If the Indians pose no threat to the rebels, why would the rebels persecute them?"

"I'll explain the best I can. The rebels have tried to forge an alliance with the Indians for years, but the Indians aren't impressed with strange notions of freedom. What do they care about free elections? For all their persecution, they are in the cruelest of senses free. They may have little, but they are self-sufficient. Dad, they are practically invisible. That is all the freedom they crave."

Mac saw real pain in Nicole's expression. He reached for his daughter, took her in his arms as he'd done since infancy, speaking softly to her as he saw Elizabeth dab at the corners of her eyes.

"There, now, baby," Mac said, soothing Nicole and himself at the same time. So much weight on her, Mac thought. When he felt his daughter recover, he held her out at arms' length, as he thought about how to say what still was entrenched in his mind. For her sake.

"Dad, no," Nicole exclaimed, as she pulled from him. "I know what you're thinking. Please don't say it. This may be the most dangerous, desolate place on the earth, but it is my home now, and it is my life, and I will not leave it."

Mac wasn't surprised he'd exposed his thoughts. Nor could he bring himself to argue with his daughter over words he'd not uttered.

Their return to Refugio was driven mostly in silence, punctuated sparingly by polite, forced conversation. Possessed of her father's persuasive power, Nicole succeeded in convincing her parents that fatigue and the occasionally pensive nature of their daughter—nothing new to either parent—were acceptable explanations for the silence joining in as a fourth passenger in the already-crowded truck.

No longer bothered by the quiet, Mac dozed off. He slept until their late arrival back in Refugio. Quick and perfunctory good nights were exchanged as Nicole let them out at the church. Mac and Elizabeth were also reminded by their daughter they should be up and ready to go at six, that another day of adventure awaited them. While Elizabeth smiled, Mac winced at the thought of anything like another one hundred and twenty-five-foot climb the following day.

Sound sleep for the lawyer soon followed, yet it would be broken by fits of restlessness throughout the night. Fatigue got him to sleep, but it wasn't enough for the rest he craved. A great debate raged within his mind. He wanted to force his daughter to leave this place; he wanted to be the good father who let go. The debate played to a draw.

––––––––––––

As her husband slept restlessly, Elizabeth prayed silently for her daughter's safety. Even as she knew of her daughter's unbounded happiness, she also knew there was much in this country an innocent such as her daughter, would be oblivious to.

Never before had she prayed so fervently, for anything.

§

The next day, and the next, they saw even more of the picturesque yet forbidding countryside. There were more ruins, more history lessons, more revelations of the fascination held by their daughter for this vast, green, still incredibly primitive place. Wherever they went, Mac was quick to notice the soldiers, who were never more than a few moments from appearing. *They're just patrolling,* Nicole continued to explain, ever quick to pick up on her father's alerted senses.

She lectured her parents a bit more. Her village was home mostly to peaceful latter-day Mayan Indians, some of pure descent, most of partly Hispanic blood brought on by centuries of mixed unions. Often referred to as *Ladinos,* the source of which was lost in antiquity, and sometimes condescendingly as *campesinos,* these fiercely proud people wore with pride the purer designation as Indians, which is what she called them. Her villagers could trace their ancestry to Tikal's ruling dynasty.

Those Indians who lived to the south, she continued, lived in straw huts, or often under the trees. They had no building skills, no tools other than what the lords of their *fincas* would furnish. After the flight from their oppressive Spaniard conquerors, the artisans and builders had settled in what became Petén, in places near rivers and in the thickness of the jungle forests. They carved out existences one tree at a time, building their homes of wood and clay and sand, converting the deforested surface into fertile farmland. They developed an infrastructure, and to this day most of the northern villages, including Refugio, sported a mayor and a congregation of elders who acted as a sort of council. These primitive types had, in just over two centuries, become self-sufficient.

The irony of it all, Nicole concluded, was she lived with and taught the same people who lived in the south, whose lot in life was decided when their ancestors migrated to lower country rather than remaining in the higher country as her villagers' ancestors had. The same peoples had diverged, become subcultures, one in peril and the other prosperous in comparison. Her parents were relieved she lived among the latter.

On their last archaeological expedition Nicole took them to the south, to her next favorite ruins, at Zaculeu. Not nearly as impressive in their grandeur as those at Tikal, the ruins at Zaculeu, found in the Department of Huehuetenango, held particular importance to Nicole, she explained, because it was here the Mayans fought the hardest against the Spanish, and paid the dearest price. Tears welled in her eyes as she spoke of atrocities heaped upon the vanquished by their captors, all, she regretted, in the name of Christianity. A different Catholic Church then, she explained, felt the need to conquer in the name of God most Holy, and to convert the heathen Indians into children of the one God. No longer would they worship Tlaloc, the rain god, and the lesser gods of war, the forest and the like, they would henceforth and thereafter worship the one God. Centuries later, she concluded, these peaceful

Indians had accepted the God of Man, but at what price? Mac and Elizabeth wisely remained silent as the words reverberated in the calm of the temple in the center of the largest plaza.

Two other visitors to the site, casual tourists coincidentally passing by at that precise moment, were struck by the strange sight of the young nun standing with outstretched arms, palms upward, surreally gesturing in an imploring posture to the two older people in front of her.

§

On their fifth day Nicole announced the touring was at an end. "I'm afraid the archdiocese needs its truck back." Mac was relieved at this news, but would never have said it aloud.

"Besides," Nicole continued, "I need to get back to work. My children have been without their teacher too long." A brief pause followed. Then, "Maybe I could interest you two in a little classroom observation." Mac could feel the anticipation coming from his daughter.

Elizabeth was quicker than Mac. "We would love to!"

Mac watched Nicole's face break into smile. "School starts at seven. Just get there when you can, and I'll introduce you to my students."

"Does this mean you won't be at our door at six in the morning?" There was a hint of sarcasm in Mac's voice.

"Bradley!" Elizabeth clearly wasn't up to her husband's attempt at wit.

"Don't worry, Mom. You both have earned the extra hour of sleep."

"We have some daylight left today. Is anything planned?" Elizabeth asked.

"I have something to do," Nicole said. "You two honeymooners are on your own the rest of the afternoon. We can meet at the church for dinner, say, around six-thirty. Sound okay?"

"Sure," Mac said. "You run on. The honeymooners will see you at six-thirty."

Nicole hugged her parents, then headed down a path Mac knew would take her south or perhaps west of the village. When she was out of sight, he turned to Elizabeth.

"It looks like we're on our own. Can I interest you in a walk? A little jaunt of our own, in search of some local flavor we might've missed?"

"Oh, Bradley, I don't know. Did you see the soldiers down by the plaza earlier? They frighten me."

Mac shrugged off her concerns. "They were only here a few minutes. Besides, you should know we have nothing to worry about, because everyone knows by now who we are, that we pose no threat. We're simple tourists. How much safer could it be?"

Relenting, Elizabeth joined him. They quickly ran into Father Art near the church, and spent a pleasant afternoon with the avuncular priest. After attending evening Mass, they enjoyed a bottle of California Chardonnay while they waited for Nicole to return for dinner. After a quiet but heavenly meal, Father Art fetched a bottle of port, Elizabeth's favorite dessert … a gift from Evan Montgomery, the priest explained.

The evening ended too quickly for Mac, who for the first time since arriving felt relaxed. When Nicole reminded them she had classes to teach, the group reluctantly called it a night. After the short walk back to their accommodations Mac and Elizabeth settled in for their first night of comfortable sleep and rest in Guatemala. The place could be gotten used to, Mac declared to his wife. But a few of life's modern conveniences wouldn't hurt much, he added.

§

The next morning, from their seats in the rear of the classroom, the parents beamed as their daughter spun a magical web over twenty-one schoolchildren. First she taught grammar, math and the Catechism in Spanish, then came an English lesson. For all their amazement as Nicole's instructions ended, Mac and Elizabeth still were not prepared for their next treat.

As soon as the books were put away, and the children were seated in rows on the ground in front of their teacher, she reached under a table and pulled out her old guitar. First she played a simple children's song they all sang in Spanish. Others Nicole sang solo.

Mac and Elizabeth watched as one rather young-looking girl moved right up next to and was all but clinging to Nicole. It was clear to them this child particularly enjoyed their daughter. Entranced by her innocent beauty, and her awe of Nicole, Mac and Elizabeth became as captivated by the child as they soon learned Nicole had. She confided in them at day's end that this one child, whose name was Maria, touched her as no other child in the village. She was her first student, the one after whom all others followed. The parents sensed that Maria brought out in their daughter a maternal instinct they suspected had always been there.

Even as Nicole put up her guitar her parents' treat was not over. They next saw their daughter exchange her sandals for a tattered pair of soccer shoes, and watched in sheer delight as Nicole joined the children in a spirited short-sided game of soccer. Scenes of standing on sidelines years earlier flooded the parents' memories, the countless miles from Pensacola to Houston they'd covered during those nine tiring but rewarding years of caravanning with the other soccer moms and dads to the endless tournaments. Those thoughts were only fleeting as both parents were snatched back to reality, observers not from chalk-lined, manicured fields with real goals and nets but on a small, sparsely carpeted field with but a single makeshift goal. The spartan appearance of the playing surface stole nothing from the real show, however—a display of their daughter's foot skills, still sharp in spite of the cumbersome nun's habit.

As with the singing, the children clamored for more when the playing was declared over for the day. There would be more tomorrow, she promised them. *The carrot hanging from the stick*, her father mused.

Two more days of this routine followed. On the third day Elizabeth joined in the teaching, working with little Maria and several of the younger children on an arts and crafts project, while Mac, feeling humbled by his lack of ability to contribute, could only watch the two women who shared a singular passion. But there was a touch of sadness in the father's heart. There would be no more moments like this for him with his daughter. He berated himself over the envy he felt toward the children, over the selfish, pitiable sadness he'd been feeling. It was time he moved on.

It was so much easier felt than done.

§

On their next-to-last day in Refugio, while Nicole and Elizabeth spent the morning at the school, Mac sought out Father Art. He pestered the ebullient padre for as much information as he could about the land, the people … and the danger.

Father Art reinforced the assurances Mac had heard from his daughter. With each comforting answer Mac felt his residual tension lessen, and the worry of his daughter's safety begin to fade. He grew to trust as well as admire the priest.

Father Art was equally as fascinated by the country lawyer from the deep South, who reciprocated by regaling him with war stories of courtroom derring-do and mischief, never letting the truth, the whole truth and nothing but the truth get in the way of a good tale.

Time became the only enemy, for it passed too quickly. On their tenth and final morning, Mac and Elizabeth said farewell to Father Art and the children, who would miss the man who hugged their Sister Nicole so much and whose eyes often brimmed mistily as she sang to them, and the woman who brought so many smiles to their teacher.

The parents' trip home was marked by relaxed silence, melancholy contentment. There had been, in Mac's case, a conspicuous absence of the irritability he'd exhibited on the trip down, what his wife silently acknowledged was a sign of grudging acceptance.

That had been only half a year ago. Yet so very long ago. A lifetime ago.

†

7

MAC DOZED INTERMITTENTLY between his recollections of the first trip to Guatemala, until sleep overtook him somewhere over the heart of the Gulf of Mexico. Turbulence from a steep descent jolted him awake. Not even the particularly rough landing would distract the quiet visitor from his business. He was here not as a tourist this time, visiting family, but to claim his daughter's body, and take her home.

He was one of the first passengers to deplane. Eager to get on with his business, he nevertheless waited to again thank the elderly couple. The strangers clasped hands a last time, exchanging well wishes. Mac watched as they melded into the throng of humanity in the terminal. A slight pang of conscience struck him after they had slipped from view: he hadn't made any offer in reciprocation for their kindness. He thought of a bumper sticker he had seen recently, one encouraging the commission of random acts of kindness. Another time, his guilt would've mattered.

As he went to claim his luggage Mac bristled at the heavily armed military. He wondered if the scene would ever change. He took pains not to draw attention to himself. His thoughts were on his objective when a sixth sense alerted him to another presence. He stopped, turned, saw nothing distinguishing, then shrugged his shoulders slightly and continued walking. Only a few steps further he had the same feeling of being watched, or followed. He stopped and again turned. Before he could scan the crowd, a man's voice startled him.

"*Señor* McHenry—*Señor* Mac—I am Miguel. I am here to take you to Refugio." Mac looked to his right, and into the face of the man whose voice had surprised him. Eyes of light brown, almost yellow, the kindest eyes he'd ever looked into, smiled up at him … penetrating eyes momentarily disarming his hostility and restoring a measure of sanity to his muddled mind. It was then Mac realized the voice came from the same man who had walked beside him from the moment he deplaned, inconspicuously until now.

Rarely at a loss for words, all Mac could muster, weakly, in response to this smiling little man was, "How do you know me?"

"You came to our village," replied the smallish brown man dressed in khaki trousers and brightly-multicolored shirt and straw hat, the typical dress of the Guatemalan natives. "You stayed in *Señor* Monty's house, while he was away. My home is near the church." He was smiling.

"Father Art introduced us one day, near the little school," he added.

Mac strained to recall, but could not place the man. He assumed *Señor* Monty was Evan Montgomery, who he and Elizabeth did not meet. He spoke again to the man beside him.

"I was told only someone I knew would meet me at customs. I did not know who it would be. I hope you will forgive me for not expecting you, or remembering you, Mr. ... Mr. ... Miguel, you say?"

"*Sí*, please call me Miguel. I am always Miguel, just Miguel." The man smiled at Mac, showing no sign of offense.

"You speak very good English, Miguel," Mac said.

"When I was young, the Church sent me here, into the capitol, for schooling. It was once thought I would enter the priesthood." Before Mac could comment, the man said, "Come with me, *Señor* Mac, I have arranged for everything. We have far to travel, many hours, and should start now, so please, come along quickly." Mac had trouble keeping up with the brisk pace.

It did not occur to Mac to question his safety, or the wisdom of latching onto a total stranger in this ominous place. Perhaps it was the uncommonly kind eyes. Whatever the reason, Mac found himself trusting a man he'd known but a moment, a man he knew only as Miguel.

§

The same battered truck bounced along the same poorly graded road Mac and Elizabeth took to Refugio such a short time ago. This time the heat was even more stifling, and it and the humidity reminded Mac of home. In several hours it would be dusk; he longed already for the respite from the oppressive sun.

Mac's thoughts turned to his daughter. This was his first solo encounter with his feelings since the news of her death. There was still confusion over the details. But it was not the details surrounding Nicole's savage murder that brought Mac to this confrontation. No, it was something more. It was his new friend—guilt. As a father, the man to whom any child should be able to count on for protection, for strength, Mac suffered his failure. This failure was the epicenter. Why hadn't he acted on his instincts?

He let her be delivered to this land of danger, and did not recognize the peril he should have. He did not intervene at the ruins, as he should have, and force his daughter's rescue. He mulled this over and over.

Miguel broke the silence. "She has been prepared for burial in the finest manner, *Señor* Mac. Someone from Guatemala City came to the village, someone trained in these things." He cautiously added, "I thought you would want to know this."

The breath was sucked right out of Mac's lungs. Setting aside his guilt, he knew instantly the man had just told him his daughter had been professionally embalmed. It was a detail Mac wished he could've been spared. In all his talks with Elizabeth, and with Father Robichaux, the subject of Nicole's burial preparation had not come up. He now realized as well he had not thought of a casket. For all he knew his daughter was wrapped in a shroud, laid out coldly on a stone slab in a vacant room in some deserted building in the village. Mac rebuked himself for his lack of attention to this detail, for his selfish carelessness. He turned to his driver, wishing he could have avoided the embarrassment of having to ask if there were a casket.

"Oh, *sí*, a fine casket." Before Mac could speak further, Miguel said, "I made it myself." He spoke neither boastfully nor with any false humility, but with a measured air of—what was it?—of satisfaction, Mac reasoned. Mac pictured a plain, rough-hewn pine box held together with dowels, hand-crafted artisan's work necessitated because mass production simply did not exist—the finished product slightly less primitive, perhaps, than a pauper's box. He made a mental note to have his daughter transferred to a more fitting casket when they returned home, although he did not tell this to Miguel. It would not do to offend the gentle man so proud of his labor of love.

Encouraged by Miguel's good-hearted exchange, Mac segued into conversation with his driver on the one subject on which he had practically no information. "Miguel," he began, foregoing anything introductory, going straight to the heart of the matter, "were you there? Did you see my daughter killed that night?" A stare like a laser trained itself on Miguel.

"I was working late, when the fighting started. When I heard noises—they sounded like explosions—I ran toward the part of the village that was burning. I stopped to help put out a fire in a friend's home. I was bringing water from the river, along with many of the villagers, when she—when it happened. Most of us did not know what was going on. We thought the electricity had caused the explosions, and the fires."

Mac had forgotten about the power the military brought to the village after his and Elizabeth's visit. Nicole wrote them about it. "Please go on, Miguel. Tell me what you know."

"*Sí, Señor* Mac. We did not learn about Sister Nicole until after we put out the fire in my friend's home. Then we rushed to the church and found her. It was already too late." Miguel crossed himself.

"I am so sorry for your loss. If I had but known she was in peril, I would have let my friend's home burn to the ground to help her. I swear this to you."

Yet another backward-looking expression of futility, the second in two days. First his priest, who would trade places with his daughter, and now this peasant who would have sacrificed his friend's home. Mac turned his gaze to the road ahead, wondering if such proffered barter ever helped the grieving. The conversation stalled as the truck bounced along.

"What about her killer? I have heard he may have been someone who lived in the village … a neighbor of yours perhaps?" Another laser-like stare.

"I knew him. He came to Refugio as a young man. We were not friends. And until that night, when the fighting started, he was nothing more than a quiet man who lived on the edge of the village. His home was very near *Señor* Monty's. That is all I know." The shimmering eyes fixed on Mac, who withdrew.

Two hours and several small villages out of the capital they were on barely more than a dirt road, rutted, Mac guessed, by heavy traffic, not by the wear one would expect from old pickup trucks such as he was now riding in, or from the carts and wagons Mac had also seen along their route. More likely by heavy trucks, he thought. Military vehicles, no doubt, such as those he'd observed since leaving Guatemala City.

Such as the one coming straight at them from around a sharp bend, for which Miguel suddenly had to veer into a safe area off the side of their road as it flew past, as if the pickup had been invisible. The old truck slammed to a stop against the embankment, dust swirling in the breezeless air. A dozen heavily armed soldiers stood in the back of the large uncovered transport, hugging the wooden side railings as the larger truck blew by. Mac noticed only one of the soldiers cast a downward glance. He wondered if the trooper cared. His face hard and expressionless, his eyes cold, he looked no more than an instant at the scene below. He appeared to be in his late teens, yet Mac knew he was probably hardened at the prospect of taking another's life, that he likely cared nothing for either passenger or driver. This was a mean, dark and unkind place in which Mac found himself. As he cleared his head from the jarring impact Mac warned himself not to underestimate the evil around him, to beware everything, to trust nothing.

Miguel stepped out of the truck, crossing himself at being spared a fatal collision. Mac quickly joined him, and played the part of the apprentice as the two men inspected for damage. Silence competed with the heat and humidity as they meticulously checked the truck. It was Miguel who spoke first.

"The soldiers, they are everywhere. They, too, are scared. No one knows what will become of this area after … after what happened." His gaze drifted away from the truck, toward the mountains for which they were headed. "These soldiers," he continued, "they have known only fighting, war, since they were born. Their whole lifetime."

Mac understood. For he already knew about such things, and had been prepared for their possible eventuality. His nation's government had seen to that.

§

The unexpected call had come while Mac was home for a spell from Elizabeth's stay at the hospital. The caller identified himself as Mr. Thomas Dillon, with the State Department in the New Orleans office, who needed a bit of Mr. McHenry's time. Mac asked the obvious.

"What could the State Department possibly want of me, Mr. Dillon?"

"Mr. McHenry, I'll get to the point. The State Department, while sorrowful over your loss, does not want your trip to Guatemala to become the springboard for an international incident. It is imperative we speak."

"We are speaking, sir. I don't have much time, but I'll give you a minute. Go ahead, tell me what's so important you would throw my government in my face at a time like this." Mac wasn't sure how the State Department could already know he was headed for Guatemala, but he saved the question.

"Not over the telephone, Mr. McHenry. I'm sure you understand. Meet me tomorrow morning at the little diner across the street from the courthouse in Covington, say, around 8:00."

Mac decided against protesting. He started to tell the man what he would be wearing, when Dillon interrupted him. "I'll know who you are," was all he said before hanging up.

Their meeting lasted barely an hour. Mac had been somewhat surprised Dillon showed up alone, even more surprised with the man's assurance their conversation would not be monitored. The intrigue was unnecessary, Dillon had assured Mac further. In his hour with Dillon, Mac received a briefing on the three-decade civil war that had ravaged Guatemala—this account pointedly different than the one he'd heard from his daughter—and of the current political instability. Dillon concluded by stating it was his country's fervent hope the present government, although not perfect, would remain in power.

"There are many efforts underway, most that will never be reported, all aimed at introducing peace and stability, and some form of democracy to Guatemala. Your daughter's tragic death could upset a delicate balance that took years to develop. While the government mourns your loss, it must insist on your cooperation."

Mac was simmering, near a boiling point. "I am outraged by this invasion, Mr. Dillon. Make no mistake, I won't forget it. I am leaving for Guatemala tomorrow, to bring my daughter home to be buried. Pardon me if I'm not too concerned at the moment about my government's efforts to interfere in the affairs of yet another country.

"Where was my government three days ago, when my daughter could have used some of its peacemaking ways? Tell me, Mr. Dillon."

"I know how you feel, Mr. McHenry. Look, let's leave it at this. Go get your daughter. Bring her home. Do it peacefully, and know you will have done your country a service."

The lawyer's courtroom sense triggered. Something in the way Dillon had just lamely given in ...

"What is it you're not telling me, Mr. Dillon? What is my government fearful of my seeing or learning while I am in Guatemala? Come on, man, level with me."

Dillon squirmed. "Fair enough, Mr. McHenry, fair enough." Dillon loosened his tie, and leaned in close. "There are concerns, both here and there, that your daughter's death might be used as a rallying cry. The peace is an uneasy one ... the slightest provocation could ignite things. Neither side is blinking."

"I don't understand. The rebels killed my daughter. What sympathy could they expect?"

Mac felt Dillon's hard gaze. "You don't know, do you?" Dillon asked.

"Don't know what?" Then realization set in. "Why won't anyone tell me what happened?"

"Your daughter was killed by a villager, Mr. McHenry, not by one of the revolutionaries.

There is no movement to strike down the Church in Guatemala. It appears your daughter may have been targeted for some other reason."

Mac was stunned. "Does the Church know this?" He thought about what Father Paul had told him: *I've been told only that one of the rebels is responsible. It's possible he also lived in the village.*

"I don't know. You'll need to ask the Church. But quietly, please. This must not become a spectacle. A tenuous peace hangs in the balance."

Suddenly only one thing mattered to Mac McHenry. "How can I get to the truth of what happened to my daughter, Mr. Dillon? Who can get me there?"

Dillon paused before answering. "Okay, Mr. McHenry, I'll give you this much … but you didn't hear it from me. Understood?"

Mac nodded.

"A villager, one of the insurrectionists, is being held in the Guatemala City prison. He appears to be the only one who joined in the uprising to have survived. The Guatemalan government will most certainly execute him, once this thing blows over. Perhaps after you've gone with your daughter, when this is all old news. But at the moment, if anyone might know why your daughter was killed, it would probably be this fellow."

"How can I get to him? Can you help me?"

"Possibly." Dillon handed him a business card. "Here, I'm giving you my private number. Call me if your own efforts fall short. I can try, Mr. McHenry, but I won't promise you anything. I'm sure you understand."

As Mac rose to leave, Dillon added, "One more thing, Mr. McHenry." His tone was more subdued. "I truly am sorry about what happened to your daughter. Truly."

Mac had wondered all the way back to the hospital if the sincerity was feigned, or genuine, and whether it mattered.

———————

Thinking back on that meeting a day earlier, Mac better understood Dillon's message. Freshly assaulted by a truckload of heavily armed, uniformed youths, he knew by nature his impulse, under other circumstances, would have been to shout and gesture obscenities at the young thugs posing as soldiers. In the present situation, that would of course have solved nothing, and could have been the spark of the very incendiary situation Dillon had been concerned about.

Miguel once again broke into Mac's thoughts. "*Señor* Mac, if you will help me with a push,

I think we can get back on the road. It is not much further before we stop for the night."

Mac exhaled a sigh of relief as he brushed aside thoughts of Dillon, of armed soldiers, of conflict. It took the two men only moments to right the truck. In less than twenty minutes back on the road, they came upon their first village since paved roads had disappeared. A small place, so typical of the rural Guatemala the McHenry family had explored six months earlier. For all Mac knew they had passed through this very same village. It held no distinguishing characteristics, nothing to mark it from the next, and the next. So barren of architecture, so void of any indicia of modern civilization, how could something like this have held any attraction to his daughter? How could the world, with its electronic, ergonomic, enlightened, information-age technology, ignore and bypass some parts? How could these people he saw walking the streets, and what passed for sidewalks in this tiny hamlet, not know there was a far better world out there? How much longer would it take progress, civilization, to reach this place?

With sunset less than an hour away, Miguel suggested they stop for the night. The truck rolled to a halt under a small tree on the way out of the village. The two men stretched, then shared a small meal Miguel unwrapped from a red bandana. Mac could tell from the yearning expression his driver wanted to talk, but he could not force himself to utter another word. Conversation had become a distraction from his mission. He closed his eyes, and did not open them until daylight.

————————

Morning's first light found the two men back on the road, passing through countless villages also awakening to what promised to be another scorching day. Mac saw his first gas station outside Guatemala City as they stopped for fuel and a stretch. He graciously accepted a share of the last of the food.

They had been traveling nearly four hours when Miguel slowed down. Ahead a few hundred meters or so Mac saw a lone figure resting under the only tree by the roadside. Apparently waiting for them, Mac guessed, as the figure rose at the sight of the truck, waving excitedly. A tinge of apprehension gripped him, but he held his calm. If he had somehow been set up for harm, this was the time and place. He was at the mercy of the man beside him, and a greater force whose existence he largely ignored these days. He waited for Miguel to speak.

"Señor Mac, we stop here. It is another six kilometers by road to Refugio, but there is a shorter way by foot, perhaps only two or three kilometers or a little bit more. It will take us longer, but I would like to take you by foot. If you will let me do this, we will let my friend Romero, the man under the tree up ahead, take the truck on to the village, while you and I walk."

Mac started to speak, when Miguel added, "It is not a hard walk for one as fit as you."

Mac ignited with apprehension, but showed calm. "I'll trust your judgment."

"Good, then it is done," Miguel said enthusiastically.

The truck pulled to a stop under the shade tree, beside the man introduced only as Romero, who did not speak to Mac except to say *Señor* as he bowed deferentially from the waist. Miguel took a canteen from Romero, then motioned him inside the truck. Mac watched the wreck churn dust in its wake as it gradually disappeared around a turn a quarter of a kilometer ahead. Mac felt a nudge at his arm as Miguel offered him a drink from the canteen.

"*Gracias,*" Mac said, smiling. He felt the satisfying coolness and wetness soothe his parched mouth and throat.

"If you are ready, we should leave now. To stay ahead of the heat."

Mac followed Miguel's lead, their path gradually thinning into the thick vegetation. He became uneasy. If this man he knew only as Miguel was not a simple villager, but a rebel or rebel sympathizer, his remains might never be found. Still, he followed the little man as closely as he could. There seemed no other choice.

Mac spoke first. "Miguel, I'm wondering. Did something happen to the stretch of road leading into Refugio, making us take this path, give up our comfortable, smooth ride in the truck?"

Miguel hesitated before he answered. "Sister Nicole, she often walked this path."

Mac had the feeling—maybe it was something in the tone of the man's voice—that a reaction was expected of him. Slightly confused, he ventured cautiously.

"Tell me," he said, "why was this path special to my daughter?"

Miguel slowed, and turned to face Mac as he stopped. "It is not something I can tell you, *Señor* Mac. It is something I must show you, something you must see for yourself.

"Come," he said as he turned and started back down the path, "it is only a little bit more." Mac once again fell into step, plunging forward, wondering even more what this was all about.

He could not have imagined what awaited him.

———————

Miguel quickened the pace, leaving Mac thirty or so paces behind. Before he could question his guide, he saw Miguel had stopped, coming to rest where the growth gave way to blue sky. He was still waiting in the same spot when Mac caught up to him. Miguel was looking straight at him, then turned his head and cast his gaze outwardly, toward an opening. Mac followed his glance, and instantly felt his knees grow weak. The beauty, the sheer grandeur of what lay before him snatched all his energy away. Mac reached out to steady himself, finding only the bony shoulder of Miguel to lend support. Words such as verdant, majestic, lush, and splendor all crossed Mac's mind, but none could do justice to the panorama before him.

He followed the view of the valley from end to end. To his left, halfway up a steep mountainside, coursed a waterfall from the side of a mountain alive with rocks and trees, spilling its slender, silvery stream to a pool below, where it turned to a near mist. To his right, where the valley sloped slightly upward, there was a sea of color—all color imaginable, from the brightest oranges and yellows, to equally radiant whites and reds … many shades of red, from maroon to crimson, the brilliant canvas framed by a dozen shades of green. Mac realized he was seeing flowers, perhaps millions of them, growing as wild as the untamed land on which he now stood. There was no sign anywhere of Man, only Nature at Her most beautiful, Her proudest.

"Miguel," he uttered. Nothing more … only the man's name. Mac watched as Miguel crossed himself, kissed his Saint Christopher medallion, and whispered a brief prayer.

Mac's gaze returned to the clearing. Below, at the foot of a winding path, he saw a flat expanse, stretching for perhaps a half dozen or more acres, bounded by exotic plants and huge trees, yet even more flowers, their effulgence in sharp contrast to the periwinkle sky and verdigris carpeting. And the birds—everywhere there were birds. Ivory-colored ones, blue-colored ones, multi-colored ones. Mac guessed the ones plumed with the emerald crests and scarlet underbellies were the *quetzals*. An endangered species, and Mac saw why. Stunning in their beauty, they were unwary trophies waiting to happen. He felt a pang of guilt at his once upon a time sarcastic reference to the naming of the country's currency after its national bird.

The cacophony drew his attention from the vegetation. It had to be the birds. Their chatter muffled any sound from the waterfall, a half-kilometer away, maybe more.

Time stood still for Mac. It was not until Miguel touched his arm that Mac became aware again of the presence of another living human.

"Was it worth giving up our comfortable ride in the truck?" The question

53

✝

carried a touch of smugness.

Mac's reply came as if time-delayed, spoken in slow motion. "Yes, Miguel, I very much approve." He dropped to the ground, needing a rest from the brisk walk, a moment to collect his thoughts. "Tell me, Miguel, how long had my daughter known of this paradise?"

"Oh, *Señor* Mac, since she came to our village. Perhaps even on her first day here." He seemed to scratch his head, as if more precision were on Mac's mind. "I am not sure, now that you ask. Maybe a little bit less. But why do you ask?"

"No reason in particular." In his lie he slumped, torn he'd never know why Nicole hadn't shared this with him and Elizabeth. Why not? Sadness knifed him in the heart.

"Where is the village from here?" His tone spoke of impatience. That and other thoughts swirled in his mind as he followed Miguel across the valley, and up the hillside into Refugio.

Nothing had changed. Nothing. Other than, Mac bitterly resented, Refugio was a few people shy of its former population. He had expected to see signs of struggle, chaos, destruction, but saw none. Only a few villagers were milling about. There were no frolicking children as before, however. There were no troops patrolling, as he would have expected. Mac found this unlikely, and asked Miguel where the soldiers were.

"*Señor* Mac, there is much to talk about, much for you to learn about. But you have traveled many miles, and now must rest. Tomorrow we will talk more."

Mac declined the kindness. "Miguel, I thank you for your offer, and for everything else today, but I am here for only one thing, and it is not rest." He cleared his throat, and with a slight tremor in his voice, continued. "I would like for you to take me to my daughter, please."

Miguel studied Mac before speaking. "*Sí*, I will take you there now, if you wish." Clearly Miguel was disappointed.

"It is. Later we can talk about where the soldiers are."

"Come with me, please." Miguel broke into stride for a point across the village square.

They entered a small, detached structure which Mac thought to be uninhabited. The outer room was completely empty. Miguel led the way through a second doorway, down a hallway into the rear area. Mac heard shuffling noises, then what he thought might be muted voices. Miguel opened yet another inside door and stepped in, Mac closely behind. Very little of the light of day made its way into this second inner room. There Mac found waiting for him his second grand surprise of the day.

Centered in the room, surrounded by four women ranging in age from perhaps twenty to sixty, was a wooden casket, a magnificently carved and sculpted wooden casket, glistening in the flickering candlelight. It, too, was breathtaking. Instantly Mac felt shameful, for assuming Miguel to have been proud of no more than the simple coffin Mac had pictured. This was truly a work of artistic proportion. He turned to thank Miguel, who held up his hand as a gesture of silence.

"It is not necessary for you to say anything. Please. I will take these women, and we will leave you alone. When you are ready, I will be down the street at the church, with Father Art. You remember where it is, *sí?*"

Mac looked squarely into the man's soulful eyes one more time, nodding in silent agreement. He made the same nodding gesture in the direction of the four women who had been standing vigil, as Miguel shooed them from the room. On his way out Miguel waved a simple good-bye. Mac went over to the doorway and watched as Miguel and the women slipped from view. He heard the outer door close a few seconds later. It was then it hit Mac. He was in a room with his daughter's body, sealed in the coffin hand-carved by this Miguel fellow. In no hurry, he just stood and looked at the casket for a moment, suppressing the host of thoughts and feelings, fighting to overcome the invisible force trying to yank the pounding heart from his chest, fighting even harder to hold back the tears he still had not shed, still wondering *why*. He did not move for over a minute. When he finally did, it was to the casket, which had been placed on a waist-high table covered by a simple white cloth. Mac bent at the waist and kissed her coffin, then touched it gently with one hand as he laid his head down on the cool wood, closed his eyes, prayed for the soul of his daughter, and begged for forgiveness he had allowed this to happen to her.

He was fatigued, and knew sleep was only the closing of his eyelids away. Yet he struggled against the full force of the aching tiredness that had all but consumed him. His arms splayed over the wooden box, his lips pressed again to the polished wooden contours whispering soft, private words to her. *Nicole, I'm here now, Daddy's here.* This time he would not let her down; this time he would be there when she needed him.

Daddy's so sorry, honey, so sorry.

He stood from his bowed stance and went to the candles, blowing out all but one. Returning to the casket, standing silently still, secure now in the satisfaction the hard part of this ordeal was at an end, he lowered himself to the floor, laid his head to rest on his forearm, closed his eyes, and yielded to his fatigue.

§

Dreams invaded Mac's slumber. Flashes of his wife, his children as youngsters, and Miguel, he of the sparkling eyes. A decoupage of these images, intermixed with Elizabeth clutching the small silver frame and the newswoman outlined by the bright light, made for a restless sleep on the hard floor. When the cool damp of the night set in, and Mac had no source of warmth, surreal, amorphous abstractions replaced more defined images. Consciousness battled subconsciousness for the rights to his thoughts; even in sleep, fear and guilt maintained their assault.

He sensed his arms were thrashing wildly, defensively at times, at other times striking out at the darkness threatening to deny him this second chance to protect her. So he fought harder still. He would recall this restlessness days later, when he sorted through the details. He would also recall the firm grip on his arms that settled their spastic flailing, and of soothing, prayer-like words spoken over him that mercifully brought calm.

Mac awoke to find a crude form of pillow under his head, and a colorful, hand-woven blanket covering him. Puddled wax remained where the candle had stood. Muted sunlight again speckled the room through the tiny cracks and openings in the walls and ceiling. How long had he been asleep? Worried he might have fallen behind schedule he bolted from the floor.

Stiff yet rested, Mac stretched his back and legs, rubbed his eyes. Grogginess yielded to sharp thoughts refocused on his mission. Taking care to fold the blanket, Mac set it and the pillow on a nearby chair, then started for the doorway. He stopped in mid-stride, and turned back to the casket. He placed a hand softly on the casket, and lowered his head. In seconds he was at the door.

The sunlight was blinding. As his eyes adjusted, he heard his name called. "Mac!" Again. "Mac, come over here." He recognized Father Art's voice. Visoring the sun with his hand, Mac's squint fell on a porch across the street, to a reclining chair in which the priest rested. Miguel sat to his right side, another man to his left. Mac started across the street, his pulse quickening.

The priest's voice was weak, but his greeting firm. "Miguel has brought me up from the church, where I could be in the sun … so I could see you first thing this morning. We gave up on you yesterday, not that you didn't need the rest." He looked ten years older to Mac, who didn't apologize for the few stolen hours of sleep.

Father Art did the introductions. "Mac, meet Evan Montgomery. He's about to leave us, but stayed to meet you. Miguel's just helped him load up for Panama City. Right, Evan?"

"Yes, that's right," the man said. He stood to greet Mac.

"The British journalist, right?" Mac shook his hand, but didn't ask about the section of shaved scalp or the stitches gruesomely standing out.

"Sorry I can't stay, but as the good padre says, I'm due in Panama City … in two days. I hope you understand."

"Certainly. Maybe someday your travels will bring you to our area, near New Orleans. You must stop in. We'd enjoy the visit."

"A kind offer. One never knows, Mr. McHenry. Perhaps I'll surprise you and the missus one day." After a casual wave of the hand, he was gone, Miguel in tow.

"Is he always that abrupt?" Mac asked, taking Montgomery's vacated chair.

"I suppose he is. He was also injured that night, you know. Deep gash on his head. You saw the stitches. It'll be a nasty scar."

Mac stared silently as the Range Rover drove away. He'd give anything to have Nicole back with just a nasty scar.

Then Miguel waved at Mac, and disappeared around a corner. Mac and Father Art were alone.

"You mustn't think unkindly of our English friend, Mac. He typically is not a social person. What happened has him as upset as the rest of us." He quickly added, "They were close, too, you know."

Mac just nodded, unsure what "close" meant, other than an impression he and Elizabeth shared that their daughter held some measure of feeling for the tall, sad-looking foreigner.

"Father," Mac began, "besides being here for my daughter, I need to learn what happened, why it happened. I'm not content with the simple explanation she met a violent death during a rebel uprising. I need your help. I'd hoped for Montgomery's help too." Mac's gaze was firm.

"My friend, I'm sure you will speak to Monty soon enough. Meantime, I'll tell you all I know. The problem is, I remember so little. Earlier, before the chaos, we'd been at the church. When the gunfire started we became separated. I was in the church tending some wounded when she came in with Pablo, a young soldier she was particularly close to. He was mortally wounded, and she was comforting him in his final minutes.

"The next thing I can recall is being outside, in the darkness, surrounded by fire and gunfire, and blurred images. The one clear vision I do have, and I am so sorry to have to say this, is seeing Sister Nicole laying not far from me, with a great deal of blood beneath her. It's all I can remember. I'm not much help. I'm so sorry, Mac."

It was not what he'd hoped for, and just hearing of his lifeless daughter in a pool of her own blood brought Mac to a state of controlled rage. He put his elbows to his knees, and buried his face into his up-reaching hands, rubbing gently his eyes, temples, forehead. He felt no need to speak, and kept his silence. He felt no need to move, and maintained his stillness.

"Mac, there's something else I must tell you. Please don't think unkindly—"

"Father, just tell me, for God's sake, whatever it is. Don't make me promise something just to hear how my daughter died."

The priest put a hand on Mac's shoulder. "Miguel would have told you himself, but I asked him to let me."

An uneasy feeling began to creep over Mac.

"Of those who rose up in rebellion, there is one who survived. He is imprisoned in Guatemala City. His name is Carlos."

"Yes, I have heard there is a rebel survivor. He is to be executed soon."

"Mac," Father Art continued, "Carlos is Miguel's son."

8

M AC WAS DEEP in thought when he heard someone nearing, and was not surprised when Miguel entered the room. "Come in, Miguel," he said, returning
his gaze to the polished wood encasing his daughter. "I've been expecting you. I can't
wait to hear your explanation."

"*Gracias, Señor* Mac, but please do not be angry … it's not as you think."

"Miguel, I am a lawyer. Lawyers are used to surprises. But I have to say, I wasn't
ready for this one."

"You must believe me, my son had nothing to do with Sister Nicole's death. Nothing. If anything, he risked his own life to prevent it."

Miguel went on. "I would have told you, but Father Art wanted to tell you himself."

Mac turned to the contrite confessor. "Say I believe what you say about your son.
What might he tell me no one else seems to know? Not even the Church."

"The rebels did everything in secrecy. No one knew. Only my son can answer your
questions. And they will not let anyone from the village see Carlos." Miguel paused.
"They tell the Church he is to be executed."

"I see." Mac knew what must be done. He returned his gaze to the coffin.

"This is a wonderful piece of work, Miguel. You are quite a craftsman."

Miguel approached tentatively. "Have you looked at the engravings?"

"A few, but not all," Mac answered truthfully. "Some are confusing."

Mac stepped aside while Miguel lit a candle and moved closer. "I had so little time,
or could have done much more. See, here, this is the church," he said, directing Mac's
attention to the first of the intricate carvings. One by one he led Mac down the wood-
en pathway of his daughter's Guatemalan life.

"Here is her guitar. These two figures are you and *Señora* McHenry. And this is
the handsome lad, with his foot on the soccer ball." Mac thought of the young soldier

Father Art told him about, who'd also died that night.

Miguel could have continued, but Mac stopped him. The last engraving spoke for itself: a small girl whose hand was being held by a taller woman in nun's habit. Mac smiled ruefully. His daughter and the child Maria. The miracle child Maria. Mac knew even less about this story than he did of Nicole's death. Under other circumstances Mac would have had many questions for Miguel and Father Art. He would save them for another time.

Mac put his arm across the artisan's shoulders. "Thank you, Miguel. From me, from my family, we all thank you. You have honored us, and Sister Nicole." His tone turned somber.

"Will you help me get her into our truck? If we leave now, and travel all night, we can make Guatemala City tomorrow with daylight remaining." Drawing a deep breath, and clasping Miguel's arm, he said, "And tomorrow, we will try to see your son." He watched for Miguel's reaction. It was not what he expected.

"*Señor* Mac, I ask that you let me make a request," Miguel pleaded.

"Can't this wait? We can talk about it on the drive. And didn't you hear what I just said, about your son?"

"*Sí*, I heard. But *Señor* Mac, what I wish to say cannot wait. I will not be going back with you … you must return without me. I would have no way of returning before next week. And I already know, even if you are allowed to see Carlos, they would not permit me to."

Mac felt a troubling uneasiness. "What are you asking of me?"

Miguel wasted no time. "This village is little more than a few homes and a church, and a few people. Before Sister Nicole came, no one knew we existed. We did not even appear on a map. Yet, in one year we are in the news around the world twice. In another month, or perhaps two, we will be forgotten again. The world will find other places for its attention, and our village will return to obscurity."

Mac could not imagine where this was headed, yet he did not interrupt. Years of trial law had told him, *Let the witness talk, you're liable to learn something.*

"What I am saying is, for the first time, the survival of our tiny village is threatened. Refugio will collapse from its guilt and shame in the death of your daughter," he blurted. "It is this simple: *Señor* Mac, she belongs here." He stopped, this time because there was no surprise, no mystery left. It was Mac's turn to speak.

At first Mac didn't understand. Then it all came home, everything from the deliberate selection of Miguel to shepherd him to the village, the extraordinary kindness of the man, the detour through Paradise, the confessed deceit regarding Carlos, then the finale: the hand-carved coffin for his daughter's burial. It all made sense now. That was the plan all along, wasn't it? Sure it was. Feeling more hurt than angry, he tried not to take too much out on the old man. He just wanted to go home, where he could bury his daughter and try to salvage a host of shattered lives.

"Miguel," he began, "my daughter will be buried near our home—her home—in Madisonville, Louisiana, where the trees grow tall and the flowers bloom freely, very much like there." He waved in the direction of the hidden valley. "I understand how the village may feel, I truly do. But what you ask, it just isn't possible. I could never—I don't expect you to accept my decision, but you must respect it."

Miguel hung his head. "Please do not think badly of me, but you must hear this. The villagers believe if you take her body from us, so also will you take her spirit, her soul. If they were true believers, it would not matter if her body is taken away. But they are superstitious in many ways, and believe there can be no soul apart from the body."

Mac started to speak, but Miguel interrupted.

"The villagers, even though innocent in Sister Nicole's death, believe they are damned for what happened, that evil will visit us unless she remains. Whether you understand this or not does not matter. What matters is that you believe me."

Mac exhaled. He summoned the strength to remain calm, to resist falling victim to the incessant assault on his privacy, longing desperately for a return to a life where his likeness, like Refugio, was obscure, unknown, as it had once before been, before his daughter's death.

"Miguel, it just isn't possible to bury my daughter here. The village will have to find some other way to hold onto its memory of her, some other means of coping with its guilt, some other way to deal with its superstitious beliefs."

Mac reminded Miguel of his schedule, making it clear he could not stay any longer. "Sí," Miguel said. "I understand. Please wait here. I will bring her to you."

Mac cleared his thoughts. This foolishness about abandoning his daughter a second time in this wretched village only strengthened his resolve not to become distracted again from his mission, and to hasten his return home. He had only one more objective to accomplish before he caught his return flight.

9

"Welcome, Señor McHenry. Please come into my office." These words, spoken by Jose Ricardo de Orellana, Deputy Minister of American Affairs, brought Mac back from the lethargy into which he had been lulled for the four hours he had sat and waited for the audience. In truth Mac had expected a much longer wait. His plea to Dillon for help brought no promises.

But this was no ordinary audience he'd been given. This was back-door politics, a favor that would no doubt call for one in return. The kind of thing Dillon surely knew about.

"I must apologize for the wait I have put you through, Señor McHenry. Perhaps if we had known more in advance of your visit ..."

"Señor de Orellana," Mac began, "I have so little time. Please pardon my American impulsiveness, but you know why I am in your country?"

"Yes, we are aware of the reason for your visit. Please let me say, and I speak for not only myself but my country as well when I tell you how saddened we are at your loss. Such a needless tragedy. We could have been of so much more assistance to you."

Mac could see the man was seeking approval. All he could think of at the moment was the troop transport that ran him and Miguel off the road. "Please don't concern yourself, Deputy Minister. It is my own fault for not seeking out the courtesy I know your government would have extended me." Mac could be diplomatic when it mattered.

"Now, Señor McHenry, what is it my country can do for you?"

He knows why I'm here. Why must we play cat-and-mouse? Mac fought to maintain his self-restraint, knowing if he lost control, didn't play the perfect part, his mission would be only half completed. He had come too far, endured too much, to be denied by his own foolhardiness. Dillon's admonitions crossed his mind as well. He answered cautiously, in a decidedly measured and well-rehearsed manner.

"Deputy Minister, there is only this one matter—for which you have most graciously given me your time—holding me from my return to America, and the burial of my daughter. And it is about this matter that I seek this audience with you, sir." The whole time he explained what he was after, Mac never relaxed direct eye contact with the official.

After a brief pause, the words Mac hoped to hear were spoken. "I believe we may be able to help you, *Señor* McHenry."

———————

An hour later Mac was seated at a table in a windowless room. Two empty chairs on the other side of the table faced him. A bulb so caked with petrified dust it resembled a rotted pear dangled from a strand of ancient electrical wire. It gave off little light. The floor was cool, made of chiseled stone set in old mortar. The walls were cracked plaster, painted in white long since yellowed with age and neglect. The room smelled of dankness, the mildewy kind that permeates leaky cellars. Even though Mac's criminal practice was limited, he knew it was not an uncommon odor in the jails of south Louisiana.

The Deputy Minister had made it clear to Mac he had half an hour with the prisoner.

Startled by the noise of the heavy metal door opening, Mac looked up to see a shackled man being led into the room by two guards, followed by a fourth man dressed in typical Latin American business dress. After the prisoner—who looked younger than Mac would have imagined—had been seated, the dapper one dismissed the two guards.

"*Señor* McHenry, I am Roberto, and am here to be your interpreter. We have only thirty minutes, so I suggest we move quickly."

"Roberto, we both know this man speaks English, at least well enough to communicate with me. You are welcome, of course, to stay, but please, in the interest of time, there is no need for your services as a translator."

Roberto grinned knowingly, and gestured with a wave of his hand for Mac to proceed.

"Very good," Mac acknowledged, turning back to the prisoner. He bore no visible marks of abuse, Mac quickly noticed. That was a plus; he needed the man to be coherent. "*Señor* Mendez—Carlos—you were there the night my daughter, Sister Nicole, was killed?"

"*Sí*," he answered.

"Did you know her killer? Do you know why she was killed?"

Carlos started to speak, then hesitated, throwing a nervous glance at Roberto. Mac understood: under a sentence of death, but apparently of some use to his captors, the man would protect himself at all cost. But Mac had no choice; he had to bear down. "*Carlos*, I need to know the facts leading up to what happened in Refugio the night my daughter was killed. Please, tell me in your own words. Don't spare any detail, however painful to me you think it might be."

The prisoner, nervously looking sideways at the well-dressed man beside him for some sign of approval, and receiving only a slow, deliberate blink of his eyes, began his account.

"Our village had always been peaceful. We knew there was war in the rest of the country, but we had never seen any sign of it. The soldiers, the guerillas, all of them had left us alone.

"One day a stranger arrived. He just appeared. He sought out only a few of us at first, one at a time, those he felt could be trusted with silence. He spoke to us of greater freedom than we already had, and promises of education—more than our simple village school had to offer—and other things. We began to listen to him."

Mac interrupted. "Who was this man?"

"We never learned his name, but we learned later he was one of the rebels. He came to our village, like many of his brothers to other villages in Petén, to unite all villages in the north to rise up against the government.

"For months," Carlos went on, "this man trained us, secretly in the night. He showed us how to aim weapons, fire and reload them. We never fired them, but we knew how. After the troops came, we knew somehow our plan had been discovered. But still the mountain villages planned their revolt. It was supposed to be a united strike, villages throughout the north rising up together, to show we were organized and willing to fight and die for our cause. All," he emphasized, "were committed to the possibility of death for our beliefs.

"Secrecy was kept at all cost. Each village had just a handful who knew. In Refugio," Carlos added, "less than twenty knew of the plan. One of these men was Juan Pedro Vega de Zea, who had been my friend since moving to the village as a young man. He did not need to be convinced to join the rest of us when the rebel stranger came to our village. Juan spoke of sacrificing his life if others might become free."

Mac heard Carlos speak of this man as a leader, not as a maniac. He wondered, without interrupting, how this obsession with freedom could have led to his daughter's death at the villager's hand. He checked his watch, fearful of losing sight of the time. Carlos noticed, and apologized for dwelling too long on things that did not matter any longer.

"Please, do not apologize. I need to know every detail."

Carlos resumed his narrative, quickly covering the details of the planned insurrection. It was hoped, he explained, that once the uprising had begun the remaining village men would join in, in a show of support, and the crude weapons they possessed—hoe, axe, machete and scythe—would be useful.

"In fact," Carlos added, "this did not happen. The village did not support us ... but we were prepared."

A nervous twitch, the broken eye contact, and Mac recognized the lie. It made sense. Perhaps Carlos knew there had been no retaliation against the village by government forces. Even if he didn't know, he was taking no chances. Mac admired his courage.

"The evening before the strike, something went wrong," resumed the prisoner, "really badly wrong in Refugio. Our leader was killed by the garrison commandant. Juan took command, and he wanted to go forward that night." Carlos glanced at the official. Mac urged him to continue.

"Juan told us we must go on, that to wait another night would jeopardize everything we had planned. The rest of us blindly followed him, and struck a full night early.

"Without our leader we had no chance, no chance." Carlos paused. Mac was wondering why when the prisoner looked up from the table, pain in his eyes.

"*Señor*, are you sure you wish me to continue? This part, it is not, it is not—"

Apprehension surged within as Mac calmly asked him to continue.

"I was in the streets, searching for soldiers from house to house and building to building. All had to be accounted for. Juan," he continued, "was also looking for more soldiers. We found three, and took them captive. Then Juan went to the church. I followed him."

Tears formed in Carlos's eyes. "The village was in flames, our real leader was dead, and Juan was like a madman. None of us had ever seen him like that before. Everything was happening so fast. We found a wounded soldier in the church. Juan shot him, and became furious at Sister Nicole for comforting him. He pulled her outside, and put her with the prisoners. I could not stop him.

"Sister Nicole, she was kneeling, praying, while this was happening, while Juan became like a wild animal. Then I saw him put his pistol to Sister Nicole's head. I could

65

†

not free myself. But I heard *Señor* Monty's voice, and watched as Juan turned and fired at him as he ran toward us. I broke free then, and threw myself at *Señor* Monty. We both went down. Afterward, all I remember is clearing my head, and looking up to see Juan's arm lifted up, holding a machete, about to strike down. I grabbed before he could. I thought I had saved her, I truly did, until I looked down and saw the blood. So much blood."

Mac was struggling to hold up. He watched as Carlos broke down uncontrollably, shoulders heaving, loud sobs choking any other sounds.

In a moment, Carlos crossed himself, and muttered a silent prayer. "You must understand. None of us knew what was happening. Death in our village had always come from disease, or old age, or evils of the jungle. Never by the sword, or by gunfire. It was in this confusion, in this moment of uncertainty, no one could react to what was happening."

He paused, fretfully confessing, "Before anyone could do anything … please, you must believe me. I would have given my life that your daughter did not lose hers." Mac could barely restrain himself; yet another wish someone else might have died besides his daughter. Didn't *anyone* know better?

"She did not suffer, this I can promise you. I was there, at her side, only a few seconds after he'd struck her, but she was already gone. There was nothing that could be done. It was over … it was over." His voice thinned.

Stillness hung as an iron shroud over the room. Beating hearts boomed like cannons, throats swallowing scraped as sandpaper on rough wood. Mac tried to move, but could not. He conjured an image of racing to his daughter, of vainly trying to throw himself between cold steel and warm tissue, between hatred and madness and beauty and innocence. Feelings of rage gave way to frustration, feelings of bitterness to confusion. Again, *why?* As it had been since the beginning, it was always back to *why?*

Mac slowly rubbed his eyes, and massaged his temples, as he found himself doing more and more these days. After what seemed an eternity he could speak, if only in a hushed tone. He asked the prisoner if she had cried out, if she had said anything, anything at all. *Nothing,* was the reply. She had said nothing. For such a violent death, she died very peacefully, he concluded.

Roberto interrupted Mac's questioning. "*Señor* McHenry, I am sorry, but our time is up. I truly am sorry."

"Please, I think there is very little left. No more than a moment or two, I give you my word," Mac pleaded. Roberto shrugged indifferently, holding up two fingers.

Mac did not have to ask Carlos to go on. He regained his composure, and resumed his story. "My father came running up. We knelt beside her. Both of us were crying. Everyone who saw it happen began to run away. I grabbed two men and ordered them to take Juan over to the building where our dead leader sat. Then my father helped me carry Sister Nicole to the church. The priest, he was also on the ground, but he was still alive. Two women tended him.

"When Sister Nicole was laid gently down, I returned to Juan. I demanded he explain why he had done this horrible thing, to one so beloved. I told him any hope of the revolution succeeding had perished with Sister Nicole, that no one, no sympathetic person or government, would condone this senseless murder. I swore at him, I damned the soul of the man who had brought disgrace on our noble effort.

"When he looked up at me, I realized he was insane, truly insane. The eyes were empty. He talked in whispers ... to himself."

Mac remained motionless, did not speak. Carlos continued.

"I looked at the other two men, and signaled they should leave. When I was alone with Juan, I loaded my last cartridge and placed the pistol on the table between us. As I left the room I told him to beg for God's mercy on his soul.

"In a few seconds the shot rang out. It was done. The troops arrived moments later. I gave myself up. I heard more shooting later, probably the soldiers finding those who ran off into the night. I think they were all killed. I believe I am the only one left."

He begged Mac for forgiveness, tears again streaming down his face.

Mac wasn't there for apologies. Only answers ... one in particular. "Carlos, think hard, please. Insane or not, this Juan must have felt hatred toward my daughter. Why? What caused it?"

"He never spoke badly of your daughter. Sometimes he had these terrible dreams, and spoke of demons in his head, but we never saw him like he was that night."

Roberto stirred uneasily. Mac pressed his luck.

"Tell me, what of your revolution? Is it to use my daughter's death as a rallying cry?"

Carlos looked worriedly at Mac. "That is not in my control. If it were, I would have all lay down their weapons, and extinguish their hatred—rebels and soldiers alike. There is already enough killing, already enough loss of innocent blood. I am so sorry it was your daughter's. Even more because of the gift of life she gave to my daughter Maria."

He looked expectantly at Mac. "You have heard of the miracle?"

Mac pushed himself from the table. Anger was building ... another deceit had surfaced. "Yes, I have heard. My wife and I have even met Maria. I have also met your father ... Maria's grandfather. Miguel. Miguel the carpenter. Let me guess: Maria lives in Refugio with your father and your wife, doesn't she?"

"*Sí.* Why do you ask this now?"

Mac looked at Roberto, coolly. "I think I'm finished now." Mac left the interview room without another word.

68

†

10

Two hours later, seated alone in first class, Mac was bound for home. None of the few other passengers seemed to register signs of recognition. He hoped it signaled a total change.

He had called Elizabeth. Yes, Nicole was with him, he was bringing her home. Had Nicole mentioned anything about a valley she frequently visited? he'd asked. No reason, he lied when Elizabeth said no and wondered why he'd asked. When her tears started, he lied again and told her it was last call to board, and speedily wished her a loving good-bye. Mac hated lying to his wife, for any reason, but her tears were not something he could handle at the moment.

His thoughts turned to the meeting with Carlos, to the details surrounding Nicole's death. For all the new information he had, there was still much unsaid, unknown. The doomed man had done his best to help. For all the hatred he felt, Mac could not hold the man responsible for Nicole's death. Yet there was another reason his life had to be spared.

In a brief, heated discussion with the Deputy Minister before he'd left for the airport, Mac had made his feelings on the subject of the prisoner quite clear: there must be no summary execution, nothing to fuel further killing. His daughter's memory would not be tarnished by the politics of murder. When Mac needed help, the timely call to Mr. Thomas Dillon at the State Department's New Orleans office had convinced the Deputy Minister the prisoner should stay put for now.

Just how long was anyone's guess.

He put Carlos Mendez out of his mind as he watched his daughter's coffin being loaded onto the plane. He'd been through much in the past three days, but nothing had prepared him for that sight. The coffin also reminded him of Miguel. Mac was torn between resentment of the man for his deceit and appreciation for the artisan's devotion to his daughter.

Mac could forgive Miguel when it came to his son Carlos. But this deceit over Maria was different. That omission had been deliberate. But it didn't fit with everything else Miguel stood for. Mac wondered if he would ever know. The search for truth was wearing thin.

———————

The deputy minister hung up the telephone. The airport official confirmed takeoff, moments earlier. Satisfied the American was gone, the minister sighed heavily. He regretted the way he'd raised his voice in anger, chiding himself. If only he hadn't been so persistent, so direct …

The American's meddling had become problematic, but the deputy minister knew when the United States of America spoke to him through its State Department, urging restraint, extending the life of a cockroach did not matter.

He reached for the telephone again. The Minister of Prisons might not understand either, but for the moment, the life of the prisoner would be spared.

———————

Mac found very little relaxation on the flight home. He had demons of another nature waiting for him when he arrived, and little time to prepare for them. There would be the matter of his daughter's quick, and very private, burial and of resuming his care of Elizabeth. And of getting on with life. That would be the hardest part.

He dozed somewhere over the place on the map where the land turns into the Gulf of Mexico. Sleep was fitful, dreams coming again in abstract, kaleidoscopic images. He felt himself running, but not moving, seeing through the dreamer's eyes, darkened, surreal scenes before him, struggling, straining, frantically trying, powerless to stop a drawn blade from its downward arc. Not knowing who held it, or the target of its sweeping motion, seeing the weapon as an extension of an outreached arm, only the glint of polished steel reflecting moonlight, for darkness was everywhere in this vision. Even in sleep the dreamer knew what the image portrayed. Try as he might, he could not move, and the blade swept downward, again and again.

He awoke in a state of terror, soaked in his own perspiration. His shirt clung like a second skin. Looking about, he was strangely comforted when he saw no one. He was thirsty, but suffered his thirst rather than draw attention to himself.

He fought sleep with all his remaining strength, but the emotional and physical fatigue bearing down on him took no prisoner. As he slipped away he prayed, for the first time in over a week. He prayed it would all just go away.

§

The knock interrupted some light reading. Mac opened the door to find a tall, nice-looking young man standing a respectful distance down the walk. Clearly not at ease, he appeared almost apologetic to the eye.

"Yes, may I help you?" asked Mac.

"Not exactly, Mr. McHenry. If I may have a moment of your time, I've come to make an apology."

Mac started to say something rude, then thought better of it. "Please, come in," he said instead.

"No, sir, if it's all the same, I'll stay out here. I won't take long."

His attempt to relax the visitor obviously had failed. "What is it I deserve an apology for, young man?" Mac asked. "I don't recognize you, and don't know of any outstanding apologies I'm due."

"You may not recognize me, sir, but you'll remember me. I came here one night about three weeks ago … in the middle of the night would be a better description." He shifted his stance, looked away, then back, and continued. "I was the cameraman behind the light in your eyes when you opened the door for Elise—the newswoman who came here to tell you, well, to—" Mac cut him off sharply.

"That was a painful memory ago. I don't care to relive it, frankly. I've just buried my daughter, and am trying to piece a bunch of lives back together. So to be quite honest, if you'll excuse me I'm pretty much fresh out of sympathy for others."

Mac watched the young man recoil. He immediately felt badly about his scornful rebuke. Mellowing, he said, "But, hey, who am I to be so unforgiving? You have come here with a heavy heart, or something like it, and want to atone. What can I do to make you feel better about what it is you've done, or think you've done, wrongfully to me?"

"Mr. McHenry, my name is Ken, Ken Randall. Until a few days ago, I had a bright future as a news cameraman. I could film a story, better than anyone else. I could capture the very essence of a person's pain, or joy, or whatever. Now, I'm basically unemployed—I quit. What happened here convinced me I'm not cut out for that line of work any longer." The young man drew a long breath.

"That night, it didn't seem right. I tried to talk her out of it, I really did. I should have walked away, but I didn't. I let her lead me right up to your front doorstep. The look on your face when she broke the news to you, I captured it on the videotape."

"What happened to the tape? I don't recall seeing it on the news."

"I destroyed it. I watched it once, one time, and then destroyed it. By all the wrong standards it was probably pretty good work. But I just didn't feel right about it. And I lied to Elise, told her the camera never started, even though I had the light on. I don't think she believed me, and she stayed on me for days, until I finally yelled at her. Told her I wasn't lying, that she'd just have to accept it. And that ended my career as her cameraman."

Mac was skeptical. "What can I do for you, Mr. Randall?"

"It's Ken, please. All I ask is your forgiveness. The image of the pain on your face may take a while to become erased from my memory, but I will feel better if you accept my apology," he said, extending his hand.

Hesitating briefly, Mac reached out and shook his hand, tentatively, still unsure how to handle this unexpected situation. He asked, more out of politeness, "What will you do?"

"I'm not sure. I have a talent, just need to feel better about the way I use it. I'm from California, but I like this area, the Jazzfest, Mardi Gras, and all the crawfish and zydeco festivals. South Louisiana is my home now, and I'm not ready to leave."

Mac asked for a business card.

"I don't have any cards. Frankly, I don't even have a new business yet."

"Why don't you send me a card when you get set up," Mac suggested.

It was not until he'd been gone for a while that Mac realized he'd forgotten to ask how the young man had entered the gated community for the second time without a call from Security.

———————

Later, when Elizabeth listened to her husband tell of the young man's visit, and casually remark on the security breakdown, she could've told her husband how it had happened the young man was invited in, but then she'd have had to tell him about the call waiting tone, and the security guard interrupting her call to Barrett Dupuis, their doctor friend, about the symptoms she'd been experiencing, and the appointment she'd scheduled, and she didn't want to do that.

§

It had been three weeks since the private service for their daughter. Father Robichaux had spoken simple, caring words at the Mass for the young woman who had given her life to God. Words of tribute, commemorative of service to the higher calling. Conspicuously missing was any reference to a life cut far too short, of lost potential; the family wanted none of that. Burial followed immediately, with even fewer words spoken at the gravesite at the old cemetery in Madisonville, in the back, wooded part, the portion reserved for special residents.

It took less than two hours to pay respects to a twenty-three year life.

Only family attended. No friends, no press, no Church officials, nothing to distract or detract. This set poorly with the locals, who used the family's desire for privacy as something to talk about. Paulette shared a comment overheard at the grocery with Mac, who dismissed his secretary's concern with a wave of the hand. If the community felt snubbed it was unimportant to him.

On a more positive note, Mac reopened his law office. It had run well enough without him, Paulette handling all but the matters calling for the lawyer's hand. Judges and opposing counsel alike generously had granted extensions to deadlines.

Even on his return Mac continued to let Paulette man the laboring oar. He sensed more than saw her caring glances, and experienced more than once her corrections of his carelessness. The melancholy gripping him refused to relax its hold, as if he were powerless to stop a burglar from looting his life.

Uninspired, Mac for the first time in his life put less than all he could into his work. Soon opposing counsel and judges alike who had been understanding and tolerant began to lose patience. Discovery deadlines began to crowd him; trial preparation fell behind. Paulette could only bail a part of the water; the ship, while still afloat, was steadily sinking. Mac suffered even more as he watched his secretary's spirits sink as low as his own.

Inevitably the first letter came. It read as termination letters often do, antiseptically and unemotionally. His services, it began, were no longer required, and, it continued, he should turn over his file in the property boundary dispute matter to another lawyer.

Mac could not fault the decision; it was the prudent thing for his client to do. It would perhaps save him having to answer a Bar complaint or, worse yet, a malpractice claim. The thought of such actions brought Mac to his senses. In a moment of righteous awakening, he summoned Paulette. "Bring the Delahoussay file, we've got a trial to prepare for," came the familiar battle cry from the interior office. Mac noticed an immediate change in Paulette.

Feelings of guilt and grief gave way, and for a while it looked like better days were on the horizon. At least it seemed so at the time.

§

One particularly restful Saturday morning in mid-October—one of those rare days in deep south Louisiana when the heat and humidity give way to a short burst of cool, western air—not so long removed from the private burial of his daughter—Mac took a call from the gate. Would he receive a Mr. Montgomery? Mac was trying to place the name when the guard told him the gentleman was in town only for the day, and was leaving for England the next.

Mac recalled the visitor's name at the mention of England. He asked the gate guard to please send the man in, with directions to the McHenry home. Mac rose from the desk in his study where he had been writing letters to his sons, and headed outside. He saw Elizabeth, who looked to be planting bulbs for her Spring garden. He waved her over, but she just smiled in his direction, and did not return his wave.

Mac was about to fetch Elizabeth when he saw the unfamiliar car turn onto Empress Drive. It rolled to a stop a respectable distance from his standing spot. The driver stepped out, a tall man dressed in khaki slacks and a short-sleeved plaid sport shirt. Head bent, slow-gaited as he walked toward Mac, the man appeared ill at ease even before he spoke.

"Mr. McHenry, I hope I'm not intruding too greatly," spoke the visitor with the obvious British accent as he extended his hand in greeting.

"On the contrary, Mr. Montgomery," replied Mac, taking his hand. Their handshake was brief but firm. "What brings you to these parts for such a short stay? Most folks who get here make a vacation of it. My invitation was meant for more than a drop-in visit."

"Oh, I'm not the holiday sort of person, not any more, anyway. Actually, I had a day between stops on a hectic schedule, and found myself with an opportunity to see this area. I'd heard so much about it from—" He stopped, and shifted his stance nervously. "Might we go inside and talk? It's a pretty day here and all, but I'd feel better if we were inside."

Mac gestured instinctively. "Please forgive my lack of manners, Mr. Montgomery. Your visit comes as a surprise, and it's not every day I get thrown off track by someone who says words like *ackshwully* and *shejule* as you," he said in an attempt to relax the foreigner. "Let's go inside, and I'll get us something cool to drink."

As he led the way to the house, Mac noticed that Elizabeth was gone. He called out to her, eager for her to meet their guest. There was no answer. Perhaps she was already inside.

Seated in the den, each with a glass of sun tea crowned with a sprig of fresh mint from the yard garden, Montgomery spoke first. "Mr. McHenry," he began, "I—"

"Please, it's Mac. You're in the South now—we're a little lax on formality."

"Very well, Mac it is. And I am Monty. Evan always seemed so formal." Mac smiled in understanding.

"This is quite awkward for me. In fact, maybe my most difficult challenge since I stopped being a drunk four years ago."

Mac thought of the tall cameraman. "Monty, whatever it is you've come here for, you need to be the one who's comfortable about it."

"Yes, of course." There was yet another pause. "You must forgive me. Despite my having been over this a thousand times, in anticipation of this moment—preparing for this moment—I still find it difficult to say what I came here to say. Please just bear with me."

"Take your time … please."

"I was in the village that night," Montgomery blurted out. "I'd returned to warn them of the rebellion. I'd heard reports … " Montgomery was noticeably distraught.

Mac's attention instantly rose to a significantly higher level. He had not lost track of the still unanswered questions, of the mystery surrounding much of what happened.

"I saw it, oh dear God, I saw it."

Mac sensed more than remorse from his visitor. Guilt, perhaps? Mac knew all about guilt.

"I watched from my hiding spot, crouched like a coward as the chaos unfolded. I could not have imagined where it was headed, how it would all end." He paused for more tea.

Mac was listening to the confession of a troubled soul; there was no mistaking this. What words of comfort did his visitor expect? … want? … need? What power of forgiveness did the journalist see in his listener, who experienced daily much the same guilt? Mac was still wrestling with his thoughts when Montgomery spoke again.

"When I saw him point the gun at Nicole, I sprang from my hiding place and ran toward them, yelling for him to stop, not to do it. He fired at me. Bullets whistled by my head … strangely none struck me. I was still running and yelling when I collided with someone. We both went down. I struggled to get up, but a ton of weight was on me. I looked up from the ground where I lay, dazed, disoriented, and saw her being struck down." Another swallow of tea. "I was too late. I could not have stopped it." His head dropped, his voice barely audible. "I might have been in time if I had run sooner, or not fallen, I know that now. I finally did manage to stand, and desperately rushed to help Nicole … but I was too late, she was already gone.

"I have carried my shame, my guilt since then. It has such a fierce hold on me. Had I not hidden for so long I might have been able to stop what happened. She deserved that from me. I wonder how I will ever again be at peace." The tea finished in a last, long swallow, the visitor looked up at his host, his expression one of begging.

Mac finally spoke. "You were not the cause of her death, and you are not charged with the failure to save my daughter's life. You need no forgiveness, no redemption, from me or from Mrs. McHenry." The mention of his wife's name reminded Mac she was not in the room, but should be. He would not stop this conversation to find her, though; they could discuss it later, when the time was better.

Mac had spoken sternly to Montgomery. There was too much guilt, too much shame, he told himself after hearing the story. He came to believe he had the power to release his visitor and all the others—the villagers, the condemned prisoner in Guatemala City, even the wretched soul of her killer—from the grasp of pain, shame, guilt. It was his own he chose to hold onto so tightly. He would consider releasing himself from the weight of these crosses he had chosen to bear only when he was ready, when whatever penance, whatever atonement he felt was required of himself was made. But others, that was another matter. His grudge-bearing was not the answer for them. Best to help them let go.

Montgomery was silent. His head was still bowed when he finally spoke. "I hope you know how difficult this has been. I know I have no right to come here like this. In a way I hope my coming is good for you and the missus as well as for me. Can you understand?"

Mac nodded in acknowledgment. Thoughts of resuming his letter-writing had already crept back into his mind when his visitor spoke again.

In the following seconds, an instant Mac would play and replay in the following months, a few words spoken more as an afterthought than anything else would haunt Mac every waking moment, would drive him daily to exhaustion.

"If only she and Father Art had left the village earlier in the day, when the truck came for them."

II

ANY THOUGHT MAC HAD of resuming his letter writing, or of concern for the forgiveness-seeking visitor, were shoved aside. Instinctively, as he did so often with a witness, Mac asked simply, "I'm sorry, could you repeat what you just said, please?" This time, however, it was not a performance for judge or jury.

"Nicole and Father Art and I were sitting at a table in the kitchen when the truck from Guatemala City arrived. I'd already told them to leave, but they ignored me. The priest from the archdiocese was more forceful. He ordered them to leave with him.

"She and Father Art told the priest they were staying. They refused to leave with him. After he'd gone, a sense of the forlorn swept our table. It may have just been me, but I suspected the same sense gripped all three of us."

Montgomery nervously clasped his hands, then wrung his fingers. "We went in different directions. I went to make certain I had film and batteries ready. While preparing for what might happen, it occurred to me that I had not seen armed conflict in many years. A fear that I had experienced so long ago, and had forgotten, crept over me. I also forgot how unforgiving fear can be.

Montgomery's Adam's apple rose and fell. "I went outside after I prepared everything. I saw Nicole walking toward little Maria's house. She was in a hurry, and didn't see me. I look back now and wonder how it is that I could have been in such fear I would have so blithely thought she was not in the same, or worse, peril."

Mac thought better of interrupting. His mind still raced with Montgomery's news. The turmoil resurfaced, but now it was a monster, with blazing eyes and fiery breath and bared fangs and talons. There had been no mention of this in Father Art's sparse account. Mac wondered why. Nor in the prisoner's, but Carlos would not likely have known of the Church's visit. Father Art was another matter. Hadn't Mac asked him precisely about what had happened that night? *Where was the Church's candor?* Self-restraint became Mac's objective as Montgomery delved deeper into the events that claimed his daughter's life.

"I watched as villagers I had known for years, men who I had never known to show a mean spirit at anything, killed every man in uniform … ruthlessly, especially those executed after the fighting had stopped. I truly believe the few villagers who died were killed in their own crossfire, and not by fire from the troops. You see, the soldiers became as neighbors to the villagers, not enemies. I lived long enough among the people of that village, soldiers and peasants alike, to be certain."

Montgomery emptied his glass. "I know this as certain as I know the very cowardice that kept me from acting as a man that night." Setting the glass down, he rubbed his forehead, wiped at his eyes. Mac was insensitive to the man's agony.

"And I know why. It all changed when your daughter came to that horrid little village. There was the most wondrous spirit in her. Everyone loved her, villager and soldier alike. I could be forgiven thinking she could fall into no harm should there actually have been bloodshed, for who would have wanted her harmed, even if the bond of peace became broken?"

"Tell me about the devil who killed her," Mac said.

Mac watched his visitor twitch nervously at the entreaty. "A quiet, even mysterious fellow. But I remember he once became enraged when Nicole tried to persuade his wife to send their children to the school. I also recall Nicole telling me how she felt uneasy around him. Something about his eyes, she said, how they directed hardness at her, for no reason she could ascertain. But she did not confront him with her feelings. She confided her sense of failure to accept the man."

A thousand questions formed in Mac's mind.

"His house, strangely enough, was the nearest one to mine. But I hardly knew him. He kept to himself. I had the impression he avoided me, frankly. I spoke often with his wife, though. Once I asked her of the screams I heard from their house during the night. She said, quite matter-of-factly, it was demons, her husband felt he was possessed by them. He often awoke, trembling, speaking of these demons as he held her tightly. It seemed odd she would share something so personal with me, a stranger, but I also sensed it was no secret in the village, that I was perhaps the last to know.

"I did not know him to be a violent man. I never heard him raise his voice in anger to his wife or children. He gave no sign of harboring the kind of hatred he displayed that night."

"Monty," Mac began after a short pause, "can you be absolutely certain the Church sent word to my daughter, and to Father Art, of the insurrection? Please, I need to know how you are so certain."

"The truck was driven by one of the priests from Guatemala City, Father Rodriguez. He often brought the mail and supplies. I knew him well."

Mac rose, and paced the distance between the fireplace wall and the bay window, deep in thought, in a losing effort to hide his feelings.

"I should be going now," Montgomery said, as one who'd overstayed his welcome.

"Yes," Mac began. "Yes, I suppose you have much left to do, far to travel," he lamely finished, in barely more than a murmur, struggling not to explode in anger. "I'll see you out."

Montgomery stopped in the doorway, his signal Mac did not need to walk him to the car. "Mr. McHenry ... Mac ... I believed earlier you had forgiven me, and I accepted the forgiveness. Yet as I leave, I am deeply concerned I have said something to change things. This troubles me. Whatever I said, allow me the chance to make it right."

There was no hesitation in Mac's reply. "It is I who owes the apology, not you. I did hear something from you a while ago I hadn't heard before, something that, yes, troubles me deeply. I do not know where it will lead me. Please don't concern yourself. You did the right thing by coming here today. I won't forget. Don't give a thought, as you leave, to having brought me anything but good. I am in your debt for your kindness." Mac held out his hand to Montgomery, who took it hesitatingly into his own before he walked the short distance to his car.

———————————

As Montgomery reached for the door handle, he felt a slight touching sensation on his right shoulder, barely more than the weight of a raindrop. Instinctively he turned, half expecting to find nothing there. What he saw caused him to draw a large deep breath, and stumble backward.

79

✝

12

I DIDN'T MEAN TO startle you," Elizabeth said to the man staring wide-eyed at her. She reached for his arm, a friendly, calming gesture.

She felt him relax at her touch. "You must be Elizabeth," he said.

"Yes. And you must be Evan, judging by your height, and your sparkling accent." In the Southern tradition, she lightly embraced the shaken journalist, her soft cheek brushing against his day-old stubble. She asked him why he'd appeared so alarmed.

"I'd heard how she resembled you, but I had no idea how deeply the resemblance ran. You must forgive me, I was only taken aback at seeing someone who so reminded me of Nicole."

She smiled. "I like that you call her Nicole. Not Sister Nicole." She glanced at his car. "Were you leaving? I saw you arrive, while I was tending to my jonquils and peonies." She quickly added, "It's probably too early, but I can always replant." She searched his face for something, asking again, "Did you say you were leaving?"

"Well, actually, I was. I have just spoken with your husband. I'm sure he will fill you in. Now, I must leave for New Orleans. I have a plane to catch in the morning. Very bright and early, as you Americans say." His feet shifted on the asphalt road. Elizabeth sensed he was nervous.

"But you must stay with us tonight," she insisted. "The drive across the lake is no more difficult in the morning as it is tonight, perhaps less so if you are feeling worn."

"I do appreciate the kind offer, but I have a guaranteed reservation at the Windsor Court, which will cost me dearly to forfeit. Besides," he added, "I believe I have somewhat overstayed my welcome with your husband."

Elizabeth frowned. "I don't understand, of course, but I'm sure he will tell me everything," she said evenly. "I doubt my husband would feel badly about someone our daughter cared so much for."

Looking around, then in the direction of the house, Elizabeth quickly turned back to the guest, who again appeared to be feeling ill at ease.

"Evan," she began, "will you follow me somewhere, right now? No questions … just on pure faith. I won't slow you long, just a short while really." Eyes wider open than normal and her forehead furrowed, she had a questioning look of near desperation, matched equally by the urgency in her voice. He didn't disappoint.

"How could I possibly refuse such an offer? But of course."

She smiled, and hugged him again. "Thank you. This will all be clear to you shortly."

———————

He followed her Saab convertible onto State Highway 21. Not far down the same road he saw a sign announcing the river he'd crossed earlier. Montgomery wondered what kind of name "Tchefuncte" was, Indian perhaps, maybe even French, and what it meant. He thought about the country club and development laying within the sheltered and gated exterior he'd just left, at how serene and secure it appeared. This family led a safe existence, nothing like the daughter had the last year of her life. He wondered how difficult it had been for her to walk away from all this, or, on further thought, how easy it had been.

Elizabeth hadn't lied. They had driven only a moment when her rear flasher signaled a right turn into the private cemetery. Three massive live oaks stood as vanguards at the entrance. A dozen more were inside, sentries standing watch over the rows of white and gray stones marking the passing of life. She stayed on the white shell road until it ended, where things became dense and darker. He pulled to a stop and watched as she started down a worn, narrow footpath.

He followed at a distance, eventually joining her where she knelt beside the headstone bearing Nicole's name, dates of birth and death, and the inscription, "Truly God's Angel." He was instantly overwhelmed by the woman's pain, and once more by his own guilt. Fresh flowers adorned the spot, their scent reminiscent of another wooded setting. He sat beside her.

She spoke softly. "I try not to let a day go by that I don't come here to talk to my daughter. If Bradley knew I talked with the spirits, even my own daughter's, he would swear I'd taken leave of my senses, so I don't tell him what I do in the afternoons while he's at his office." She appeared quite smug in her deception. Montgomery said nothing, just listened.

"I know about you," she said next, turning to face him. "I know, for instance, you were in love with my daughter."

Montgomery lowered his head, a silent confession. She returned her gaze to the headstone and earthen plot marking her daughter's resting place.

"Do I make you feel uncomfortable?" she asked next. "Maybe I have lost my senses, and my husband would be right about me. Do you think he's right?"

"Elizabeth," he began, "there was no time I spoke to your daughter of my feelings for her. That was something I kept entirely to myself." He picked at the grass, dropping it a blade at a time as he fought not to say anything with a ring of bitterness.

"But I came to realize it was not a physical love. Too late, I knew it as a spiritual love. Before I knew the difference, I was tortured by my feelings for your daughter. Strangely, almost, it was because of your daughter," he continued, "I grew to know the difference. I think, if I had to define my feelings for her more precisely, I should be more inclined to think of myself as wanting to protect her, to care for her. And I failed so miserably . . ." He began to weep. "I told myself I would not let this happen," he said, reaching for a handkerchief.

He'd made his confession, but there was more. "Your coming here is not a bad thing, Elizabeth. You mustn't think Mac would think so. Your daughter is gone; that is a sorrow no parent should endure. If spending time with her like this will help you get by, then this is where you belong." He reached out his hand to touch her shoulder.

"She spoke so lovingly of you. She called you her dearest friend."

Elizabeth tilted her head where her temple brushed against his hand. Her recognition of his kindness complete, he withdrew his hand. They were on even ground.

"I'm having a bit of a tough go of it myself without her." He looked at Elizabeth, apology written into his expression. "I have no right to say that, especially here, now." Another unspoken plea for forgiveness. He wished hers would make him feel better than her husband's had. Mac's almost hostile response was still fresh.

He'd have to wait. Elizabeth took a detour, forgiveness perhaps not on her mind at the time.

"Tell me what it was like to know my daughter as you did. I know so little of her life down there. Only a few letters, and the short visit last year, when my husband and I stayed in your house. And of course your wonderful stories on her. But what was it like, to be her friend?"

Montgomery obliged Elizabeth with all he knew of the last year of her daughter's life. She probed for and soaked up the tiniest of details. "So many lives," he lamented, "that could have gained from her wondrous, marvelous spirit. So much wasted." The words forbidden at her memorial service, now sounding so right, so dignifying to her memory.

Then it was Montgomery who listened in awe as the mother reciprocated with stories of her own … of Nicole's happy childhood, growing up small-town with a worldly flair, of her ambition to master everything—even the soccer her larger, more athletic younger brother Chris excelled in naturally. Elizabeth referred to her daughter once as the poster child for the word *driven*. The mood sunk briefly as Elizabeth spoke of a boy named Tommy, Nicole's only beau, ever. *Ever* spoken with such finality. Young love begun in the seventh grade, continued throughout graduation from high school, then even to the first years of college. A nice boy, she said as her voice faded.

"We had always thought they would marry," she continued, her voice picking up. "Things just sort of unraveled for them during her third year away at college, and then, of course, Nicole came home and, next thing we knew, she was off to become a nun. Just like that, no warning. It crushed Tommy," she added, "just devastated him. I don't think he's over it yet. With Nicole gone, we don't see much of him anymore."

She gathered her skirt under her legs, running her fingers over the grass. "The miracle. What can you tell me about the miracle? The Church hushed it up so, we never had a chance to talk to her about it."

"Was it really—? I mean, did she …?" The probing expression again …

He flushed with the recollection. He still had his own unresolved conflict. "I was there … I saw what I saw. I'm not much of a believer, but I stood there as the doctor pronounced the child dead, and saw with my own eyes as she recovered as Nicole held her."

"But did you sense, *feel*, you'd witnessed a miracle?" Her eyes penetrated layers of acquired disbelief.

"I wrote of the miracle in the mountains, but I'm not sure. There was no heavenly sign, if that's what you mean. It was just a conclusion we all reached. Maria was gone, then she wasn't. I'm told the Church is still investigating it, unsure it was not some medical abnormality."

"As a Catholic I want to believe. As her mother, I am not sure what to think. Do you find that strange?"

"Elizabeth, I'm a terribly poor source for the answer to that one. But I suppose you should remember her the way it brings you the most joy. Hold onto what's dear, and let the others struggle with the uncertainty."

"Yes, I suppose."

Melancholy emanating from her voice, Montgomery knew it was time to leave. What little cheer there'd been must not be allowed to give way to less. He reached for her hand.

"You so remind me so of her. I feel you have been cheated today because of that."

"How so?" she asked. "I don't understand."

"I feel I have had extra moments with her today, vicariously through you," he replied. He caught the sparkle in her eyes before she spoke.

"Evan, what a beautiful thing for you to say. I am so moved by your words." She affectionately pressed his hand between hers as she spoke. "Yet it is you who have brought me joy today. I've been such a prattling old crone." She swatted her hand in the air, as if at a pesky insect.

"I shall miss talking with you when I am here tomorrow," she lamented. "Will you come back someday, please?" She looked away, fearful of the answer.

"How could I possibly refuse such a splendid offer?" He was smiling broadly at her. She gushed like a teenager.

Elizabeth stayed, business with her daughter unfinished. Montgomery left slowly, glancing in the rear view mirror until the cemetery was no longer visible. He reflected on the day as he drove through the sleepy little river town, with its curious drawbridge that did not raise two sides up from the middle, but to the side, on a swivel. He went over in his mind how he had come for one purpose, his own, and had left only partly succeeding. But he had accomplished far more healing of his own soul in the past hour with Elizabeth than the time he'd spent with her husband. *How curious,* he thought, *the differences between them.* Whatever common interests had driven their lives before the death of their daughter was not clear to the journalist. The only common bond was their sadness. Yet even in grief they were different. It had not occurred to him before that grief could wear more than one hat. Perhaps the answer lay in personality type; he didn't know. But whatever the reason, after nearly four hours with Mac and Elizabeth McHenry, he knew this much: Elizabeth had no interest in the darker side of her daughter's passing—that was Mac's wont. While the gracious mother thrived on and fervently grasped each shred of her daughter's life, the intense father was inclined to probe into the bottomless pit of uncertainty surrounding her death. *There may be hope for her,* he thought, as he drove onto the long bridge that would deliver him across the twenty-six mile expanse of Lake Pontchartrain, to a hotel room and a night's rest before an early trip to the airport, and the refuge waiting in his home country.

_____

Even as the journalist walked toward his car Mac wrestled with his resurrected torment. The visitor's words came so unexpectedly, so chillingly. Not in his most desperate moment had he considered the Church could be *responsible* for her death. Not until now, until a chance encounter with not much more than a total stranger had Mac even theorized his daughter's death could have been preventable. Until now, Mac had been resigned to accept a madman had randomly killed his daughter, for some reason he might never learn. Things were different now. An eyewitness to the Church's culpability had come forward, innocently and by all outward appearance truthfully. It wasn't just culpability Mac was dealing with. To the trained lawyer, the Church's lack of action bordered on criminal neglect, a half-rung on the legal ladder from intent. To make it worse, the Church seemed indifferent to it all. Something known to a down-and-out journalist surely was known to the Church. Why had the Church not stepped forward with something, anything? Forget apologies; why not a simple explanation? What appeared to be an attempt at secrecy took on a more sinister air, became something grimy even holy water could not cleanse.

He had always insisted each committed wrong called for—deserved—accountability. He'd preached it to his children, he'd counseled numerous clients with the same diatribe. Thinking back over what had happened, been said or left unsaid, Mac began to form certain conclusions. This freshly-gained knowledge kindled fires of anger. There was born in the lawyer an intensity, an offspring conceived of malevolence for a father and unforgiveness as a mother, and the child was delivered with a vengeance.

Accountability would have its price.

He dialed a familiar number. "Father, I have just heard something that disturbs me greatly, something I need you to confirm. I cannot accept no one knows the answer. Will you help me?"

Robichaux unhesitatingly agreed.

§

The confirmation of Montgomery's account Father Robichaux dutifully delivered within a week was irrelevant. Mac wanted to pray, to ask God for guidance and strength and the ability to turn a blind eye. But that would have been like the survivors calling the killers back, wouldn't it? He silently cursed the Church for its robbery and plunder of his life, his lust for life. Now he had no choice but to contend with this new knowledge. The yellow tape that had only a short time ago come down was back up again, wrapped tighter than before. Mac hunkered down, readying himself to get on with what must be done.

The trademark passion with which he led his life, as a husband, father and lawyer, knew no bounds. It was this passion spilling over from his personal into his professional life that guided him on a pathway of distinction, over the years earning the respect of his clientele, his peers, and judges in whose courtrooms he practiced. Mac subscribed to the maxim, "Always give three hundred per cent: one hundred percent *inspir*ation, one hundred percent *perspir*ation, and one hundred percent *prepar*ation". His passion wore down many an adversary. He never fatigued in the final quarter, when everything rode on fourth-and-goal.

He also inventoried his finances. To his surprise he had attained modest, comfortable wealth. Enough to allow him more leisure in the last few years, certainly for the remainder of his and Elizabeth's lives. To embark on his new mission clearly meant shutting down his law practice. He needed to survive for an extended time on current resources; there might be no others for a time to come, if ever. Litigation was expensive. Mac's checklist required his commitment to exhaust his savings, if need be. Again, there was no choice; it was all or nothing, no middle ground, no compromising.

Then there was Elizabeth. She would never side with him in this effort. He was prepared to go this alone.

Secure in the righteousness of his task, aware of its likely outcome and the consequences, he unhesitatingly made his decision. It was the first decision of any import in over twenty-seven years he had made without consulting Elizabeth. A twenty-seven year unbroken promise. Until now.

I 3

P AULETTE WASN'T EXPECTING anyone, unless it might be her friend Desiree
Landry dropping by on the way home from Sunday night bingo, as she had on
occasion. Putting down the photo album she was updating for her son and daughter-
in-law, she headed for the door. Expecting her friend as she opened the door to her
Twenty-Third Street bungalow, Paulette was all the more surprised to see her boss
standing there, more long of face than he had been since the awful events of recent
past. Her immediate embarrassment was over her ragged appearance: T-shirt and
cutoffs, hair a mess, no makeup. Her worst nightmare.

She knew this was no ordinary social call. In all their years, Mac had never appeared
at her doorstep. She prepared for the unwanted, wishing she'd not answered the door.

"Mac, excuse the way I look, please. I wasn't expecting anyone. I thought you might
be that daffy Desiree, on her way home from bingo or something. Is everything all
right? Is Elizabeth okay? Please, won't you come in."

She hoped this was not what it appeared.

Mac thanked her, and stepped inside. He wasted no time. His words materialized
her worst fear, yet also calmed her. There is often a relief accompanying bad news,
perversely a welcome respite from the gnarled entanglement apprehension causes.
"Paulette," he spoke in a hushed tone, "I'm closing the office."

Paulette thought this possible in the weeks following Nicole's death, when Mac fell
into such a dismal state. She even prepared herself for the news. It seemed inevitable:
no father was more devoted to a child, and, in Nicole's case, even Paulette conceded
there was more at issue than blood and the bonds of family. Nicole truly had been a
gift, so full of life and happiness. A staple at the law office for as long as memory served,
a source of enormous pride for her father—and, in a curious way, for Paulette as well—
Nicole would one day surely have carried on in the McHenry tradition. Given all that,

her father could easily have been excused for simply walking away at her death, to sequester himself, to become mired in self-pity. But Mac chose a different path. He had stumbled, yes, but she had seen a resurgence in the man these past few weeks, a reemergence of his former self. The Delahoussay trial a few days earlier resulted in a favorable outcome, easily a springboard for more and better to come. It was as if the worst was over, the old Mac was somehow back. This announcement killed that myth.

"I owe you an explanation," he said.

"Paulette, you know this tragedy with Nicole devastated Elizabeth and me, just as it has you. I've tried to regain my life, and to be there for Elizabeth, who has not recovered as well as I have, not yet, anyway. And we were making progress, slowly, but at least it wasn't like we were moving backward." Paulette agreed.

"A few days ago I learned something that changed everything. It's too painful for me to talk about right now, but you'll know about it soon enough. There is something I need to do, something that will take every moment of my time. Nicole," he went on, "deserves this from me. Her memory deserves it. Please try to understand."

Paulette of course did not understand. Putting aside her own selfish concerns, she simply waited for Mac to say what had him so bothered. Years with this man had taught her sometimes it was better to let him speak, to listen. Now, she realized, it was probably more important than ever that she did.

The telephone rang, but Paulette made no move to answer it. She was still chewing on the gristly piece of meat Mac had just fed her; even if she could swallow the morsel, she doubted she'd be able to digest it. She just stood still, mute, struggling to make some sense of what she'd heard.

She began to weep. Before her stood the man who, years before, had won her wrongful death case against her late husband's company, and, because of the enormous heart in him, made a life possible for her and her children far beyond her dreams. This same man was now bringing an end to the dream. A sure excuse for tears … but her tears were not only for herself, and she suspected Mac knew as much.

"You know I've provided for you. Your retirement should see you through a long life, unless," he added with a twinkle, "you take up with a man of low repute."

Paulette tried to smile, but it was useless. She barely heard Mac thank her for the years of devotion, for the very breath of professionalism she had brought to his law office.

When he stood to leave, Paulette spoke solemnly. "Mac, I know there is much you haven't told me. I don't know where you are headed, but I won't put you through an inquisition. You deserve better. Your news leaves me saddened, which should be expected." Mac lowered his head at these last words.

"I'm saddened because we won't be working together any more, and I'm saddened because I'm going to have to totally rearrange my life. My only wish, my prayer, is for you keep following your heart, like you've always done. It's your most endearing quality, the one I've tried to emulate, the one I tried to instill in my children. You have taken on cases no one else would, and won a fair number of them, because you believed in what was right. So, what can I say as we pull the plug? 'It's been loads of fun' doesn't seem enough. Nothing seems enough, frankly.

"Mac, whatever it is you are planning, just make sure it is right. I have a funny feeling about this decision."

He was looking deeply into her eyes. She was waiting. He took neither the high road nor the low one, opting for the safe middle ground of indifference. He told his devoted assistant simply there was no need for her concern, it was just something he had to do. Paulette didn't force the issue further.

"Should I come in tomorrow morning to clean out my desk and go over your docket with you? I know you'll be needing to find new homes for your clients." She wiped her eyes dry.

Mac hesitated, a dead giveaway. The final realization struck hard. "I take it if we were to walk out to your car right now, we would find my things, what, boxed up, or worse yet, in some of those horrible plastic bags they give you at the grocery?"

"Paulette," he started, "it's better this way. I have brought your things with me, but only because I was able to go through every open file, every matter on my docket. No sense putting you through more than necessary. You have always been so organized, there was really no effort in it for me. And I'll be taking steps to transfer the files to new counsel." He reached for her hand. "It's really better this way," he repeated.

"And I wouldn't have dared put your things in those plastic bags, you know better."

"So this is it?" she said, starting to weep again. "Oh, Mac," she went on, feeling sadly for herself, and the intense need to say something light for his sake as well, "you certainly know how to make a small town gal's Sunday night." She brushed her eyes dry, forced a smile, gave ground. "Okay, counselor, let's get it over with. Let's go get my stuff and wrap up this show."

When they'd brought her things in from the car, Paulette thought to ask the one question thus far eluding her. "Mac, what about Elizabeth, how does she feel about this?"

The heavy sigh and the quick, averted glance gave him away. She took a hard step to her right, positioning herself directly in front of him, forcing his attention on her. "Mac," she began, in full earnest, "you can't possibly mean you've redone your entire life, and Elizabeth doesn't even know?" Her mouth still open, she waited for his answer.

"Paulette, I don't think Elizabeth is ready for this yet. I don't want to put it to her as a decision she must make when I do tell her what I—we—will be doing. All in good time." He added, "You must trust me on this, I know what I am doing."

My trust in you isn't the issue, Mac. Paulette shook her head disbelievingly.

After the promises of lunches to be shared and the occasional visit, and as she watched the shiny Lincoln make the turn at the corner and disappear from sight, Paulette held tightly to the St. Christopher hung on the fine gold link chain around her neck—a Christmas gift from Mac and Elizabeth years ago—and whispered a prayer for Mac McHenry.

The vaguely familiar voice from the front office broke the Monday morning quiet. The young black man checked his watch—seven twenty-three—and looked up from the work spread before him, toward the doorway. He heard the same words again. "Hello, is anybody here? Hello?" Rising from his desk, Matthew Courvillon went to see who had come in more than an hour before his law office officially opened for business.

"Mr. Courvillon, good morning, sir," said Mac McHenry to the young man. Trying to suppress his surprise, the younger lawyer shook the hand Mac extended to him and said good morning in return. He also asked if his visitor would care for a cup of coffee.

"That would be fine, Matthew," he replied, "cream if you have it, no sugar."

"How is powdered? I don't have a refrigerator yet, so I can't keep the real stuff cold."

"Artificial's fine, thanks," Mac answered. "I don't like putting anything in it—ruins a good cup of coffee. But I need something to cut the acid. Too hard on the stomach at my age."

Handing the giveaway mug from the local bank to the man now seated before him, and taking his own seat behind the desk, Matthew Courvillon, fresh-from-the-packing-crate lawyer he was, asked the inevitable. "What brings a man of your stature to my humble office at such an early hour?" He followed the polite question with one of an equally pleasing tone, a smile across his face. "Didn't you put the britches on me well enough in the Delahoussay case?"

Mac returned the smile. "Your first jury trial, was it?"

"Did I do that poorly?" There was still a smile, but fewer teeth were showing.

Ignoring the opportunity to reply, Mac got to the point. "Matthew, I'm here on business, but not past business. Only future business." He took a sip from the steaming mug. "I'm resigning my practice, young man, and, as you know our code of professional responsibility requires, I must see to it my clients are not prejudiced by the resignation. You know, no missed filing deadlines, that sort of thing."

"But how does this affect me?"

"Matthew, if you're interested, and I don't mean to force any of this on you, but as I say, if you are interested, I am prepared to recommend to my clients they engage your services … So, are you interested?" He took another sip, his last.

Matthew Courvillon stared into Mac's eyes, saw a little sadness, yet as well a little gleam in them. *Was this a joke? A test of some cruel proportion?* These and many other questions raced through his mind as he searched for the right response, to make sure he got it right.

"Mr. McHenry, if you are indeed closing your practice, why me? Me, a lawyer with little more than two years' experience, and a black lawyer in the heart of white folks country at that, still paying for law school, no secretary. And this office, just look at it, man, would a client of yours want to come in here?

"And you are offering me, and I am taking on faith this is for real—and not some hoax—your law practice? What can I possibly have to cause you to even think of making me this offer?"

"Matthew, we are not total strangers. We go way back, but you would have no way of knowing. Not important at the moment. What is important, and the only thing I need to know, is, are you interested in my offer? There are no strings here. No unearned fees thrown under the table back to me, no back-door anything. I didn't run my practice, or my life that way, and I know you don't either. For whatever reasons I have come here, it is you I believe will do the best job for my clients, most of whom are friends of mine as well. So I will ask you once more, are you interested?"

"I take it you need an answer now, it's not something I can think about?"

"Matthew, what's to think about? Either you want to practice law, or you don't. I think you do. Don't make me think I've misjudged you."

While Matthew Courvillon digested the mild rebuke, his visitor continued. "Look, if you think you won't be working harder than any other of your classmates, and longer hours, and doing more research than you ever dreamed you'd be doing over the next few years, on points of law so obscure you'll wonder if law school ever prepared you for anything, you are, as they say, sadly mistaken. But if you don't mind the extra effort, you may just rediscover what set you on the course to begin with."

Mac followed with another burst. "You spoke of our Delahoussay trial, in Judge Mouton's court, where the jury ruled in my client's favor. What you don't know is Judge Mouton, who is a close personal friend of mine, but a straight arrow all the way, told me he had been surprised by the jury verdict in my client's favor. But I already knew."

Mac rose and walked to the young lawyer's inexpensively framed certificate. "What the judge told me, what I knew after the trial had concluded, is in another year it's a good bet you'd win that trial. Same facts, same jury, same everything, only another year's experience in the courtroom, and your argument persuades the jury in your client's favor.

"When I shook your hand after the verdict, I meant it when I said it could have gone either way, that you had nothing to hang your head about. Do you remember?"

"I remember it proudly. It was a small but meaningful consolation to me at the time."

"So, what's it going to be, young fellow? Are you up to the task? Oh, and one last thing, before your answer. Drop the black man bit. Now, and from here on. Your skin color might mean something to you, but don't let it mean something to anyone you do business for, or with. Just be a man, Matthew, a good man, and the respect will come your way for being a good man, not a good black man. And don't apologize for this office, or the lack of help. I started in far less than this, and most of my clients don't like the idea of paying for expensive space and furnishings anyway.

"So, for the last time, in or out? I don't have all day, and I do have a lot to do, so it's now or never, as the saying goes."

Matthew Courvillon walked over to Mac, squaring himself before the older, enigmatic man. "Mr. McHenry, I'm overwhelmed by all of this. It would have made my day for you to just walk in here this morning and have a cup of coffee and a short conversation about the weather, or your family, with me, nothing more. Instead, you lay before me an opportunity you believe I have somehow earned, me without the slightest clue how, other than I almost—you say—won a trial I might win 'next year,' all things being equal." He turned his head, looking about the spartan surroundings, then again faced the man who had come calling this otherwise uneventful morning.

"I accept your proposal, Mr. McHenry. It would seem I must. You know why I must probably better than I, but, hey, this is something bigger than both of us, isn't it? It's something I will know one day, when … when what? when I win my first really big case, or when I stumble across something in the deep recesses of a file you are handing over to me?"

"It's nothing so complicated, Matthew. There will come a time all this will clear up for you. Things will happen in the near future to explain my decision. Now's not the time to dwell on it."

"So what do I do next?" Matthew Courvillon asked, still confused by it all.

"The files are at my office. It's no more complicated than your coming by—the sooner the better—and our spending the time necessary going over the high points."

"Wouldn't it make more sense to meet my new clients first, before going over the files?"

Mac smiled, and said, "Oh, that detail. I've already talked to them. Yesterday, called 'em at home. I didn't mention this sooner, because it might have distracted you from the decision I asked you to make. Bottom line, you'll wind up with about half of my clients. Not too bad, if you ask me. And I wouldn't worry about the other half if I were you."

"How do I thank you for this, Mr. McHenry? How can I?"

"Young man, you already have. The rest is up to you. But make no mistake," he added, "don't call me for help with any legal issues, don't ask me to intercede if you get crossways with one of these prima donna clients, and don't call me up to thank me, or curse me, either, after today. You are on your own now, all I've done is give you a little wind behind your sail. Understand?"

"Yes, sir, perfectly."

"Good. Now there's only one or two small details left. Do we have any more time? When's your first appointment this morning?" Mac asked in rapid succession.

"Please, don't embarrass me too much. I could tell you differently, but truth is, I've got all the time you need."

"Good. Since you don't have an assistant, and I just retired mine, and you are, whether you realize it yet or not, going to need some skilled help, I'd like to suggest a good person for you to consider hiring. She's so organized it will cut your load in half, and she knows the clients already. Only one possible problem: she is awfully independent, so if you have any notions of this gender superiority thing, it just wouldn't work between you. Interested?"

"How would I afford her? I'm barely making ends meet, you must realize that."

"Shouldn't be a problem, Matthew. I've, shall we say, taken good care of her, and since she would keep your books as she kept mine, she would know when it was time for her to start drawing her salary."

"That sounds like something I can handle. Do I need to know anything more about her?"

"A fair question. She came to my office many years ago, a young widow, husband killed working on an offshore oil rig. Not a penny to her name, two small kids, rent overdue. But the case was a winner, and she was bright, so we made a deal. She started working in my office, first as a file clerk, then light typing, then gradually whatever needed doing. She excelled at everything. After a time, long after she'd received a full settlement for her husband's death, which included college funds for her children, she just stayed on. There was always a purpose in it for both of us, I'm convinced of that."

Matthew had heard coffee shop talk of how generous Mac McHenry had been to the needy and deserving. This was confirmation. He felt warm inside.

"Paulette Sonnier. That's the lady's name. Her address and home number are in the files somewhere; you'll find them easily enough. So think about it, okay? Meanwhile, when can I expect you to come pick up the files?"

"I have two calls to make, and one small detail to tend to, so I need about thirty minutes. Does that work for you?"

Mac shook the young man's hand, and started for the door. "I'll have things ready when you get there."

"Mr. McHenry," Matthew Courvillon called over his shoulder.

Mac stopped and turned slowly, head down, looking to young Matthew as if he were expecting bad news. "Yes?"

"I'm sorry about Nicole. I'm real sorry. I went to school with her, all through junior high and high school in Mandeville. She was very special to me, sir. I just wanted you to know."

"Yes, she was special," Mac said, turning again for the door.

Pushing it as far as he dared, the younger lawyer added, "She was my friend, Mr. McHenry."

"I know," said the father, pulling the door shut.

§

While Matthew Courvillon dove for the telephone to call out with the news, first to his mother, and then to his fiancée, Mac called Paulette with news of his arrangement with Matthew Courvillon.

Paulette was predictably home, predictably loyal. "Mac, of course I'll help him if he calls." But there was a more important matter lingering on her mind.

"You still haven't told me about Elizabeth. How is she handling this?"

"Paulette, I—" He wouldn't lie to her, so he simply said nothing.

"Oh, Mac, I hope you know what you're doing. You do, right?"

"Yes. Yes, I do."

He was no more convinced than Paulette was.

———————

That night, comfortably seated in his study as he waited for the dinner Elizabeth was preparing, Mac reflected on the developments of the past twenty-four hours. He'd closed his office, protecting Paulette and his clients in the process. And he had helped a deserving young man. He felt good.

Almost.

His eyes wandered over to the bright blue book on the corner of the desk in his study. It had been less than a day since he'd last read the passage. Still, he reached for the book again, opening to the inside of the back cover. Nicole's Sophomore yearbook from Mandeville High. One inscription after another, in every color of ink, in flowery and illegible hand alike, filled its pages. Each message no more or no less prominent than another. But one in particular stood out, the same one upon which his eyes now rested. Written by the child of a woman he had once represented in a legal matter, and to whom he had done nothing more than lend a helping hand at a time of dire need, the child now a grown, proud young man and probably oblivious to a dark chapter in his family's past, it had recaptured Mac's attention. Reading it again, he thought back, to a time many years earlier.

The frightened black woman had come to his office right after he'd opened it. She was being battered by a drunk and philandering husband. Her four young sons were also being terrorized by the abusive man. *What can I do?* she had asked Mac in desperation.

Long before laws to protect against such domestic violence had been the subject of debate, even longer than before a white sheriff's office would set foot in the colored part of town to deal with such matters, or the district attorney's office might have out of sense of duty spread justice equally across the color barrier, Mac had taken action … quick, decisive action to put the woman and her sons under the protection of the court. Another form of justice was soon rendered, for within six months the man was dead, a shooting victim in a saloon fight. Once again Mac had been there to help.

Functionally illiterate at the time, the woman was equipped for no more than cooking and cleaning. But she excelled at both, and Mac and Elizabeth found friends who needed housework done, and cafeterias needing a cook for the public school lunch program. The woman completed her high school education and never let her boys settle for second best.

Early on Mac would drop in to see how she was managing. On one visit the third boy, the one she had named Matthew, probably no older than six at the time, had hugged Mac, clutching his leg with all the force and might of a snapping turtle. Mac had not forgotten the desperate affection of the young boy. On a hunch years later, Mac asked the woman not to reveal to her sons he had a hand in any part of their lives. She deserved the credit, not he. Arguing that wasn't so, she nevertheless promised to honor Mac's wish.

She would never know it was Mac who wrote letters of recommendation to help with scholarships and grants to enable her sons, each an honors student, to attend college, and, in young Matthew's case, law school. Mac had always reasoned the lads could have done it on their own, but what was the harm in a gentle nudge?

Years later, his daughter freshly away at Dartmouth College, as he one evening nostalgically reviewed her accomplishments in the "Skipper," Mandeville High's yearbook—Homecoming Maid, Sophomore Class President, Honors class upon Honors class, varsity soccer—he also noticed in the inscriptions a familiar name. He found a Senior photograph to complement the name and inscription. He'd never thought about the ages of his daughter and the young man being so close.

Now, as he sat in his study, the words took on their most meaningful import to Mac. He read them again.

It was so eloquently simple. *Dear Nicole,* the message read, *I hope when you read this, in a week, or even twenty years from now, you will remember me. You have been so nice to me, all these years we have been in school together. You have always been my friend, and talked to me when not many other white kids would. Thank you for being my friend. I'm now going on to college, while you stay here for two more years. I hope they are great years for you. I hope all your dreams come true. My dream is to be a lawyer. My momma has always told me being a lawyer is the most honorable thing a man can be. I hope I can be the kind of lawyer your daddy is. Good luck, Nicole. Your friend, Matthew Courvillon.*

14

Two and a half hours earlier, Mac had been resting comfortably in his study, reading high school yearbook inscriptions while reflecting on his decision-making … and gathering the courage to face his wife. Now, again in the privacy of the same room, things weren't so good.

Elizabeth had been preparing chicken and andouille sausage jambalaya, the first Cajun dish she had mastered as a new wife. He recalled her pride the first time she'd served it, how much he'd enjoyed the rich and delightful flavor. It had gotten better through the years, as family recipes do.

He also recalled his pledge not to ever again make a decision affecting the family without including her. He was not surprised she'd remembered. The price tag for his broken promise was almost unaffordable.

When her anger subsided, and the tears had dried, Elizabeth stood firmly. She would have no part of his lawsuit against their Church. The marriage would continue, but he was not to bring the lawsuit into their home. Mac had no doubt of the outcome if he violated the condition.

He walked away from the clash with a bittersweet win. The decks clear, it was time to start work. He reached for the stack of papers on the corner of his desk, and began reading.

In no time he was pounding away at his keyboard.

———

Solomon Lieber sat motionless at his desk. He was alone in the room. The quiet of the past ten minutes was broken as the grandfather clock chimed six times. He subconsciously made the count as he thought about, again, what had just happened. It *had just happened, hadn't it? Oh, yes, it had. Sol, Sol, what have you done?*

He glanced at his appointment book. There it was, confirmation, on his daily planner, neatly inscribed by his secretary: *4:45. Mac McHenry. Wants last appointment of the day. Needs about an hour of your time. Said just a visit from an old friend.* Lieber recalled the initial surge of excitement at the thought of seeing Mac again, nearly seven months since they'd last gotten together. He thought back over the many years the two of them had practiced law on the North Shore, more often as adversaries. In St. Tammany Parish, when Mac and Sol teed it up, other lawyers closed shop and went to the courthouse. Early. Seats weren't available if you waited too long. That was back before the silk-stocking New Orleans firms had deported some of their inner-city partners and associates to startup offices in Covington and Mandeville, back when it was just the usual group of Parish Bar members. The good old days.

The mutual respect had developed into friendship. There were still the inevitable confrontations, but in the past half dozen years or so, they'd seemed to settle their cases more often than trying them. Whether a matter settled or not, their friendship stood at the courthouse doorway, no matter what. The client's interests always came first. Their oath demanded as much, and that's how it was.

Mac had arrived punctually, and asked Sol to dispense with the amenities. He was gaunt, the eyes that had always shone with such brilliance now dim, set into sockets sunken in colorless cheekbones.

His new client wanted the time clock turned on. Sol knew better than to argue.

Mac began with the loss of his daughter, then his desperate attempts to learn why her life had been taken, first from Father Art, then from Carlos the prisoner.

With a noticeable shift in temperament Mac next told Sol what he'd learned from Evan Montgomery of the Church's warning. He'd picked up the cut glass paperweight on Sol's desk, gripping it with white-knuckled force, as he jumped from fact to legal contention that a warning was not enough, that the Church owed his daughter the duty, forcibly if necessary, to remove her from harm's way. It was a simple precept, one they'd learned in their first year of law school: a master owes a duty to his servant to keep the servant from harm. Regardless of whether he ever learned why his daughter had died, Mac wanted the Church held accountable for what had happened.

Sol knew Mac well enough to understand how he would not let one senseless act be attenuated by an equally senseless inaction.

Mac had handed him a stack of documents, and walked him through each, beginning with the complaint, and the rough draft of a response to the inevitable Rule 12b6 defense motion. Then a memorandum of authorities drawn from cases, law review articles, statutes, news stories, texts of every imaginable kind and source. Sol had questions. Mac had the answers. All neatly packaged, as logically presented as it could be for such a novel undertaking. Then, finished, he'd asked Sol to represent him. Vainly trying to inject the only levity into their meeting Mac had mumbled the "lawyer who represents himself has a fool for a client" maxim.

He'd said *yes*, impulsively, because it made more sense for him to have carefully made his own objective review first … like the one he was conducting at the moment.

He measured every conceivable angle, he extended every hypothesis to some presumed end point. In the final analysis, Mac's case probably would survive the early dismissal motion, and might even one day find its way to a trial setting date. There was no precedent for what Mac sought, only analogous authority. Uncertain, certainly challenging, but not impossible.

The simplicity was impressive. So was filing in federal court, rather than in a state district court. State court cases dragged on for years, often lifetimes, but such delays no longer were tolerated in the federal system.

Next came the personal considerations: there were probably just as many reasons why he would not want to take on this representation as there were why he would. The irony of the situation had not escaped him, either: a Jew, representing a Catholic, against the Catholic Church, in federal court in New Orleans, where only two of the sitting judges were non-Catholic. The fundamental "good faith" requirement was there; Sol could sign his name to the complaint without fear of the dreaded sanction for the filing a frivolous suit. *No*, he told himself, *this suit is not frivolous*. It had force, and could gain momentum if a few preliminary hurdles could be cleared.

The big unknown, the one giving him the most trouble, was how well he would hold up when the going got rough. His own measure of grief over Nicole's death could weaken the effort.

There was one final, inescapable observation the learned trial lawyer made: the case was doomed from the start. It hadn't a prayer of success. He suspected Mac knew as much.

In the end, he decided against calling his newest client and resigning. He made a second decision as well: this would be his swan song. Time to call it a career. He had enough fight in him for the struggle. He was healthy, fit. There was just he, with Sophie gone.

So Sol Lieber, lawyer, friend to his client, dictated a message to his secretary to set up a new file, J. Bradley McHenry, Plaintiff, versus The Roman Catholic Church, through its representative, the Archdiocese of New Orleans, Defendant, and to make the deposit of Mr. McHenry's retainer check into the firm's trust account at the first opportunity. She should bill at the firm's standard rate, and make an extra effort to keep him current on his time slips. He would explain everything in due course, the memo concluded.

It was not until he'd turned out his office light, and dropped the microcassette dictation tape and check on his secretary's desk he first realized Elizabeth's name appeared nowhere on the pleadings, and at no point in their meeting had her name been mentioned.

§

Rich Quisenberry exited the revolving glass door, and instantly slammed into the wall of heat and humidity. The office building's air conditioning replaced by a blast furnace, in seconds his French-cuffed shirt was one with the soaked undershirt, both laminated to his skin. His thoughts weren't on the heat as he briskly covered the few blocks in the CBD—the Central Business District of the city of New Orleans—to the office of what he hoped would become his firm's newest client. Normally accompanied by a phalanx of his firm's top litigation associates, this time he walked alone. He'd been told to come alone.

Quisenberry was the head of the Commercial Litigation Section of Phillips, Dawson. Fifty-seven years old, the veteran of forty-one trials as first chair, steel-nerved and feared as an adversary. He took no prisoners. The engraved brass plaque on his desk read simply: *No quarter asked, none given.* It was his mantra.

The head of any litigation section usually delegates to subordinates, reserving the highest profile cases for himself or the rising stars. Rarely are they held accountable as rainmakers. Quisenberry prided himself in his ability to handle both responsibilities, and had, in rising to the top position in one of the city's largest law firms, distinguished himself through the years by harvesting scores of new clients. In addition to his courtroom prowess, he was also quite personable. He liked to think of himself as multi-dimensional, which he translated, loosely, as not only possessing the qualities of a good lawyer, but of a real fine person as well. Viewing himself as the standard, he had a hard time with the public's general disdain of the legal profession, believing instead lawyers weren't such a bad species.

The call from Monsignor Zachary at the Roman Catholic Archdiocese had, however, caught him unaware. Quisenberry, a staunch Catholic, attended Mass at the cathedral, where the monsignor occasionally conducted the service, and over the past few years the two men had become social acquaintances outside the Church's somewhat narrow ecclesiastical confines. In fact, the two men enjoyed a good round of golf whenever their harried schedules permitted. Rainmaker he deservedly considered himself to be, it had never occurred to Quisenberry to pursue the archdiocese as a client.

Sometimes business was better not mixed with pleasure.

But, he reflected as he trudged along in the stifling heat and humidity, *business is business.*

While Rich Quisenberry made his way along the sidewalks of the CBD, Archbishop Thomas Ryan watched quietly from inside his office. Pensively he studied the courtyard below, then the wall around the manor housing the New Orleans Archdiocese. And at this particular moment, as he looked out the ten-foot window three stories above ground level, he was thinking of more carefree days many years earlier, when he was but a young parish priest in Opelousas, marrying parishioners and baptizing their babies, hearing confessions and occasionally conducting a burial mass. Having risen above such stature, he had also risen to accept the responsibility of caring for all parishioners, and all parish priests, young and old alike, in his diocese. At times it was a nearly impossible burden. Yet his faith, and prayer, had delivered him more than once from situations seemingly unmanageable, situations the gravity of which tested his faith daily.

Now he was faced with perhaps his gravest test yet. This was not the first time the Church had been sued. It was, however, the first time the Church would be faced with accountability for the death of one of its own. A few days earlier, when his secretary had handed him the court papers, he had been distraught at seeing Sister Nicole's father named as the plaintiff. The young nun had spent several months at the archdiocese before going on to her Guatemalan mission. He'd grown quite attached to her, and her death had affected him as deeply as the death years earlier of his own sister, his last living relative. He had called to console Sister Nicole's parents, but had never received a return call. There was unfinished business here, he had thought then; he was forced to think the same thing now.

Deep in thought, he was startled when his secretary's voice announced his visitor's arrival. He crossed the room to make the acquaintance of the man he had been assured was the best trial lawyer the New Orleans defense bar had to offer. He hoped the man's character was as impeccable as his professional reputation.

Quisenberry followed the archbishop to a small seating area in an adjoining study, a comfortably sized room adorned with rich, dark wood paneling from floor to ten-foot high ceiling, and books, thousands of books, neatly shelved on three of its walls. Neither austere nor ostentatious, Quisenberry noted, but impressively comfortable. As he motioned his guest to take a seat, the prelate encouraged Quisenberry to remove his coat, and to cool off with some iced tea.

"Mr. Quisenberry, I shall, as some say, 'cut to the chase' if you don't mind. Your time is certainly not best spent by engaging in idle conversation. By now you have had a chance to review the complaint Mr. McHenry filed against the Church?"

Quisenberry smiled. *Awfully presumptuous of you, Eminence. You asked me over, but didn't tell me why. It was sheer talent that prompted me to send runners to the state and federal courthouses. The rest was easy, finding the complaint, analyzing it, preparing for this meeting.* The rules were clear to Quisenberry: flattery and games-manship were to remain unstated and understood. It was time to get to the business at hand. Quisenberry answered, "Yes, your Eminence, I have."

"You have also done some legal research, I may presume? And please, while I appreciate the respectful thought, the position of archbishop does not entitle me to be addressed as 'Eminence' or 'Your Eminence'. Perhaps if I am one day made Cardinal you may then choose to call me by that title. 'Your Excellence' is politically correct for my current position, but I would prefer you not use it either. Please, I insist you call me Tom. I'm quite comfortable with Tom."

"Fine, Tom it is. And I am Rich. Mr. Quisenberry, rest his soul, is buried in the small town of Springhill, up in the northern part of the state. And, yes, some preliminary research has been done. May I get to that now, or do you have other questions first?"

"Let's wait a moment, shall we, before we discuss the research. I'm interested in some more background first. I understand you have locked horns with Mr. McHenry before, when he was representing some rural people against one of your oil company clients. Am I right? Maybe on other occasions as well?"

"Only once, and once was plenty. I might as well tell you, up front, Tom, Mac McHenry fairly well schooled me. I thought I had a rock solid defense, but he prevailed at every step. My clients—there were a number of oil companies, not just one—all caved when he prevailed at the Third Circuit Court of Appeal. Even though there was the right to a higher appeal, they did not want a Louisiana Supreme Court decision to result. They paid, dearly."

"Do I need to know about the case?"

"Not so much the nature of the case as about the lawyer we were up against. My firm threw a half-dozen lawyers at him, a one-man shop, and he never once asked for a continuance of a court date, or an extension of a filing deadline. Not once. Tom, that just doesn't happen in my line of work. And he's tireless. When he's working a case, I can tell you he becomes consumed by it. I am the same way, frankly, much to the chagrin of my wife and the frequent disappointment of our children. The thought crossed everyone's minds more than once a settlement was the only way out. I think if the case had been lost, one of us—the loser, of course—might have gone over the edge. Not something I care to relive, frankly.

"Anyway, it ended well for both of us. McHenry made enough to retire a dozen times. But I must tell you, if that case was any indication of what Mac McHenry would be like in another case, even one in which he's the plaintiff instead of the plaintiff's lawyer, I can assure you we will have a real fight on our hands in this new one. And I apologize for being presumptuous, Tom, by saying 'we'. I know Phillips, Dawson hasn't been hired yet."

"A formality, Rich, a formality. And thank you for the insightful view of Mac McHenry. Now let's talk about the complaint, shall we?"

"Certainly. Where would you like to begin?"

"He is suing the Catholic Church, over the death of his daughter, a nun killed while serving in Guatemala. I take it you know of the unfortunate event?"

"I do. I doubt there are many who don't. As a father myself, I can understand the grief he must feel. I'm not sure why he holds the Catholic Church responsible, however. The complaint is a bit unclear. It just says she was killed as a result of the failure of the Church to adequately safeguard her. Ordinarily in Louisiana, in cases of injury, even death, the legal remedy is to file suit under worker's compensation statutes, which are state laws carrying certain recovery limits. In Louisiana, the remedy isn't available: the Church is an eleemosynary institution, not susceptible to worker's compensation laws. That left the door wide open for McHenry to sue in state court for a fortune in money damages. But he hasn't."

"Why do you suppose he is not suing for money?"

"You understand it would only be a presumption on my part?"

"Of course. But I need to know what you think."

For the first time since the two men had met, one of them smiled. It was Quisenberry, who looked at the cleric through a smile, and said, "Tom, this might take a while. It gets a little complicated. How much time do we have?"

Archbishop Thomas Ryan rose from his chair. "Come," he said, and motioned for Quisenberry to follow him. "Bring your tea and leave your coat."

The archbishop led Quisenberry down two flights of stairs and through an ornate doorway into a secluded garden area, shaded from the sun and cooled by ceiling fans hanging under the veranda. It was quiet and serene, and, as Quisenberry quickly learned, a place where the two could relax and be on even keel.

"This is my sanctuary, Rich. My private little place where I can come and escape the pressures of my job. It may be warmer out here, but the ceiling fans should help. If you get too warm we can go back inside. For now, if you're ready, the meeting is yours to conduct."

"Thank you, Tom. I'm okay out here. It's nice. This really isn't heat, by the way. Heat is what radiates off the pavement outside this lovely garden area that soaked my shirt on the walk over." *Or what I lived in for a year back in Sixty-Seven and Sixty-Eight, as a forward observer way north of the Mekong Delta.* He smiled again, getting one in return from the archbishop.

"Now where were we? Oh, yes, why I think Mac didn't take the conventional route in this lawsuit. Two reasons, really, and a single result. One, Mac isn't interested in money. I don't think he wants a dime from the Catholic Church. And two, which is clearly the more obvious, he wants to be in federal court." Quisenberry paused to let things settle in with the archbishop.

"I'm afraid you've lost me, Rich." The archbishop sipped his tea and waited for a reply.

"Mac could easily have sued for money in state court. Yet he chose not to. I'll get to why he didn't in a minute. He can't sue under what's known as diversity jurisdiction in federal court, because his domicile is the same as the Church's: Louisiana. He's left with what's known as federal question jurisdiction if he wants to be in federal court. Domicile of the parties is not a factor, nor is any damages amount. His lawsuit is filed under the Occupational Health and Safety Act, which is administered by the Occupational Health and Safety Administration, or what folks call OSHA, which is a federal law, which gets him into federal court without regard to money damages. Here is where it gets dicey. He is suing the Catholic Church, as a private citizen, under a federal law dictating safety in the workplace. It is quite simple, for all its seeming complexity."

"What does this OSHA Act say about a situation such as the one we are faced with, where a nun has been killed?"

"Not surprisingly, Tom, there is no precedent for this kind of claim, or lawsuit. We're on new ground here. To begin with, the usual way for an OSHA claim to make its way into court is through the agency itself, or some aggrieved business licking its wounds and appealing a fine or penalty levied against it in an agency proceeding. Listen carefully to me Tom: there is no record of a private citizen bringing a direct action against an institution under the framework of the OSHA Act. Not a single case turned up in our preliminary research. I'm not saying it can't be done, but I will tell you it seems most unlikely a federal judge will countenance such a bizarre notion."

"Say he persuades a judge his approach is valid. What would an adverse decision mean to the Church? If he's not suing for money, what does he win if he wins?"

"I'm coming to that, Tom. Bear with me."

"I'm sorry, Rich. I have this tendency to speak when I should be listening."

"Don't apologize. You ask good questions, for which I may not have good answers. This is all speculative, mind you, but I think I see where he's headed. Stay with me a bit more.

"Now, where was I? Oh, yes, the lawsuit. It hangs by a very thin thread. No express language in the statute for a private citizen to bring it, no precedent enlarging the statutory framework—clearly an uphill climb for our plaintiff."

"Can he succeed? Or is the best we can do is try to predict a likely outcome?"

"All we can do is look to cases decided on similar points of law, and by analogy draw a likely outcome. Just exactly like the courts do it."

Quisenberry didn't wait for another question. "First, and most importantly, as I just said, no private citizen has ever sued under the OSHA statute. Usually an exclusive right of the government. But the government has delegated the right to the individual states, which it can, but it has never delegated to private citizens. This is the first hurdle McHenry must clear."

"What do I want to know next? His other hurdles, or whether he can clear this one?"

"I'll give you both. Can he clear this hurdle? I don't know the answer for sure, but I do know it will not be easy. There are certain federal laws providing for private citizens to sue under. The lawsuits they bring are known as *qui tam* actions. They've been around since Reconstruction, put in place as an enticement to prevent fraud

105

✝

by government contractors. If a law is susceptible to an action, that is, a private litigant's right to sue in place of a governmental entity, any citizen can bring the lawsuit, so long as the basic requirements are met. Theoretically, in this case, even though a *qui tam* type action is not expressly authorized, there may still be an argument it's implied in the statutory scheme, and literally any John Doe walking the streets could bring such a lawsuit."

A noticeably perplexed look appeared on the archbishop's face. "So you are saying Mr. McHenry might meet the requirements of bringing a *qui tam* lawsuit under the OSHA Act?"

"Not *per se* a *qui tam* action, but on the same general legal principle. His first hurdle is to avoid dismissal from what we call a Rule 12b6 motion, in this case on the issue of whether he has the right to sue—we call it standing—under the OSHA Act. If—big *if* here, Tom—he convinces our judge he has a right to sue in this capacity, he must then establish, among a number of other things under the OSHA Act, first, there was an unsafe condition, next, the Church was aware of it and did nothing or next to nothing to correct it, and last, an injury resulted."

"And if he gets that far, the remedy would be what? A fine?"

"Well, the court usually requires the offender take corrective action."

"What kind of corrective action?"

"The big question, Tom. When it's factories, the penalty is a fine and more training, more awareness, less apathy on the part of management. Those are the usual means. In this case, who knows? We won't know for sure what he has in mind until we get into discovery. But I won't kid you, Tom. I don't think Mac McHenry is at all interested in corrective action where the Church is concerned, at least not the kind most folks would think of as corrective."

The prelate frowned deeply. "I sense you're valiantly trying to protect me from something you think I'm not prepared to hear. Do you hold back like this with all your clients?"

Quisenberry stirred restlessly in his seat, and drank the last of his tea. "You don't mince words, do you? I suppose I do owe you my full opinion. When you hear it, you may think mine is the product of way too much caffeine, an imagination spoiled by too many years of desperate people doing desperate things to each other in and out of court. I'd rather you viewed it as nothing more than a theory. Do we have this understanding?"

"Yes, of course. And Rich, the Church does not kill its messengers."

The lawyer smiled again. The door was wide open for him, so he stepped through. He was at his best. At his brilliant best. And he had carte blanche.

"I'll get to the point. Mac McHenry had the right to sue the Church under state law for a king's ransom under both wrongful death and survivor actions when he couldn't sue under Worker's Compensation laws, which traditionally yield lesser, structured recoveries. He didn't. Another point: he's tight with nearly every judge in St. Tammany Parish, and the Church is susceptible to suit there. He could have safely sued in his back yard, literally. Yet he came to New Orleans, to sue in federal court where most of the judges are Catholic, and who probably don't have a clue who Mac McHenry is. And under an obscure statutory framework many people feel has outlived its usefulness in today's world. Most people in the know conclude the agency administering the OSHA laws is scheduled for extinction. But I digress. We have to ask ourselves why Mac McHenry chose this particular vehicle to bring suit. I believe there is only one clear answer."

He loosened his tie, and continued. "Mac doesn't want money for his daughter's death. That would cheapen everything. Plus he doesn't need the money. His daughter's memory has to mean something to the man. I believe what he wants is accountability. If I heard him use that word once, I heard it a hundred times during our previous lawsuit: accountability. How does Mac get accountability from the Catholic Church in this lawsuit? He doesn't get it by a token fine the OSHA Act provides, which is nothing more than a slap on the wrist. No, he does it by the ultimate penalty most lawyers and legal commentators believe the OSHA Act provides for, written between the lines, something never before attempted except in the pages of scholarly treatises or law school exams … what is referred to as the death knell: he closes down the factory. He shuts the doors of the plant that has ignored the safety needs of its employees so repeatedly as to evidence a wanton and reckless disregard for their safety and well-being."

Catching his breath quickly, he concluded. "In this case, there is no factory, or plant. There is only the Church, the Holy Roman Catholic Church.

"Tom, I believe it is Mac's intention to put on a case designed, ultimately, to close the doors to, and bring about the shutting down of the Catholic Church in this country, or at least most of it."

15

ARCHBISHOP RYAN WAS TOO stunned to speak. Such a thought was unimaginable. He'd conditioned himself for bad news, but not catastrophic news. The heat, ignored before, now threatened to suffocate him. He wiped his forehead free of the ribbons of perspiration.

He struggled to recover. "I also suspect you have formed an opinion on whether or not our friend can succeed. I need to know your assessment of this likelihood as well."

"Tom, you know I cannot give you any kind of guarantee, or even a simple assurance, one way or another, on the outcome of this lawsuit. But I can share with you what I think is a likely outcome of the case. If you'd like."

"We've come this far; why leave the opera before the last aria?"

"Splendid. Let me see if I can break it down in some kind of orderly fashion. Let's go through the hurdles, as we've taken to calling them. One at a time. First, while I personally don't think Mac has the law on his side, there is a chance the court will not dismiss his case for want of standing. Incidentally, there is no jury. Cases such as this are not tried to juries, but to the court. Which is a strong reason why our federal judge will probably not toss it out, to give the plaintiff his day in court. It's a new strain of justice in the American courts; we affectionately refer to it as 'results oriented.' Very unpredictable, as its name suggests.

"But getting back to our first hurdle, while we will certainly frame a compelling argument against it, and I feel an appellate court will reverse a lower court finding adverse to our position, I believe there is at least a fair chance the district court judge may ultimately decide to hear this case. Thus, Mac has at least a snowball's chance of clearing this first hurdle."

Quisenberry forged ahead. "Assuming he gets over the first hurdle, we'll get into discovery. I doubt Mac will spend the kind of serious money on discovery this case dictates before he gets a ruling on standing. The good news about discovery is it's where we'll learn how strong his case is. We get to see his evidence."

The archbishop leaned forward. "Unfortunately, I'm familiar with the discovery process." He also had a question. "Earlier you said there is no precedent for this type of case. What might persuade a judge, or later an appellate court, to make a particular ruling on a point of law undecided in prior court decisions?"

Quisenberry paused before answering. "I think I can explain it this way. Our laws in this country are largely based on the English common law. In fact, until the late eighteenth century our American jurisprudence was little more than a restatement of the common law of merry old England. But ours has always been a restless society, and changes in custom, in the way we as Americans thought and felt about certain commercial and societal issues, soon gave way to a need to develop what I must loosely refer to as a hybrid form of jurisprudence. Remember, most of the major changes in the world occurred in this country after the late eighteenth century. It was only natural we develop our own body of law.

"Perhaps the best illustrative example I can give you of this phenomenon is in the history of death claims where minor children were concerned. Today, in this country, there is no second thought given to a large money damages claim in what we call a wrongful death lawsuit, specifically where the deceased is a minor child. The parents or surviving next of kin sue for, and quite often recover, great sums of money for the loss of love and affection for the deceased child. In old England, this never occurred; any recovery was predicated purely on the child's earning capacity. For a deceased child of, say, the ripe old age of eight or nine, whose earning capacity under an extant child labor regime might have equaled or even exceeded an adult's, the parents might have recovered generously. But for the wrongful death of an infant, or a toddler, neither of whose future earning capacities was defined yet, there was no recovery. As you would expect, this never set well with the practicing plaintiffs' bar in old England, yet it withstood attack for centuries. Well, it didn't set too well with the newcomers to this untamed land we call America, either, yet for three and a half centuries it remained the law here as well, despite relentless determination by the plaintiffs' bar to tear down the barrier on our own shores.

"Finally, in what we call a landmark case—I remember it well enough from my first year of law school, as it was a fairly recent case back then—the case of *Wycko versus Gnodtke*, the Michigan court broke from *stare decisis*, or court precedent, and rec-

r . r .   b r y a n

ognized a child's life had a far greater measure than the traditional earning capacity notion. It's been gaining momentum ever since. Eventually even England succumbed to the same change, I might add. Suffice it to say there is virtually no reluctance today for a trial judge to let an infant death claim go to the jury.

"The *Wycko* example may be a bad one, since this case has as its premise a federal law. The Federal District Court in New Orleans will be dealing with a brand new situation, not contemplated by the OSHA statutory or legislative scheme. The court will analytically resolve the issue in a manner not unlike the analytical framework used in the *Wycko* case. This is where a results-oriented ruling might enter the picture.

"What I'm saying, Tom, is that change in the law, even in our federal system of justice, is inexorable. Glacial, but inexorable. The mark Mac will leave, even if he is unsuccessful—which he will be, ultimately—is an easier path for others to follow. Today's *McHenry* case could very well become tomorrow's new *Wycko* case. Mac knows this; he knows other lawyers who would follow his lead will chip away at whatever weakness each previous reported case leaves, until the pressure gets too great, and the wall crumbles."

The lawyer thought for a moment more, then added, "Make no mistake. This isn't an academic exercise we're dealing with. Mac doesn't care about seeing his name in some lawbook, either as a lawyer or as a plaintiff. To him, this is a mission. We'd be seriously underestimating the man if we were to think ego played any part in his bringing this lawsuit."

The archbishop rose from his chair, and walked the few paces to the statuette of the Virgin, offering comfort and compassion. He spoke over his shoulder to the lawyer who, still seated, had decided it was time to truncate his presentation. He'd made his point.

"I see. The bastion, while formidable, is not unassailable. Maybe it does not crumble today, maybe not in our lifetimes, but eventually … if the pressure is as relentless as you so vividly describe in your explanation of the *Wycko versus Gnodtke* case."

Quisenberry nodded. "Yes, possibly. Much will depend on our particular facts. For instance, how many times does something like this happen? How many nuns, priests even, die each year in the service of the Catholic Church? Is this a widespread situation? And are the facts similar enough where it might factor against us later? You will have to help me with the answer to these questions. I have an idea this information will become crucial before the case is resolved."

The archbishop had turned and was again looking at the statuette. A long silence passed. Quisenberry grew uncomfortable. If this was a signal for him to leave, he had one more point to make first.

"Tom, there's something else I'd offer you here, another personal opinion. It's based on years of experience, and knowing a bit about Mac McHenry.

He folded his arms across his chest, body language suggesting strength. "I don't believe this case will ever come to trial. It may get nasty, and harsh rulings may result along the way, but odds are it will not go to trial. We can't even be sure it's a trial Mac McHenry wants. We know it isn't money, so we're left with only some concession from the Church. Assuming I'm right.

"I'm of course talking about a settlement. Statistically, over ninety percent of the lawsuits filed in this country settle without a trial. No matter how grief-stricken or angry he is, I'm betting Mac McHenry wouldn't want his church to be subjected to the harsh penalty we're discussing here. He's still a decent man, and if it ever comes to a point Mac holds the upper hand, I believe he will be raveceptive to some gesture that gives him his accountability.

"If I'm right, it's our job to find out what he's willing to accept as a tradeoff under his 'accountability' standard."

After another moment, the archbishop spoke again. "I believe you have given me a most insightful account, Rich. I have much to tell my superiors, but I do have the authority, which I now exercise, to retain your services to defend this lawsuit. On our way out my secretary will give you my private telephone and fax machine numbers, and my schedule over the next several months. I will be on the move quite a bit, and must therefore rely on your judgment. I have the utmost confidence in your ability to do what is in the best interest of the Church, and I empower you to act in her best interests accordingly."

He continued. "We have a lawyer of our own here at the archdiocese. She no longer practices trial law, but she is a valuable asset from experience and reliability standpoints. I believe you may even be acquainted with her—she was once associated with your firm. You might direct copies of correspondence and court filings to her, rather than to me. Also, if I am ever unavailable, and it is imperative you obtain guidance or authorization, you may rely on her. Her name is Sister Katherine, and she is, as I say, a nun assigned to our archdiocese. You will meet her in due course, I'm sure. My secretary will also provide you with her numbers."

Quisenberry knew the meeting was over. He stood to receive the archbishop's handshake. "Rich, thank you for coming over. Monsignor Zachary has done his Church a valuable service in recognizing your capability, I am convinced of it. Our meeting has been a good one. I will see you back to my office now."

In less than a single hour, at the billable rate of two hundred fifty dollars per hour, Rich Quisenberry had charted the courses of more lives than he could have imagined at the time.

§

Mac poured Elizabeth a glass of *pinot noir* and set it beside her as she slowly stirred the pot. The gumbo would ruin if it burned to the bottom, even slightly. He wanted her to turn and face him, but knew she couldn't. He began slowly.

"I thought you should know, I hired Sol Lieber, and he filed—" He caught himself before he said *our*. "—the lawsuit on Monday." Before she could reply, he added, "I just thought you needed to know."

She spoke into the pot of crawfish gumbo. "I thought we'd agreed not to discuss your lawsuit in this house. And why Sol? Did it have to be someone else who's suffered a recent family death? Or just someone you could control? Which is it?"

"You don't believe any of that, Elizabeth. Not a single word."

"Then tell me why you picked Sol."

"There isn't a better lawyer in these parts. Or one less connected to the Catholic Church. And Sol is his own man, he wouldn't any more let me control him than I would the reverse. If anything, he will keep my objectivity focused." He sounded so clinical, even to himself.

She set the spoon down, and sipped the wine. She almost turned to face Mac, then resumed her stirring. "I'm as against Sol's involvement as I am your lawsuit, but for your sake, I am glad the unending days and nights of you being cooped up in the study are at an end, and now it can get down to just … what? Just the usual, run-of-the-mill litigation?"

No, it's a little more than that. If you'd be a little more tolerant, I'd explain it to you. Maybe then you'd understand. "Elizabeth, let's don't argue, please. Why don't we have our dinner out on the back porch. It's nice out this evening."

"Now that is the first sensible thing you've said in longer than I care to remember. This needs a few more minutes. Why don't you set the table, and I'll call you when it's ready." She handed him the Tabasco. "Here, you always forget this." There was so much sadness in her eyes.

Half an hour later he was on his second bowl; she'd hardly touched her first. "I should've put my foot down when you first told me about your lawsuit, but I didn't. Now I have the feeling I'm going to regret my earlier decision. Tell me, Bradley, what is it you haven't told me about your lawsuit? What do I need to prepare myself for?"

He patted the napkin to his lips, then gingerly set it next to the empty bowl. "If I tell you, and I will if it's what you truly want, then you must accept it. That's my condition. I am beyond being discouraged." *Be careful here, Mac.* "So is it a deal?" he added.

"It's so bad you must impose on me a condition of 'keep my opinions to myself'?"

"You'll see it differently than I see it. You always see things differently than I do."

"Does that mean you see things clearly, and I don't, or won't? Is that it?"

"That's a possibility, but it isn't what I'm saying. I see a wrong. I see something needing to be set right. You know me, how I demand accountability. In this particular instance, I have my idea what that should be. If you were completely honest with yourself, you might actually view what the Church did as a wrong also. But you would never expect the same measure of accountability I do. You would settle for less, perhaps none at all, and our daughter's death will in the end be a forgotten, wasteful thing. I won't allow that to happen. Nicole's death will not fade into oblivion, not if I can help it."

"Bradley, how drastic is this measure of your revenge? You may as well tell me, I will see it soon enough in the papers or hear about it from some stranger while I am on some grocery errand, or down at the Shell, filling the tank. Everyone knows us now, I won't be able to hide behind anonymity, so you may as well tell me, what is it you are after, this accountability you seek?"

He told her what she demanded.

When two are together for so long, and experience the daily highs and lows as marrieds do, and share the many deeply personal moments, there is very little left to know about each other. This was a truth; this was the sun coming up in the east, seven-day weeks, the reality of death and taxes. Mac accepted such truths, always had. Because he knew such, and accepted it, he knew as soon as he told Elizabeth he'd just as surely taken the knife at their table and plunged it into her heart. No matter what she'd thought before he spelled it all out, it paled to the whole truth. The look in her eyes, the frozen expression on her face, everything from revulsion to horror showed.

He'd been a fool to think she'd react differently. It was a strong marriage, but his wife had her limits. He'd gone too far. His wife just sat at the table, staring blankly at first, then bowing her head onto folded arms. Mac could hear the muffled sobbing.

"It will be all right," he whispered to her, running his hand along the smoothness of her arm, across her shoulders, softly down her back. As much as he despised himself for what he'd done to his wife, he remained resolute.

This was something else for which the Church would be held accountable, he silently vowed.

————————

Barely a day after he'd met with the archbishop, the Phillips, Dawson firm's senior trial lawyer called the meeting to order. Before him in the War Room on an upper floor in one of New Orleans' tallest buildings was gathered his seven-person trial team: his second chair, a junior partner, two young associates, a chief and associate paralegal, and one office services minion. In the silk stocking firm mentality, it takes a village to try a lawsuit. All listened attentively to Quisenberry.

"Group, we've got a big one here. Before you is a copy of the complaint lodged four days ago in the Eastern District. You can, rather you will read it later, but for now, you only need to know we are representing the Catholic Church in a hybrid form of *qui tam* action clearly non-existent under the OSHA act and legislation." Noting their amazement, he quickly added, "Don't worry, this is new to me also. We'll work through it together. It still just distills down to being a lawsuit, fellas," and, turning to his right, "and lady. We've done lawsuits before, right?

"Let's start by returning the Rule 4 waivers, and entering our appearance. I don't want to request the usual extension; I want our answer filed within the twenty days required by the rules. Everything according to the book on this one, group. Any questions yet? Good," he said, not even pausing, "then let's move on.

"I've been up against the plaintiff before, in his capacity as a trial counsel, not as a litigant. Most of you know this. Marsha knows him well." He paused to gauge her reaction. There was nothing more than a slight shoulder shrug. Good; no damage there … no preconceived notions of too much headache ahead. He stampeded on.

"As I was saying, this time he's the plaintiff. He also happens to be, for those of you who have been in a coma the past eight months, the father of the nun who was killed by the rebel guys down in Guatemala. It's hardly been out of the news since it happened. Anyone here not know about it? Good." Nearly everything Rich Quisenberry said was followed by some note of affirmation. *Good* was his word of choice. You either got used to it, or you moved on.

He continued with his opening salvo. "After you've finished reading the complaint, I want a memorandum from each of you, complete with all the authority you can muster, on our defense. Don't just parse with me here, group, stick your collective necks out, and be aggressive. If I'm right in my analysis, and in all modesty I believe I am, we have a huge undertaking ahead of us. The future of the Catholic Church in this state, perhaps this country, might hang in the balance. We'll meet again in a week. I want your memos by then. Got it? Good.

"There's more. Nothing we do will wear him down. He's just one man, and he's got a storefront lawyer as counsel of record, but make no mistake, we're up against the real deal here. He will expect us to try to paper him to death, the way we tried the last time. It won't work. We're going to try a new approach this time around. For now, anyway, I want him to dictate not only the pace, but the direction this suit is headed. We will speak when spoken to, and rest when he rests. We can turn up the heat later, but for now, no scorched earth. We plant instead of burn. And even though he has loads of money, we're not going to waste it. That would mean we're also wasting our client's money, which we're not going to do. Got that everyone?" Unanimous nods came quickly. "Good." That word again.

"And another thing. This one stays here, inside these office walls. There is no exception to this rule, understand? None. This suit was filed quietly. The plaintiff isn't trying it in the press, and neither are we. It will not be discussed with family, friends, third parties, and, most of all, any nosy representatives of the media. I don't care who it is, you break this rule and you are out of here, zip, gone. And if you're still wanting to practice law, you'll be lucky to be clerking for the deputy associate junior legal assistant to the dogcatcher in Igloo, Alaska … and believe me, I can make it happen." *Is that perfectly understood?* he'd asked next.

They knew it was coming. "Good."

It had started. Not a runaway yet, but the train was definitely out of the roundhouse. Quisenberry detected the presence of adrenaline in the morning, and liked it.

16

Mac!" The voice came at him as if an air bubble from the depths, straining to surface. Again: "Mac!" He turned to see Father Robichaux approaching, all smiles and waving arms. His reminiscing could stand the interruption.

"I've been calling you from across the green," the priest said, beads of perspiration glistening across his forehead. "You were trancelike. I have obviously interrupted some serious thought."

Mac was embarrassed. "I confess, I was in deep thought. So much is on my mind right now, I hope you'll forgive me." He checked his watch. The Celebration would begin in half an hour. The nerves were restless again ...

"No apology needed, Mac, you know better. Actually, I just came over to see how you were holding up. I've been chatting with Mary Alice Simpson and her friend Bertha Roberts—you know them, of course, from St. Joseph—and they absolutely wore me out. But, bless their Catholic souls, we now know who is responsible for this lovely setting. They hired those two homeless men we see every so often foraging for cans and bottles along the old Ponchatoula highway to set up the chairs and the stage. Paid them handsomely. They also got help from our local police chief and his sole prisoner. Quite nice of them, wouldn't you say?"

"I'd say." Mac wasn't up for more small talk.

"The invited have started arriving. Are you okay? Anything I can help you with, a comforting bit of prayer, perhaps?"

"No, thanks, Father. I'm doing fine. I wish Elizabeth were here, but I've at least got my boys. I do have my boys, don't I?" he asked, looking in the general direction of the rope swing.

"Oh, yes. You needn't worry about them. Mac, I must say, they are so handsome. They're over there spending a little brotherly time with each other, and I believe some of their friends who showed up early. Believe me, they're fine."

"It's good they've got friends here. I needed this time to myself."

"I can take the hint, my friend. I'll be back in a bit, to wake you from the next phase of your trance. Sound okay to you?"

"It would be just fine, Father, I'd be grateful."

"It's settled, then. Let me see if I can find a way to go spark some more Mass attendance out of the crew over there with your boys. Assuming I can dodge Mary Alice and Bertha.

"And," he added with a mischievous eye-twinkling, over-the-shoulder glance, "you did not hear me say that."

Mac watched the priest head toward his sons. Always in motion, it seemed. Always aimed in the direction of souls to save. Like this thing today, this Celebration, a product of their collaborative effort. Mac once again looked around, at nothing in particular, at everything, and wondered again if this wasn't just a bad idea. It had seemed so positive, so called for. A healing thing. *What could not be good about that?*

Across the river, an egret swooped down next to one of the plentiful cypress knees poking from the brackish water like so many cut cornstalks. Motionless, silent, the spindly-legged creature began its vigil. Mac held these curiously magnificent birds in such fascination. Often he would drive by the same spot he'd driven by the previous day, and would see the same creature seemingly unmoved from its perch. He'd wondered if they remained fixed until anything in particular happened. *Was it only food they sought? Did they crave rest? Attention? Were they in hiding?* These questions crowded his packed subconscious.

The living statue across the river remained motionless for only a moment. Under Mac's watchful gaze, it poked and probed at the water's surface with its sharp beak, raising its head to look around every so often. He knew they were prey for the hawks and alligators, worse yet, the poachers lurking in the backwater reaches of this river. But he also knew they were plentiful and, their delicate frames notwithstanding, possessed of sensory powers of preservation. In a world of such fragile existence, curious and helpless as they seemed, they were survivors.

The egret rose from its perch and flew up river, barely above the current, effortlessly, gracefully, silently. A ballerina with wings … just the sort of creature Nicole had always cared for.

As the egret alighted further upstream, and again assumed its rigid pose, Mac's thoughts resumed their own flight, carrying him back along the odyssey delivering him—finally—to this day.

———————

Mac answered the phone. It hadn't rung in days. He'd become listless, even giving up his therapeutic sailing excursions. Nerves were wearing thin. Hooked by a relentless malaise, he was ready for something, anything, to reel him in.

The familiar voice was like a finger snap waking him from the hypnotic lethargy. "You were supposed to call me yesterday."

"I know, Sol. I'm sorry. I wanted to give it one more day."

"Well, you're the client, my friend, but this calls for some attention, don't you think? I mean, they filed an answer in record time, no request for an extension or anything, and boom! … nothing. Nearly three months now, and nothing. Where's the mass of discovery you said they'd hit us with? You sure you have this figured out all right?"

"Maybe I misjudged, okay? They hired Rich Quisenberry, and we both know he knows my style, if I have a style."

"Mac, you have both—style, and a style," Sol quipped.

"Cute, Sol. Humor I don't need right now. We're supposed to be up to our foreheads in the swamp, and we're instead in some lockdown. Whatever happened to the defendants taking the initiative?"

"They heard that one already, pal. Hey, what say we load up the cannons ourselves? Take the fight to them. Come on, either we attack, or I'm heading south."

"Sol, where do you think you are? You are south."

"No, I mean really south. Miami, or someplace in the Caribbean. Somewhere south as in really nice to be there south."

"File our discovery, Sol. And all the deposition notices, and the subpoenas. Go ahead, file it all. Call Quisenberry with our suggested pre-trial schedule—he'll go along with it, maybe make a few changes, nothing more—then we wait for them to crank things up. We go to Plan B. They win Round One in the war of nerves. No big loss."

"You, my friend, you're the one who always said you take your victories in small steps, then add them up and measure how far you've come. Remember?"

"With you around as a constant reminder, how could I forget? This is all they win … it ends here. After you talk to Quisenberry, and get everything filed, then you might as well head south. Check in with me from time to time, though. You know they'll file their own discovery, once they see ours. When that happens, we'll need you back to get our responses in. Got it?"

"You sure?"

"I'm sure. Go, and have fun. Just come back, safe and sound. Promise? I need you, Sol, you can put off retirement for a while longer."

Sol answered only, "I promise," and hung up.

Mac placed the receiver in the cradle. This was an interesting development, one he'd not considered. He'd drafted an initial set of discovery, and had outlined a pre-trial schedule, but hadn't intended to file anything until after the plaintiff had filed its discovery first. Defense lawyers always jumped into the discovery phase first, as was their style. The show of righteous indignation, of strength. Not to mention the opportunity to do some serious billing before the client got too involved in settlement thoughts. Mac had considered the possibility, had even prepared for it. He'd hoped their false sense of security would lull them into underestimating him. But something different was happening. Why? How had he misjudged? Mac suspected his former adversary was responsible for this turn. *Fine*, he thought. That was one-on-one, may the best man win. Rich Quisenberry, he could deal with.

The decision to move forward was sound. Not one that fit with the game plan, but sound nevertheless. A temporary detour from Plan A, but easily handled. The train was still on track. All was well. No harm done. He could relax again.

It was time to take out the *Nepenthe*. Facing thirty days of respite, it was time to seek out and restore some order to things. Pleased with his decision, he went to find Elizabeth, his lone remnant of reason. If only momentary, life was once again manageable for Mac McHenry.

He was still troubled. Three months after meeting with his lawyer, the archbishop was not satisfied the best course was a traditional lawsuit defense. This was not a case of black and white, of good versus evil, of fight fire with more fire. There were grays, and much was wedged between good and evil. And fire-fighting—open, hostile judicial warfare—just didn't seem in the Church's best interests. Instinct and years of working at saving souls tugged and tore at him.

There was no denying he made the right decision to hire seasoned defense counsel. The alternative was to capitulate, an unacceptable option. But did he have to participate in this litigation process under conventional rules of engagement? Did he not have options? Maybe his lawyer didn't, but Rich Quisenberry was bound by a different set of laws and rules than the archbishop was. Quisenberry answered to the court of Man, but when souls were at stake, as here, the archbishop answered to the ultimate Court.

He had prayed mightily. And he'd listened to his lawyer carefully, concluding no matter what the outcome, the Catholic Church would be left with a gaping wound. Intact, but wounded. The Church had enough open wounds at the present; every day, it seemed, there were fresh allegations of misconduct. Isolated incidents, to be sure, but alarming, portending perhaps of worse. More than one legislature had rewritten limitations laws. And Rome was not happy.

It was common knowledge a sharp division in the Church was developing. The shame and disgrace brought on by the uncovering of a half-century of abusive practices in this country by priests and nuns alike had created a rift. It was not the way to end a glorious millennium. And there was the current movement by a growing number of renegade American priests and nuns to abrogate the requirement of celibacy, even to the point of marriage, which had not gone unnoticed by Rome. There had been talk, very silent at first, but gaining volume and momentum, that perhaps a separate American Catholic Church was called for. The subject now only of infrequent conjecture, but who could say when it might gain momentum? He was reminded of, in a historical context, seemingly insignificant events often preceding radical change.

This case must be—*will be*—stopped, Archbishop Thomas Ryan silently vowed.

The archbishop reached for the folder on his desk. He opened it again: the complete dossier on Sister Nicole Michelle McHenry. The same message he'd initially taken from the contents of the folder was still, inescapably, right in front of him. There was hope, not a great deal, but enough to lift his spirits. It was time to act. He picked up the receiver, pressed the three numbers with which he was now quite familiar, and waited for the answer.

"Sister," he began, "could I impose on you to come to my office, please. We have a situation. I need you to counsel me on *Wycko versus Gnodtke.*"

The civil servant perused again the classified report he'd held long enough for the headline news on his office television set to run through another half-hour cycle. Stamped "Eyes Only" just above the name Thomas Dillon, it had a foreboding air of solemnity. Long ago calloused to such mystique, he thought now only of reporting to his superiors further intervention was unnecessary, even risky.

Much had happened since he met with McHenry, and *encouraged*—clever agency vernacular—him to observe a certain protocol while retrieving his daughter's remains. He had not been totally surprised the lawyer found a way to meet with the condemned man. *Quite a resourceful fellow.*

The ordeal left the agency on edge. A precarious equilibrium hung in the balance. At stake were many American families, expatriates some, but taxpayers for the most part. The majority were without influence in higher circles, but a few, an important few, had connections to the very top. All of them in any event worthy of protection by their homeland. A thirty-plus year civil war affecting only the nationals was of minor significance, so long as those American interests remained unaffected. But when a full-scale overthrow attempt meandered onto the radar screen, his agency took note. Which meant Dillon took note.

The lawyer's visit, surprisingly, had not attracted appreciable attention. The press thankfully missed it. Bells of rebellion against oppression no longer rang in the countryside. A well-placed call to the highest echelon had assured the execution of the condemned prisoner would not occur. Quiet reigned everywhere, it seemed. To the cautious, such as Dillon, the quiet deserved a watchful eye. Best to be vigilant, and avoid surprises.

On the domestic front, there was this tricky business of the lawsuit. McHenry seemingly withdrew into a state of hibernation, only to emerge vengefully. State's lawyers had theorized a bit, but eventually wrote the suit off as the desperate act of a grieving, albeit misguided father. It had no eventual outcome other than ignominy. Thus it bore no high-level attention.

Still, Dillon knew, from his years of encountering the unlikely, the disjointed pieces of this puzzle could be assembled in a way that jeopardized the balance. It was his call, whether or not to intervene. He pondered choices, and outcomes. The end result? Too much was beyond his control. He would have to fly blind, and trust his instincts. For now he could only watch …

Yes, he was quite resourceful, this McHenry fellow.

17

IT WAS LATE ON a particularly uneventful and boring Friday. Seated in the center area of one of those time-shared office arrangements so common in the fringe business district of New Orleans, the young receptionist wondered why she had to stay until the regular closing time, just because *he* felt the need to stay. *I mean, couldn't he, like, just answer his own phone? Would that really, like, be so difficult? He* was Ken Randall, the owner-proprietor of Randall Video Productions, the newest tenant. In over a month, he hadn't had more than a call a day, and as nearly as she could tell, only one small assignment, and at a deeply discounted rate. Her antagonism was broken by the ring of the telephone … a call coming in on the Randall line! She subconsciously adjusted her posture as she punched the button for Suite 125.

"Randall Video Productions," she answered. "How may I direct your call?"

"Ken Randall, please," was the reply.

"May I tell Mr. Randall who is calling, please?"

"You may tell him Mr. McHenry would like to discuss retaining his services, if you would be so kind."

Excitedly, the eager voice gushed, "Just a minute, please, while I transfer your call." Then, "Ken! Ken! Pick up line one, it's someone who wants to hire you. A Mr. McHenry."

Across the hall, the young man motioned she forgot to place the caller on hold before she shouted her message. He smiled at her embarrassment before he picked up. "Mr. McHenry? From the North Shore?" She kept her ear to the receiver.

"Hello, young man. I got the business card you mailed me. How'd you like some work? The pay's not bad. Might involve some travel, expenses paid of course. Interested?"

Quietly mouthing a *Yes!* with the pumped clenched fist, Ken Randall calmly answered. "Yes, sir, Mr. McHenry. I'm ready. What are we looking at?"

His eavesdropping receptionist also pumped her clenched fist.

"I need a videographer, for some depositions to be taken in a lawsuit. It's important we capture the very essence of the persons being deposed." He let the last part soak in for a second. "Sound familiar to you?"

"Very much so. I'm into private productions now, but I still have my touch. I'd be pleased to help you out. When did you want to start?" He crossed his fingers. "I'm asking only because I have one small project to get out of the way, a two or three day filming down at Marsh Island, starting next week. It's for the state wildlife department. Will that be a problem?"

"No, just give me a call when you're finished. I'll fill you in on the details then."

"Sounds good. Thanks, Mr. McHenry. I do believe you just made my day."

The tone at the other end turned somber. "There's some hard work ahead, Ken. How strong are you at staying with a job? Don't answer, just think about it while you're down at Marsh. You'll be tested on this one. I need you to come through for me. Still interested?"

"More than ever. I'll call you, Mr. McHenry." Before he could say anything further, the connection was broken. No good-byes, no nothing. Strange.

"Sherrie," he called out across the hall as she was making her own disconnect, "you have to remember the little red button gets pushed down as soon as you say to the caller, 'I'll transfer your call.' Okay?"

Not much younger than Randall, but vastly less mature, the receptionist apologized, clearly ill at ease for her error. Randall waved her off, saying things had worked out anyway.

"Who is this Mr. McHenry?" she asked, curious at who might be responsible for part of her salary in the near term. Randall told her.

"I remember when that happened. That was so tragic. Why do you think he's hired you?"

"To videotape depositions, he said."

"Depositions?" she asked. "As in lawsuits?" She did hear him say lawsuit, didn't she?

"As in a lawsuit, would be my guess. I'll know soon enough. I think I'm going to head out for the day, Sherrie. Will you close up for us?"

"Sure, Ken." She began to clear her desktop. "Gosh, that's still so sad and all, like, his daughter being killed, a nun and all." There was no reply from across the hall. She looked up, and saw he was gone. She shrugged her shoulders, finished her tidying, and closed up the small office. By the time she'd driven the two miles to the nearest watering hole frequented by the younger set, she'd forgotten all about Mac McHenry and his slain daughter.

Elizabeth brushed away the pine straw with her hand, as she did most every day this time of year. It made a fine ground cover for the colorful yard gardens so plentifully dotting the area, but right now it was fouling her daughter's resting place. She cleared the last of it.

She was alone, as always. Truth was, she preferred being alone at her daughter's side. It gave her time to herself—quiet time, she called it—to meditate, to call her own. She came here to pray as much as anything else. Today, Elizabeth was praying for her husband.

124

†

His obsession, which is what she'd come to call it, was taking a toll on their marriage. She thought back to when he'd first told her of Evan Montgomery's revelation, and how things were different because of it. At first, she'd thought his fervor would exhaust itself. As the days passed she found out differently. One evening, when he did not answer her call to their supper, she'd become concerned, and headed down the darkened hallway toward his study. As she got near enough to see into the room, she gasped, covering her mouth with her hand. There sat her husband, surrounded by stacks of papers, others strewn everywhere, typing away, muttering to himself in little more than grunts. The dim light cruelly distorted his face, portraying a monstrous image. That this man, who could still make her laugh, who still shared their bed, could now have the appearance of one so possessed, both frightened and concerned her. She'd withdrawn into the shadows, vowing never to venture back to the study again while he was working.

He'd eventually emerged from his exile, and life had seemingly returned to normal. But last night, when he'd broken the news to her about his lawsuit, she'd realized there was nothing at all normal in their lives.

She and Bradley had never used their children as sounding boards against each other; their lives would be complicated enough without the added burden of playing arbiter in parental matters. But today was different, and Elizabeth found herself crossing a line out of desperation. Her words, spoken aloud, were directed to her daughter as confidante.

"Nicole, I can't stay long. So much is happening, and I have been powerless to control it. I think more than anything I need your forgiveness, where your father is concerned. We miss you so much. Our lives will never be what they were. I in my own way deal with losing you by coming here. I know you are here with me. A mother knows. And I know you see what is happening."

She cleared her throat, searching, groping, for the words to free her from the torment. "Am I to just let your father continue on this course? Do I trust that his eyes will open in time? Do I look for some sign of what to do?

"This isn't just for me. I have stood by your father for over twenty-seven years; I will do so until I die. But I cannot bear the thought of his throwing away both our lives, and destroying your precious memory in the process. He is after his blessed 'accountability'. Will he not rest until he has succeeded in destroying the Church, your memory and our marriage at the same time?

"We go through motions in our lives. The same strength that always kept us together also threatens to divide us. I cannot stand up against your father right now … give him a 'me or it' ultimatum. There has to be another way. My heart, weakened as it is, believes there is another way. If there is something I should do, please guide me. Just this once I ask you to help me, please."

She stretched her lithe body its full length on the ground over her daughter. She laid on her back, eyes closed, and extended her arms outwardly, cross-like. The coolness of the shaded grass felt good as it bathed her body. The grieving woman still lay there even after the first few cleansing, nourishing droplets of rain found their way through the boughs and onto her and the soft ground around her.

§

The news from the archdiocese of Mac's lawsuit left Father Robichaux stunned and saddened. He used the news to prepare the homily, in his characteristic spirit of optimism.

"Our scriptures this morning speak to our faith. Our faith, just as our Lord's was, is assailed by forces that may not be of evil origin, but may instead be rooted in misgivings, confusion, any number of human feelings and emotions. God asks us to keep our faith; he tells us our faith will sustain us even through the darkest of times. God may even test our faith. Does He expect us today to have the faith of Abraham? Probably not. No, our God is a benevolent God, a caring and judicious God. He says to us, 'Here, lay your hands on Me, give Me your pain. Suffer no more. Have faith in Me.' It is up to us to accept this offer.

"And what a wonderful offer it is. It is the cornerstone, the very foundation of our religion. It is what this Church is built on: faith. Faith of those who said 'yes' to His offer. Faith," he continued, "built from the sacrifices of many, through the centuries.

"Years ago, when I first came to St. Joseph, I spoke one Sunday from this very spot of the colorful history of this wonderful parish. Think back with me. This was the very first parish outside New Orleans in the land known as the Louisiana Purchase. It was founded by a small group of Jesuit priests who canoed across twenty miles of often treacherous lake waters. These intrepid missionaries were met by peaceful Indians, who for the most part embraced their new robe-clad, crucifix-bearing visitors, but who on occasion became displeased at the new religion being thrust on them. Our devout Jesuits faced uncertain peril. There are accounts of savage reprisals. Yet others still came here even as their predecessors were being laid to rest in our little town cemetery.

"It is reported the first nuns arrived in the 1830s. They were young girls, freshly ordained, when they arrived from Alsace, Burgundy, Provence and other rural areas of France. Full of faith, full of spirit, of dedication to purpose. Their faith was soon to be tested as well."

Before he would tell the congregation a number of the young nuns met the same fate as their fellow priests, he glanced in Mac's direction, hoping he was still seated beside Elizabeth. His eyes met Mac's. It was too late. The punch had been telegraphed, and Mac knew what was coming. Averting the priest's eyes, Mac made his way to the aisle, kneeled and crossed himself, and headed to the rear door. He did not stop for the Holy Water in the vestibule.

Alone in the rectory at day's end, Robichaux thought about his choice, and defended it. To himself, and his God. It was the thing to have done. Save one soul, he'd been taught, and it got you to Heaven and a place at the right hand of the Father. Robichaux, however, was worried about more earthly concerns at the moment. His thoughts were on his friend. How would he now reach him? The question lingered as he prepared his evening meal.

Robichaux's thoughts drifted to the catechismal story of the shepherd whose attention was focused not on the ninety-nine of his flock that were safe, but of the one still in harm's way. An amazingly simple story, yet forceful enough to keep him focused.

§

The deputy minister pulled his office door closed, and sat down heavily. Cabinet meetings, once concluded, were usually forgotten once the orders from on high were passed along. Those he parceled out with ease and indifference. But on this day he received only one order: the execution of the political prisoner, Mendez, was to be postponed—again. This time indefinitely. The look from *El Presidente* had said it all:

ALL THE ANGELS AND SAINTS

do not question this command. The deputy cared less if one more prisoner lived or died. Still, the reprieve brought him pause.

The rebellion had never begun. The remaining insurgents were in hiding, their silly boldness replaced by cold fear. To his amazement the government had declared there would be no reprisals, so long as peace reigned. So far it had. He suspected it was due to short memories, fresh with recollections of the death squads' work the last time fires of rebelliousness burned. But he also suspected more subtle influences were being exerted. Peace, and the end of all human rights violations, were being thrust upon Guatemala by its American ally to the north. And by old and new players, such as the International Red Cross, and Amnesty International, whose substantial political weight bore minding. This much was to be expected. But surely, the Americans and these others would appreciate the execution of a murdering criminal, to serve as an example for others. Even the *Americanos* executed their criminals, didn't they? Of course they did, although usually not until after years of incarceration. A waste of good opportunity, he reasoned.

18

M AC, MY FRIEND, I'M hungry, and I think we're as ready as we're going to be. We've got a strong brief, and the equities lean our way. I'm feeling pretty good about our chances." He shut his trial notebook and looked at his client.

"As good as any Jewish lawyer who's trying to convince a Catholic federal judge in the predominantly Catholic Eastern District his client has standing to bring a lawsuit aimed at closing the doors of the Catholic Church could feel under the circumstances, anyway," he added.

"Suppress the pedant in you tomorrow, Sol, and we'll do all right," Mac kidded. "Keep the argument pellucid. Give the judge credit for having some sense."

Sol noted it was Mac's first display of concern since they'd immersed themselves in preparation for the hearing. "I give us a vote of confidence and all of a sudden I'm pedantic? Whoa, boy, one of us might be wound a little too tight."

"You've done a good job, Sol … put up with a lot from me. I'm grateful. I know you'll give it your best tomorrow. Feeling good going in is better than the converse."

"Let's get some rest," Sol said with a yawn that seemed to last a full minute. "Why don't we leave from my office at six-thirty, beat most of the Causeway traffic?"

"I like your plan," Mac said.

Sol remained after Mac left. Hundreds of times, he recollected, he'd been through preparation like this. Arguing before the bench was his strongest suit. For the most part, judges liked his style. He might not always get there, but if there were any way to get past the first hurdle every lawsuit faced, he'd usually been able to find it. Tomorrow, though, Sol ruminated dejectedly, he was going down. In flames. *Big time*, he thought, shaking his head side to side, *major flames*.

His false bravado to Mac notwithstanding, Sol knew even if the Eastern District bought Mac's argument, the Fifth Circuit would shred the holding with little more than a cursory reading of the briefs. For all its equitable appeal, there just wasn't enough hard law. It didn't help matters they'd argued in one part of the brief the Church was an eleemosynary institution—a charitable entity—and not subject to worker's compensation as a sole remedy, only to turn about and argue in another part the Catholic Church is nevertheless a business regulated by OSHA. In one breath, a charitable institution not subject to the laws governing businesses, yet in another breath, a business subject to possibly the harshest laws regulating businesses that existed. Sol quivered when he thought of the court's reaction to such a fence-riding position.

He'd done it for his friend. He'd have done just about anything his friend would've asked him to do, though. They were two old warriors, from a different time, with different values than the younger breed, often than even some of their peers who'd sold out to compromised values along the way. He would never have caused his friend to look elsewhere for legal counsel to represent him in this lawsuit, doomed as it was. He'd come to Sol, and the search would end there. It wasn't the money, either; Sol had no intention of keeping Mac's money. The file was being billed, just as he'd promised, and the retainer replenished regularly. No client of Sol's had ever paid as punctually as Mac. But Sol would be depositing the money in Mac's account as he headed south for the last time. Mac would just have to accept it's never money when it's between friends.

Not a bad ending, Sol thought. It could have been worse: obscurity, or worse yet, ignominy, the career's end several of his brethren had suffered. The finish, the race's end, maybe it would be a different matter after all. *Just retire to the south of Florida, take an occasional pleasure boat over to Jamaica, or one of those really ritzy spots like St. Kitts, and live out your years with a bunch of other old retired Jewish lawyers. Tell them how you, in a moment of desperate loyalty, for a goyim no less, took on the Catholic Church and tried to get its doors locked. They'll get a real hoot and a howl out of that one.* On second thought, maybe he'd keep this one to himself. He'd also just have to hope news of severe judicial whippings in Louisiana's Eastern District didn't make the south Florida retirement community newsletters.

Meanwhile, Sol, old boy, pack your brief case, buckle your chin strap, and be ready for what happens tomorrow. Give it your best shot, for your old friend.

§

Rich Quisenberry walked toward the elevator without his usual swagger. He wondered if his adversaries were still at it. It was eleven, which made the morning's hearing less than a good night's rest away. He'd gotten by on little sleep before. And the year behind enemy lines in the Sixties had steeled his nerves for anything he could ever expect to encounter in a court of law. He loved the fight, always had. Better when no lives would be lost in this kind of fighting, but he remained grateful in a perverse way the service for his country had unlocked the puzzlement in him, through the restless years, of what lay ahead. After his discharge, he'd made it straight for law school, and hadn't looked back.

This is what he was put here for, this gentleman's combat, this civilized form of warfare. He regaled in the opportunity to attack, and defend, the next morning.

For months of sixteen-hour days, and countless miles of travel, ever since he'd taken on the defense in the McHenry case, he'd worked tirelessly to get to this point. To the first hurdle, the one he'd told the archbishop the plaintiff's standing to bring the lawsuit would be tested.

Tomorrow's hearing was a *fait accompli*, a done deal, a laydown. He'd craftily led the plaintiff and his lawyer into the heart of the battlefield as he warily sealed the escape routes. They were now trapped, hamstrung with their argument—he would characterize it as disingenuous to the court—that the Catholic Church both was and was not a business for purposes of this lawsuit, how it possessed an identity of convenience. Quisenberry was confident McHenry's double-edged position would not play well to Judge Maurice Daigre.

Quisenberry turned his attention to the man on the bench. Maurice Daigre had been his law school classmate, a moot court opponent. He had showed, at best, average skill as an advocate. After graduation, while he—Order of the Coif and Law Review—had taken the bait offered by the large, silk-stocking firm of Phillips, Dawson, Maurice Daigre had gone the way of moving to one of the deep southern coastal parishes, and had set up shop as a solo. He'd done well enough, usually representing insurance companies and corporations sued by the local populace. His *curriculum vitae* as complete as it would ever be at the attorney's level, he got himself elected as a state court judge first, then lobbied for the first available federal bench opening to come along in his district. Timing being right politically, he was virtually unopposed, and went through the confirmation process unimpeded. So far, he'd done a good job on the bench. Even if the facts and the law were not so overwhelmingly favorable to his client, Quisenberry knew this judge would be inclined to toss the suit, perhaps even to impose a sanction on the old coot of a lawyer representing

Mac McHenry. *Just where had Mac found the old man, anyway?*

As good as his argument was, there was always the possibility the court might reject it. He wasn't worried. His team had researched the issues to the depths and breadths of extant jurisprudence; if the Eastern District ruled against his 12b6 motion, the Fifth Circuit could apply the final blow on appeal. The eventual outcome was not in doubt. He would stake his name on it.

Feeling supremely confident, Rich Quisenberry pushed the button to take him to the lower level parking garage, and smiled the smile of the victor as he sets in for the kill.

§

In a small, sparsely decorated candlelit room no more than a mile from where Rich Quisenberry operated the remote keyless entry on his Lexus sedan, one decidedly more concerned than he about the outcome of the next day's hearing grasped the necklace-like object between the first and second fingers of her right hand as she prayed silently. Saying the rosary each night was a matter of routine for the nun. Tonight, there was a controlled anxiety as she prayed, for she suspected the next day would bring about a different outcome than the one the archbishop had relayed to her from Rich Quisenberry. She'd monitored the case from the shadows, her attention focused on the elusive creature at issue in most lawsuits: *justice*.

As a lawyer she had to acknowledge the "results oriented" phenomenon in the courts of America. Legend had it some silk stocking firm invented the term after losing an unlosable case. Regardless of the expression's origin, any lawyer who viewed justice in this day and age as the scales tipping in one direction or the other based purely on jurisprudential weight was out of touch with reality.

As a nun she understood there was a grieving father with no outlet for the pain at his loss. There was nothing more than accountability sought: he only wanted someone to pay. Not money, but penance. Was that not the very thread of the Church's fabric? Penance as a means of absolution? The irony was too real not to be in Quisenberry's face. A good Catholic, no doubt, but perhaps too much the lawyer and not enough in touch with the spiritual side.

Put together, she saw it would be no step too great for even a federal judge to deny the motion by the defendant and to allow the suit to proceed. She had a strong feeling the outcome of tomorrow's hearing was preordained.

The source of her concern lay not in the suit continuing, but what it would do to those who were involved … including herself.

Not long ago, she'd done her best to explain to the archbishop how this might play out. He'd seemed to understand, but had left her with the nagging feeling there was more. She'd been given his file on the lawsuit, and asked to keep abreast of its progress, to advise him when she thought it necessary. The archbishop had funneled Quisenberry's correspondence to her, and shared the phone conversations, yet four months into the case she had still not met with the Church's lawyer. They hadn't been face-to-face since she'd worked as an associate in his firm years earlier, in another life. She wondered if Quisenberry even knew who Sister Katherine was. She reckoned he would know soon enough.

Tonight, she'd met again with the archbishop. She'd briefed him with her thoughts on the outcome, noting almost apologetically her observation of Quisenberry's one critical flaw. He'd thanked her for her candor, and, seemingly as an afterthought as she had turned to leave his office, had asked her to return, to have a seat. He had something to discuss with her, he'd said, a thought or two on expanding her role in the lawsuit.

As she knelt now, in prayerful repose before her God, the same God of all the angels and saints and sinners alike, setting aside the pain she felt personally, she asked for courage and strength to meet the challenge laying ahead, and for the wisdom to do what was in His best interest first, and in those whose lives and souls were at stake second.

§

He sat alone on the lanai out back, in the dark of a moonless night. They'd eaten later than usual, inside, while an evening shower christened western St. Tammany Parish. The rain stopped at about the same time the dishes had been put away. It was Elizabeth who'd suggested they move outside. Mac's work done for the day, he'd jumped at the chance to be anywhere with his wife.

The air was heavy with the dankness following the short bursts of rain after the heat of a summer's day. Mist rose from the ground, from the flowers, from their lawn table and chairs. She wiped down the table and chairs while Mac poured their after dinner coffee. Elizabeth was atypically loquacious this night, at times almost giddy, as she shared a humorous account of an encounter with a raccoon family earlier in the day. Normally nocturnal, it seems the rascals had braved up to the house in broad daylight, and had helped themselves to their garbage. Almost as if they'd known it was pickup day, they'd hidden in the wooded lot across the street until she'd filled the cans, then had brazenly gone for the loot when Elizabeth returned to the house.

When she'd returned momentarily with another bag, she'd found them rooting in the cans. She laughed as she told her husband how they'd scampered off in their fright, only to return and challenge her for the rights to the booty. Elizabeth's compassion for the critters ended the standoff; she'd given in.

Mac had long ago quit caring for the cuteness of scavenging varmints. He was more concerned with the mess they invariably made, and set about to raccoon-proof their garbage cans. He'd prided himself in succeeding where lesser men before him hadn't. For years now they'd had no more encounters with the wily creatures. Until today. And for some reason it had struck Elizabeth as funny she'd had to fight over her garbage with a raccoon family. Mac was not amused. But he did enjoy seeing the revitalized spirit in his wife, so he let her have her fun. He sensed Elizabeth's airiness had more to do with her satisfaction the animals had outsmarted him than anything else. His guard down, he'd become caught in his wife's giddiness, and had actually laughed, a good old-fashioned belly laugh. Then Elizabeth grew weary, as she seemed to do earlier and earlier most evenings these days. They embraced as she excused herself. Mac made a point to ask later about her painful wince from his hug.

Elizabeth had gone inside an hour ago, leaving him to his solitude. While she knew nothing of the hearing in the morning, Mac suspected she knew him well enough to know when he was feigning sincerity. He had to concede she'd become quite accustomed to it the past six months. Still, it had not come to a question of his love for her. Only his devotion. It was obvious to him she missed the old, plain and simple affection he'd always shown her. It was the same with him. He missed his wife, his wonderful, satisfying life with her. For months now he'd all but deserted her, doling out only bits and pieces of himself, expecting the leftovers to be enough, but knowing they weren't. He wasn't fooled by his own illusion; why should he expect her to be?

Mac paused in his thoughts. He cautiously allowed himself to think about what lay ahead the following morning. Rich Quisenberry had forged a strong motion, but it roiled within itself, its very legal core muddled by its intransigence. It had no heart, no soul. Still, if this case was to move forward, Sol had to believe in it.

Tomorrow would test Sol's belief in their cause. He would need to rise to a higher level, to argue passionately. To those who would say the federal bench is immune to spirited, passionate oral argument, Mac had only one response: rubbish. All judges, federal and state alike, expected and were disappointed when they received less than conviction from an advocate. Ordinary lawyers, those without the passion or the conviction of their clients' interests, made only for good excuses. No, make that bad excuses.

Mac kept a close watch on Sol these past few months. Their pace had been a wicked one, and the last thing he needed to do was be the cause of a stroke, or a heart attack, for his lawyer. But he'd been pleasantly surprised at the older man's resilience. Sol had stayed with Mac stride for stride, hour for hour. Once Mac suggested they rest for a week or so. The idea had infuriated Sol, who in a burst of sanctimoniousness, questioned his client's motivation. Not another word about resting had been spoken afterward.

Once the flow of paper started, discovery took them on a whirlwind ride. After Sol prepared, filed and served deposition notices and subpoenas, Mac called his young videographer, made the requisite number of plane and lodging reservations, and the plaintiff commenced taking depositions. True to young Mr. Randall's modest boast, he had captured on videotape enough of the pathos of each witness's shame and misery to have secured plenty of money damages from even the most unwilling of jurors, had that been the objective. The witnesses were the selectively chosen group of priests and nuns who had disgraced themselves and their Church in a number of celebrated abuse cases in the past two dozen years, the miscreants whose cases Mac had found while doing his online research.

Each witness testified he, or she, engaged in the actions which brought about their dismissal from the service of the Church, and at no time had a superior so much as spoken a word of concern over their aberrant behavior. Parents' complaints were ignored, injuries with suspicious origins were passed off as quirky accidents, and on and on, *ad infinitum*. The earlier pain of the transgressors was nothing when compared to the agony Sol led each one through as he probed their faithlessness, the Church's disregard of their deceit, the hushed transfers, the denial when confronted with the truth.

It had been like shooting fish in the proverbial rain barrel.

As he reviewed their videotaped testimony later, Mac saw how well Ken Randall had done his job. Mac knew any judge viewing these pitiful stories of what amounted to total and absolute neglect by the Catholic Church would be compelled to feel the same way, would find it very difficult to deny the spirit of the law had been violated. It was the letter of the law part posing the big, unanswerable question.

In spite of the videotapes and the compelling nature of the case, Mac prepared himself for failure. If tomorrow did not work for him, if the court ruled to dismiss his lawsuit, Mac would accept the ruling and would not appeal. The thought brought him down, but his despair was short-lived. Courage, stamina, and belief in his undertaking were called for. Another time, he might have prayed for these things; the hypocrisy of his indulging in a prayerful moment hung large, like a grand chandelier. While he did not give in to the urge, he leveled his thoughts in the general direction of such a notion. He had not stopped believing. God was still in his life, but God was more than the Church. The Church, not God, had done wrong. Should Mac have left the punishment to only God? Was he wrong to take on the responsibility, the commitment, to be the punisher? These same questions still haunted him. More than six months along, and the only progress, if it could be called progress, was that in a few hours a man would hear other men argue the fate of the extension of God in the Catholic society. *Extraordinary*, Mac thought, one man with so much power, comfortable dealing with such an overwhelmingly unknown and critical issue.

As he headed for his two hours' restless sleep, he nodded in the vague direction south, where, in New Orleans' Garden District, Judge Daigre lived. The nod was a simple gesture, intended only to convey a single, simple message: *do what you must, but be guided by your heart as well as your head.*

As sleep overtook him, Mac called to mind another thought, one lurking deeply within, safe from the thrusts and parries of the litigation, but gaining in momentum. He began to feel better about it now. Its time was nearing.

BOOK TWO

19

Exhilaration stirred within the passenger as her plane circled the airstrip. Toward the northern horizon lay endless green forestation, stretching into Mexico. To the far east were the seas, their blue-green blending with the robin's egg blue of a cloudless sky, as far as the eye could see. She checked her map again. To the near east lay Belize, a vacationer's paradise, home of vast stretches of beach. In a former life she might have fretted over the pilot overshooting his landing. But it was not Belize she should be over. She cringed with excitement as she said the word: *Guatemala*. Again: *Guatemala*. This is where she should be. It was no mistake.

As the plane descended toward the geometric arrangement of runways below that crisscrossed like so many pick-up sticks, Nicole's fingers deftly searched out the crucifix hung from her neck. Holding a quick breath she prayerfully closed her eyes for only seconds. She had arrived. This was her destination, her new home. A brightening smile formed as she opened her eyes and let go of the small, golden cross.

Nearly twenty-three, newly ordained, she'd gone straight into field mission work. It was the culmination of the yearning that had quietly awakened one day in a private moment in her small south Louisiana parish church. This would be the fulfillment of her calling.

In moments she would meet Father Art Hurkinen, the priest in Refugio. She knew little of him, but it was all favorable. He'd been in the village for seven years, and for all of those seven years he'd pleaded for help. That translated as, *Please send me nuns, preferably American*. She warmed at the thought of meeting the other nun she would share duties with, a girl from Boston.

As her plane taxied there were fleeting last minute thoughts of and prayers for loved ones, family and friends alike. It was clear enough to her that once she arrived in her little hamlet, there would be far less time to meander through her past life.

Work would begin in the morning.

She could hardly wait.

Nicole was greeted warmly by Father Art, who introduced her to Miguel Mendez, a diminutive native possessed of the most sparkling eyes she'd ever seen. They glowed as polished amber and begged you to like the man the instant he smiled.

"Miguel speaks a good deal of English," Father Art said. "I'm afraid my Spanish is still pitiful, so, I must say, I could not have managed without him."

Miguel beamed proudly. "I will go for your things, Sister," he said. It was as if he was on cue. Nicole instantly liked him.

"Thank you, Miguel. All I have is a large brown trunk and one dark brown suitcase. Oh, and a guitar, in a hard case." She handed him the claim receipts. "Here, you might need these."

"Thank you, Sister. I will bring everything." He left hurriedly, still smiling.

Nicole frowned as she watched the small man head toward the luggage area.

"Does he worry you?" said Father Art.

"Oh, no, Father. I just hope he'll be careful with my guitar." Her eyes stayed fixed on Miguel as he disappeared into the crowd.

"Believe me, you needn't worry," Father Art said. "He will treat all of your things with the greatest of care."

Nicole turned to Father Art. "I'm so sorry. I realize how judgmental what I just said—"

He waved her off. "Not necessary. You will see for yourself soon enough."

Nicole needed a change of subject. "Where is Sister Renee? Or is she already in Refugio?"

Father Art put his hand on her shoulder. "I'm afraid Sister Renee changed her mind. It may be awhile before we can find a replacement. I'm sorry. However," he continued, "the decision is yours whether you want to go on alone. If you prefer not to, the archdiocese will put you up here in Guatemala City until we find a replacement … or even put you on a plane back home."

Nicole felt a mixture of surprise and disappointment. "I came to serve, Father. I'm not bothered at all to go on alone. If you're not."

That was the last mention ever made of either Sister Renee or help for Nicole.

It took the three of them to load her belongings into the bed of the old pickup truck. Nicole started to say something clever to Father Art about the truck, but thought better. Maybe when she got to know him better, and vice versa. One apology to him was enough for the first day.

An hour into the trip Father Art began Nicole's orientation. Refugio, he explained, was Spanish for "safe haven," literally "refuge". The Mayan spelling of Refugio's equivalent had long ago given way to the current Spanish spelling. Then the conversation turned to the more serious nature of what she might expect in her new life.

"Whatever you were told about primitive conditions, poverty, illiteracy, disease, danger, you will experience far worse. Notions you might have of the allure and romance of a laid-back existence will wreck you, my dear. And just in case you thought we had the use of this fine carriage we're so comfortably seated in, think again. It goes back to the archdiocese, in Guatemala City, in two days."

Nicole let herself smile inwardly. She wouldn't have called it a fine carriage, but the point she'd have made would've been the same.

Nicole hadn't been concerned about trucks, or contact with the outside. She would deal with living conditions as she encountered them. Meanwhile, she had only one thought. Breathlessly she asked, "Father, what of the school? I was told I would be teaching the village children."

"Ah, I suspected we would get around to that. I've been forewarned of this infectious desire of yours to bring literacy to our youngsters."

For the first time since she'd met Father Art she felt uncomfortable. His piercing gaze penetrated the façade of their fledgling camaraderie as he asked, "Is it a charming little red schoolhouse, with a cupola and a nice bell for you to ring in the little fellows and ladies that you're expecting?"

"I don't understand, Father, I—"

"Our 'school' is an open-air structure, not much more than four corner posts with a poor excuse for a roof attached to them. There are crude benches for the students, and a table at one end, for the teacher, which was me for the first four years I've been here. But I make a bad teacher, Sister, which is why you are here." He looked away.

"We haven't had school for three years now. I regret to tell you that this is a start up program you've come into." Something about the way he was averting her eyes …

So it was a sense of failure he was feeling, she realized. His carefully confessed fallibility touched her.

"Father," she began, gently patting the back of his hand, "did they not tell you I am probably the best start up person in the Western Hemisphere? And," she added, "that I knew what this mission involved—and I mean everything about it—before I asked for it?"

His head turned back. She saw the relief in his eyes, then warmed to his smile.

"Bless you, Sister. I suspect you will work out nicely. But make no mistake, your work is cut out for you." This time it was the priest who patted the back of her hand.

Livelier conversation resumed. Father Art mixed his stories well, disarming Nicole's residual nervousness with his unique style of humor. She liked his informality, and more than once laughed aloud at his wit. In return, he drew much about her, and her story-telling ability rivaled his own. With each account of something slightly more than ordinary, he would exclaim, "Well, now, I've seen it all." It was a foible she would become accustomed to.

As the miles and conversation rolled on, over roads that grew progressively worse, she heard from him the vagaries of nearly all the villagers she would be meeting in the days to come. It was Father Art's way of humanizing these strangers who'd never seen a nun. The men, he told her, would at first be standoffish—as they would be with any Western woman—but would eventually warm up, once their women realized that the young nun posed no threat, that her beauty was not a curse upon the village.

"Why do you flush and stiffen at the mention of your beauty, which is most obvious even to this old priest?" She was sure from his smile that he meant no offense.

She was prepared. All her life she'd heard how lovely and pretty she was, so this was nothing new. Unexpected, but familiar nevertheless. She answered straightforwardly. "Just an old part of me that I'm still a little sensitive about, that's all. It's nothing. And I am counting on you, Father, to let these villagers know I am but a simple nun, here to do God's work, and to be their servant. Any physical qualities I have should not get in the way of that message, don't you agree?"

"Perfectly, Sister Nicole." She caught a twinkle in his eye.

Almost as if the road disappeared from beneath, the truck crashed down hard, causing the occupants to bump heads on the cab's roof. Father Art yelped the loudest.

"Miguel, my back, please. Try to miss at least one of these blessed ruts."

Nicole smiled. Even in rebuke Father Art was gentle. He reminded her somewhat of her own father. It became something to hope for, that they should meet.

Conversation took a break, and Nicole used the respite to scan the surroundings. The thick forestation of her native Louisiana was a distant runner up to the imposing jungles. She began to form an image of what Refugio would look like. She'd been cautioned not to fantasize, but by the time Father Art spoke next she'd already painted the canvas. She liked what she saw, or rather what she expected lay ahead.

"How's your Spanish, Sister? I was told you are fluent. Sister?"

Nicole blushed, as if she'd been caught daydreaming in class. "I did well in school, and have been told I should do well here also. I suppose I won't know until I put it to the test."

"You'll do fine, I'm sure. What you lack I know our friend Miguel will be pleased to help you with. Right, Miguel?"

"Sí, padre. I help *Señor* Monty, I can help Sister Nicole also."

"Who is *Señor* Monty?" she asked.

"Miguel," Father Art interjected, "we forgot to tell Sister Nicole about our friend *Señor* Monty. What's wrong with us?

"Sister," the priest began, "*Señor* Monty, is Evan Montgomery, a British journalist who lives in our village, at least part of the time. He works for a news service, and travels throughout Central America. He follows the strife in Guatemala—that's why you saw gun-carrying troops at the airport, by the way, just in case they forgot to tell you.

"A very interesting fellow, though," he added. His expression gave away nothing. Nicole was already forming an impression of the journalist.

"Is he Catholic?" She wondered as soon as she'd asked why it seemed important.

"Wel-l-l-l," Father Art drawled, "let's just say he's not quite the practicing Catholic he might otherwise be. But there's hope, always hope, for his poor soul. Right, Miguel?"

"Sí, padre, right."

"He sounds fascinating, this *Señor* Monty. I am looking forward to meeting him."

They stopped for the night in a small village, where she experienced her first taste of Guatemalan cuisine. The family that shared its small home and meager blessings was plainly entranced by Nicole's presence. She was at once taken by their generosity and friendliness, and pleased that poverty had not stifled their happiness.

––––––––

The next morning Father Art held Mass before they left their stopover point. Nicole flawlessly assisted him at the altar. When the Mass was over Father Art explained there was a dreadful shortage of priests in Guatemala, as nearly everywhere else, and that he said the Mass whenever he came here. That might be once a month or two, he told her. He lamented on the sad fact that these folk, who were hungry for the teachings of their faith, had to wait so long in between for the blessings of God. She could see that he cared deeply for these natives. That thought stayed on her mind as they loaded up for the remainder of the upland trek to Refugio, now only a few short hours of bad road ahead.

Nicole asked Miguel if she might drive the rest of the way. "Please," she urged, "I haven't driven in so long. This may be my last opportunity for a while."

She caught Father Art nodding at Miguel, who grinned broadly as he assumed the center position in the front seat.

"Why are you smiling so big, Miguel? I would have driven yesterday if I'd known it would make you this happy."

"I did not mind the driving. It is that you are the first woman I have ever seen drive."

Nicole looked over at Father Art, who just shrugged. "Well, Miguel, then I am honored. I only hope I can do as well as you did yesterday in finding the deepest ruts in the road." She winked at Father Art, who rolled his eyes in return.

Miguel just frowned.

"Miguel, my friend, I think our Sister Nicole makes a little fun. I'm sure she means no harm. Right, Sister?"

Nicole studied the pleading expression on Miguel's face, and realized Refugio might not be ready for her style of humor. "Oh, most certainly, Father." She turned her eyes on Miguel. "Father Art is right, Miguel … I meant nothing offensive. Will you please forgive me?"

No one saw the washout. Before Miguel could speak, before anyone could brace for the jolt, the truck rose and fell violently, stalling as it came down on a ridge. Arms and legs were tangled inside as the three occupants looked at each other for an explanation. The humor struck Nicole first. She started laughing, and the two men quickly joined in. No one had been hurt, only a little pride.

"Miguel," Nicole wheezed between breaths, "remind me never again to make fun of your driving. I have no right to make fun of anyone's driving."

One turn of the key and they were on the road again, this time Nicole's attention fixed intently on the road. She practiced her Spanish on Miguel. She grew comfortable in the informality. Better yet, she liked these men. They were good men, nice men.

Not unlike her own father, she was thinking as she coaxed the old truck another half kilometer up the last hill and into the village of Refugio.

20

I
T WAS STILL DAYLIGHT as she came to a stop in front of the church. Mouth agog, she glided from behind the wheel and into the street, eyes transfixed on everything at once: the ornate cross, the bell tower, the arches, the ivy-tressed masonry, the massive iron-hinged doors, the stained glass window, all bursting with an Old World charm that made her feel instantly welcome.

Father Art's voice broke the stillness. "Miguel and I will leave you alone for a moment." There was a knowing look in his eyes. "I will be back shortly to help with your things."

"Thank you, Father," Nicole somehow mumbled.

Her first church. Overcome with emotion, with the edges of her index fingers she swept back the trickle running down her cheeks. As she reached into the pocket of her habit for a kerchief she felt a comforting hand on her shoulder. She expected to find Father Art, and was surprised to see a lovely woman of perhaps her same age shoring her up.

The woman, noticeably concerned, asked her in Spanish if she was all right.

Nicole answered in Spanish. "Yes, thank you, I'm fine. I just didn't know the church would be so beautiful." She wiped her eyes dry. "You understand, these are tears of happiness. I hope you do not think me silly."

One look in the woman's eyes convincingly dispelled that notion. Nicole sighed in relief. *I have my first woman friend here.*

"I am Teresa," the woman said in Spanish, "the daughter-in-law of Miguel, who brought you here, wife to his son Carlos, mother to his granddaughter Maria and grandson Tomas."

Nicole introduced herself simply as Nicole.

"*Sí*, Sister Nicole," smiled the other woman.

Nicole smiled in return as she lightly embraced Teresa. "I feel as if I already know you, from all Father Art and Miguel have told me. Except how beautiful you are."

Teresa blushed. "It is you who are the beautiful one, Sister."

For the only time in memory this sounded good to hear. Nicole straightened her habit, composed herself, and asked Teresa if she knew where her room was.

"*Sí*. Come, Sister, I will show you to your room." Teresa picked up the larger of Nicole's two bags and was on her way inside the small church before Nicole could argue.

As they walked, Nicole formed images of a tiny room with a single cot and, perhaps, at best, a small vanity, surely not even a closet. Another thought surfaced as well, of this being the end of a lengthy trek that began with the relative comfort of a spacious and grand room in the home of her parents, to slightly less in her sorority house at Dartmouth, then to more spartan quarters at Sister Teresa of Avila Convent in New Orleans. And now to this. She wondered if homelessness was her next stop, lying on the bare earth somewhere, clutching and straining for warmth and comfort. She mildly rebuked herself as she rethought her vow of poverty. She should not be so foolish as to attach significance to her living quarters; there were things of much more importance to be considered.

She needn't have worried. As Teresa pushed open the door at the end of the long corridor behind the altar, Nicole was astonished to see a spacious room with two beds, each adorned with a magnificent headboard, complete with a beautifully tooled set of matching wooden furniture.

"Oh, Teresa, this is lovely. The beds ... the rest of the furniture ... I would never have expected anything so grand."

"It is all made by Miguel. He is a carpenter of great skill."

Nicole's eyes stayed fixed on the surroundings. "This is truly the most wonderful room I've ever been able to call my own." Teresa proudly accepted the thanks for her father-in-law, and said she would pass them along.

Nicole politely declined her new friend's offer to help with the unpacking, explaining she was quite tired, and would be getting to bed early after a light supper with Father Art and some prayerful time. "I have a long day ahead of me tomorrow, Teresa. I am going to begin the work of starting up our school again." She spoke with unmistakable determination.

Teresa smiled anxiously. "My Maria ... I hope she will be able to attend the school."

"How old is Maria?"

"She is barely five, but she is such a smart and wonderful child. You will see tomorrow."

Nicole knew six was the minimum age, but now was not the time to make an issue of the age requirement. She tactfully told Teresa how anxious she was to meet Maria.

"You will see, Sister," Teresa repeated, "how wonderful my Maria is."

Nicole smiled at the mother's love.

Nicole readied for her first supper with Father Art. By dinner's end, he promised, the fabled cooking of her native South Louisiana would be a distant yearning. Their hosts would be the mayor and his wife, and, if he had returned from Costa Rica, Monty would also join the group.

She was treated to turkey—*pavo*—prepared in a stew-like concoction possessed of a heavenly fragrance ... a bit on the spicy side, courtesy of one of the local peppers, with fresh corn and a delightful flat bread, like tortillas but thicker, still warm from the open earth oven. The most interesting aspect of the evening, however, had been Evan Montgomery. She'd been entranced by his worldly wit and charm. Montgomery had been the reticent speaker, but being the perfect gentleman, had yielded to the pleadings of the newest village resident. When the evening finally ended, she apologized for her persistence, which of course he'd rejected out of hand.

Montgomery made it clear it was the most pleasurable evening he'd experienced in quite some time, that it was the least he could have done to welcome her to this remote spot so near the earth's very edge. She'd sensed there was a touch more of sadness than cynicism in his voice.

Father Art escorted her back to the church. She was not surprised he did not lock the doors, or secure the altar. His calm put her at ease. She followed him into the rectory. He pointed out that his room was at the opposite end of the hallway, and that if anything frightened or disturbed her during the night, he was but a shout away. She told him she would be ready the next morning promptly at five-thirty. She knew already long days that began at early hours lay ahead.

Alone later and readied for bed, she ran through the last two day's events in her head. From the previous morning's sendoff by her parents in New Orleans, to the seemingly lightspeed flight, to the drive with Father Art and Miguel, to her meeting with Teresa, and, at last, the evening meal with Father Art, the mayor and his wife, and Mr. Montgomery—Monty, he'd insisted—she couldn't recall a fuller two days in her life. It was time to bring the odyssey to a close. She fell into prayer. Her life had changed radically when she'd entered her order, but in no way more pronounced than prayer. Prayer became her connection to all things spiritual. More than implorings and thanks to the Almighty, more than a means of seeking forgiveness for the venial sins of her day, prayer became for her the means of communicating with God from deeply within her soul. Prayer filled the void that so troubled her youth. Not a path for all, she knew, but when it all opened up for her, as it had after a particularly trying time within, she'd been amazed at how simple it all became. This night she had much to be thankful and hopeful for. Somewhere between thanks for a safe arrival, and for being blessed with such warm new friends and a caring priest and wishes for strength and guidance in re-opening the school, Sister Nicole Michelle McHenry slipped off into a deep, restful, but altogether too short sleep.

✝

21

Absorbed in the minor repair of a kneeler in one of the pews in the small chapel, he barely noticed the movement to his side. "Hello? Is someone there?" First in Spanish, then in English.

The meek voice of his new charge wafted from around the corner of the nearby doorway. "It is just me, Father. I am sorry to bother you like this, but even though I know there is no tub, and no indoor plumbing, I can find no washbasin or outdoor plumbing. Could you perhaps steer me in the direction of both?"

"Oh, Sister, I am so sorry," quickly came the reply. "As I told you, it will take awhile before we can make arrangements to bring in a new tub for your own private bath. I have none either, by the way."

"Then how do you bathe?" she brazenly asked.

"Occasionally I borrow the tub in Monty's place, when he's away. Most days, I just freshen up with a washbasin of water that I keep in my room. A French bath, my mother used to call it. Takes some getting used to, but it becomes routine. I can have Carlos bring you a washbasin when he arrives later this morning. If you like." There was no immediate answer.

"Sister," he continued, "I fear they forgot to tell you before you left America that bathing here is, shall we say, not an everyday thing?"

Dead silence. "Sister?" The priest rose from his labor and headed for the doorway.

"I'm not dressed, Father. Please. I know what I was told of the, the—" She hesitated, her voice quickening, hesitating at the word *conditions*. "I'm not sure what to do. I had looked forward to cleaning up for my first day. The trip left me coated in road grime. I knew there would be no running water, no shower … but I'd hoped to at least freshen up. I would very much appreciate a washbasin. When will Carlos get here?"

"Any moment. And Sister, no matter how long it takes to get you a tub of your own,

I assure you, neither I nor the villagers will judge you on when you last bathed."

Inwardly she accepted the news with all the zeal of one facing a root canal; outwardly she hid her disappointment. "I understand," she replied. "And the outdoor facilities? Please tell me where I, well, you know …" She was uncomfortable from a bladder expanded to capacity.

"Ah, Sister," came the hesitant reply, "perhaps you might find Teresa, who is probably in the kitchen right now. She can show you to the facilities."

"Father, why do I have this dreaded feeling that I am in for an even greater surprise where my other personal needs are concerned?"

"Sister, Teresa can fill you in on everything you need to know. I suggest that you seek her very capable assistance. She should be, as I said earlier, in the kitchen. You'll find it—"

She cut him off. "I know where the kitchen is. I'll find her. Thank you, Father."

Moments later, returning from the outdoor facility Teresa had so nonchalantly sent her to, Nicole ruminated on the first of her first day's developments. *If my friends could see me now,* she hummed on the way back to her quarters. Her first real outhouse experience. It would take getting used to, but she would, in time, come to accept it as unworthy of a second thought. But bathing, that was different. She vowed that before the day was up she would, by God, take that basin bath.

§

There were fifteen villagers at the morning Mass. Father Art introduced Nicole to the faithful, and urged them to welcome her. To her joy, they'd greeted her warmly. Thoughts of how they might have rejected her for her state of uncleanliness, not to mention their first contact with a female of the cloth, quickly dissipated when their warm smiles and handshakes bathed her in the most cleansing soap of all—acceptance. After they'd left, she thanked Father Art, and vowed not to be such a problem to him again. He dismissed her apology, explaining he, too, had encountered the same conditions on his arrival. The adjustment he'd made years ago was now a way of life, as it would become for her. So much for creature comforts.

Next he gave her a verbal tour of the surroundings. "The village spreads outwardly from the church in all directions. Most of the homes are to the east," he motioned, "with a few to the southeast, where Evan Montgomery lives. And to the west there is a water pool at the base of a waterfall that falls from a steep drop-off to a hidden valley below. There is also water in the river to the northeast, a half-mile away. The villagers fish and bathe in the river.

"A word of caution: I would suggest you do not venture that way near day's end if you want to avoid the possible unpleasantness of encountering naked Indian families, who, despite my teachings tend to disdain anything resembling modesty when it comes to bathing. They do stay clothed while in the village," he assured her.

"They also haul water from the river for drinking and cooking, in large handmade pottery urns set on homemade wagons. Only in exceptional situations will they bathe in, or bring water from the pool in the valley below," he explained. "The climb is too steep to carry much, for one thing, but more importantly the valley can be a treacherous place. Villagers have fallen prey to marauders of all sorts: carnivores, vipers and other deadly creatures that do not hesitate to strike." Nicole shivered with dread.

Father Art continued. "Families live in small homes with few rooms. Only our church has an indoor kitchen. All other cooking in Refugio is done outside the homes, often under hand-fashioned canopies to shut out the rain.

"Refugio has a number of empty structures, from homes to small shops where craftsmen show off their woodworks and women their hand-sewn bolts of colorful cloth. On an irregular basis, as nearly as I can tell when the mood strikes them, the villagers hold a bazaar of sorts, where they barter foodstuffs, textiles and other crafts. There is merriment for a few days, then a return to normalcy until the next festive whim strikes." She smiled. It might be more like south Louisiana than she'd thought.

"There's even a deserted garrison, built over twenty years ago when war in the region seemed imminent. The conflict never materialized, but the military installation has stood all these years. It is off limits to our villagers, who gladly give it a wide berth. Doubtless it is overrun with every imaginable form of wild and unruly vegetation and vermin."

Something he'd said earlier had caught her attention. "Did you say something about a hidden valley?"

"That's something you'll need to see for yourself … being mindful not to go alone," he cautioned. She made it a point to explore the valley at the first opportunity.

The tour concluded, Father Art led her to the open schoolhouse, pointing along the way to the places and things he'd just told her about, giving mental images a certain reality. They reached the school quickly. Its simple thatched roof covered a dozen rows of long tables, with short benches that could neatly seat as many as thirty.

"You should not expect a large turnout this first day," Father Art explained. "Our friends will probably need time to adjust to your presence."

Nicole frowned, and started to speak.

Father Art never slowed. "You might be viewed with skepticism at first, but," he calmly reassured her, "in time you will surely need additional benches." She smiled at the compliment.

"I'm up to the challenge," she replied as she took her seat at the head of the class.

An hour later, then two hours later, they were still alone. Not one child had shown. There is only so much small talk two people can make in the space of an hour or two, especially when they are, for all practical purposes, virtual strangers, moreso when they are of the cloth. It becomes more problematic when, as here, expectations run so high and are totally unrealized. But somehow Nicole managed to find enough common ground with Father Art to weather the awkward situation. If anything, it drew them closer. He kept her focused not on what could have been perceived as failure, but on the positive side: that she had shown up, and was prepared to teach. He assured her, the school would eventually fill.

She believed him. With his help, she would get this school started, and would make it a place where the children would want to come, a place where parents would encourage their children to go. Just a bump in the road. She smiled at that thought. It was something her father had always said, when things got tough.

When ten-thirty arrived uneventfully, even Nicole was ready to concede the first day's failure. "Sister, despite my advance notice to these fine folk that today was to be the first day for the new school, they have apparently chosen to test our resolve. I can't imagine why the reluctance. Nevertheless, we shall have to try it again tomorrow."

"They will come around, in time," he said, patting her shoulder as they trudged back to the church.

She looked over at him. Confidence featured prominently in her voice. "Father, I am more determined now than ever. I have no intention of giving up."

"That's the spirit. Now, while I go back to the church to attend to some priestly matters, what will you do?"

"I'd like to look around, if I may. Any suggestions where I might begin?"

"Certainly." Then he smiled at her, a Cheshire kind of grin that neither did nor didn't answer, and swept his arm over the panorama that lay before them. With that silent, sweeping gesture he headed back to the church.

She watched him walk away, head erect, a strong gait, a certain quiet power radiating outwardly. In the space of less than forty-eight hours she had learned much about him, yet still knew so little. But she had come to trust him. When there is trust, the rest can wait.

She struck out to the northwest, away from what Father Art had told her was the most developed part of the village, hoping the course would take her toward the mysteriously inviting valley. A winding path led the way. Its dried, matted grass spoke comfortingly of heavy traffic. Until she conquered her inchoate fear of the unknown in this new world, her sense of adventure would take a back seat to a stronger sense of awareness and self-protection. She'd been warned to beware of certain venomous snakes, the *fer-de-lance* in particular, with a bite that led to agonizing death, and the jungle animals that preyed, albeit rarely, on humans. There was no substitute for caution when straying from the village.

Nicole saw she was alone. It was a small village, but to be deserted at this time of day didn't seem right. She halted, a sense of anticipation building. Her spine tingled, producing a shivering chill. Inexplicable unease crowded her thoughts. Was someone watching?

She shrugged off such a foolish notion, and forged on. This day was too precious to dwell on such wildness.

The tremulous feeling was a reminder of the care she'd been told to take. But this day was so gloriously beautiful, the heat barely noticeable and the light blue sky dotted with soft brush strokes of white, fluffy clouds that for once did not portend rain, even in this rainy season, that a certain amount of caution could be thrown to the wind. Forcing herself to relax, Nicole continued ahead on the path as it meandered away from the village perimeter. Soon she stood in a small clearing at the edge of an area of thick growth. Once she stepped into the denseness, the village would pass from view.

The temptation to explore was irresistible; fear of the unknown took a back seat to her sense of adventure. She stepped through the invisible curtain that separated safety from uncertainty.

She stopped abruptly after a few paces. A chill again raced the length of her spine; telltale gooseflesh appeared on her forearms. Her earlier feeling of unease tightened its grip. She looked quickly over her right shoulder, hoping there would be nothing there but fearful that something would be. Nothing. With half-squinted eyes trained on the row of houses nearest her, she could also see far enough in the distance to make out the back of the church. There was no movement, no sign of anything out of the ordinary. Chiding herself, she shrugged off the sense of alarm and went on.

But the eyes that had remained fixed on the nun kept their silent, menacing watch, until she was out of sight.

After two more days of empty benches, Nicole decided that it was time for her to take the message to the villagers. Visions of herself, withered and worn two years hence, still sitting alone, watching and waiting for students who never came, flashed through her mind. This would not do. Impressed with her initiative, Father Art encouraged her.

Armed with the locations of the houses with school age children, she went calling. In three days, she visited all but two families on her list. Making the most of her Spanish-speaking ability, she explained to a surprisingly skeptical group of parents that their children needed and deserved to learn to read and write, and to learn the catechism, and that she was there to do the work of God to bring these things to their children. They, as parents, wanted this for their children, *sí*? *Sí*, they unanimously replied, all agreeing that bright and early in two days their child or children would be in attendance at the school. Pleased with her success, she reported to Father Art.

"A fine effort," he told her. "Now you must also prepare yourself," he cautioned, "for the possibility some, maybe even most of these new students, might not actually show up as promised."

"I don't understand, Father. I was told—"

"And it may yet happen. I just don't want you to become discouraged if it doesn't."

"Father, why am I getting the impression there is more to this? What haven't I been told?"

He looked away, sighing heavily. Slowly he pulled off his reading glasses, and rubbed the bridge of his nose, chafed from the frames' tightness. Uncharacteristically pensive for a brief time, he cleared his throat, then spoke. "I suppose it's time you knew a few things. Why don't we go for a stroll and I'll try to explain."

She didn't know what to expect, but had no intention of putting him off.

Standing in the small patch of earth beside the church that once had been a flourishing garden, now desiccated from neglect, she heard things her training had left her unprepared for. "The war," he began, "it's this blessed war. Isolated as we are up here, word still gets around. They have no television, or radio, or even a telephone, yet our villagers know what is happening in the rest of their country.

"For centuries, ever since the earliest priest-missionaries came and converted them to Catholicism, the Indians have taken on blind faith that the Church would serve their every spiritual need, which would in turn spill over into their every worldly need. And for centuries these poor, uneducated people have accepted their lot, staying illiterate, poor and downtrodden. The Church, steadfastly apolitical, has merely preached Salvation, and has neglected to cultivate ambition in the natives by which they might escape from their misery. Somewhere along the way," he told her, "the Indians—not all of them, but a fair number—have begun to question the role of the Catholic Church in Guatemala."

He looked squarely at Nicole. "And you know what? They're right. The Church has been content to teach about God and the gospels, but it has not led these people into the modern world, into the miracle cures of medicine, into modern education, into electricity or even indoor plumbing. Despite its outward efforts, the Church has turned a blind eye to the welfare of these unfortunates. It would have taken so little over the centuries," he continued, "if the Church had had the foresight. Now, well, things are so far in arrears a turnaround seems next to impossible. It could take centuries to catch up.

"To make matters worse," he added, "there are stories that have filtered through the community, accounts from outside sources, that priests, and even nuns, should not be trusted. I'm speaking of things best left unspoken. It is quite possible, Sister, and you should consider this wisely, that your arrival might have stirred in the minds of the villagers visions of things potentially unpleasant." He paused.

Nicole digested the news. She'd heard of such things in her own country, stories that were beginning to surface, of abuses by the clergy, priests mainly ... but not entirely. She wasn't sure exactly what to say.

"I see." But she didn't, not really. "Father, forgive me if I seem confrontational, but why haven't I been told this before now?"

"I suppose you should have. Frankly I didn't want to tell you something like this unless it was necessary. For all I knew they would flock to your school. They did to mine, but times were different when I first came. There has always been a priest in this village. Not always a school, and never a nun. But I was not faced, as you apparently are, with having to prove myself to these people. A whole new dread chokes this country, apparently even our peaceful village. Your arrival has not come at the best of times."

She straightened her skirt, then looked up, in the direction of voices coming from over the rooftops. The oyster shell sky promised rain within the hour. She started to bite her lip, a bad habit kicked long ago, then thought better. She took a step closer to Father Art before speaking.

"I came here for a reason. I knew it wouldn't be easy. What you're telling me, I suppose if I let it, could discourage me. But I won't. I'll just have to work harder to earn their trust. At least I know what I'm up against." Father Art had the look of one who felt better, but the wrinkle on his forehead suggested there was more.

A slight breeze picked up, tossing her veil across her eyes. She swept it aside. "Father, while we're talking, is there anything else that I should know?"

"My, you catch on quickly. Yes, I suppose there is."

She bristled noticeably with alarm. Father Art smiled as he raised both hands in a gesture of self-defense. "No, no, Sister, it's not what you think. I was going to tell you this today anyway. And it's not related to what we were just discussing, so please relax, and let me explain.

"Refugio is for the time being not my only village. It is yours on a full-time basis, but for now, until additional help comes, I serve two nearby villages as well, on a rotating basis: eight weeks in Refugio, then two weeks each in the other two villages before I return to Refugio. Next week," he continued, "I must leave for a month. All this means is that for four weeks you will be on your own. Teresa will look after you, and you may always rely on the mayor and on Miguel."

It was one thing to have one's faith tested; it was entirely another to have it abused. Feelings of hurt and anger stirred as she considered this latest development. Yet as she thought more carefully she saw opportunity. Here was a chance to accomplish her goal entirely on her own. Already she was calming. Her thoughts were interrupted by Father Art.

"I hadn't intended to hold you hostage this long, Sister. I'm afraid we'll have to finish this later. Evening Mass is but moments away. I truly am sorry we don't have more time ... I know you have more questions." She smiled, and kept silent.

The evening Mass took on a different cast to Nicole, who saw the familiar worshippers in a new light. She needed a generous dose of inspiration at the moment, and found it right before her, in the weary, weathered faces of these loyal parishioners. Letting go of the pettiness of her own problems, she prayed for the souls of the faithful who crowded before the altar to receive the body and blood of Jesus Christ.

———————————

She was once again in her room, readied for bed, fatigue and the lateness of the hour reminders of another long day. What had she walked into? What if Father Art's suspicions were well-grounded, and she was looked upon as a person not to be

154

trusted, or worse yet, a person to be despised? This simply would not do; her time was now. What divine inspiration or intervention would make these people know that she was here to help? Her first concern, the one above all else, was of course the school. The political intrigue, she would leave to others. Her efforts would be on attracting the three dozen or so village children to her school; the rest, all the mundane exigencies of a day in the life of a nun, must take second place for a while.

The stillness and quiet enveloped her as she groped for something, anything, she could use to penetrate the barrier separating her from those whose lives she hoped to better. She found it disturbingly ironic that these native villagers were shutting her out from one of the very things for which Father Art held their Church blameworthy—a course of betterment. It was imperative she find a way to gain their trust.

———————

The cries awakened him again. Judging by the hour, they were the screams of one trapped in a bad dream. The third night in a row. If it were like the last two nights, quiet would be restored in seconds. He made it a point to make a proper inquiry of his neighbors in the morning. Shaking off his torpor, the journalist rose from bed and made use of the chamber pot. *Thanks*, he grumbled to the one who'd robbed him of the full night's rest. He stepped outside and sat on one of the chairs Miguel had crafted for him. He settled comfortably into the soft cushion Teresa had sewn. It had been a restless sleep anyway, and the night air felt good. Faced with a deadline in two days, and an empty carriage in his Corona, this was a good time and setting to deal with the nagging problem he couldn't shake: his lack of creativity.

This could be his last stop. It had been a long, slow fall from grace for the once-heralded journalist, from Pulitzer quality work in Southeast Asia in the Sixties to this. "This" was Central America, where he'd managed to land on a trial basis as a freelancer with Reuters two years earlier. With most of the world's attention focused on war and ethnic cleansing in the former Balkan states, unrest in the People's Republic of China and the eastern curve of the Mediterranean—rich assignments for journalists whose holds on their lives were not as precarious as his—he was told he should feel fortunate there was a war on drugs being waged in Central America, and a civil war in Guatemala thrown in for good measure, for him to use as a springboard to salvage a wrecked career and life. Out of respect for his brilliance in an earlier time, under far different conditions, they'd not spoken of his excessive drinking; that had been left understood. He'd simply been shown the corporate policy on drugs and alcohol, and encouraged to carefully read it. Emphasis on *carefully*.

Out of desperation, and a healthy measure of fear, he'd taken the provisional assignment, and had begun to write again, not top quality stuff at first, but acceptable. The past year had seen his work approaching the caliber of his halcyon days; all it lacked was inspiration—what he usually found embedded in human interest. His two Pulitzer nominations had not been for reporting on the ravages of a political war dividing a country, but for knowing the names of the home town and wife or sweetheart of the soldier who'd given all in some rice paddy. Evan Montgomery, the journalist with a heart, some said. To him, far too much credit had been given for

possessing some character trait he didn't possess. He wondered if guilt over some undeserved accolade might've caused his downslide. Soon the liquor, and the uncertainty of his own motivation, ran their course. He vanished from the landscape, only to emerge from obscurity in Central and South America. Those peers who still remembered Evan Montgomery joked of his inability to find his way out of the jungles of the world.

He'd struck up a friendship with the padre instantly, in time managing to slow down a bit on the drinking. There were times when the old curse held him in its grip, and pulled him under, often enough that Reuters had not relaxed his probationary status. Thus he lived from day to day, certain only that if he crossed the line once too often what his next step would be. There was much incentive to hold onto what he had.

As if on cue, the fitful noises next door stopped abruptly. He heard muted voices from within the house. The man and woman who lived there with their two small children seemed ordinary enough. The man, Juan, or something like Juan, tended a few goats, managed a small garden, barely got by from outward appearance. A likeable enough fellow, but quiet, with dark, brooding eyes. Probably nightmares, as he'd thought earlier. He made another mental note to inquire on it.

He'd seen Sister Nicole again today. It had been three, maybe four nights since they'd dined at the mayor's home. Her youth hid maturity and intelligence well. Guiltily, he'd also been taken by her beauty, and beguiled by her fascination of what had become all too common to him. She'd been relentless to get from him what lay outside this village. Had he visited the many ruins? Was Costa Rica as beautiful as it appeared to be in the books and post cards? Just how fierce was the war to the south? What hope for peace was there? Had he ever seen the Manchester United team play? Where did she have to go in Guatemala to see a soccer match? Captivated by her innocent energy, Montgomery stumbled in conversation more than once. She obviously thought way too highly of him. It was not so much a loss of face he feared. No, it was this confusing feeling that his insides, long ago sapped of warmth, were aglow in the span of time it took to consume an evening meal, revealing what some had debated years ago existed at all: a spark of decency in the man.

His deadline crept back into view, along with it the nervous tension of one grasping at something just out of reach. Montgomery slipped into his cottage, lit the lantern, and sat at his desk. He knew what he must write, just not how to go about it. Too much about her still lay unknown. As the dew settled on the ground outside, he made his decision.

She was worth the risk of a missed deadline, if that's what was necessary.

———————

This place defied description, begged for poems and songs to ring its grandeur. Selfishly she hoarded it in these private moments. But it was not in her to put up a NO TRESPASSING sign, real or imaginary. She would've shared it with anyone. Fortunately, no one intruded. Selfishly or not, she liked it that way.

The psychology of it all was perplexing. She was like her mother, surrounding herself with nature like this. That part was understandable. The seclusion, the aroma of the earth and its vegetation, it would hold the same attraction for Elizabeth McHenry as it held for her daughter. Here she could plan ahead—the next day's attempt to find pupils for the school, the various errands and missions for Father Art or her neighbors whom she thought of as family now—or she could relax, and let a weary mind and body drift aimlessly. Free time, she fondly recalled it from her preschool days. Time to do anything she wanted. A perfect opportunity to reminisce.

It was near the end of her first year at convent. She'd been summoned to Sister Agnes Ann's office. Not the first time she'd been called to appear before the Mother Superior, or Mother Hen as Nicole had called her, but, as it turned out, the most unpleasant.

"Sister Nicole," the elder nun had begun, "I think it's time we talked about your future." The lines around Sister Agnes Ann's mouth were more prominent than usual. Nicole knew something wasn't right. Still, to the postulate these had been magical words, signaling an end to eleven tough months of near thankless toil and study. There had been that jolt of internal elation at Sister Agnes Ann's words. It was to be short-lived.

"And by your future, I of course am referring to what it is you'll be doing after you leave St. Theresa of Avila Convent, and you return to a civilian life."

Had she heard right? It hadn't sounded like her vows were about to be solemnized, that she was to be moving on to her first assignment. "Excuse me, Sister Agnes Ann, I don't understand. I have no plans to leave the convent. I actually had thought I was nearing the point I could take my final vows. I am still quite determined to be a nun, Sister. What are you telling me?"

"I'm telling you we don't see you making progress here, as we'd hoped, and the hesitation we—that is, I—spoke to you of upon your entering our convent, because of your youth, and presumed immaturity, well, I'm afraid we should have relied more on our experienced judgment.

"I'm sorry to have to break this to you, for we had such high hopes. You must realize, we are not branding you as a failure, or a bad person. Quite the opposite, really; there isn't a single one of us who hasn't been absolutely charmed by your vivacity and your wit. But there are other qualities we look for. We are not looking for someone to simply brighten our day. It's more than that. We look for those who will adhere to our strict regimen, who will learn and bear obedience to our Order. And that person does not appear to be found in you."

Nicole couldn't believe what she was hearing. She couldn't speak; breathing was even difficult. Surely this was not happening.

"Sister Nicole, a little merriment around here, so long as it isn't distracting, is always welcome. But I fear you have carried things a bit too far."

The accused spoke next, through tears spilling from reddened eyes. "Oh, Mother Superior, you can't mean the prank with the pizzas. That was harmless fun. It hurt no one. Even you laughed afterward."

"It isn't just the pizza incident, although I cannot imagine for the life of me what would have inspired you to order a dozen pizzas in my name at ten o'clock last Saturday night. That poor delivery boy, I felt for him so … the undeserving victim of your prank."

"But," Nicole broke in, "he told you that wasn't the first time it had happened to him. And he was grateful to be paid, remember? Not like the other times when he wasn't."

"You're not getting the point. This isn't a girl's dormitory at some exclusive school back East, where such things might be carried on routinely. This is a convent, where we work hard, and train women in the service of our Lord. There is such a huge difference. We don't think you've learned the difference."

"I suppose I have too much of my brothers in me."

"I'm sorry, I don't understand. What did you say?"

"It's nothing. Just thinking out loud. I should have said something about how hard I've tried, in my work, in my studies. Haven't I done everything I said I'd do when you so very reluctantly admitted me a year ago? Haven't I?"

"I must admit you have excelled. But this is not a university, and just being an honors student isn't enough. We are looking for more. Call it spiritual, call it whatever you wish, but there is something lacking. If we don't see the whole picture the way we feel it should be, it is our choice to open the darkroom door and expose the negative—if you'll pardon my metaphor ... And it isn't as if we haven't cautioned you before," she concluded.

"Sister Agnes Ann, I am beginning to feel no matter what I say, your mind is made up. Is there no second chance for me?"

"I'm afraid not, dear. I'm sorry, I really am. It's late now, I'm afraid I prayed on this decision far too long not to make it final tonight. In the morning, after we've all rested, Sister Mary Frances will help you pack, and with all the paperwork. It won't take long.

"And Sister Nicole, I do mean it, you should not take this as a sign you have failed at life. This experience will hopefully enrich you, lead you to some other pursuit that will bring you true happiness." She rose to embrace Nicole. There was little comfort in that act of mercy.

Nicole returned to her room in tears. Her crying was loud enough to disturb Sister Katherine next door, who came to see about her friend.

Katherine just held Nicole, soothingly telling her that at times God operated unpredictably. She'd brushed Nicole's tears aside, and they'd talked long into the night, Nicole unburdening a lifetime's weight from her heart with the older woman, who carried her own heavy load. It was as if the last barrier had been penetrated, and a hidden treasure was found. Confessions flowed like water from the burst dam; pleas of many sounds and shapes made their way out, broken loose from their Gordian bonds at last. Nicole did not sleep until sunrise.

She'd awakened mid-morning, startled that she was still in full dress. Her habit was rumpled, her veil askew and hair spilling out everywhere. She began straightening herself, until she remembered she might just as well have started removing the clothing that signaled her life as a nun. Her mind still hazy from the emotional trauma and lack of sleep, she was sitting motionless when Sister Agnes Ann entered her room. Regimentally, as if there had been no evening before, Nicole sprang to her feet, addressing the mother superior with all due respect.

Sister Agnes Ann spoke as if she'd heard nothing from Nicole. "I'll make this brief, Sister. Very brief. I've reconsidered. It is possible I may have overlooked some redeeming quality in you. I give you your second chance. There will be no others. You either know or will never know what is expected of you … what being a nun involves. And if I suspect for an instant that I have made an error in judgment, you will simply find your clothes neatly folded on your bed, and the door open for your prompt exit. Is that completely understood, Sister Nicole?"

Through the astonishment at the complete turnaround, she managed to say "Yes, Mother Superior, I understand completely. Thank you, Mother Superior."

Her entire outlook changed after that wake up call. She noticed, in small ways at first, how she perceived the instructions she was receiving, how she went about her duties. It became a new source of pride and inspiration to her. Conspicuously gone were the juvenile urges to make light.

She grew to know the change in her by name: humility. Her spirit hadn't been broken, it had simply taken on a new and far better form. She felt residual tension slip away, as remnants of her life outside the convent took on a lesser importance. In a sense she was relearning her existence. If she'd been told that was something she needed to do when she'd first arrived at the convent, she'd somehow missed the message. Whether she had or hadn't heard it then, she was living it now, and finding in it the enrichment her life had always been lacking. Her gift was to serve, and to serve one must first be a servant. A painful lesson for one of such independent and strong will to learn, but once the knowledge was hers, it became second nature to put all else first, and herself next in line.

The last months went by as a blur. Her friendship with Katherine became more spiritual than before the incident with Sister Agnes Ann. And as for the mother superior, Nicole at first kept her distance, but gradually loosened up as the days passed. The incident between them was never again mentioned.

What had been, she'd realized, a commitment lacking totality became a second epiphany. It had been one thing to realize she was meant to be a nun, another to make the full commitment.

Sitting here in her Sanctuary, as she'd named it, the memory was as fresh as if it had happened today. She was totally commited to her mission in Refugio, to Father Art, to God.

She would put discouragement over the school behind, and commitment to purpose back where it belonged. This struggle was far from over.

Nicole was becoming accustomed to the French baths, but had not given up hope of taking a real bath again. She went to see Carlos after morning Mass, to ask about the tub. Expecting Carlos to appear at the door, she was greeted by his wife instead.

Teresa's greeting was warm. She invited Nicole into her small but tidy home. Carlos was away, she explained, and she did not know of the tub, but would ask him when he returned. But as she was here, would Sister Nicole care for some freshly made tortillas and *cochinito pibil*, a tasty roasted pig dish, left from the evening before?

Nicole stared at the proffer. While not looking all that appetizing, it had a mouthwatering aroma. She graciously said yes to a small portion. As Teresa fetched a plate, Nicole caught Maria peering from the doorway. She smiled at the pretty girl, she of the porcelain skin and large, radiant, dark eyes, and held out her hand in a welcoming gesture. Looking in her mother's direction first, and receiving a nod, Maria dashed to Nicole.

Teresa explained. "She watches you as you walk about the village during the day, to and from the school, toward the valley. Your clothing fascinates her."

It made sense to Nicole, whose own fascination with the child was forming.

Maria clutched at the bottom of Nicole's habit. "Teresa, may I hold your daughter?"

"*Sí, Sí,*" Teresa answered.

In a rapid motion Nicole swept the young girl up from the ground, cradling her to her bosom, eye to eye. Maria was clearly enjoying the moment. Nicole forgot about the food, wondering if the same thought had crossed Teresa's mind. Nicole spoke first.

"Teresa, do you still wish her to go to school?"

Excitedly crossing herself, speaking in rapid Spanish, the mother said, "*Sí,* I do, very much. I almost walked Maria to the school during the past two days, when the other children had stayed away, but thought better of it. I did not want to upset Father Art, or cause problems for you, Sister."

Nicole had made her decision. "Tomorrow morning, then, I will take her to the school. I will work it out with Father Art later. But tomorrow I teach school, Teresa.

And little Maria here," Nicole continued, "will be my star pupil." She smiled, and hugged Maria tightly.

"Sister," began Teresa, "you must not worry about the other children. They will come, too. Give their parents time. It is only that they are frightened at something new and unknown, and nothing more. They have not learned to read or write, and do not know what good that will be when it comes to working in fields, or in garment-making. It is nothing more."

"Teresa, I don't care if every child comes tomorrow, I still want Maria to be there. May I come for her in the morning?"

As Nicole combed back Maria's hair with her fingers, looking at the child as lovingly as any mother might, Teresa again said *sí*. And with that, the Refugio children's school had its first student. Things were looking up for Sister Nicole.

22

TEACHER AND PUPIL WALKED hand in hand to the school. Nicole was impressed; she hadn't expected such a young child to willingly leave home without a parent. She was also pleasantly surprised as Maria began to speak … not the usual broken, shy talk of small children, but that suggesting maturity beyond her years. Even a little English she'd picked up from her grandfather and father. Father Art just had to see that Maria was ready for school.

Father Art was leaving on his sojourn the following day. Nicole thought of returning to the church to plead her case for admitting the underage pupil, but thought better of it as Maria began leafing through one of the textbooks. Nicole noted it was a second grade level reader, written in Spanish with English subtitles. Maria was pointing at the pictures, proudly calling each figure by name. Father Art could wait. If this were deceit, it could wait until her next confession.

Anxious to begin, Nicole reached for the reader. Maria stubbornly refused to give it up, immersed in her world of fantasy and delight. Amused, but needing to make a point, Nicole praised Maria's achievement, then let her know there were rules to be followed. She spoke in a stern and authoritative voice … a mother's voice. Reluctantly the child gave up her prize. Nicole recalled her own youthful stubbornness, the patience her own parents and teachers had shown.

Nicole handed Maria a pre-school reader—more pictures, less text. Maria excitedly began naming every object that colorfully graced each page. Such excitement! She ignored Nicole's instruction to close the book, to listen. Sterner measures were now called for.

Nicole placed her hand on the book, so that Maria could no longer turn the pages. She looked into the young girl's eyes, raising an index finger to her lips in a *shhh* gesture at the first sign Maria might argue. Maria understood the gesture. Nicole calmly explained, *I teach, you learn. You listen when I teach, you talk when I ask you to talk. Those are the rules.* Nicole was forceful, without scolding. Their eyes locked. If this was to be a battle of wills, Nicole had to emerge the victor. She knew it was more important that she establish herself as the teacher first, and the friend later.

Maria became silent also. Their eyes remained locked. It was Maria who blinked first. Then it was Maria who relaxed her hold on the pages, and Nicole who slowly pulled the book back. When Maria started to protest, the nun's index finger went gently back to the child's lips. Maria became quiet. Nicole withdrew her index finger, then spoke. She patiently explained, again, that Maria must let her, Sister Nicole, lead her through the book, and explain the pictures and words to Maria. When Maria asked what words were, Nicole's first test of wills was won. All learning truly begins with questions.

Nicole had taken a step toward becoming a teacher. She reflected on this time and again as the morning flew by, as teacher taught and student learned.

§

Teresa looked up to see Maria walking toward her with Nicole. The image of the nun and her daughter gaily traipsing along the dusty walk, set against the backdrop of the village and the magnificent blue ceramic sky over the distant treetops, brought a surge of spiritual warmth to the mother. She broke from her cooking, and went to the street to greet them. Maria had a book in her hand. Although she could not read, Teresa knew of books, and was pleased to see her daughter, so young and already tightly clutching the font of knowledge. Mother and daughter hugged first, then Teresa warmly embraced Nicole. Teresa received a glowing report on her daughter's first day of school, with special emphasis on how bright she indeed was. Teresa beamed when the nun asked if Maria might come again the following day.

They walked into Teresa's home. In the front room, Nicole placed her hand on Maria's head as she spoke to Teresa. "I had become discouraged thinking these villagers would forbid their children to attend school, without even giving it a chance. I have prayed for guidance, for strength and wisdom, and for help from God to make this happen." Nicole shifted her gaze to the child. "I believe God has led me to Maria."

The moment quickly passed from joyful to much more. Teresa made the sign of the cross; Nicole followed. Maria had gone to a nearby chair, and was turning pages in her book as quiet swept the room. Teresa again thanked Sister Nicole as she turned to leave.

Nicole smiled. "I expect Maria in class promptly at eight in the morning."

Returning to the church, Nicole rejoiced in the events of the morning. It was a small step, to be sure, but it was a step. She prayed that Father Art would relax his age requirement. For the first time she could remember in a long while she actually dreaded an encounter.

As she entered the church, there was a noticeable, eerie quiet. She called out to Father Art from the nave, but got no reply. She tried the rectory, and again found no sign of the priest. Walking down the hall toward her own room, she saw what appeared to be a note on her door. The best surprise of her day was yet to come. She smiled broadly as she read the few words penned by Father Art. *Sister, I had to leave a day early. Sorry for the lack of a more formal good-bye. Remember, you know who to get help from, if you should need it. But you will do fine. You are adjusting well here, and are strong. And, as I saw this morning, your school is flourishing. Your star pupil looked quite young. I suppose I'll have to lower the age requirement. We can't have our school breaking its own rules, now can we? Good-bye for now, I shall return in four weeks. God be with you, Sister. Father Art.*

She folded the note and placed it in the small wooden box in which she kept her other treasures. She bowed her head and said a simple, "Thank you."

The next morning, the same faithful few showed up for the morning Mass. They knew, of course, that Father Art would be gone, and that Sister Nicole would only be saying the prayers and dispensing Holy Communion. Which suited Nicole— she had a more urgent agenda. She rushed from the church after the final prayer, apologizing to the congregation for her haste and bad manners. She sprinted for the school, carrying two personal items, something she hoped would be special to her young pupil. As she neared the clearing, she noticed a small gathering of villagers, perhaps a dozen to fifteen feet from the school. Maria was not seated at her place, she could see that much. Maternally, she worried for Maria's safety. She quickened her pace.

She saw four adults—three women and a man. Timidly behind them were five children, all neatly and cleanly dressed, poised and watching as she approached. Nicole's heart raced with eagerness. She stopped a few feet from the man. Speaking in Spanish, he told Nicole his name was Eduardo. He nudged a young girl forward.

"This is Bonita, my daughter," he said. The girl, perhaps eight or nine years of age, dropped her head shyly. Eduardo asked if Nicole would please accept his daughter into the school, and those other children of his neighbors, as he motioned to them with his free hand. Nicole knew this was no time to be speechless, but she found herself working hard to find the right words. In the end, she said very simply that these, and all other children of the village, were most welcome in the school. She thanked the parents for bringing the children this morning. This greatly pleased the parents, who immediately began giving last-minute admonitions on respect and behavior to the five new students.

One boy listened to his mother, but his eyes were clearly fixed on the round object under Sister Nicole's left arm. She noticed his gaze, and, when the mother had finished, she held the ball out to the boy, who took it and held it gingerly, admiringly.

Nicole asked his name. "Enrique," his mother answered. Nicole bent down and asked Enrique if he'd ever played *futbol*. He said, no, he hadn't. Smiling at him, fondly thinking back so many years to a far distant place and time, she told the boy they would certainly see to it that he would, if his parents did not object. The mother said Sister Nicole could teach the boy both his lessons and *futbol*. When Nicole asked the same of the girls' parents, the reaction was different, however. Nicole assured them *futbol* was just as much a sport for girls as it was for boys. Still they were not convinced. "Watch," she said.

Asking Enrique for the ball, she dropped it to the ground, and began dribbling. A few basic touches, and then some fancy juggling, on the foot, then foot to foot, next up to the knee, back to the foot, then up to her head and a few bounces, drawing gasps from her visitors all, then releasing the ball onto the ground. The parents glanced back and forth to each other, nodding approvingly. She now had five students, and a good start on a small-sided soccer match. Life was glorious.

As the parents left their children in her charge, Nicole noticed Maria had arrived. Teresa stood to the side, looking worried.

"Teresa, is something wrong?"

"Sí. Now there are other children who are coming to your school, and when even more come, you will be sending Maria home, because she is too young. This makes me sad."

Nicole laughed, and grasped the shoulders of the worried woman. "Teresa, I have good news for you. No longer is Maria too young for the school. God has answered many prayers since we last spoke. Maria is as welcome as any other child. You have nothing to fear."

Jubilant, Teresa thanked Nicole, and flashed a warm smile at her daughter, who was proudly showing her book to the other children.

As Nicole watched Teresa and the other parents drift away, she triumphantly decided it was time to get down to the serious business of teaching. She turned to her six students.

Yes, life was quite glorious.

Within a week the school was full. Each day became like the one before … lessons first, then the catechism, then as a reward music and *futbol*. They were voracious learners. There was no threat of boredom.

All eyes of the village were on Nicole … those of the parents, those of the elderly few who came zealously to morning mass, even those of Evan Montgomery, when he was in the village. All watched, at first skeptically, then gradually in awe as life in the village took on a new cast. Eyes that had at first dimmed in her direction were now open wide in adoration and respect. All who witnessed her at work or at play saw in her a woman of God, of tender and compassionate spirit, and of raw, tireless and boundless energy. All eyes saw beauty in her, not just of the physical kind, but of the spiritual as well. All eyes saw the next thing to an angel on earth.

All eyes save two.

Two eyes saw a different vision, framing this trespasser as a demon, a force of evil. Malevolence roiled in these eyes. And they kept constant vigil on the unsuspecting nun.

23

Near the end of the third week of Father Art's absence, on an especially warm day, Nicole had just returned to the church. Her habit clung like a second skin, soaked with perspiration and caked with mud from the dusty surface of her improvised soccer field. Her first thought was of the fun she'd had playing soccer with her children.

Her second thought was how in heaven's name she would ever make herself and her habit clean again. Uncharacteristically, she found herself craving: what she would give for the cool, cleansing water of a bath. She was beginning to question Father Art's prohibition against bathing in the nearby river when she stepped into her room and found the porcelain treasure.

A claw-footed heirloom, as white and unstained as it must have been when brand new, the tub sat invitingly in the far corner, near the window. Miguel and Carlos were grinning broadly, obviously proud of their accomplishment.

Miguel excitedly demonstrated how the tub functioned. The water would come from a holding tank on the roof, rainwater-fed and heated by the sun. He'd built a shield over it, to keep debris out. He also proudly let her know that his neighbors had hand-carried enough water to fill the tank; she did not need to wait for the next rainfall for her first bath. He showed her where the fill line was hidden from view behind her headboard, and how the stopcock regulated the water flow.

She was too dehydrated for tears. The men fidgeted to the side as she placed her hands on the rim, leaving muddy prints on the glistening whiteness. By the time she looked up to thank them, they were gone. It was just as well. The sponge that had been in Carlos's hand was on the floor beside her. She turned the stopcock, and watched the water spill into the smooth curve of the tub.

The next hour was spent in luxury as Nicole bathed from head to toe for the first time in nearly three months. Before Refugio, a day without a bath was unthinkable. One of life's simplest pleasures, taken for granted as so many others, unappreciated until lost. In this light, she bathed as if it might be her last.

The water, at first warm, was now cooling to the touch. She didn't care; warm or cool, it was refreshing, cleansing, relaxing. Lifting her arms, she slowly squeezed both hands around the sponge, freeing its interstitial content. She followed the current as it trickled down her wrists, twisting in rivulets further on down her arms, shoulders next, then down her front and into the tub. The water massaged, soothed her tired and aching muscles, sinewy again, as they had been in her youth. Twice more she repeated the therapeutic procedure.

Tomorrow's lessons could wait. Cleaning her habit could wait. Everything could wait. She would savor this moment. Time stopped, and her life held in blissful abeyance. Old memories, long since pushed deep into cortical folds and recesses by newer ones, clawed and kicked like the diver with depleted lungs straining to break the surface for the precious light and air above.

Showtime ... everyone quiet. Roll the cameras.

The Life of Nicole Michelle McHenry played on the imaginary screen behind her closed eyes, images flickering like a vintage thirty-five millimeter black-and-white reel. Starring Mac and Elizabeth, the lawyer and the schoolteacher, and their three perfect children. One in particular.

Let's have a close-up, please, the unseen moderator says. There she is, the girl sandwiched between the two boys—she's the one morphing from the ballerina slippers to the soccer cleats, to the sandals beneath her nun's habit. Share with us, Nicole, the moderator continues, a few vignettes of your life ... a few special moments.

Sure, here's a favorite. We'd moved out of New Orleans when I was very young, across Lake Pontchartrain to Madisonville, on the North Shore, to a quaint bedroom community nestled in an enchanted forest. I remember my first day at school, at Madisonville Elementary. My favorite teacher was Miss Jenny. I don't remember her last name. No one ever called adults by their last name. Custom in that area, I learned. I loved Miss Jenny. I loved every minute at that school.

Besides school, ballet became my life. Danny fished and hunted with his friends, and Chris played soccer ... but from the first day I'd gone with my mother to her ballet class, when I was only three and we still lived in the city, I knew I was meant to be a ballerina. Six years I went to classes and recitals. Then, a week before my twelfth

169

✝

birthday it all ended for me. They didn't understand, of course, and I didn't want to tell them about it. But you know how relentless parents can be. A solid two days of gentle coaxing from my concerned mother wore me down. It's like this: one day after practice I'd overheard my instructor discussing who would dance the part of the Sylph Maiden in the spring recital. You have to know, the Sylph Maiden was the choicest part, the dream of every aspiring ballerina at our studio. It was my part; I'd worked harder than everyone else, and I knew every step blindfolded, even the toe part.

But it was not to be. My entire eleven-and-a-half-year-old world crumbled as I overheard my instructor say that another girl fit the part, that I was not tall and lithe, and did not have the graceful features of a classic ballerina. No, I was short, my thighs and shoulders were too thick, my face too round. Whoever danced the Sylph Maiden must not look the part of some common athlete.

If I did not look like a ballerina, I did not want to be one. If I looked like an athlete, then I would be one.

It was the first time in my life I'd ever experienced disappointment. Yes, I can look back now and honestly say I was overprotected.

I saw a new and different side to my mother when we went to the studio to get my things.

"Why Miss Elizabeth," the instructor began, "I don't understand. Nicole is one of our most gifted young ballerinas. She is on the verge of great things. Are you certain you want to pull her?"

"At our home," my mother began, "my husband and I are more concerned with character development than we are accomplishment. We tell our children it is never failure when they don't succeed, as long as they try, that it is only failure when they do not make the effort."

"Yes, well, that is very much the same thing we try to teach our students at this studio."

I watched as my mother leaned in close to the instructor, and said something I could not hear. I watched the color run from the woman's face, which had more bony features to it than I'd noticed before. The icy, rigid features on my mother's face were also new to me. Then, swiftly and decisively, Mom took my hand and marched the both of us to the door. I turned to watch the struggling woman.

"Wha—I—but Miss Elizabeth ... " She just stood there, all but mute. I knew, somehow, a measure of justice had just been exacted.

"What did you say to her, Mom?"

At first there was no answer, just my mother's warm squeeze of my hand. Then, in her wonderfully flourishing way, she'd swept away all things tormenting and confusing with a simple proclamation. "Let's go find some soccer shoes, my dear," Mom said.

Very good, Nicole, the hidden voice says. *We see that early in life you suffered an image-shattering experience. Which is why you, a) took up soccer, and b) became a nun, right? Is that how the credits will roll at the end of this little film?*

Well, it's more complicated than that. There was school, where I was the classic overachiever … straight As, which everyone thought came so effortlessly to me, but which kept me up past midnight most nights. Only my parents knew the late hours part. They worried about me. But I had to make those grades. I don't know why I was so possessed with the drive to excel, I just was. If I'd ever made a "B" I couldn't have shown my face at school.

There were other obsessions. Maturity came early to me. While some friends were still content to savor childhood, I chose to distance myself from it. I felt a restlessness my friends didn't, stirrings I could not share even with Mom. Growing up became an obsession.

Enter Tommy—my first and only boyfriend. I was seventh grade, he eighth. Tommy Hebert was the captain and quarterback of the Mandeville Junior High football team … voted most popular boy in school. I liked Tommy, which was good, but it was more that I had to have him, you know. You do know, don't you? Like my straight As, and being the best, I had to have the best boy. I was allowed to car date at fourteen. I pushed them hard on that one, but my parents trusted me. And I rewarded their trust. Not one broken curfew. Ever.

The voice again. *Anything else you're remembering?*

Yes, but for the life of me I don't know why. There was a boy at school … a black boy. Matthew Courvillon. I think I met him the first day of school at Madisonville Elementary. He was two years older. We always spoke in the halls, but that was it. He was so shy. But I'd always liked him. I remember the first time I did speak to him outside of school. It was the summer before seventh grade, and he was bagging our groceries at the old Delchamp's market. I felt comfortable in his awkward, quiet smile that said more than words.

Later, when I was a freshman, I saw more of him … still the loner, very much a studious type, all but invisible in the halls of the formidable, mostly white Mandeville High School. It was a strained peace. Black athletes, especially the better ones, received a conditional acceptance; non-athletes and loner types like Matthew were left alone but left out. Those few blacks who ran in packs and displayed inner-city culture were dared to cross a line, and left to know there would be consequences if they did. There were no incidents, only glaring looks and pent-up feelings.

Matthew and I shared a class that year. He set the curve on the first test, something I wasn't used to, so I sought him out. It wasn't about the color of his skin, I explained. I just wasn't used to making the second-highest grade. How imperious I must have sounded. Matthew was almost apologetic, when he had every right to stuff me in the nearest trash can. He explained that his only hope for college was to earn an academic scholarship. He had to make the best grades he could; surely I could understand that.

I felt ashamed, for the first time I could remember. Deeply so. My grade became insignificant. I grew to respect and admire Matthew Courvillon, for his goals and ambition and perseverance. There was something else, too, something less definable, his clarity of vision perhaps. We became friends. It was something most of my friends counseled against, but in time they acquiesced. Even Tommy grew to like him. We used to spend an occasional Sunday afternoon with Matthew humoring my star athlete by running pass patterns at Pelican Park while I fretted over my math. The beginner glided with a swift, natural grace as he ran routes Tommy drew by finger on his palm, which was necessary because Matthew had never played a sport in his life and had no clue what a pass pattern was otherwise. But his hands were like baskets as each throw was caught, even the bad ones. Tommy asked why Matthew had not played football. His reply broke my heart.

Matthew came from a single-parent home, had more brothers than Tommy could count, and had worked an after-school job since he was old enough to get a work permit. Before that, he'd cared for his younger brothers, so that his mother could work a second job. Back then both of his older brothers worked at student jobs, so it fell on him to help out at home. There just wasn't time or opportunity for extracurricular activities. Tommy was surprised to learn that Matthew's mother had been one of the cooks at the junior high. That Matthew had no time for sports, or for any of the normal childhood activities was not something Tommy could relate to. It struck me as a shallowness on Tommy's part. An opportunity for an awakening in him slipped by.

I think it was then I realized Tommy had become only a convenience for me. Calls for dates from the upperclassmen had stopped … I was Tommy's girl. He was my shield from commitment.

Okay, Nicole, is that about it? We're nearly out of film.

Not quite. There's one more part of me I think is important. It's about my faith.

Oh, sure, we can't forget your faith. What is it about your faith that's special?

In all of my pursuits, I was consumed by the quest for perfection. But when it came to my faith, I was less involved, less driven. Like many of my Catholic friends, I attended Mass and RCIA classes, went to confession once a month—when prodded, and not until—and helped occasionally with the various parish bazaars and fairs and food and clothing drives. Mostly whatever my parents found for me to do. Never as a leader, always as a follower.

Outwardly I led, I gave, I exemplified, expecting nothing in return. Within, though, where it was just me to myself, it was different. Inside, there lived another, one who did not possess such an indomitable spirit, such self-effacing commitment and courage, who crept up on me in moments when I was alone, and became me. This other person cried herself to sleep most nights, after the studies were finally ended, after the long telephone conversations late into the night with friends and Tommy were over. Doubt and uncertainty from an unknown source filled me to the brink of overflowing. The overachiever by day, the frightened child when alone at night. Even fatigue was no ally. A certain force had hold of me, and dwelled within my soul. It had no name, no identifiable origin.

It was like a voice I couldn't hear. An instruction manual I couldn't read. It was scary. Whatever it was, it dominated me. It would not let go …

24

THE KNOCK STARTLED HER. She reached for her towel, smiling as she saw the water wrinkles on her fingers and toes. She'd lost all track of time. Who was there?

Shaking her head free of watery snarls of hair and the dormant memories, she wrapped herself in the towel and went to the door. There would be time later for more baths and reminiscing. For now it was, as they say, back to reality.

Peering through the crack in the doorway, Nicole's eyes met those of Evan Montgomery. She brightened at once. "Evan! I've been in the bath. I finally got my tub! I'd let you in, but I'm not dressed. Please, can you give me a minute?"

"I should go. I'll come back later. I had no right—"

"Don't be silly. I'll just be a moment. Wait for me inside the church."

In moments, wet hair and all, she joined Montgomery. She found him staring curiously at the Madonna and Child on the wall beside the altar. "I've seen this depiction so many times in my life," he began, "but until this very minute I have never wondered why the glorification of the Mother of Christ by the Catholic Church. No other Christian faith elevates Mary to such a position of exaltation. Why so the Catholic Church?"

"Why not the others?" she countered.

"And why isn't Joseph, his father, in the picture?" he added, avoiding her riddle.

"Evan, is it a religious instruction you've come for, or was there something else on your mind? We can talk about who Christ's real Father is, and how he is quite present in the Catholic Church's picture if you like, but I have a feeling you're here for something else."

"Interesting," he said, his gaze still fixed on the Madonna.

"Actually, you are right," he continued, turning to Nicole. "Something entirely different than a discussion of the faith. I'm here to ask you to go for a walk with me. I have some free time, and I would most appreciate the pleasure of your company on a walk through this paradise I am stuck in. I can take only so much of my journalistic duties before I need companionship, preferably with another educated person. Poor Miguel doesn't quite get me there, I'm afraid.

"Meaning no disrespect to Miguel," he added, noting her furrowed brow.

"I'll let your comment slide," she said. "But I can't believe you said what you did."

"Miguel is held in my highest esteem, I assure you, right up there with Father Art. This isn't about Miguel. It's about whether or not you'd like to accompany me on a stroll, that is, if you've nothing else to do right now. So do we walk or not, Sister?"

She eyed him uncertainly, then shrugged. "A walk would be nice."

"Shall we go?" He was beaming.

She laughed. "Lead the way," she said, reaching for his arm.

"You're laughing," he said. Not a question, but asking one.

"I'm laughing because I am not the least bit concerned at the moment about my wet hair, and I have just stepped out of a tub after my first real bath in weeks, and my fingers and toes are still all wrinkly. See?" She held out her hands, and extended a sandaled foot.

"There was a time not so long ago I wouldn't have let anyone see me like this. It's funny how vanity has faded, no, vanished from my life. I actually am relieved by the loss of the very thing that troubled me for so long." She looked up at him, still smiling.

"I'm familiar with the concept of a woman's vanity. Never had much use for it myself, as you can plainly see. I've been in this same shirt for days, and may shave and bathe tonight for the first time in as long. With me, though, it's not a question of lack of vanity. I always thought of it as a sort of laziness on my part, frankly. Do you find that odd?"

"What I find odd is this conversation." Noticing him recoil at her statement, she quickly added, "What I mean is, I haven't had a one-on-one social conversation like this in as long as I can remember. My whole world is wrapped up in the Church, and my teaching, and before I came here it was preparation for my vows. What we're talking about, my lack of vanity, your whatever-you-want-to-call-it regarding your personal hygiene, is what I find odd."

She paused. "Am I making sense? No, of course not. I'm making a fool of myself."

"You shouldn't be so hard on yourself. I actually find you quite charming. But more importantly, I do see, quite possibly, we might both benefit from conversation."

"I think I'd like that," she said.

They walked down a path clearly familiar to her, equally as unfamiliar to him. She broke the silence first. "I take this walk nearly every day. I've even come down this path on days when it rains. It's become a part of my daily regimen. I remember the very first time I started down this way, long before it became so familiar to me." She stopped, but did not turn her head to meet his eyes fixed so intently on the side of her face. "I'll never forget the feeling of unease, maybe even a kind of fear, that came over me. You know the kind of feeling, when the bogeyman—" She laughed again, quietly, embarrassed by her confession. "—when you have a feeling there is someone, or something, lurking in the shadows … hiding … watching you?" She caught her breath. "I had such a feeling the first day I came down here. I had to force myself to continue, so great was my urge to turn and run back to the safety of the chapel.

"I could feel a presence, and it wasn't a kind presence either. At first, I thought one of the villagers might have been following me, more out of curiosity than anything else. I was new then. It would have been a natural thing, their curiosity. But I remember turning, and expecting to see one of the children peeking around a building or tree, or one of the older villagers, maybe, keeping a watchful eye on me. It even crossed my mind you might have been following me, as we had just met a night or two before. But there was nothing. That's when the feeling crept over me I was being watched, and not protectively. It felt—" She groped for the right word. "—menacing. I'll bet you think I'm a silly child, pretending to be all grown up in a nun's habit." She began walking again, before he replied.

Montgomery was thinking hard on a reply when he realized she'd left him behind. He quickened his pace to catch up before he spoke. "I can't deny your feelings. They're after all yours. But I think I can safely say there is nothing in this tiny village you need to fear. I would wager anything on it. Now, the wildlife around here, that's something altogether different."

She thanked him for his words of comfort and assurance, but did not tell him that nearly every time she started her walk down this path the same feelings enveloped her. She did not tell Evan Montgomery she had begun to fear for her safety.

It was unthinkable her life might be in danger.

They stood at the precipice, the quiet majesty spread before them. Impressive even to the calloused Montgomery. He whistled softly.

"This has been here the entire time I have?"

"I'm sure even longer than that, Evan," she replied with a hint of sarcasm. "You should get out more, you know." She headed along the rim while he digested her last remark.

He followed as she made her way down a narrow path leading to the base of the escarpment. "Do the villagers know about this place? Surely they can't have lived here all their lives and not have discovered it."

"Of course they do. Some of them come down here on occasion, to fetch small amounts of water when they don't have time to walk to the river. I suppose it's nothing special to them. As long as I lived in south Louisiana, only thirty miles from the French Quarter and all the mystique of New Orleans, I took it for granted. It was just there ... it had always been there. I suspect to our quiet villagers this place is also just here, as it always has been. It's their familiar. To you and me, it is special. To them," she repeated, "it's just here."

He looked up from the base of the facies. Montgomery gauged the height to be just under one hundred feet, all of it almost straight up. The walk down had surprisingly not tired him. He would normally have wanted a smoke by now. But this was different. This was like a holy place. He would not foul it with tobacco.

Staying close while she wound through the dense forest, he noticed the effortlessness with which she made her way. He was all clumsiness, she, grace personified. It was as if her feet were on air, and the branches that reached and tugged at him parted in her way. It was mystical. Though he towered over her by a foot, he felt strangely small.

In moments they were nearing a vaguely familiar sound. Even before he saw it he pictured the waterfall, its cascading stream plunging into a pond. And when he did see it, he was once more struck by the beauty and majesty of nature at Her best. Again he whistled.

He was taken by the sheer simplicity of her happiness at showing him this secret place. A part of him felt guilt for the invasion of privacy, another reveled in the honor of having been selected. His eyes were not on the falls, or the pond, or the colorful flowers encircling this paradise; they were on her. Feelings within him began stretching after their long nap. A heart that had sunken so deeply into the mire of self-pity and despair was buoyed by the sight before him of so beautiful a young woman, so completely given to faith and purpose, possessed of a refreshing naiveté. In another time, he might have pictured her dressed in gauze and a flower headband, gesturing with the peace sign as she twirled around and around to the music of some protest song on some college campus. But this was no flower child before him. This was a woman of God, spoken for in every sense, and as he watched her a sense of shame for his feelings tempered the other feelings, those that made him weak in the knees, dizzy and weightless.

He was relieved that she did not speak, for he'd become as speechless as the dumb.

Evan Montgomery listened as Nicole explained she was in Refugio because she wanted to be a nun, not because she didn't want to be her father's law partner. Certain it made sense to her, he wasn't inclined to probe, less concerned with what she might answer than he was with controlling the fierce desire to pull her to him, to hold her, to smother her with his love.

"It's not as if one day I said to myself, 'Nicole, you can never be like your father, so find something else to be and someone else to be like.' No, it took something else entirely for me to know what course I needed to take. I suppose I had known all my life, but—what's the old saying, 'Can't see the forest for the trees'? That was me. Big-time denial, trying to be something I thought everyone else thought I should be. I would be a lawyer, like my dad. Period, end of story.

"That was me, though, putting that pressure on myself. My parents never pushed me in that direction. They supported me as long as they thought it was my goal, but they didn't push. There's a difference, you know." He nodded. *Don't be a fool, Evan. She'll see right through you.*

"During the light of day, I was happy making others happy, but at night, when it was just me, I became a scared child, afraid of the unknown. I froze at the thought of getting to college, and taking courses that would lead me eventually to law, when I knew within me that I did not want to be a lawyer. It just sounded good, saying the words, 'I want to be a lawyer like my father.' And I loved working with my dad, I really did, but I knew that it didn't fulfill my every desire. Just like I loved being Tommy's girlfriend, because it took other dating pressures off me and it was less complicated, but I knew that it wasn't a forever thing. I always knew that.

"Then one day, after I'd left Dartmouth and gone home to the safety net of caring parents, it all came home to me. I'll tell you the story sometime, not now. For now, just know that one day I saw it all so clearly, what and who I was, and I knew this is who I was, this is where I should be. And my life has been the richer for it since, every day.

"I know it sounds so corny, but it's true. I had a religious experience, and it brought me the only true feeling of accomplishment I've ever known. It's not like I didn't know happiness before I became a nun … my life overflowed with happiness. And it's not like all I've known since I became a nun is happiness, because that's not the case either. I've had my moments of doubt. But I truly believe they've made me more devout. I would not be here otherwise.

"I never wanted to bear children. I always liked children, and was filled with a nurturing instinct each time I held a baby. I don't know how, or why, but I always knew I would never become a mother. I thought I could see myself married, and a good wife, but my commitment would never have been total. Tommy knew, I know he did, and probably would've settled for it. He loved me that much. But my lack of commitment would've eventually taken a toll even on him. I broke his heart, the day I left him at Dartmouth, but it was the only way."

He waited for a lull, sensitive to her plaintive expressions of endearment for a young man he now foolishly thought of as a rival. "So here you are, thriving in a northern extremity of Guatemala, in a hidden paradise no less, while what? Tommy pines over his lost love?"

"Evan, stop, you're cruel, you know. Tommy is fine … we still write. He left Dartmouth at the end of the semester after I did, transferred to LSU, and changed his major from pre-law. He should graduate next year, as a licensed physical therapist. Plus, I hear he's found a girl in Baton Rouge. He's told a few people he's thinking of proposing. Things worked out for both of us. There's no pining away. Shame on you," she chided.

He let it pass. He was intent on hearing more from this girl who was stealing his heart. With every detail of her life, he became more swept up in his own emotion. He felt himself flush.

She was staring at him. "Are you all right? Is the heat getting to you?" A slight breeze caused the wind chime she'd hung in a nearby branch to ring its calming sounds. Not exactly like being saved by the bell, but instrumental in helping him regain his composure.

"I'm afraid I may have gotten a bit dehydrated, that's all." He reached into the pool of the clear, fresh water, and scooped a handful into his mouth. And another, and another. Hiding his deceit, he thanked her for the concern, and commented on the lovely ringing. The conversation became upbeat and lively as she entertained him with stories of life at convent, and of the nuns who tried to mold her into their idea of a true nun, only to settle for what they got in young Sister Nicole instead. Her attempt at self-deprecation failed. Then came stories of growing up, fun times with her friends, her brothers. Amused and charmed, he caught himself laughing aloud. He couldn't remember the last time he'd laughed. He wondered if hers was a bottomless grab bag of memories. He hoped so. He hoped the day would never end.

"Evan," she began, ending the moment, "we've nearly lost daylight. We should head back. There's a home cooked meal waiting. Please come to supper at the church, as my guest."

"How could I possibly refuse such an offer?" he managed, silently wishing for just a few more moments with her, where they were, like they were.

She stood, ready to leave. "Thank you for coming here with me."

He would have said something, a well-chosen expression of his own, but he went stage struck when she gave him the electrifying embrace. Later, he thought, after regaining his composure, he would tell her just how much the day meant to him. How much she meant to him. Not now though. Now was not a good time.

25

I F HE HAD FANTASIZED a quiet dinner alone, just the two of them, Evan Mont-gomery could not have been more surprised or disappointed. When he showed up at the church's kitchen, promptly at seven as he'd promised, he was greeted by the startling beauty of a small child who, in perfect English, introduced herself as Maria and invited him in. At once discomfited, the dinner guest casually lowered the bottle of red wine he'd been holding in his right arm to his side in a cradling fashion, then tried to hide it behind his back. The child smiled. "*Señor* Monty brought sangria, Sister," she yelled toward the kitchen. His face flushed for what he thought was the hundredth time that day.

"Please tell *Señor* Montgomery to bring himself, and his bottle of wine, into the kitchen," came the familiar voice from around the doorway.

Montgomery followed Maria into the kitchen, where he was greeted by Nicole and Miguel, the carpenter, and three others he did not know who were introduced as Maria's parents and a younger brother.

Nicole was working furiously beside Maria's mother—her name, he learned, was Teresa—as the two women formed and shaped tortillas on the *comal*, the flat cast-iron griddle that sat atop the open fire. He could also see the chicken and corn stew simmering in the kettle. The stew was a local dish he had come to appreciate. The aroma was overpowering, giving him the sensation he hadn't eaten in days. It robbed him of the disappointment of the quiet meal for two he would miss.

"May I help with anything?" he asked.

"Everything is under control, but thank you for offering. You should sit and visit with the men. That would be the culturally right thing to do." She was radiant, he thought.

Nicole paused from her labor at the *comal* long enough to guide him to his chair beside the other men. "How nice of you to bring wine," she said, taking the bottle from him.

"Oh, it's nothing, really." He lied. It was his last bottle of an estate-bottled red from the private cellar of one of the finest vineyards in all of Bordeaux.

To his surprise, he was quite impressed with the company of the two men. In Miguel he found a doting grandfather and a proud parent, in Carlos a devoted son and a kind heart. The two men probed him for stories of places near and far, forcing him to become the reluctant yarn-spinner. His awkwardness lessened as he caught Nicole more than once looking over with a smile.

The meal was worth the wait. Nicole explained that this was something she did every week on this night. She had set out to learn all she could of these exceptional people, their cuisine included. The church provided the food, in return for the cooking lessons, and the official tasters. "I hope you know, Mr. Montgomery," she started, "that this is my first time to try cooking this stew. But Teresa was here to help, and I haven't made anyone sick from the other things I've cooked, so you really were quite safe."

"I never doubted for my safety, Sister," he said. "This meal ranks right up there with the best I've had since I coming to Guatemala, I must say."

"I think you are being too kind," Nicole said, "but the credit should go to Teresa. She is the real cook in this kitchen." Nicole repeated herself in Spanish for Teresa.

Teresa smiled, little Maria hugged her, and the men followed Montgomery's applause.

"And you, you bring this bottle of very fine wine," she said, holding the empty bottle aloft, "to a simple family gathering. How sweet of you."

She knows. I am such a shallow, one-dimensional pig.

It was time to leave, before things went from pretty good to hopelessly bad. The meal officially over, Montgomery excused himself quickly, explaining to his hostess that he had work to do. He thought he detected a trace of disappointment in her expression, but said nothing about it. He thanked her for the lovely dinner, and again for the day's walk and conversation, and headed for the door. She followed him.

"Evan, thank you for this wonderful day. I know you have work to do, and that you don't often stay here very long, but do come by when you can. Come see my school, if you can, if you care to. The children are so fun, and they would love it if you came to see them." No reaction. "But I warn you, they'll steal your heart."

"More than the little one in there already has? She has 'angel' written all over, you know."

"She's my pet," was the whispered reply.

"I might surprise you one day and drop by. I've been known to drop in unannounced," he began, catching her beginnings of a smile, "but only on those for whom I care greatly."

"I'm honored to be in that exclusive company."

"Now it is my turn, to thank you, again, for a splendid meal, and a most memorable day. I should think myself a lunatic if I did not come back for more. And I shall," he continued, "come back for more, that is, whenever I can, until I wear out my welcome, which I always do, sooner or later. It's my curse."

"False modesty is not a virtue, Evan," she chided. "I expect you to come visit my school.

"Good night, sweet Evan," she said, when he had been swallowed whole by the blackness of the moonless night.

§

In the darkness around the corner from the Mendez home was one not so taken by the pleasantries of this night. Pulsing, pounding waves struck at the temples of the watcher, whose eyes and temples were covered by hands trembling with rage. Uncontrollable rage.

†

26

Evan Montgomery stared blankly at the typewriter carriage, motionless for the thirty minutes he'd sat before it. It wasn't writer's block. And it wasn't burnout. No, it was her. Nicole. Thoughts of her, images of her were all he could think of. Maybe it was time to return to England and that corner bookstore he'd always dreamed of opening one day. He'd saved some money, not a great deal, but enough, he reasoned, to get himself started.

Leaning back in his chair, he mulled over the day's events once more. Why had he sought her out upon his return to Refugio? He'd been quite taken by her when they'd first met, but there had been no overpowering urge to fall at her feet, for God's sake. Was it idle curiosity? That didn't seem right. It certainly wasn't lust; that thought rankled him.

No smile had ever captivated him, no laughter had ever awakened his spirit as hers had. She had wit. She had the most refreshing naiveté he'd ever encountered. She was fun. She was pure. He was impressed. He was entranced. He was in love.

He was also practical. This was never to be, this love for a girl less than half his age, a nun at that. He would control his urges; dignity would be maintained, his and hers. This would be no shipboard romance. If it had to have a name, this would be a secret.

He reached across the small wooden worktable for a ballpoint pen, and put it to the tablet he carried in his shirt pocket. He wrote her name: Nicole. Nicole. Nicole Michelle. Sister Nicole Michelle. He struck through the last entry, then, having second thoughts, rewrote it. He stared at the variations. All described a thing of beauty, all prompted feelings of tenderness. All provoked in him vivid images of green eyes, smiles, laughter, and warmth. He set down pen and paper. His fingers moved to the keyboard. Effortlessly, he began to type. The force bearing down upon him moments earlier lifted. He was weightless again, as he had been at the pond only hours ago. He wrote passionately, composing sentence after sentence, filling three pages seemingly before he drew a second breath. Editing quickly, he condensed his effort to a page and a half.

He pushed his chair back. Missing from his thoughts was the urge to reach for the tumbler at the table's corner that held his nightly panacea and sedative all rolled into one. He read, slowly, the words she'd made possible.

> High in the northern extremity of tiny Guatemala, Mexico's less fortunate neighbor to the south, in the department of Petén sits the tiny village of Refugio. There are no indoor toilets in Refugio; nor is there electricity. Its inhabitants are mostly brown-skinned Indians of almost pure Mayan descent. Spanish is a second language; precious few speak any English. There are ten head of cattle and a herd of goats whose number changes daily; the village owns the cattle and goats communally. Farmers, goatherds and a few artisans make up the workforce. The women cook, give birth, and care for the young inhabiting the village. There are no doctors, no hospitals. The pastoral setting of this small village should not conjure images of green pastures, or of fertile soil. There are no cash crops—everything harvested is shared by the families while any excess is put back for lean times.

He put himself vicariously in the mind of the reader, searching for missing information. Thankfully, he'd left out nothing. Nearing the end, he slowed his pace. It was important he got this part right.

> There is a spirit in mankind that escapes definition, defies explanation. Amidst chaos, there arises the leader who exalts others to remain calm. Amidst war, there emerge heroes who others follow into battle, who set by their example the will to conquer a foe. Such leaders and heroes are not born, they are made, usually from situations not of their making.
>
> And here in Refugio, keenly perched atop a mountainous ridge and overlooking an expanse of forest and jungle as far as the eye can see in any direction, such a leader and hero lives. Here, unlike further south, there is no chaos, there is no war, but there is condition enough calling for leadership, and a hero. But who is this heroic figure?
>
> She is Sister Nicole, of the Sister Teresa of Avila Order, a Roman Catholic nun, hailing from the bayou country of south Louisiana. Born into comfort none in Refugio could possibly imagine, sacrificing the comforts of a world that takes for granted what the native villagers will in all likelihood never in their lives experience, she has brought with her the tools to forge knowledge from illiteracy, and the will to succeed at whatever the cost. Turning her back on a life of luxury in America, she has come to Refugio, to sew light where there is darkness, to spin silken cloth from the coarse fibers of humanity inhabiting this region. She is paid less for a year's work here than the average wage earner in her

185

✝

native America would make at a drive-up fast food chain restaurant in a week, and she will give that to the villagers through her needful purchases. She asks nothing, and gives all. She smiles when the harsh reality around her would bring tears to the eyes of the most hardened of men. She steps forward when others of less conviction would surely run. She is strong, when grown men would certainly cower before the strain of a day in the life of these hapless villagers. She has established a school, where she teaches eager children every day.

Pray for her tonight as your waiter clears the dishes from your bountiful feast, or as you seek the comfort of your spacious beds. Pray for her tomorrow as well, and in the days to come. Never stop praying for her, and others like her, no matter what your personal beliefs. For they are our real leaders, our real heroes.

✝

He knew it would baffle the chief correspondent in Mexico City. This was not the usual travel guide drivel he'd churned out the past three years; this had an element of passion. He also betrayed his own feelings, but so be it. That was no price to pay. There was something now to write about, something he could again take pride in. Let anyone try to take this from him, just let them.

He pulled the last page from the typewriter, put it with the other one, and sealed both in an envelope marked for delivery to his section chief in Mexico City. It would be posted tomorrow, once the courier returned to the capital city, his first deadline missed in a long while. He was content in that as well. But his contentment was short-lived. The same nagging thought that had bothered him earlier in the evening resurfaced. The feeling of incompleteness.

Interlacing and twisting his fingers, as was his habit when young nuns weren't clasping his hands between theirs, he recounted the conversation with Nicole at the pond, how she had begun to open up to him about her past, and how uncomfortable it had made him. He had so abruptly cut her off, hadn't he? Why had he done that? Surely it was a defensive strike, some mechanism to keep her at an emotional distance, for familiarity was not a good thing in this relationship. Now he realized that there had been much left unsaid, and he wanted to know it all. He was no longer fearful of being drawn close to Nicole; it was too late for that. What he felt bore not on what he didn't know of her, only what he did know and feel, what more he yearned to know. She'd left the door open for him, hadn't she, compelling his attendance at her school, telling him to drop by any time he cared to? What further invitation did he need? Weren't her penultimate words as he left her doorway at the church, *I expect you to come visit my school?*

The words she spoke just before she said, *Good night, sweet Evan?*

"Jerry, you're not going to believe this." Jerry Carpenter, section chief for Reuters in Mexico City, looked up from his desk at the sound of Bob Wagner's voice. He disliked Wagner. He disliked everybody, really. But particularly Wagner. He listened while Wagner threw a few vulgar epithets on top of the earlier comment as he tossed the envelope on his desk.

"Montgomery's gone over the edge this time. Bet on it: he's on the sauce again."

As he read the contents of the envelope, Carpenter ignored everything else Wagner said, until Wagner got the message and left the room muttering to himself. "Hmmpf," Carpenter said, after he'd finished. He'd seen a lot worse from Montgomery. This was different—not exactly world-class stuff, but different. Refreshing, something to take the heavy bite out of a revolution that had become old news to most. The coverage of the internal strife was necessary, for as every newsman knew, today's local rebel uprising might be tomorrow's Castro-overthrows-Batista headline, and folks didn't like surprises when they opened their morning papers. They liked continuity, even when it became a little boring.

But this was a rose in the thorn brush. It had promise. His newsman's intuition— he truly disliked the phrase "nose for news;" what idiot dreamed that one up, anyway?—took over, and gave him reason enough to give printed life to this most recent effort from his grizzled old friend.

"Wagner, get in here," he demanded. Handing the copy over his desk, he said, "Go with this. Run it across the wire. Let's see who picks it up."

Ignoring the surprised look on Wagner's face, Carpenter continued. "And another thing: Evan Montgomery's a friend of mine, you got that? He may not have a lot of miles left in him, but he's been at this business since Christ was a corporal. He's working an angle here, I'm sure of it; I've seen him do it before. I squeeze this, and he never makes another deadline, goes back to that dreary and Godforsaken English town of his and fails at a crummy little used bookstore. That's not the way it's going to end for Monty, not if I have anything to do with it.

"Now go put that over the wire like I told you!"

Chewing hard on a soggy cigar, the news chief slowly shook his head from side to side. "Monty, whatever are you up to? Hmmm? Why do I think this is going to cause me trouble?"

27

CLASSES NEARED AN END, still there was no sign of Evan. She'd felt a schoolgirl's giddiness at the thought, no, the expectation, of him coming to her school. Her usual flair was missing, which hadn't gone unnoticed by her students, whose participation level had been as weak as her own. Maria's asking if she felt sick exposed the lethargy, and sparked a burst of energy. If Evan hadn't shown, then there was good reason for it. She knew he would, sooner or later.

He didn't appear the next day, either. After delivering Maria home, Nicole asked Miguel if he'd seen *Señor* Monty. The old carpenter shook his head.

It was time to pay a visit. Skipping her daily walk, she headed for Evan's cottage.

There was no answer to her knock, to her calling out his name either. The door was locked. She peered through the windows, and circled the house. Nothing.

As she turned to leave, she caught sight of a woman looking at her through the window of the house nearest Evan's. Nicole smiled at her, and waved. She'd never seen the woman before. She also noticed two young children playing in the dirt beside the house, a boy and a girl, he perhaps as old as seven or eight, she five or six. She'd never seen either of them before either, and wondered why they weren't in school. She turned back to where she'd met the woman's gaze a few seconds earlier and found her gone. Nicole walked toward the window, stopping when she heard a commotion from the back of the house. She changed course, heading for the sounds. When she rounded the corner, there was no one. No children, no one. She heard a door close. She found the door, and knocked. Speaking in Spanish she identified herself, and asked to speak to the woman in the home. There was no answer, no sound from within. She knocked twice more. Still nothing.

Nicole had no doubt there was someone in the house. She made it a point to ask Teresa and Miguel about the woman, and the house. Something wasn't right.

Strange behavior, strange indeed.

———————

A day later there still was no sign of Evan. It was as if he had vanished. Nicole tried not to worry; he was, after all, a grown man and had done well enough for himself before she'd appeared. But he was at an age when things such as heart attacks, or strokes, or a myriad of other ailments might target him. She found herself praying intently for his safe return. Soon Father Art would be back. Perhaps he would know something.

Her life took on a new dimension when she struck up the friendship with Evan Montgomery. For a week after their first sojourn into her private Sanctuary they met in the afternoon, after classes and extracurricular activities were over. They'd gone in his Range Rover to several of the ancient ruins. She'd even coaxed him into the chapel. He'd balked at the notion of reacquainting himself with prayer, but she stayed hopeful.

The excursions to the ruins had been the most fun she'd had since school days back home. She'd volunteered to be their tour guide, and made picnic lunches in exchange for the fuel and transportation. One afternoon—the last she'd seen of Evan—he'd been a bit morose, but refused to tell her why. She'd given up on the explanation. But he did say he would try to come by the school the next day. She hadn't sensed anything was wrong, and had eagerly looked forward to another day's adventure. But he hadn't showed, and now, three days later, was nowhere to be found.

She did receive some good news: a message from Father Art telling her he would be returning on schedule. Six days. Time enough for the archdiocese to fill her order for the food, wine, and beer, and soft drinks for the children. She meant to throw a grand welcome home celebration … an old-fashioned surprise party. She mentioned her idea to Miguel and Teresa, who spread the word throughout Refugio. In no time Nicole had a volunteer work force. She all but forgot about the absentee Evan Montgomery.

Two days before Father Art's return Nicole gathered her children. She reminded them there had been no school when Father Art had left. He would be returning to a village with a school, with wonderful students who had learned much, and who one day would all read and write in at least two languages. That made them very special, she explained. Nicole asked what the children wanted to do for Father Art, to show him how much they'd learned, how happy they were to be in school.

Faced with the very first decision to make ever given them by an adult, the children returned the highly expectant look of glee from their teacher with stone blank expressions. Unwilling to settle for failure, Nicole persevered. "Children," she began, in her very best Spanish, "what do you do when you honor your parents, and grandparents, on a special occasion? Have you ever put on a play, or made something special?"

Again, blankness. Then Maria spoke up. "Sister, maybe we could invite Father Art to come to our school. He can watch us learn from you. And we will be very good. We will dress nice, and Jorge and Hector won't fight, and Manuel will stay awake, and we will all read our very best, and color and work our problems our very best, and we will sing songs our very best, and show Father how well we can play *futbol* now. Can't we just do this?"

An old expression of her mother's came to mind: *from the mouths of babes.* "Class, what Maria says, do you all think that's a good plan? Is that something you would like to do for Father?"

A chorus of yeses rang out, and little hands clapped. It was set. The children would do no more than they had done since Father Art had left, only this time it would be a special class day just for him. Their teacher could not have been prouder. The special place in her heart for Maria grew even larger.

Her heavy heart lightened. Concern for Evan Montgomery faded. For now, there were preparations to be made.

§

The day before Father Art's scheduled return, Nicole received another surprise, an unexpected and wondrous surprise. Clutching a letter in her hand, she raced into Teresa's house without knocking, exclaiming, "My parents are coming! My mother and father—*mi madre y mi padre*—they are coming to visit me!"

Nicole grabbed a surprised, wide-eyed and open-mouthed Maria, joined hands and danced a circle around the dining table. The commotion awoke a napping Tomas, who walked into the room, rubbing his eyes, looking confused. He, too, was swept into the merriment as Nicole scooped him into a free arm, and together with Maria twirled some more.

The frolicking soon ended, and a breathless Nicole sprinted for the church, much to do. Evan Montgomery slipped from her mind.

Nicole slept restlessly that night. It seemed as soon as she dozed, she awoke to a new concern. Where would her parents stay? The letters she'd written them had never mentioned the lack of lodging. This called for action. First, though, she must take care of Father Art's return; her parents' needs would wait.

Refugio was magnificently alive the day of Father Art's return. It was nearly noon when he arrived, seated in the familiar courier truck. Nicole embraced him as an old friend, Southern style. With that expression, the last vestige of formality between priest and nun slipped away.

The merriment began. The driver unloaded the cases of soda for the children, and beer and wine for the adults. Nicole admonished Father Art against complaining about the fuss. Predictably, he exclaimed more than once that he'd seen it all now, as the children reveled in the mystery of the fizz that tickled and the sweetness that bathed their tongues from the curious containers Sister Nicole called *cans*. Father Art was led to the tables set up beside the church for the feast, a Guatemalan equivalent to a covered dish supper. It lacked for nothing in the way of local cuisine. Eating became a serious issue. Father Art shamelessly overate, promising to confess his gluttony at the first opportunity. He complained of bad food during the past month, but Nicole pointed out how he didn't look as if he'd missed any meals since he'd left Refugio. The priest patted his expanded midsection, then raised his hands in mock defeat as everyone laughed at her quick wit.

There was music, and dancing. Nicole sang and played with two of the men who also had guitars, then stopped to dance with Maria. Father Art watched as the two made turn after turn, hands joined in circular fashion, as if they'd danced together many times before. The bond did not go unnoticed by the priest.

The revelry lasted until there was nothing left to drink, and little left to eat. The children had rushed off to play games as the adults sat and talked. Nicole watched in awe at the scene before her. How many crawfish festivals had she been to, from Gueydan to Houma, Lafayette to Grand Isle, all with live zydeco music, songs sung in pure Cajun, as good folk ate and danced merrily for hours, then broke into groups to catch their collective breath? For the first time since she'd arrived in her new home, she felt the pangs of homesickness. Luckily, home was coming to see her, and soon.

As tables were being cleared, and the last of the partyers prepared to leave, Father Art and Nicole were seated alone. He thanked her for this fine homecoming, which she shrugged off as a group effort. Then he got serious.

"Were you all right while I was away? I worried, you know. I was afraid I'd left you with too much responsibility for one so new to this place. So, were you okay?"

"Father, I wanted for nothing. Teresa has taught me to cook many tasty dishes, and I have had Miguel and Carlos at my beck and call. They even installed my tub right after you left, so I've been able to bathe. What more could I have wanted or needed?"

"Just the same, it was probably unwise of me to have left you alone. Thank the Lord nothing bad happened while I was away. I could not have forgiven myself.

"By the way," he said, "what did you find to do while I was away? With only one pupil at your school, which, I must say, I will again try to help you put together now that I'm returned, you must have been enormously bored. Whatever did you do with all the time on your hands?"

"Oh, I managed to stay busy," she coyly replied. "I've taken to long walks, and I read the books you left me on the ruins. And Evan Montgomery came back, just after you left. He was kind enough to furnish his Range Rover for the two of us to explore a goodly number of the ruins I'd read about. He is a most fascinating man, Father. You were right about him. But despite all the free time I had, there were still enough hours in the day to do God's work, Father.

"And speaking of free time," she quickly added, "I may need a little more from you. I have some exciting news. My parents will be here in about ten days. Isn't that wonderful?"

"Yes, how wonderful. But are they prepared for what they'll find here?"

"You don't know my parents. They can handle anything for ten days."

"Excellent. I suppose you've made arrangements for them?"

"I'm still working on that part. I suppose they can have my room, and I can sleep under the stars." The thought made her shiver.

"Nonsense, Sister. Something will turn up, it always does. Now let's say good night to our few remaining guests, and see what we can do about preparing for tomorrow's Mass. Have the faithful showed up every morning in my absence?"

"Oh, yes," she replied. "Every day, the faithful."

§

That night, as she did most nights, she wrote letters. Tonight, to her brothers. They'd been on her mind lately. She missed them. She felt a nurturing instinct when it came to her brothers. And it ran deep, always had. She wrote of their parents' impending visit. She shared much of her new life. She unceremoniously stripped herself of habit and veil, and became once again their sister. Her candle burned long into the night.

———————

In another room, down the hall and around a corner, two men, old friends, talked. Rather, one talked, and the other mostly listened. When it came time to talk, Father Art—as the priest, not the friend—spoke to Evan Montgomery in the hushed tone one might expect from the other side of the confessional. Words of solace, words of encouragement; words of prayer as well. There was no long good-bye when the time came, no high moment of drama. Each man understood what was best, what was required. They shook hands, and the taller man left.

The priest made ready for bed, dwelling on the talk with the journalist. He worried about his troubled friend, and about his young charge. This was a delicate situation, calling for wisdom and resolve. It called for prayer. His prayer lasted well into the night.

193

✝

28

MORNING CAME SOONER THAN either wanted. Despite the lack of sleep, Nicole and Father Art were in cheerful spirit when they met in the chapel for the morning Mass. But not all heads were clear that morning. There were *looks* from the wives at the husbands who'd overindulged the evening before. Father Art spoke of compassion, understanding and forgiveness in his brief homily. God's words had a temporarily softening effect, as sharp elbows gave way to strained but at least peaceful coexistence. Husbands said *gracias* rather than *amen* as they received the host during Holy Communion. A knowing priest smiled as he blessed them all.

When the Mass had ended and the blessedly forgiven had left, Nicole waited for the right opportunity. Timidly she began. "Father, I wonder if you might delay your work here at the church for a bit, and come with me. There is something I think you might like to see."

"I think my work can wait," he replied unquestioningly.

There was surprisingly little conversation between them as they walked. She hoped he would remain this aloof until they turned the next corner.

He did, and the seemingly never-ending walk finally brought them to the edge of the clearing, where Father Art was greeted by more than two dozen children, dressed in clean, smart clothes, seated at their benches, backs straight, proud, ready. All eyes were on the adults dressed in black. The few parents who'd stayed to see them arrive waved a good-bye, leaving the children to put on their show.

"What have we here?" said Father Art. "I see you've been busy while I was away, Sister. I believe you had but one student, and an underage one at that, when I left."

"Oh, Father, I do have so much to tell you, but we wanted this to be a surprise. I hope you don't mind. I couldn't bring myself to tell you and spoil their moment."

He smiled at her. "Well, now I've seen it all. I am not sure what to say. Am I invited to stay and watch the classes?"

"Father, your seat is right over there. Jorge," she said to the nearest boy, "please take Father to the seat we have selected for him." A tall, thin lad with a huge smile took the priest by the hand, and led him to the far side of the classroom, to a seat adorned with small gifts and ornamentations, handmade endearments from the children. Visibly touched, he thanked them all, and asked if he could look at everything later, that he now would much prefer to see them at work in their classroom. On cue, Nicole took over, and the lessons began.

He watched with split measures of awe and adulation. It was obvious these children had been schooled well, and enjoyed their studies. Their enthusiasm was genuine, their attentiveness remarkable. Beyond that was their devotion to the instructor. She was no charmer, no snake oil peddler. This was something almost symbiotic, host and symbiont, one nurturing, another being nourished. *How does she do it?* Hers was a divine calling, he concluded. This woman … chaste, obedient, living in poverty … fulfilling her vows. His worry at hearing one man's profession of love for her the night before took on a lesser import. Her devotion to this chosen life would withstand any turmoil brought on by vagaries of the flesh.

A saddened and embarrassingly tearful Evan Montgomery just hours earlier had sought help with the sensitive matter of his feelings for Nicole. In the end, it was not the priest's counsel that set the journalist on his course; rather ironically, Father Art mused, it was love that drove Monty away. For here, before him, was everything decent, all that was pure and unspoiled, and only a fool would overlook it … or risk spoiling it. His denouement was simply to leave. It was time for a much-needed holiday. When a clear head could overpower a weak heart, he would return. There had been no argument from the priest.

"What do I tell her, when she asks what happened to you?" Father Art asked.

"Tell her I'm on assignment. She'll understand," Montgomery replied.

So as he watched her now—Montgomery having departed in the night to an appointment with deliverance, salvation perhaps—Father Art knew that, for the moment, there would be no turmoil surrounding the unrequited, forbidden love. He would do as asked, while Monty went on his quest for redemption.

Twice he was pulled into the lessons, quite the willing participant. Then, to his further amazement, she imperceptibly segued into the catechism. They had learned much in a short time. He wondered if she would try to reach the young minds with the intricacies of the Holy Trinity and such. She was up to the task. He'd seen it all. Almost.

"You are quite the soccer player, Sister," he said as they walked back to the church. "The product of a misspent youth, no doubt," he chortled. He made a mental note to speak to the archbishop about more equipment—shoes, balls, regulation goals. He knew little about this sport that united even this conflict-ravaged nation, but he knew that it had a future in Refugio. It was a good thing, and it deserved nurturing. He would see to it.

"Sister," he started, "I believe I have a solution to your parents' lodging dilemma. Something quite unexpected, a Godsend, really."

"Tell me, Father," she said.

"Monty has gone off, on assignment. Indefinitely, I believe. His place is open. It should accommodate your parents quite well."

She studied his face, hesitating before speaking. "How—How do you know this, Father? He's been gone for days now, no word to anyone, no word at all from him."

"He came to see me last night." Catching her look of dismay, he quickly added, "Very late, long after you had retired, I'm certain. He said to give you his regards, and to apologize for cutting class, as I believe he put it. But he was called away. Something he just couldn't say no to."

Nicole spoke next. "We had such a wonderful time, those days while you were away. I felt as if I had found a new friend, Father, a very special friend. It disappointed me so when he didn't show up at the school, as he'd promised … he didn't even send word he was leaving. I went to his cottage, to see if he'd fallen ill, or worse. There was no sign at all he'd been there. It was as if he'd never been there."

"Well, not to worry, Sister, he'll be back. He wanted me to tell you that, and not to worry for him. We didn't talk about the use of his cottage, but I know he'd be honored if your parents would stay there. Please trust me on this one." He could see her mind was elsewhere. "You will trust me on this, Sister?"

She mumbled something like a *yes*. It was good enough for now, he thought.

———————

Gone scarcely an hour, she missed them already. There was a time it would have been impossible to spend ten days with her parents … but not this time. She'd so enjoyed their company. Especially her mother's. Her father had aged. His signature spark had dimmed; he seemed tired. He and Father Art hit it off quite well, though. Their bond freed up time with her mother, still lively and beautiful as ever. Nicole wondered if the family genes would preserve her as well. She hadn't wrinkled at twenty-two, but who knew what she might look like at thirty?

They'd brought news of her old friends, and of Tommy, who would be graduating LSU soon. Her brothers were well, they sent their love. They enjoyed getting her letters, and hoped she understood that they are not much at writing. They would call, but, of course, they can't. She should be a nun in a place where there are phones, Chris says. All this was passed on to her, this and more, and for a brief moment she longed for the comfort of the once familiar. But as memories of the days with her parents would pass, so would that feeling. She was where she wanted to be, and that's all there was to it. She was at peace.

Yet she kept an important part of herself from her parents. She had hoped to take them to her Sanctuary, her paradise, to show them the tranquility that surrounded her, the peace she'd discovered in a land so raw and savage. She'd held back, though. The unease she felt where her father was concerned, his lack of acceptance, stopped her. Until her father came around, this deepest recess of her spirituality would remain guarded. This one would be played by her rules.

Her parents left in late April; the military came in mid-May. On a typically quiet morning, the rumbling of three heavy trucks, the clank of armaments, and hammering of nails posting signs disturbed the silence and calm, signifying a new, ominous presence. The schoolchildren were frightened. Nicole did her best to console them, but settled on letting class out early. She met Father Art at the church after delivering Maria to a worried Teresa, who held her child closely, looking to draw as much comfort from the youngster as Maria did from the mother. Nicole assured both of them there was nothing to fear, and hoped she was right.

Nicole listened as Father Art spoke with a soldier who bore the insignia of an officer. He ignored her presence.

"Padre, I and my men will occupy the barracks in the garrison. There is no cause for alarm. We are here to protect against reported guerilla activity in the region, nothing more. The other larger villages will also receive military protection," he added. His manner was as crisp as his uniform.

"You will see, as time will tell, that my men will be as neighbors, even as friends. I will personally see that harmony reigns. I pledge this much to you and your village."

The officer was smiling broadly. Father Art shook his hand and thanked him.

"Oh, I almost forgot to tell you. The village will derive yet another benefit from our presence, something that should convince you of our sincerity." Still smiling, the officer continued. "We are bringing electricity into the village. First the garrison, then the homes and other structures. Please pass this along to your parishioners. Most will not know about electricity, but as you know, it can change their lives—for the better. No telephones yet, just electricity. You will excuse me now, Padre." Touching his fingertips to his cap he bowed in Nicole's direction. "Sister."

He turned and left, before Nicole or Father Art could react to the news.

A full ten minutes after the officer had excused himself Nicole and Father Art were still standing in front of the church, watching as the soldiers continued unloading their trucks. Father Art spoke first.

"Do you really suppose we will soon have electricity? I barely remember what it's like, I've been so long without it."

"Oh, Father, I don't know. I feel uneasy about the soldiers coming here. I don't think the villagers will welcome them with quite the open arms as our commandant would like to believe. But a selfish part of me would like to have electricity. Think what it could mean."

"I am. I'm not sure the price we'll all pay isn't too great, that's all." She watched as he turned and went into the church, shaking his head as he walked away.

Nicole thought about the day's development for another moment. It struck her as a monument to her own insignificance that such a thing could have happened so quickly, so totally without warning, and so resolutely. Idyll and tranquility shattered by truck engines, the nearly soundless patter of mostly bare feet soon to be drowned out by marching boots, all in the name of, of what? peace and protection? Somehow the political strife in this country had been in the backwash of other villages, other people, leaving her untouched in the relatively short time she'd now been here. In barely more than an instant that had changed. There was nothing on the horizon to portend such a happening. No great debate, no vote, not even an invitation or advance notice. Reduced to its simplest form, it could be said everything happened after grammar, before math.

Later she would visit with Father Art more on the subject. Perhaps there would be word from the archdiocese, some guidance. There must be a protocol in matters even of this sort, she reasoned. It just couldn't happen so suddenly like this, it simply couldn't.

———————————

In all, eighteen men were eventually garrisoned in Refugio. Nicole steeled herself for the sounds of hostility, but the crack of gunfire and the barking of close-order drill commands never came. After two weeks, true to the commandant's assurances, the military's presence was uneventfully felt by the village. They were there, yes, but they kept to themselves. A few of the soldiers ventured out of the garrison from time to time, but for their uniforms and shouldered rifles drew no extraordinary attention. They could just as well have been out for a stroll as on a reconnaissance mission.

Still, Nicole was asked the same questions over and over: *Why are they here? Do they mean us harm? Are we to change the way we live?* She deferred to Father Art, who appealed to Christian values as he urged his parishioners to maintain calm and respect.

Life as usual gradually resumed. Controversy gave way to the daily grind. The monster was not a monster, only men who dressed differently, and carried different tools of a trade. Then, after just over two months' occupation, the commandant's second promise was kept and Refugio was introduced to the wonder of electricity. It took several weeks for the soldiers to set the poles and run the lines, and a few more to wire each of the homes and shops. Father Art was still unsure whether it was worth the bother, but put aside his own predilection in favor of calming his wary and superstitious parishioners. Not surprisingly, the church was nearly last in line. The priest held out to the bitter end, still unsure if having electrical power was worth it, or if the price to pay was too dear. Nicole was not so unsure, however; to her it was a gift from Heaven. With the convenience came opportunity, and she intended to take full advantage.

With the guile of a Middle Eastern merchant Nicole set about persuading the commandant to wire her school. To the frightened children, she cajoled, electricity meant learning, the opportunity to experience something as simple as a radio. She held back on a greater dream of television and personal computers. Baby steps were needed, not a world record triple jump.

"Please, Commandant Major, think of your own children before you say no to me." She forced him to look her squarely eye-to-eye. His barely perceptible nod was all she needed. Throwing both arms around the startled Major, she thanked him and God in the same breath. The rest of her day was spent planning, scheming ... there were parents and

199

✝

friends who would be getting letters soon, requests for things electric, large and small. Her excitement overcame the urge to sleep. She once more wrote long into the night.

———————

As Refugio looked less warily at the intruders, the soldiers no longer patrolled with drawn weapons. Nicole theorized the gruff commandant with the soft heart had seen the villagers posed no threat, that a nice balance indeed had been achieved. The soldiers were young, probably away from their homes for the first time. Thus it was a welcome sight as Father Art gave communion to several of the young soldiers one Sunday at Mass. The number grew with each passing week. It was no surprise when one morning a young soldier stood beside the school dressed in soccer gear, dribbling a fine new ball from foot to knee, knee to head, head to toe, and so on, with the skill of one obviously able and appearing ready to play. Nicole approached the young man, who gave his name as Pablo Vasquez, who told her he'd played soccer all his life … before he became Private Vasquez.

"I have watched you play with the children. Your side always wins, unless you allow the other to win." He grinned. "I could be the equalizer."

Nicole polled the class. The boys were ecstatic; Pablo was already their hero. The decision was made: Pablo was the newest team member. The first day he was tentative; by the second even the skilled Nicole knew she was nowhere near his equal.

"Pablo," Nicole began, after the third day, "we are no match for you. I believe you could easily defeat all of us." She smiled engagingly as she paid him the simple compliment.

The young man's face reddened. "Should I not come here any more? If I am not welcome, then I should stay away."

"Oh, Pablo, no, you misunderstand. Of course you are still welcome. What I was trying to say is I fear we are so poor a match for you that we cannot be much fun for you. Which would be sad, because they have so much more fun when you are here."

Pablo's smile was quick and large, answer enough. It was not until after he'd gone that she realized how much he reminded her of Chris. She again caught herself missing home, and family.

29

THE WOMAN WAS NEAR hysteria, beckoning Nicole to follow. What Nicole found at the woman's home was a man delirious with fever. The woman collapsed beside him, doubling the patient count. Nicole wet down a rag and applied the coolness to the two foreheads that gave off heat like small radiators. As she treated the couple she could hear the frightened villagers exclaiming *"La fiebre! La fiebre!"* Even if Nicole wasn't sure what she was dealing with, there were those around her with no doubt whatsoever. *The fever!*

In moments Father Art arrived. "One of our flock tells me we may have a problem, Sister." His understatement somehow calmed her.

Nicole told the breathless priest all she knew. "What are we dealing with? Are they right about this being the fever?" She dipped the compresses into fresh water and wiped foreheads, necks, wrists. The body heat was increasing.

"I don't know," he answered. "I haven't seen any sign of it during my stay here. I'm not sure even what the symptoms are. I am certain of one thing, however—we must not let panic overtake this village. I suggest we tell everyone to return to their homes, and take inventory of who's feeling poorly, and who's not. I also think we would be well advised to consider a quarantine, don't you, until we're sure what it is we're facing?"

"Yes I do, Father."

He was staring at the old couple. "We should think of setting up a field hospital. Any suggestion where?"

In unison they both said, *"The schoolhouse!"*

Evening had fallen in the space of little more than the hour it took thirty-nine villagers to be delivered to the makeshift hospital. All were fever-ridden; many unconscious. Rags were boiled, then cooled by waving them in the evening air. The cooled compresses were applied to burning extremities, and listless heads were lifted so water and broth could be force-fed. Throughout the night Nicole and Father Art and a dozen volunteers tended the sick. Despite the heroic efforts, by morning the fever had claimed its first victim. Death came to the older woman who had first summoned Nicole. Not long after, the husband followed. Nicole paused in her nursing labor only long enough to pray for the souls of the couple, and to wish for the safety of her own parents.

This was Nicole's first face-to-face encounter with death. Still, there was no time to dwell on the loss of life, only time to tend the ill.

Miguel helped Father Art carry off the dead couple. Their spaces were quickly taken by other patients. Nicole methodically divided the labor effort among the volunteers. She became concerned when Father Art and Miguel did not return for over an hour. *Where are they?* she wondered. Soon enough she knew.

Mid morning of the second day, Father Art came to her with the news she had dreaded. Teresa, Maria and Tomas had been stricken; strangely, Miguel and Carlos had not, not yet anyway. They were at their home, where Miguel was caring for them.

Father Art had scarcely finished with his news before Nicole abruptly rose and wordlessly left, handing him the damp compress. There would be no use in trying to dissuade her. He knelt to the near lifeless figure, and continued applying the cool, damp relief.

§

It was an unusually warm morning. Perhaps, he thought, that was why the streets were empty. But how could that be? These people were always wandering about, warm or not. *Where are the villagers?* The commandant called for his aide, and ordered the young soldier to reconnoiter the village. He urged caution.

The explanation came soon enough. The aide, breathless, caught up to his commandant in the mess room. The aide reported fever had struck the village, and seven were already dead.

Acting quickly, the commandant ordered the radio operator to call for the surgeon from San Luis, a full three hours' drive away. "Tell the doctor there is probably an outbreak of the fever." At that instant, young Pablo slumped to the floor. The commandant saw fear frozen on his men's faces.

"What are you afraid of?" he barked. "Our surgeon will know what to do." He turned to the two men at his side. "You two, take Private Vasquez to his room, wrap him in a dampened cloth, then wash your hands." He felt Pablo's forehead; yes, it was the fever.

"Sergeant, you and the corporal there, come with me now to the village." When they hesitated, he snapped hard at their reluctance. "Behave as soldiers, not scared children!" Fearing him more than the fever, they fell in quickly.

After a systematic search, he found the priest at the school, tending as many as fifty afflicted villagers. He rushed to the priest's side. "Father, I have ordered the surgeon. He will be here in three hours or less. He is equipped to treat this disease." The Major placed a caring hand on the priest's shoulder. "I have heard of seven already. Are there others?"

"Still just seven, but I fear I am about to lose at least that many more within the hour. I do not know how to treat this fever, Major; all that we are able to do is comfort the dying."

"My surgeon will know. I will put him at your disposal. I am sorry I did not know of this sooner. You should have come to me. I would not have refused your needs. I am hurt that you did not think me humane enough to help," he added, softening the rebuke with compassion in his voice.

He watched Father Art's eyes fall downward, his lips part. Only silence followed.

The commandant again grasped the priest's shoulder. "It is all right, my friend. We will talk later. Now we must prepare for the arrival of my surgeon."

While the priest stood in stunned and worn silence, the commandant instructed a small group of villagers in what must be done to prepare for the arrival of help. Unquestioningly they obeyed the man who had such a short time before been the source of fear and doubt. This was no time for such feelings. Now was the time to learn strength.

"Where is your nun?" asked the Major, alarm in his tone. "She has not fallen ill?"

A villager spoke up. "She is at Miguel's home, next to the church. The child Maria—"

The Major interrupted. "You men stay here and do what you can to help. Come for me when the surgeon arrives."

He found Nicole tending to Maria. The child reminded him of his own daughter, who he would see when his time in this village was up. Nicole turned, surprise in her expression. "Commandant," she said. "I have a very sick child on my hands. Two very sick children," correcting herself as she glanced at young Tomas. "And a sick parent as well. Is it the fever?"

"Sí. That is all we call it. It strikes like the jungle cat, silently, quickly, deadly. Only the very strongest can survive without medication."

She reacted quickly. "There is medication? This can be treated?" Her elation was as if in slow motion. He could see the warning signs.

"Medication is on the way." He saw relief creep across her tired face. "I have called my surgeon. He will be here soon. We must hope," he said, taking a knee beside the exhausted nun, "that it is not too late."

He caught her just before she hit the floor. She spoke weakly, begging that he not let anything happen to Maria, please, that he see to her, protect her. Her voice trickled off into silence. He cradled her limp head into the fold of his arm and carried her to the church. He found the room that could only have been hers. He gently laid her on the bed. His arms were wet from her perspiration-soaked clothing. He wished there were a woman to leave her with. Looking down on the exhausted woman before him, he could find no reason not to admire her. Hardened in the military way, his feelings surprised him. He touched his fingers to the strand of hair that protruded from her veil, whispering, "I will care for your Maria, I will watch her and protect her for you. Rest now, my little angel."

He left the room, and went looking for a woman of the village, someone to come and care for the young girl he'd just called *his* little angel. It would be after this peril had subsided, when the moments of acting in crisis had passed, that he would call into question the images and thoughts that had so altered the man's very core, if only momentarily. But for now, there was help to be found for the young woman, and a surgeon whose arrival was imminent. Familiar juices were flowing. He was the commandant again.

§

Something wasn't right. It was as if she were suspended in fog. But she wasn't back home, where early winter fog shrouded all of St. Tammany Parish some days, often until well after noon. No, she was in Refugio. There was no fog here. Smoke . . . was it smoke she was staggering through? There was no acrid, burning sensation tearing at her eyes and nostrils, so it was not smoke either. She fought to free herself from the tethering force, to move forward at a more quickened pace. It was as if she were anchored on a glacier.

Ahead, there was a shimmering of light. Ribbonlike, it glowed behind the shroud of cloudiness in which she found herself. Dazzling rays of brilliant white light spread around her.

The light source stayed barely out of reach. She relaxed in her pursuit, for the light was not running from, but leading her.

A familiar voice was near. She could not make out the words, but she knew the voice. Father Art. She spoke his name. What was happening to her? Why could she not move?

More voices. One familiar, the rest not. She was spinning. Her feet slipped from beneath her. She was no longer walking, no longer anchored to the glacier. She had wings … she was flying. Her flight was away from the light. The light was fading. A single sound rushed to her lips, borne of the impending sense of darkness ready to swallow her. She muttered but one clear sound, one noise before everything went blank. *Maria.* And as all was turning dark, she reached toward a child, somewhere out there, a child who needed her, who she needed. *Maria,* she said again.

And then the darkness took her.

✝

30

OPENING HER EYES, SHE saw Father Art standing over her. The Major was standing beside him. Trancelike and weak, she asked where she was.

"You fell ill, Sister," said the priest. "We've kept you in your room while you mended."

"The fever," said the Major.

Father Art spoke again. "You've been out for three days. You had us quite worried. See here, even Monty caught word of you being down." She saw him gesture to the side, where the familiar figure of one Evan Montgomery stood, safely at a distance.

"Hello, Evan," she managed. "Nice to see you again."

"And you, Sister," he replied shyly. "Don't try to talk. You should rest."

She was listless, drained of all strength. As her thoughts began to clear, they turned first to Maria. She spoke with some difficulty. "Is Maria all right? And Teresa, and Tomas, and Carlos? And the rest?"

All eyes in the room were on Father Art. He laid a hand on Nicole's shoulder. "All in good time, Sister," he said. "Do as Monty says now, and rest. Then we'll talk."

"I must know how Maria is. She's not—she didn't—oh, Father, please don't put me through this, just tell me, tell me how Maria is, I have to know."

"Maria is alive, but she is terribly weak. She may be in a coma, the doctor isn't sure. Carlos, Teresa and little Tomas, they're doing all right, weak and still in bed, but they will recover. But we lost seventeen of our flock, Sister. Seventeen of our friends and neighbors are with God now." As he crossed himself she reflexively did the same. "My other children, Father. What of them? Are they safe?" Even weakened she could come up with tough questions.

"We've not lost any of the children. Most took ill, but they're safe now. Only Maria is still in harm's way."

There was no disguising her reaction. He spoke quickly. "You must not let Maria's condition keep you from your rest. You are still in danger yourself. You'll be no good to Maria or any of us if …" She wasn't listening.

"As your superior, I must insist you rest." It was the first time he had pulled rank on her. She forced a weak smile, turned her head to the wall and said nothing. Soon she slept.

The priest smiled one of those invisible smiles, the kind that doesn't show itself to anyone, that only the smiler knows about. He'd been stern, but to what end? If she'd had any strength she'd have risen from her sickbed and marched to Maria's, and stayed until hell froze over if that's how long it took. He'd talked to her father enough to know this lass had a strong, independent mind. He'd seen as much himself. Fortunately he would not have to contend with a stubborn streak this day, for she was thankfully asleep.

Monty and the commandant had excused themselves, leaving him alone with her. It was a time for prayer. Neither the journalist nor the military man was equipped for that task, and neither was troubled at stepping aside in favor of the man who was. Father Art pulled up a chair to Nicole's bedside, prepared to stay the entire night if necessary.

She stirred restlessly. Adrenaline pumped through his system as he felt her forehead for any sign of the fever. She was almost cool to the touch, a good sign according to the doctor. He called out through her window. "Enrique, go get the doctor. Hurry!" Young Enrique sprinted off to the garrison. He'd sat outside the window all night, waiting. Father Art was not at all surprised by the lad's devotion to Sister Nicole.

The doctor arrived just as she was awakening. He checked her vital signs, nodding his head. "You are out of danger now, Sister. In a few days you'll be back on your feet again."

Stronger from the night's rest, Nicole could prop herself up on an elbow. With her first words she asked the surgeon of Maria.

"She is still resting, but she slips in and out. She was so weak when I arrived. The commandant instructed me to treat her first, which I did, which is probably all that saved her. I cannot say that she will for sure recover, Sister, although I wish for your sake I could, but she is truly in God's hands now. I have done all I can. Only time—" Stopping himself, recognizing whose presence he was in, he changed course. "—and prayer will tell."

Nicole thanked him, and the doctor left. She heard him greet Father Art and the Major outside her window, and the three of them head off to check on Pablo. Her sweet Pablo. She waited until she was sure they were gone. There was somewhere she had to go, something she must do.

207

✝

3 1

S HE'D ALMOST MADE IT when Father Art's voice resounded over her shoulder. "I thought you'd try something like this."

She stopped in mid stride. Not turning, she hung her head and shrugged her shoulders, preparing for a battle she did not want to fight. She was surprised when the priest took her by the elbow and said, "Why don't we go in there together?"

"Thank you, Father," she said. "What a wonderful idea. I can use the help. I've been ill, you know." They both smiled at her weak attempt at humor.

He guided her through the doorway, into Maria's room, where two of the village women sat watching over her. They crossed themselves when the nun and priest entered the room. Nicole knew them both; their children attended the school. Both women assured Nicole that their children were safe, that the fever had spared them. They thanked her.

She asked how Maria was. One woman told her it was as if she was permanently asleep. This might have been encouraging to the village women, but it was not what Nicole wanted to hear.

Nicole asked them to leave her alone with Maria. When they were gone, Nicole knelt beside her small friend. She stroked her cheeks with soft fingertips, and kissed her closed eyelids, the same way she knew her own parents had fretted over her so many growing up years earlier. Nurturing came easily. She bent in close, and whispered. "Little Maria, I am here to watch over you. I had to be away for a while, but I am here now. I am here to bring you back. Your mama and your papa, and little Tomas, they miss you too. Baby Jesus misses you. Maria, come to me. Come to Sister Nicole, my little angel."

There was no movement, not then, not for the next twenty-four hours, and not for another twenty-four hours after that. It was not until more than two days later that

Maria moved, at a point when Nicole was again near exhaustion from her constant vigil. It was not a peaceful movement, but a restless one. The doctor, who had stayed over as a kindness to the commandant, was summoned. He administered more medication.

"Sister, I need to prepare you. The child is not responding. You, the padre here, maybe you should consider last rites. I am sorry. This is not easy for me either."

Refusing to accept the news, she redoubled her prayer vigil efforts.

Nicole collapsed on the sixth day, not from the fever but from sheer exhaustion. Father Art found her sprawled on the floor beside Maria. He was frightened, but her strong pulse calmed him. He and Carlos, who was now recovered, carried her back to her own room, her own bed. Teresa watched over her through the night, while Carlos and Miguel stood over Maria.

———————

She awoke with a start, squinting. The morning sun's rays stabbed painfully through her eyelids. Teresa was asleep in the chair beside her bed. Nicole didn't bother to wake her. Instead, she bounded from bed and made for the church's front door. She must get to Maria; it was urgent she get to Maria.

She was halfway across the street when she met the doctor and Father Art. Their expressions … without a word being spoken, Nicole knew. She raised a hand to her mouth. "No!" she screamed, pushing the men aside as she broke full stride for the child. Father Art grabbed her by the arm as she flew past, spinning her around wildly. She tugged, twisting her arm.

"Let me go! Father, let go of me!" His grip remained firm.

"Sister! Listen to me. There was nothing more we could do. She just slipped away, only a moment ago. Our Father has called his little lamb. You must accept this as His will, Sister."

Nicole heard none of this. She had turned stone deaf to even the thought that Maria might die. She feigned relaxation. When the priest relaxed in kind, she broke free, and ran on.

Entering the house, she found Carlos and Teresa in each other's arms, Teresa crying aloud, Carlos silent, his tear-stained cheeks sign enough of his grief. Maria lay on the bed before them. Nicole rushed to her, ignoring the parents. Maria's skin was cool to the touch. She was pale, as lifeless as the rag doll beside her. Nicole stroked her face, and held her hand, squeezing it as she resumed the prayers. There was nothing. The steady breathing that once had served up so much hope was gone. The little chest moved no more. Nicole shrieked, and grabbed Maria with what strength she could muster, pulling the limp body to her bosom, rocking her gently, patting her back, saying her name over and over and over, kissing her cheek, cupping her head, each small affection a desperate attempt to reach the girl who simply could not hear, or feel.

Trancelike, Nicole settled into a steady rocking motion as she walked a small circle, still patting Maria's back, speaking her name softly. She began to weep. The crying became louder, and as it did, her rocking motion became stronger. Her prayers continued. She begged God to intercede, to take her own life for Maria's. She never saw Father Art and Evan Montgomery enter the room.

She felt Father Art trying to take Maria. "Here, child," he was saying to her, "you must let go. Please, Nicole, let me take Maria." He called her Nicole. He'd never called her by her given name. She held tighter than ever. He pulled harder. Maria's fragile body was jerked around as if it were weightless.

It was when Nicole spun Maria's body from Father Art's attempt to take her that Teresa gasped in horror. Or was it something else? Carlos followed his wife's gaze to his daughter's face. His daughter's eyelids were open slightly, not just open and fixed in death, but open and fluttering. Carlos grabbed Nicole's shoulders from behind while he stared into his daughter's eyes. They moved! They were dull and listless, but they had moved, and as he looked into them, straining to see more, her eyes moved again, and met his, straight on. Then they blinked. Carlos could not believe his own eyes. Teresa saw it, too. As Father Art moved again toward Sister Nicole both parents shouted for him to stop, to come round and see. Confused, he blindly obeyed. He froze in stunned amazement.

"Dear God," Father Art murmured, crossing himself. Evan Montgomery leaned in, and his eyes, too, grew wide. Maria's colorless, chapped lips were parted, struggling to close again. Her lids fluttered weakly. But these were no involuntary reflexes of the dead. Something unexplainable was happening before their disbelieving but hopeful eyes. Carlos released his grip on Nicole's shoulders. Oblivious to what was happening, she kept pacing, rocking Maria gently as she invoked the power of the Almighty.

Montgomery had seen enough to know the doctor's services were needed. As he fled the room he left a scene worthy of remembrance: one trance-like nun who continued to caress a once dead but now very alive child, a priest who had not seen it all, and the incredulous, joyful parents.

In seconds an apprehensive doctor entered the room, followed closely by the Major and Evan Montgomery. Hypnotically Nicole still paced, and rocked, and prayed. The physician, quickly diagnosing the situation, realized that somehow—he would reconcile the how part later—this child was indeed quite alive. He moved in front of Nicole, whose own blank and expressionless eyes told him to act with care. He coaxed her to release her tightened grip on Maria, as gently as he knew how, until she understood, and handed Maria into the physician's arms.

While Maria received immediate medical attention, Father Art and Evan Montgomery tended to Nicole. They guided her to an empty bed in the same small room, where she laid down. In seconds she slept.

Across the room from Nicole, Maria, too, would sleep until morning. She was breathing steadily, the wisp of moonlight shining on her face accentuating her innocent, youthful beauty. A lone figure sat on the floor, between the remarkable woman and child. His eyes did not close; they never left Nicole. He could not explain what he'd witnessed, but it did not matter to him. His mind worked differently than most. Sometimes an explanation was better left unsaid, to the imagination; others, well, others required slightly more, a power of suggestion. In that he excelled. He was a journalist, and still a good one. His station in life, as he saw it—had always seen it—was to take the complicated and make it simple. Here, right now, was no exception. Already he knew what must be done.

She was worried. He'd left with the courier two days ago, with no word before or since. That wasn't like Father Art. She could manage, that was not the issue. It was the uncertainty that bothered her. She said a short prayer for his safe return.

Three weeks had passed since Maria recovered from the fever. Nicole had awakened in the room with the girl and rushed to her bedside, elated and grateful to find her breathing normally, her skin again warm and vibrant to the touch. She'd opened her eyes when Nicole kissed her forehead, smiling up at the face of the woman she loved as dearly as her own mother. "Good morning, Sister," she'd said, as if nothing had happened.

"Good morning, my little angel." Nicole's soothing hand brushed Maria's forehead.

"Am I late for school?" Maria's eyes blazed anxiously.

Nicole smiled. How much this child reminded her of herself. "You must rest now. You are not quite well yet. School will come later."

Maria looked ready to question the puzzling words when Teresa came into the room, and, seeing her daughter awake, rushed to her. Overwhelming Maria with affection, prayerfully and tearfully holding her much the same way as Nicole had the evening before, Teresa unwittingly robbed her daughter of nearly all the strength she had left. Nicole cautioned the overindulgent mother, who understood less was better. She released her hold, laying Maria's head onto the tiny pillow. "Rest … you must rest now," the mother said quietly.

"That's what Sister Nicole told me," Maria said.

"And Sister Nicole is right. I will be here with you." A last hug for her darling, and the mother rose to leave.

Nicole left the room with Teresa, who grabbed her in a particularly tight embrace as they stepped into the kitchen. Teresa gushed with thanks and praise, and crossed herself a half dozen times or more, speaking so rapidly everything became lost in the translation. Nicole almost had to struggle to break away from Teresa.

Gratitude for what? Nicole wondered as she said good-bye to Teresa.

For days Nicole sensed that everyone knew something she didn't. Father Art hadn't helped with her unease. "Sister," he began, "what do you recall of the past few days? Anything?"

The anxious expression on his face told her he knew something. "I remember the fever and … my Maria … I'm sorry, Father, that's all I can remember. No, wait, I remember bright light, walking into bright light. Not walking, almost like floating. Please tell me, what is it everyone else knows that I do not? Why is everyone in the village looking at me so strangely, smiling and bowing so, so *weirdly?*"

"Maybe it will come to you, in time," he replied. Nicole struggled with the vacuum her memory had become.

She resumed classes as soon as the burials were over. She had known the victims, all of them. They were some of the most faithful in Refugio. So many lives, she lamented, so many called home. This was not a part of her calling in which she could take comfort. If she never attended another funeral Mass it would be too soon.

It was on these thoughts she reflected this Saturday morning, while waiting and wondering on Father Art. Wondering even more what had happened to Evan Montgomery, whose presence she felt strongly while she apparently was in the grip of the fever. But it was more than just a feeling …

Yet another unexplained mystery.

Thinking of Evan, and feeling stronger now, she felt able to resume her daily walks to her Sanctuary. It had been too long. It was like an old friend that she longed for. Hurriedly, she headed down the familiar path. Maybe when she got there all this confusion would sort itself out. There was too much left unsaid, too much still unknown.

———————

Nicole did not have to wait much longer for her explanation. It was brought home in a most disturbing way upon Father Art's return. Her feeling of relief on seeing him was short-lived.

"Sister," he began, after their perfunctory embrace, "I'm afraid we have some unpleasant business at hand. What might have been better left to run a natural course is of necessity on, shall we say, the front burner. Come, let's go inside, where I can sit and rest while we talk. This has been a trying two days for me," he added.

Obediently she followed him into the church, where he motioned her to sit in the front row pew. There was little light outside, and darkness would be settling in soon. Father Art still would not let himself use the electrical outlet to light the chapel; he likely never would. Before sitting next to Nicole he walked to the altar, knelt, and went out into the vestibule. He returned with a booklet of matches, and lit the two altar candles. The flame flickered in the semi-darkness, casting dancing, distorted shadows around the room. Nicole felt a chill. She waited for Father Art to speak.

"Am I safe is presuming you still have no recollection of what happened after the fever struck our blessed little village? You haven't regained a memory of the time you were ill by any chance, have you? It's been over three weeks."

"I don't suppose I have, Father. If it weren't for your telling me, and my calendar I suppose, I would not know those days of my life are unaccounted for. Why is it that you ask? Did I do something wrong, Father? Something dreadful, something the Church is unhappy about? Please tell me, I need to know."

Her unease continued as he studied her before speaking. She could sense his struggle, as he might if a soul hung delicately in the balance. "Sister," he said, "something quite—" He groped for a word. "Something quite unusual happened while you were ill, something in which you played an instrumental part. You apparently do not know, and may never remember, so it has now fallen upon me to tell you what that was. I hope you're ready for this."

He told her what had happened.

She was speechless. It was unfathomable anything like that could have happened, much less she would have no recollection. She told Father Art as much.

"I have no doubt you are being truthful with me, Sister. I would never question that."

"Then tell me, Father, what is the problem with what has happened? There must be something more."

"There is much more, I'm afraid." The ominous tenor of his reply was not lost on her.

He reached into his pocket. He handed her the folded scrap of paper, and said only, "Here, read this."

She unfolded what was a clipping from a newspaper. There was no date, and the name of the paper did not appear anywhere, but she quickly recognized the byline. Fingers trembled slightly as they pinched the corners of the clipping, taking special care not to tear or smudge the paper. She read quickly.

MIRACLE IN THE MOUNTAINS

Special Correspondent Evan Thomas Montgomery

(Guatemala City—REUTERS) In ravaged, war-torn Guatemala there still exists hope. This reporter has written of the courage of a people downtrodden for centuries, their homeland confiscated, their ancestors beaten into submission by a government of outsiders. Yet these people manage. They do not give in; they have the will to survive. They will survive.

Nowhere is the microcosm of this society more aptly personified, nowhere is its spirit of hope more prevalent than in the tiny village of Refugio, in the northern department of Petén. As much has been featured in two prior accounts by this reporter. Today, in the aftermath of that village's very recent escape from certain death at the hands of a dreaded killer fever, there reigns hope more eternal, more fierce, than in all the history of the country of Guatemala for this people, for they have witnessed a miracle, a miracle of epic proportion. Most assuredly, this is no secondhand account; this reporter can bear witness to it. He was there; he saw it all.

Maria, age five, took ill early the second day. She was but one of the more than eighty of the villagers who would eventually be held in the fever's vicious grasp. Sister Nicole, featured in this reporter's last account, had collapsed after nearly twenty-four hours without rest in treating the afflicted. She was unconscious and feverish when Maria became ill.

Before Sister Nicole would regain consciousness, a military doctor—a hero in his own right—would watch as little Maria lost her valiant struggle, as had seventeen other villagers. As the grieving parents stood overlooking their daughter's lifeless figure, there appeared Sister Nicole, who lifted the child into her arms, drawing Maria tightly to her bosom, swaying and praying before the astonished parents, clutching the dear child so tightly as to nearly crush her fragile bones. Those who thought these the actions of the grief-stricken nun soon realized it was much more, for after no more than a few minutes of such powerful embrace, Maria—declared clinically dead only minutes before—came to. She lives today, healthy and active as ever. Touched by the hand of God through Sister Nicole, Maria miraculously—yes, miraculously—was restored to life.

Sister Nicole has no recollection of the experience. She quickly slipped back into unconsciousness after Maria's lifeless form again drew breath, and did not rise herself for another day. She has resumed her life as teacher, nurse and nun to the villagers, who are proclaiming her a saint and an angel, and Maria's healing a miracle. This reporter finds no fault in any of these premises.

✝

Nicole lowered the clipping. "Father, I don't know what to say. I almost don't want to believe this. I remember none of it, and feel embarrassed at the spectacle of it all." She did not tell him of her wondering of Evan's presence. That question had now been answered. It was the only blank filled in so far.

"Sister, have you any idea of the magnitude of the spectacle—to use your word— this has brought on?"

"I can only imagine. But you're going to tell me, aren't you?"

"Let me put it this way. Monty has written three pieces on Refugio so far. I'm sorry I don't have them to show you. I'm certain you know nothing about the other two?" he asked.

"Nothing. I've never read a word he's written, about anything. Until this," she added.

"Well, he apparently has cultivated a following out there for you in readerland, and what had been a modest volume of what?—fan mail, is that what it would be called?—has become unmanageable by his office. He's told me there are bags of letters waiting for him. He's almost afraid to return to his office."

"You've seen Evan? When? What—tell me, Father. Tell me everything, please."

His reply was as urgent as her question. "Sister, I've just returned from Guatemala City, where the archbishop requested my—and Monty's, too, I might add—presence, to discuss the events of three weeks ago. The article was the first report he'd received of what had happened, and he wasn't too pleased at having been kept in the dark. Frankly, I'd thought of couriering him a note, but I didn't know quite how to put things.

"Archbishop Santiago needed assurance Monty was acting alone … without collaboration, or an accomplice. He wanted to see Monty's face when confronted with the veiled accusation. My choice of words … so you'll know."

"Accomplice? Collaboration? Veiled accusation? What does all this mean?"

His expression revealed everything.

"Oh God, Father, no, you can't be serious. He could not have thought that. Please tell me I am imagining this entire episode." Valiantly she tried to stop the tears.

"I would give anything if I could, dear child. I am as shocked as you, maybe even more, and certainly disappointed at this turn. But the archbishop made me promise to confront you. The Church cannot afford to be compromised if there is any margin something such as this was—what?—staged.

"It was not my choice, you must know that."

"Confront me about what? That Evan and I aren't running some carnival side-show up here in this veritable paradise, some little con game we've cooked up to fleece these wealthy natives? Better yet, the Catholic Church? Forgive me, but is his high-ness worried about his job down there in the capital?" She was quite furious. Along with her earlier tears, every trace of humility had departed. She paused to collect her thoughts, catch her breath. "You're smiling, Father. I don't understand."

"I suppose I'm seeing the assertive woman of strong will and quick temper I heard of from your father." He smiled at her. "Calm yourself, Sister, please. That's not it at all."

"Easy for you to say. 'Calm yourself.' The archbishop's not gunning for you."

"He's not gunning for you. I can try to explain, but my problem is the explanation doesn't make sense to me, which makes it hard to feel any conviction. Do I make sense?"

"Try me," she said, far too flippantly, regretting it quickly, apologizing profusely.

"It's okay, my dear Sister, no apology necessary. Let me try to answer you this way. The archbishop does not fear you seek personal gratification from the healing of our Maria. He is concerned first at the authenticity of what happened, secondly at the timing. The Church would have preferred to be the purveyor of the news of a mira-cle"—he made the little quote marks with his fingers around the words *a miracle*—"rather than what the archbishop considers a hack journalist. This potentially puts the Church in an embarrassing position."

"I don't understand. Obviously I am missing something. I'm not the smartest person who ever took vows, but I'd fancy I'm not the dumbest, either." She sounded like her father. She thought of him for an instant. She wanted to see him. He would know what to do.

"This is the hard part, and I shall do my best to explain. The missing parts you'll have to fill in with that superior intellect of yours."

Her eyes blazed.

"I meant the superior intellect part as a compliment."

She calmed.

He continued. "The Church, indeed the entire world, is watching, waiting as an-other nun nears her end, in another faraway, ravaged land. She hasn't much time left. She is a healer, like you, a worker of miracles in her own right."

"You're speaking of Mother Theresa?"

"Yes, I am."

"I don't understand. How does anything about her relate to me, and what hap-pened with Maria? Are we somehow competitors?"

"In the archbishop's eyes, eyes that by imprimatur are the Church's as well, yes, you are. The archbishop sees Mother Theresa as the Church's rallying point, its redemption at a time when there is so much uncertainty, so little cohesion within the ranks. She is a living saint. She stands above all else, save the Holy Father of the Church, our Pope. Archbishop Santiago tells me the Church prefers that she maintain that special mys-tique, that she not have a rival for the attention of the masses. What's happened with you has changed everything. He believes the Church is not prepared to handle this situ-ation. Because of Monty's story, the Church can't very well say what happened did not happen. Nor can it risk a gain in momentum. The sanctity of Mother Theresa's place must remain intact. Does any of this make sense to you?" He sat back, sighing heavily.

"It would be far too easy for me to say I simply don't care a whit about receiving any attention, wouldn't it? That won't be enough, will it?"

"I don't think so. There's more. You see, the Church has received numerous formal requests for interviews, press conferences, and the like. With you. Yes, Sister, with you. Everyone wants you, it seems. The Church is plagued with requests. Not only from the United States, but all over the world. This has become something bigger than either of us might imagine, I'm afraid.

"Let me put it this way. Mother Theresa"— This time, at the mention of her name, they both crossed."—never brought a single dead person back to life. I'm sorry to put it so bluntly, but this calls for bluntness. She has healed many sick, and is most certainly a living saint, but she never brought back the dead. Frankly, Sister, you're only the second one to do that, and we both know the first one." The implication was unmistakable.

Nicole saw an opportunity. "Skipping for the moment I have absolutely no conscious recollection of anything I've heard of the … the incident with Maria, we both know miracle is an abstraction. Every day doctors massage hearts and perform organ transplants, and ordinary citizens apply CPR. Every day people stop breathing and are resuscitated. Patients on the operating table are brought back to life after being 'clinically dead'. The Church can't ignore this. Those experiences aren't called miracles."

"So it's a debate you want, is it? Well, here is the Church's position, as I hear it from the archbishop. Those are all medically explainable situations, not involving a clinically diagnosed death. What you've done stands alone. It is inescapably something miraculous. The villagers know it, Monty knows it, the doctor who was there knows it, I even know it—but my opinion is off the record. Sadly, for all the good something like this could accomplish, the intrigue and backdrop within our Church puts things in a state of unease."

"Do you believe I brought Maria back to life from the dead? Did I really do that?" She was calm now, pensive, calculating.

"I suppose what you are really asking me is if I think Maria was really dead when you entered the room. I don't know. I thought she was, but I have no basis for my opinion other than I was only accepting what I'd been told. I did not question what the physician told us.

"But I do have a question for you, Sister. When you are able, please explain to me how it was you rose from your bed, not once but twice, in your state of delirium. You didn't know that, did you? I see from your expression you didn't. You rose one other time, and on your own managed to walk in a state of total unconsciousness halfway across your room, to your doorway, where you called out Maria's name twice before you passed out. Did you know that? I didn't think so. And did you also know at the very moment you were calling out her name she was slipping into unconsciousness herself? Explain that to me, and while you're at it, also explain to me how you again rose from your own bed two days later, still quite delirious, and made your way to Maria as she was leaving, or had left us. How would you have known what was happening, at the instant it was happening? Tell me, Sister, while you are tossing this other stuff around in your mind, as you are searching for answers. I spoke all of this to the archbishop two days ago. I became your most staunch advocate, and did little more than ask questions and recite facts. I didn't need to voice my opinions; the facts spoke for themselves. In my opinion the archbishop should desperately want to believe in your miracle. Only he knows why he chooses not to. So the water running downhill makes its way to you. Such a heavy burden to bear. I fear we will lose you because of this test of your faith."

She ignored his last comment. "What do I do, Father? I of course am not interested in press conferences, interviews, publicity of any kind. Just leave me to my simple life here. I suppose I could deny what happened, but too many others were there, I take it. I could say that I knew Maria was only breathing shallow, and I did no more than administer CPR. Whatever it takes, just tell me and I will do it. I have no desire to battle my sister in India for media or any other attention, especially within our own Church."

"I have an idea the purity in your soul might have a better answer to all of this than anything I or the rest of the Church might devise. It would likely be the simplest and the most honest way of handling things. So, tell me what you would do. Let me add something," he continued, "before you say anything." He leaned in closer, where she could feel the soft air from his very breath. "I believe you have been chosen by God, Sister, I really do. Surely He has reached out and placed His hands on you. He has plans for you. This is but a test, a simple test. He tests all of us, some considerably more than others. I have failed so many I cannot recall them all. But you, Sister, you have failed not one. I have been around you enough these past eleven months to know that. I mean it when I say your soul is pure. Your heart, too. This simple village needs you. This world needs you. When I think on it, I see there have been two miracles at Refugio. Maria's recovery is surely the one that will receive the most attention. But the one perhaps more deserving is your being here. You are the more important miracle. While you will most certainly not think so, there are those of us who see you in no other light. Find within yourself the peace you must make to shoulder this burden, and this controversy over our precious Maria will fade. Accept from me that you must not cower before this pressure, but stand firmly in the face of it all. Give the meaning to your life it deserves."

She sat silently, motionless, then spoke with effort. "Thank you, Father. I am most humbled. I confess I do not see myself in the same light you do. As to the matter at hand, I would like to pray on it. May we talk more in the morning? I am rather tired at the moment."

"That's very wise of you. I'm a bit tired myself. We can talk about it when you're ready."

"I think by morning will be fine. And Father," she added, "I'm sorry for saying what I did about the archbishop. I had no right. I'm truly sorry."

"I'll hear your confession in the morning. Personally, who am I to sit in judgment of you where your opinions are concerned? However, when it comes to Church business, I can help, that's my job. Confession promptly at six-fifteen. I expect you to be there."

Message received, loud and clear. "Certainly, Father. I won't be late. Good night."

Long after the priest had extinguished the twin flames perched atop the altar, as light darkened outside and the dew squeezed from the thick air was spread over the earth, Nicole's work was done. And she was ready. Ready to tell Father Art what was best in handling this miracle situation, ready for her confession, and ready to resume life as it had been before all this confusion.

Before she was thought of by others as a miracle performer.

Before she had to think of herself as one.

So much to put upon her, he reflected. Would she be up to the task? Would she look to Him for comfort? Would He make her way more clearly known? Too many questions, too few answers.

He paused, drew a fresh breath, and looked around the chapel. The flickering candlelight extinguished, only night shadows graced the walls, the altar. He recalled the trials of his Lord, and wondered if Christ could have had something like this in mind when He made the ultimate sacrifice. He wondered if that sacrifice would be enough.

§

In another part of the village, under cover of the same darkness, the small group of men spoke in hushed tones, for fear of detection. The business of the miracle was not their agenda. These men schemed. They spoke against tyranny, as revolutionaries do. They were not so much idealists as hungry and poor. They had the same ultimate goal as the idealist, however: freedom.

The word was spoken as a rallying cry. The leader, one not of the village, had trained in Cuba and was a combat veteran, a true revolutionary. He commanded attention, respect. Skilled in the art of persuasion, he forged an alliance with those in the darkened and crowded room who would fight back against the government that sent soldiers, not teachers, that denied medical care until it was too late for friends and neighbors, that made no provision for the elderly and the infirm.

Two in the group were village leaders. Each was similar, each was different. Both husbands and fathers, neither formally educated. But only one was even-tempered. His counterpart was filled with rage and hatred. He was chosen by the visitor from the south as the leader of the group. The others voiced no objection. They pledged their absolute secrecy, and to meet again.

Soon.

§

Most of Refugio was engulfed in a foreboding stillness that night. The kind of calm signaling the advent of something dreaded, like the red sky and flat sea before a typhoon, or the eye of a storm just before the havoc worsens. All was peaceful, quiet, save for one place, near the eastern edge of town, where, on most nights the low guttural screams and howls echoed eerily beyond earshot of the rest.

To the man who savagely clung to the woman beside him, as the two small children huddled in a similar fashion watched, frightened and wanting, this night signaled a coming change. He whispered to his wife about demons to be cast out, while she nodded fearfully, and kept a mother's watchful eye on their quivering young. Bitterness roiled within the husband, as it did each time the demons mocked him. Hatred was born of this bitterness, a hatred he knew would boil over into unreachable limits of insanity unless he took action. *Until* he took action. He would show them he was in control. When the time came—and time was nigh—the nightmares would also stop, the demons would be silenced, and nights like this would become as forgotten bad memories. He longed for the day the demons that tormented and scorned him would be silenced.

He told his wife it would be soon. Very soon.

32

Refugio had electricity, but no telephones. *A blessing, perhaps,* Nicole thought, as she stared at the mail sacks. The usual one or two letter delivery from the courier sat before her in two bagsful. There was only one answer, one overwhelming explanation. All she could think of was, *What if everyone who wrote had tried to call?* It was too great a riddle to ponder as she opened the first bag and sifted through the hundreds upon hundreds of letters, all addressed to her. She thought of closing the bag, of leaving the contents unread, of turning her back on those who chose to pay homage, for whatever reason, but dismissed the thought as quickly as it had surfaced. For, if she left the bags unopened, how would she ever know which letters might be from those she knew, like her parents, or Katherine, or quite impossibly even her brothers? It followed, only logically, that she must open the bags, and the letters inside them. All of them.

The letters came from everywhere imaginable. There were postmarks from Italy, Norway, Great Britain, Australia, of course the United States, many, many of the individual states—Kentucky, Rhode Island, Florida, Minnesota, and more—and from the Orient, from Hong Kong, Japan, Singapore, even South Korea. An Israeli postmark drew a larger smile than most. She opened it first. The smile turned to amazement, not because the letter was written in Hebrew, but that it contained currency. Someone had written her a note, in a language she would never be able to read, and had included what she could only presume was a charitable donation. She set it aside, and opened one from Dallas, Texas, and another from Shreveport, Louisiana, close to home. Two more notes, two more contributions. She didn't know how much the bill in the envelope from Jerusalem was in dollars, but the currency from the Jewish family in Shreveport and the check from the Methodist family in Dallas were easy enough to sum up: seventy dollars, a princely sum in Guatemala. There were notes from every donor ... very touching messages from total strangers. She set the notes aside, to answer later, to thank the donors for their generosity. She returned to opening the multitude of envelopes. Where to next? She picked out the blue one with a smudged postmark that looked like Fairbanks. As the blue flap gave way she received yet another prize, this one from distant, frozen Alaska.

Father Art was in the rectory when he heard her shouts. Before he could worry that she was in danger she stood breathlessly in the doorway, shaking her fist in his direction, a fist clearly full of currency, a great deal of currency. He could feel her excitement.

"Oh Father, you won't believe this. Look at this money ... cash, checks, big checks—" She paused to show him a check made out in her name, the amount unmistakably one hundred dollars. "Have you ever seen money from The Netherlands? or Hungary? At least I think this is from Hungary. Look." She showed him what was compressed into one hand, spilling it onto his desk. "This may be over a thousand dollars."

Bewildered, he could only grasp for words. "Where did you get this?"

"The mail sacks the courier left this morning; two of them, both filled with letters. This is only one handful. There is so very much more."

"I've seen it all now," he said.

"Not yet you haven't. Come with me. Set what you were doing aside, it can wait 'til later. You must see this. *This* is a miracle, Father," she said over her shoulder as she danced down the hallway.

What he saw in her room, littered everywhere, were thousands of envelopes. She hadn't exaggerated. There was a neat stack of letters on her small nightstand, and another pile of currency on her bed, greater than the one in her hand. He bent closer, and saw it was foreign. He sat on the edge of the bed, his thoughts muddled. There was but one explanation for this largesse. It had not occurred to him, or to Archbishop Santiago, this could happen. He was still in his quandary when she squealed with delight at another large bill from the next envelope. He could see it was only going to get worse. An inspiration came to him.

"Sister, we should let the archdiocese handle this. There are people in the capital city who will be able to sort through it all, record donation with donor, and see to it the proper thanks are written. That would be best, don't you think?"

"Someone else answer my mail? How could I allow that? It wouldn't be right."

"And who would run the school, and assist me with daily Mass for the year or two it would take you to answer these thousands of letters?"

He'd prevailed. He knew it the moment she did not have a quick response.

"I suppose you're right. But it saddens me to think so many people have gone to this much effort, and I won't be able to thank them personally."

"The Church will make sure these generous people know why it was not possible for you to answer their individual kindnesses. Put your trust in the Church."

Together they carefully returned the many donations to their proper envelopes, and re-bundled the bags. It took an hour. They talked all the while, their conversation uplifting, the stress of the prior week seemingly forgotten. He'd worried for her. He'd prayed for her. His prayers were that what had happened would not create a rift—between her and the Church, between her and him—that she would not suffer a loss of faith. In their line of work, faith was at the heart of the ability to function. Without faith, it was just going through the motions, and leaving the service of the Lord was only a matter of time. With Nicole, that must not happen.

She'd come to him the morning after he'd returned from his visit to the archdiocese, when he'd told of his conversation with the archbishop. Without her saying so, he knew she'd had a sleepless night. No mortal confronted with the news he had shared with her could have been unaffected afterward. The strongest men of the Church he knew would have struggled with pressure of such enormous proportion. She was still so young, barely a year removed from taking her final vows. How could she handle this, even comprehend it?

He needn't have worried.

A day later he'd ridden into the capital city with the courier and, unannounced, interrupted the archbishop's meeting with some of the local gentry. Archbishop Santiago wisely cut short his meeting, and called in Refugio's priest.

"And this is so important that you would disturb my fundraising? Any one of those patrons could have made a contribution sufficient to run your mission an entire year. Did you think about that before you barged in here? No, of course not. This must be an American thing, yes?"

"Actually, Excellence, I am here to follow up on the Sister Nicole matter. I felt this could not wait. I thought I understood from you we must act quickly. Did I misunderstand?"

The archbishop ignored his question. "Were you able to accomplish anything? Will Sister Nicole disclaim any participation in a miracle?"

"I presented no such option to her, Excellence." He watched as the archbishop hung his head and shook it.

"Excellence, I felt there was a much deeper issue than a simple denial would have addressed. Such a ridiculous disclaimer would have disgraced us all. The world is not inhabited entirely with the ignorant."

"I see. Only those of our cloth in Rome, perhaps? For it is they you have stood against in your foo—in your *devotion* to this Nicole child, not I. Surely you realize that."

"I never even considered it. It doesn't matter. Theirs is a different agenda than mine. We have the same mission, mind you—saving souls, spreading God's word, making good Catholics of the world—but you know that isn't at issue here, Excellence."

"What I know does not matter. I am not at liberty to question what I am told. I did not think you were either."

"Then maybe I have learned something from—what did you call her?—this Nicole child."

"Father, we are not fencing here. This is not gamesmanship. We are talking the very serious business of the Church, the *Holy* Roman Catholic Church. Do you quite understand?"

Father Art stood firmly. "We finally agree on something, Excellence. That is precisely what I am talking about."

It became a standstill. They exchanged hard glares, borne not of rancor but passionate differences of opinion. The archbishop spoke first. "Tell me what you propose. Tell me what I am somehow going to communicate to Rome after you leave, after you return to your mission, which may be the last time we ever see each other, as I may be the only archbishop on his way back to a humble beginning as a simple parish priest. Perhaps even in the village next to yours."

When the explanation was done, even Archbishop Santiago was convinced it was the right thing for the Church. Nicole's stock had risen even with this man, who had little use for women in the service of the Church in the first place.

—————————

The fever and the funerals had passed from recent memory for most of Refugio. For Nicole, however, each day she walked Maria to school, each day she spent teaching and tending in Refugio, she was reminded of how perilous life could be in this place. Death was a rogue jungle cat, snakebite or maverick fever away. She became even more protective of Maria.

The school continued to flourish. Nicole could see potential in several of her older students, and already was grooming Father Art and the parents of her more gifted students for the next step—boarding in Guatemala City, and advanced studies. Jorge, who also excelled on the soccer pitch, and Estella, the oldest girl in the school, were the brightest. They, and several others, deserved the opportunity to further their education. Nicole pledged to these trusting students that education meant a better life for them, and, in the end, a better Guatemala.

Her mind on these other matters as she walked toward her Sanctuary one exceptionally lovely afternoon, she paid no conscious heed to the ball slowly rolling in front of her feet. Instinctively she hitched her habit up to knee length as she placed one heel in front of and locked the toe of her trailing shoe at the base of the ball and, ever so effortlessly, rolled it over her heel and over her shoulder and onto her awaiting knee—a perfectly executed rainbow—where it bounced just as effortlessly until she held it. She turned and realized there was no one else around.

"Jorge," she called out, for she'd missed him at school that morning. It would not be unlike him to play with her like this. "Jorge," she called again, leaning to check around the corners of the nearest buildings, "I know it's you. Come out and let me see you."

The emptiness and the silence confounded her. Cradling the soccer ball in her arm, she noticed that it was new, not the worn one she'd been playing with for nearly a year. She looked behind her, at the deserted street and the vacant corridors between the buildings, she heard a voice, a familiar voice, a reminder of her life's passing in a fleeting instant.

"That was an awesome rainbow. When did you finally learn to do one?"

She turned to the grin, the dimples, his arms outstretched in her direction.

Only primates are capable of shedding tears. None can do so as quickly as the female species of *homo sapiens*, and, it could be argued, none quicker than the older sister of one William Christian McHenry, who stood before her at this very moment. She sprinted to him, hurtling herself into his outstretched arms. Just simple tears at first, then an uncontrolled stream. He stood ground dutifully, until she let go her embrace long enough to look up at the face of the brother she had been missing so much of late.

"What—how—Chris—" She couldn't start or finish a sentence. She grabbed him again and held him as tightly as she could, draining the color quickly from his face.

"Hey, brat, easy on the squeeze … the ribs, the ribs." The mock painful wince and the grin were such a welcome sight. A feeling of immense relief flooded her. "And when did you learn to finish a rainbow like that?"

"I'll have you know I don't just kneel and pray twelve hours a day. They give us soccer breaks down here. In fact, to be a senior nun you have to be able to do three perfect rainbows in a row."

"Yeah, right. The one in a row I just saw is all you'll ever manage, so forget being a senior nun, whatever that is."

They both laughed, and hugged again. Their laughter carried up and down the silent, empty streets of the village. Nicole knew that more than one person would pause to wonder at the disturbance. She smiled. They would know soon enough.

"What are you doing? How did you get here?"

"We can talk about all that later," he replied. "You looked in a hurry to get somewhere when I tossed you the ball. Do you still need to go?"

She smiled coyly at Chris. "Don't ask any more questions, okay? Just come along with me. You'll see."

✝

33

I DON'T BELIEVE THIS place." Chris sat on the bank of the small pond, squinting as he raised his head to savor the mist. The cool wetness soothed him from the day's cruel warmth.

Nicole keenly eyed her brother with that look of part pride, part vanity. She gave him his communal moment with Nature before speaking. "You don't know how much I've missed you ... how much I've been thinking about you lately. It's so ironic you'd show up now, when my thoughts have been the strongest."

"Call it killing time before starting back to school—up in Colorado this time, by the way—and besides, it's been kind of odd for me lately, having a miracle worker for a sister. How could I not come to see you? I tried to get Danny to come, but he couldn't get away. He's right in the middle of some flight-training thing. Desertion wasn't really an option, so he took a rain check. I'm supposed to give you a huge hug from him too." She endured the crushing squeeze, as Chris paid his older brother's debt.

Still devoted, as always. She glowed, even as she ignored the remark about the miracle. They'd get to that soon enough, she figured. "What about soccer? UCLA? The tryout with the Under-20 National Team? Mom and Dad told me bits and pieces. I want it all. C'mon, give."

"I know Mom and Dad told you about me flunking out at UCLA. Great coach, the soccer was good, but that was it. I just didn't fit in. Did the U-20 tryout thing. I came out goalkeeper number three, but they only needed two. Anyway, I was lost, needing to get myself back on track. College seemed the right place to start. So for me it's 'Hello Fort Lewis College and Durango' and the Fourteeners of Colorado ... and getting my life back in order."

"Fourteeners?"

"It's what they call the collection of mountains over fourteen thousand feet. There's a bunch of them. Very appealing to a flatlander like me."

She reached for his hand, as she had another's in this same place not so long ago, and held it tightly. He could try, but masking his disappointment with his sister was not going to happen this day. "If you did your best, then it's just one of those things not meant to be. Accept it, and move on. It isn't the end of the world."

He looked deeply into her eyes. "It's all I know, Nic. It's who I am. But hey, I didn't come down here to cry on your shoulder, honest I didn't. I came to see my sister. My world-famous sister. I couldn't believe it when the news was filled for days about this nun, this Sister Nicole down in Guatemala, who'd brought this little village girl back to life. What's that all about? Did you really do that?"

There was more, before she could answer. "And now, after you've been all over the news, the story seems to have changed. Now the Church is saying that maybe it wasn't a miracle, that the doctor *maybe* misdiagnosed a faint heartbeat, some kind of medical thing where the patient's heart is still beating, but so faintly it can't be picked up with a stethoscope. Sounds pretty hokey to me. What's our Catholic Church got against a good ol' miracle?"

"This is just me and you, Chris, right?" she asked. "What I say doesn't go outside this valley. I want your word."

The wrinkled smile, cocked eye and frown reminded her of their father. "I'm your brother, for God's sake, how could you say something like that?"

"I know, I know. I'm sorry. It's just become so complicated, and I'm still a little bit nervous about everything. No, I'm a lot nervous. There are things you don't know, things that could become troublesome if what I say ever gets out. I'm telling you this so you'll know how important it is nothing I tell you is shared with anyone else, not even Mom and Dad, or Danny. I'm just asking you to respect that, not accusing you of anything."

He smiled at her. Shaking his hand free of hers, he raised a curled little finger in her direction. "How 'bout I pinky swear, then. For old times' sake."

"Pinky swear." She smiled in return, locking her little finger in his, their bond sealed.

Nicole told him the whole story, all she knew of it anyway. There was much still unaccounted for; even the missing parts Father Art had filled in were not enough. She realized when she'd finished it was the first time she'd discussed anything that had happened with anyone other than Father Art. She could tell Chris saw her confusion.

"You don't remember anything? I mean, like nothing at all?"

"A total blank. I have only the vaguest recall of floating, and haze, or fog, and bright light and distant voices, but nothing else."

"Doesn't that tell you something? I mean, if what other people tell you really happened, and you don't remember it, doesn't it start to sound like something a little more than ordinary to you?" He paused. "It sure does to me. Pretty much like a miracle, in fact. I don't know about miracles, and it's just bizarre I'm even having this conversation with anyone, even more my own sister. But Nic, if there are people who saw it, and there's, like, medical proof the girl was dead, how else can you explain what's happened? Have you thought about that?"

"Every day of my life." She dropped her gaze to the ground. "Being a nun, a teacher, a nurse, those things I can deal with on a daily basis. But this other, how am I supposed to handle it?"

"Why do I get the feeling that the Church is more than a little disbelieving about this thing? One minute it's all over the news, and the next thing—nothing. For about a week, not another word. And never anything from the Church. Then, out of the same nowhere it all vanished into, here comes another news flash, this time from the Church." He put his hands together, then spread them outwardly, forming a banner. "*Flash, it wasn't a real miracle. The medical evidence is under review, and an official proclamation will be made as soon as the review is complete.*" Before she could say anything, he followed with the most telling remark. "I suppose I should tell you, I've talked to Dad about this, and he's not too happy about what's going on. You should also know he and Mom were headed this way when Dad got a call from Father Robichaux asking him not to, telling him you were all right and didn't need the distraction right now. Dad canceled the flight, but he wasn't happy about it. Think about it—you wouldn't be either if it was your child splashed all over the world news and you couldn't even talk to her. Man."

Chris had always said *Man* to emphasize a point. He said *Hey* a lot, too. He'd changed so little … "But he didn't ask me to come here, and doesn't even know I'm here," he continued, "and would not be happy about it if he did find out."

"Your secret's safe with me." Hearing that her father knew, and was concerned, brought her mixed feelings of relief and anguish. "Nothing gets by our Dad," she threw in for good measure.

"So what's the deal with the Church? Now can you tell me?"

She sidestepped the part about the icon in the faraway hemisphere. "The Church just has to be sure, that's all. And I'm not much help, okay? If I could remember anything at all, the Church might acknowledge what happened. But until I can come up with more than *I'm sorry, I was unconscious the whole time*, what option does it have?"

"So the follow up bit about the Church checking on the medical evidence, that's routine? You gonna tell me that?"

She grimaced. After a moment's pause, she answered. "That was my idea. I asked the Church to make that statement. Chris, listen, I don't want to become some spectacle, and that's what would happen. It wouldn't do for me, and it wouldn't do for our Church if political pressure from some source we can't even imagine right now caused the doctor, for instance, to change his story, or the garrison commandant his. Even the villagers, who saw very little, maybe they all of a sudden remember something. Before you know it, what was a really good thing, becomes tawdry, and tarnished. Forever.

"I don't want any of that, Chris, it isn't worth it to me. Hey, I'm still your simple big sis, who doesn't have a clue about anything, remember? This is way over my head. I just want to be a good nun. I love being a nun. It's my life, baby brother. It's who I am, what I do."

Echo-like her words draped over her brother. He shrugged his shoulders, the old *What can you say?* gesture. She smiled, plucking petals from an unlucky bloom.

Chris pulled his sister over, removed her veil and smoothed her head as they held each other. There were a few tears in both their eyes, the moment overpowering for brother and sister alike. If not for her habit, a stranger onto the scene would have thought them more as lovers, as she sat back against his chest, nestled into the comfort of his arms.

Chris mulled over his sister's words. He was young, but not stupid. He could figure things out. One day when the fickle mind of the collective public was stilled, and voided of any current recollection of "the miracle in the mountains," there would be some obscure, yet very official pronouncement from the Church the evidence had been considered, and it was inconclusive. In the end there would be no miracle.

This saddened him. Not because his sister yearned for such recognition, but because she deserved it, and it would be withheld. The similarities of both their predicaments was not lost on him; but he was shamed in his own mind for wanting the recognition of his ability, and being denied more than once in favor of inferior talent, when his sister was willing to walk away from her just reward simply because it was not something she wanted. Both deserving, neither attaining, yet hers was the purer heart. It was a lesson he would ponder for some time.

They talked on, Chris hearing of Maria's recovery, of the thousands and thousands of letters and contributions that had poured in from around the world. He bristled with alarm as she downplayed a niggling fear of being watched by something sinister, not always but often enough. She refused to stop talking long enough for him to press her on the subject. He relaxed and let her continue. It occurred to him their childhood's innocence was gone. Until this moment, he could always have fantasized from wherever he was that nothing had changed, or would ever change, that he was still the baby brother to his big sister, and life had always been one way and could always and forever be this way. He felt his heart go heavy. His was a child's fantasy whose time had come and gone. She was sister to many more than him and Danny now. How he envied those who could, on any given day, afford the luxury of taking her for granted, as he'd done all their lives together. Part of him wanted to cry out to her, to beg her to come home, where she could teach in any of the local parochial schools, where electricity wasn't a magical force, where indoor plumbing and running water weren't unheard of. Selfishly he harbored this fleeting wish, impatiently waiting for her to finish telling him about some derelict old British reporter and some schoolchildren she'd taught to read so he could say the words to bring her to her senses, back to her home and family.

It was her serenity that eventually disarmed him. His fervor was no match for the commitment his sister communicated in the simple softness of her voice. He felt a sense of tranquility as resistance gave way. Immobilized by the kinetics of something of higher origin, Chris gave up the fight within, and settled for the peacefulness that comes with acceptance.

He felt her fingers touch the object hanging from the chain around his neck. It had draped onto her shoulder. "You still wear this?" she asked. A simple medallion, a trophy from a youth soccer tournament awarded so long ago.

"Not since high school. Honestly, I'm not sure why I wore it down here. It just seemed like the thing to do. Something special for you, maybe."

"I'm honored." She smoothed it onto his shirt, patted it softly.

Silence descended momentarily. Then she spoke, tentatively. "How long can you stay?"

"I might have to play that one by ear. My return flight's open, but I need to get back in time for registration. Hey, I give you a few days … you'll be asking me to leave."

"I doubt that."

"We'll see, okay?" He gave her a reassuring hug.

"Yeah. Meanwhile, you write Mom and Dad, tell them you're here so they won't worry."

"Danny's probably told them by now. But I will, I promise. Pinky swear."

Without looking she raised her little finger overhead, where his hooked into it just as nonchalantly. Nicole lay her cheek on Chris's chest. "I'm so glad you're here."

"Me, too." He wrapped his arms around her, and squeezed lightly. He felt her relax. "I love you, Nic."

"I love you, too, Chris."

In a moment she was asleep. He had an idea, convinced it would result in fortune for this place, these people. It felt good. All his life he'd had trouble fitting into the adult world. Now, he was thinking like one, and come tomorrow, would begin acting like one. He drifted off, tired, but confident.

Chris felt his sister jerk upright. "Chris! We've let it get dark. This is not good. We need to get back, and in a hurry."

He didn't ask questions. He followed her down the path leading to the steep climb, barely able to see. He became a bit unnerved. To Chris they were Jem and Scout, threading their way home in the dark in some mythical Southern woods, frightened of the unknown, the bogeyman, comforting one another as they stumbled along. It was not until they were safe at the church that they laughed long and loud at their foolishness, for, they boasted, there were no bogeymen to fear.

233

✝

For the next three days Nicole had a roommate. She shared the small room with her brother, who slept in Sister Renee's empty bed. Chris was offered the same accommodations his parents had just vacated, but chose instead to spend the time with his sister. Father Art of course approved.

Chris immersed himself in the his sister's daily existence. Mornings he'd risen early, even attended Mass. He'd delighted in the soccer matches with the schoolchildren. On the second day, Pablo had shown up, and the two young men had put on an awesome display of talent. Brother and soldier bonded briefly, the cultural chasm notwithstanding.

Chris even helped with the cooking, and the cleanup afterward. Brother and sister shared another long afternoon at her Sanctuary, where he probed deeper and wider into the interaction of the archdiocese. She was surprised at the depth of his curiosity. An even bigger surprise awaited.

"What if I spent the day with Father Art tomorrow, instead of in first grade?"

She gave him a look. "I know how you are about your Catholic beliefs. Tell me I don't have to worry about what you might say to my boss." She thought back to when Chris had to be cajoled into attending catechism, and later first communion classes. Now he was asking to spend a day with Father Art. What would Father Robichaux think?

Now *she'd* seen it all.

"You haven't asked why I'm asking all these questions. I'll tell you anyway. I've seen something around here, and I've got an idea. Maybe it's a bad one, but I needed to get a grasp of how the system operates before I say something that might get hopes up, you know, the kind of thing our dad would do. Like he always said, 'Get your ducks all lined up,' whatever that means. Except I suppose we always knew what it meant."

"Can you tell me what it is you're thinking about? Does it involve me?"

Be patient, he told her. First he wanted to talk to Father Art, then he'd meet her at the Sanctuary. If all went well, he would share his idea with her.

He was already there when she arrived, waiting, dangling bare feet in the cool, clear pond, as pensive as she'd ever seen him. Always the carefree and fun-loving brother, in three days Chris presented a more mature, focused image. She liked the change, and told him so, before he unfolded his plan.

And what a grand plan it was.

"Wow. And he went for it?"

"Let's just say I made some serious progress. Besides, when you think about it, doesn't it just make plain, common sense? If you weren't so involved, you'd have seen it. Basically, it was a no-brainer."

"For three days you listened to me tell you how fulfilled I am at teaching young minds, and how frustrated I get at the same time that it will all be for naught because there's no future for these kids except the fields, or raising a few chickens or pigs, or working at little arts and crafts trades like their fathers and mothers and theirs before them, and you say it's just some natural thing to start a scholarship fund with the money the archdiocese has counted up—how much did you say Father Art told you it was, over twenty thousand dollars in American money?—like it's as plain as the noses on our faces? False modesty was never one of your redeeming qualities, William Christian McHenry."

"There's more," he said. "You need to hear the second part, too."

And she did, attentively at first, until she'd heard enough. "Chris," she began, holding back on the urge to unload, "how could you possibly even think of disturbing this place? When have you ever seen anything so wonderful? I almost feel betrayed. I can't believe what I've just heard."

"Hear me out, Nic. Have you ever walked this entire valley floor?"

"Not all of it, no. Why?"

"I didn't think so. But I did, yesterday. Do you know this valley stretches nearly three-quarters of a mile across, until it reaches an embankment on the other side? It's a short, steep climb to the top, and another half mile or so to a road, and I'll bet it's the same road that winds along the ridge all the way to your little village. Tree-lined the whole way, that's why no one would even notice this place."

"I've walked to that road many, many times. What does it have to do with anything?"

"Okay, did you also know that the valley extends for a mile or more from end to end? This waterfall," now gesturing with an outstretched hand, "this waterfall is just past the midpoint of the valley. The same valley winds on hundreds of yards further, then wraps around the back of the village on the northwest side. The rest of the ground rises up ever so gradually to meet that back ridge. There's nothing spectacular in the view, and the rock facies aren't conducive to tree growth. Basically the only way anyone would ever see this place is from the air, if they were low enough to the ground, or completely by accident. Did you know that Father Art didn't know this place was here his first year, and even then he didn't really think it was all that special?"

She smiled at her brother. "Guess he never had a rope swing on the river when he was a kid, huh? Doesn't have that bond to the water we've always had?"

"Whatever." There was a somber character in his voice, something she hadn't known. Time to stop kidding around …

He went on. "Listen to me, because there is something in this for everyone. You get to keep your valley, and the village makes a great gain." Chris went through it again, more deliberately the second time.

"Remember Pelican Park, in Mandeville, where we played youth soccer?" This time she nodded yes. "That was all forest until the trees were cleared for the fields. And is your recollection of that place one of a scarred landscape, or lush fields of green, surrounded by trees of majestic height and splendor … Nature in harmony with Man?" He was hamming it up, but was also making headway. "The best part is, the trees they cut paid for most of the park. Those old pines, the hardwoods with the twenty-plus foot bases … I can't begin to tell you what that wood was worth. Think what it would be worth today, fifteen years later."

His gaze moved outward, dragging hers along. "Look. What do you see, Nic?" He waved his arm outwardly, gesturing. "Where we sit, right now, will be protected, secure. All I'm talking about is clearing several hundred trees from the valley floor, leaving what is the most incredibly rich earth—no, make that flat, rich earth—in this entire countryside. Just imagine," he said, pointing, "imagine the playing field, right over there. And Mom's azaleas at the far end. Imagine a habitat. Do you know how few birds there are in this valley right now? It's too dense, and what natural food there is isn't accessible enough. That could all change—for the better."

She let him go on. "I have no idea how much the timber would fetch on the open market, but I know good, quality hardwood when I see it, and I know this is premium oak. Dealers will pay a fortune for this timber. Hey, you're talking to someone who worked two summers for one of Dad's timber clients, remember?

"Think what the money could mean to the village. Water wells, for one thing. No more catching rain water, or pulling crude wagons carrying river water in leaking urns and hoping it doesn't become foul before the next rain. Think about some improvement to the sanitation system. I don't even want to talk about how worried I am about your health, using outdoor toilets and all. What about your simple privacy? Better yet, how about a few other conveniences? A truck, for instance, for you and the good padre. Maybe if you had a truck you and I could go for a drive some afternoon, see the sights maybe. I don't know, lots of things come to mind. Hey, God may have brought you to this place, and shown you poverty and ignorance and all things primitive, but did you ever stop to think that it's your calling to deliver these people from this, and into something more meaningful? Where is it said God wants his flock to live this way?"

"What did Father Art say when you told him of your plans?" Her question cut right to the heart of things. Chris wasn't ready to answer.

"Does that mean you're won over?"

"No, it just means I want to know what my boss said when you laid out everything."

"Okay, okay, it's like this. He went for the scholarship fund idea, big time. I have an idea that one will work." When he paused, she saw what was coming next.

"I didn't talk to him about the second idea. I saved it just for you."

"Well you know I can't—"

He cut her off quickly. "C'mon, Nic. This one isn't for Father Art. He doesn't own this village. Or this valley. It's not his decision. It's really not even yours, but I wouldn't take it to the next step without your approval. You don't like the idea, it dies on the vine, right here, right now."

She shut her eyes and massaged the slight pounding in her temples. Even her brother being here had become a complication. What he said made some sense; she couldn't argue that. Nor could she disregard his comment on why God had perhaps chosen this place for her. That remained a mystery to her. But even though Chris's was such a grand plan, it remained an intrusion on her privacy, and that of the community as well. She held no misgivings over the simple life she'd chosen, despite its inconveniences. And the village, while far from prosperous, was content. She saw ahead gradual change, in due course. Chris was suggesting abrupt change, and that would surely bring more abrupt change, and almost certainly an upsetting of balance, possibly even discontent. She pondered it all and chose her words carefully.

"Chris, you do know how to sweep a sister off her feet. You are the sweetest, kindest, most loving brother any girl could hope to have. I am so proud of the man you're becoming. I wish our parents were here, to see what I have just seen. They would also be proud."

"Please don't let the next word from your lips be *but*."

She went right at him, without hesitation. "*But,* my dear brother, what you now ask of me, I cannot give. You want me to make a decision that would affect the lives of the entire village. Father Art isn't the only one who doesn't have such power."

It was a *But,* all right, just not the one he expected.

He cleared his throat. "I couldn't begin to sacrifice what you have, not for a single day, and you continue on day after day. I see things you contend with, but I also see ways to help you deal with them. How to handle the money, that was nothing. I thought to myself when you first told me about it, 'She can't see the forest for the trees.' And you know what? That's when the other idea hit me. That's the really big one, Nic. A chance for this village to pull itself out of the Stone Age. It's the real miracle here … waiting to happen. It's so obvious, and you can't see it. Give it purpose. Let these people see there is another way. With the money from the sale of the timber, they can buy what they need to make a better way for their children, and their children's children. They will listen to you, and to Father Art."

Chris watched her closely. He'd seen that expression before. She was thinking.

I just might have done it, he thought.

34

CHRIS CAUGHT THE shuttle the following morning. He told his sister he would return in a day or two, three at the most, and to expect good news. When he did not return in five, she began to worry. Father Art did his best to console.

"I have a feeling your brother is able to look after himself. You needn't worry," he offered.

"Why do I get the feeling that you and my brother know so much more about what's going on around here than I?"

"I suppose I could be evasive and say to you, 'Why, whatever are you talking about?' but I also suppose I should answer your question truthfully."

"Will someone please tell me what's going on?"

"Let me put it this way. I had the most spirited discussion with Chris a few days ago. Remember the morning he and I spent together? Yes, I'm sure you do. No doubt you two talked about Maria, and what happened. Anyway, he knew about the donations that had flooded in from around the world."

She interrupted him. "Father, I told him about the money but—"

He waved her off. "That's immaterial. I would have expected you to share that with him. I'm certain you didn't share the Church's private business with him ... I can be certain of that, can't I, Sister?" He cast a non-accusatory, harmlessly inquisitive glance her way.

"You can be certain of that, Father." *A white lie is a venial sin ... right?*

"Good. Now where were we? Oh, yes, we were having this spirited discussion, your brother and I, about the money, the donations. He asked me how much I thought it totaled, and I told him perhaps as much as fifteen or twenty thousand dollars American, with more still coming in. Then he asked me what would become of the money. I frankly hadn't given it much thought, and told him so. He asked me what I thought of the idea the money could be used for educational scholarships for the village children, and some medical supplies and an occasional visit from a physician. I again told him I hadn't given it much thought, but it seemed like a good enough idea.

"He rather surprised me with what he said next." The priest was smiling now, curiously, Nicole noted. "He looked me straight in the eye and said, and I won't ever forget what he said or how he said it; he said, 'Father, you don't understand. The money was sent to my sister for those purposes, and it is not open to question. That is the use the donors wanted to be made of that money, and I shall look to you to see that is exactly the way the money is used.' And he never took his eyes off mine, and his voice didn't waver a bit."

He swallowed hard, and continued. "I'll tell you, that was the most persuasive 'advice' I've received from anyone since my own father—and I do mean my biological father, God rest his soul—lectured me on the evils of alcohol and tobacco at a tender age. I didn't feel threatened," he continued, sensing alarm from Nicole, and feeling the need to ease her qualm, "nor should you impute a threatening tone to what was said. No, it was so much more. It was a pronouncement, the kind of thing to which the only answer is action. I tell you, my only thought was to tell the archbishop the money would be used in exactly that manner. It was not my station to question any of it. And I can visualize myself standing before Archbishop Santiago, who is already tiring of me I'm sure, and saying it to him just as young Chris said it to me, hopefully with equal conviction."

Her smile was so totally inward even the furthest corners of her lips didn't move. Chris had used one of their father's trial tactics. Maybe he would be the lawyer she would not.

"Is that how you wish the money to be spent, Sister? I presume Chris had your blessing before he cajoled my willingness."

"Father, I apologize for my impetuous brother. I—"

"An apology is not necessary. I think we have a case of a young man driven to do the right thing, by his sister as well as the Church. I don't see that calling for an apology."

"It must be your decision, Father. But thank you for putting it so well. I'm sure Chris will be gratified to learn he made such a favorable impression."

"Since we're on the subject of your brother, and his good intentions, was it his idea to do the landscaping in the valley? Or yours? A surprising notion whichever. I rather like the idea."

"I must confess, Father, the idea was entirely his. But how did you learn?"

"I would hope the day never comes in our village that anyone can gather the elders together and present such a grand plan without my hearing of it."

"And you are not upset he didn't include you?"

"Perhaps a little. But when one considers everything, it was not your brother's place to invite me … it was the village's. Chris's was the politically correct way."

Nicole released a heavy sigh of relief. "Nobody loses, right Father?"

The priest's silence was only a little more upsetting than her brother's overdue presence.

240

✝

35

CHRIS RETURNED AFTER a week's absence. Two Hispanic men accompanied him, one a well-dressed, nicely groomed younger man, the other older and wearing traditional work clothes. He introduced them hurriedly to Nicole and Father Art, then insisted that they all go to the valley, so the visitors would have plenty of daylight to look things over before their long drive back. Father Art declined, but shooed Nicole along, telling her to take whatever time she needed.

"Okay, Nic, here's the deal. I found a buyer for the cut timber. The only requirement is the buyer's local representative must approve. No approval, no deal. But," he grinned, "if these guys like it, it's a done deal."

"How do you know you can trust these two?"

Chris smiled. "You'll see soon enough."

Nicole's apprehension was short-lived. The better-dressed gentleman was Raphael Palomar, a graduate of the University of Pennsylvania, a sister Ivy League school to the Dartmouth College she had attended. He obviously came from wealth, yet took no pain to lord his status over his host and hostess. They relaxed in the small chatter of new acquaintances while the group made its way to the valley floor.

"My family has traded in everything from sugar and textiles to exotic birds—until that trade was outlawed—but primarily timber. Our timber business has fallen off," he explained, "due to the hostilities in the southern part of the country.

"There has not been much trade here in the north, because of the lack of adequate roads, and the treacherous terrain. But this area," he continued, "is different than most of the northern region. I am not familiar with it, and am surprised that it has escaped my family's detection for so long. We had not known such fine quality timber to exist in these parts."

Nicole watched as Palomar's eyes greedily scanned the surroundings. She had an alarming feeling from the way he spoke.

In less than an hour Raphael and his foreman had been to the far side of the valley and back. Chris walked over to Nicole's side as the scion and his helper went ahead, to view the spectacle of the waterfall. Chris assured her it had been made abundantly clear there would be no trees cut within fifty yards of the pond. The falls would remain only partially visible from any direction. Her Sanctuary would not be damaged.

"They will report to the people I called that the timber is acceptable, and the price we discussed is more than fair." Chris beamed with accomplishment.

"You've already discussed price?" Nicole asked. "Before you've talked with the village?"

"I learned enough along the way to make the price contingent upon the approval of the village. Give me a little credit, please." It wasn't annoyance so much as arrogance in his tone that bothered her. A little voice sounded from within. This was moving too fast. Shouldn't this take more time? Her morning tea, when she was fortunate enough to enjoy it, steeped longer than this was taking. She asked Chris to fill her in on the details, like where he'd been for the past week, and how it had come to this. Could these people be trusted?

"What's not to trust? Papers will have to be signed, and work will be carried on right in front of the villagers' own eyes. This is no sneak-in-under-cover-of-dark-ness-and-clear-cut-the-forest kind of operation. The operation requires care, so as not to damage healthy standing timber. And the stumps will be removed safely, dy-namiting only if no other way works. We don't want to open some fissure that might drain our pool, now do we?"

She ignored him. "Chris, I'm really getting nervous. How can we be sure this man will honor Refugio's privacy? Why should I believe his interests coincide with my village's?"

"Because I told you so." He gave her that Mac McHenry *You don't have an option* look. No grin this time, only the hard stare. It translated as, *Nic, this is under control.* She wondered where the shrinking violet side of her had all of a sudden appeared. She'd never let her father get away with that stare; why should she let her brother?

"Chris, listen, I know you have put your very best into this. My only hope is Refugio doesn't get hurt. Tell me, how could we stop that from happening?"

"Because I have told you so."

She could not hold his stare, and dropped her gaze to the ground, holding his arm tentatively with one hand. "Okay, you win." She did not look up to see his scowl at her wry smile.

Chris had visited a lawyer in Guatemala City. The two of them checked the property records, determining the village of Refugio owned all of the land for over a dozen miles in every direction. Ownership extended to all rights, from deep into the earth to as far into the sky as the eye could see and beyond even that. A dictate of Old Spanish law, unchanged over the centuries, applicable to the conquered *Ladinos*. Chris was satisfied the government had no claim to the land or the fruits of that land. Armed with this knowledge, and a purpose, it became a simple matter of finding a businessman he could trust to finance the transaction.

Pat and Sean Miller had been Chris's close friends since the third grade. Heirs to fortunes at age twenty-one, legacy of a land baron of a grandfather, but few knew. Chris did not learn until one quiet night the summer after graduation from Mandeville High, when their dates had been taken home and the three of them lay sprawled on the ground near the rope swing, under the starlight, the beer gone, and talk of their imminent parting having run their high spirits aground. They'd quietly told him that while he was off chasing his dream of playing soccer for school and country, they'd be learning the family business. They told Chris his father, the great Mac McHenry himself, remarkably enough, was legal counsel to their family business, yet another revelation to Chris. They'd ended up working together that summer and the next, on family-owned forest land in Washington and Tangipahoa parishes. Chris learned the forestry business in those two summers.

And when he needed help to get from Colorado to Guatemala, Chris and Sean had been there for him. They, too, wanted to know more about Nicole's recent brush with worldly fame. Without question, the ticket money and more, was in his hands within hours.

He called with the tantalizing prospect of timber riches down Guatemala way. After hearing the details, they'd gone straight to the bottom line on him: What would he want from the deal?

"Me? Nothing. This isn't for me. You should know me better than that. But the village, it gets a third. One third of the net." He let it settle in. "So, do we have a deal?" He was quickly learning this business deal stuff.

They agreed. The money part was good. But the deal depended on final approval from a family in Guatemala City they'd done business with in the past. If they were good with it, Sean and Pat would be too.

"How do I know we can trust these friends of yours?"

Chris quickly regretted his question.

"Because we don't do business with people we don't trust."

Nicole didn't need to know any of this. It was a simple notion to begin with. The actual plan of operation was no more difficult than the idea. While not a huge deal to his friends, it did stand to make them nearly a half million dollars. A gift, a total right-on-their-doorstep gift, after labor had been paid, after the land had been reclaimed from the temporary carnage, after the percentage to Raphael's family for brokering and fronting the hard costs of the deal, and after the village received its two-hundred-fifty-thousand dollars share. Chris had done what he'd set out to do. He looked at his sister, the worried expression still on her face, and massaged her wrinkled brow with his thumb. His way of saying, *Let me do the worrying.* She relaxed the frown, and reached to hug him, mumbling words of thanks and prayer simultaneously, as Chris looked up to see Raphael and Javier walking toward them with expressions of incredulity on their faces.

He could already taste the sweet nectar of success.

———

First it was electricity. Now heavy industry visited Refugio. Routines were disrupted; superstition and fear shook up the bucolic idyll. Roads that saw only occasional traffic, the archdiocesan courier and an occasional military transport, now rutted deeper under the wheels and tracks of mammoth machinery. The noise alone was enough to frighten.

Concerned villagers crowded into the church. This was more than they'd expected.

Chris was prepared. With Raphael translating, and his own superior knowledge of timber clearing, calm was maintained while they heard, again, how this would help them once it was done. The noise and inconvenience were only temporary, he explained.

Blessed with favorable weather, the work progressed quickly. The noise became tolerable. Fear gave way to acceptance. Life returned to normal. Tentative trust strengthened. Sister Nicole's brother was hailed as an instrument of goodness.

Chris had endeared himself to the Major as well. The military had no concern one way or another in the village bettering itself, he learned. The consummate schmoozer, Chris persuaded Raphael to bring him two bottles of fine Caribbean rum, a gift to a surprised commandant. The grateful officer shared one with Chris that same night. A disapproving sister nursed her brother back to wellness the following day, admonishing him to refrain from such foolishness in the name of a good business deal. Chris needed no lectures. Through the pounding in his temples and the roiling in his gut he took satisfaction in knowing he had taken care of any problem that might arise where the military was concerned.

Through it all Chris settled for nothing less than perfection in the quest to harvest a bountiful timber crop without the loss of any of the solitude and tranquility his sister cherished so dearly. Before the cutting was through, because of the care taken, sprouts of native grass already could be seen here and there. A full meadow was not far away. Better yet, the waterfall still fell magnificently, and, as he sat on the banks of the pond a last time, he nodded with great satisfaction that the tranquil setting was undisturbed. A promise kept; a good moment.

He was packing his small bag when she walked into her room. It was a moment they'd both known would eventually come, but reality often strikes cruelly. He stiffened defensively as he heard her catch her breath at the total unexpectedness of it all.

"I thought it would be better this way," he said, without looking up.

"This is so surreal. It's as if we're some couple splitting up. You're packing and I'm the last to know. They don't prepare you how to handle this in nun school." She moved toward him, sitting on the edge of the bed as he stuffed his bag.

"Hey, Nic, c'mon, I'm vested in this place now. I'll be back. I've got soccer to play on our new field, when the grass is in, and kids to coach, and your butt to run ragged around the goal. You think I'd give that up? Get real." The grin was back.

"I guess not, but that doesn't make it any easier on me." She was biting her lip again. "So, when do you leave?"

"Raphael left yesterday to get the papers and the money ready in Guatemala City. Javier will be here for me in half an hour."

He stopped cramming dirty clothes into the bag. "Hey, I have a timber sale to conclude in Guatemala City tomorrow. And a quick trip to the States … but I'll be right back, I promise. Do I need to remind you that two-hundred-fifty-thousand American dollars will be in a bank account for the village of Refugio in a matter of days? That alone should make at least some of the people around here happy to see me go."

"Were you going to say any goodbyes?" She couldn't stop biting her lip.

"What do you think? Like I'm going to just leave without telling you good-bye? How can you say something like that? Besides, it's only for a few days. And I already paid the good padre my respects. We're tight."

"I don't mean just me and Father Art. The people have grown to accept you as one of them. You're family now, too." She paused. "It's a tough responsibility, isn't it?"

This was becoming harder. "Okay, where can I find Maria? And Pablo? Oh, and Enrique and Jorge. That would do it for me, Nic. Any more than that and I lose my edge, I get sappy. And these people don't need me to get sappy when I'm about to wheel and deal with their future."

"Sappy? Rough and tumble Chris has a sensitive side?"

"Enough, already. I'm running out of time." He slung the small bag over his shoulder, and said, "Now, take me to your children." Slipping his free arm around her, they walked toward the only other good-byes he would say.

"Oh, I almost forgot. The ball … keep it, it's yours 'til I get back. It's on the little table by your bed, along with something else. Something special for you."

Cradlng a softly sobbing Maria in her arms an hour later, she waved at the muddy sport utility vehicle. Chris's arm extended from the passenger window in reply, staying visible until the truck was around the curve and out of sight. Maria's crying stopped as she played with the curious metal object newly hung around Sister's neck along with her Saint Christopher. Then it was Sister Nicole's turn to wipe the drops from her eyes, then from her cheeks. As quickly as he'd arrived, he'd gone. Like a bad dream, the thought entered her mind that she might not see her brother for a long time … maybe ever. She'd never thought of being here as being alone before, but at this moment, as she held the child of her heart in her arms, feeling the small fingers wiping the wetness from her face, wondering what this child of God thought at wiping away a nun's tears, she knew for a while at least she would be alone.

There was an air of joyous apprehension in Refugio the night Chris left for the capital. No one other than Miguel, Father Art and Nicole had the slightest notion what an American dollar was, but everyone knew that the missing trees would be replaced by American dollars, enough of them to make good things happen. For years Miguel had described to his neighbors things such as water coming out of spigots, special rooms for bathing and toileting, boxes that kept food cold and even made ice, and devices you held in your hand while you spoke into one part and listened into another. When electricity came to the village, and Nicole unfurled the wonder of videocassette movies on a television monitor, and the townsfolk were shown such unimaginable things really did exist, certain expectations began to form in their minds. It was exciting, thinking of such things.

Father Art and Nicole did their best to temper their parishioners' expectations, but it seemed not enough. Miguel tried to help, reminding his people what Chris had said, it would be weeks, maybe months before all could be arranged. Even Miguel struck out. He explained to Nicole and Father Art such excitement was only natural for people who were about to see something for the first time. Miguel made sense, they concluded.

The revolutionary dreamer found it difficult to compete with the intoxicating effect capitalism had had on these men. He saw a different kind of fire in their eyes, and his efforts to rekindle the blaze of liberty, justice and freedom might just as well have been wasted on the garrisoned soldiers. He persisted, believing if but one more would break from under the spell, another, then another would follow. But it was not to be. Not this night. He looked hard at those who ignored, forcing them to meet his incendiary glare squarely, eye to eye, and hastened them to know that their absurd notions of ever seeing any sign of the wealth they expected was nothing more than pure folly, that it was they who would remember this night, come the time when regret and disappointment reigned over their empty pockets and dashed hopes. He struck hard at their strength, their hopes, and made fear of unfulfillment his strength, their point of weakness. He planted the small seeds of doubt, nothing more. And when he was finished, he stormed from the small room, cursing them as cowards and old women. His insults took some purchase.

It was the one named Juan who spoke first. The only one who had not been swayed by the young American's vision and promise of money and fine things, the one among the group who took up where their leader had left off. Juan reminded his neighbors of the government that betrayed and enslaved them every day of their lives. Did they really believe that this government would allow their tiny village to acquire anything close to wealth, or finery? They were bigger fools than they'd just heard from their departed leader.

He berated them for their lost conviction, their selfishness. He hit hard at the latter point. Would these good men abandon their brothers in arms in other scattered villages … *over American dollars?* Would they bring such shame to themselves? How dare they.

He rose to leave. He, too, had planted small seeds. The men who filed out after the first two were now more cautious. Doubt crept into their minds.

As other men with dark thoughts and darker intentions made their ways home on the shadowless night, the commandant re-read the communiqué he'd just been handed by his radio operator. The major was not accustomed to being awakened in the night. The message forebode unease. He dismissed the messenger; the orders needed no clarification.

Following the orders wouldn't bother him much. He was a soldier first, which compelled obedience. Duty wasn't troublesome to him … but betrayal was. Performance of his duty would, to these villagers, be seen as a betrayal of their trust, and their friendship.

He took a last look at the message before returning to bed. The words still chilled.

Rebel movement in northern region. Exercise extreme caution. All garrisons in Petén commence two-man armed patrols immediately, repeat, armed. Investigate and report suspicious behavior. Impose and maintain eight o'clock curfew. Arrest and detain violators. Continue until further notice.

§

Five months earlier, when he'd come to this curious place, it had been to discourage the very thing with which he must now contend. The unrest to the south, missing from this peaceful northern region, had taken a heavy toll for over a generation. He'd lost friends to the conflict, been party to acts he struggled to keep suppressed in a clouded memory. Acts of retribution, many of them savage and unspeakable, demanded in the name of the same duty he must again obey, hopefully this time with a different outcome. The mountain people he tended, they were not like their warlike countrymen to the south. These folk were a simple lot, singular in purpose: weave and dye enough cloth and harvest enough to sustain them. It was nothing more than that. Now that would change. Any chance at preserving the way of life in this village had just been lost. The message he'd read guaranteed it.

If the movement from the lower region had indeed spread to this place, he would know soon enough. He would see it in their faces. He was skilled in such art of perception. Subtle changes in daily habit would be the first telltale signs. While he could not picture these people as the sort to sympathize with the guerilla movement, he also realized men can dream of something better. Once the first seeds take root, the quiet, simple man who was once his friend, a man he was charged even with defending, becomes his enemy. Allegiance is a two-way proposition. Be with me, or you are my enemy. There was no room in this equation for sympathy or argument.

A warning had been issued, and it must be heeded, regardless of his personal feelings.

He wondered how it would affect the balance that had been struck between his small garrison and the villagers. There could be no further fraternization. The weapons that had been missing—at his directive—would reappear. Even attendance at the Masses must be forbidden. He thought of young Pablo, who'd become as a lamb to the nun, as devoted to her as to his own mother no doubt. The effect on his men perhaps would be as difficult as on the villagers. In the morning, at dawn's call, he would inform his men, and in soldierly fashion would compel their obedience to the same order to which he was bound. They would take it harder than he, but that was youth questioning experience, which he could tame.

He thought of the nun. What an interesting phenomenon, he reflected. It pained him to think of her in harm's way. The innocents often do suffer the fates of the damned, he lamented. He'd witnessed the remarkable happening only a few months earlier, and had wrestled with it since. He might never fully know or understand what he witnessed. It was not to be forgotten, however; suppressed, maybe, until a better time.

He closed his eyes, envisioning his return to home and family. He had only three more months left to serve at this desolate station. After that, he was due for a promotion, and a softer existence, a rotation into the administrative services, closer to civilization, closer to Guatemala City, to his family. They'd sacrificed much during his absence this year for the extra pay, and the opportunity to advance in rank. Would any of this be realized? When all was said and done, would it have been worth it? For the first time in his career, he began to have doubts.

§

Even the best-laid plans go astray, literature and life tell us. In today's parlance, that message translates simply as Murphy's Law. The image of a crude bumper sticker to this same end registered in Chris's mind as he sat in the office of some low-ranking deputy official in Guatemala City, the ceiling fan barely rotating, nothing resembling air conditioning anywhere. More prominent in his thoughts was the concern, once the news of the catastrophe worked its way back to Refugio, his sister would be in danger.

This was a charade, that was easy enough to figure. Where it had originated was not clear at the moment. All he knew was that his timber shipment had been confiscated.

By the government, he was being told—the government of this wretched, backward, corrupt, third world ghetto, he angrily uttered under his breath. The "official" pretense he'd been witness to earlier, that the shipment was being held up indefinitely pending inspection, wouldn't have fooled the village idiot. This much was also clear: one, it was too late to call his father for help; and two, when Pat and Sean got wind of what had happened they would pull the plug, cut their losses. Meanwhile, Chris was being handed his passport and return ticket to America by the official, who was telling him not to make trouble, and not to return. Chris, drenched in perspiration, felt an icy chill. He was powerless to do anything but follow the official to the car waiting for the drive to the airport. Fear of failing his friends, and himself, took a distant second to Chris's gnawing fear that Nicole, unknowing and defenseless, stood centered in the crosshairs of his screw-up.

———————

While Chris agonized somewhere over the Gulf of Mexico on his flight back home, Raphael sat across a rather impressive scrolled mahogany desk from his father, who looked scornfully at his son.

"Raphael, you insult and shame me, our family. Why is it that you crawl before me today, begging that we settle for the crumbs that your American acquaintances—" He omitted any reference to *friends or partners.* "—are willing to dole out to us? Do you not see what we are facing here? They would have us be the broker and work gang of a rich timber deal. We make a meager profit on our out of pocket expenses, while they reap a vast sum of money. You are not concerned?"

"Father," Raphael began, "do we sacrifice our family honor and reputation for the possibility you can find a buyer for the timber? Do we not risk far more than we stand to gain?"

"Raphael, my son, this family has done business for centuries without the help of the Americans. Just because you and I went to school in that wicked country doesn't mean we owe anyone from America anything. There is no one up there who would step forward if you or your family had needs. You may think differently, but if candor were within your thoughts, you would know this." He crossed himself, and kissed the eighteen-karat St. Christopher medallion that hung from the gold braided chain around his neck.

"That is not the issue, Father. The issue is that we made a deal to harvest the timber, haul it to the shipping docks, load it, and send it to my friends to be sold in America.

There is a signed agreement. We gave our word."

"In our culture, as you well know, such a writing means only that we will honor it if nothing better comes along. Your American friends should have known better. This will be a valuable lesson for them. They are out no money. We have paid for everything so far, they nothing. This is right, and in time you will come to know it is right."

"Our customs may very well apply to those of our own culture with whom we deal. With our own, it is expected. But we deal now with strangers to our custom, who rely on such things as honor and trust." He swallowed hard. "Father, I ask you, please, make this right. Let me conclude the transaction as I have told my friends in Louisiana—our partners—I would do."

The father eyed the son craftily. "You have much to learn of the ways of our family business. And," he continued, sharply, "we shall not even discuss the matter of putting the perceived interests of others ahead of those of your own family.

"The timber will be sold in Panama in a few days. There will be no trail, no documents to tie us to any of this. That, my son, is how to successfully broker a deal."

He again looked hard at his son. "I consider this matter closed, Raphael."

The boy stood erect before his father, questioning his respect for the man for the first time, but fully accepting there was no changing the course of events. He also sensed something besides a timber deal was lost, something even the position of his family for generations in the highest social and business circles of his native land would be unable to rectify. He wondered if any amount of influence would be able to redeem the family from this callous act of his father.

He would tell Sean and Pat Miller the harvest had been confiscated by some official, who claimed sovereign rights over those of the villagers, then sold to a dealer in Panama. If he were to openly confess to them what had happened, the result would be the same, only he would also betray his father and family in the process. He was damned and doomed in both events. Ignoring his conscience, he decided to tell his friends the awful lie, and hope for the best. With a lie, there was always hope that it would not be exposed.

36

S HE TORE OPEN THE envelope. It was her first word from Chris in the two weeks since he'd left. A hopeful, tremulous voice within her spoke words of calm as she unfolded the single sheet of a schoolchild's lined tablet paper.

Nicole, the letter began, *Raphael has betrayed us. He has stolen our timber, under the pretense of "government confiscation." Some guy in a uniform forced me on a plane and sent me back to the States before I found out what happened. He wouldn't let me return to Refugio, or write you. I couldn't speak enough of the language to get one of those Guatemalans to deliver a note to you sooner. I'm sorry, Nic. I'm back home, working with Pat and Sean to get the money. We'll make it right, I promise. Don't let anyone blame you, tell them it was my fault. I dropped the ball. It was me who didn't make the save. I'll be back soon, with the money. I promise. Love, Chris.*

So caring, she lamented. She'd not learned first hand until this moment, but she'd been in the country long enough to know betrayal was a way of life, a routine part of the culture, not uncommon even within families. She was not surprised at his news … only disappointed for her brother, who'd done what was for him the first noble adult act in his young life. She prayed he would be spared grief, turmoil.

She turned her thoughts to Raphael's betrayal. If there were those in Refugio whose disappointment rose over their heightened expectations, whose anger at the deceit rivaled her brother's, there might be a problem. She had no way of knowing how they would receive the news. That knowledge would come when the unfortunate, inevitable truth was disclosed.

Moments later she stood at a familiar doorway. "Come in, Sister," Father Art said. "What brings you to my office this fine afternoon?" He sounded in unusually high spirits and didn't wait for her to answer. "I was just mulling over a plan I'd devised years ago to tap into the water reservoir running below the ground we walk on. It must, you know," he continued, motioning her to his desk, spreading some hand-sketched diagrams for her to see. "The falls at which you spend so much of your free time," he said as he looked up from the papers, smiling at her, "don't just appear at the rock face. They come from an underground source, perhaps several, and we should be able to tap into that supply. It would only take the simplest kind of water well drilling equipment to prove this up. Once we have the windfall your enterprising younger broth[e]   our own water supply. No more trips to the riv   more fear of disease that comes with pu-trefac   nning to relish the thought of improving condi

It   any expectation he'd held over the timber sale.   wer, as the boughs of the pines back home woul   ng cones in the early fall of the year. The alert   er every expression to know when some-thing   ntal brow.

"

H

B   lined school paper, and to bite her lower lip.

bec   you are, in a way of your own that I have

was   self for what has happened." She sensed he

                    once, speechless.

H   d told her to sit. "There is no blame here. What has happened is still a   of us anyway. Let's analyze it, shall we?" He sat back, and clasped his hands behind his head. She was already beginning to feel better, and found herself wanting some wise counsel.

"The worst thing that can happen is that our friends will question whether your brother stole their property. What I'm saying is, if they don't believe the government confiscated the timber, as Chris tells us, what choice do they have left? Only that Chris stole it, right?"

Nicole nodded *yes*.

"In my most imaginative, inspired state of mind I cannot conceive that our friends would believe that. And I think you cannot either." He sounded very convincing—rational and convincing. His words brought comfort and hope. She was desperate for relief of any kind.

"But Father, what about their dashed hopes? And now, what about your own high hopes? We've heard so much from Teresa, and Carlos, and our other friends, about how much they were looking forward to the things the money would bring them. We encouraged those hopes and expectations. *I* did, I mean. This was my doing, Father. *I* built up their hopes. And now, what's to be said about their lost hope, and disappointment? Where will that blame fall? What—"

"Sister," he broke in, unclasping his hands and putting one out in front of her in a halting manner, "we get nowhere placing blame. Ours is a very forgiving religion, and these are fine people, who've been taught that forgiveness transcends all else. If there is among them one who looks for a place to attach blame, we shall but remind him, or her, of this lesson. But I feel your fears are misplaced. I think they will surprise you. Yes, there will be disappointment, and there will be anger toward the government that stole from them, but it is the same government that has stolen from them all their lives. They will simply add this latest theft to the list, and accept it in the spirit of the forgiveness we have come here to teach. But there will be no anger toward us, for we had nothing to do with this. They may be illiterate and even a bit superstitious at times, but they are a kind-hearted and understanding people, and it is not our cloth that will inspire their anger or distrust. You've been here long enough to know this."

"I suppose you are right, Father. I hope so, anyway."

She asked when they should break the news, and how it should be presented..

"It's not something we want to overemphasize to them. I will report it to Miguel and Carlos in the morning, and together we will take it to our mayor, and from there, it will run its own course, I'd imagine."

"I want to be with you when you tell them. Please. I still feel responsible, and want to see how they react to the news. For me, Father. For Chris, too. It's important to me."

"Yes, I suspect it is. That will be fine, Sister. Tomorrow morning, after Mass, before your school, we'll call on our friends the Mendezes. There now, it's settled. You must relax. This will all be okay. You'll see, it will be forgotten in no time." He patted her arm.

She forced a smile, and excused herself. It was time for meditation, and she longed for the peace and quiet that awaited her below the village. She tried hard not to think of it as a crime scene.

After she left the room the priest reflected further, wondering if he'd succeeded in convincing even himself that there was no need for worry. He gathered up his sketches, and put them back into the folder they'd been stored in long enough for the pages to yellow and curl at their corners. With a touch of dismay he replaced the folder into its slot in his desk. He wondered if it would see the light of day again. He chided himself for the fleeting thought of disappointment that perhaps it might not.

She did not recognize the man. He was a stranger to the village. From a distance, he looked to be of Indian descent, but his manner and dress were different than the villagers. If looks could tell such, he looked educated. And purposeful. If he were lost, he did not look it. Nothing suggested lack of self-confidence, or confusion of his whereabouts. He meant to be where he was, she concluded.

He was leaning against a tree beside the pond. His eyes had watched her every step along the familiar path. She felt no fear of the stranger, only curiosity. He was nice-looking, with a pleasant expression on his face. "Hello," she spoke in Spanish. "I am Sister Nicole, from the village." She held out her hand in greeting.

He smiled, and bent at the waist as he returned her handshake. He introduced himself only as Raul. He was from the south; nothing more than that, just the south. She did not press him for more. If he'd wanted her to know more, she reasoned, he would have told her more. He spoke English, though, which added to the mystique.

"What brings you to Refugio? We don't see many strangers here."

"I'm only passing through, a wanderer in these parts," he answered. His final destination was farther to the north and west, he told her, his English crisp, his manner pleasant. "I stopped to rest on the road, parked my truck under a large tree, and started walking. I found my way to the valley quite by accident, and spotted the falls from the clearing on the ledge. Do you know the clearing and ledge I speak of?"

"Oh, quite well," she answered, feeling even more at ease with the stranger. She guessed him to be in his late twenties or early thirties, no more. He eyed her curiously, prompting Nicole to flush in embarrassment. "Why do you look at me like that?"

"Like what? What about the way I am looking at you?"

"Oh, I think you know what I mean, Raul." She moved around him to the edge of the pond, where she bent and scooped the cool water onto her neck and face.

"Actually, I was wondering what I had done to encounter a most beautiful, obviously American woman—and a nun, no less—in the middle of a jungle forest in Petén, on this particularly fine day. My thoughts have not always been so transparent. You are wise beyond your years, Sister. I should do better to keep my expressions a little less obvious." He took a step nearer to her.

"I apologize for having offended you." He held out his hand again. "Forgiven?"

She took the olive branch … but she did not thank him for his compliment, and remained wary. He moved a respectful distance away. "This valley, it is lovely. But it is not entirely natural, I see." He motioned over his shoulder. "The clearing, it looks to have been freshly cut. The grass isn't completely in yet. There are many places that look to have been where trees stood. There is no explanation why the trees just suddenly stop, on both sides of the valley. Someone," he shrugged, "has been making changes to the landscape. And, it looks, for the better."

She frowned. "Yes, but at a price, I'm afraid." Perhaps sharing her weighted conscience with a stranger would be cathartic. If, that is, he cared to know.

He did.

"I am sorry, Sister. How do you mean, 'at a price?' How can such beauty, matched only by your own, be at any price? I do not understand."

"Please," she said, "I thank you for the second compliment, but I am not so comfortable with any physical attractiveness I possess. If you find it there, and it pleases you, that is fine. Share it with anyone else, but, please, not with me."

"That is fair enough," he said. "Twice now I have offended. Not a good start for me."

"It is forgotten. Now, what were we talking about before I scolded you?"

"You were going to tell me how this valley has created some kind of problem for you. That is the feeling I had." He leaned in slightly. "You owe me no explanation, Sister. We can talk about anything else you like for the few moments I have left here."

"No, no, it's all right," she said. "It's really nothing, yet it is," her words making little sense, but suggesting more. "It all began," she said, and the entire story unfolded. When she'd finished, Raul, who'd sat silent and expressionless throughout, stood quickly, and dismissed her concerns with a cavalier wave of his hand.

"What is there to worry about? These people would not expect one so young and inexperienced as you to be a match for the deceit that nearly always enters a business deal in this country. In every likelihood it was not even the government, but the very businessmen with whom your brother had been dealing who made off with the harvest, then blamed it on the government. The important thing, you must realize, is that no one was hurt. No lives were injured, or worse yet, lost, and for that, when such sums of money are concerned, you should be grateful. And you certainly have no reason to bear any guilt or despair for what happened."

Before she could reply, Raul excused himself. "I have far to travel before dark, and, as you know, traveling after dark is unwise in these parts."

Nicole felt there was unfinished business with this traveler, but did not try to slow him. She would draw comfort from his words, and make do with that. The rest would be dealt with in the morning. She gave a warm farewell handshake to Raul, whose mood seemed to have changed. She shrugged off her perception of a distant look on his face. Earlier she'd had the feeling he could see straight through her; now he was looking far beyond her.

She wished him a safe conclusion to his journey, and the peace of God along the way.

As he walked away she felt the strange sensation that this might not have been a chance meeting, and even stranger yet, that it would not be her last with Raul.

_____

While Nicole wondered if she'd seen the last of Raul, thoughts of an altogether different kind collided in a chain reaction in the young revolutionary's mind as he made his way back to his hidden vehicle. How fortunate he had come early today, and took the time to visit this site of the source of his disappointing last visit to tiny Refugio. How fortunate indeed.

A chance meeting with the young nun who unknowingly had stood in his way to the strike against tyranny, and he was now primed to turn things around the way they should be.

Fresh from his deceit, he felt giddy with delight at being able to share with his small group tonight the news that their dreams had been robbed by those who sought only to keep them oppressed and downtrodden, as they had been always at the feet of the Spaniards, the intruders. It made no difference whether it was by the government or by the very scoundrels these men had worked beside in clearing the land, the result was the same. What was rightfully theirs had been taken, and that was wrong and should be made right. He would show them what was right. The inroads he'd failed to make these past few weeks, the elation he'd been unable to overcome in these foolish dreamers, would all change.

He, Raul, revolutionary, purveyor of a different kind of hope—the hope of freedom—would show them tonight.

_____

There were two of them, armed and marching. She recognized the one closest to her. "Pablo! Pablo!" She started to call out a third time, but the young soldier turned his head in her direction before she could. The sad, crooked smile he forced after she'd run across the street to greet him, along with the carbine slung over his shoulder, were enough to alert her to a change. She bristled with apprehension, but reached out to Pablo as always.

It was when he withdrew from her attempted embrace that she noticed for the first time their steely eyes and set jaws. The other fellow was a stranger to her, but Pablo was like family. This was all wrong. What had she done to deserve this?

He whispered harshly, "Sister, I cannot! It is forbidden by the commandant's order. You must understand. I can be in bad trouble for even talking to you like this. Please." His look was one of a pleading child, not of the hardened soldier it had been seconds earlier. She understood. But understanding never got in the way of Nicole having her way. Regrouping, she instructed Pablo and the other man to fall into line and continue their patrol. She would walk beside them. All Pablo had to do was listen. He wasn't required to talk. That way she could spare him a reprimand.

The three of them walked along the side of the street in the square, moving away from the garrison, toward the church. Nicole folded her arms as they walked, wishing she might have been allowed to walk arm in arm with Pablo. She thought of Danny, who flew high-speed fighters on peacetime missions, and wondered if he was as rigid as Pablo when he was all military and following orders. She could accept duty as an excuse.

"We haven't seen you. The children miss you, and so do I. We understand—you have a duty, and orders to obey. You are a soldier first, but when the time for soldiering is over—" She stopped, turned, and faced him squarely. "—you come back to the school. Please come back, Pablo. I know you cannot answer me. I understand. I just wanted you to know you are always welcome."

She turned and headed toward the church. She heard him, *sotto voce*, over her shoulder. "I will come back, Sister."

§

She could never tire of this place. Here, in her Sanctuary, where the shade was cool and the water cooler, where solitude reigned over chaos and indecision, nothing could defeat her. This was her hot iron to smooth the wrinkles, her cleansing soap. This place fortified her. She needed the strength, especially now—she'd taken on too much. Her link to a chain of events over which she had no control had become a distraction. Bound to all that was worldly and not spiritual, she had lost the acuity that kept her focused on God's work. What had happened with Chris and Raphael would be resolved for sure, but in God's way, and in God's time. The unsettledness among the villagers would be resolved, in the same fashion. As would be the divine intervention with Maria. The other distractions, the money that still trickled in from donors in places far away, the tightened grip of the military presence, with it Pablo's dilemma, and the still nagging feeling that she was being constantly watched by some sinister force, these, too, would be taken care of by God. The explanation was now clear to her. The same kinds of distractions faced her in this life as they had in her earlier one, and the way to their demise today was the same as it had been that day she knelt before Him in St. Joseph Catholic Church: total acceptance. Take hold of His hand, let all else go. Follow His lead, be guided in His way. When the mind is uncluttered, and the heart has a strong beat, the way becomes clear. It was all so simple.

She broke into song. One of her own, written in high school. The lyrics simple, but full of a deep meaning, full of history with her.

She goes on

> *Like nothing's wrong*
>> *Hides her pain*
>>> *'Neath the sweet refrain*
>>>> *Of her melancholy song*

> *But she knows,*
>> *Yes, she knows*
>>> *It's there*
>>>> *Just over there*

A melody for the soul, comforting her, quieting despair, finally trailing off into a whisper. Then there was total quiet, and peace.

From behind a tree at the edge of the clearing the listener thought about saying nothing. He'd intruded on a very private moment. But silence wasn't an option … he had important work ahead.

"I don't know whether to applaud or just quietly savor the moment."

She spoke his name before turning. "Evan," she said, smiling as she flew across the clearing.

"Oh, Evan," he heard her say again, above the pounding of his heart, as she held him fiercely. Just before she lit into him.

37

WHERE HAVE YOU BEEN? How could you leave like that, without a word? Nun or not, you owed me the respect of a proper good-bye, and at least an occasional word so I wouldn't have to worry about you." She was actually shaking her finger in his face.

And she wasn't finished. "As for your truancy, I have no choice but to make you repeat fourth grade." He hoped her grin was real. They were going to need the levity.

"May I interrupt? I was so enjoying that scolding, but do prefer your humorous side. Besides, I've returned for a reason." He motioned her to sit. It was time for business.

"I bring troubling news. Something you must pay attention to."

Concern showed in her expression, and she grabbed his arm. "Is my family all right?"

"It has nothing to do with your family … but with you, I'm afraid." He sat beside her.

"Evan, I don't understand."

"There is very reliable information about a rebellion, an organized uprising from 'the peaceful north,' to serve as a unification of the anti-government forces that have been operating mostly as splinter groups." He was surprised at her lack of reaction. The next piece of information would surely get her attention. "You are in danger."

She didn't seem too upset. "While you were away, the military moved in. We have the military to protect us from the rebels."

"You can't be that naïve. The soldiers are in Refugio because there are villagers who will be a part of the conflict. There are no marauding rebels up here, only infiltrators who are preaching sedition. They are trained revolutionaries. Trust me, your peaceful villagers are plotting an uprising as you sing your songs and teach their children.

"This will be an armed insurrection," he continued. "Peaceful natives, such as your villagers here in Refugio, will be armed with guns. Innocent blood inevitably will be shed." He gripped her hand. "I have my favorite innocent to protect; I hope you understand."

"Evan," she began, "yes, I see the soldiers with their hard stares and rigid jaws patrol with their rifles, my dear young Pablo among them—Pablo who can no longer spend his time at the school and is not even allowed to talk with me socially—but I do not see the fires of rebellion in the eyes of my neighbors, and there is no talk of any uprising. If there were, I'd certainly have heard it. Or certainly Father Art would have."

"My sources say differently."

"It's useless to debate this. I'm sure you have your reliable sources. If they are correct, then my mission here will be more critical than ever. It will be these peaceful natives who are the targets, not a nun. Or a priest either."

"The same trust that led to the problem with the trees," he said, pointing beyond her, in the direction of the new clearing, "will cost you again, if you are not more careful." He spoke with a sterner tone … authoritative, parental. He must get her attention.

"What do you know of the problem with the trees? You haven't been here in over a month."

"There is talk everywhere. I was in Panama when I first heard of it, quite by chance. That's where the timber is headed, in case you were wondering. The local merchants your brother dealt with are to blame, not the government."

Her reaction was immediate, an expression of suppressed hurt. "Are you all right?" he asked.

"I was just thinking. I suppose one never knows who can be trusted. Is that how they think of me now? Someone who can't be trusted?"

He didn't answer. Instead, he delicately lifted the object hanging from the chain, resting just below her throat. "This is unusual. Something new?"

"It's Chris's. A medallion from a tournament a hundred years ago, back when he was invincible and never questioned it. Before he let doubt take hold."

Montgomery released the medallion. "Ah, yes, Chris the younger brother, the soccer marvel if I recall correctly. What, he just appeared?"

"Yes. He'd heard of the, the—" She was groping.

"Let me guess: the miracle in the mountains. Your brother came down to see his sister the miracle worker."

"Evan, that sounds almost disingenuous the way you say it. It was, I am told, you who brought it to the attention of the entire world in the first place. Now you put such a sarcastic spin on it when you speak of the very thing. I don't understand."

"Let's just say what started out as quite the heartfelt tribute has plagued me from the moment Reuters decided to run with it. It's almost cost me this job, because I refused to retract it when pressured to do so."

"By whom?" she asked.

"*Whom* do you think?"

"I suppose I have an idea, but maybe you should tell me."

"I fear I have spoken too much about it already. I should not have brought it up. Let's just drop it, shall we?"

"My, aren't we touchy."

"Let's don't press it, my dear. It's too fresh a bad memory for me. Maybe later. For now, let's head back to the village. I think Father Art should hear about the state of unrest in these parts. Maybe he can realize that caution and sensibility are called for. Unlike some others who haven't a clue," he added lightly, masking concern.

Through his attempt at humor he was, different from prior form, wary and protective, his other feelings for her put on hold.

———————

Unlike previous reunions, this one was far from lively. The three of them huddled around Father Art's desk in the rectory, framed in bad light and worry over the uncontrollable. Montgomery brought up what he knew about the rebellion, then what he'd overheard in Panama.

Nicole continued to ignore the warnings, clinging instead to the notion of mankind's goodness. "I'm sorry, Evan, but I still don't think Raphael came in here and cold-bloodedly stole the timber. I spent enough time with him, and just don't see that heartless, calculating side. I believe something else happened, something over which he had no control. I'm not sure it matters, really, what actually happened, but I feel better believing Raphael isn't a bad person."

Finally, something Montgomery didn't have to argue with her about. "Regrettably the only thing I can agree with is it doesn't really matter, all the background intrigue, Raphael's character. The sad fact is the timber is gone, and whatever gain this village might have expected gone with it."

He furrowed his forehead. "We need to forget about Raphael. More importantly, have you noticed a change in the village since the news of the timber theft reached them?"

Both Nicole and Father Art had to admit there had been a change. Not only with the villagers, but with the military detachment as well. Father Art told him of the resumption of the armed patrols, Nicole of Pablo's dutifully brusque treatment and the children other than Maria who no longer came to school.

Montgomery repeated the news of a looming insurgence. The dour moment worsened as he added, "There is no horror like war. Forget the uselessness of it all … the elusive peace always just out of reach … the politics. Forget everything except taking whatever precaution you must to evacuate those villagers who are at risk—by that I mean, of course, the women and children—and flee this place until it is safe to return. I am dead earnest."

Nicole and Father Art turned to look at one another. Father Art spoke first. "Monty, I'm sure you mean well, but we can't leave this place just because there is a threat of war. We wouldn't leave if the fighting were right outside that door," he said, pointing toward the church's entrance.

"He's right," Nicole echoed.

"Besides," Father Art continued, "when would we leave? Tomorrow? Right now, perhaps? Think about it, Monty. We can't just uproot ourselves from this mission. That would be the worst form of deserting our responsibility."

Nicole rose. "I'll get us something to eat. It sounds as if we still have a lot to talk about, and I, for one, am starved."

After she'd left the room, Montgomery looked at Father Art. "She doesn't take anything I'm saying seriously. You need to take charge, Art. What if I told you my sources also say everything happens in three days. Would that make a difference?"

The priest's eyes looked past him.

Montgomery followed the priest's gaze to the doorway. Nicole was standing there, her expression momentarily frozen. She stepped back into the room and retook her seat.

"Why did you keep this from us until after I'd left the room? Evan, I—I …" He saw pure disappointment in her downcast look. There wasn't time to plead, to be nice about this.

"Does it make a difference? It shouldn't. You ought to be gathering your schoolchildren up right now, herding them to safety. Bring them here until I can get back with a fleet of trucks."

"Three days, Evan? What happens in three days? And skip the histrionics. I can handle it."

"Yes, very well," he said, making it a point to bare the sharp edge of irritation in his voice. "It seems the army is convinced that is when the strike will take place. It's to be a coordinated effort, all of the northern villages on the same night, a giant rallying cry for the rest of the country to follow. Lest I not make myself quite clear, that means your garrison here is ready and waiting for your peasant group. It will be nothing less than a slaughter, I assure you. Right here in Refugio, and in every other village where men take up arms. The snare is set everywhere."

Her hurtful expression was replaced by one of fright. She stood quickly. "We must warn them. We can't allow this to happen. We—"

"Stop, Sister," interrupted Father Art. "Bring yourself under control. It's not so simple."

"What do you mean, it's not that simple? It is no more complicated than we are not going to let our friends, our parishioners, the parents of my schoolchildren, walk into a bloody ambush. What's not simple about that, Father?"

"Nicole," interrupted Montgomery, "Art—Father Art—is right. You haven't thought of the consequences. Sit down, and listen. If we warn the villagers, the slaughter will still take place, only it's the garrison that will be ambushed. The major and his men will be killed in their sleep, no doubt. It's a no-win situation. We can't meddle. We should just grab the children and go, let what will happen just happen."

She was astonished. It showed in her expression, and it unnerved Montgomery. "You would," she began, "choose the lives of the soldiers over those of the villagers? Are you playing God here, Evan?"

He tossed the challenge back at her, only harder. "And you would let these young soldiers, one of whom Father Art tells me is like a brother to you, die instead? Who is playing God now, Sister?" Anger showed in his voice, and in the red that painted his face and ears.

"Well, we can't just—"

"Sister, calm yourself," Father Art interjected. "The Church, as you know, simply cannot involve itself in the political struggles of these people."

Nicole didn't hesitate. "If I have to, I will report this to the garrison commandant, and our major friend will simply arrest and detain everyone until the threat of this revolution all blows over. Hey, no fighters, no war, right Evan?"

"It's not that easy either. If you report anything to the garrison's commandant, he will call in more troops, and the retribution in this village will be like nothing you can imagine. I venture your wonderful garrison commandant has handled similar uprisings in the south. That's why he was sent here, you can be sure. What these soldiers do to rebels and peasants, you really don't want to know, much less be held responsible for.

"Right now," he continued, "the Church is in the thick of the controversy, because of that stupid idea about the timber. Do you want to make it far worse, like where the Church is held responsible for the loss of life instead of money no one here had any idea about in the first place? Think, Nicole, you're an intelligent woman. Don't make such a rash move. The price would be too dear for even one who prays for a living to bear, I assure you." He looked imploringly at her, searching for some sign that he was getting through.

"That stupid idea was my brother's, I'll have you know. And just so you know the full story, he stood to gain nothing from it. Only the satisfaction of helping out some-one, me included. He had a vision of something better for these 'peasants' as you call them. After only a couple of days here he saw two ways to help them better them-selves. What have you done for them lately, Evan?" Her voice was tremulous.

"Hopefully," he began, "I've given you enough information to save most of their lives. That's what I've done, or at least tried to do for them today." The red was now gone from his face and ears, and all he felt was dismay. "I apologize for the comment about the stu-pidity of the idea. I didn't know it was Chris's, but that's no excuse. I am sorry, Sister."

"Oh, Evan," she said, "that isn't important any more. Truth is, maybe it was a bad idea. We all learned from it, I suppose. But it is important you know my brother's heart was pure. I haven't seen or spoken to him since he left here, but I can promise you that there is no one in this world right now who feels worse than he does about what's happened. And I also know that he will not rest until either it is made right, or he has exhausted every opportunity to make it right."

"Sister," Father Art said, "there is something else we need to consider. Monty has given us some very sensitive information, known to only a few. Certainly not to those the information is designed to bring down." It didn't take long to solve the riddle.

"Let me finish that for you, Father," Nicole said. "You're saying that if I rush to warn our friends, and they move up the timetable a day or two based on an anonymous tip, then Evan is compromised. Is that it, Father?"

Both men were staring at her. The silence in the room was deafening. Nobody moved.

"I'm still hungry," Nicole finally said. "Promise me you two won't hold a secret con-versation while I've gone for food."

As she stood, they heard the loud knock, and a familiar voice. A day early ....

265

†

38

"It's late," Father Art said. "We should all try to get some sleep. Tomorrow morning we can work this out."

"Art's right. I haven't slept in two days ... rushing back here from Panama, with this unheeded—this terribly unheeded—warning," Montgomery added, without looking in any particular direction.

"Tomorrow morning, then," Nicole said with her glare exclusively in Montgomery's direction. "Five o'clock. Before Mass. Good night." She cleared off the desk and left.

When she was gone, Montgomery pleaded. "Make her listen, Art. She will, for you."

"You don't know her very well, Monty. If she doesn't want to leave, the Pope himself couldn't make it happen."

"I hope we don't live to regret this, Art," Montgomery said, pulling the door to the rectory shut.

———————

She knew the answer without having to wait until five the next morning. She could not leave. She could not warn anyone. There was risk in every option. Everyone she cared for could be hurt, or worse, no matter which decision they made.

Surrounded by impossibility, choking with desperate anxiety, she was near collapse with worry. Three days. That's all the time she had. She thought of the two men at the table. The same worried and frightful expressions on her face showed on theirs. There was still time, she told herself. And as long as there was still time, there was hope. Three days to stop the calamity.

Three days to work another miracle.

§

Even as a journalist, a priest and a nun wrestled with their choices, one man in another part of the same hamlet drew strength with each new breath as he instilled inspiration in others who were gathered with him, men who, like he, wanted to strike down tyranny and oppression and had already made their choice. It was time, Raul was telling the group, to set aside fear, it was time to overcome any thought they had at not succeeding, for fear and lack of conviction were worse enemies than the few soldiers they would be attacking tomorrow night.

Yes, he told them, it must be the next night. The many months of preparation, of sharing the dream of freedom, of stories of abuses to the south, of promising a new government, and of showing them how to use the few weapons he'd provided, all of this mix had now come to a boil. They must strike on the following night, he explained, because men allied with their cause had let it be known to the government they would rise up in not one, but three nights, and they would catch their enemy off guard, unprepared for their early attack.

Raul gauged the group's reaction to be favorable at this news. He knew they were frightened, these men who'd never fired a weapon, who'd never taken a life or seen one taken in combat. They needed inspiration, and he was giving it to them. His work tonight only just begun, he bore on. There was much to do yet.

––––––––––––

Major Arturo de los Santos was disturbed. No, it was more than that—he was quite angry. His call for reinforcements had been summarily denied, under the flimsiest of reasons. Two days ago, when he'd first learned from headquarters in the capital city that a rebel strike would be made simultaneously in three days, he had asked for reinforcements. He'd just received a rejection.

He was told to make do with his present complement. No other commandant had requested reinforcements, and he'd given no compelling reason to grant his request.

He'd been faced with this arrogance many times in his career. His ability to overcome its demoralizing effect had served him well. He was undermanned, and cautious enough to let headquarters know it.

He was troubled that word had been leaked that the revolt would commence in three days. These new rebels were not stupid. He was convinced, quite to the contrary, they were more organized than ever. In the few months he'd been in this quiet village, there'd been no sign at all of any insurgent buildup—not a single gunshot fired as a training exercise, not a single gathering of the villagers, and, most importantly, no change in the daily patterns of these meek people ... except for attendance at the school—but that was over the timber deal. All of his careful observations told him there was a new kind of revolutionary leading this group, and that he had best be on close watch.

The major moved quickly at the radio communiqué, summoning his first sergeant, ordering him to assemble the men to ranks in fifteen minutes.

Looking them over, the major for the first time was faced with the prospect of commanding these young men in a battle. He saw them as boys, not yet soldiers. The daily exercises he and the sergeant had led them through were barely a start on the training they should have had. There was no honed edge. Its absence alarmed him, but it was too late. The hands were dealt, bets down.

He gave his orders and, as was his style, words of praise and encouragement. Maybe the extra touch would make a difference. He turned to the First Sergeant. "Sergeant, you may dismiss the men."

His sergeant waited until after the troops had scattered to their posts, the lucky half back to their cots, before he approached the commandant. "Permission to speak, Major?"

"Certainly, Sergeant. You know I always welcome you to speak your mind." He had an idea what was on the sergeant's mind.

"Major, why are we assuming a passive position? Why not grab some of the villagers and make examples of them in front of the others … as we have many times before. Very effectively, as the major will recall." Message received.

"A fine thought, Sergeant. But I am afraid our hands are tied these days, not like before. There are groups, not just the International Red Cross, but others as well, who stake out wars and rebellions and carry great weight with the governments on whose soil they come to monitor activity. They influence such things as how much aid a country will receive, and how much trade a country will be permitted, and, more importantly, whether governments will be recognized officially. These groups, they demand obedience to their rules. They say we cannot make examples of innocent citizens, as the First Sergeant correctly points out we have done in the past. We are to respect what they call 'human rights.' These rights state it is still permissible to kill, but only under the rules of engagement. Yes, it is strange, isn't it? Killing is still acceptable, so long as it is humane, within some set of new rules." The irony hung heavy in the air, like the tension.

The commandant shrugged. "I am sorry, but that is the best explanation I can give."

"I understand, Major. I do not agree with these new rules, but I understand it is not for us to question them. Thank you, Major, sir."

"Will that be all, Sergeant?" The sergeant saluted over his perfunctory *Yes, sir*, and left.

The major felt badly for not being truthful with the first sergeant, who deserved more in the way of an explanation. The major could have told the sergeant why they were here, in Refugio, instead of patrolling the countryside—that headquarters decided to garrison troops in suspected lairs, to lure the rebels into smaller skirmishes rather than allow them to gather numbers and build momentum. Military strategy his sergeant would understand—they would take the fight to the enemy, on the enemy's turf.

He had to admit the idea was sound. If only he had a few more men …

The major weighed his options. He had no idea when, or even if the suspected uprising would take place, or if this particular village was to take part. His soldier's instincts told him he could not rely on the sketchy information from headquarters. What he needed was more complete, more reliable information, the sort of which he had obtained in other places before this one by stealth and cunning. He hoped there was time to exact the kind of intelligence a soldier must have, whether it be to attack his enemy or to defend his position.

Thus as Major Arturo de los Santos was readying for another sortie, his third in as many nights, his thoughts were on finding the enemy. This he was trained to do, and this he would do.

As the military man furtively slipped out a rear door, ready to blend with the shadows in a search for an unknown foe, Raul was winding down his final instructions to the patriots gathered before him, the men he would lead to glory the next night. *They're ready*, he told himself. Their conviction was readily visible; they now joined him in his barely audible exaltations of *Freedom!* and *Down with tyranny!* He'd trained them to use the sidearms and rifles, without firing a shot. Each man could load and reload, even though there were not enough guns for all. Some men would carry their tools—the weapons of true revolutionaries, he'd told them. Hammer and scythe, hoe and pickaxe, machete and pitchfork—his reminders of the true revolutionaries, Lenin, Mao, Castro. He made the patriots feel proud to carry those weapons. But he also knew that success of this operation depended on which men could be counted on to hold up best under fire, which of them could handle the real weapons of warfare, the guns and rifles.

Raul had selected Juan, the most fervent of the lot, to carry a pistol like his own, and Carlos, less intense than Juan but more intelligent, to carry the automatic rifle.

The two carbines were handed to the young men who had spoken the loudest of their anger at having worked for five weeks cutting the large trees, only to forfeit the riches that by rights should have belonged to the village. He counted again; they numbered a dozen faithful. They would have the element of surprise, the equalizer to their lack of arms. They would strike when their enemy was fat and sleeping.

———————

The commandant crept among the homes, as silently as the night air blowing gently through their open windows, his eyes as watchful as those of the forest around him. An unusually quiet night, he thought, and not much light. The little light there was stayed hidden behind clouds filling up for a soft morning rain. The darkness hid him well, but it also slowed him. He encouraged himself to remain patient, attentive. There were lives at stake, his own included.

Tonight there must be no careless rush; this must be done right.

The major persevered, ducking in and out of narrow spaces between homes, careful not to awaken anyone, watchful of the dogs protecting against the snakes hunting their prey at night. Tonight he, too, was a snake.

After reconnoitering for an hour he was convinced there was no force to strike in this village. He'd seen no sign anything was amiss, only the movement through the village of the tall journalist, headed in the direction of his cottage. The major watched as the man stopped and turned in his direction, chiding himself for being spotted by one so untrained in the way of stealth. He did not move until the Englishman was out of sight. The slightest carelessness could be costly.

All was peaceful and quiet. There was only one area left, a small enclave of homes and outbuildings right on the forest's edge, not far from the home of the British journalist. What he sought would be there, or it would not exist. He made way for the last remaining possibility.

———————

It was almost time for the group to break for the night. It was late, and he wanted them rested for tomorrow's work. He needed little sleep, and no comfort from a wife or children, but understood these men did. He would in time, when the business of freedom was settled, but for now would settle for comfort under a convenient tree, and the warmth of his bedroll.

He let the others talk. They were inspired. As he'd been taught, the spirit of freedom is infectious, and here was proof. He broke in only when the noise from the group threatened to rise above a safe level. It was good they fed on each other's inspiration, that his was no longer the only voice they listened to. He took pride in this.

The uninvited visitor silently watched in hiding as Raul savored his accomplishment. Major Arturo de los Santos squinted through a small crack in a back window shutter, then pressed his ear against the cool wood, straining to hear the hushed undertones. There was no mistaking it—the unconfirmed plot was indeed a reality. The few mutterings he could make out were proof this was the unseen enemy, the men who would rise up against his government, do him and his men harm. The unmistakable air of bloodlust radiated from their midst, giving the hardened veteran of many conflicts a chill. Armed with such passion, even an untrained opponent would make a formidable foe.

He counted their number at no more than thirteen, including one he recognized as the likely infiltrator. No doubt trained abroad in revolutionary tactics and the art of subversion, he stood at the head of the group and arrogantly watched the rest work themselves into a silent frenzy. A certain nervousness crowded into the commandant as he listened and watched. While it made sense for him to hasten to the garrison and return with a squad of men, there was also the distinct possibility they would not be here when he returned. He would be no better off once they had scattered. He did have an option. It was risky, but if his plan worked, the rebellious effort in this village would be crushed before it began. If it failed, his men would be leaderless, and would likely fall victim to an attack. There was no time to dwell on it. He decided quickly.

The major stayed put, in the fringe of the shadows, to keep watch over his adversary. He scoffed—these careless fools had not even posted a sentry. How could they expect to run a country?

Raul quieted his group. He told them not to not expend all their passion before the fight. He led them in prayer next, assuring them God was on their side against tyranny. This was their final gathering as slaves. By this time the next day they would be freedom fighters, free men. As they filed quietly from the door to the hutch, Raul gave each a last parting handclasp, a firm, silent reminder of the task only hours ahead.

He gloated triumphantly in the knowledge his compatriots had leaked reports of the rebellion commencing in three days. The preemptive strike would surely catch the military unprepared. He allowed himself a brief moment of smug satisfaction.

r . r .   b r y a n

He knew some would die, perhaps even himself. At twenty-nine, he had already experienced much death in his life. First an older brother, a dreamer such as he and, shot down not in battle but in a crowd while another spoke out against oppression. As a boy of twelve he had held the bloodied body of his dead brother in his arms, vowing revenge. Raul was not afraid to die. Because of this, his followers, too, were prepared to sacrifice their lives.

He'd trained them well.

Every uprising in every village would not be successful. But he knew his would be. There had been no discovery of his group, no infiltration by an informant, of that he was certain. Sidetracked only momentarily by, as it had turned out, the most fortuitous of circumstances, their zealousness had returned with a heightened intensity even greater than he'd hoped for. Word had spread in the region of the government's deceitful treatment of Refugio's timber harvest, and it had served as a rallying cry. How ironic, he smiled, that his coincidental encounter with the nun had served as a source of his rejuvenated effort. Of course he knew that there had been no underhanded theft by the government, but in this game one took advantage of opportunity. First in this village, then in the others as he spread the word to his colleagues the news that would further their cause.

His mind still on the thoughts that drew him from the caution he was trained never, ever to relax, Raul stepped from the doorway, and pulled the door shut. Wary that discovery of even the slightest disturbance to routine—even in the form of a door to an empty house inexplicably left ajar—might spell doom to the effort, Raul took pains to guard against any such discovery. He reached for the branch that he would sweep the telltale footprints from the ground. He would leave no sign that anyone had been there.

The tight grip he felt overtake him came so quickly, so unexpectedly. Before he could react, the hand over his mouth jerked back, and the piercing pain in his back froze him in terror. His eyes opened widely. He could not cry out. He could not resist, the paralysis of the pain and the grip entirely subduing him. *What was happening?* He tried vainly to collect his thoughts. Warmth ebbed within, and the piercing was not as painful, yielding to a turning, twisting kind of pressure instead. He wanted to resist, but had lost the strength. His thoughts cleared enough to know this was a nightmare, that he must fight it, not succumb to it. But his strength was gone, and the warmth he felt was the blood flowing from his body. His life was draining and he could only struggle mentally to stop it. *How had this happened? What had gone wrong? Why?*

———————

As these questions raced through the dying man's mind, the soldier kept the pressure on the hilt, turning and twisting, destroying the man's liver. A sure kill, just not as clean as the throat. But the man had bent toward something—a branch?—before he could strike the jugular, leaving only a split second to reverse course, to instinctively plunge the tip of the blade into his back instead. It struck bone and cartilage first, then yielded to vulnerable tissue. Death would be as silent, just not as quick. It would be just as effective when the man's lifeless form was dragged into the center of the village, to serve as an example. He pressed harder, and as he did, leaned in closely to the man's ear, whispering, "You swine. You shriveled excuse for a man, you are no soldier, you are hardly worth this killing effort. You are a pathetic waste of even a dreamer. You never had any chance, none of you. Rot in hell, and know that even as you die, so shall your comrades."

He did not hear the steps behind him, and had no time to react as the cold steel pressed to the back of his head and the steel alloy hammer simultaneously made contact with the cartridge's brass percussion cap, taking the slug's short trajectory straight through the thin layer of epidermis and into his brain, through the cerebral hemisphere and into and through the corpus callosum, bringing instantaneous death. A lifetime of memories became splattered matter, the exiting projectile cleanly erasing the blackboard.

Raul fell to the ground as his killer's grip on the knife handle loosened. The major's body followed, slumping onto the revolutionary's.

Juan Pedro de la Zea viciously pushed the soldier aside as he reached for his fallen comrade. He did not even know the young man's name. He held his compatriot in his arms, and pulled him to a spot in the dew-wet grass. There was much blood … too much blood. What little life remained would not serve their cause. He whispered gently to the man.

"My leader, I came back to thank you for entrusting your confidence in me. I am too late to stop this cowardly dog from attacking you from behind, but he will attack no one again. He is gone, and I spit on his worthless body."

"Good friend," Raul struggled to say, "you must get me to our men." Juan urged the man to save his strength, not to talk, but to listen. Juan Pedro de la Zea, descendant of the mighty Mayan dynasty that once ruled this land, would carry on. The soldiers would pay for this cowardly act.

The dying man smiled at Juan's words, too weak to say anything more, the warmth of the earlier moment now giving way to a coldness spreading quickly. Raul blinked silent encouragement with eyelids that would soon not move at all. He would not live to see it, but he would die in the serenity of knowing that his devoted disciple would carry on, would be victorious.

He could barely hear now. It was as if the man speaking to him were far away, and the words were taking forever to reach him. Passionately they still flowed, and he could see the fire in the man's eyes, feel the strength in the arms that held him. The last sounds he heard in life, the ones that froze and dilated his eyes at the instant of death, were not those consoling words of passion and purpose, not a send-off draping him in the peaceful security of knowing that they would succeed. No, the words that froze him in death were unmistakable—his comrade would seize this moment to call his brothers to arms, not the next night, but this very night.

Juan Pedro de la Zea, revolutionary, would lead them in victory *tonight.*

39

Evan Montgomery instantly recognized the all too familiar sound of a gunshot. He'd heard very few since the Sixties, in his other lifetime. But this one was unmistakable, and it was ominous. He sprang from bed, where he'd lain awake and tormented since leaving Nicole and Father Art. He'd finally left the church when it became obvious he could not convince them their lives were in peril if they stayed. His own life, he told them, was not, as the revolutionary movement would need journalists to spread their cause, to report on their successes. Priests and nuns were expendable; they did not even count when it came to protections from war crimes mandated by the human rights watch groups—look what had just happened in Rwanda.

They had still been arguing when Father Suarez, the archdiocesan courier, entered the church at ten-thirty.

"Father Suarez, you're not due until tomorrow. And it's so late," Father Art said. "Come in, have a seat. We have some food if you're hungry."

"There isn't time. Your lives are in danger, and—"

"We've heard, from our friend Monty here," Father Art said. "We were just discussing it."

"Good, that saves precious time. Father, Sister, the archbishop has sent me to fetch you to safety until the threat of rebellion is over. Hurry, there's no time to lose. We have other churches to evacuate." Father Suarez was motioning them to the door when Nicole spoke up.

"Father Suarez, it is precisely because of the rebellion that we cannot leave. We will be needed … there will be wounded to tend to, children to comfort."

Father Art supported her. "She's right, Father. We can't leave."

The messenger told them it was not their option to stay, the Holy Roman Catholic Church, through him, the archbishop's own messenger, was ordering them to leave, and to do so immediately. It was, he admonished, not their choice.

Neither priest nor nun could be persuaded to leave.

"I cannot condone this willful disobedience of the Church," Father Suarez said, "but neither can I tarry here and risk getting others to safety. May God have mercy on you." And he was gone, leaving an enraged Evan Montgomery to continue.

"I cannot for the life of me understand what it is that moves you to stay here. You will not be doing God's work to die innocently, worse yet viciously at the hand of some outraged, warmongering rebel, or some miscreant villager who might somehow hold you responsible for that bedeviled thing with the trees.

"Those Godawful trees," he finished, slamming his hand on the desk before him. Neither the noise nor the sudden movement startled either Nicole or Father Art, who were quickly becoming numbed to the events around them. They had cast their lot, and were not looking back, and Montgomery knew as much. His perturbation was exceeded only by his growing anger.

After nibbling at the cold snack Nicole served the group, and agreeing to meet in the morning, he'd headed home, pausing only long enough on the way to glance over his shoulder at some shadowy apparition. Satisfied it was just the product of a hyperextended imagination, he'd gone on, not stopping again until he'd reached his small house and begun his watch, a watch that he knew might last until dawn, and if not this next dawn then the next, or the next. He felt powerless to do anything except wait.

The gunshot had changed all that. Still dressed, he needed only to slip on his boots before he was out the door, and on his way to protect a loved one.

§

Juan lifted his comrade onto his shoulders. He would not leave him here, in ignominy beside the wretched commandant. Juan knew where his leader belonged.

He'd traveled only a few paces before he met two group members who had heard the gunshot. Juan hastily told them what had happened. Before doubt could take hold, he reined them back in, authoritatively, decisively, telling them to quickly gather the others and meet at his house, before darkness gave way to light. *Before you lose your passion and return to being the cowards you were.*

When one of them hesitated, Juan unleashed a torrent of well-chosen words, challenging him in the name of their fallen comrade to do his duty. As the fire lit in the man's eyes, Juan passed his first test as a leader.

He carried Raul to the village center and set him upon the porch of a home near the garrison. "Watch from here," Juan said. "You will see great things tonight."

While evil spread throughout Refugio, Evan Montgomery warily made his way to the church. The total darkness came and went as the cloud cover parted, then resealed, providing just enough light. Slipping from house to house, not knowing what was out there, only that the air was heavy with signs of danger, he took care to avoid detection. He stopped, paralyzed with fear, when he saw others also quietly moving about. Whatever was to have happened in three days was not destined for the wait. It was happening now. And he was in the middle of it, trapped between the safety of his own cottage and the church, vulnerable to the whim of some equally fear-riddled villager who might mistake him for an enemy. He was not prepared to die. The need to warn the young woman he loved strangely did not override his innate need for self-preservation. His heart raced, the beads of perspiration that earlier dotted his forehead and arms now a torrential river of sweat. He slunk back into the darkest shadows, his back pressed against a cool wall, his arms outstretched downward, fingers splayed against the wall, frantically clawing into the adobe, as if some medieval alchemy might magically blend his flesh and bone into the hardened mud. He feared his heart would explode through his chest, that the pounding in his head would signal his hiding place.

Go to her, you coward. She needs your help.

The dancing shadows were gone. He peeled himself from the wall, felt the stinging pain in his fingertips. He wiped the oozing, sticky wetness onto his pant legs, and readied for the sprint. *Don't be afraid, Nicole. I'm coming for you.*

In seconds he was gasping at the church door. It was unlocked. He let himself in. The chapel was eerily quiet, and pitch black. Warily he tiptoed through the pews, headed for her room. He would alert her first, then the priest. Twice he banged his shins. He ignored the pain. Sweat reappeared, the torrents again running into his eyes. He was too close to stop now. She was just around the next corner. Ambient light shone through a crack in a nearby window, illuminating the hallway. When he reached it, he rushed for her doorway. Candlelight flickered through the partly opened door. He whispered her name aloud. Again. There was no answer. A third time, he spoke her name into the doorway space. Fearing the worst when she still did not answer, he bolted into the room.

It was empty. She was gone.

r . r .   b r y a n

Cradling Tomas in one arm, her free hand clasped in Maria's, she led the others along the treeline, in a direction away from the village center. Whatever was happening—and she knew something was; she'd known it the instant the shot rang out—she would guide her children to safety. The game of war the men would fight would not claim her babies as victims. Welcome expressions of relief had graced the faces of the parents at the sight of the nun at their doorways. Few words had been spoken. Far too much was already understood. She'd told those parents who wanted to come with their children they must not, that a large group would draw too much attention. They must trust her, she pleaded.

No parent stood in her way.

She saw ahead to the small hut, the one that stayed empty. It would make a safe haven while she went for the others. Jorge could watch over this first group. He was the elder, the one she must count on. She urged them on with equal measures of praise and patience. They were almost there.

They were gathered in hiding not far from the entrance to the garrison. The group knew of their fallen leader, and the major. Miraculously the garrison was still quiet. Juan told his followers that the soldiers were asleep, or inattentive. *Now is the time to strike!* Grabbing each man by an arm or shoulder, fiercely urging his full devotion, the new leader prepared them. They must move quickly; daylight was their worst enemy.

Coolly, he surveyed the fortress. Its front entrance was well lit. There must be a sentry posted inside the locked door, perhaps even two. Once they were through the doorway they could not be stopped. But storming the door would cost them surprise, precious lives, could jeopardize the mission. Juan glanced over to his fallen comrade. *How had he planned to get us inside?*

As he tormented over the unexpected, a thought came to mind. He gathered his men in closely, and told them to remain hidden in the shadows. He would return in moments. Sensing doubt, he pressed them for obedience. He demanded it. Then he was off to see an old enemy.

Something ahead made her stop. Through the darkness she saw a form on the ground, in front of the small house. It could only be one thing. She put a finger to her lips, and the children became silent. She set Maria down, placing Jorge's hand on the child's shoulder, motioning her group to stay put. They should not be afraid, she whispered, promising to keep them in sight.

Dismay wrestled with fright as she inched her way forward, crouching as she gained ground on the motionless body. She prayed her fear would not be realized.

She leaned cautiously over the uniformed body, laying face down. As she tremulously knelt beside the form, she caught the unmistakable scent of fresh blood. It made her nauseous, her legs wobbly. Touching the body, she knew instantly it was lifeless. She made the sign of the cross and kissed her crucifix. There was blood on the ground, on the back of his head, more yet on his outstretched hand. Nicole pulled him toward her, gasping in horror to see the commandant's face. A man she knew only briefly, a good man, gone now. She rested both her hands on his arm, wondering what brought this on. How did such a seasoned soldier become trapped in death, murdered so savagely? Who had done this? Fear turned to anger.

She thought of the children, who must not see the sight of this man with the gaping wound to his head. She tried to drag the major away, to get him around to the side of the house, out of sight of the front doorway. But pulling with all her strength was not enough; he was too heavy. There was no choice but to walk the children around his body. Absorbed in her thoughts, she was surprised by the snarl.

"What are you doing!" Not a question, but a command, it demanded she stop. Turning, she found herself staring into Juan's maddened gaze. She recognized him as the strange fellow whose looks always averted her own, who refused even the most ordinary conversation, whose shy wife remained silently behind the door and windows of their home … the one whose cold, empty eyes brought chills to her skin. *What is he doing here?*

"Get away from him!" he snapped, shoving her aside. The abrupt sweep of his arm knocked her to the ground. He did not apologize, or help Nicole to her feet. Bewildered, anger building, she stood, smoothed her habit, brushed the dirt from its folds. She watched him bend over the dead soldier and rummage through his pockets. When he finished, it was obvious he hadn't found what he was looking for. He stood, his legs straddling the corpse, hands on hips. He was in deep thought. Then he jerked almost impulsively, and quickly bent down again. She watched, aghast as he unhooked the dead man's belt and tugged at his trousers. Now it was her turn to intervene in another's work over the lifeless form.

"Juan, is it? And just what are you doing? You leave this man alone!" She pushed hard, barely knocking him off balance.

He recovered, and caught himself before striking her again. His menacing eyes pierced right through her. Nicole was filled with terror. She was face to face with a crazed madman.

He reached into his belt for something. The darkness obscured the object he withdrew, until he raised it to her face and she stared into the borehole of a handgun. She saw frothing at the corners of his mouth as his eyes, widened enough already to suit her, grew even wider.

She reacted instantly. "Juan, you may kill me before this night ends, but even you, father of two small children yourself, would not take my life before the eyes of those children who stand over there, not a dozen paces from us." She motioned to his side, where the six children were frozen in their own terror. He replaced the gun in the front of his pants.

"I need this man's clothes. I came for a key, but there is none. So I will have his uniform instead. Now stay out of my way, and I will leave you alone." He hesitated, then added, "For now, anyway."

"I will not let you take the clothes from this man. Not while these children watch. You will have to kill me first, Juan."

Another menacing smile crossed his lips. "I have no time for your defiance. Either help me pull this pig out of their sight, where I will have his clothing and you may then return to the children, or I shall put a bullet through your heart, and while you lay dead on the ground I will strip this coward right in front of them. Decide, *now!*" he said, reaching again for the gun.

Choose your battles wisely, her father always said. She looked at the huddled group. It was not a difficult choice.

"I will help you move him. And I will not stand in your way."

"Be thankful, woman. Now grab his other leg," he said, lifting one himself, "and help me pull him to the side of the house. I only need a minute to get what I want, then you may return to your precious children. And when you do," he added, "I do not want to see you again this night. A great battle will be won by our friends, a victory for freedom. People will die. Pity you might be one of them."

Nicole didn't respond, doing her best to pull her part of the major's weight. Once the body was safely out of the children's sight she ran back to her flock. She was comforting the children when Juan tore by, dressed in the major's uniform, eyes blazing with fury.

He was talking to himself.

§

"Wake up, Art!" Evan Montgomery shook the priest hard. Desperation rivaled urgency in his voice. When all he succeeded in arousing was mumbles from the sleeping priest, he rushed for the doorway, a rescue mission in mind. Leaving, he heard something over his shoulder.

"What's happened, Monty? What is it?"

"It's begun, Art. Something's changed, or maybe the plan all along was to deceive. Regardless, the revolt has begun. Come on, man, there's work to be done!"

Father Art rose quickly, dressing while Montgomery fidgeted. "Did you alert Sister Nicole?"

"I tried. She wasn't in her room. I don't know where she is."

Something Montgomery saw alarmed him. "Art, are you all right?"

"Just a slight pain, here," he said, pointing to his chest. "And I'm a little short of breath."

Montgomery hesitated. He thought to suggest his friend lay down, but shrugged off the idea. There were lives to protect. One in particular.

§

Elsewhere the group of fighters encircled their new leader, nodding with approval at his ingenuity.

Juan whispered instructions. When he was certain they all understood and each man was still prepared for what lay ahead—for there was no turning back now, he assured them—he stepped into the street and made for the dim light of the garrison's doorlamp.

He stopped suddenly, placing his hands over his ears. The demons were awakening. Howling, they beckoned him to do what must be done. *Forget the revolution! Get back to her!* Their screeching pounded in his head. How much longer could he deny them?

§

Peering cautiously, the two sentries glanced through the eyehole. The light tap on the garrison door seconds earlier had alerted them. They saw the silhouette of their commandant, holding a pistol in one hand while he stomped an impatient foot and waved the sentries outside with hurried circular motions of his free hand.

They watched closely. The major left through the rear door to do his reconnoitering. They'd heard the shot. Concluding he was in danger, and did not want to risk reentering the compound through the rear door, the two men instinctively snapped into action, freed the bolted door, and stepped outside to rescue their commandant.

Death was swift and silent.

Juan was surprised at the ease with which he could kill, and not be bothered by death.

He waved the men over, and told them to hide the newest casualties.

Then he led his men inside the garrison. Nothing would stop them.

§

With three more children safely in tow, Nicole rushed to the next familiar home. Obsessed with concern for their safety, she moved almost mechanically. She was beyond fear. Slowed only by her cargo, she hastened to the doorway a few paces ahead. She expected to find two more there.

The sudden eruption of gunfire rocked the night's stillness. Nicole froze, picturing armed soldiers opening fire on the villagers. *Pablo!* There wasn't time to worry about him. Her children must come first. She held her group steady, unsure if it was safe to move.

An incandescent glow framed them a fraction of a second before the blast. The shock from the explosion spread a tingling sensation over her. *This is insane. What is happening? Heavenly Father, please guide us to safety. Please protect these children.* Nicole wrapped her arms around the youngsters. She whispered soft words of comfort over their whimpering cries, urging them not to be afraid, to stay with her—she would lead them to safety. She held them close, crouched low to the ground, calming them as only a loving mother can.

The gunshots continued and the sky flickered more menacingly. Nicole heard the soft cries of her children, saw their trusting expressions. At the door, Nicole shouted above the noise, begging to let her take the children inside to safety. The door opened slowly. Firm assurances were given to more parents, and five more of them headed for the rendezvous with Jorge and the others.

Afternoons on their tiny soccer pitch gave them the strength and stamina for this nighttime flight from peril. She marveled as well at their teamwork, evident each time a grip came loose and the group waited for the straggler. Gradually, the frightened but courageous group made its way to the small house where six others anxiously awaited.

Nicole surveyed the group. There were eleven of them, as calm and settled as could be expected. The explosions had stopped—only an occasional gunshot pierced the air—a good time to go after more children. She looked at brave young Jorge, whose eyes pleaded with her to trust him to protect the others.

The next explosion came just as she reached to pat his head and say *yes*.

40

THE DOOR CRASHED OPEN, banging against the inside wall, slamming with such force it snapped back shut. Almost. The door stopped shy enough of the jamb to leave a narrow opening. She swallowed her breath as the children yelped in fear. The sky shone a bright red-orange through the doorway slit. Trembling, Nicole inched her way forward. She reached out gingerly for the clasp, just out of reach … fingertips barely touching it … almost within her grasp … so close …

The door burst open again, her delicate, fingertip hold helpless to slow it. She shrieked. The children shrieked. The air rang with the thud of boot heels at the doorstep. The group huddled in terror. A sense of helplessness overpowered them all. Eyes shut, Nicole prayed again.

The heavy but unmistakable accent of Evan Montgomery ended their desperation. Relief swallowed fear whole as she looked up into his eyes and saw he held two children in his arms, and had three more in tether. He spoke hurriedly.

"Take these five, Sister, and stay here. I'll bring others as I find them!"

"I don't understand, Evan. What—where—"

"There's no time to talk. Look, Father Art and I were searching for you when the fighting started. When I saw you headed for this hut, I knew you'd be safe here, so I reported back to Father Art."

Montgomery put a hand on Nicole's shoulder. "I think he's had a heart attack, or is about to." He kept a strong hand on her shoulder as she tried to rush past him. "No, Nicole, it isn't safe. Besides, I took these children from Teresa and another woman, who have gone for more. They know to bring them here. There is no need for you to search for others."

"But what about Father Art? I can't just leave him out there. I must go and help him."

"Father Art set up a temporary hospital in the church. He's in pain, but he is able to care for the wounded. They will not bother him."

"They will not bother me, either, Evan. I've heard enough. I am going to my priest, and will tend to any wounded." She turned to Jorge and the two oldest girls.

"Jorge, you and these two, stay here and watch the younger ones until Teresa comes. Do you understand me?"

Jorge convincingly nodded yes, the two girls less so. Jorge made leaving easier. "Sister, go and help others. We will be safe." She saw the fierce determination of a much older boy in his expression. Her way became clear. Nicole rushed to Maria, gave her a special look, and a special hug, and returned to the doorway, where she met the weak resistance offered by her British friend.

Montgomery refused to move aside. Glare met glare. Neither spoke, but her unspoken words filled volumes. She defiantly twisted her way around him. He stood no chance of success.

As she reached the doorway, he grabbed her arm and spun her around. He spoke harshly. "You listen to me. This is so utterly irresponsible and foolish, but I know there's no stopping you. If you must go, then do it my way. You stay with me, understand? Do not let me out of your sight, do not argue with me if I stop, and do everything I tell you to do. Is that understood?"

There was something vaguely like a muffled *Yes* as she bolted through the doorway, headed straight for the church. She nearly collided with Teresa, who brought three more children.

"Maria and Tomas are safe in the house. Evan and I are going to the village, to help Father Art, and the wounded." Teresa grabbed her arm. Fear showed in the woman's face as she spoke.

"Sister, Carlos—my Carlos—he is among those who have brought this war to our village tonight. Watch for him, Sister. Please watch for him."

This news chilled and numbed Nicole. It seemed inconceivable Carlos would be a part of this. That thought slowed her for a moment. She thought of her father, who'd often said you could know someone all your life, but never really know them. This was no time, no way, to experience that lesson.

"I will watch for Carlos, don't worry. And I will tell him where you, Maria and Tomas are, and that you're safe." She hugged her friend. "Now I must go."

She raced beside Montgomery for the church. Her greatest fears were for her priest and young Pablo. The thought of Father Art in danger, suffering perhaps from a heart attack, brought home even more the sheer lunacy of this night. Innocent children put in harm's way, a caring, fine man dead, his corpse vilified by a madman, and Father Art imperiled. She wondered who else she might find wounded, or in worse condition. Would this night end with this village intact, or would the burning fires ahead level it to the ground by morning? This was more uncertainty than she could deal with until she reached the church.

She ran even harder, easily outdistancing Montgomery, who was too winded to keep up ... who failed to see the overhang on the building. Carelessly, he would regret for the rest of his life, that in the instant he took his eyes from Nicole and put them on the path the overhang met his forehead. The force knocked him unconscious.

Nicole, a full thirty paces ahead, never heard his shout, never saw him collapse.

She would never know that he had tried to slow her.

She would never know of his sense of failure.

She would never know of his love for her.

41

AHEAD, FIGURES RAN IN all directions. More bodies lay on the ground. For the first time she saw the flames rising. They came from within the garrison. She turned, looking for Evan, but he was not there. She started back for him, but a familiar voice stopped her in mid-stride.

"Sister," the voice weakly hailed. She looked all around, but saw no one, no hint from where the voice called out. She called back.

"Pablo?"

"Yes. Over here."

She found Pablo hidden in some of the same shadows in which she'd earlier taken temporary refuge. He sat upright, his legs propped against a wall. She bent down to him. The flickering light from the blaze exposed a wet, crimson-colored chest, and the pale face of one who had lost much blood.

"Oh, my Pablo," she said, gingerly brushing away the lock of hair hanging into his eyes. "Can you walk?"

"I don't know, Sister. I am so weak. And I hurt all over."

A sense of morbid hopelessness overcame her as she held the lovely boy. His wound was mortal. The compress she fashioned with her veil was useless to stop the life oozing from his chest. The weight of it all began crashing around her. She had so bravely stood in the face of danger this night. She had exceeded any personal expectation, any duty imposed by her Church. She'd been thrust into a war that made no sense, was surrounded by violent death because of it. She wanted to cry, to let the tears flow freely down her face, as she had when she was a child, when her father would, mysteriously somehow, make the bad go away.

She thought of just giving up. There was a quiet place she knew, just a short distance away, where the water stayed cool and fresh and the wind soothed and made music with her chimes, where she could be safe and pretend this was not happening, and when it was over she could crawl out and pretend it had not happened.

Pablo's crying brought her back. He sobbed softly, repeating *Mama, Mama*. Incited, Nicole stood, urging Pablo to try as hard as he could to stand. If he would try, she would help him to the church; it was only a few paces across the way. She promised him they would be safe there.

If it were death he would encounter this night, it would be with dignity.

The walk seemed to take forever. A weary Father Art met them at the door. Together he and Nicole guided Pablo to one of the pews, where they laid him down. Nicole folded a blanket and placed it under his head. The boy smiled up at her, and started to speak.

"Shhh," she whispered, her forefinger to his lips. She wiped his brow, and sang softly.

His eyelids drooped, and he turned his head into the pew. His breathing was shallow.

Nicole looked around the church. There were wounded everywhere, being tended by sisters, wives and mothers. Other groups gathered around lifeless forms covered in white sheets stained deep red. Several women knelt beside the crimson-stained covers, their shoulders noticeably shaking. She would tend to them in a moment, when Pablo no longer needed comfort.

For now, she sat with the young man who'd come to her in friendship, and who'd brought so much enjoyment to her children. He began coughing. Pain registered on his face. She lifted his head onto her lap, sliding the blanket under the dampened coal black hair, and began to run her fingers smoothly over his forehead. She whispered soft, comforting words as she felt his skin growing cool, his breath shortening. Drops from her eyes ran down her face, and fell onto his.

She bent slightly, kissed his forehead., and whispered her prayer. "God bless you, my sweet Pablo."

———————

Father Art sat down beside Nicole after concluding Pablo's last rites. "Sister, I am sorry you must endure this, but I am relieved to see you are safe. I have been so worried about you." He patted down Pablo's chest, then dropped the bloody rag into a pile of many others. Air whistled from the wound as Pablo's lungs filled. Father Art returned Nicole's saddened look with a light pat on her shoulder. She spared him the burden of making light deathbed conversation.

"Evan told me you might have had a heart attack. Are you doing all right?"

"I'm fine, just some shortness of breath, that's all. And a bit of a sharp pain, but I'm fine, really."

He lied. The truth would have served no purpose. He watched Nicole comfort the lad. A curious irony occurred to him. Here lay a boy, death so close, and she gave him the same nurturing comfort she had young Maria. One child survived; another would not. Was it to be a one miracle performance? He was dwelling on this mystery when he heard a commotion in the vestibule. He turned to see Juan, Carlos and a group of men enter, the angry look of death on their faces. The gripping pain in his chest returned. He fought to breathe. Nausea set in.

§

"It is finished," spoke Juan to the gathering in the church. "We are victorious! We have conquered our foe. He is vanquished! Long live freedom! Long live liberty!"

The followers echoed his chant. Their adrenaline still flowing, Juan and his followers were in high spirits, celebrating exuberantly. Busy tending the wounded, the others in the church did not react.

This was the leader's crowning moment. He craved the victor's validation. "Will none of you share in the glory?" He scanned the room, but found no takers. Disappointed, he turned to leave and had all but stepped through the doorway when he saw Nicole in the shadows. Rage seethed within him as he saw her administering aid to the enemy. Brandishing his weapon, he strutted to her, intoxicated with his own sense of accomplishment. She looked up at him with tired, imploring eyes, and spoke.

"Savor your moment, enjoy whatever sweetness you may from the night's butchery, but let it end now." She continued smoothing Pablo's forehead.

Juan knew the look she gave him. He understood the message perfectly, but had no intention of leaving the church until his work was finished.

He stood over them, squinting at the wound. The boy had no color, and was all but finished. Still, the soldier breathed, and Juan had vowed none of the soldiers would breathe after this night. The three captives waiting outside would know the meaning of death very soon, he told those in the church. But first, this boy must be given up, to join his comrades outside in a soldier's death. Nicole held tighter.

"Sister," Juan said through clenched teeth, "let him go. Allow my men to take him outside with his fellow vermin. Let him die honorably, not at the hem of your soiled habit!" *Kill her! Kill her now!* the voices hammered at him from within.

"Do not harm this boy," she said, a menacing look of a different kind coming from her eyes. "You can see that he is dying. He will not live long enough to be dragged by your men into the street. Allow him this final dignity. Please."

She looked at Carlos, standing next to the menacing madman. "Carlos, your family is safe. Teresa and your children are safe. Speak to Juan, tell him this is wrong. I beg you."

Rage erupted from the leader. "Take them both!" he screamed. "Take them both outside! Do as I say!" The demons were still chanting. *Kill her! Kill her!*

There was no movement at all from the few men who stood beside Juan. Carlos was a statue. There was no glory in this for him.

Juan turned to his followers. "She is our enemy too. Don't you see that for yourselves? She stole our future, now she aids our enemy. This makes her our enemy! She must also pay a price for opposing us." The demons were hard at work.

"Take her!" he shouted again, more forcefully this time. "Take them both outside with the others!" The madness was nearly complete.

Still no one stepped forward. Juan's expression changed to one of bewilderment. *It should not be this way. Why don't they obey? Why don't they honor their leader's command?*

Ignoring Juan, Nicole continued to comfort Pablo. The boy was murmuring something, a final prayer perhaps. She put her ear next to his lips, still cradling his head in her lap, still gently brushing her fingertips across his brow. The movement was too quick for her to see, to defend.

"Cowards! If you will not follow orders, I will do it myself!" Juan reached for the dying soldier, grabbing his arm, pulling him from the nun's grasp.

"No!" she screamed. "Stop, do not do this!" She held as tightly as she could.

Juan's grasp of the soldier's arm slipped, and he stumbled backward. Regaining his balance, the humiliated madman said nothing, only stepped forward, his arm extended with the instrument of death pointed at the source of his anger. One step, then another, toward the target that was deathly still but for the gentle rocking of the comforting arms.

42

THE NOISE FROM THE shot reverberated throughout the small church. Nicole felt the impact from the slug into Pablo's heart, and a searing, sharp pain crease her leg. Paralyzed by a tidal wave of thoughts cresting in her mind, before any sense could be made of the terror of the instant, she numbly held firm her embrace. As the noise died and the warmth of the liquid began to soak the gown of her habit, the body in her arms sagged lifelessly and reality set in.

She looked up, into the eyes of the madman. The pistol, its barrel still emitting a wisp of smoke, was shaking in his hand, still outstretched, still pointing at the boy whose life was mercifully ended. Her gaze followed the trajectory's path, and came to rest on Pablo's heart, the organ that once beat so strongly, that knew the joy of life, and youth, and happiness. Images of Pablo, gliding effortlessly across their small *futbol* pitch, expertly dribbling the ball, of that wondrous day when he and Chris had spellbound a group of children with their magic, flashed across her mind. She looked down, and saw a different Pablo, his eyes half-closed in death, and a surge of relief mixed with anger overcame her.

"May Almighty God forgive you for the cowardly murder of this innocent boy." Droplets of her grief fell onto the blood-soaked chest still resting on her lap. She continued to gently rock the body of the fallen youth.

"Murder, you say?" came the guttural, spittle-spraying response. The gun was still pointed, the hand holding it shaking as he spoke. "Murder? It is not murder to strike down one's enemy, to fight for freedom!" He searched his comrades for a sign of approval. There was none. There were only the astonished, wide-eyed expressions of men unaccustomed to such things. The madman's gaze shifted to the gun, then to the dead soldier, then to the nun. The rage returned. To hell with these cowards who stood around him; he would do what must be done. He, Juan Pedro de la Zea, would finish this.

Grabbing Nicole's arm, driven by voices within him shrieking and howling as banshees, he yanked her slight frame from under Pablo's body. The terrorist pulled her close, pressing his face to hers. "We shall see now, Sister, who your God shall protect." He spun and lunged for the open door, dragging Nicole behind him.

———————

Strangely Nicole felt no pain from the wound to her leg. She felt powerless to combat the force that controlled her, that caused the body of her young soldier to be dumped onto the floor, not far from where Father Art lay, clutching his own chest. The surreal image of the priest sprawled under the pew stayed with her as Juan shoved her into the street.

The night was still ablaze with the red-orange glow of flames rising skyward. A crowd stood in the center of the street, encircling three uniformed men. Nicole knew them by sight, but not their names. Juan threw her onto the ground beside the men. She heard only muted sounds. She looked up once and saw the face of de la Zea, his fiery eyes trained on her. Pulling herself to her knees, she began praying. Fear pounded at her breast.

It was at that moment she realized Death might be staring at its next victim, right through the crazed eyes of the madman who glared at her.

§

Evan Montgomery opened his eyes. He felt the dull ache and the sharp pain in his head simultaneously. Barely conscious, groggy from the blow, he tried to sort things. Why was he crumpled on the ground like this? *Where is Nicole?*

He gently touched the wound on his forehead. Rubbing the coagulating droplets between his fingers, he listened for sounds, anything to orient him. He saw the flickering sky, and remembered the fire from the garrison. He strained to hear more, but heard nothing except the faraway sounds of a roaring fire, sounding curiously like waves softly lapping at a sandy shoreline, one on which he'd once lain, he was certain, but at this moment a memory so far recessed it was all but lost.

Then he heard someone shouting … an unfamiliar voice, but recognizably angry. Warning sensors went off.

He stood, his head throbbing and his legs wobbly, and shakily followed the sound.

§

Her head bowed, hands clasped at her lips and eyes closed, she prayed. Lips moving, words soundlessly coming from them, she spoke the prayers by rote.

Our Father, Who art in heaven, hallowed be Thy name. Thy kingdom come, Thy will be done, on earth as it is in heaven. She was trembling.

§

As Evan Montgomery stumbled toward an unimaginable destiny, the priest's eyes opened. His chest felt as if it were being pressed under the weight of a mountain. He tried to move, but the pain was too great. He became aware of two women trying to help him up. The church was quiet but for their urging words. He fought the sharp pain as he tried to move. The women were telling him something. Excitement and alarm from their voices registered. Sister Nicole was in trouble. He must help her. He must get up and go help her.

He staggered to his feet, draping his arms over the women's shoulders.

§

The demons were harder at work. *Kill her! Kill her!* they howled, drowning out everything else around the madman.

§

Her prayer continued. *Thy Kingdom come, Thy will be done, on Earth as it is in Heaven.*

She was in God's hands now.

§

Father Art was at the doorway. He caught a glimpse of the boy's crumpled body. He remembered Sister Nicole holding the lad just before losing consciousness. A chill ran down his spine.

Hoarsely, he managed a single word to his helpers. "Hurry." Silently he added another: *Please.*

§

"These are your enemies!" Juan shouted, surveying the gathered villagers. He could tell that many were still confused, hesitant. He ignored their worry of the reprisal they faced because his preemptive strike would alert the military, not frighten it. More importantly, he ignored the radioman's distress call they'd been unable to stop, which meant help was surely coming. He must not show fear. He must remain in control. He pressed on.

The voices within him made sure of that. Their destiny would be encountered tonight.

"Hear me, my friends. Our small village is not in this alone. We will be joined by our brothers and sisters, in other villages here in the north, who will also rise up and strike down the corrupt government. This is just the beginning."

Raul's cold, motionless form perched across the square would have, if not so very dead, told the madman there were no other villages rising up against tyranny that night.

Juan searched the throng for any sign of encouragement, but found none. There was no inspiring, tumultuous cry—only silence and stares from disbelievers. Of the stalwart group that months earlier committed to the course, only six remained before him. Even these men appeared tentative. He was becoming a band of One, and that reality struck deep. The man so possessed with the fire and passion of a cause lost his capacity to reason, and slipped into the grasping clutches of dementia.

§

Nicole neither saw nor heard anything around her. Her head remained bowed; she was encased in the protective shell of prayer. *Give us this day our daily bread, and forgive us our sins, as we forgive those who have sinned against us.* Fleeting thoughts of her childhood, of home and family and friends, of convent, of her friend Katherine, crowded her mind. She was bleeding, yet felt no pain. She was kneeling in the presence of a madman, yet felt no fear.

Some would later swear an aura illuminated her, a radiating luster not of the ordinary.

… Lead us not into temptation, but deliver us from evil …

§

Venomous drivel splattered from Juan's mouth as he cursed and berated those who would not honor their cause. Words spoken with such volume that he did not hear the old priest's first shout. But he did hear the second shout. He turned to face the man with the white collar.

§

"Juan, what has come over you?" The priest made his way closer to the leader, still leaning on the women for support. "You must stop this before there is any more killing. Oh, God, what has happened here?" he asked, surveying the carnage. Uniformed and native-dressed bodies alike lay scattered in the street. The fires still burned brightly. The corpse of a young man he did not recognize sat in a chair on the porch to his left. But he did know the pure evil standing before him, and, by God, such madness must be stopped.

"People, good people, go back to your homes! This crime will not go unpunished, but do not make it worse. Let those who are responsible face their fate." Father Art spoke convincingly. Some turned to leave.

Juan turned on the priest. "Be silent, old man." To the crowd, he said, "Do not listen to him. He is just as much your enemy as these three men." He motioned toward the captives. "He wears a different uniform of the government. Yes, the government! Do not be misled by his words," he said, pointing at Father Art. Turning to Nicole, he added, "Or hers either!"

All who turned to where he gestured saw Sister Nicole kneeling, silently, peacefully.

Father Art broke free from the women. He lunged toward Juan, who shoved him to the ground with a laugh.

"Listen to me, people. We must show our brothers and sisters in the neighboring villages what it is to fight for liberty. Our enemy must know we are mighty, fearless, and will fight to our own deaths if we must." He turned to the three prisoners. "These men took your comrades' lives tonight. They must pay. They must pay with their lives."

He spoke to an armed man. "Take them to that wall. Show them we serve no one but the cause of liberty." The last words, spoken often by their former leader, echoed from the self-proclaimed successor with little effect.

Carlos declared, "Juan, to fight and die in battle is one thing, but to kill these men mercilessly …" Carlos pointed at the captives. "As prisoners, do they not serve us well?"

"You would challenge me on this?" Juan moved within a breath's distance, the heat from his body noticeable on Carlos's skin. "You speak now for our mortal enemies?"

"Do not misjudge me, Juan. My lot is cast with yours, and you know it. We shall all surely live or die together as free men. But we must not kill unarmed captives. That is not warfare, that is cold-blooded murder!"

The two men were squared off, neither giving ground. Juan spoke first. "Hector," he said to the man to his right, "shoot them. At once!"

"Hector—" Carlos called, but it was no use. Hector turned from where he was standing, and fired point-blank at the three men, the bullets tearing into their clothing and flesh before Carlos could utter another word.

The noise drowned out Father Art's painful shout. A ricocheting slug had struck him in the shoulder. He stumbled at the impact, but held his balance and did not fall.

The gathering stood in shock. All but Father Art, who started toward the slain men. In his weakened and wounded state he would not have made a second step on his own power in any event. The butt of Juan's pistol cracked his skull before he could fall on his own.

Hector turned to his leader. "Why waste time? Why listen to them whine and beg for their lives? It was better like this." Hector ejected the empty magazine and loaded a full one.

§

Montgomery's head felt as if it would split open any second. He heard more shouts, then a burst of gunfire. He staggered to the edge of the clearing and peered around the corner.

He saw a circle of villagers, and bodies scattered everywhere. He tried, but could not focus. The pungent smell of burning wood and spent powder hung heavily in the air. The odor dulled his senses, and turned his stomach. He leaned to vomit. Bile followed what little food he had left in his stomach. Only a short time ago, he remembered hazily, Nicole was apologizing for serving cold food. *Nicole!* Panic overtook him. He rubbed his eyes, straining to see her. He prayed not to see her gray habit piled in a heap.

One man—he looked familiar—seemed to be leading the others. That man, brandishing a pistol, pointing it downward, shaking it as he did, angrily, at whoever knelt on the ground to his side. He strained harder to see, and sunk to his knees when his greatest fear materialized.

Every muscle and tendon in his body locked and stiffened in terror unlike any he had known, in the jungles of a past life or in life since, as he watched the man point the pistol at Nicole's head.

§

I confess to Almighty God, and to you, my brothers and sisters, that I have sinned through my own fault, in my thoughts and in my words, in what I have done, and in what I have failed to do; and I ask blessed Mary, ever Virgin, all the angels and saints, and you, my brothers and sisters, to pray for me to the Lord our God.

§

"Do you hear me?" he yelled. "Stand up! Stop your foolish praying!"

§

Lord, make me an instrument of your peace: where there is hatred, let me sow love; where there is injury, pardon; where there is doubt, faith; where there is despair, hope; …

Juan turned to those few who were still gathered at the clearing. The others had fled after the execution. He remained unrelenting.

"She, too, must pay! She is our enemy as well as those who wear the uniform of the military. Don't you see that?"

The voices were in total control …

… Where there is darkness, light; where there is sadness, joy. O divine Master, grant that I may not so much seek to be consoled as to console, to be understood as to understand, to be loved as to love …

§

His eyes vainly searched theirs for a sign of acceptance. There was none to be found. His moment was nearing its end.

Carlos stepped forward, moving in close to Juan, and spoke quietly, defiantly, where only the two could know what was being said. "If you are thinking of harming this woman, you will have to kill me first. Do you understand?"

§

… For it is in giving that we receive, it is in pardoning that we are pardoned, it is in dying that we are born to eternal life …

§

Cocking his head in some vague gesture of condescension, Juan stared coldly into the eyes of his friend. He then gestured at Hector, who was inching forward, poised and ready at the command. As Carlos waited for words of assurance, Juan struck out, clubbing Carlos across the jaw with his pistol. The blow knocked him backward, senseless, into Hector's firm hold.

Juan commanded his lone follower, "Hold him! He would betray us." Hector locked Carlos to his own body with the automatic rifle.

Juan returned his madness to Nicole. The dense layer of sweat on his face glistened with the reddish-orange sheen of the flames, and his eyes reflected light from the fires of hell itself as the vitriol intensified. His desiccated lips begged for moisture. The tongue that washed over them spread only a foamy slaver. The veins in his forehead and neck distended to the point of certain rupture. He was beyond any point of return. The voices, the unexorcised demons owned him. They clasped hands and sang and danced in a ring inside his head. The muted shades of black and white and red whirled and twirled and spun until all the host could do was stare at the kneeling figure before him. There were no more words left to be hurled at the defenseless form. There was nothing more the man could do except yield to his rage.

§

Hail Mary, full of grace, the Lord is with you! ...
... Blessed are you among women and blessed is the fruit of your womb, Jesus ...
Daddy, where are you? I need you, Daddy. I'm scared. I'm so scared.

§

Recovering from the blow to his head, Carlos saw the hideous creature with the gun swaying, gentle movements back and forth, as he again raised his arm, the instrument of death still clutched in its willing hand, still warm from the shots only moments earlier. Carlos cried out.

§

... Holy Mary, Mother of God, pray for us sinners, now and at the hour of our death. Amen.

§

Carlos's cries were drowned by the hysterical singing and laughter of the demons. Not so the voice of Evan Montgomery, who was sprinting headlong at this surreal scene, waving his arms, shouting *No! No!* as he ran, half-stumbling, straining against some invisible force that would hold him back, stop him from protecting the one pure thing in his world.

§

Juan turned to the soul that would deny him. Unblinking, he trained the bore on the man he knew only as a foreigner and sometimes neighbor. Effortlessly he squeezed the trigger once, then a second time. He felt the recoil as his arm shot upward, the first time, then again, as he unleashed the pistol's fury in the direction of the charging man.

§

Montgomery was aware only of a hissing sound that passed inches from his head, then quickly another, before the greater, booming sound caught up an instant later. He had stumbled again, fortuitously, and did not fall to either of the first two shots. Plodding forward relentlessly, he yelled even louder, *No! Stop! No!*

§

Carlos felt Hector's restraint loosen, and seized the opportunity. The journalist was only a few feet away, Juan much further. In a split second he made a decision, a choice he would regret forever. He grabbed at the rifle, snatching it from the grasp of his captor, and flung it into the night. In the same motion he lunged at the journalist, knocking him down, falling himself as the third shot, the one fired at point-blank range, narrowly missed its mark.

§

† Puzzled by the distraction no more than an instant, Juan returned to the business at hand. He looked down at the supplicant figure, praying her ridiculous prayers, in absolute fear of her subjugator. How he had yearned for this moment, for so long. The torture would be avenged by one more slight pull on the piece of curved steel his finger pressed against. Then it would be over. The demons would be cast out—the images, the nightmares, the endless nights of broken sleep would all be gone. He placed the tip of the barrel to her head, whispered *Go to hell*, and pulled the trigger.

43

THERE WAS ONLY A sharp click, and no recoil. He pulled again, and again, but each click was followed only by another. It was not supposed to be this way. There should have been noise, and a jerk in his arm. He pulled the weapon to his face, looking at it as an inquisitive child would some foreign object. He opened the cylinder, and emptied the spent casings. Reflexively, dispassionately, he rummaged through his pockets for more cartridges, fingers probing, wriggling until they scraped an empty bottom. He looked to Hector for more of the brass missiles, but Hector was on the ground, on his hands and knees. Why was Hector crawling on the ground like that? And where was Hector's rifle? That would do. Yes, that would do nicely. He looked for the rifle, but it was not there either. Hector was looking at him in a strange way, as were the others. They were saying things, all of them, and waving their hands and arms in his direction, gesturing, imploring, but he heard nothing from them, only the laughter and singing inside his head that kept growing louder, drowning out all else. He could not bear the noise.

§

… Pray for us sinners, now and at the hour of our death. Amen.

Daddy, Daddy … help me, Daddy.

Oh, merciful God, give me strength. Make me brave. Give me courage. Please, I pray, Please.

Oh, Daddy, where are you?

§

He dropped the revolver, and returned his hands to his ears. The guttural noise from the deepest part of his throat was building, rising to meet the thick air stifling his breathing, threatening to suffocate him. The noise reacted with the force and fury of pure phosphorus against air in a cacophonous explosion of sound, blinding the man into delirium.

The scream pierced the darkness, a night sound unlike those to which the village was accustomed. There were those fleeing the village, heading deep into the lowland forest, others further out, who swore later that the haunting, accursed sound was the cry of the Devil himself.

The frightening howl drove them further, faster along their escape routes. None would recall ever hearing a more terrifying sound. Until the second one, that is, which was far more frightful, far more satanic. Yes, the second one, the one that followed only a moment later.

§

The Lord is my shepherd, I shall not want ...

§

Those who stood closest to the deranged figure covered their own ears, until the sound no longer came from within the man, long before the last reverberation died down.

§

... He maketh me to lie down in green pastures; he leadeth me beside the still waters ...

§

They listened and watched in their own private horror as the madman's arms swung and lashed out and flailed aimlessly at everything, yet at nothing ...

§

... He restoreth my soul ...

§

He stopped his jagged movements to reach for the object suspended benignly in one of the onlooker's hands, to wrench from its grasp another kind of steel, sharpened for peaceful labor but the fruit of a different labor this night still crimson and warm on its honed edge ...

§

... Yea, though I walk through the valley of the shadow of death, I will fear no evil ...

§

The demons urged him on, their commands more urgent ...

§

... For Thou art with me ...

§

… Lifting it to his face, turning its handle side to side, inspecting it, its shiny surface reflecting reddish light into the black eyes of pure horror, savoring it, brandishing it, raising it …

§

… *Thou preparest a table for me in the presence of mine enemies* …

§

… Slowly … higher, higher yet, eye level, still higher …

§

The words. Forgetting the words. Mustn't forget the words. … *my cup runneth over … Oh, heavenly Father, protect me now … at this the hour of my death … my death … oh, Daddy, Daddy …* Tears began to fall.

§

… Black and white and red images in his head flashing, swirling, laughing, louder …

§

… *Surely goodness and mercy … Don't stop praying. Don't stop.*

§

… Another burst of sound beginning, building from the same depths, deeper even, building with ferocity, exploding, deafening, the tip of the blade nearly at its apex, demons lustily applauding …

§

… *Shall follow me* …

§

… The arm fully raised, fully extended …

§

… *All the days of my life* …

§

… Its swift descent beginning …

§

… *And I shall dwell in the house of the Lord forever. Amen* …

§

… Gaining momentum, sharpened steel silently, swiftly splitting air heavy with violence …

§

... Help me, Daddy, please Da—

§

... Blurred, glinting metal surging, striking ...

§

... Her muted scream ... his screams quieted ... his arm no longer taut ... arc stopped ... no longer plunging ... gasping for breath ... the demons shrieking even louder, *More! More! More!* the yelling continuing, louder ...

... time to obey again ...

... once more lifting, the arm extending upward, the instrument heavier this time ...

... the voices commanding, *Yes, Yes, plunge harder, plunge deeper!* Screaming ...

... obediently serving ...

... the arm raised, ready again ...

... something wrong ...

... the arm locked, heavy, weighted, unable to move ...

... another grip, another force, much greater ...

... binding him ... *Stop him!* ...

... ah, Carlos, my friend ...

... *Make him let go! ... Don't you understand? ... Can't you hear the voices?* ...

... they must be silenced ... *Carlos, don't you understand?* ...

... Carlos isn't listening ...

... his grip, tightening more, his own on the cold instrument now weakening, letting go ...

... resisting weakly, the voices murmuring in their mockery of him, his work unfinished, shame and reckoning facing him ...

... being led away, the clump of white and black and gray, and spreading, fluid redness, laying still, silenced, but still haunting him, forever to haunt him ...

§

He sat alone in the small room, in his hands the pistol Carlos had placed on the crudely-fashioned wooden table. The cries in his head were louder than ever. He knew they would never be silenced. Too far gone to realize what was happening to him, he was experiencing wisdom at the moment of one's death, gained too late for the living, taken into whatever afterlife awaited. Only one thing was clear to him at this moment, as he cocked the steel hammer, touched the barrel to his temple, and for the final time pulled his index finger toward the palm of his hand.

His demons were silenced forever.

The light was back. Something about it was familiar. She'd seen this light before. Another time, not so clear in her memory, but not so long ago. But just as comforting. It adorned her in its protective, brilliant glow, and basked her in a sensation of weightlessness. Warmth replaced the cold, and serenity returned. She'd felt as one waiting for a final destination, or perhaps a final destiny. No matter, it had been a short wait. A hand extended through the light, beckoning her. There was nothing to fear. One light touch, and it was all so clear. In that instant, meaning attached to all that had been her life. There was no more doubt, only clarity. Every question answered, every care, every decision validated. She slipped her hand into His, and unquestioningly followed the light …

†

BOOK THREE

44

MAC LOOKED OUT THE large window, taking in the panoramic view of the Mississippi River thirty-one stories below. Ol' Man River's commerce moved to and from destinations as far north as Minnesota, a whole world away, but here, New Orleans, was the stopping point. Another time, such a splendid view would have held for him a deeper meaning. But today, near the top of this tall office building in New Orleans's CBD, business—lawsuit business—was at hand, and there was no time for reflection.

He sauntered to the far wall of the twenty-foot ceilinged room, with its twin sixteen-foot doors, to view the four paintings. The firm's founders. Nearly two hundred years earlier they'd formed the firm to represent cotton merchants and plantation owners alike. Today, such a dual representation would constitute the classic conflict of interest. Then, it was a necessity, for there were few lawyers who ventured into the fledgling territory bought for pennies on the acre from a financially desperate emperor who saw France's hold on the New World slip away when Haiti drove them from the small island. History sees it as a politician who made a bad business deal. The politician saw it differently in 1803, without the benefit of hindsight. To him, it was a loss that needed cutting. A poor choice in retrospect, but the life of the diminutive emperor was as tenuous as his hold on the land he sold as the Louisiana Purchase. Perhaps it was the most made of an inevitable situation after all.

With the exit of French rule came adventuresome sorts inexorably drawn to the new American frontier, a few lawyers among them. Whether there was no work in the cities from which these men emigrated or whether they were visionaries was still debated by a few who cared of such historical minutia. To J. Bradley McHenry, on this day there was not a care for the reason or the men. His focus was on the gathering about to convene in this room in a matter of moments, and on the featured event.

Today marked the commencement of his deposition.

His deposition. Mac could not stop thinking about it. He'd known it would come, its inevitability as certain as the grudging acceptance of his daughter's death. He stood over the conference table around which a court reporter and a half dozen lawyers and paralegals and other support staff would soon be seated, their sights on him. He ran his fingers over the smooth glass covering the restored blond cypress underneath, salvaged from a sunken flatboat from the Tchefuncte River, or so the engraving read. It cost, he was certain, more than the contents of his former law office.

With clients such as the Archdiocese of New Orleans, not to mention shipping lines, the largest financial institution in all of Louisiana, a number of energy companies, the regional utility, and countless insurers, the Phillips, Dawson firm could well afford such trappings.

Sol Lieber sat at one end of the table, riffling through papers, trying to look busy. Mac smiled in Sol's direction, knowing there was little he'd needed to prepare for today's proceeding. Sol would only be defending, not taking the deposition. He was there to make objections to questions trying to penetrate the shield of the attorney and client privilege, or not in the form prescribed by the Federal Rules. Otherwise, Sol might just as well spend the day looking through the travel brochures in the outer pocket of his briefcase.

Five weeks had passed since the hearing on the Church's 12b6 motion. Sol argued well, not so much brilliantly on the law, but passionately. With little caselaw to support their position, Mac and Sol were pleased the court took the motion under advisement. It was anybody's guess how long the ruling might take. The court only promised it *shortly*.

There had not been much to do these past five weeks. Most of their discovery had been completed with the video depositions. Mac thought back to those depositions, almost feeling sorry for the former clerics who'd disgraced their cloth. *Almost*.

Sol's voice interrupted Mac's thoughts. "Did you get my message yesterday?" He was peering over the reading glasses resting halfway down the ridge of his ample nose. Mac liked the way the lenses made Sol look distinguished, from a distance anyway. The effect was entirely lost up close, when they called one's attention to the crop of wiry hair sprigging wildly from the tip of his nose and the insides of his nostrils. So many times he'd thought of saying something clever (*Hey, Sol, you ever think of braiding that stuff?*), each time passing on it. A line best left uncrossed, even with a good friend.

"I didn't get your message, Sol. I haven't been in my office for two days. Was it anything important?"

"We got some new requests in from Quisenberry, and something else a little curious. There's a—"

Sol was stopped by the knock, and the door opening to let in the court reporter. A woman entered, neatly dressed in a casual business suit, a welcome relief to Mac, who detested the sheer blouses and daring displays of cleavage so many of the younger reporters seemed to be sporting. He appreciated this woman's taste, and complimented her on a nice outfit. Elizabeth would've approved.

To be polite, Sol and Mac helped the lady set up. It was a small thing, but it enabled Mac to select where he chose to sit. In the litigation game they were playing, he hoped, somewhat uncharacteristically, the side of the table he selected would irritate Rich Quisenberry.

Ten o'clock came and went with no Rich Quisenberry or his minions. Sol looked at his client. "Mac, they're more than fifteen minutes late. We can leave if you want to."

"No, let's wait. What's to gain?"

Sol snapped his fingers. "Mac, I was about to tell you about some papers we got from Quisenberry—"

Before Sol could finish the doors opened again. This time the well-groomed and very familiar Rich Quisenberry trailed a tall, slender woman, dressed in a dark, fashionable business suit, with the telltale briefcase in her hand.

The day's first surprise was standing no more than ten feet from Mac.

§

"Hello, Mac. Sol. Sorry we're running a little late, but we had some orchestrational things to discuss. Hope you haven't minded the wait."

Something unusual was up, for Rich Quisenberry was never late, and never trailed another living soul into the deposition room. A grand entrance at the head of the line, followed by his supporting cast, was his style. Sol shrugged at Mac, who returned the same.

"Oh, Sol, did you get the new papers we sent? I had our courier deliver it, in case the mail might've been delayed."

"Late yesterday, Rich," Sol replied. *As I suspect you intended, just before I left my office, so I wouldn't have time to raise an argument.*

"What papers, Sol?" asked Mac, moving toward Quisenberry for the customary handshake.

Quisenberry answered before Sol had a chance. "Oh, just some renenewed requests for production—and an entry of appearance for our new co-counsel here," he continued, a noticeably vapid smile on his face as he motioned toward the tall woman standing silently at his side. "Gentlemen, please allow me to introduce you to Ms. Katherine Carson, who has entered an appearance in this matter. Sol, I trust the service copy was included in the papers our courier dropped off yesterday."

"Yes, Rich, I saw it. I haven't had a chance to tell my client about it yet. We drove over in separate cars, and, wouldn't you know it, I was just about to mention it when you made your grand entrance a moment ago."

Mac cut off any quick retort by Quisenberry. "I'm Mac McHenry, Ms. Carson," he said, extending his hand to the newest lawyer. "Pleased to meet you."

"Likewise, Mr. McHenry," she replied, taking his hand. If there was any discomfort on either lawyer's part it didn't show in the handshake.

"And I'm Sol Lieber, Ms. Carson—it is *Ms.*, right? I want to be politically correct here, and I thought I heard our friend Rich here say *Ms.*, as opposed to *Miss.*" Sol gave her the more traditional, ladylike fingertip handshake.

"It's either, Mr. Lieber. I have no husband, and am certainly past any age of caring about the political propriety of a social title. And, frankly, since it's 'Rich' among you fellows, I'd feel more comfortable if you also called me Katherine."

Sol was about to lamely agree when Mac broke in. "Let's give that some time to develop, shall we, Ms. Carson. No offense, but Mr. Quisenberry and I go back a ways, and Sol here, why, he's so old he's just Sol to everybody. You understand, don't you, Ms. Carson?"

"That's certainly fair enough, Mr. McHenry, I would probably do the same thing if our positions were reversed," she coolly replied, spooning Mac a taste of his own medicine.

"Shall we get started, gentlemen?" boomed Quisenberry. "We've got a lot of ground to cover, and I'm sure we all want to get our reporter out of here at a reasonable hour."

"Suits us, Rich," Sol replied. "Mac, why don't you take your seat up there, where we set you up."

Quisenberry uttered a muffled *Wha*— sound, but a silent, frowning nod from his new counsel—a show of control Mac and Sol caught at the same time—ended any protestation. Mac gave Sol a *This could be interesting* look. Sol winked in reply.

A visibly rattled Quisenberry moved to the beige leather armchair across from Mac, as if to seat himself. Hesitating awkwardly, he moved over one chair, leaving the first chair for Katherine Carson. Lacking his usual enthusiasm, he said, "Ms. Carson will be taking this deposition, gentlemen." Clearly, Quisenberry was off to a good start on a bad day.

Mac waited for the attractive, thirtysomething-looking woman to begin, more anxious than ever to get on with it. Nothing could have spelled more relief to him than not having to endure a day under examination from Rich Quisenberry. Nothing.

The reporter administered the oath to Mac, and the deposition was underway.

"Mr. McHenry," Katherine Carson began, all business, "we are here today pursuant to a notice of deposition in the matter of *McHenry versus the Roman Catholic Church, through the Archdiocese of New Orleans*, Case Number CIV-94-A1146D, in the United States District Court for the Eastern District of Louisiana. A copy of the notice was served on your counsel," she said, nodding in Sol's direction, "compelling your attendance today. Is that your understanding, sir?"

He wondered if she was a baby lawyer, one of those older types who went back to law school as a second career, looking far more mature than they really were, or in-house, possibly with the Church's insurer, with little or no litigation or trial experience. She didn't appear to have the hardened persona of an in-the-trenches trial lawyer. Catching her wondering expression, he realized she wanted something from him. "Yes, that's my understanding," he answered.

"The notice, which I've asked our reporter here to mark as Deposition Exhibit One, specifies you were to bring certain documents with you today—well, let me stop here, and first ask you, Mr. McHenry, have you seen a copy of the notice of your deposition?"

"Yes, ma'am, I have seen a copy of the notice, and the *duces tecum* part as well."

"Then may I presume you've brought the documents with you, the ones we requested in the *duces tecum* portion of your notice?"

"Yes, ma'am, you may so presume."

Sol opened his valise and pulled out a stack of envelopes wrapped in a pink ribbon. He tossed them midway across the table. Mac noticed a touch of both arrogance and resentment.

"Solomon Lieber, Ms. Carson, representing Mr. McHenry to my left. May the record please reflect Mr. McHenry has indeed brought the documents responsive to Exhibit A to the notice—the *duces tecum* part—and those responsive documents are on the table right in front of you, Ms. Carson, at this time." Sol cleared his throat. "Before we continue, we have prepared an application for protective order, to make sure these documents are kept in the strictest of confidence, not disclosed outside the courtroom, the usual sort of thing. It's all here in the PO," Sol concluded, laying the five-page document on the table beside the stack of envelopes. "Please, take your time," Sol went on, "read the application and form of PO, and let us know if there is a problem with executing it on behalf of your client."

Sol was showing a smug side, lacking thus far. He'd done this on his own. Now he sat back in his chair, expressionless.

Katherine Carson read the double-spaced document quickly, the prolonged silence broken only when she flipped the pages. "That won't be necessary, Mr. Lieber," she said, sliding the document over to Rich Quisenberry, onetime lead lawyer. "Unless Mr. Quisenberry sees something I missed, this application meets with the defendant's approval. Mr. Quisenberry will sign and return it to you. And, if you like," she added, "we can have one of the firm's runners take it over for filing right now … save you the trouble, and get a jump on the court's approval."

"Fine, Ms. Carson, but we don't go forward with any part of this deposition dealing with these protected documents until the PO is signed by the court. Let me make our position very clear. We've not delayed once in this case, and don't intend to start. You—yes, you, Ms. Carson—come in at the last minute as additional counsel of record, and next thing we know this deposition of my client is noticed up in far less than the courteous, and, I might add, acceptable length of time countenanced by the Eastern District, and now you good folks want to view the very private letters my client and his wife received from their daughter … deeply personal letters which must never make their way into the press or become known to the public. And you expect this depo to continue, or at least the part of it dealing with these letters, without my client enjoying the protection of a signed court order? Ms. Carson, dear woman, and you, too, Rich, that just isn't going to happen. Not today, not ever. We can move on, and we can talk about anything you want to, so long as it's within the scope of the notice and not privileged, but we are not going to dig into those letters until we have a signed PO. Am I getting through to you all?"

Mac smiled at the contrast between his lawyer's poker face and the stunned expressions of the lawyers sitting across the table. Except for Katherine Carson, who wore a poker face of her own.

"Mr. Lieber, we can do it this way, if you like." Her response was a radical departure from the outburst Quisenberry would have made for staff and court reporter. She didn't stop there.

"Of course, there is little doubt our magistrate judge will sign the order—and you are also aware we could simply place a call to him right now if we wanted to, and he would give us a verbal—but in the spirit of moving things along, and not troubling the court, we are prepared to wait for a signed order before we open any line of questioning regarding the letters. Letters we also recognize are deeply personal, and would never be made public by the defendant. The Church has no malevolent purpose in mind."

Mac watched her closely as she spoke. Cool, even-handed, self-assured, poised, and totally in control. This was her show, not Rich Quisenberry's. *What's going on?*

Sol spoke. "Let me have a moment with my client, please. This will only take a second or two." Mac followed his lawyer to the hallway outside the conference room.

Sol pulled him in close. "I know what I'm doing. This is bizarre, them switching lawyers like this. It's pretty lame, using the PO as a test, but what else did we have? You know we need to know the lay of the land. We don't need to be wasting our time wondering what's coming next. With Rich, hey, we had predictability. Our new player, who she is, what she brings to the show, we don't know. But it's in our best interest to know, wouldn't you agree?"

"I'm with you, Sol. You know I am." Mac patted his friend's arm in a display of confidence. "So, did we learn anything?"

"Naw," Sol replied, "probably not. We're just better informed."

"What do we do about the letters, after she's made a pretty embarrassing record for us in there?"

"That's what we came out here to talk about, my friend, at least that's what they believe, anyway. I'm ready to go back in there, with your approval of course, and eat a large helping of southern crow, you know, give them what they want. She was right, of course. It's a given our magistrate will sign the PO."

"Sol, let's play this one out. You did good, and it had an effect on them. They're not going to embarrass us with the court. So let's see where this leads, buddy, what do you say?"

"Your call. Let's go tell 'em we've talked things over, and prefer to wait. They'll know we're up to something, but then we're both guessing. Not a great plan, but it's good enough."

When they'd taken their seats, Sol announced briefly the plaintiff would stand on his objection, and was ready to go forward, with the understanding the letters would be saved for another time, when the court had signed off on the PO.

Rich Quisenberry spoke. "I presume, Sol, you'd have no objection if we start reading through the letters, while we're waiting for the court to act." It was a question, made in statement form, as most lawyers do. It was a control tactic, and Sol would have no part of it.

"You presume wrong, counselor. Those letters stay right there, wrapped in that pretty pink ribbon Mrs. McHenry tied them in, tearfully I might add, until the court signs off on the PO."

Quisenberry was speechless for the second time in a short span of time, highly unusual for the man. His day wasn't getting any better.

"Very well," Katherine Carson said, "let's resume the deposition with that understanding."

She stayed all business. Taking him through the usual preliminary matters—"Have you ever given your deposition before, Mr. McHenry?"—"If I ask you a question you don't understand, please ask me to repeat it, to make sure our reporter records an informed, accurate response."—"Please give our reporter speaking answers, as she cannot record nods of the head or mumbles as responsive one way or another."—"Even if you believe you know what I am about to ask you, please let me finish my question, so we aren't both talking while the reporter is trying to accurately record what's being said, not to mention you may inadvertently give an incorrect response."—before she got into the substance of the deposition. Mac was more than ready to get started after the thorough ground rules session. Always a game ... the same one he played from the other side of the table.

She handed the reporter a copy of the complaint, the written expression of the plaintiff's case against the defendant. The reporter applied a small, rectangular yellow sticker, numbered it with a "2", and handed it back to Katherine Carson, who in turn handed it to Mac.

"Mr. McHenry, I've handed you what our reporter has marked as Defendant's Exhibit Two, and ask if you can identify it as the complaint filed in this case."

"Yes, I can." The strange detour now over, it was back to answer-the-question-only.

Mac saw she had no yellow tablet from which to lead him through a series of scripted questions. Just a very thin stack of papers—the documents she'd be questioning him on. Where were the numerous boxes of files and records?

"Mr. McHenry, in paragraph six of the complaint, sir, you have alleged the defendant was aware it placed Sister Nicole in a perilous position, and took no reasonable steps to remove her from said perilous position, which resulted in her death. Is that a fair summary of the allegations in paragraph six?"

"Objection to the form of the question," Sol interjected, "as the complaint speaks for itself." Sol then turned to Mac and advised him he could go ahead and answer the question.

It was a valid objection to a wasted question. *Why don't you ask about the facts, Ms. Katherine Carson? I'll give you all you can handle.* But Mac noticed something unusual. When reading from the complaint, Katherine Carson had substituted "Sister Nicole" for "the decedent," a noticeably sensitive touch. But why? Mac could dwell on that later; for now, his answer was due. He replied, "As my counsel has stated, the allegation in the complaint does speak for itself, but yes, it's a fair summary."

"Very well, would you now tell the court the facts upon which you have based your allegations? Please start with the allegation the Church knowingly placed Sister Nicole in a position of peril."

I'll give you facts now, Ms. Carson. Thanks for asking.

It was a good question. Inexperienced parties to litigation rarely understand that, while the lawyers draw up the court papers containing the plaintiff's allegations and the defendant's excuses, it is the parties who must defend the allegations and excuses in court. A deposition is just like being in court—taken under oath, with real questions from lawyers and real answers from deponents taken down by a court reporter. It's not for the timid, Mac had often advised his clients. Now it was his turn; it was time for Mac to explain why he was after the Catholic Church.

The trouble was, he didn't have his story all put together yet. There were still gaps in places, key places, and he wasn't ready to answer questions such as this one before he had all the facts. But he was prepared for the question.

"I want to make it clear, Ms. Carson, we do not have all the facts gathered just yet—as you know, discovery is ongoing, and we need to follow up on new information we glean from our discovery—but at this time we do have certain initial, somewhat broad conclusions I could share with you."

And you won't believe your ears, Ms. Carson …

"The defendant recognizes that your answer will be subject to change once new information becomes known. In that regard," she paused, "may I have the agreement of your counsel, on the record, we may reconvene this deposition when new facts that would change your response are known, and that your counsel will inform Mr. Quisenberry when such facts are known. May we have such an agreement, Mr. Lieber?"

Sol answered. "Yes, ma'am, we can have such an agreement."

Mac didn't wait to be prompted again. "I believe I was prepared to give you some factual bases for the allegations in the complaint, Ms. Carson, as they relate to how my daughter was placed in and allowed to remain in a position of peril. My daughter volunteered to do mission work in Guatemala after she took her vows. Why she chose Guatemala remains unknown to me, but I do know she was persuaded by some influence of the Church."

"May I interrupt your response, Mr. McHenry?" she asked.

"Certainly."

"When you say 'persuaded by some influence of the Church,' are you suggesting it was a coercive influence, or something more passive? You shouldn't necessarily rely on my choice of words, please feel free to use your own."

"I do not think the Church forced my daughter to go to Guatemala, like the Marines forced her older brother to go to boot camp at Quantico, if that's what you mean. But I do believe she was influenced by the Church, perhaps to the point it may not have been an entirely willing decision on my daughter's part."

"I see. Are you suggesting the influence of the Church was in any way improper?"

"Yes, Ms. Carson, I am."

She stared a large hole right through him. He was uncomfortable with the gaze, but maintained eye contact. She seemed almost speechless, but he knew better. Even a baby lawyer could recover from a defiant response such as he'd just delivered.

"Do you have facts to support your belief, Mr. McHenry?"

"I do not have anything in writing, or anything from a live witness, not yet anyway, if that's what you mean, but I do have over twenty-three years of being her father to know a little something about my daughter. I tell you, and this court, that I believe my daughter was improperly influenced by the Catholic Church to take a mission assignment in Guatemala, and the Church knew full well that it was an unsafe place to be, and the Church did not take the steps it should have to protect the life of my daughter. I would add that this failure on the part of the Church to take even the most reasonable step to protect my daughter's life surely resulted in her death."

"Please tell the court what the Church did not do that resulted in your daughter's death."

"Ms. Carson, you're new to this case. If you had been involved before today, you would know from our depositions of Father Art Hurkinen and the young priest—Father Suarez, I believe his name is—depositions taken about two months ago in Guatemala City, that the very night of the rebel uprising, the night my daughter was butchered by a madman, the Church came to take her away, to a place of safety, a place of refuge, and left her instead to die. You would know the Church knew the rebel uprising was set to happen at any time, and that the safety of the Church's priests and nuns should have been of paramount importance. You would know that, because it is the very reason—admitted in a videotaped deposition—the Church sent its truck to evacuate its people from the northern region where my daughter lived. You would know that Father Suarez left without my daughter and Father Art, in spite of his command to return with them. You would also know that Father Suarez and the other priests from the archdiocese who went to Petén on the rescue mission left with every other priest and nun they were sent to save. Only my daughter and Father Hurkinen were left to die. Miraculously Father Hurkinen survived. My daughter didn't. You would know all this, Ms. Carson, and would not have to ask it of me."

"Objection, not responsive," she said, sticking with the rules. "Mr. McHenry, I may have come into this case as counsel of record a bit late, but I am very aware of the content of both of those depositions, and all the others as well. Questions and answers. In that regard, I have heard, and seen, Father Suarez's testimony he did all he could to convince Sister Nicole the Church literally *commanded* she leave the village with him, and even then she refused. I heard Father Suarez say he felt powerless to change her mind when she refused, despite being told of the danger. Yes, Mr. McHenry, I've heard—and have *seen*—everything that's been said in response to Mr. Lieber's very probing questions, questions designed to present your side of this case. Now it's the Catholic Church's turn, and I want to hear what you have to say. So let me rephrase the question, make it easier for you to answer. Is there something the Church should have done differently that night?"

"Objection to the form of the question," chimed in Sol. "Go ahead and answer, Mac."

Mac stared incredulously at her. Quisenberry would've shown more tact; she went right for the jugular. She was asking him point-blank to say the Church should have somehow forced Nicole to go. There was but a single answer, and it was the weakest part of his case. Better to get it out there now, and deal with it.

"Yes, there is."

"Would you please tell the court what that is."

"Ms. Carson, my daughter was a strong-willed young woman. I believe she resisted authority that night. But I also know there is—rather, was—a point at which my daughter would have given in to authority, a turning point even for her. For example, as strange as it might seem now to talk about, sometimes, as her father, I had to raise my voice at my daughter to get her attention. I used good, old-fashioned parenting tactics to compel her to do things she was just too strong-willed, or obstinate, or whatever, to do without my resorting to the heavy-handed approach. But it worked. And it would've worked that night, too, if the Church had taken its responsibility with my daughter's life as seriously as it should have."

"How so, Mr. McHenry?"

"Do you mean ... are you asking me if I think Father Suarez should have yelled at my daughter? Or Father Hurkinen? Or that both of them, if need be, should have physically forced her into the truck and left the village if nothing else worked? You bet I do. I think the least the Church should have done was use whatever means it could to force my daughter into the truck, and then to have driven her as far away and as fast as possible. I know my daughter well enough to know, however stubborn she could be, even she had her breaking point." He paused, then added, "That's how so, Ms. Carson."

She was still staring a hole through him. She paused briefly before moving on to the next allegation in the complaint. Mac got through the tough part. Nobody had won, but he had not lost … which was about all he could hope for at this stage.

The questioning continued for another hour. Katherine Carson painstakingly led Mac through more allegations in the complaint, probing him for the all-elusive facts to support his claims of wrongdoing. Stress cracks were showing by late morning.

"Let's take a short break, shall we?" Rich Quisenberry said, sparing the two adversaries the discomfort of holding out to see who blinked first. Quisenberry's voice startled Mac. How long had it been since Rich Quisenberry went over an hour without saying anything? He conjured an image of Rich in the womb, but even then he imagined a mouth moving. *Poor Rich*, Mac thought. *Relegated to second chair. What could have brought this on?*

Sol left for the restroom. Quisenberry sat at the table, reading from what was no doubt a position memorandum from the newest minion assigned to the case, while the rest scattered. Mac walked to the large window, and once again looked down on the brown current below. He was thirsty. Amazing, he thought, that the muddy water would trigger his thirst.

Mac found the crystal pitcher on the antique sideboard next to the window, nestled among the many soft drinks, the gourmet coffee and tea, and fresh fruit and pastry. He poured one glass, then another. The water was a welcome quencher for his parched throat and mouth. *Cottonmouth*, his high school coaches called it, when the saliva dried up the tongue and gums, and the roof of your mouth got all sticky and made breathing more difficult. The dryness in his mouth quickly soaked up the nourishment. Just as importantly, the water soothed his nerves. He'd fared well enough so far, but it wasn't over yet.

"Are you going to drink the whole pitcher?"

It was Katherine Carson. She held an empty glass. He still had the pitcher. It took him a second to add two plus two.

"I'm sorry. Can I fill your glass?"

"Please." He emptied the pitcher into her glass.

"Thank you." She took a long swallow, her eyes scanning the room, then the high-rise view of New Orleans. "Listen, I don't mean to intrude. If you like, I'll leave you alone."

Mac smiled at her. "Are you saying you'd like to talk, what, off the record? You feel like you need to ask me first, instead of just saying something about the heat, or how 'bout them Saints?"

She shook her head side to side, smiling. "That's a little too analytical for me, Mr. McHenry. No hidden agenda, just polite conversation while we're on break. I can see I've intruded, though. My mistake." She turned to walk away. He reached out, a light hand on her shoulder.

"Say what you came over to say, okay? Don't mind me, I'm just a guy whose daughter is dead, who hasn't come to terms yet."

"Mr. McHenry, I really didn't come over to talk about the case. That's for when we go back on the record, when the reporter can take it all down and we can all feast on what you say into the late hours of the night. Nothing in the rules says we have to be uncivil just because we're on opposite sides of a lawsuit. Besides, word has it you regard professionalism as one of the most redeeming qualities in a lawyer."

"There's some truth to that, Ms. Carson," Mac said. "What else do they say about me?"

"You're a good lawyer, a good man, a good father and husband, and," pausing, "a good Catholic."

"Whoa, now. You're out of bounds with the 'good Catholic' part. We can be civil, but leave the personal out of it."

"Maybe you ought to be more careful what you ask me. I was only answering your question."

Move on, Mac, before you lose your edge. "So what brings you to our neighborhood, Ms. Carson? Neither Sol nor I know you, or where you came from, anything at all about you, really. I figure Sol is out looking you up in Martindale-Hubbell or on Westlaw as we speak. Why don't you tell me, so I can surprise my old friend when he gets back. As they say in these parts, where ya from, Ms. Katherine?"

She looked at her watch. "Maybe some other time, Mr. McHenry. We should get back to business now."

Ouch! "Okay, have it your way. *Again.* When you're ready, Ms. Carson."

Mac walked beside her until they split company at the end of the table. He stopped to say something else, something inane, but she kept on walking to her chair, sat down, and waited until he did the same.

45

M R. McHenry, please answer the question. Your counsel's objection is noted, but I am entitled to an answer. Tell the court upon what facts you base the
allegation in paragraph nine of your complaint, which states the Catholic Church has
acted and continues to act with a pattern of total, conscious, and callous disregard for
its employees, Sister Nicole among them, over an extended time and area, such that
the health and safety of all of the Church's employees is threatened."

It was near noon, and they'd been at it hard since the break ended an hour and a
half earlier. Mac was right, Sol had gone down several floors, to the law office of an old
friend, and had searched Katherine Carson's background, strangely turning up nothing. There hadn't been time to call the Louisiana State Bar Association to check the roll
of attorneys. Sol told Mac there wasn't much else to do except defend his complaint—
something he and Mac had been over countless times in preparation for this day.

The walk through the complaint had been uneventful until they reached paragraph
nine. Katherine Carson was bearing down on him with full force on the "total, conscious, and callous disregard for its employees" allegation, and wasn't buying into
the objection her inquiry invaded the area protected by the attorney's work product
doctrine. She wasn't settling for lame.

Mac was prepared for this, if Rich Quisenberry had come to the same point. "Ms.
Carson, we have compiled, from reputable authenticated sources, every reported,
thus we presume, every known, incident of abuse—be it physical or sexual—the
Catholic Church has been accused of in this country for the past thirty years. You
might be surprised to know there are more than one thousand of these documented
reports of abuse, and many hundreds of confirmations. In the past twenty years, just
as an illustration, the Church has paid out tens of millions of dollars to victims of
this abuse, and their families. It is remarkable, truly remarkable, the degree of callous

indifference the Church has shown over this period.

"And this compilation does not include the other examples of the Church's callous disregard, the incidents of harm, and worse, that have fallen upon others besides my daughter."

Now it was Mac's turn to gauge her reaction. It was surprisingly nonplused. "Can you be more specific, Mr. McHenry?"

"More specific than the Church doesn't care, you mean?"

"Objection, non-responsive. I think you know perfectly well what I mean. I mean can you give the court some specific examples of how the Catholic Church, the defendant in this case, showed a callous and total disregard for those persons upon whom the Church's clergy effected their physical and sexual abuse for the past hundred years, or somehow led to the harm you speak of?"

Mac leaned forward in his chair for effect. "That's not what I said. I never said that the callous indifference was shown, or rather not shown, for the victims. In fact, Ms. Carson, it is shown toward the Church's own. You know how this lawsuit is pleaded. I have no standing to bring suit on behalf of the victims of this pervasive abuse. But I believe I have standing to bring this lawsuit for the Church's continued neglect of its own. It's all in the statistics, Ms. Carson. Instance after instance of abuse by the Church of its clergy, which led to the clergy's further abuses on the innocent and unsuspecting. It isn't just the abuse of others we're talking about. We've also documented a significant number of deaths in only the past fifty years of priests and nuns who were left in peril by a Church too wrapped up in its own sense of mystique, or whatever, to take care of them. They, like my own daughter, were left unprotected, in positions of peril, often to die, usually at the hands of those whose homicidal, or worse yet, maniacal tendencies were known far in advance of the actions themselves. Uganda, Southeast Asia, the Congo, Rwanda, Colombia, and even Guatemala. I call that a pattern, Ms. Carson, and I believe the finder of fact, our judge, will also. Now, is that answer enough for you?"

The only sound in the room came from the slight ticking noise of the reporter's keypad, her inscription trailing Mac's words by only a few seconds. Then came total, almost eerie quiet. Katherine Carson's hands were clasped on the tabletop, fidgeting slightly, thumbs tapping silently on the shiny, smooth glass surface. A paralegal cleared her throat. Mac waited only a few seconds more before he spoke again.

"If you're waiting for more, there isn't any. I believe I've answered your question. Do you have others?"

She looked at her watch, and turned in the direction of the reporter. "Off the record, please." She then directed her attention to the other side of the table. "Gentlemen," she began, "it's a quarter past noon. May we suggest a break for lunch? Resume at one-thirty?"

Mac nodded at Sol, who said they would return at one-thirty. The reporter logged off, and Mac and Sol rose to leave. Rich Quisenberry and his staff sat rigidly and quietly as the two men left. The last thing Mac saw as he exited the tall, stately doorway was Katherine Carson bowing her head, her eyes closed, and her hands still clasped on the table. The fingers were no longer interlaced. They were stretched out, with palms pressed together. For an instant Mac wondered if she were praying.

It was actually cooler at noontime, she thought to herself, than it was later in the day. The heat from the afternoon sun seemed to beat down less forgivingly than it did morning and noon, which made working in the garden easier early than late. Since she'd stopped teaching when the children reached an age they needed a full-time mom, Elizabeth had spent her leisure time building a garden in the family yard. The one-acre expanse of broad-bladed St. Augustine covering the yard when they bought the house had given way over the years to more than half an acre of flowers, plants and trees that bloomed, blossomed and prospered year 'round. Like a receding hairline, where the baldness was replaced by rich, bountiful color. Only the yardman really cared about the gradual erosion of the greenbelt, the rate he charged for his mowing and edging services becoming less each time a portion of yard was reclaimed.

The gardening was her knitting, her game of chess, her ballroom dancing. Elizabeth believed digging in the earth was healthy for the body and the soul. It gave her a connection to Nature much as sailing did for her husband. It was good, she'd always thought, they had separate interests for their idle time, what little of it there was—good for her, good for her family. She dwelled on this while digging, making places in the soil for the irises and glads. The earth turned easily, thanks to the daybreak shower. She rarely used gloves, which made for a host of constantly split nails and damaged cuticles. But vanity was not an issue with Elizabeth. Never had been.

The same earth was now home to her daughter, she reminded herself. Her daughter's physical remains, that is, for her spirit, her soul, were everywhere, unconstrained. Nicole's presence was strong all around her, in the trees, in the flowers, in the very air that wrapped itself heavily, moistly around her. She missed her daughter. No amount of gardening could fill the void of the loss of her child. That was an emptiness nothing filled. She felt physically empty inside as well, as if there were a vast chamber where a heart used to beat and organs once functioned. Most days, her only sense of life was the feel of the earth as it oozed and trickled through her fingers. The sadness was not getting better, as she'd been assured it would. It was actually getting worse.

Today was a good day for digging and planting, but it was not a good day for her. Too much else was on her mind as she wiped the rich mud from her fingers onto the rag and carefully placed the veiny, spiny bulb in its sarcophagus. For one, her husband was across the lake, sitting in some room no doubt surrounded by lawyers with talons bared, clawing out at him, trying to rip the flesh off the body of his legal argument against the Catholic Church. For another, the pain was back, and it was worse this morning. While she worried for her husband, whose lawsuit she neither understood nor condoned, she knew he was a worthy match for his foe. Not so for her.

Elizabeth winced from another of the lightning-like pains, her alarm clock-less wakeup to reality. The frequency and intensity of the pains had increased in the past month. All her years of proper diet, exercise, plenty of rest, total abstinence from tobacco and near total abstinence from alcohol, all seemed like so much squandered opportunity. Her friends who drank and smoked heavily, and whose weight had soared after fewer births, and whose only exercise consisted of watching the newest aerobic infomercial, they would, she knew, have the last laugh. Everything she'd heard and read about was upon her. She fit the profile: multiple births; over the age of forty-five; her babies nourished at her bosom; in the genes. The last one hit home the hardest—her own mother a victim at almost the same age.

She'd gone to see Barrett Dupuis, under the ruse of a last check on the after effects of the concussion. He'd noticed her grimace at a routine fingertip probe of the abdomen, and, because he was a good physician, probed her just as thoroughly with some hard questions. Her answers, truthful only to a point, had given him cause to conduct a few tests, then a few more. Just last week she went for her results. The news wasn't unexpected.

"Elizabeth, you are very sick. But you don't need me to tell you that. I suspect you've been in pain for quite some time, perhaps even before the concussion."

He was right. The pains began about a week after Nicole's burial. At first minor, not much more than ordinary indigestion, but they had gradually worsened. "What's the prognosis, Doc?" she jokingly asked, fearful of but prepared for what was coming.

"I'll be as honest as I can with you, Elizabeth. It's bad. I don't know if we've caught it in time, frankly if we ever would have. The only protocol we have at the present is a full spate of radiation treatments and comprehensive chemotherapy. Even at that, there is a limited survival rate." He waited a second, then continued.

"On the positive side, you fit the profile for survival. You are quite healthy otherwise, and have a strong physique, which would serve you well on the program I recommend we start immediately."

A thought came to mind as she weighed options, pondered choices. "If I were to wait, say, a month or two, before we started these treatments, how might that affect my chances?"

"Let me make something clear. This is serious. I am telling you we need to start this protocol tomorrow, if not today. One or two months from now, I cannot guarantee you won't be bedridden, with no hope of survival. This thing spreads quickly. It's insidious, takes no prisoners."

"Barrett," she began, "I need a day to think about it. Just one. I'll either be at the hospital tomorrow to start your protocol, or let you know otherwise. That's the best I can do on—what's the old saying—on such short notice. Now isn't that a pathetic play on words?"

"Tell me what you're thinking. Forget the patient-physician thing for now. You and Mac have been my friends for too many years to remember. I delivered your oldest when I was in residence. What's going on with you in your personal life? Tell me what it is that's got you thinking you might give up, leave Mac a widower and the boys without the world's best mother."

"My but you do have a way with the words, Doctor. That calls it all home, doesn't it? Is it fair of you to put that guilt trip on me? Don't answer that, you don't have to." She stood, moving from the exam room gurney over to the small window. Across the street was a public elementary school. Children were playing. *Recess, it must be recess.* Old memories surfaced. How nice it must be to live so carefree, where the only worry was whether a classmate broke in line for the slide, or you went out first in a game of dodge ball. She smiled as the young girls jumped rope, black and white alike, dressed in the new uniforms required in even the public schools. She could not hear the children, but knew they were squealing with laughter, gaiety, lost in the momentary innocence and happiness of childhood. It called to mind what she would share with her doctor, not as a friend, but as her doctor. She would not embarrass him by commenting on the distinction she would draw between the two.

ALL THE ANGELS AND SAINTS

"Barrett, I suspected it would be bad news. Maybe not this bad, but what difference does the degree make? I am almost fifty. It will be years before my boys give a thought toward making me a grandmother. My daughter brought home the same reality even sooner than her brothers. I'm an out-of-work mother, with no prospects for grandbaby nurturing in sight. It sounds pathetic—that's twice, in a space of only a minute, I've described myself as pathetic, isn't it?—but I think Nicole's death has left me with more of a void than I can handle. I can't help my husband with this crusade or whatever it is he's on. Being a wife and mother is what I was meant for. I've outlived my usefulness, I think. God and Nature, which by the way I've always felt were more the same than not, have other plans for me. I miss my daughter, and I think it's my time to go, to be with her again. That's why I would think about not partaking of your protocol.

"I don't relish the idea of dying," she continued. "I am not suicidal. If you gave me more of a chance of survival, I wouldn't hesitate to grab the ring. But the thought of living my last days so shriveled up and weak that the dearest people in my life would wish my time would come quicker is not much of an option, not to me anyway. I might die in more pain, if I understand what you're telling me, but it will be swift, and I will keep my hair, and won't be a burden for long. That's what I have to look forward to, isn't it?"

A hard look and a shake of his head were all she would get from her doctor.

She'd called her sons, and probed only as much as she dared into their personal lives. Neither had a serious romance going. Flying jets and preparing to tackle English Lit and world history classes occupied their time. Her decision was that much easier.

Barely twenty-four hours earlier she'd called Barrett Dupuis with her decision. "Barrett, I'm going to see my boys. I'll be gone two weeks, so I'll need a strong painkiller … I don't want them seeing anything to give me away. It might be awhile before I break the news to them or Bradley. Please don't argue with me, my mind is made up." He'd argued of course, but her decision was final.

This morning she couldn't will away the pain, and took her first pain capsule as she dressed. She wretched afterward, supper from the evening before and breakfast freshly on top. She would settle down, the pharmacist had told her, in a day, two at most. For all the emptiness caused from the voided meals, and the other kind, there was something else now—an invader, the unwanted—that had found its way inside her. How odd the irony, she mused, the one thing alive inside her was something that didn't belong. She felt it, imagined its horrible, ugly shape, housed in some crevasse where healthy parts of her used to be. Ignoring it was not possible, its periodic messages too harsh a reminder of being in there all right. Denial was not part of her makeup; Elizabeth McHenry's strong suit was in confrontation.

She confronted a nice-looking young student who obviously would never succeed as a pencil salesman over twenty-seven years ago, and made a dream life with him ever since, confronting challenges by the score throughout their years together. This was different. This was a silent, unseeable thing, a form she could not confront verbally or eye to eye. For now, it was best to position herself erect, adjust the right body parts, head, shoulders, attitude, and say, *Look, whoever or whatever you are, this is me, Elizabeth Rogers McHenry, wife and mother of three, yes, three, I will always be a mother of three, and I don't like you inside my body, and either you leave, or we're going to have problems.* Yes, that was confrontation enough for now.

46

Whats happened to us, Mac? We're at a salad bar, for God's sake. What happened to the days we could slip into Mother's, or the Bon Ton, and enjoy a two thousand calorie lunch, something swimming in a decadent sauce—a hundred or more fat grams' worth of pure delight? And a cold beer? Is aging something we have to fight so hard we forget how to live, and enjoy living, especially the feasting part? Tell me, my friend, is this plate of greens what we've worked so hard for all these years?" He made a face as he took in another bite of the salad.

Picking at the cold asparagus spear with his salad fork, eyeing the mound of spinach leaves, bean sprouts, fresh mushroom slices, and Feta crumbles topped with balsamic vinaigrette dressing, Mac wasn't up to the reply Sol set him up for. His mind was so elsewhere he and Sol might just as well have been at separate tables, if not in separate worlds. He was thinking of his daughter, as he did most days, thinking of how her death would never—*could* never—be reconciled, no matter what he accomplished in this lawsuit. The morning's encounter left him uneasy; it was all out in the open, the plot hatched for all to see. The countless days and nights of research, the information gathered from sources guarded by a maze of privacy walls, but out there on the information highway for anyone perseverant enough to back up from the blind endings and try again, and again, until the clearing appeared. Added up it presented a daunting task for the Church to respond to. If Mac's case theory was solid, the Church might never overcome the staggering force of its past behavior. There was just too much to contend with, all of it documented, all of it unassailable. It was almost frightening to Mac, to have so much evidence on the crucial issue. It was the same overwhelming kind of evidence he'd had in his big case years earlier against the oil companies. Lawyers rarely held all the trump cards, but he had in that case, and he did in this one, too. Such a display of strength would only firm the resolve of the Church. The real fight had not begun.

Expressions can deceive, but those he saw on the defense lawyers' faces hid nothing. Especially Katherine Carson's.

What a strange one she was. There was more to her than met the eye, he was sure. She was adequate enough a lawyer to take his deposition, but there was something else about her, about her demeanor, how intently focused she was, how unyielding her position had been. All of it suggested something else behind those penetrating looks. She might be new to the case, but she knew much more than the cold words appearing on the pages of the court papers. Whatever the connection, it was not likely to bear on the outcome of this lawsuit. Lawyers rarely affected outcomes of lawsuits at this level; judges, the law and a dash of fortune did. If Katherine Carson were perchance a hidden ace up Rich Quisenberry's or the Catholic Church's sleeve, the most it might count for would be a surprise gulp. *No hill for a climber*, Mac always said. No, it wasn't her that had Mac riled at the moment, and it wasn't Sol complaining about fat grams and calories and a better lunch they might have enjoyed in days past at old haunts. It was a feeling Mac had about saying aloud what he had in store for the Church, a parade of horribles airing every fiber and thread of the Church's dirty laundry for a third of a century, every smelly, dark secret he'd unearthed from every venue in the country, all neatly packaged into a buffet serving that would choke the heartiest appetite. That's what had Mac worried.

Worried maybe his case was too strong.

§

Promptly at 1:30 the reporter reminded the witness he was still under oath, and a composed Katherine Carson resumed the deposition of Joseph Bradley McHenry, attorney, plaintiff, father of Sister Nicole Michelle McHenry, deceased.

"Mr. McHenry, I'm going to hand your counsel this document." She handed a multi-page document to Sol, and spoke again to Mac. "While he verifies the signature, I will represent to you the document I just handed to your lawyer is a copy of the signed protective order. Our magistrate was kind enough to sign it over his lunch hour."

Sol showed the copy to Mac, who nodded in acknowledgment. There was obviously some hurry on the Church's part, some agenda calling for immediacy. He made a mental note, certain Sol was doing the same thing. He waited for Katherine Carson to resume; this was her show.

"Before we continue with your deposition, Mr. McHenry, I would ask that the letters we requested be handed over."

Sol reached into his valise and withdrew the same bundle of letters, still neatly tied with the pink ribbon, the mother's touch. He handed them to Katherine Carson, who gingerly placed the packet on the table a few inches from her hands, which she once again clasped, index fingers pointing across the table straight at Mac.

Katherine Carson spoke first. "We have no other questions at this time. However, we do reserve our right to continue the deposition in accordance with our earlier understanding."

"That suits us, Ms. Carson," Sol replied, concealing his surprise at this newest strange turn.

It was all so anticlimactic, Mac thought as he and Sol packed to leave. There would be more to come, to be sure; today's start was, looking back over it, little more than a skirmish, but he felt comfortable in having emerged unscathed. It was not a time for a false sense of security, but a long, slow exhale was in order.

Outside the large conference room, in the sterile corridors of Phillips, Dawson's offices, Mac and Sol were saying their good-byes when they were approached by Katherine Carson. From a respectful distance she demurely asked if she might interrupt. Sol invited her over, saying he was just leaving, that he had other business on this side of the lake, but didn't mind delaying long enough to talk to *Ms.* Carson.

"Actually I was hoping to speak for a moment with Mr. McHenry, alone, if that was agreeable to both of you. You know I can't approach him outside your consent, Mr. Lieber, and I would not do so even if it weren't part of our professional responsibility code."

"I appreciate that, Ms. Carson. My client and I, as you know, are in separate cars, and I have other business in the city. I don't know his schedule. So it's his choice. Mac?"

"I don't have other business like my counsel, Ms. Carson. I'd be pleased to stay for a moment or two and visit with you, although I hope you understand, I won't discuss this case with you outside my lawyer's presence."

"I wouldn't expect you to. I'll just keep you for a minute."

Sol and Mac shook hands as the elevator arrived. After his friend was gone, Mac turned to Katherine Carson and asked what she had in mind.

"Mr. McHenry, I have something for you. Actually, the Church has something for you. It's related to the lawsuit, but it's not part of the lawsuit." Noting his quizzical expression, she quickly cut to the chase.

Reaching inside her valise, she pulled out a plain manila envelope, clasped shut, bulging at the middle. There was no label, no inscription on the outside. It was as nondescript as any other office supply article.

"What is this, Ms. Carson?" Mac asked. "Better yet, am I going to regret accepting an unmarked envelope from you—from the Church?"

"I will tell you what's in the envelope, Mr. McHenry, and let you decide. They're letters. Nine of them, to be exact. They were written by your daughter to some of the sisters at the convent, from her mission in Guatemala."

"I don't understand. We haven't—"

"No," she began, cutting him off, "you haven't asked for them. We—the Church—thought you might, and gathered them for you. They needn't be treated as responsive to lawsuit discovery. The sisters who received them are quite happy to gift them to you, and to Mrs. McHenry. If you don't want them, no feelings will be hurt."

Mac took the envelope in his hand, slowly twisting it side to side, perplexed at the unexpected turn. He was still in thought when she spoke again.

"Mr. McHenry, the Church asked to see the letters your daughter wrote home to you. There was a great reluctance on the part of some to that request, but—"

"Ms. Carson, I really don't want to get into the lawsuit—"

"You're right. I'm sorry. I don't mean to. Please, it isn't that complicated. Your daughter was a prolific letter writer, it appears. Others kept her letters just as you and her mother have. Take it at that—take what you will from this gift. If it turns out you take nothing, that's fine. There are no strings attached."

"Are you sure, Ms. Carson? My experience has been there is a string attached to everything. My wife, by the way, is devastated at the Church taking our daughter's letters. I am not very popular at my home right now. I'm to blame, you see, for her having to give them up. I have assured my wife she will get them back, as soon as copies are made. She wouldn't let me copy them. She made me promise not to copy them. I made, and I will keep that promise, but I hope you will see to it the originals are returned as quickly as possible."

"The originals will be couriered to Mr. Lieber this afternoon. Or you can wait here a few moments longer while I have them copied. Which do you prefer?"

"I do need to run. Send them to Sol. Too bad he was in such a hurry." He paused. "You say the letters are written to the nuns at the convent?"

"Yes, that's right. To three of them, anyway. What I am telling you is, these letters were written to three of the nuns who knew Nicole while she was at convent. They are willing to give them to you and Mrs. McHenry, if you would like to have them."

"You called my daughter by her first name, Ms. Carson. Did—"

Her face flushed. She interrupted him quickly. "I apologize, Mr. McHenry. That wasn't proper of me. I meant no offense." She bowed her head, Oriental-style, in humble contrition.

Mac did not reply to the apology. He twisted the envelope in his hand a few more times, like an unopened gift, wrapped and mysteriously inviting.

"I accept your offer, Ms. Carson. I'll take this gift, as you call it, and share it with my wife. I'm sure she will appreciate it too."

"Wonderful," she said, more an expression of relief than glee. "Remember, they are yours to keep, if you like. If you decide not to keep them, the nuns would like them back."

"That's understood. Now, I really do need to head home, if you don't mind. May I drop you somewhere?" He punched the button for the elevator.

"No, thank you. It was very kind of you to ask, but I have some more work to do here, and I don't live far. I'll be fine. Thank you again for the offer."

"Certainly. 'Til next time, Ms. Carson," he said in parting.

§

She kept her gaze on the elevator doors even after they'd closed and Mac was well into his descent. She'd made the trade. It was up to him now, and to his wife. If there was to be peace at all, this was how it would begin, with healing.

———————

Elizabeth surprised him with an announcement during their quiet dinner at The Dakota Restaurant, their favorite. Between the corn-crusted tilapia lightly covered with a special dill-and-caper meuniere sauce, garlic whipped potatoes and vegetable medley garnished with roasted pine nuts, and the light espresso they called dessert, she told him of her travel plans.

"Bradley, I've got the yard and garden taken care of, and I miss my boys." She always called them *my boys*. "I've booked a flight to San Diego, day after tomorrow, and another to Durango, a week later. I'm going visiting."

"That's a wonderful idea, Elizabeth. Maybe I could meet you there in a few d—"

"No, I'm going by myself. This will be my trip. I'll spend a week with each boy, then come home. Danny is due to ship out to advanced flight training in a few months, and I won't have another chance for a long while to spend the time with him. Chris is adjusting to mountain living in Colorado, so what better time to pay him a motherly visit? Besides, they need a good spoiling. You'd just be all business, and ... " She stopped in midsentence, the message clear enough.

Another time Mac would have been mystified, hurt even, at her not consulting him first. But things were different. He'd changed the rules. The wound he'd created was still open; his wife's retaliation was better left unchallenged. "Okay, that's fine." The weak capitulation was not his usual way, yet another reminder of how so many things had changed. It also called to mind the day's earlier development he'd not shared with Elizabeth. The letters. He had opened the manila envelope, and glanced inside, where he'd seen three bundles of envelopes, each bound by a simple rubber band. No mother's touch, no pretty ribbons. He'd intended to mention it to Elizabeth later, thinking a nice dinner was in order first. In the instant she sprung her travel plans on him he made the decision to leave it that way, sparing Elizabeth the potential sorrow of seeing another sad reminder of their daughter.

Mac smiled at his wife, took her hands in his, and said, "I think this is a marvelous idea, Elizabeth. I've been too wrapped up in myself lately—I'm not telling you anything you don't already know—and there's no reason for you to just hang around here while I … well, you know, keep on doing what I've been doing. You might just as well go spend some time with your boys. It's a great idea. I'm actually quite envious. I wish I were going."

"Good, then it's settled."

They made small talk until the espresso was gone. As Mac paid their tab, he looked up to see the proprietor, their dear friend, standing beside the table. After the usual pleasantries were exchanged, and compliments to the chef passed along, their host's tone changed. His voice was more subdued, almost apologetic.

"Mac, Elizabeth, I waited until you were finished before I came over tonight. There's something I'd like to show you, something I'd like to talk to you about, before you leave. Don't let me rush you—you know you're welcome to stay as long as you like, and I can even have Shelly bring you another espresso, on the house even, if you'd like to stay longer …"

"No, no," Mac and Elizabeth said in unison, hands on stomachs in a show of gluttony, "there's no room left." Mac spoke next for the both of them. "We were just about to leave, actually. Is it something we can do on the way out, or did you want to come over to the house?"

He said, "Can we go to my office? It'll just take a minute."

Mac and Elizabeth followed him into the crowded, littered office. When they were all in, their friend closed the door, then fidgeted a bit before he picked up a large, rectangular object resting against his small desk. It was loosely wrapped in brown paper. He removed the paper, showing the back of a frame. The restaurant was known for displaying works of local artists, many who had developed regional acclaim. Mac and Elizabeth were no doubt to be treated to a preview of another fabulous work by one of their favorites.

"I would like your permission to hang this in the entry," he said, holding up an exquisite oil of their daughter … an exact likeness. Beyond the unimaginable cost, the painting's impact on Mac and Elizabeth was one of total surprise, almost shock. Elizabeth put a hand to her mouth as she sucked in a deep breath, and touched her other hand to the canvas, probing it lightly for the feel of her daughter's warm skin, for some sign of life. At seeing the likeness of his daughter Mac faced the rage he'd fought to control for the past ten months. Feelings for his daughter surfaced even as he reached out a hand to cover his wife's, protectively, knowing what her fingers searched for … wanting to find it himself, knowing it could not be. Their friend spared them further torture.

"Listen," he began, "I can see this has upset you, but I hadn't, I mean, I thought maybe enough time might have passed where this wouldn't happen. I'm sorry, both of you, really I am. It's still painful for me, too. I watched your lovely child grow up, you know. And those summer evenings Nicole worked here as our hostess, before she left for Dartmouth, those first two summers when she came home, she became like family here. I miss her too. Everyone who works here does. I speak for a lot of other people who do as well. So I'm asking you, could I please honor her, her memory, with this portrait?

"You know the bare spot on the wall in the entry, just behind the reservation stand, that's where it would hang. A small light on it, that's all, nothing more."

Elizabeth had already pulled back her hands, folding them together across her abdomen. She tried to say something but made no sound. Mac spoke. "May we have some time to think about it? It's a little much right now, we're tired, and Elizabeth has a long trip to pack for. I promise, we'll let you know soon."

"I understand. I feel so badly for imposing. I should've known better."

"No, no, it's all right," Mac replied, doing all he could to save their friend's feelings, Elizabeth saying nothing, hiding behind the same mask she had worn since, since …

––––––––––

They didn't speak on the drive home. The couple together so many years, taking pride in always sharing, never keeping secrets, was bound in turmoil over secret-keeping. The artist's likeness of their daughter, missing only the warmth of her living flesh, called their deceit into focus, Mac's hidden agenda, Elizabeth's silence about her deadly intruder.

To Elizabeth it was a lawsuit with an unthinkable objective. Mac concealed from her its outward purpose, just as he hid it from Sol. The secrecy now included a collection of letters from Nicole to strangers he was withholding, letters possibly holding great meaning to his wife. Even Sol didn't know about the letters. What would his lawyer make of it?

As these thoughts pinballed their way through Mac's head Elizabeth sat just as silently and tormented in the seat next to him, wondering if the meal she'd just finished would make it through the night, wondering if she would be able to sleep the night without waking and needing more medication, wondering when her husband would notice the jumpy movements she could not hide or control and ask her about them, or the painful winces at his slightest touch, wondering further if she would lie to his face instead of only by her silence, wondering if she would live out the year, wondering if the end would ever justify the means.

47

WHAT DO YOU MAKE of it, Sol? We're not looking at some Trojan horse are we?" Mac sat across the desk from his lawyer, who inspected the packet much the same inquisitive way Mac did. Thumbing through the envelopes quickly, Sol saw the handwriting was unmistakably Nicole's. He wondered what Mac was thinking as he held them.

"Mac, if these letters present us with a problem in this lawsuit, I don't know what it could be. We'll just have to find out the hard way, unless you want me to return them."

"No, I don't think so. I guess I'll go back to my study and start reading them. I've managed to wait four days. I don't know what's kept me from reading them up to this point … maybe it was waiting 'til Elizabeth left on her trip." It was not really Sol Mac was talking to.

"Go on home, Mac, get comfortable, read the letters. That's step one. Step two will take care of itself. And step three, and four, and so on." Sol, always the practical one. Easier when you're the lawyer and not the client, plus in this instance Mac needed the gentle, reassuring prod.

"You know where I'll be if you see something …"

It was still early on a quiet Saturday morning when Mac left Sol's office. Sleepy little Covington had not awakened yet, its quaint shops and galleries several hours from opening. The slow drive through the small downtown, past the old and architecturally disastrous courthouse, the renovated buildings here and there, across the small bridge that spanned the fetid Bogue Falaya River, then onto Highway 190 heading south, toward the Interstate 12 exit that would take him home. Traffic was sparse at the moment, but soon enough it would strangle any movement. Mac was not one to be judgmental when even the slightest intention was pointed in a meaningful direction, but each time he ventured onto the roads of the trio of bedroom communities at the north edge of the Lake he allowed himself to wonder if whoever took on the responsibility of traffic management in this part of St. Tammany Parish had any idea at all what he was doing.

He leisurely drove down Highway 190, opting on the spur of the moment to pass the exit ramp to Interstate 12 that would have taken him straight home. He would take the longer route this morning, the trip through Mandeville and Madisonville. He headed south, passing a surfeit of subdivisions housing the commuters who worked across the lake but opted for the higher quality of life the North Shore provided. Twenty-six miles each way. The drive across the Pontchartrain Bridge eventually wore him down, made leaving his corporate job and entering private practice an easy decision. Now, it seemed civilization was muscling him out. He wondered how long he might've stayed with his practice if not for his mission, if he still would have magnanimously handed it over to the young and hungry Matthew Courvillon. Mac reminded himself to check with Paulette on Matthew's progress.

His thoughts returned to the possibility of leaving the area. Despite his own misgivings, change seemed agreeable to most everyone else. Along with a five-fold increase in the population had come more commerce, and more opportunity. Crime had somehow stayed virtually non-existent, but how much longer could that be expected to last? With his children and his business gone, there was very little to keep him there. He wondered if Elizabeth would feel the same.

He turned onto Highway 22. The five-mile drive to Madisonville was especially pleasant this morning. Mac shut off the air conditioning and opened the windows and sunroof. The fresh air was exhilarating. Elizabeth would've approvingly sighed one of her large, emphatic sighs. He missed her. A familiar ache returned, a feeling missing for some time, but not forgotten. He'd never shared with anyone there were times, many of them, he felt the ache of longing for her from no further away than his office, or from some courthouse in a neighboring parish. It didn't have to be on a special occasion, and most of the time it wasn't; he would just find himself thinking of and missing his wife. Twenty-seven years hadn't changed his feelings for her.

He'd not fought her decision to visit her boys. That he hadn't surprised him as he thought about it. He could not recall an earlier time in their life together such a thing might have happened. If ever a trip to see the boys, or their sister, had come up in all those years, it would have been both of them who'd gone. Not that they were conjoined at the hip, or tethered needlessly, it just would never have occurred to either of them to want to go without the other. His thoughts again turned to change. For Elizabeth to have made her plans, and acted on them to the point of scheduling the travel, without discussing even the idea with him signaled change. More than congested traffic and another new subdivision close to home, this hit right in the home. It caused Mac some worry.

He had been preoccupied with his lawsuit for well over half a year, but every attempt to involve Elizabeth had been rejected. Although they were physically together, they had become emotionally estranged. His doing, though, not hers. The trip without him must have been the culmination of her long, losing battle to hold things with her husband together. Nothing else made sense. It brought home a deep sense of regret. His choice had put at risk the harmony of a life together. He'd still not overcome his own feelings of guilt at losing Nicole, and was faced with yet more feelings of recrimination for foolishly thinking he could balance a strong marriage with devotion to a mistress whose name was Lawsuit. Elizabeth had taken the morally high road, yet her denouement was not without its benefit: for two weeks he was free of any distraction, to put everything he had into his quest for accountability. He intended to make the most of the time. He would start the healing process with his wife when she returned.

He came to a slow, rolling stop, taking his place in a long line of cars, a quarter mile from the south side of the drawbridge. The warmth of the late fall extended the boating season, and river traffic rivaled the summertime peak. Every half hour the bridge swiveled, like a maestro's swipe of the arm inviting all to the grand show inside the big top, and remained open until the boats stacked up in queue on both sides of the bridge had passed. Mac could recall times when the bridge stayed open more than closed during a given hour.

He propped his head with the palm of his hand. Terns and gulls hovered overhead, searching for food. The Gulf winds calmly blew in the tepid salt air that, for once, did not reek of dead fish or worse. Ahead, as far as he could see around the winding line of cars and pickup trucks, masts of the sailboats and upper decks of the pleasure craft crisscrossed, some headed inland while others made for the lake, possibly further, into the Gulf. Mac missed the water. He thought of the last time out, when he and Elizabeth kept on going, as far east as the Mississippi coast, dotted with all its brightly lit casinos. It was the last time he'd seen her truly happy. Maybe when she returned they could go again. That would be nice.

335

A horn tap startled Mac. The traffic was moving. He waved an apologetic thank-you and caught up with the slow line. In a minute he was across the bridge and into Madisonville. He was ten minutes from home, but not beckoned at all by the emptiness awaiting him. His thoughts settled instead on the reason he took the long drive home instead of the short one. *Don't even try to fool yourself, Mac.* Ahead a quarter mile, just past the old cemetery, St. Joseph Catholic Church, the Madisonville Branch of the St. Tammany Parish Library, the feed store and the turn-of-the-century family home on Covington Street, were the familiar live oaks that stood vigil over his daughter's final resting place.

Mac had not visited Nicole's plot since the small service. Once he'd let Elizabeth talk him into going, only to falter emotionally and send Elizabeth on without him. She had not understood, of course, but had relented, and hadn't asked him again. He knew she went to the place, nearly every day, but he still found it an unmanageable strain, so he stayed away. His only contact with Nicole's memory was in his work with Sol. Today, though, things seemed a little lighter on him, with Elizabeth away, and every development in the lawsuit going his way. It seemed a time to confront one's own weakness, to deal with the undealable. The doubt that crept in, late at night, when he was alone in his study, mulling over evidence, charting the next step, the indecision visiting him more and more of late, had a home, and he knew where the home was.

Mac pulled to a stop at the end of the dried shell road, where the public part of the cemetery ended and the more private area deeper into the trees began. The loose shell crunched under his feet and the whitish powder stirred enough to settle as a film on his loafers. He walked to where the smooth headstone was surrounded by bedding plants and bushes, an unmistakable sign of his wife's presence. The sight of his daughter's name and the years she lived on earth chiseled into the gray marble sucked the breath from him. Not even the tranquility of the morning, or the solitude of this place softened the impact. Almost a year later, still so much pain, but he had to do this.

He sat to the side. Some inner voice whispered for him not to sit on the ground over her. He wasn't sure why, but did not question the silent admonition. He sat silently, fingering the blades of grass, and the leaves of the flowering plants, as he thought of something to say. It was important to choose his words carefully. It might be his last chance to make things right.

It took him forever to begin. He started clumsily. "Hey, honey, it's me, Dad. I've been away for a while, doing some things. We'll talk about them later. I just wanted you to know, even though I've been away, I haven't stopped, not even for a second, thinking of you. Besides, your mom's been here a lot, probably enough for the both of us. I know, that's a weak excuse, but if Mom hadn't been here, I would have. Somehow we'll see to it that you're never alone. That's the main thing, you not being alone. You need to know Mom and I will always be close by.

"Like when you were little, remember? When the thunder came, and you crawled into bed with us, not because you were afraid of the noise, but because you didn't want to face it alone. All those growing up years, we watched you, and listened, and your mom and I would say to each other, no matter how much you grew and matured, the one thing you never seemed to get used to was being alone. We tried so hard to always be there for you.

"When it counted the most, we let you down, didn't we? It haunts me every day. Forcing you back East to school … then your junior year, when you came home, lost and alone like the little girl awakened by the thunder, I should've known it was from school pressure. You needed me to make it better, not worse."

The memory was still fresh. He and Elizabeth had just come home from a nice evening out to find Nicole's car in the drive. A full six weeks until the end of the semester, no warning, but unmistakably her car, heavy with road grime.

It took her four days to come out of her room. Elizabeth ventured in only once, emerging to tell her husband their daughter just needed some time to sort out a few things.

The music that played incessantly, and the dirty dishes she left outside her door were the only signs she was there. Whatever healing his daughter was enjoying took a toll on Mac. Each time he threatened to play the parent Elizabeth coaxed him into patience, understanding.

She finally emerged. She was ready to spend some time with her parents, her mother first, girl stuff, then, if he'd have her, she wanted her old job back at her dad's office. There were no arguments.

For those next several days Mac marveled when he saw his wife and daughter together, inseparable it seemed. Their laughter filled the room wherever they were, and brought joy to what had become a quiet house where two empty-nesters lived. Whatever had troubled Nicole seemed in the past. Her gaiety caught on with Elizabeth, whose color returned, whose eyes shone as they hadn't since her daughter left home. Something close to envy fleetingly tugged at Mac.

A week later Nicole reported to the law office of J. Bradley McHenry. She kept a respectful distance during the first few days, sticking close to a joyous Paulette. To Mac's chagrin the two women formed a curious alliance. Mac's hopes for the reunion with his daughter took a back seat to her helping more with the clerical work than the research, the writing and the other more lawyerly work. Mac held back. Patience may not have been his best suit, but he knew his strong-willed daughter. She would let him know when it was his turn—in her own way, in her own time.

Nicole came home just after Mac was hired to draft the wills of a wealthy childless couple. They desired to leave their fortune, which included large parcels of land in both Orleans and St. Tammany parishes, to St. Joseph Church and the New Orleans Archdiocese. Mac was busy with other business, which left Nicole available to be his liaison with his clients and Father Robichaux, who told Mac daily how he delighted in the refreshing exuberance Nicole brought to the tedious process.

Mac and Nicole often worked well into the evening, more than once being greeted by an annoyed Elizabeth, grousing about warming cold meals for her workaholic husband and daughter. Mac sensed it had become the mother's time to envy.

Through the frenetic pace, Mac and Nicole shared lighter moments, usually after Paulette had gone home and they were alone in the office, the phone lines forwarded to an answering service. Mac held off questioning her decision to leave school; Nicole could tell him when she was ready.

One evening his patience was rewarded. Conversation centered on the latest news of her brothers—Danny was near graduation from Marine flight school and Chris was struggling with school and soccer. Nicole spoke so admiringly of her brothers, almost too much so, Mac thought. He asked if she felt they were too much of an act to follow. Her answer surprised him.

"It's not that I can't compete with my overachieving older brother or my undera-chieving younger brother—I simply haven't found my own niche. I'm not sure who I am ... what I am supposed to do."

Mac was stunned. *How could she feel that way? Of my three children, she has always been the one most together. How could she say such a thing?*

"Growing up," she continued, "who I was usually was measured in how other people saw me, what they expected of me."

Mac felt the stinging hurt of rebuke, but he listened. His daughter was baring her soul. He felt inadequate to the task, and wished Elizabeth were there. Talking one on one with his boys was easy; with his daughter, he was in uncharted waters. She had to know his discomfort. He feared where she was headed.

"I always seemed to know what everyone expected of me. In school, it was grades … nothing less than straight As would do. In sports, soccer, if I didn't make the big play …" She stopped herself. "With my classmates, I was everybody's friend. My life wasn't my own … I had to be there when this or that friend had a problem. I'm not complaining, Daddy. I know it sounds like it, but I'm really not. I liked making good grades. I loved soccer, being everyone's friend. Somewhere, I'm not sure where, but somewhere I stopped having my own life. Does any of this make sense?"

Mac swallowed hard. "Once I get past the shock, yes, I suppose it does. Your mom and me, we never—"

"Daddy, I'm not blaming you or Mom for anything. It was always up to me to be who I was meant to be."

Mac smiled at his daughter, and warmed when she smiled in return.

"Tommy became my escape. You can imagine how big I thought I was … seventh grade, dating the most popular boy in the school. To this day, the only boy I've ever kissed."

Mac squirmed.

"Except for you and my brothers, of course. There were other nice boys, and at times I wondered what dating them might be like. It was easier to stay with Tommy than to dig into the whole dating thing. So, while you and Mom were worrying we were getting too serious, I was using Tommy as a shield. I knew at the time how terribly unfair it was, but I wasn't sure what else to do. I thought when we went off to Dartmouth things would become clearer. They didn't. He was always so good to me, always the perfect gentleman." She was looking him square in the eye. "You know what I'm saying, right?"

Mac squirmed again. "I think I get the picture. Look, Nicole, we don't—"

"No, Daddy, I want to do this. Just listen, okay." She didn't wait for a response. "Near the end of my first year, Tommy started getting impatient with me. I didn't blame him. We'd been dating five years, and, well, nothing … nothing below the neck or above the knees. Like I said, he was always the perfect gentleman. Anyway, Tommy started talking about getting married, having children. And for the first time, I had to confront my deception. I couldn't bear to tell him what I'd known for so long, that I didn't really love him, didn't want to be married. Not to Tommy, not to anyone. I never saw myself as a mother, a parent.

"I started going to Mass. And to confession, and talking to a priest. We talked for hours sometimes. He showed me how I could open up to myself, and be truthful with Tommy at the same time. I made up my mind to do what had to be done. I knew Dartmouth wasn't for me. And I knew Tommy would get along fine without me. He must have suspected something—about that time we had our first real fight. We said hurtful things. I left his apartment and went back to mine. I knew then what I had to do. But I needed to say good-bye first, so I went back to Tommy's. My car was already packed. He started crying, apologizing for saying what he'd said. He built us a nice fire, and made soup. We talked some more. I tried, but the words just would not come. We fell asleep, in front of the fire.

"I took the cowardly way out. I left him a note ... used the old 'it's me, not you' excuse."

Mac's throat was parched. Odd, since it was his daughter who'd been doing the talking. But he had his explanation. The very thing he'd patiently waited for had been gift-wrapped and delivered with as much love as a daughter might share with her father.

He was still in thought when she spoke again. "Daddy," she'd begun, "there's more. I've always tried so hard, you know I have, as your little girl, to do the right thing, to be a good person. I want to—no, I need to tell you something else, about that last night with Tommy." She was biting her lip, looking deeply into his eyes, the crystalline green of hers searching out the aquatic blue of his, the thought so heavy on her heart cutting in line and speaking silently ahead of the words on her lips. Mac instantly saw through it all, knew what was next. He saw it in the painful look on his daughter's face, felt it from the sadness in her voice. He knew, from the wisdom of his own years reaching far beyond hers, wisdom that was now an uncharitable teacher. While she fumbled on the unnecessary confession, he felt only the need to make her pain go away, however he might, and to spare her this moment. His pain served them both. He would not put her to this.

He looked down at his watch. "Oh, honey, look at the time. I promised your mother we would not be late for supper again tonight. Can this please wait? First thing tomorrow, okay? We can finish then, I promise." God he despised himself for this, but what else could he have done?

Nicole's hands were trembling. Mac took his daughter into his arms. "There now, dear heart, everything will be all right. Tommy will be fine. You will be fine. You've done the right thing, coming home." He squeezed tighter. As he straightened his arms and held her in front of him, she'd avoided his eyes, averting her own, and he knew the unfinished business he'd stolen from his daughter was still on her mind. What shame or penance she felt was a hard enough lesson, not something for which she should batter herself further, least of all for his sake. In time she would come to know this. The same wisdom that gave him such clarity moments earlier now dictated what was best. Her pain would eventually subside; if necessary, he would carry his as long as need be.

A father's compassion for his children is tested often. Not something that can be practiced, it must flow freely from the heart. Having compassion doesn't stop even the well-intentioned father from making mistakes. The best a father can hope for is that his mistakes are inconsequential. As he and Nicole readied for their quick ride home, to a surprised Elizabeth who had no meal waiting, Mac hoped the one he'd just made would not come back to haunt him.

It was now but a blur of a recollection. Days later Nicole announced she intended to enter the convent at Sister Teresa. It had all happened so fast: one minute she had left school, but was adjusting to life at home and working at his office, the next she was leaving everything to pursue a calling she'd never once in her life spoken of. The mystery went unsolved.

That seemed so long ago. Here, seated at her grave, the same thoughts still rumbled in his head. Mac looked down at the mound where the earth had been disturbed to make room for his daughter. He'd visited so few cemeteries in his life, without a thought before about when the plots smoothed out. It was yet another jumbled thought to cross his mind. He had come this morning to face some issues, spend some quiet time with his daughter. It wasn't such a strange notion, to talk with the departed. It just bothered him it was his daughter. Acceptance was a ways off for Mac McHenry, and he didn't seem to be in all that much of a hurry for it to arrive.

Speaking aloud to her in death, for the first time, his thoughts were on the present. "Nicole, am I doing the right thing? Not the popular thing, but the right thing? You know the difference. If it were me, or your mom, or one of your brothers, wouldn't you be doing the same thing I am? There's a lot going on here," he continued. "Now that's an understatement, isn't it? Bet you're having fun with that one."

He turned serious, the gravity of his tone cascading much as the heavy humidity would be in an hour or so. "I'm in this all alone, honey. I've put a real strain on your mother, and on myself. But I can't not do this. Do you understand? I must go through this, even though it's the hardest thing I've ever done. You do know that, don't you?

"I could accept your death as an accident, a pure freak of circumstance, until I learned what happened was not just foreseeable, but expected. That's the most troubling part." The question plaguing him from the beginning forced itself out. "Why didn't you leave? What made you risk your life, ultimately give up your life? Whatever it was, I hope it was worth it. Wherever you are now, whatever it is you're doing, I pray it's much better for you than still being here with us, me, your mom, your brothers, your kids. Because, and I know I'm scolding, and I don't mean to, but I hurt so, and I can't stop hurting, but the rest of us here miss you so much. So very much."

Mac had locked his hands around his legs, much the same as Elizabeth had that stillness-shattering night. Now it was Mac's turn to gently rock in the upright fetal position, forehead pressed against his knees as he searched for answers.

"I figure you're pretty upset with me. I would expect you to be. But you know your daddy, and you know I'm going to do what I believe is the right thing. For almost as long as you were alive I worked for people who wanted to right the wrongs others had done to them. I'm in that same position now. If I'm doing the wrong thing I'll have to live with it. Just like I have to live with my own thought that you did the wrong thing. I pray you aren't regretting your decision, like I'm prepared to regret mine."

He stopped the slow, rocking motion and relaxed, painfully aware there would be no answer, no sign his daughter had heard, no sign even that she disapproved.

The words dried up. Whatever Mac had hoped to accomplish was unsettlingly unaccomplished. He felt no lightness in his spirits, felt no redemption in his efforts, felt no forgiveness or understanding from his daughter. Yes, he'd hoped after he shared this time with her that Nicole would somehow let him know she understood. He wanted more, of course, but would have settled for understanding. Like a rock cast at the sun, his effort would fall far short of its mark.

As he rose, wondering what he would say to his daughter in farewell, if he would return, how much longer his torment would continue, he saw on the ground beside him the packet of letters from Katherine Carson. He was puzzled; how did they get here? He'd left them in the passenger seat, hadn't he? Certain he had, as he picked them off the warm ground he instinctively looked around, certain he would see another person there, the one who'd quietly brought him the letters from the car. But there was no one. One envelope near the middle slipped out of the stack, and would have fallen to the ground if he hadn't caught it. He recognized his daughter's flawless cursive. Unease gripped him.

It was addressed to Sr. Mary Ann Richmond, in care of the Sr. Theresa of Avila

Convent in New Orleans. Mac set the others back on the ground as he inspected the slightly yellowed envelope. There was a jagged edge where it had been opened. He lifted the flap, exposing the folded letter. He weighed the consequences of reading it. Slowly he ran his finger along the fold, back and forth, as if to find some Braille-like clue, anything to spare him ... but of what? Pain perhaps? Or might it be more confusion? Was Katherine Carson playing him for the fool? Mac harbored no doubt she had read the letters, and knew full well their contents. She had not given him these letters as a goodwill gesture. There was mischief afoot, Mac was certain. His only question was, did it matter? What might he see in this group of letters to affect him, or his lawsuit?

Never one to shy from the unknown, Mac pulled the folded content from the envelope, opened it and began reading. Mac McHenry, plaintiff, father of the deceased, now voyeur, had much to learn.

48

It was Elizabeth, calling from San Diego. She was having a great time with Danny. Today he had liberty, and he'd escorted her on a special tour of the city. Yesterday he'd shown her his jet. She would show him the photographs when she returned. What had he been doing while she was gone?

Oh, nothing really, he lied. He would set the record straight when she returned, for it would not do to spring on her he'd just finished reading and re-reading nine letters their daughter wrote to three of the nuns she'd known at convent—letters leaving Mac sapped of spirit, saddened beyond even the death of his daughter. He would not disrupt his wife's trip with such news. It could wait … 'til she got home, maybe not even then. He wasn't sure.

Mac talked to Danny before saying good-bye to Elizabeth. He promised his son he'd come visit as soon as he could. Then he told his wife he loved her deeply, something he hadn't done in a while. It was important she know.

It was nearly ten o'clock when he hung up. The knot in his stomach from the letters had grown tighter. He was debating making a call himself. Against all better judgment, he reached for the phone. He punched the first six numbers in rapid succession, hesitating only on the seventh and final one. He closed his eyes, as if in prayer, as he depressed the seventh number and locked in the call. The first ring had barely begun when she answered.

"Hello, this is Katherine."

"Ms. Carson," he began nervously, "Mac McHenry here. I hope I've not disturbed anything important. It's late, I know, and it's Saturday. Actually, I'd not expected you to answer; I was going to leave a message on your machine—"

"Mr. McHenry, I don't have a machine, and it's all right you called. Now, what can I do for you?" She sounded as if everyone called her at the office late on Saturday night.

"I have a request. I have not discussed it with Sol yet, but he won't object to what I am about to ask. Are you okay with that?"

"Go on, Mr. McHenry. What do you have in mind?"

"I—I've read the letters you passed along to me. I'm sure you've done the same with the ones we turned over." He instantly regretted his last statement. Why procrastinate? She probably knew the reason for the call anyway … "I should get to the point. Would your client object to my talking with the three nuns?" He thought he heard a gasp at the other end. "Are you all right?"

"Yes, yes, of course. Mr. McHenry, you know you don't need my permission, or the Church's, to talk to any of the nuns to whom your daughter sent those letters. They don't come within the cloak of protection of the attorney-client privilege. I do appreciate your courtesy in asking, but—"

"Look, this isn't easy. I thought hard on this before I called. Spare me the legal opinion, please, and just let me know how I need to go about this."

For a moment there was only silence. He'd been rude. Maybe he should hang up. This was all so bizarre. Finally, "I assume you know where the convent is, on Hyacinth. You should feel free to drop by at any time. No appointment is necessary."

"How candid can I expect these ladies to be with me? I mean, have they been prepped to give me sterile answers to my questions, you know, the party line? Will they want counsel present? Tell me, Ms. Carson, so I don't waste my time."

"Actually, the nuns I suspect you wish to speak to have no idea you'll be calling. In fact, they have no idea you are suing the Catholic Church, so unless you tell them— and I impose no such requirement on you—they won't know why you are asking them any questions."

"What, just swing by and ask for Sister Mary Ann, Sister Josephine and Sister Veronica, and that's all there is to it?"

"That's all there is to it, Mr. McHenry." Another pause. "Will there be anything else?"

"No. Nothing else. Thank you for your time this evening, Ms. Carson, and for the okay to speak to the nuns. I'll—we'll be in touch. Good night."

"Good night, Mr. McHenry."

After he'd hung up, Mac gathered up the stack of letters. He would need them in a week or so, when he headed back across the lake into New Orleans, and an appointment with a hitherto unknown part of his daughter's life. First he had to tend to some personal matters: a boat that sorely needed attention, unprepared tax returns approaching an expiring extension, some unfinished business with Sol.

The unease was still there after he did the mental checklist. What was causing it? Fear? Dread? Both? Maybe in a week or so he would get an answer.

───────────

It was midnight before she finished her day's labors. Prayer the last hour, before that almost two hours with the archbishop, he of the unquenchable thirst for news of the lawsuit. She'd reported on the deposition. He had frowned deeply as he learned how pervasive the man's case against the Church was. It was their worst fear. Just as Rich Quisenberry predicted, McHenry was striving to close the Church's doors. But it was worse than even Rich had imagined. The Church's neglect extended far beyond Sister Nicole's death. McHenry had documented its blind eye at its clergy as well, and scores of years of abuse its own had heaped upon the defenseless. Not just the few documented abuses in this diocese, but in them all. It reflected a pattern, a pattern imputable to the Church as a whole, if the court were so inclined. If their judge were to rule against them on the standing issue the way would be opened up to pursue the entire case, everything the plaintiff wanted. She reported sanguinely to the archbishop, as any good lawyer would to a client.

He wanted to know if she'd handed over the letters … all of them. No, she answered, not all of them. Only nine, not the other three. The cleric studied her keenly, asking if it was wise to conceal such an important piece of information. While he would support her decision, he also felt it his duty to question its wisdom.

It was the only way, she'd told him.

An hour ago the archbishop had accepted her decision, empowering her to continue as she felt. As she lay in her small cot, in a seldom-used wing of the massive building housing the Archdiocese of New Orleans, Sister Katherine Carson prayed she was right.

Her first prayer, the obligatory one, was to God; the second one, the one she put her heart and soul into, was to an old friend.

───────────

He seemed to be rising earlier as he grew older, or so he thought while he watered the small houseplants Sophie had nurtured all those years. It was left up to him now. He'd named them, all fifteen of them. Most days he forgot the names, and made up new ones. What did they care anyway? A little water, a little sunlight, what more could they expect? Sophie had fretted over them, though, and treated them with kindness and respect. Sol Lieber, widower and plant caretaker, lawyer and confidante, did his best to follow his wife's lead.

Mac's cryptic message on the office recorder left him confused. *I won't be at your office today as we'd planned, Sol, so don't go in unless you have other business there.* Nothing more, nothing less … not like Mac. But Mac had gotten a bit strange lately, which gave his lawyer something to worry about. Maybe he would fill him in later, and the explanation would make perfect sense.

§

As Sol tended to the English Ivy, Boston ferns and the blooming Peace Lily—Maggie, Jo and, not surprisingly, Lilly, respectively—Mac was coming to a stop in the "VISITORS ONLY" space of Sister Teresa of Avila Convent. The thought of making the unannounced visit had gone into hibernation, awakening yesterday when Elizabeth called from Chris's apartment in Durango. She would be home tomorrow.

He'd come, hoping to find answers. It was half past eight on a Monday morning marked by a light shower and the promise of heat and humidity in the high nineties. The whole city wondered how much longer the heat could last, a strange question on anyone's lips in mid December, even in south Louisiana. Mac didn't let the heat keep him from dressing in suit and tie, out of habit. The walk to the entrance took him through a courtyard, into a world immersed in two and a half centuries of tradition. The statuary on the grounds, the Old World architecture, the magnificence of it all was impressive even to a Catholic like Mac. If it weren't for the painful memory …

There were no signs or markings to guide him to an office. Taking a chance, he entered the tallest of the three sets of doors facing the street. The cool was refreshing. The spacious room was dimly lit, the trappings old. The lone sofa was practically threadbare, and the two easy chairs neither matched each other nor the décor. Mac was almost embarrassed for the occupants. Despite the grandeur of the outside, judging by the inner contents they obviously took the vow of poverty quite seriously.

He looked about, but saw or heard no one. The place was quiet and empty. The wood floors were polished to a high gloss, and were covered by a massive woven rug that Mac guessed to be either Turkish or Persian. It, too, was threadbare, but worn as it was the rug gave off a grand presence. Mac was admiring its intricate designs when he realized he was no longer alone. He turned to see a rather pretty, smiling nun he judged to be about sixty years old, watching him intently. She spoke first.

"I see you know quality work when you see it. It's been a part of the convent for almost a hundred and fifty years. It's from somewhere in the Far East, I believe."

"Actually, Sister, I was admiring the rug, and couldn't help but notice how worn it is.

I'd always thought they were indestructible. Goes to show what little I know."

She extended her hand in greeting. "I'm Sister Agnes Ann, and I am more or less in charge of the office functions here at the Convent. How can I help you, Mr. …?"

"I am Mac McHenry, Sister. I'm here on some personal business."

Her expression changed to one of indecisive expectation. "You wouldn't be Sister Nicole's father, would you?"

"I am." He volunteered nothing else.

"What is it we can do for you, Mr. McHenry? I speak for us all here. We dearly loved your daughter. There isn't anything anyone here would not do for you. Please, just name it."

"Thank you, Sister, that's very kind of you. I'm here to talk to some of the nuns who my daughter stayed in touch with.

"From Guatemala," he added. "Their names are Sister Mary Ann, Sister Josephine and Sister Veronica. I believe they all live here. Or so I'm told, anyway."

"Oh, yes, they are all here. Do you wish to speak to them together, or one at a time?"

"Actually, one at a time, and I really would like some privacy while we're talking, if that's not asking too much of you, or them."

She smiled. "I'm sure whatever your needs, the sisters will do all they can to help. Come with me, Mr. McHenry, we're not far from Sister Veronica." Mac fell in step.

A short walk later through a series of hallways and corridors, then outside through several of the many arches, and they were entering an old building that had the unmistakable air of the sickly. It was not unlike a dormitory, other than the smell of hospital. At the far end of the hallway, Sister Agnes Ann stopped in front of a closed door, and motioned a *Shhh* with a forefinger to her lips. She tapped lightly on the door, and entered when a soft, faint *Come in* answered. Mac heard whispering. In seconds, Sister Agnes Ann motioned him in. He entered a room bright with sunlight, the flimsy curtains on the single window drawn back, exposing a giant magnolia in the courtyard. The fragrance of the tree's white blooms permeated the small room, overpowering the medicinal odor, ridding Mac of a queasy feeling the air of sickness brought on.

Propped up in the cot was a woman Mac judged to be in her late seventies, maybe even older. She had the frail look of one very near death. But she smiled at Mac, and in a surprisingly strong voice invited him to her bedside. "Come over here, Mr. McHenry. Let me get a better look at you, and shake your hand properly."

Mac approached the bedridden nun cautiously, gingerly taking her hand and completing the formal introduction. "I'm Mac McHenry, Sister Veronica. I was hoping to chat with you this morning, but I didn't know you were feeling poorly. Perhaps I should come back, when you're feeling better." Southern polite—genuine, though, and spread on marmalade thick.

"I haven't felt this good in days, Mr. McHenry, so you'd best make it today. Might not be a tomorrow."

This unsettled Mac. He hadn't come here to deal with yet another death … only one.

Sister Agnes Ann interrupted his thoughts. "Mr. McHenry, if you'd be so kind as to give me a hand lifting Sister Veronica into her wheelchair, I'll be on my way and let you two visit. She'll want to sit outside, in the shade of her magnolia, but where it's still warm. She likes the warmth."

Mac thought once more about the stifling heat, but didn't object. He gladly offered his help, and carefully lifted Sister Veronica into the wheelchair beside her cot. She was feather-light, her aged body ravaged by an assortment of cancers, but her spirits were high. Mac could tell from her giddiness she was delighted at all the attention.

Sister Agnes Ann walked with them to the doorway. "I'll have someone here in an hour to take Sister Veronica back inside, Mr. McHenry. If you'll meet me right over there," she continued, motioning toward the nearest building to their left, "in the doorway right under the balcony, at ten-thirty, we'll go next to see Sister Mary Ann."

Mac thanked her, and turned his attention to the ailing nun as Sister Agnes Ann whisked off. "Do you have a favorite spot under the tree, Sister?" he asked as he pushed the wheelchair along a narrow sidewalk as cracked with age as the face of the nun he was guiding.

"Right over there would be nice, under the largest limb," she said, pointing in the direction of a limb Mac guessed was at least three feet in diameter. Mac wondered what kept it from breaking off under its own weight. He saw a small wrought iron bench nestled underneath. It would be a hard seat, but better than standing for an hour, or sitting on the grass so cluttered with debris from the tree and the array of small birds chirping and flitting around.

He stopped when they were well under the limb, and shielded from the brightness of the early sun. He turned the wheelchair to face the statue of a prayerful Virgin in an adjoining courtyard, then draped his coat over the bench. He sat in front of the withered nun, who crossed herself, mumbled a short prayer and crossed herself again before she looked up at Mac, still smiling at him as if he were an old best friend come to visit. "You've come to talk to me about Sister Nicole, I'd bet. Sister Agnes Ann told me you're her father."

"Well, you're right, on both counts. I am her father, and I did come here to talk to you about Nicole, and maybe some other things that just come up, if you know what I mean." She nodded.

"Sister, you'll forgive me, but I had no idea what to expect before I got here. I'm a bit surprised to find you bedridden, and not teaching class. I thought you were a teacher."

"Oh, I am, or was, I suppose is more accurate. For over forty years. But I've been retired from teaching for over fifteen years. I'm out to pasture, as they say."

"I don't understand. In my daughter's letters—wait, I'm getting ahead of myself. Let me slow down, and start from the beginning.

"I have some letters my daughter wrote to you. They were given to me recently by the Church, and I presume they came from you." She nodded again, and he continued. "I'm grateful you shared them with me, even if you didn't know it was me they'd be loaned to." He stressed the word "loaned."

"Mr. McHenry, what may I do, or say, to bring you comfort this morning?"

My, but aren't we direct, for such an old gal? "Sister, I don't know exactly. I've read the letters, a number of times, and I've also read the ones she sent to Sister Josephine and Sister Mary Ann. I'll be talking to them later, after they've finished with their classes this morning. And—and—" He stammered, unsure where he wanted to go, how to get there. "I think, more than anything, I'd like to hear what you have to say about my daughter. I have such a void in my life, with her being gone. My memories are clouded, no longer the vivid, colorful images they used to be. I miss that clarity. What can you tell me about her? Tell me anything you can remember, please."

If it were possible, her smile widened. "Oh, Mr. McHenry, that will take us much longer than the hour we have. I could spend a year or more talking to you of your daughter. She was special, that one."

The compliment brought Mac no relief. He'd become accustomed—"accustomed" being a euphemism for immune—to the incessant platitudes of praise heaped upon Nicole. He made no point of it with Sister Veronica, however. "Well, tell me this, first. If you haven't taught in over fifteen years, how did you come to teach Nicole? I don't understand."

"I didn't teach her in the traditional sense of teaching, you understand. Sister Nicole was assigned to me as a very new postulate, just as the young nun you'll meet in an hour, when she comes here to take me back inside. I do love to be outside, even in this heat, but too much of a good thing is not so good for me." This time Mac nodded.

She continued. "Sister Nicole became my aide her first week. We're supposed to rotate my aides every term, but in her case we didn't. She stayed with me the entire time she was here. It was her choice, and it was mine. No one seemed to mind, so we just left it that way."

When he said nothing she continued. "You probably already figured it out, Mr. McHenry, but not only is this beautiful place a convent for the teaching of aspiring nuns, it is also a rest home for us old goats. In my case, it's also my final resting place. Very soon, I suspect, I'll be over there." She motioned to a place out of their sight, beyond the buildings on the south periphery of the convent's grounds. "Where so many others rest peacefully." Mac wondered if it was the same place the Church buried *its own*, as the two priests had put it. *Would Nicole prefer there?*

"Those like me who can't get along entirely on their own, well, we get taken care of by a young postulate, as I was saying. I was fortunate to draw your daughter when she arrived. My life has been blessed ever since by that simple luck of the draw."

Nicole's letters said much the same. Passage after passage recited the joy this old woman brought her, the clearer meaning she'd given her life, the thanks for keeping her on the straight and narrow. Nicole spoke to her as teacher, not as shut in or invalid, and as friend, not as burden.

"What do you want to know about her? It might help if you could be more specific."

"I'm not sure, Sister Veronica. Maybe for starters you could tell me what she was like here, what it is you saw in my daughter."

"I can tell you what she was like when it was just the two of us, Mr. McHenry. I can't help you beyond that. You see, I've been confined to a wheelchair and bed for nearly six years. They didn't think I'd make it this long, but I've held on. Sister Nicole came not long after I became too weak to get around on my own. I was pretty cranky back then, as I recall, feeling sorry for myself, that sort of thing. I'd always been a nun, a servant of God, a teacher, and I'd never thought of the day I wouldn't be able to continue my work. I never thought of retiring.

"Anyway, here I was, just looking for some excuse to vent my frustrations on something, or someone. I'd had two other postulates before Sister Nicole, and I'm certain they were as relieved as I was their tour of duty with me was up. I was sweltering in self-absorption. You know, I can't put my finger on it, not for sure, but I would like to think I saw something special in her the first time we met. Goodness she was such a pretty girl, but it was her smile, I believe, that just lit up everything around her. The first thing she did when she came to my room was to open my curtains, then my window. She brought me outside, nearly every day, for the two years she was here. She'd sit right where you are seated. It's like we never stopped talking and laughing."

Mac felt a tingling sensation. It was one thing just to be here, another altogether to be sitting literally where she sat, serving in a crudely twisted fashion the same purpose Nicole had. He struggled to hide his discomfort. "What did you talk about, you and my daughter?"

"We discussed everything imaginable, I think. But you're not interested in such. I can tell from just sitting here next to you. I have an idea what you might want to hear. Something about why your daughter came here in the first place." She was watching him for a sign of recognition.

"I'd say you're getting warm, Sister." *So am I*, he thought, as the perspiration beaded on his forehead. "Go on, please, as long as you feel up to it."

"Oh, I'm fine, Mr. McHenry. In fact, I'm quite rested today. Last night was a good one for me. Not like some I've had lately." She made a slight smacking noise with her mouth, the way Mac had seen so many of his older clients do. He imagined the saliva glands were drying up as much as the rest of her body. He offered her some water from the container on the wheelchair. She took several small swallows, and thanked him. She squirmed in the chair, positioning herself to her liking. Mac thought better of asking her if she were in pain, imagining what it would feel like someday for him to feel his own sharp bones poking into what little of his flesh might still be clinging to them. The thought brought on a warm shiver.

"Enough about my problems. When I was a young girl," she began, "living in small towns like Plaquemines and Buras, and later in Morgan City—my father worked the oilfields, which meant we moved around quite a bit—I took care of three younger brothers and four younger sisters. Daddy worked seven days a week and momma took in ironing and did some cooking for folks. It was a hard life, but it was the only life any of us knew. I was a happy child. I wasn't the only one on our block who had responsibility like that, mind you. We all came from Catholic families, so there were lots of babies, and there were lots of 'big sisters' and 'big brothers' helping out. We weren't poor, either. We had what we needed, a roof over us, food on the table, and we had each other. That's the way it was back then."

Mac wondered when "back then" was, but didn't ask, figuring it had to be in the forties and fifties. Before his time, but not out of memory's reach where accounts of his own parents' earlier lives struck a familiar chord. The entire post-war country must have been like this.

"None of us thought about things like going off to college back then. We thought about life after school, but that meant grammar school. Most of my friends stopped after sixth grade, the rest after eighth. Few went on to high school. When we became of age, we went to work. For most of us, that meant fifteen, sixteen at the oldest." She paused, Mac figuring she wanted him to take special note of something.

"Like I said, Mr. McHenry, that's just the way it was back then. With me, it was a little bit different. I knew from the day I set foot in church in Opelousas, when I saw Sister Mary Margaret and Sister Lucille kneeling at the altar, I wanted to be a nun. They became my friends as well as my teachers for the year or so we lived there. It was my eighth grade year—I remember it like it was yesterday. And when it came time for me to choose between work and high school, they influenced me to stay in school, as long as I wanted to travel in God's path as a nun."

She took more water from Mac. He was content to just listen. Mac, the good listener, at his best.

"I stayed with it, became a nun, and in my entire life have never for an instant regretted the decision. To this day, I know it was why I was put on earth. The joy I have felt at serving God and Church, and leading a life of piety and sacrifice, it's what I was meant to do."

It was nearly a minute before Mac realized she'd stopped, and was not going to say anything else. The bewildered expression on his face betrayed him badly.

"Mr. McHenry, I see by the look on your face I have left you confused, or wanting more from me. Which is it?"

"I am a little bit confused, Sister. Yours is a wonderful story of awakening, commitment, service. But how does it relate to my daughter? You knew from an early age, but my daughter made a spur of the moment decision when she was in her third year of college. I don't see the similarity, or, as she said in her letters to you, how much alike you were."

"I'm sorry, but I've grown very tired, Mr. McHenry. Our time isn't due to be up for a while, but I think it would be a good idea if we went back inside. Would you mind helping me?"

"What about the nun who is supposed to meet us here? What will she think?"

"Oh, I wouldn't worry, she'll come find us. Where else would we be, anyway?" A thin smile creased her cheeks, and the twinkle returned to her eyes, if only for an instant.

She was silent as he wheeled her back to her room. They exchanged small talk as he helped her into her bed. Once again Mac shivered at her frail, emaciated frame.

Her eyes closed as he set her head onto the pillow. He stepped to the window overlooking the setting they'd just left. Images of his daughter sitting with this aged nun under the massive tree, of talking over the things that kept them bound together, whatever those things might have been, crossed his mind as he searched for meaning from the few words she'd been able to share with him. He was still deep in thought when he heard her weak voice.

"Don't worry, Mr. McHenry, it will come to you. What you seek is right before you."

As Mac turned to ask her for more, a young nun walked pertly into the room and headed straight for Sister Veronica. She checked her pulse, and spoke closely into her ear, softly, saying, "Sister Veronica, it's Sister Noreen, I'm here. Can I get you anything?"

The only sound to come from the bedridden nun was a stifled utterance that Mac found unintelligible. The postulate responded as if what she'd heard was plainly decipherable: "Very well, Sister, but please let me know if you change your mind. I'll be right here. It's time for your visitor to leave. Would you like to say good-bye to him?"

Sister Veronica propped herself up weakly on a twig of a forearm. Her fingers moved ever so slowly, beckoning him over. Her voice was whisper soft.

Mac walked to the bedside and took the withered hand in his. He bent to the same ear as the younger nun had moments before, whispered his thanks, and wished her God's blessing. He felt the slight squeeze of the nun's fingers before he lowered her hand to the bed. He imagined she was already asleep. He pushed from his mind any thought of it as a final sleep, which would surely come soon.

The postulate ushered Mac to the doorway, pointing across the expanse of the courtyard at the figure of another nun who waited by an archway. "That would be Sister Josephine. She will wait there for you." Mac thanked Sister Noreen, took a last glance at Sister Veronica, and headed toward his next encounter with the curious combination of history and destiny.

§

Sister Josephine Rudiger hailed from Friedberg, Germany, a small village near Frankfurt. She came to America as a child with her mother to rejoin her father, a war prisoner. They had been granted citizenship, largely on the strength of her father's engineering background. He had joined the upstart Westinghouse Corporation, and quickly established himself as a gifted technician, later as one of its leading engineers.

She entered an all girls' parochial school in upstate Connecticut as soon as her parents settled there, and was schooled by their Order of the Virgin Mary. By the time she'd graduated high school, it was virtually ordained she would take her vows. She did not disappoint her parents or her teachers. She served her first five years in Germany, and returned to America when her parents became too old to care for themselves. After their deaths she came to the Sister Teresa of Avila Convent in New Orleans, where she'd taught religion for twenty years.

She and Mac were the same age. Mac listened attentively as the woman began and ended her life's story in a matter of ten minutes. He wondered if he could—and hoped he couldn't—encapsulate his own existence in the same brief period of time. He found himself again waiting patiently for the connection this nun, like the one before, had with his daughter. He told her about reading the letters from his daughter, about being touched at the expressions of love he'd found in them. She'd held a stoic appearance, her expression showing no sign of emotion. He wondered what he might learn from this woman.

Once more Mac was mystified. Where was the connection? *Why is everything such a riddle?* He tried a different approach. "Sister Josephine, I know my daughter was immensely fond of you, from her letters. I'm certain she meant much to you as well. But tell me, what was the bond you felt with my daughter?"

She became fidgety, and rose from the chair in a small anteroom where they'd been seated. She paced the floor and walked to the window. "Mr. McHenry," she began, "only Sister Agnes Ann knows what I am about to tell you. It is not something in which I take any pride, and in fact, as you hear me out, you will no doubt recognize the shame I feel. But you have a right to know what I am about to tell you. While we have all suffered a loss, it is yours that is the greatest, and for whatever reason you are here, if I can bring you comfort then I will sacrifice my own feelings."

Are they all so pious? "Please, if it's not asking too much."

She re-seated herself, and started another story, this one with a marked difference in tone and energy. The other had been from the head; this one came straight from the heart.

"At about the time your daughter came here, as a postulate, I was experiencing what the Church calls a dilemma of faith. You would call it an identity crisis, I believe. Either way, it's the same thing: I wasn't sure I wanted to live out my days as a nun. It was not a sudden realization I was faced with, it had been building for years. My life had been planned for me, and it was never a thing to be questioned. I would never have shamed my parents by leaving the Order while they were alive. I knew, inside me, I was not happy, but I also knew that while they lived I would endure what I had to. I was a very unhappy nun, Mr. McHenry.

"Momentum kept me going for years after their deaths, even long after returning to America and moving to New Orleans. At about the time your daughter arrived I had all but decided to renounce my vows, leave the Convent and the Order, and to make my way in the outside world. I was within days, maybe even hours of announcing this to Sister Agnes Ann.

"But I met your daughter. The first day she walked into my classroom there was something that attracted me to her, something that made me want to know why a girl who was so lovely and with an upper-class upbringing chose to become a nun. Can you see the fascination with which I would have held your daughter, given what I have told you of myself?" She looked expectantly for his answer.

Mac stammered a weak *Yes* even though he didn't see anything yet.

"I held back on making my announcement to Sister Agnes Ann. There are perhaps an infinite number of reasons why I did, and perhaps it is only one. You know the one I mean, Mr. McHenry, the one running along the line of *the Lord working in mysterious ways*, as the old saw goes. For whatever reason, I stayed my course, and each and every day watched and listened as your daughter absorbed what I taught from my head with her heart. I saw in her the spirit I lacked in myself, and it had a profound effect on me."

She sat back in her chair, clearly more relaxed than moments earlier. Mac, too, showed a comparable sign of relaxation. He sensed where this was heading, but could not make the connection where his daughter was concerned.

"Classes that had, I'm sure, been terrifically boring for my students for years, because of my hypocrisy, became interesting. Not just to the students; they became interesting to me as well. Your daughter had a voracious appetite for learning. In short time, I found myself becoming as much her student as she was mine. It became fun to teach. It became a thrill to see what learning could be like. Frankly, she rescued me from my pathetic self-pity.

"At night, when I readied for bed and took to my knees, I found a new dedication to God. There was an awakening within me. It may have been the only true calling to God I ever experienced, I'm ashamed to say. But it was such a glorious feeling. There were times I trembled as I prayed, and times my eyes filled with tears. My heart so heavy I could not even take my loss of faith into the confessional became as light as the fresh air that always surrounded your daughter.

"One day Sister Agnes Ann called me to her office. She had this stern expression on her face as she motioned for me to take a seat in her office. Very official, not like Sister Agnes Ann. She got straight to the point, asked me if I were carrying on with a man. Can you imagine my reaction, the horrified expression on my face? She told me later her first thought was that my shocked reaction was a confirmation of her suspicion, but my quick answer was of course not, I was as chaste and pure as the day I first took my vows. I demanded she explain the accusation, and she gave me the most wonderful answer. It seems that not only she, but everyone else around the convent, had noticed a dramatic change in me, and my usual dour mood had been replaced with another, one of exuberance … and no one knew why. Until Sister Agnes Ann explained it to me I had no idea such mood swings seem to take effect when—when—well, I'm sure you know much better than I do of such matters of the flesh, Mr. McHenry, so let's leave it at that, shall we?"

Mac flushed, nodding weakly.

"So, confronted as I was with my noticeable personality change, I unloaded everything on Sister Agnes Ann. She listened patiently, and seemed convinced of my explanation, yet I sensed there was something else, something about which she remained worried. I recall asking her about it, but she begged off an explanation, and it was forgotten.

"It was never mentioned again. I have never regretted my decision to stay, which I credit your daughter with as much as anything else." She looked deeply into Mac's eyes at this point, and, taking his hand in hers, said, "I must tell you, in all my years, there has never been another one like her. It wasn't just me, she made us all feel proud and happy to be nuns, and, strange as it may sound to you, she was one of us long before she became one of us. Do you understand this, Mr. McHenry?"

"Yes," he replied quickly, unhesitatingly. He didn't, of course, but was powerless to say so.

"There came a day, very near the time Sister Nicole was to leave us for her mission work in Guatemala, that I thought might make a good time for me to drop a little bit of the holier-than-thou convent mystique. You know, where we could speak on the same level. I called her to my office, and told her what I would be saying must be taken in the strictest confidence. She of course agreed. I told her the impact she had on me, pretty much what I have shared with you today, and how I had also shared it with Sister Agnes Ann. I wanted her to know, from me directly, how great an influence on my life she had been. I think it is an understatement she was speechless by the time I'd finished, probably the only time I'd ever been around her when she didn't have something to say. I could see she was quite humbled by the whole thing, and more than a little bit embarrassed. Not wanting to add to her feelings of awkwardness, I then shared with her something I believe is the source of why you are here, Mr. McHenry, my lengthy story having a point after all. You see, I then told her of all my students she was the one most ideally suited to teach. I think that made her the happiest I ever saw her the entire time she was here with us, I truly do. She hugged me so tightly, and told me she loved me dearly, that someday she might understand better how it was she had been an influence on me. She promised me she would be the very best teacher God would allow, and it would be me she would give thanks and credit to. There were tears in her eyes, and in mine, as she smiled upon me that day.

"Mr. McHenry, in all my years I have never been so touched. Not by anything else, not by anyone else. I will live out my days here, endlessly happy to be a teacher of young women who choose a life of service to God. I owe so much to your daughter. I keep her picture on my desk, as a reminder.

"We are taught not to grieve for our own, because the departed are with God. I cannot take issue with that teaching. Yet I grieve nevertheless, and each and every time I enter the confessional I begin by saying I have sinned by wishing the life of Sister Nicole had been spared. I miss her so, as I know you do. And I am sorry if I have brought sadness to you."

Mac was overwhelmed, drained again. The hand still in the nun's grasp gave a firm squeeze that all was well, words of apology unnecessary.

She spoke again. "The letters she sent me, I treasure them. When Sister Agnes Ann asked us for letters from Sister Nicole, I had no idea why. I see now it had something to do with you. I'm not sure what, but whatever it is, I hope it's been good for you. As much as I treasure those letters from your daughter, you may keep them. I entrust them to your heart."

It had been awhile since Mac had to fight the burning lump rising in his throat, and the droplets welling in the corners of his eyes. He was not prepared for it. This was more than he'd bargained for. Mac began to detest himself. It was good his time with this nun was over, for he had grown tired of his charade, tired of himself. Truth was, he had simply grown tired.

He almost skipped the session with the third and last nun.

49

THE BUZZ FROM THE intercom startled him. How long had he been sitting, frozen in thought, staring from the window with the Dictaphone's microphone in his hand? Twenty minutes? Longer? He shook his head, snapped into gear. "Yes?" he said to his secretary.

"It's your wife, Judge. She says it's really important, won't take but a second."

"Thank you, Sylvia. Put her through, please." Judge Maurice Daigre for once didn't mind the forbidden interruption. He picked up the phone wondering what major social catastrophe had befallen her this time.

She'd forgotten to tell him they were having dinner guests over. Councilman Russell and her husband, the interesting literature professor at Loyola, would be there for cocktails at six-thirty, dinner at seven. Just the four of them. Grilled salmon, herbed red potatoes and glazed carrots, after a nice salad. Their favorite white wine. Didn't that sound just heavenly? Sure, he told her, sounds nice. She could scarcely contain her delight when he said he'd even be home early. In fact, he was ready to leave right then. Just one small detail to take care of first. Some last-minute perusing before he turned over some dictation to Sylvia. Dear? Dear? He'd been rambling, and hadn't realized his wife had already hung up. Well, that certainly was important, wasn't it?

Where was he? Oh, yes, the *McHenry* matter. Back to wrapping up his dictation. He'd worked on this one for a week, after his law clerk had researched and briefed it for him. Not an easy one. In fact, a particularly mean one. Bad cases make bad law, as the old saying went. This one would be no exception.

A truly novel approach, he mused. Not many lawyers would've approached it as the plaintiffs' lawyer had, but then again, when money wasn't the objective, and there was a message to deliver, you grabbed at what you could. But a federal statute with few real teeth in it? The OSHA Act? Now that was a stretch, and not just of the imagination. Still, the plaintiffs' argument had been compelling. Inspired even, he recalled. Shot more from the hip than through the crosshairs, but effective. On the other hand, as the defense had aptly pointed out, there was no precedent, only the wildest assortment of "analogous holdings" from other federal jurisdictions hanging by the thinnest of threads. Of course Rich Quisenberry would adopt that position. He's always thought the law was inflexible, inelastic, even when they were moot court adversaries in law school. He smiled in his recollection of those halcyon days. Rich was a good student, and became a good lawyer, a fearless and tenacious advocate for his client, but he still didn't get it, did he? The law was all too often an unwilling bride, yet a wonderfully tolerant mistress, something the Rich Quisenberrys hadn't figured out yet and the Sol Liebers somehow knew instinctively. Interesting, wasn't it?

Musings aside, it was his, Judge Maurice Daigre's, job to "do the law," to cast aside personalities and prejudices, to preserve and maintain trust in the federal judiciary. He'd never adopted the simplistic view some of his colleagues had that it didn't matter what effort he put into a decision since it would be appealed by the loser anyway. That style of play didn't suit him. Even on the rarest of occasions when there was a tossup, and he could go either way, he never flipped a coin. No, on those few occasions he simply started over, and took a look at the case from a different slant. The answer was there; it was just a matter of finding it.

This one had been tougher. Each time he'd come up with as compelling an argument one way as the other. The briefing had been as good as it gets from both sides, and the additional research by his law clerk turned up nothing giving either side the edge. His own research failed to reveal anything persuasive either. He'd even set it all aside for a night while he reflected on the social implications, a consideration within his province in first impression matters such as this one. Again, it was an evenly divided issue.

In the end, he'd gone with what he thought was right. With little law to guide him, what was right seemed as compelling a basis upon which to rule as anything else. The best part was, he felt good with his decision. He would not be troubled by what a higher court did with it.

He finished the dictation. He instructed Sylvia to advise the parties he would announce his ruling in open court. A bit extraordinary, but warranted under the circumstance of this case.

This *McHenry* case had worn him out. It was time to relax. He was already looking forward to dinner with the councilwoman, the lady from the projects, her party's hope for something better one day. Hopefully tonight's conversation would be a change from the usual pointless banter about the troubled casino, or New Orleans attracting a professional basketball franchise. Turning out his desk lamp and grabbing his brief case, he quickly forgot about *McHenry versus The Catholic Church*, and thought about stimulating dinner conversation.

———

The receiver was more than a foot from her ear, and she could still hear him shouting. Besides the sheer noise, Katherine Carson was enduring a second form of discomfort early this particular evening: she was being scolded. Not since she was a grade-schooler and her own father had erupted over some triviality could she recall a man's voice being raised at her so harshly. Much more than a lawyer's civility and professionalism restrained her from shutting down the tirade from Mac McHenry. This was something she had foreseen, but had hoped against hope would not happen. *Foolish woman, foolish hope.*

"I mean, how could you!" he bellowed. "This is so low, even by the Church's elastic standards. And I mean you personally, *Sister* Katherine Carson," the emphasis on *Sister* unmistakable. "How do you live within *either* set of rules you are sworn to uphold? If not the letter, at least the spirit of both your oath of attorney, and your vows, tell me, where does deceit fit in? Tell me, *Sister*."

He wasn't quite finished yet. "I don't mean some simple strain of deceit. I mean of the most virulent kind. In all my years, never have I been subjected to anything such as this. The Church put you up to this, didn't it? Don't waste a single breath trying to convince me you weren't brought into this because of your relationship with my daughter. Oh, God, this isn't just deceit. It borders on sordid. It is beyond shameful. I am sickened."

Unsure whether he was just drawing a breath and coming back at her with more, she remained silent. She pressed the receiver to her ear. He was breathing hard. When he didn't speak, she began. Measured and unrehearsed, from a heart no less heavy than his own … a plea, really, not some useless, meaningless apology.

"Mr. McHenry, it's time you met Sister Katherine. Not the person you know as Katherine Carson the lawyer. Sister Katherine will be in the courtyard of the archdiocese in one hour. She will be alone. Nothing we discuss will ever become a part of the lawsuit. You have my word."

"How can I possibly trust anything you say? My every moment since we spoke last has been provoked by an act of betrayal. And the worst part is, I can see through it all.

That's the easy one. I'm the bad guy here, so do what it takes to lose the bad guy. But what about Nicole? This so cheapens and erodes her memory, it—" He stopped. She could feel him swallowing hard.

She had but one response. This was no time, no way to conduct an argument with her friend's father. The mention of Nicole's name had evoked a certain and painful response in Katherine Carson, nun and lawyer alike. "You wouldn't have asked unless there were doubt on your part. My invitation stands. I will be there in one hour, and I will stay there until morning if it takes … and as long as it takes after you get there.

"There is a private entrance to the courtyard from the south side of the archdiocese, the one on St. Matthew Street. I will leave the door unlocked for you. One hour from now."

Seconds later she heard the click, then the dial tone. She held on to the phone, praying silently for the souls of her friend, and those of her friend's parents. If he would just come, and listen, the rest would work out, be fine. God would somehow make everything better. But Mac McHenry had to show up first. So she prayed extra hard for her invitation to be accepted.

Even nuns have to grab at straws once in a while.

§

Darkness descends on downtown New Orleans differently than most cities. Below sea level to begin with, encircled by an elaborate system of dikes and berms that mechanically rid the city of its sea water, fully operational around the clock even when there are no high water events such as hurricanes and heavy rains, the city looks up rather than out at a sunset. All available land was claimed over a century ago, and the city was built upward after it could no longer spread outward. Buildings hid the day in the heart of New Orleans. Revelers in the city were known to lose track of time. In its defense, in the French Quarter few cared to keep track of it.

While shards of daylight still peered through empty patches in a clouded sky stopping just short of the far horizon, where the red sun dipped halfway into the far western end of Lake Pontchartrain, darkness had already set in where Sister Katherine Carson sat in the center courtyard of the New Orleans Archdiocese. The heat and humidity of the day gave way to a welcome coolness mingling with the slight breeze brought by the storm-boding clouds overhead. The ambient conditions were not on her mind, however.

She clutched her treasure in trembling fingers. *Some treasure*, others might scoff. Three letters. Three pages. Just over one thousand one hundred words. They were the only tangible remnants of her friend. She had lost others, but their memories were of another kind. With Nicole, it had been different and special, from the beginning. When would she tire of reliving the memories, give up and move on? It was the one prayer that she'd never made. Two tests of faith put her at the center of a tug-of-war. By what right did Mac McHenry believe he had an exclusive on memories and grief? Wouldn't he be surprised to hear there were moments, dark moments, when she wanted to tell him he was right to bear down on the Church, that the Church did have an accountability for the loss of his child? Wouldn't that just freeze an expression of incredulity on his face? She tried to picture it, and even came close, but there was no smile on her face at the irony.

The light moment passed, as had the hour she set as their meeting time, and another. She waited on, as promised. She hadn't asked where he was calling from, and he hadn't told her. It was a far shorter trip from the outskirts of the city, from where he might've called her, than it was his home. It hadn't seemed important enough to bother with at the time. Now it loomed as a critical oversight on her part. Maybe she should've given him more time, or possibly less time. Why hadn't she just asked him how long it might take him to get there? She berated herself for the slipup, realizing he could be there now if she'd handled it differently. She'd given him an ultimatum, a veiled ultimatum, but he would know it for what it was. Upset with herself, she turned her attention to devising some other way to make Mac McHenry confront her. He had a right to, and she desperately wanted him to exercise the right.

Absorbed in thought she did not hear him walk up from behind.

Only the flickering flame from a single candle splintered the darkness in the courtyard. Standing beside a trellis adorned with English ivy and sweetly aromatic jasmine he was safe from telltale shadows. He watched her for a while before he spoke. She didn't seem quite as tall or lawyerly sitting there, dressed in nun's habit. She looked vulnerable, much as the sacrificial lamb might. He pictured his own daughter dressed in the same fashion, and wondered if others saw the same vulnerability in her. How had the murdering coward pictured her before he cleaved cold steel into her warm, soft flesh? Had he considered for so much as an instant the after effects of his actions? Did he consider that there might be an accountability for him to face? Did he care?

The same questions, over and over again. In a different setting this time, but always the same questions. How would this nun help him with the answers? How would anything she might have to say bring some element of peace back to his life? How would she heal his crumbling marriage, surely as broken as the torn and ravaged sinew in his daughter's body? What mystery did she hope to solve for him?

He'd hung up with no thought at making this visit. *No way*, he'd said out loud after setting the phone in its cradle, *not a way in hell*. He'd vowed even harder that the Church would pay, and Sister Katherine Carson too. Still enraged to learn what he had from his third visit, the one with Sister Josephine, concluded only hours earlier, an eternity ago, he quivered with shock at the thought of meeting with the person who had so expertly manipulated him, who had put out the bait, set the hook and was no doubt relishing the thought of filleting her catch. And the audacity with which she had presumed he would heel to her beck and call. His fire that had begun to burn out earlier, after meeting the first two nuns—the same fire that burned slower as time had worn on in the case of *McHenry versus The Catholic Church*—reignited and threatened to rage uncontrollably.

Then Elizabeth called. She was ecstatic from a wonderful visit with Chris in Durango. He was fine, sent his love, and, oh yes, one more thing, she would return the next day, as scheduled. Mac had lost track of the time, but hadn't let on as much. She'd had more to say.

"Don't come to the airport. Patti Moreau is picking me up, and will bring me home. It was her idea … we have some catching up to do." Mac had been relieved to hear from Elizabeth, and thought nothing of the arrangement she'd made with her good friend Patti, the oncologist. Mac was too wrapped up in himself to pay attention to the details that would make more sense later …

His anger at Katherine Carson had lessened by the time Elizabeth said good-bye. She'd been especially tender near the close of the call, reminiscent of times gone by and sorely missed. His spirits were lifted by her words of intimacy, of longing. As he stood in this darkened courtyard, far behind enemy lines of the battleground on which his private war raged, he no longer harbored the hatred and longed only to get this over with. He owed his daughter that much. He stepped from the shadows to meet Nicole's friend, the lawyer who would deny him his justice, who would fight against the accountability the Church owed him.

"Mr. McHenry, I prayed you would come."

"I almost didn't. If your prayer included a separate wish that my wife would call after I just said out loud there was no way in hell I would make this meeting, then be thankful talking to her would change my mind. So, here I am, *Sister*."

"I'll take that as an expression you are here because you want to be. I feel my prayer has been answered, however so."

They sat down. Mac spoke first.

"I can see why my daughter would have liked you. Let me guess, it was probably an instantaneous thing, probably the moment you met."

"It was," she said, almost questioningly. "With both of us, really."

"Don't ask me how I know; I just know. I suppose my daughter would've seen in you everything she wanted to be, in one package. You're tall, slender, attractive, and a lawyer."

The look in her eyes pierced the darkness between them and then some, penetrating to the core. Mac fidgeted uncomfortably. "I've said something wrong?"

"What makes you sure I was a lawyer when I met your daughter?"

"Add it up. You only met three or so years ago. You've got a little more savvy than someone who would've just passed the bar exam." He smiled. "Besides, your bar roll number is an older one, putting you in the ten to fifteen year range."

"Ah, undone by my bar roll number. Thirteen years ago. Vanity prevents me from sacrificing the extra two years."

Mac smiled at the attempt at humor. *Give her credit; she wants to make this easy on both of us.* Soberly he cut through the chitchat. "What do we do now, Sister?"

"We start by you calling me Katherine, as I asked when we first met. I would like that more, right now, than anything else."

"You ask too much for starters. I'm not too far removed from Ms. Carson, and in all my years I've yet to speak to a person of the cloth by his or her first name. But I'll work on it. And that puts us back to where I started a second ago. What do we do now?"

"That's fair. I suppose I'd have trouble calling you Mac."

He smiled again.

"We began our stay at the convent on the same day. Nicole and I were thrown together in our humble little dormitory. We had private rooms, but shared a small bathroom area, and there was another door joining our two rooms. We might as well have bunked together. The walls are paper-thin, and even with the door closed we could hear even the lightest sound coming from each other's rooms. It became so comical. We eventually just left the doors open. We were already sisters by then."

She looked across at him again, differently this time. "I mean sisters as in the blood kind, not the religious Order kind. Just in case you didn't catch my meaning."

"I'm a quick study. I caught it the first go-round." Mac recalled how much Nicole had always wanted a sister. It wasn't until she'd gotten older he and Elizabeth told her about the complications from Chris's birth, how there would be no more children. For years she brought home pictures clipped from this publication or that with the sadly pathetic face of some orphan girl from Korea or Ethiopia or Mexico, begging her parents to adopt. Mac had no trouble believing Nicole found in Katherine Carson the sister she'd always wanted.

"No foul intended, Mr. McHenry. I forget you know nothing of me. I'm a little surprised Nicole never said anything to you about me, but I can understand it."

"How is that?"

"I'm not entirely sure. Let's just keep on talking. Maybe we'll figure it out together. Anyway, where was I? Oh, yes, our doors were open. Long before that we had become fast friends. We worked and studied hard, but we had fun too. She was so full of life, and I wasn't when we met. I was as lonely and as desperate as a person could be, running from unhappiness, and there she was, my light. Almost fourteen years younger than me, but wise far beyond her years. She was not without her own emotional baggage, as she shared later. We brought a balance to one another. It would have been easy for me to just take from her, she had so much to give. She asked for nothing, not from me, not from anybody."

"Tell me about her emotional baggage, please. It's the part I don't know about my daughter. It's the part I need to know. Her letters, to the nuns, the ones you gave me, they showed another side to Nicole, a person I don't think I knew. Does that make sense?" He set the bundle of letters on the table between them, and nudged it her way, as if to give them back.

She put her hands to her face, fingers pressed together over her mouth, as if in prayer. An eternity passed between them.

"Oh, God," Mac said, "of course. That's what it was all about, isn't it? 'Here, Mr. McHenry, learn all about your daughter. Forget twenty-three years of preconceived thoughts of who she was, what she stood for. See her in this new light. See her as she really was.' That's it, isn't it? My God, I'm such a fool."

"You are no fool, Mr. McHenry. You are the most loving father a girl could hope for. There is no cause for you to feel as you do. There is a very happy ending waiting for you here, if you'll just see it through the distraction."

"I can't accept that. You don't know how many times since Nicole's death I've admitted my failure to protect her, how many times I've had to admit to myself I let her down. Do you know the feeling, Sister? Can you begin to relate to the guilt and shame I feel?"

"For what? Guilt and shame for what reason? You dishonor her memory if you feel that way. Look what she stood for. Look what she—"

Mac quickly cut her off. "My daughter quit on life. She walked away from everything, a future, a good future as a lawyer, someday as a wife and mother, to what? To become a nun. What is that? Will she serve any purpose, any cause to better herself? It only proves she was a good person. We all knew that about her without the need for her to take up wearing a nun's habit."

"Out of respect for Nicole, I'll ignore the insult."

"I'm sorry, Sister, I meant no insult to you. I deeply respect you for what and who you are. I do, really. I'm very sorry for saying what I did."

"What you're really saying, isn't it, is it's all right for someone else's daughters to become nuns, just not yours? Because you had such grand plans for her, plans never considering she might have chosen a path of her own. Right?"

"My daughter had low self-esteem … even though I never understood it. She was always so vulnerable to things that reduced her self-esteem even further."

"And your point is?"

"Look, my daughter fell to the pressure of a difficult third year of college. I happen to know her relationship with Tommy, her boyfriend, had reached a point he was putting pressure on her, and in a moment of weakness she gave in. In a moment of confusion and desperation. The guilt was so great she just walked away from it all. She came home, to be with her mother and me. Home, where it's safe and warm and loving and forgiving." He cleared his throat.

"After about three or four days in her room, playing her guitar, keeping to herself, she came out, good as new, and life began to pick up for her. She began to work at my office, and we dug right in, father and daughter, just like it had been in high school, and summer days when she was home from college. She was always going to be my partner, my successor."

"What do you know about her feelings of low self-esteem, Mr. McHenry?"

"I know, for one thing, my daughter was self-conscious about her height. She wanted to be tall and lithe like her mother, like you, even, not thick like me. It never mattered to her she was drop dead beautiful, and no one even noticed that she was five feet four inches tall and not five feet ten inches tall, and would never have a model's slender frame.

†

No one could convince her it didn't matter. She never got over her physical limitations.

"She dug in, and became obsessed with excellence. I've never known such an overachiever. Nothing less than an A suited her, nothing less than being captain of this team or that, or holding the highest office in that organization was acceptable. She strove for perfection, and usually attained it. Still there was the nagging reality she would never be what she wanted. Even I had to accept she was settling for a second choice where becoming my law partner was concerned. When things fell apart at Dartmouth, and she came home, all the pressure and turmoil built up and made her vulnerable to anything offering a safe haven.

"I put her to work helping me with some business dealings at our parish church. You've probably heard her talk about Father Paul Robichaux at St. Joseph. She was spending a lot of time at the church. She talked at great lengths with Father Paul, and before anybody knew what had happened, she announced she was entering the convent. Just like that. Nothing at all to warn us. Her mind was made up. There was no talking her out of it. It all happened so fast … one minute she was here, the next she was dressed in a habit."

He paused. His listener spoke next, before he could continue. "And what? You think the Church tricked her, preyed on her in a moment of vulnerability? Is that it?"

"What other explanation is there? We are talking about a girl who had never given a thought to becoming a nun, who one day, out of the blue, not in the most stable frame of mind, just ups and enters the convent, and you'd suggest to me the Church didn't have a hand in it somehow? Don't patronize me, Sister. It happens every day in other organizations. Look at the way recruiters in the military do it, promising a life of romance and intrigue to impressionable young men barely old enough to shave. Once in, they learn it's just another hard work, no pay job, only with the added bonus that you also get to lay your life on the line for two or three hundred million people, too many of whom could care less. Why should I believe the Catholic Church would operate any differently? Did you ever consider that?"

"Every day of my life. And you are so right about the hard work, no pay part. There is no day in the life of a nun she does not work hard, and the pay, well, I'm sure I don't need to explain how that works. The physical danger aspect, yes, it's there too, unfortunately. We can talk about that if you want to. But I am intrigued at your idea that somehow the Church, what, hoodwinked, or took advantage of Nicole, is that a better way of saying it? And she blindly one day entered the service to God and

Church? Never once questioned it afterward? Never had the opportunity to walk away, no questions asked?"

"My daughter never quit at anything. She didn't know the meaning of quit. She wouldn't have walked away once she started."

"Do you hear yourself? Do you understand what you just said? In one breath you say she did just that—walked away from the life you had all neatly packaged for her, quit it stone cold, and then entered something you regard as little more than a cult following. Yet she never quit anything? That doesn't compute well, Mr. McHenry."

"My daughter was impressionable, okay? She easily could have made a spur of the moment decision, and would have stayed with it long past the point others would have walked away. She would eventually know when it was time to walk away; it would just take longer for her."

"I ask you again, do you hear yourself? Just think about what you are saying. Don't make me say the words that you know are inside you. Don't make me say the things that will hurt, for it is healing I am most after. You have read these letters." She touched the packet. "You would not be here unless you saw something … something about your daughter to make you want to learn more."

"The letters you used to lead me into a new state of awareness about my daughter? I'm still not right with that. The rawest form of deceit imaginable, and from a person of the cloth. And a lawyer on top. I must tell you, I've never been as dumbstruck as I was when, near the end of my time with Sister Mary Ann, I learned who you really are. It was an eye-opener, believe me.

"Sister Mary Ann was apparently the disciplinarian for you postulates, the poor soul put in charge of making sure everyone followed the rules. Like the other two nuns I spoke with before her, she had a real fondness for Nicole, as she told me my daughter was so high-spirited and fun-loving. The woman had a twinkle in her eye as she spoke of Nicole's mischievous streak, how she wasn't above a few pranks just to keep things loose. In all of Sister Mary Ann's years, she told me, no other candidate had spread cellophane wrap across the bowl under her toilet seat, or short-sheeted her bed, or ordered a dozen pizzas in Sister Agnes Ann's name, or a few well-chosen other juvenile pranks the likes of which she and some of the other nuns at the convent had to endure. Not 'til my Nicole came along, anyway. She even had me cracking up. Every barrier was coming down by then; I was ready to walk away from this whole lawsuit thing, just quit and go on, never learning the answers I still so desperately seek, but not wishing any further harm to the Church. So imagine how I felt when Sister Mary Ann said to me if I really wanted to know just how mischievous my daughter was, why didn't I just ask her best friend, her roommate, her partner in crime: Sister Katherine? I didn't think anything about the name similarity. After all, there are more Sister Mary Anns than one can count, as I understand it, so what's one more Sister Katherine? So I asked where I might find this friend and roommate, this Sister Katherine, and to my great surprise I am told she is right here in New Orleans, an archdiocesan lawyer, living in the north wing of the archdiocese.

"I got a bit of a chill up and down my spine at that point, Sister. I described you to Sister Mary Ann—tall, light brown hair, hazel eyes, slender, attractive, maybe? *Why, yes, it sounds just like her*, Sister Mary Ann told me. *And it was she who asked Mother Superior for the letters*, she just threw in as an afterthought."

Mac bit his lip, controlling the temper that had flared earlier. "Suddenly I feel the perfect idiot. What a sap I am." He looked across at her. "Do you have any idea how much this hurt?"

"You know I meant no hurt. More importantly, you know exactly why I did what I did, or you would not be here. We both know that."

"You still have some serious explaining to do."

"Do I really? Isn't it you who has the explaining to do? Not to me ... to yourself."

"I don't understand. That's misdirection at its worst on your part."

"Mr. McHenry, your daughter entered the convent because she wanted to, not because she was vulnerable to some recruiter's ploy to get her in—and we don't have recruiters, by the way, in case it matters. Read the letters again, Mr. McHenry." She pushed the stack back at him. "They have told you what you need to know about your daughter. You see it now, I know you do.

"Nicole was never happy trying to be what she thought everyone else wanted her to be. She lived to please everyone else, most of all you. To your credit, you never pushed her in any direction, you only supported what you thought were her wants and needs. You were a wonderful father to your daughter, the very best. But she was lost, Mr. McHenry, she was drifting aimlessly. She wanted something from her life, but wasn't sure what it was. And when the realization finally struck her, and she knew what it was, one day, alone in prayer in little St. Joseph Church, the weight of the whole world eased off her. She knew, had always known, what she *didn't* want, she just wasn't sure what it was she *did* want. That day, everything become clear."

"What didn't my daughter want?"

"It may surprise you to know that she never wanted to be a lawyer. She respected you greatly for being one, but she was never happy doing anything in the law except helping you. Not for her, but for you, because it made you happy."

"But I—"

"She would never have told you. She wanted you to just realize it. You were the smartest man she'd ever known; she figured you had to know. She gave you credit for knowing it was the reason she came home from Dartmouth."

"That was because Tommy pressured her into …" He could not bring himself to finish.

A look of compassion came across her face. "Nicole told me about that too. I can share it with you, if you like. It's very personal, girl stuff, but I think she would understand. I think she would even want me to."

Mac offered no response, a sure invitation for her to continue.

"When it all sank in that spring, and Nicole knew she couldn't continue to live the lie, she went to Tommy one night, knowing he would understand. He didn't, yet he loved her enough to not stand in her way. That made it even worse for her. Kindness disarms more than anger, as we both well know. Anyway, Nicole knew long before then she would never marry Tommy."

She paused. "That was another thing about your daughter I bet you didn't know. She had no desire to marry anyone. Or to have children. It bothered her so much to feel that way, being the daughter of such loving and happily married parents. She felt there was something wrong with her. She often cried herself to sleep bearing that heavy cross, sometimes others as well.

"Does that surprise you?" she asked. "You knew she used to cry herself to sleep in the wee hours of the morning when she was much younger. She told me you woke up more than once to the sounds of her crying. She knew it when you stood outside her doorway and listened. At first, you went in and talked to her. Did your dead level best to be a good dad, right? Find out what the problem was, fix it and make everything better."

All he could do was blink in her direction.

"Don't misunderstand me," she went on, "you did it the right way. How easy it would have been for you to bust in and tell her to quit crying, to blame it on the relationship with Tommy, but you never did. Nicole didn't realize until after we had been at convent, and we'd spent hours talking about it, what was eating away at her. Back then, when it was really tough, when you stood outside her doorway and thought about

371

going into her room one more time, she learned that it was something she would need to go alone. She learned to bury her face in a pillow to muffle the crying, and to carry the full weight of it all on her own shoulders. She loved you so much, she couldn't bear to drag you into her pit any more."

"I don't understand. You are talking about my daughter, who, yes, for a short time did have a growing up-type adjustment she had to go through. What young girl doesn't? Her mother and I never turned a deaf ear or blind eye to her needs. We saw her struggling with some growing pains, and we walked through those times with her. Yes, there was a period of time she cried at night—again, what teenage girl doesn't?—but we're not talking about an every night thing. I refuse to believe that."

She just stared at him. The look spoke volumes. He hung his head. "Is this the part where the father learns just how stupid he was?"

"It doesn't have to be that way. This doesn't have to be a guilt trip or latter-day awakening for you. But you do have much to learn about your daughter."

He rubbed his chin, looked up again, and asked with pleading eyes for more.

"Things eventually caught up with Nicole. Years of carrying around her burden reached a point where she could no longer deny it was time to confront things. That was around the time you and her mother returned home from a nice outing, and found her car parked in the driveway at your home. You remember that, don't you?"

"Sure I do." His reply sounded too glib, and he apologized for it. "I didn't mean that the way it came out. Forgive me."

"Nothing to forgive. This is not going to work if we're going to spend our time walking on eggshells."

"You're right. I'm okay with that."

"Nicole needed the comfort of home, and family. You and Elizabeth, you were her rock. She needed you both. She was an emotional wreck. School … expectations … her relationship with Tommy … everything had worn her down. She felt trapped, with nowhere to turn, except home and family. None of this should come as a surprise to you."

"Why do you say that? All of it comes as a surprise to me. Except the part about her family being there for her."

"That's not my point. Are you certain you did not know she was struggling? Can you honestly say you suspected nothing? Not even with Tommy?"

Mac had already crossed this bridge, when Nicole came home from Dartmouth. He'd known something was upsetting his daughter. He'd suspected it was a spat with

Tommy. Elizabeth told him flatly there had been no spat, that their daughter just needed time to sort out a few things. Mac gave her space, first her time with Elizabeth, then his turn. Afterward, things had been fine. He told Katherine Carson all of this. He left out the one episode, though, the one that had ripped his insides out at seeing his daughter so torn over a confession she felt obligated to make … something he could not bear to put her through. Now a stranger was telling him there was more to that episode. It was going to hurt; he got ready.

"Mr. McHenry? Are you still with us?" She had concern in her eyes.

"I slipped into thought. I do it a lot. I'm sorry. Please go on."

"That night, her last in Hanover, Nicole went to Tommy to say good-bye. She had been his girl for nearly seven years, and other than one little petting episode in junior high they had never … well, you know. Nicole kept him at bay through those years a young man has typical yearnings, and eventually Tommy accepted it. Nicole just wasn't interested in sex, as she explained it to me. The biological impulses somehow passed her by. She even wondered whether she was abnormal for a while, but had nothing to compare normal with. She couldn't explain it, not to herself, not to anybody. She just carried it inside, all the while deceiving Tommy. He was convenient. That's exactly the way she put it. As long as Tommy was there, Mr. All-American Guy, there was no pressure for her to be dating around, and to have to contend with the same problems with other boys. As the years with Tommy went by, it became harder for her to carry on the deceit. It finally wore her down.

"That night, with all the despair and confusion inside her, she thought of Tommy, and how good he'd always been to her. She wanted to make good-bye something less than heartbreaking to him. There was only one way she could do that. She even thought if she gave herself to him it might make a difference, awaken in her those things other girls found normal, exciting. She was willing to try anything. When Tommy figured out what she had in mind—'the great seduction' she called it—and you may find this very hard to believe, I know I did, he actually tried to talk her out of it. He knew something wasn't right. He was kind and compassionate enough to say no, to stop it from happening, never suspecting she might leave the next day. That made her want to go through with it all the more. And of course it happened, on a cold, early spring night, in front of a fire, and it was a most beautiful experience for her. I should think every girl would wish for her first time to be like that. I know it wasn't for me, and if I had been prone to envy when I heard the story from Nicole I'm sure I would have envied her the experience."

She eyed him curiously. "I can sense what you're thinking. I'm not a virgin, Mr. McHenry. I have known the carnal side of life. My experiences were mostly good ones, luckily, but that's another story. As for what I am telling you, you should harbor no unkind thoughts toward Tommy. He was the gentleman, the picture of chivalry. Nicole left him a letter, explaining 'why' the best she could. She doubted he'd understand, but there was no turning back for her."

"I'm so uncomfortable with this, Sister. I guess I knew they had—how can I say it —consummated the relationship. Is that acceptable for a father to say about his daughter? I've blamed Tommy for it happening. Now I suppose this changes that. Why was she in such inner turmoil? What was it that kept her from being as happy on the inside as she appeared to all of us to be on the outside? In your time together, did you two ever figure that out? I would be happy now just to know the answer to that question."

"We sure worked on it enough. I'm not certain the answer we came up with will be acceptable to you, though. It's quite extraordinary when you think about it."

"What, I'm good only for ordinary explanations? You can do better than that."

"Ouch. Okay, let's see what you make of it. It goes something like this: your daughter never quite fit in. Her earliest recollections were of seeing things differently, of feeling differently about the things that wrap us in our everyday existences. She felt God made her special. She truly felt God had touched her. Once she tried to talk to you about it. You gave her the stock parental answer, that she was special in God's eyes. But she wasn't looking for some stock answer children get from their parents. She knew, beyond a doubt, that God truly had touched her … she just didn't know how to deal with it. I'm not sure any child would."

"I don't recall the conversation. I wish I could."

"I wouldn't worry. It's not the point, anyway. What is important is Nicole trying afterward to figure out what God had in store for her. She searched for anything to unlock the mystery, and all she could come up with was the notion if she was good, and stayed good, and made her parents proud and happy, that had to be the answer. The problem was, no matter how hard she tried, and how well she did, the void was still there. Praise from her parents and from others wasn't enough. She became lost in a sense of failure.

"Did you know Nicole loved going to Mass? It was where God protected her. She didn't allow unrestfulness to follow her into the sanctuary of the church. It was peace she didn't know anywhere else. Every other aspect of her life was a struggle, and things—things such as peer pressure, and the fear she would hurt you and her

374
✝

mother and those others who loved and cared for her—if she didn't conform to their expectations, those things distracted her, pulled her form the refuge the Church gave her. After she'd fought it all she could, one day she walked into your little church in Madisonville, took to her knees, and gave herself up to Him. The part you are having trouble accepting is Nicole was never happier in her life than when she took that step. As corny as it sounds, the bonds slipped that day, and she was set free. Her life, and the lives she touched after that day, are infinitely richer for that experience. It had nothing to do with her height, her physique, or any feeling of low self-esteem.

"I believe Nicole was touched by the hand of God, Mr. McHenry. It used to be a passing thought, but I know it for certain now. Your daughter was chosen for something none of us could understand. It pains me so to think it meant she should sacrifice her life, but I can no longer question even that. I miss her so, I truly do. I was telling myself before you got here you have no right to the corner on the grief market. We who knew Nicole are richer for knowing her, poorer yet at her loss. There is no way to explain what happened other than it was God's will. As hard as that is to accept, it's the way it must be."

Mac was shaking his head. "I can't accept your explanation. I don't see what happened to Nicole as a sign of His will. I understand now, I really do, she gave herself to God, and her life was the better for it. I can even accept Nicole did not cave in to the pressure of a life of seclusion as a means of escaping reality. I never wanted to think that of her. But," he went on, "I cannot excuse the Church for its neglect of her safety, and for its inaction leading to her death. Neither the father nor the lawyer in me is so forgiving. The Church hasn't earned that much from me."

"And you think Nicole would approve? Is that what she stood for?"

"This isn't her decision to make. The lawsuit isn't Sister Nicole versus the Catholic Church. It's me, her father, who's the plaintiff. I'm the guy who represents all those priests and nuns who the Church has used and ignored for the past half-century or so, who deserved better. My daughter's is just one part in the story."

She glared at him. "That's the most pitiable case of rationalization I've ever heard."

"That's awfully judgmental of you, Sister. Where do you get off judging me? Your past pleasures of the flesh notwithstanding, until you've suffered a loss such as I have, I suggest you stick to what you know, not what you think. It isn't you who will never hold your child again, or see her smile, or get to tell her to clean her room, or turn down her music."

She looked down at the table, sighing heavily. With one hand she held the collection of envelopes on the table top while she traced the rectangular border of the package with her other forefinger. Mac watched her nervousness, certain she was about to say something, certain he'd said enough for the moment.

"Perhaps you are right. In spite of what you may think, my purpose in giving you these letters was not to entice you to drop your lawsuit. I intended to do nothing more than what I hope I have done … help open your eyes to who your daughter really was, let you see she had moved on. You know from reading her letters to the Sisters—even if you don't believe a word I've just told you—she freely gave her life to God, and every day of her life she was happy for it. She lived for those people in her tiny village, and accepted every risk that came with the job. You've seen it in her own hand, heard it from me and the others. Of course, if you want to continue believing the Church somehow brainwashed her into such a state of mind, I can't stop you. I think you're wise beyond that. Your daughter gave you credit for being so, anyway."

There was more. "I understand how you feel. You'll have to take what I say on faith. But you need to accept something, Mr. McHenry, as hard as it might seem. Your daughter, the one with the messy room, and the loud music … she left home. Never your heart, but most certainly your home. There is no good to come of holding onto that memory any longer."

There was both hurt and anger in her voice. Mac knew it was time to quit. This would move on to another day, another time. Before tempers flared, and things that needlessly hurt were said, he thought it best to leave. "Sister, we've talked way past midnight, and my wife is coming home tomorrow afternoon. It's probably best I head home."

"I went too far, didn't I, with my last statement? You know I meant no—"

"Don't apologize. The truth is, it is late, I am very tired. I've got some house cleaning to do, and could use a little rest. But I'm glad I called you, and that you met with me. Thank you."

"Me, too. Do I need to worry about you on the long drive back home?"

"I'll be fine," Mac said, as he rose from his chair. "I can see myself out."

"Godspeed," she whispered as he walked away.

———————

A silent prayer followed. It was still being said as the door to the outside world clicked shut behind him. When it was finished, she picked up the packet from the table, and placed it in her front pocket, right alongside the three letters of her own.

50

He overslept. Last night was painful. So much of what Katherine Carson said made sense, explained much ... but he still felt empty. Had he been so much the ogre his daughter could not come to him, share with him all she had with her new friend? How should he feel now, having so poorly known his daughter?

He made coffee, and began straightening the house. Elizabeth would be home in less than an hour, and there was still much to do. Recollections of his conversation with Katherine Carson persisted, would not let go. His daughter, so troubled, so in need. What could he and Elizabeth have done differently?

If Katherine Carson was right, becoming a nun ended Nicole's despair, made her life complete. Mac couldn't argue it; he'd read it in her letters. Her happiness in Refugio was no act. Sadness of a different kind was on Mac's mind this morning. It tore at him, this feeling others saw in her what he failed to see. How could he have been so blind?

He missed her more than ever. His grief was overwhelming. He began to pray.

I need one more chance ... please, let me have one more minute with my daughter, to tell her how blind, how wrong I was. I need this more than anything I've ever needed in my life. Please, please, I am begging You. You can make it happen, I know You can. You gave my daughter a miracle, now give me one. I gave up my daughter for You, all I want is a small piece back, just for a moment. I'll stop all my foolishness, I'll go away ...

The ringing interrupted his prayer. He wasn't near enough to the phone to catch it before the answering machine picked up. Sol's voice came over the speaker.

"Mac, Sol. Listen, I just opened my mail. I had my investigator friend look into our new lawyer, Ms. Katherine Carson, when you and I couldn't find anything. I just got the report. You're not gonna believe this. She's a nun. I'm serious, Mac, a nun. *Sister Katherine.* Can you believe that? Carson was her maiden name, which she took back when she became a nun. She's carried on the roll of attorneys as Katherine Meadows. That was her married name. Meadows, got that? Ring a bell? It gets kind of messy here. She was a brilliant associate down at Phillips, Dawson—our friend Quisenberry's firm. Seems she had a husband, a doctor, and a son, not quite two. They were killed by a drunk driver about six or seven years ago. Remember Billy Sheene? He was that securities lawyer with the Conrad, Dupre firm, the guy who got soused after the big deal they closed, and ran over the guy out jogging with his kid in the stroller? You guessed right, it was her husband and kid. Big news, bad news, made worse when Sheene got off with the "involuntary intoxication" story the jury bought. She dropped under the radar after that. Until now. Look, I'll fax you the report. Call me." Click. Dead silence.

Except for his trembling hands, Mac was motionless. He felt small, shriveled, dirty. He despised himself. She'd just sat there last night as he sanctimoniously ripped into her.

She knew his sadness.

He needed to be some place where he could go and hide and wish away the mound of dirt he'd covered himself with. He also had a prayer to finish.

Something pushed and pulled him up the familiar flight of stairs to the second floor, down the hall to the closed door. He hadn't been in her room since the service. He turned the knob, entered tentatively, searching. He walked in, as softly as he had when she slept in her crib. The room was antiseptically clean. He looked around, finding the Dartmouth and Mandeville High pennants where they still hung on the walls, the framed photographs on her dresser, the souvenir blanket from a family trip to Disney World at the foot of her bed.

Thoughts of Katherine Carson crowded in with thoughts of his daughter. He was still trembling. He couldn't shake the shakes. He groped for the prayer he was in the middle of when the phone rang. He tried to bring it back, to finish what he'd started. He *needed* to finish that prayer. He was here now, giving in to whatever force had delivered him to his daughter's room. This was a message, wasn't it? He was willing to let go, he had already let go; couldn't God see? He would open his eyes and his heart to whatever else God had in store for him, this he promised, if just this one prayer would be answered.

Through watery eyes he searched the room for his daughter. She was there, he knew it. He could feel her. A father knows. His prayer was answered. He looked over his shoulder. Toward the closet. At the bed. At the walls, the adornments everywhere.

He clicked on her stereo. A compact disc she'd played over and over was still in. A familiar song filled the room.

He was spinning. The room was spinning. Everywhere he turned she was not there. Why wouldn't things be still? He wanted to see her, talk to her, one more time, tell her how sorry he was, tell her so many other things. Couldn't she just let him? "I'm sorry, Nicole. I'm so sorry, baby. Please forgive your daddy. Where are you honey?"

Words could no longer choke their way from his throat. Only throaty spasms yielding to heaving cries. Tears so long suppressed flowed freely. The room spun wildly. All was a blur of color, a spinning top with him at the epicenter. Walls were misshapen, bent as funhouse mirrors. Then he saw her. Through it all he saw his daughter. *Oh, God, he cried, Oh, dear God, Oh thank you, dear merciful Lord, Oh my Nicole, oh baby,* he cried out, reaching for her. She was right there, right in front of him, barely out of reach. He strained, his feet bolted to the floor, grabbing at the space between them as he fell, while the room kept spinning, and the haunting melody continued, and he was uncontrollably crying, and crying out for her as everything in the universe imploded into a dark mass and came crashing down on him.

379

†

51

B<small>RADLEY! BRADLEY! TALK TO</small> me, Bradley!"

He opened his eyes to Elizabeth. His head was in her lap, her face lined with worry. "Bradley, are you all right? I'm calling for help if you don't answer me right now."

"Elizabeth, I saw her. It's Nicole. She was just here." He moved his head side to side, scanning the room for her. "You must have seen her."

"Oh, Bradley, oh, dear, dear Bradley. Please don't have gone mad on me while I was gone. Don't do that to me. It's the one thing I don't think I could bear."

"No, you don't understand. She was here. I really saw her." She wiped his cheeks dry.

"I prayed to see her, Elizabeth. I asked God to give me a chance to tell her how sorry I am, and he answered my prayer. Don't you understand?"

She pressed his head to her bosom. She spoke when he was settled.

"Bradley, tell me what's happened. Tell me what's gone on while I was away. I fear there's much you haven't told me when I called."

They talked into the night, huddled on the floor of their daughter's room, holding on as young lovers might have, drawing strength from each other as they had all their lives together. She saw his tears for the first time, drying each carefully, tenderly. When he finally fell asleep, hours later, she covered him with a blanket and put one of Nicole's pillows under his head. She kissed him on the forehead and rose to leave. Standing at the doorway, looking back on him in the half darkness, she knew the ordeal was over. Whatever this was, whatever strange thing she had walked into earlier, it was a sign, a good sign. It would end soon, soon enough for her she hoped. This nun, this exceptional woman her husband had talked about, she would find her and talk to her. She owed her much. There would still be time for them to meet and talk.

She paused at the doorway, a curious energy forming within her at the sight of her husband lying asleep on the floor. The man who would put all he had and all he was on the line for a belief, an unpopular and divisive conviction, and then slug it out to the bitter end, looked no more imposing than a frightened child. A turning point, a true watershed, so long overdue. Whatever emotional upheaval she had just witnessed had done more good than harm, that much seemed certain. The rest would take care of itself.

She left him sleeping on the floor, heading quickly downstairs to their bedroom, just long enough to change into some drawshorts and a T-shirt and walk back upstairs to take her place once again beside him. As she had years ago to their infants, who slept just as soundlessly as her husband now did, she gently stroked her fingertips across the furrowed forehead, until it smoothed. There would be restless sleep this night, and sore backs in the morning, but it would be all right. *Everything will be all right from here on*, she told herself. The healing had begun.

§

He stared straight up from the floor. The slow orbit of the ceiling fan had a mesmerizing effect, momentarily diverting his thoughts from his stiff joints and aching lower back.

He'd awakened to find Elizabeth beside him, snuggled in close, sharing a blanket and the pillow from Nicole's bed. Fighting through his torpor as fiercely as he did the lower back spasms, Mac tried to sort things out, searching for an explanation why they were in Nicole's room cuddled together like puppies. Elizabeth awoke, and anxiously told him about his collapse, what he'd shared with her afterward. Then he'd filled in the gaps for her, the ones he could anyway. When there was nothing more he could offer, she'd gotten up and headed for the kitchen. A breakfast omelet, with grits, toast and juice, would be ready in a half hour, and he'd better be downstairs when it was ready. She wouldn't have him looking so hollow any longer. Mac hadn't argued.

What had happened last night was shrouded in mystery. He'd so desperately wanted his prayer to be answered. He'd thought it had been. Through some kind of haze he'd seen her, he just knew he'd seen his daughter. More than that, he had *felt* her there. It was the answer to his prayer … it was the sign from Nicole he'd asked for. But it had been Elizabeth, not Nicole. Was he mad? That prospect left him chilled … made moving on to other matters practically effortless.

There was time before breakfast to think things over. He was thinking about *McHenry versus the Catholic Church. What's next?* he asked himself. The outcome he'd set out to accomplish was still possible, but he was beginning to question if the result was worth the effort.

He had told himself if the doubts ever overcame the conviction, he would walk away. Knowing his case was strong, and there was more than a slim possibility he might succeed, a different kind of doubt crept into his mind. The words of Father Art Hurkinen prophetically came to mind: *Be careful what you pray for; your prayer might just get answered.*

He was on his feet, stretching out the kinks and the knots as best he could as he took one more look around the room. He didn't want to leave it, its warmth so comforting. It was getting late, and time was no longer an ally.

He had turned to leave when he saw it, protruding from under Nicole's bed, partly concealed by the dust ruffle. A corner of a piece of paper, harmless enough looking. She'd stored her whole life under her bed, he smiled in remembrance. Every magazine, every school note, every scrap of her life. No amount of coaxing or cajoling had gotten her to clean up the firetrap before she left for Dartmouth. It had all stayed there, gathering dust. Funny, he hadn't noticed it the night before. He bent, soreness and all, and pulled it out from under the bed, a page from a child's coloring book, a drawing of a shepherd, young David perhaps, a lamb slung along his shoulders, staff in hand, brilliantly colored in crayon. From a catechism class, Mac guessed. There was no date on it. He lifted the edge of the bedskirt to see if the rest of the book was there. No, only stacks of other books and papers. This was just a stray page. He smiled at it. Those were such wonderful days, he reminisced, when their children hung on the parents' every word and he and Elizabeth could do no wrong. It was all so fun back then. That fun was gone now, though, he realized as he reached to set the coloring on Nicole's bed. It would've stayed there, but for the draft from the ceiling fan. The page caught the edge of the bed, and slid back down to the floor, flipping over, revealing a glimpse of the other side. Mac strained to reach down a second time, picking up the paper, straightening it to look at the reverse side, the one he'd neglected seconds ago.

He could hear Elizabeth calling him down for breakfast. What he couldn't do was move. His feet were as stuck to the floor as they had been the night before. He wobbled at the sight of the drawing before him, and then his knees weakened as he edged his way onto the bed, his eyes never leaving the page. For an eternity he stared at it, while he questioned every movement he'd made since he walked into the room, last night, this morning, it didn't matter, everything had to be questioned. And when there were no explanations, of the logical kind anyway, nothing but his own beliefs to guide him, he bowed his head in understanding, and in total acceptance.

A different prayer was on Mac McHenry's lips as he pulled the door closed.

"Sister, we need to talk again. Please." There was a sense of urgency, of needfulness, in the "please." Katherine Carson lowered the receiver and closed her eyes.

"When and where, Mr. McHenry? Or right now, over the telephone?" A second chance was a divine and eggshelly fragile opportunity she didn't want to risk losing.

"Can we meet somewhere else this time?" he asked. "The other night, at the archdiocese, was okay, but not today. Today ..."

"I understand, Mr. McHenry. If you have no other preference, mine would be Audubon Park. As crowded as it is, it's quiet, and—"

"The park's fine. I'll meet you there in an hour, at the museum entrance." He hung up before she could answer.

As presumptuous as he'd been, she hadn't questioned it. She was already there, waiting, when he arrived a few minutes early. He looked tired, dark circles deeply recessed under his eyes. They started walking, oblivious to the joggers and sunbathers and baby strollers. Mac wasted no time.

"Why didn't you tell me? Twice now, in less than a week, you've held back, letting me stumble all over myself. What, do you just delight in watching me make a fool of myself?"

He took her hand. "I am deeply sorry about your husband and son," he added, the look in his eyes showing he meant it. "The one thing you *can* relate to when it comes to my own situation and I practically accuse you of being insensitive. There's some measure of irony, I'm sure, but it's not much help to either of us right now."

"You don't have to tread so lightly around my feelings, Mr. McHenry. I have been at peace for a long time over the loss of my husband and son. Yes, I was angry and disappointed when the man who took them from me walked away, but even if he hadn't, the loss was there just the same. No punishment the law could have imposed would have changed a thing where John and my son Kyle were concerned."

"That's the party line, isn't it? What the support groups preach, what the self-help books and talk shows and columns teach. 'Say good-bye, get on with your life, forgive, forget.' You may find this really hard to believe, but that's just what I was prepared to do." Mac had stopped the slackened pace, and was facing her straight on. She felt the heat of his breath in her face. "As grief-stricken as I was about Nicole's death, I had no thought of vengeance. When the official reports were all in, it was a case of her death at the hand of a madman, some berserk anarchist who for some reason had it in for my daughter. But he was dead too. What was left? Did I dig up his body and scatter his remains, and pray his soul never find rest? I may be misguided, Sister, but I am not so vengeful. No, what was done was done. What was left? Believe it or not, just to go on living. Maybe even clean out her room some day.

"But something unexpected happened one day. We had a visitor, a man we'd never met. You've heard his name: Evan Montgomery. You know, the foreign correspondent who wrote the nice pieces on Nicole, who first reported on the miracle. The man who made our daughter a worldwide topic of conversation. He came to our house, blaming himself, filled with guilt over being unable to stop what had happened. Even that gave me no reason to change the way I felt. He felt no different than I, really. I was still blaming myself for letting Nicole down so badly she took refuge in a convent, of all places. Not even Evan Montgomery's confession of cowardice changed my thinking. No, it was what he said on his way out the door, no doubt an innocuous afterthought, but it shattered the peace, and has driven me ever since. It was Evan Montgomery who lamented if only she'd left earlier in the evening, when Father Suarez came for her and Father Art, then none of it would've happened."

He wiped away the beads of perspiration from his forehead. The morning's coolness was giving way to the mid afternoon heat, while heat of another kind was building inside him. "I was dumbstruck. I couldn't believe what I'd heard. The Church sent a rescue party, and took *No* for an answer? That made no sense to me. It still doesn't. My daughter is dead, and for what reason? So the great Holy Roman Catholic Church could have another martyr? Is that it? See how this sounds: 'Okay, guys, let's sacrifice another lamb, why don't we? We haven't had a good sacrifice lately. It's good for the whole mystique thing; it keeps us holy within ourselves, makes better Catholics of the masses.' Get the picture, Sister? Do you see how this looks? When there's a fire, and the firemen go into the house, do you think they ask the occupants, 'Uh, hello, would you like for us to rescue you?' Pardon my being so flippant, but the shoe fits. See how ridiculous it sounds?"

The sweat was beginning to run into blazing eyes. This was no closing argument, but it was as passionate.

"We see Nicole differently. You see her as a trapped occupant. I see her as the fireman. Firemen lose their lives too. When they go into those burning homes they do so to save lives, at the risk of their own."

Mac's lips began to quiver. This was no argument they were having, but whatever it was he was losing it badly. She was feasting on a buffet of his stupidity and arrogance. Tears he could not blink back mixed with the sweat, forming tiny salty rivers that searched out the lines in his face, lines of age and weariness guiding the currents downward, where they finally dropped from his chin and cheeks onto the small square checks of his shirt, dotting them as freshly fallen raindrops might have. He stood there as she reached to wipe the rivulets from his cheeks.

He spoke slowly, evenly. "I'm trying to let go, Sister, I really am. Surely you believe me. Thoughts, images of my daughter, kneeling before a madman who is about to strike her dead, I can't rid myself of them. She was defenseless, innocent. Was she courageous? Was she afraid? Did she suffer? What were her last thoughts? Did she say anything before she died? Oh, dear God, I crave answers to these questions, and know I will never, ever have them. All I have to give me any comfort is what the law can give me. It's all I know, all I can invoke to keep me sane. Can you not see that?"

"This isn't about the law, Mr. McHenry," she began softly, "it's got nothing to do with your lawsuit. It never did. And my being in this case was never about taking advantage of my friendship with Nicole. You may choose not to believe me, but it is God's truth. There was nothing to be gained by bringing another lawyer into the case, especially one who hadn't practiced law in years, and who had walked away from that life.

"This is about *you*; it has always been about you. As you've just admitted to me, it's your soul that's steeped in agony, and it doesn't have to be. You know I'm right. I know you do. Open your eyes, open your heart again. Give Nicole's death the peace and dignity it deserves. You don't believe the wicked scene you just painted, about the Catholic Church capitalizing on her death. That's a trial lawyer's performance, not a father who loved and misses his daughter. There is no one in the Church, from the very top on down, who does not truly mourn the loss of your daughter." She gripped both of his arms, and shook him lightly, almost maternally. It startled Mac, who regained some of his footing.

"The Church has an unusual way of showing it," he replied. It was a crack, a small one, but enough for starters, and she seized the opportunity to pry it open further.

"How so? Explain to me why would you think the Church would be uncaring."

"Would it surprise you to learn the Church would not even let me see my daughter after the reports on the miracle? Can you imagine opening the morning newspaper, of all things, and reading something like that about your own flesh and blood? We were on our way out the door, to the village in the middle of nowhere, to see our daughter who was recovering from a deadly fever, mind you, when Father Paul at St.

Joseph called, and said we shouldn't go, not yet anyway … the Church felt it would create a problem. Then, receiving a letter from her, not the usual two-week old date, but one scarcely days old, telling her mother and me not to come see her, to stay at home until things settled down. She did tell us she was over the fever, but the only thing in her letter about the miracle was her instruction for us to not give it a second thought. You've seen it, in one of the last letters we received from her.

"How extraordinary of the Church to muzzle something as potentially wondrous as a miracle! Do you have any idea of the toll on her mother and me? What kind of Church would do such a thing? Don't even try to convince me it was my daughter telling her parents to stay home."

She studied him momentarily, curiously. "I respect what you feel, Mr. McHenry, I really do. And I won't try to change your mind. But you haven't answered my question yet. What makes you think the Church is uncaring when it comes to your daughter's death?"

The lawyer in him fought tenaciously to keep quiet, to not say the words that would be so damaging as trial testimony, when the time came. If he spoke them now, the lawyers could prepare for them, soften their impact, even negate their usefulness to him. Better to stay mum. Better for his soul to stay in tortured agony.

Her long, watchful silence demanded something from him. "It's not a matter of caring or not," he said finally. An admirable effort to break the tension, yet an incredibly weak response. It was all he could muster. His strength was draining.

She could see him struggling, in his face, in his movements. "Talk to me, Mr. McHenry. Get this out in the open. Forget the lawsuit. There is no court reporter here. This is just you and me, and I am not a lawyer right now. I am a friend of your daughter's. I will not betray you."

She moved to within a few inches of his face. Her challenge cut through all the clutter. "What is it you want from the Church, Mr. McHenry?"

"You won't believe me, but the lawsuit wasn't about punishing the Church. I still love my faith, my church."

"Then what?"

"She'll be forgotten." His tears were back. The deep ache too. "A year from now, no one will know her name. Her death another useless, forgotten memory."

"No, you're—"

"Wrong? I don't think so."

"Then tell me, what is it you want?" She searched his expression for something, anything, everything. A telltale sign, just a little head start, a teeny push in the right direction. Her eyes pleaded with his. She started to speak again, to ask for the hint he would not volunteer, but he put a finger to her lips, silencing her before she could utter a sound.

With his free hand he reached for the folded paper in his pocket, then handed it to her. He placed her right hand over his heart as she held the paper in her left. He pressed down gently, firmly, on her hand, closing his eyes, clearing away the static, opening his heart up to her, and let all the pain out, the whole torrent of strife purged in the same instant it took her to blink once, as she felt his heartbeat and saw what was on the paper, and looked into his eyes, and in that instant it became clear. Hearts became conjoined, what was dense became thin, and when she made the gasping sound he knew all knowledge was hers.

387

✝

52

"MAC, SOL. YOU THERE? Pick up if you are, it's important." Mac could hear his friend's voice as he walked down the hall. Before the "Leave your message at the tone" reminder could sound, Mac switched it off, and picked up the receiver. "Sol, I just walked in. What's up?"

"Got a notice in the mail today. Judge Daigre wants us all in court in three weeks. Seems he's reached a decision on the 12b6 motion, and will announce it in open court. A bit unorthodox but, when you think about it, probably the best way to do it. I told you this guy has a flair for the dramatic."

Mac couldn't recall being told their judge had any theatrical notions, but he knew the significance of the court's notice.

"I've marked it on my calendar, Sol. Look, if you need to do anything between now and then, it's probably a good time. Take some time off for one of your trips to points further south, or just hang out if you like."

Sol interrupted before Mac could say anything else. "We haven't spoken for a while. You all right? You never got back to me on the information about our new lawyer."

Mac held back on the whole truth. "I'm fine. I got your message, but a lot's going on with me right now. Haven't had time to get back to you. All I'm saying is there's nothing for us to do 'til the hearing, and I know how restless you get, so why not make the most of the time the court's given us. That's all I'm saying."

"Sounds okay with me, old friend. I'll be at the same place down in the Keys. You still have the number?"

"I still have it. I'll stay in touch, Sol, don't worry."

"See you in a few weeks, Mac. I'll be thinking of you." And he was gone.

Mac was grateful his friend hadn't exposed his charade. It was a testament of faith in a way, for Sol to trust him not to mess up their fine lawsuit, everything they'd worked on so hard for so long. The die was cast, as far as the court's decision on the motion was concerned, but Sol was no dummy, he knew there were other factors at work.

But Mac really did have things under control. There was nothing to do except wait. He could wait awhile longer. Suddenly it had all become worth waiting for.

§

At the other end of the phone, Sol just smiled. He'd been down this road before. Mac couldn't hide it any better than any of his other clients. He smelled a walkaway. *He's lost the urge, the edge. The old killer instinct isn't there, is it Mac my friend?* He wondered what had happened, but wouldn't toil or tarry waiting to find out.

Hello, Florida Keys. Here comes your old buddy Sol.

✝

"How can you be absolutely certain? It is even more strange than the way he has pursued this legal matter against us, don't you agree?" The archbishop leveled his gaze at Katherine Carson in a way more imposing than she was prepared to deal with. "You tell me he didn't even ask for it, yet you somehow just know it's what he wants?"

"Yes. I just know. He would never say those words aloud, it would be beneath him, and would turn this into a cheap negotiation. Which is not how he wants his daughter's memory honored. You have to trust me on this. You put me into this to save a soul, and this is the way it can be done."

"Might I inquire, 'off the record' as you lawyers put it, how you feel about the request, if it can be called a request? You were quite close to her. I know this hasn't been easy for you. But put all that aside, Sister, and tell me, how does it strike you, what he wants?"

With every ounce of conviction her own weary body and mind could manage, without the slightest hesitation, she fired back in earnest. "It's the most right thing conceivable, Excellence. I believe in it, and it needs to happen." She never took her eyes off his.

"Very well. You are to accompany Father Reneau to the Holy See, and present this as my emissary."

Always the unexpected from this man. "Excellence, I am hardly the one to—"

"There will be no debating this, Sister. It is done. There is no one else but you who could do this the justice it deserves. A favor owed me will get you in with as little delay as possible. You will need to learn the various protocols, but Father Reneau is quite familiar with them. The rest must come from your heart. This is as much your tribute to her as what I hope ours is, if you get my full meaning. Now go, you have much to do, and so little time. I pray there is enough time." They both knew his concern was over the pending court date, three weeks hence.

It was a long shot, but it could work.

She took her leave, strangely thanking him as she left the room. Nerves already shot just got more frayed, she lamented. A current of excitement was winding its way through her, and with it surged a new hope. *This will work*, she promised herself.

§

After she'd gone, Archbishop Thomas Ryan walked over to his window of choice, to look out over the grounds of the fine home housing the New Orleans Archdiocese. He recalled the other conversation earlier in the day on the matter of *McHenry versus the Catholic Church*, the one with Rich Quisenberry. He rather liked Quisenberry. The fellow would have made a fine priest. All the right qualities. He'd made his pitch to the court, as had McHenry's lawyer. His had been the more reasoned, the more logical; Lieber's more the emotional, tugging-on-the-heartstrings variety. In three weeks, which argument will it be the court bought? That was anybody's guess. It was a dead heat, Quisenberry had confided. Too close to call. A photo finish.

The Church had faced adversity worse than this. This was all the more manageable because it had been kept out of the press. How, he couldn't imagine, but it wasn't important at the moment. Once the ruling was made, there would be no way to stop it from spreading. While it was doubtful there would be panic among the faithful, there would be a demoralizing impact on the Church if McHenry's motion were successful, which it apparently had at least a fifty-fifty opportunity of being. Those weren't the best of odds, an obvious fact to even a non-gambler.

He'd waited until Quisenberry left before calling in Sister Katherine. No sense in pitting one against the other. Hers was a different perspective. The archbishop had hoped for good news from her private efforts with McHenry.

She brought hope. Of sorts, anyway. A bit complicated, but intriguing. He'd trusted her intuitive ability implicitly. He couldn't afford not to. There was probably not enough time, but he had help up the ladder, which made it possible. The rift between the Roman Church and the American one existed in policy matters, not in matters affecting the unity of the whole body. If Rome would just step back and look at the larger picture …

All things considered, this was a good thing, sainthood for the young nun. Fitting for her, good for the Church, good for the lawsuit, good for the tortured soul of her father.

Saint Nicole. Was this something the Holy Father could embrace? It all would depend on Sister Katherine.

The pain was worse today than yesterday. It was a mean, cruel tumor, this one. She would talk to Patti about a stronger prescription, but the call could wait until tomorrow. For now, she could make do by doubling the dosage on the refill she'd picked up yesterday. She wasn't worried about addiction; she'd be gone before what was left of her could develop an insatiable craving for the narcotic. A few more months, five, maybe, at the most. More like three or four, though. She was also getting weaker, a sure sign it would be sooner than later.

Bradley, poor blessed Bradley, aloof to it all. She'd never intended to wait this long to tell him, but things just got too confusing. One minute, it would've been ideal— the time they slept on Nicole's floor, after his experience in her room. She should've done it then, over breakfast, when he was so mysteriously upbeat, when she was flush with happiness at spending time with her boys. The thought had formed, but he'd surprised her with the rather nonchalant announcement he was going to meet with the Church in an hour or so, and if all went well, the nasty business of the lawsuit would be ended. *Isn't that swell news?* he'd said.

She had managed only to bite her tongue at breaking her own news, and told her husband the best way she knew how that she was pleased for him.

He'd turned sullen the next day, tense and irritable, as much a bundle of nerves as he was before a trial. There was no trial, he'd told her, only a routine appearance in a few weeks. Yes, it was important, but not something to fret over in the meantime. The work was done, and it would only be a routine announcement from the court. Somehow she didn't think it was the full story, but she held back from forcing the issue. So many things were different. There was a time not long ago when he would've gushed forth everything to her, down to the smallest detail, omitting nothing. Under their new arrangement, she didn't know where to begin when it came to asking questions. She settled on asking a few, and letting it drop. She settled for token interest. He had his secret, she hers.

That was over a week ago, and now, with the pain increasing, and coming on more frequently, it had become more than a little game of *Who can keep the secret the longest?* Plans had to be made. Arrangements and such. Present and future, future meaning *after*—as in after she was gone. At first the thought paralyzed her with fear, but not any longer. She was to the point she just wanted it over with. It brought her closer to her daughter, which was better than what she was leaving here. Bitter? You bet she was bitter. But it wasn't all Bradley's doing, and pointing the finger of blame was not her way. Criticism rarely fixed a problem, it only hurt feelings or made things worse. No, her way was to counsel, to foster the positive. And, she could say with some measure of pride and accomplishment, she'd done quite well with her way.

The bitterness was mostly random, directed at nothing in particular, borne of losing her daughter. What was unusual about that? Bitterness under such a circumstance was very understandable, very normal. Maybe not the healthiest way of dealing, but good enough for starters. Her husband went to war with the Catholic Church, and left her at home to tend the garden. They'd avoided completely falling apart by staying distant, patronizing one another as a quick fix, falling into the slipstream of inertia. They were to the point of walking on ice so thin it would break with the slightest additional weight. Telling her husband she was dying would break the ice, and doom what little they had left of their marriage. Whatever else happened, she owed him the right to pursue this thing, this unholy war on the Church, if that's what he still wanted. She wasn't sure; one minute it seemed all but over, the next, full speed ahead. Keeping her secret allowed him the perquisite of his vacillation. For her part, there was no longer any need to question if it was the right decision. It had been made, and that was that, and when the day came she could no longer conceal her pain, and he would find her crumpled on the floor somewhere, comatose possibly, then he would know, and would understand. He'd get over his anger. He could bury her next to their daughter, grieve a little more, then get back to his war. He was well-suited for that, she'd learned.

Trouble was, she was a terrible liar, and she was scared to death, and sentenced to death, and she desperately needed him in the little time she had left. She prayed most of all for guidance.

———————

Twelve days, without any word from Katherine Carson. Frayed nerves were getting the better of him. Here he was, ready to make peace with his archenemy, forgive and forget, in exchange for this one small concession. Rarely does such an ideal solution come along. So why hadn't he heard from her? Twelve days was pushing it.

Why was he so knotted up? She was in Rome, working on sainthood for his daughter, what he'd wanted all along. It was right, wasn't it? He'd read of far less deserving than Nicole who had been given the exalted recognition by the Catholic Church. In the realm of those who deserve, Nicole emerged the victor. If the Church agreed, the only remaining barrier was the court. If the court bought into his case too strongly, it was possible the settlement and dismissal would be disapproved. His only downside … too strong a case.

Calling Rich Quisenberry hadn't helped—he was still operating under the presumption Mac didn't know she was a nun. Mac was beginning to feel deceived again. Paranoia wasn't his long suit, so he decided against dwelling on something he had no control over, and sat back in his chair for a long look at things. When one or two of them emerged with some degree of clarity, he forgot about the others, and rose from the desk in his study with an assortment of things to do.

The first one was to sneak up to his wife, who stood in front of the kitchen sink washing freshly-picked organically grown snap beans, and throw his arms around her. It was time to start winding down, preparing for the end of this long campaign. Become his old self again, for starters. He squeezed her as he had countless times before, expecting the customary squeal of delight.

Her scream shook him to the core. It was not from fright, but pain, unmistakable pain. She went limp in his arms.

"Elizabeth!" Feeling useless and helpless at the same time, all he could do was stammer. "What's wrong? I barely squeezed you."

"It's a slight infection … a female thing. I didn't want to worry you. I'm taking medication. It should be gone in a few days."

"Do you need some water? Can I get your medication? Anything?"

"Just give me a minute," she said. "I'm over the pain; it's the fright I need to get over."

He stood there, holding her. He didn't need any special training for that, thank goodness. He could handle being a post until the pain, or fright, whichever it was, passed. He could feel the life reenter her as the wet dishrag limpness gradually gave way. Better, much better.

"Can you move? Don't let me rush you." He smiled at her, the smile of the past.

"Another minute or two of this might be nice," she said. "Does this mean romance is back in our kitchen?"

He smiled at the humor, and patted her arm, the one holding on so tightly.

"Bradley, what were you coming in here to tell me? Was it good news? I hope so. Tell me some good news, please."

"I suppose it was good news. I've been thinking. How'd you like to go for a sail tomorrow, an overnighter? Remember how much fun we had the last one? It's supposed to be perfect weather the next week or so. If you feel up to it. I didn't know you were feeling down, or I'd have been tending to you. I should be upset with you for not telling me, but I'm the last one around here with the right to get upset with anyone. I've been a terrible husband to you, Elizabeth. That's changing, right now. I was coming in here to tell you. Let's just slip away for a few days, forget about everything, have some fun. Sail, snorkel, fish, listen to the waves lap the boat at anchor every night." His mouth curled in a mischievous smile.

"Bradley, that sounds wonderful. I can't think of anything else I'd rather do. I'll be fine in the morning. Can we leave early?"

"I wanted to stop in and visit with young Matthew Courvillon first, see if he's doing all right. I haven't followed up with him like I said I would—I don't even know if Paulette is helping him. Anyway, that was the only other thing on my list to do tomorrow. Can you manage to pack us up while I pay my visit first thing?"

"Oh, I bet I can probably manage."

"Then it's settled." He hugged her again, a little softer this time.

———————

If love is truly blind, her husband needed a litter of Seeing Eye dogs. How could he not know?

His little reassuring hug hurt, but she didn't let on, and stifled the grimace well. Another double dosage would deliver her from the bonds of this pain, and she would have the excursion with her husband. Maybe it was not too late to enjoy some happiness with him before she died.

Bradley, that sounds wonderful. I can't think of anything else I'd rather do. I'll be fine in the morning. Can we leave early? Four sentences. One truthful, two outright lies, one fence rider. It was time to come clean. She hated living this lie.

In a few months it wouldn't matter; it would be forgotten. Or he could be bitter if it's what he chose instead.

53

THE SMALL GATHERING SAT in stony silence as the prefect studied the sheaf of papers. A single volume, held together with a simple clasp, it paled in appearance to the more voluminous, elegantly bound presentations he was used to. As the head of the Congregation for the Causes of Saints, he, Cardinal Bertolucci, had seen his share of presentations. This one was the orphan, the pound puppy needing a home more than any of the others. Fortunately for the nun who sat across the table from him, the first of her gender to appear before him as a postulator, the *Divinus perfectionis magister*—authored by the Pope many years earlier—did not specify *by whom* such a presentation should be made, only what it should contain. This tidy creation contained the requisite biographical narrative, a medical report, a few witness's statements, what looked to be a dozen or so letters, and some videocassettes in a plain manila envelope. The eager, pleading expression on the nun's face told him, apologetically, this was all there was. *So be it,* he shrugged, setting about his task.

His job at the moment was studying a report submitted by Sister Katherine Carson in behalf of the Archdiocese of New Orleans in support of the sainthood of one Sister Nicole Michelle McHenry. Sister Katherine was the sponsor, or postulator, of the cause. Once he completed his review of the submission, he alone would make the decision whether to present the candidate for sainthood to the Holy Father. If he found things in order to submit the candidate for beatification or canonization, he would do so through a relator, someone other than himself. He would most likely select the young priest at his side, Father Luigi. If it did turn out to be him, he would be working with the American nun in the preparation of the *positio*, the name given to the detailed argument presented to the Pope in support of the beatification, or in Sister Nicole's case, full canonization. Instant sainthood. But this one had some complications …

§

A half dozen gilded sconces cast their cherubic shadows across walls stretching twenty feet from floor to ceiling. Windows covered with brocaded curtains, royal purple and gold, majestic and regal, delivered a message of quiet power. The room, however, was not nearly as imposing as the man in the scarlet and cream robe, stitched with golden thread, who sat a few feet away.

She watched his every movement, searching for a sign. She frowned each time he did. She averted his glances when he looked up. The silence was deafening. Time was slipping away …

Time was her biggest enemy. There was not much of it left before the small group of litigants would stand before a judge in a cold courtroom in a colder courthouse ten thousand miles away to learn the fate of a lawsuit threatening to rip the very fabric from the Church's mighty altar.

It was still within her grasp to save a soul and her Church, if only this process would not bog down in the mire of the Catholic Church's own occasional imperiousness. She'd refamiliarized herself with the process of sainthood. The processes of beatification—a sort of preliminary stage to canonization, or sainthood—requires a single miracle. The process is complete after a second miracle is confirmed. There is only one straight shot at the brass ring: martyrdom. No miracles are required; canonization is virtually guaranteed.

The current Pope had beatified and canonized more candidates than any other before him. Not since Alexander in the twelfth century had reserved unto the Holy Roman See the privilege of canonization had a Pontiff taken such a hands-on approach.

She'd learned a candidate's life did not have to be perfect, only an exemplar of holiness and, perhaps above all else, heroism. The word heroism kept appearing in all the reference materials she'd been given by Father Reneau to prepare her for this meeting.

It seemed perfect. Nicole had been martyred. Forget she had performed a single miracle; that would only result in beatification, and the uncertainty of a second miracle. Nicole had died young, after only a short time as a nun, yet there was no age requirement for sainthood, no minimum years of service requirement. If only the Church could overlook she ran around in soccer cleats, once wore a skimpy bathing suit, talked back to her parents, and, sin of all sins, ordered a dozen pizzas delivered to Sister Agnes Ann at the Sister Theresa of Avila Convent.

There was the delicate matter of purity. She dreaded the question if it came. The Catholic Church put great stock in its women saints being, or at least being recognized as, virgins. The earliest women saints were those Christian women martyred as virgins in the Roman arenas, served up as delicacies for wild beasts in the arenas, as spectator amusement. It seemed too much to believe as she read historical account after account, but it was so engrained in the Catholic Church's order of things that, fable, folklore or fact, it was now fact. The Church simply revered its virginal martyrs. It presented an obstacle, but not an insurmountable one. When the time came, she would be truthful, yet she would fight on this point if she had to. One night would not stand in the way of *Sister* Nicole becoming *Saint* Nicole.

"Is this all there is?" Cardinal Bertolucci broke the uneasy silence. "Have you anything further to submit, after today?" He held the entire report aloft, as if to use it to fan away a wisp of smoke or a meddlesome insect. Katherine held her tongue at the show of disrespect.

"No, Your Eminence, there will be nothing else. You must realize there was so little time to prepare this for you. Please do not react unfavorably for its lack of weight or a fine binder, embossed as the others I see before you. I assure you, even in its abbreviated form there is a full biography of the candidate."

"I note there is nothing from the parents. Was she an orphan?"

"Her parents are both living, Eminence. There was not time to seek their input. Also, there is the somewhat delicate matter of her father pursuing legal action against the Church."

"I beg your pardon. Are we to understand her father is taking the Church to court? Whatever for?"

"It's very complicated, Eminence. In the interest of time we felt it was not necessary to add anything from the parents. However," she continued, "in spite of her father's legal action, we know he would support this action the Church is taking." She slightly bowed her head, a sure sign there was more to the story. It did not escape detection by the prefect.

"Sister Katherine," he began, "the Congregation will not rush this matter through. We have all the time it takes to give it our full attention." There was an irritated tone to his voice. "Perhaps you will share the remainder of the story with us."

"Very well, your Eminence." And she did. The whole story, from start to finish, no detail spared. He remained silent throughout the long narrative, his only reactions an occasional frown or, oppositely, a raised and wrinkled forehead.

"So her father, you believe, would end this siege of the Church if we would proclaim his daughter a martyr, a saint? Is that what you are telling us?"

It had an awful ring to it, she had to admit. It sounded as blackmail, and if left in that light, the outcome was predictable. In her haste to put this matter before the

Congregation, she had presumed too much. No one would see this through her eyes; no one could be expected to.

"Eminence, it is not so simple. If I may speak candidly, please."

"You may. This is a formal procedure, but we are not so ceremonial that the truth should not find its way into the process."

"I quite agree. It is that same truth I also want to be known." She swallowed hard and bore down harder while she had his full attention.

"First, on the matter of her father—and I leave out her mother, because I know so very little of her, except she does not participate in the lawsuit and would be a good source for this cause—please realize he did not ask me to come here and do this. I should be here regardless. But he did, and I use this word guardedly, intimate to me there was a way he could give in, and walk away from the lawsuit. He does not ask it, because he believes, as I, that it is the only right thing to do. His daughter truly deserves this recognition. The Church owes it to her, Eminence."

"Just the same," he began, "does the father not make the request even though he says nothing? You understand what I am asking, do you not?"

She thought a moment before answering. She saw a way, maybe. "Let me put it this way. If there were no lawsuit, if it were just the matter of this Congregation considering Sister Nicole, how would the Congregation hold? Is there not enough before you to make a decision? Do you not see a true martyr here, one of our own no less, who gave her life for the Church? Should anything else matter?"

"My dear Sister Katherine, you oversimplify here. True, there are those saints from the past whose martyrdom would today be questionable. That we cannot deny. Your nun, did she truly die for her faith? Can you tell us she was told by her assassin to renounce her faith, and refused on pain of her own death? Or did her assassin persecute her on account of her faith? If you can tell me yes to either of these questions, then yes, I believe we have a true martyr here. You have not so written in your report. In fact, there is nothing in this report telling us why she died at the madman's hand. It is a mystery, it seems, why the man took her life, and just as great a mystery whether he demanded her to renounce her faith before he struck her dead. Correct me if I am wrong, Sister, but the priest, Father Hurkinen, he was unconscious during the last moments. And this journalist fellow, he was apparently out of earshot. You weren't there. A handful of villagers may have witnessed her death, but your report does not identify them. Only one, and he is apparently condemned to death, perhaps by now even executed.

So, you have no conclusive proof her death was a result of her refusal to give up her faith, do you? Her death could have been a murder with no faith-based reason?"

The long silence and stare between them was answer enough. The reality was painful, but it was not unexpected. With the Pope's energetic movement to recognize as many candidates as he could for sainthood, there was still the burden of meeting the formal requirements. There was no evidence Nicole was asked to renounce her faith. Just as importantly, there was no question she would never have renounced it, which Katherine told the official. The same held true where the cause of her death was concerned. It was unexplained, perhaps unexplainable.

"Yes, Sister, I believe that as well. Despite my hard questions, and my harder demeanor, you present a compelling case. I must present an even more compelling one for His Holiness. We cannot build conjecture on top of conjecture, you understand. There must be something more concrete. If we were to bestow sainthood on every one of us who died at the hand of another while wearing the habit, priest and nun alike, then the true purpose of the sainting of martyrs would be lost. We simply cannot proclaim all of us who fall prey to bandits and blackguards as saints. In the past ten years alone, we have lost dozens of our numbers, most of them in your country I would add, to rogues who murder for the change from the Poor Box, or less. Even the priest who was killed while riding his bicycle in the New Orleans French Quarter not too long ago, would we call him to sainthood as well? Surely his life was also a model of heroism, and piety. Consider while you ponder your reply, he had been a priest, tending to the poor and homeless in the sewers and alleys of your own city for over twenty years. Why do you not champion his cause, if you believe what you tell me about your friend Sister Nicole?"

Her head hung in disappointment. "Yes, Eminence, I understand." Stillness, the kind surrounding a frozen pond in the dead of winter in the thick of a forest, set heavily upon the table. Until, that is, a new voice was heard.

"Eminence, while martyrdom may be questionable at this juncture, there is nevertheless a strong case for beatification. We do, after all, have the one miracle. And this would seem an ideal instance for waiving the after death requirement, do you not agree?" These words were spoken by the Italian priest who sat beside the prefect. He looked straight at Katherine as he spoke to his superior. She caught the gleam in his eye.

"Ah, Father Luigi, my great compromiser. Yes, I suppose you are right. We have the miracle of life given to the little village girl. I am not surprised her name is Maria, by the way. Did anyone else take note?" He seemed quite proud in his own observation.

"Sister, may we presume in your role as postulator you have no objection to pursuing sainthood through another route? If what you have presented to us bears out after a full investigation, I believe we might just make a case for beatification to His Holiness. As father Luigi points out, it would not seem too much for us to relax the requirement that the miracles occur after the candidate's death. That would, as you know, put Sister Nicole in line for immediate canonization when a second miracle can be confirmed."

The words *after a full investigation* took their toll. Inevitability often carries with it a message of doom; it seemed so this time.

"You do not look pleased, Sister."

Of course it pleased her. But it probably was not going to be enough to stop J. Bradley McHenry from pushing forward with his lawsuit, the outcome of which bode unfavorably for the Church. There was no use in forcing the issue; a strategic retreat was called for.

"Eminence, it does please me. You understand, what matters most to me, both as postulator and friend to Sister Nicole, is she take her rightful place alongside the other saints of our faith. As hard as it is for me to accept that what I have brought before this Congregation does not show conclusively she has been martyred, I can still rejoice in knowing she may yet attain sainthood through beatification. Of course this pleases me, Eminence. I am most grateful."

"Do you, and does Sister Nicole's father, understand there is a five-year wait for beatification, or canonization as a martyr?"

"Yes, Emminence. He will understand the wait if he knows what lies at its end."

Cardinal Bertolucci frowned again.

A strange quiet descended on the group. Katherine thought the conference was over, and awaited the benediction, the last item of business to be recorded by the transcriber. The Cardinal was obviously not ready to bring things to an end just yet, however. He continued to read in the materials … something else—overlooked earlier, possibly? He squinted as he rubbed the bridge of his nose, his large fingers raising his glasses to where they covered eyebrows as white as the hair on his head.

Katherine held her silence.

The prefect slowly slid the report to Father Luigi. "We shall immediately commence our investigation into this 'miracle in the mountains' as it was called by the journalist. An interesting account, Sister, quite an interesting account. Father Luigi will leave as soon as he can make the arrangements. He will of course visit the village, talk to the priest and the villagers, and he will speak with the archbishop in the capital. His investigation will be most thorough, I assure you. If there is any way he can substantiate this account of the miracle, Father Luigi will do it. He will also need to speak to the military physician who was there, which I presume the archbishop can help arrange. And then he will travel to your country, where he will conclude his investigation by speaking with the nuns at the convent, her family priest, and, lastly, her parents.

"Do not worry, Sister. It is required when the parents are alive that they be consulted. And if they refuse to see Father Luigi, it will not result in the undoing of the cause. Our Church is not nearly so unforgiving or lacking in understanding."

The question was on her lips, but she could not bring herself to ask.

"Ah, the matter of the lawsuit, it still troubles you, yes? Let me further assure you, while it might have some impact on our decision, I cannot say it would be the undoing. Let us move forward presuming it will not." He smiled at her. "Good Sister, trust in God."

The room rose with the prefect. He walked to where Katherine Carson stood. Bending at the waist, she kissed his ring, and thanked him. "Continue in your faith, Sister. God's will *will* be done."

He invited her to accompany him to the Holy Father's private chapel in the Vatican that evening for what he called a private Mass, after her evening meal. It was something, he said, she should do before she left the following morning. As distraught as she was, she accepted the offer. Few were invited to such private services, and only the ridiculously foolish declined.

§

When it seems not possible, light somehow manages to shine through even in the darkest of places—much the same as water seeks its own level—and a photosynthetic bridge is built by which living things can take root and flourish.

For without light, all except that which serves darkness would eventually wither and perish.

So it is also with souls in times of darkness, where light of another kind claws and scratches its way to the surface to sustain and nourish.

For souls need such illumination no less than all other living things.

As she knelt at her bedside, a very tired yet spiritually uplifted Sister Katherine prayed that the light of all wisdom and understanding would find its way into the hearts of two men, one a young priest setting out on a mission, the other a broken-hearted father.

It was a simple prayer, that light would find its way through the darkness.

54

THE EASTERLIES DELIVERING THEM so quickly to anchorage off the Alabama coastal town of Point Clear had calmed. They blew teasingly as whispers into the sailor's face. He let the anchor down slowly, taking care not to snag it in some fisherman's trap. He felt the line tug, a sure sign the gulf currents were strong, fierce even, six fathoms below the sturdy keel. But on the surface they made for no more than an occasional wave lapping at bow and stern, and a gentle rocking motion. The boat would be as a hammock tonight. Sleep for the captain and his passenger would be restful.

Scanning the sky for any sign of a storm—even though fair weather was still forecast—he saw only the shimmering starlight of a quarter moon's doing, light tracing erratic lines on the water's surface, scribbling a message in some iridescent, invisible ink here one instant, gone the next. It had been a good day, ever since they'd left the waters off Biloxi. It would have been a perfect day but for the torment inside him, the running debate cutting silently into not only his communion with the sea but the time with his wife as well. He'd hoped to shut it out, and rekindle a flame too long buried in cooling ashes, to escape to the water, let the wind and the waves take them both away. The last time, months ago, he'd taken the boat out for Elizabeth, or so he'd told himself, to let her know nothing had changed between them, but his lie then had fooled no one. This time, he'd tried, really, he had, but even his best intentions weren't enough. Handling the boat had been mechanical, the thrill subdued, as his thoughts dwelled more on things other than the beauty around him. He felt ashamed again. He'd cheated himself, and his wife, out of the fun he'd promised. He'd try harder to make it up to her, if not tomorrow then the next day. Or the next.

Another day would get them to Florida, to Destin and its brilliant white sand beaches, to perhaps as far south as St. George Island if they pushed hard. He laughed softly at his own euphemism: pushed hard. If he kept running, trying to escape, was more like it. Mired in this thought he was oblivious to the sound and movement behind him, until he heard her voice.

"Bet I know somebody with a lot on his mind," she said, startling him. "I've been waiting in the loft. I know how long it takes you to set anchor and rig down. So, I figure you're still up here caught up in whatever it is that's been on your mind ever since we left yesterday. Don't you think it's time we talked?" She walked up beside him, slipping her arms around his waist. "You seemed so upbeat two days ago, I thought you had everything under control. What's changed? Come on, Bradley, talk to me. It's a beautiful night, let's make the most of it. Let's hear it, right here, under the stars. Right now."

He shrugged. Time to confront. "I was just telling myself maybe if I ran from it tomorrow, one more day, I'd be able to confront it the next. Or maybe the next, even though I hadn't gotten that far yet." He turned, and faced her, looking down at the perfect face that could reduce him on sight to molten slag, still radiant and unwrinkled, still looking back at him the same way it did that first time, when she was on her pencil-buying spree. "I had us making it down to St. George Island. Who knows, maybe we'd even get to St. Barts before I could sort things out." It wasn't like him to be glib. He started to apologize, but she stopped him.

"Let's not think about tomorrow or the next day. Why not just concentrate on here, and now. I know that sounds pitifully trite, but things are complicated enough without trying to be clever at the moment.

"So, what do you say?" Playfully tugging at him, she forced the issue a bit more, urging him the way a wife might, when familiarity is a license, and boundaries are long ago settled. "Come on, you know you'll feel better. I don't know what's going on inside you. What's got you so emotionally wrung out? Here we are, on your favorite highway. It's not like you to drag along baggage." She tugged some more, and smiled some more.

Resistances and barriers shut down, the urge to clear the air overpowered the urge not to. He took her hand, and they walked without speaking to the stern, where the cushioned seats waited. Her husband found the words to fill in most of the blanks for her, until the air got chilly, and they went below, where they talked until she was certain she knew everything. Still, she had a few questions.

"What softened you? Why did you just all of a sudden mellow and begin to question what you were doing? Was it just Sister Katherine?"

"I suppose it was the letters she showed me." He dropped his head, eyes to the floor. Body language betrayed him.

"I don't remember you saying anything about letters. What letters?"

"Oh, some letters from Nicole to the nuns I told you about." *Oh, God, here it comes.* "I guess I forgot to mention them. I'm sorry, I—"

"Letters from Nicole? You saw letters from our daughter? To the nuns?" She was agitated, something he didn't want to deal with.

"Yes, Elizabeth, letters from Nicole to her teachers, or some of them anyway. I meant to tell you. But to answer your question," he continued, "I think it was the letters more than anything else." He would've gone on, but she was homing in on a smaller target.

"Bradley, where are they? I want to see them. I can't believe you haven't shown them to me already. And what about my letters, the ones I gave to you? Where are they?"

"Yours are safe, at Sol's office. I just need to pick them up. As for these new ones, well, there's a reason you haven't seen them. They were given to me while you were away, visiting the boys. Sister Katherine needed them back. I wasn't trying to keep them from you."

She sailed around the troubled waters. "I understand. I do understand. And it doesn't matter. None of it matters, really. I shouldn't get so riled like I am. Forgive me. But I do want to see the letters. Can you ask her to let me read them, your new nun friend?"

It was a curious reference to her as his new nun friend, almost challenging in the way she so casually laid it before him. It begged for a response; it also begged for a wide berth. He chose the latter. "Of course, and I will. As soon as we get home, okay?"

"Okay. Now tell me about this other business, the part about the Church and Nicole. You kind of skipped over that part, right at the end."

"I can't."

"What do you mean you can't? What's not to tell me?"

"Elizabeth, I haven't sorted it out myself yet. It's what's been on my mind these past two days. I haven't been able to think about much else. I love you with all my heart, but for two days, you, the boat, the great seas, nothing could pull me away from the question of what I'm supposed to do. I've started something, and I'm pretty sure I don't want to go through with it, not the way I started out anyway, but beyond that, I don't have a clue what to do."

"You mentioned that the Church might do something for Nicole. What's left for the Church to do?"

He'd hoped Elizabeth would see right through the haze, all the way down the tunnel to where the light was not much bigger than a speck, and it would all be clear, and she would accept it, embrace it, stand beside him. *It wasn't that hard to figure,* he said over and over again to himself, *if your heart is pure, and if you really knew her. It would be almost the same thing as your idea, and I'll gladly share it with you.* But his wife wasn't getting it. *Sister Katherine got it. Her heart was pure enough; she understood. Why hadn't he heard from her? Where was she? Why couldn't his own wife understand?*

"Bradley, you're keeping something from me. Either your lawsuit goes away, or it doesn't. What does Nicole have to do with it? What does the Church doing something for her have to do with it? What am I missing?"

He looked at Elizabeth the same way he had a few days ago at Sister Katherine Carson, knowing she, too, would see inside him, to the core, to the very essence of the man, and know what had to be done, the only way he could rid himself of guilt and shame, the Church of its culpability.

She looked back at him with the most puzzled of looks. "I have the feeling I'm supposed to look into your eyes, and somehow know what you aren't telling me, and slap my forehead and exclaim something silly like 'Of course, it's right in front of my eyes'. Trouble is, I am totally lost. I don't have any idea what you're not telling me. If you want to keep us both up all night—because I'm not going to bed until you tell me what's going on—then stay silent, and keep me guessing. I can't imagine not being able to handle it." She was showing her sterner side, the one Mac tried to avoid. "Why don't you give me the benefit of a doubt?"

He had nowhere to run. He stretched on the bunk in the aft cabin, clasped his hands behind his head, and started stringing one word after another the best he could, hoping it would all come out right. "I started to say something the other night, in Nicole's room, when you'd just come home, but we fell asleep before I could."

"If you keep up like this it'll happen again. Come on, Bradley, just let it out. It will be a big load off your shoulders, you'll feel great."

Hoping she was right, he put a toe out and tested the water. "All I wanted when I filed the lawsuit was accountability from the Church. She was gone, I knew that would never change. I didn't target anyone in particular, just the Church. It took a lot of digging and research, and a novel legal theory, but I found a way to get the attention of the Catholic Church. We had that discussion, remember?"

"I remember you telling me it wasn't money you were suing for, it was some notion of the court closing the doors to the Church. I don't remember you saying anything so benign as just wanting to get the Church's attention."

"You're right. I always had something else in mind. A way to honor our daughter. Then I met Katherine Carson, the nun I just told you about, Nicole's friend. Through her I found the three nuns at the convent. The more I dug into what they put in front of me, the more I learned about our daughter, and about myself, and before I knew it, I realized what I was doing wasn't right. It wasn't a question of 'Nicole wouldn't have wanted it', it was much simpler. It boiled down to an issue of right versus wrong ... and I was wrong. So by the time you got home I had decided to just drop the whole thing, just walk away. I would have, Elizabeth, I promise I would have. Except the morning we woke up on Nicole's floor, while you were downstairs fixing breakfast, I came across something under her bed, something not there the night before. I wouldn't have overlooked it. It was partly under the bed, partly sticking out, so inviting, so findable.

"Do you understand what I am saying? Do you, Elizabeth?" He was searching her eyes ...

"Oh, Bradley, please don't ask me to answer. Leave it as rhetorical, and keep going."

He nervously combed a hand through his hair, and reached into his pocket. He handed her the folded piece of paper. As she nervously unfolded it he finished what he had to say.

"I found this, under her bed. And it changed things. I saw it as a message, something I'm supposed to do for Nicole. Something besides walk away. It's the accountability I had in mind from the very beginning, but I was never sure how to turn the thought into reality. Now I do. It cleared up for me that morning, in her room."

She finished unfolding the paper, and took a quick breath as she saw the partly colored picture, the one on the reverse side of the brightly-colored one. "Oh, Bradley, she must have been a grade-schooler in Catechism when she did this."

"I figure she was about eight or nine."

"But I don't get it. I mean, I see the picture, and it's as precious to me now as I'm sure it was even back then, but how does this fit in with what we're talking about?"

"Our faith recognizes its most special people in most special ways. Right?"

"That's another riddle, Bradley. I see this coloring, and I know in my heart our daughter is with God, and—" The color drained from her face. "Bradley, you're not thinking what I'm thinking? You wouldn't—you—oh, Bradley, no, you must not do this."

"What? Let the Church know our daughter deserves to be recognized as a saint? See how hard it is to say? Even you can't. Now you know why I was struggling with it."

"I—I don't know what to say. There are no words. This is way too much ... give

406
†

me a minute, please."

He ignored her. "Elizabeth, why is this so hard on you? It's the easiest thing I've ever done. It's as if some divine guidance reached down and pried open my eyes where I could really see. In the beginning, I wanted this for Nicole because I refused to let the Church not recognize her memory. Without this, she'd have been forgotten in a year, her life wasted. She deserved more.

"I was reconsidering. It didn't seem to matter anymore. Then I found this. It's as if she was sending me a message." *Or answering my prayer.*

Mac continued, "Our daughter no longer belonged to us, Elizabeth. She was gone to us long before she arrived in Guatemala. She'd taken a path neither of us knew was there for her, but that she'd always, somehow, known was there. It was very difficult for her, but in her heart she always knew she would find her way. We are the ones whose feelings she tried to protect, until the burden on her became too great. She came home to us, but we still didn't see what was troubling her. 'It was Tommy.' Or 'It was school pressure.' Or 'It was doubts about a career path.' How many other possibilities did we exhaust?

"Wake up, Elizabeth. It was none of those. It was Nicole reaching out, all right, but the perfect parents just didn't connect with her. We put her right back into a life she'd walked away from even before she went off to college, and never bothered to ask what was in her heart. We never once listened, to her words, to the resounding crescendo of her silence."

He stopped long enough to brush a tear from his wife's cheek. "Don't. It's all right. It isn't our fault. She chose a life we wouldn't have chosen for her, but she was never happier. We just have to accept it."

"What do you think I've been doing this past ten months, while you've been researching, and filing your lawsuit, and globetrotting? Every single day I live with the decision our daughter made. I still am. I will until I die. But what you are doing here, that makes a mockery out of her, and what she stood for. How could you, Bradley?"

"A mockery? I don't understand. Sainthood is the highest honor the Church—"

"Bradley, if it's something the Catholic Church *wants* to do, fine. But you are meddling. Let me guess: you told this Sister Katherine you would drop your lawsuit if the Church would make Nicole a saint, didn't you? That's why you had a tough time telling me, isn't it? Not because it's what the Church wants to do, but because it's a, what, a settlement? Something as beautiful as our daughter's memory, a bargaining chit?"

"Don't talk like this, Elizabeth. You don't know what you're saying. If there were any way Nicole could voice an opinion, any way at all, it would not be for this recognition of her to be stopped. If anything she would shrug it off, but she would not forbid it."

"How can you possibly think she would say nothing to stop this foolishness?"

"Because I know my daughter."

"And I don't? What makes you think you know more than I do about our daughter?"

"It's not a question of which of us knows more. It's—it's—" He fumbled for words.

"You don't know everything about her, Bradley. Not nearly everything. There are things she shared with me that missed even your attention. Incredibly important, personal things. Woman things, Mother and daughter things." Tears formed again.

"Like her and Tommy. There, I said it. Don't make me say more, you know what I'm getting at. You didn't know, did you? Just once in her life, Bradley, just one night. There, I've betrayed her. I swore I never would. Not to her, to myself. Don't you go and tell me you knew it, Joseph Bradley McHenry, don't you dare say those words. I shall never forgive you if you do."

Only the fool would have taken that dare. Mac was foolhardy at times, but he was no fool. "It's not the sort of thing a daughter would open up to her father about. And you didn't need to, either, especially at a time like this." He hoped it was ended.

He never got to hear her reply. "I feel sick, Bradley." She ran toward the head.

"Elizabeth, please—wait!" He started after her, but she was in the head before he could stop her. The door was shut, but not locked.

"Elizabeth?"

He heard a retching sound, then a noise sounding like she'd slumped to the floor. He opened the door, found her doubled up, moaning, one hand on her abdomen, the other clutching at the air …

§

Elizabeth was apoplectic. The relief from the last dosage wore off much sooner than expected, and the pain was back. This was not the time to let a little thing like her terminal cancer and the unbearable pain tagging along with it get in the way of trying to head off a terrible wrong. She suddenly regretted ever relenting in his course of action against their Church, wishing she'd instead fought him every step of the way. This could have been avoided, this, this unholiest desecration of her daughter's memory.

Her husband would undo this wrong. When she got better, he would hear about it from her. He'd gone too far.

She clutched at the porcelain bowl, the pain drowning her thoughts.

ALL THE ANGELS AND SAINTS

"Well, Sister, how was Rome?" Archbishop Thomas Ryan seemed particularly anxious. Her flight had landed at ten the night before. His call woke her a half hour earlier. It was not yet seven.

"Rome was quite an experience. The Congregation is very busy right now, it seems. Our official was Cardinal Bertolucci, by the way, in case you didn't know already."

"A good man. Stern, but a good man. Not likely to be our next Holy Father, but up there with the best of the candidates." He sipped his coffee, and offered her a cup.

"No, thank you … I might like to return to my room after we're through. I've been up most of the night, and need the rest."

He got down to business. "What decision was made, Sister?"

"I'm afraid Cardinal Bertolucci rejected the idea of martyrdom. I thought it was a bit of a stretch myself, although even in our times there are cases for martyrdom with less support. But," she added, "they were men and women with a lifetime of service to the Church. Nicole's was also a lifetime of service; it just didn't quite measure up time-wise."

"Yes, I see. Well, what then? Were you rejected out of hand?"

"Not quite. The Cardinal's younger assistant, Father Luigi, came up with a sort of compromise. He suggested we should pursue beatification, in the process sanctifying the miracle. I thought it wasn't a bad result. It won't appease her father."

"It doesn't help you with the timing problem, does it? The court rules in a few days, I believe."

"I'm afraid so. No, the timing couldn't be worse. All I can do is call Mr. McHenry, and tell him we did our best, and there is still hope."

"Are you certain it's what he wanted? This was the tradeoff?"

"He wouldn't have put it that way, Excellence. But, yes, it's what he wants for his daughter. I don't know the impact my telling him it might not ever happen will have. Telling him 'the Church is trying' is only as good as he will let it be."

"When will you tell him?"

"I'll call him today. I think he should know as soon as possible."

"Yes, as soon as possible. You'll of course let me know what he says?"

"Yes, certainly," she said. "You know I won't plead with him, try to convince him one way or another. That would be an insult."

"The soul, Sister. Save the soul." Pausing at the doorway he turned and said, "Mr. McHenry needs his faith. Don't lose sight of that, either."

55

IHAVE THREE CRIMINAL MATTERS this morning, before we get to the civil docket. Two arraignments and a sentencing. I am filling in for the magistrate judge, who is happily vacationing somewhere. Those of you with other business are welcome to remain in the courtroom, and equally welcome to leave if you prefer.

"I don't expect the criminal matters to take more than an hour, quite possibly less," he added.

Judge Maurice Daigre's announcement paradoxically spelled both relief and greater tension for Katherine Carson. She was relieved for the reprieve, however slight it was. She imagined a condemned man would make the most of such a stay, each moment of life becoming more precious when the air of finality had set in.

The tension was due to the unexplained and notable absence of Mac McHenry.

She'd called Sol Lieber when her telephone messages to Mac went unreturned. Sol was in Florida, but she'd learned from his answering service Mac had gone sailing. A week passed. There had been no bad weather, no reports of a distress signal—no word from Mac McHenry or his wife.

She listened as Judge Daigre took on the two arraignments. The first, a drug offense, was a quick *not guilty* plea and a hearing set for another day. The next arraignment took the very breath from her. Her mouth dropped open in amazement as the orange-clad prisoner was led into the courtroom in shackles by the U. S. Marshall. As she whispered his name on her lips, the bailiff was saying aloud, "Next case, Your Honor. The United States of America versus William Andrew Sheene." He looked so pitiful. He'd been so smug, so arrogant, during his trial for the negligent deaths of her husband and son. Now he looked a shriveled rag of a man. He was charged with racketeering and money laundering. The man standing beside him entered his appearance for the accused as court-appointed counsel. Times had not been good for

Mr. Billy Sheene, she guessed. She was still watching him, her eyes fixed on his back, when he turned to look over his right shoulder. Her eyes followed his, to a woman and two small girls seated in the front bench. A wife and daughters? Odd, she'd never thought to question if he were married. The woman's shoulders rose and fell and her head shook in telltale fashion, arms around the girls.

He entered a guilty plea. Katherine was surprised. He took two lives once, and was as legally and morally guilty as any criminal had ever been, yet he disclaimed guilt, and on a novel defense walked away a free man. Here, only money was at stake, and he was accepting full responsibility for his crime. Strict federal sentencing guidelines would mandate a fixed prison term; there would be no early release for good behavior. No doubt he had bargained for a reduced charge—and a concomitant reduced sentence—in exchange for his guilty plea. Still the slick one.

The judge accepted his plea, and deferred sentencing until the presentencing report was complete. The prisoner was remanded to the custody of the Marshall pending sentencing in six weeks' time. Next case.

The marshal pulled at his arm. Only for an instant did he look at the threesome huddled in despair. The rest of his gaze spread over the courtroom. Katherine knew the look of humiliation. She glanced around to see if there were others here to see his degradation. Her eyes met his. They did not even blink while passing over her, barely fifteen feet away.

Numbed at the unexpected reckoning, she missed seeing the judge's secretary hand him a message slip as the next prisoner was brought before the bench. She also missed the judge's motion to his law clerk, who stepped to the bench for a whispered comment. She was still absorbed in a mirage of thought as the next criminal matter—a routine sentencing in a tax evasion case—was handed down to the poor wretch who'd only tried to start a small business, and who'd failed in the effort. The tax money he'd spent had not gone to profligate ways, but to the care of an invalid child. No matter, the sentence was meted out dispassionately, and today's Jean Valjean was led away in handcuffs while his tearful wife and their wheelchair-bound nine-year-old son watched.

The only thing missing was the stern lecture judges gave once upon a time before the mandatory sentencing guidelines.

All in all, it was not a good morning in federal criminal court for the families of the accused.

Katherine was brought back to reality as the gavel sounded twice, one harsh rap followed by another. "Court will be in recess for fifteen minutes. When we return we will hear *Stokes versus McAffrey*, on the motion for leave to amend the court's scheduling order. Also, are the parties here on the matter of *McHenry versus The Catholic Church?* Can I see a show of hands?"

"Katherine Carson here, Judge, for the archdiocese. I can get Mr. Lieber, counsel for the plaintiff, if the court would like."

"That won't be necessary, Ms. Carson. If you would please pass along to Mr. Lieber, and of course your co-counsel—I did see Mr. Quisenberry lurking about, didn't I?—that my secretary just received a telephone call from Mr. McHenry, who asked if we might put this matter off 'til last. It seems he is on his way, and will be an hour late. I instructed my secretary to tell him the court would grant his request. Actually, the court had intended to take this matter up last anyway.

"You'll pass this along, won't you, Ms. Carson?" he asked.

"Yes, Judge, thank you, I will."

"Fine. Court is in recess." The gavel cracked again.

"All rise. Court is in recess," the bailiff boomed.

———————

She was standing in the hallway, in front of the twin courtroom doors, as he stepped off the elevator and turned in her direction. She seemed startled to see him. She met him halfway between the two sets of doors.

"Mr. McHenry, is everything all right? We've been concerned—"

"Sister, you'll forgive me, but I've driven at breakneck speed to get here, from Point Clear, Alabama no less, and I don't want to keep the court waiting any longer." He started around her when she did not move quickly enough out of his way.

"Mr. McHenry," she called after him, "the court is in recess. Besides," she paused, "there is something I need to tell you. Please, it's important."

"Later, please," he said, moving past her as he might have a panhandler on a crowded French Quarter street corner. He entered the courtroom on the fly, a rebuffed Katherine Carson trailing by a short distance but fading as he quickened his pace.

She'd been right, he quickly discovered. Court was in recess. Not all bad, he needed the respite. It lasted all of seventy-five seconds, until the door to chambers opened and the procession reentered the courtroom, bailiff first, followed by the reporter and the law clerk.

"All rise, court's now in session. The United States District Court for the Eastern

12
✝

District of Louisiana, the Honorable Maurice Daigre presiding."

The judge entered next, authority in the form of a black robe emanating throughout the room. "Be seated, please," he said, taking his own seat in routine style. He made a quick notation on some papers before he spoke. His voice echoed clearly in the room. "I am advised the parties in the *Stokes* matter have worked out their differences, so the court is ready to proceed in the *McHenry* matter. Are all parties present?" He looked down at Mac. "Good morning Mr. McHenry. I trust everything is fine now."

Rising from his chair at counsel table, Mac answered. "Good morning, Your Honor. Yes, things are fine. We thank the court for the brief continuance."

"Quite all right, sir, I assure you. I presume we are ready to proceed?" It was an invitation for an objection, a typical formality. It was also a signal to begin.

The courtroom was clear except for the judge, his law clerk, the reporter and the bailiff, and of course the cast of characters seated at the counsel tables. Sol and Mac sat alone on the plaintiff's side, while the entourage from Phillips, Dawson sat stoically around the defendant's table. Rich Quisenberry was dressed in yet another Italian creation, but the ridiculous bow tie drew all attention from the suit's stylishness.

At the invitation from the bench, Mac stood slowly, and began his address to the court. "Your Honor, I apologize most humbly to the court, and," turning to the defendants' counsel table in time to see Katherine Carson inconspicuously seating herself, "to counsel for the archdiocese. I also owe an apology to my own counsel," he said next, reversing his field of vision to catch Sol's return nod.

"May it please the court, I have a statement to make. I realize this is somewhat unorthodox, but the court is aware I am a lawyer. As such, I understand the ramifications of my actions."

"Mr. McHenry, does the court understand you are somehow asking to be enrolled as counsel of record in this case, for if you so desire, I must tell you—"

"No, sir, that is exactly what I am not doing. I do not wish to speak to the court as a lawyer, but as the plaintiff in this matter, charged with full knowledge of the import and content of my address to the court. Said differently, I am fully aware that I as the plaintiff in this lawsuit will be bound by what I say, the same as if it were Mr. Lieber who said it."

"If counsel, including even your own counsel, Mr. McHenry, have no objection, the court will hear what you have to say. Especially under the foundation you have laid. I presume you wish the reporter to take everything down, as she has everything else thus far?"

"That's correct, Your Honor."

Before Rich Quisenberry could stand and speak, Katherine Carson was on her feet. "No objection by the defense, Your Honor." She sat down as quickly as she'd stood. Quisenberry sat quietly, a thin smile forming.

"Thank you," Mac said to both counsel tables, and again to the court. "Your Honor, I wish to dismiss this lawsuit. That is, I will instruct Mr. Lieber to file, contemporaneously with the conclusion of my remarks, a written motion to dismiss this lawsuit." While Sol smiled all-knowingly, and Katherine Carson's eyelids slowly closed and her lips barely moved, the phalanx of Phillips, Dawson lawyers and support staff were open-jawed, their thoughts ranging from the lost billable time and bonuses to the sweat and grit already put into the effort.

"Your Honor, there's more. I would like to apologize to the court in particular, and again to counsel, for the inconvenience endured by all. It concerns me some might think that my actions in filing this lawsuit were not properly motivated. On the contrary, until now the decision to file this lawsuit was the hardest decision I'd ever made. Now I make an even harder one, for the dismissal I am requesting, or rather that my lawyer will be requesting, is with prejudice, Your Honor." For full effect he added: "This lawsuit will not be refiled by me.

"I know the court was prepared today to issue its ruling on the defendant's motion. The court no doubt put forth great effort in its preparation, for which I am both grateful and again apologetic. It was not my intention to hold the court hostage to some Machiavellian ploy to extract a concession from the defendants. And I state, for the record, this dismissal with prejudice carries with it no settlement, no compromise of any kind, or nature." He turned to look at Katherine Carson. "There are, in the vernacular, no strings attached, Your Honor. It's a clean walkaway by the plaintiff, should the court permit it."

He looked back up at Judge Daigre, who appeared mildly amused at the unfurling scene. "I also ask the court to keep sealed the written reasons which were to be read into the record today. It would serve no useful purpose for them to be made public, Your Honor.

"Lastly, Judge, if there are any costs, the plaintiff will assume the responsibility and the obligation to pay them. We—Mr. Lieber and I—will prepare the appropriate dismissal papers, and, again, assume all costs in connection with the dismissal. I presume that meets with counsels' approval?" He looked again at Katherine Carson.

She respectfully rose to address the court. "The defendant has no objection, Judge."

Judge Daigre spoke next. "We're all big boys and girls, and lawsuits do get dismissed. The court will consider your motion, when it is received in writing. I can state now the court will not be inclined to deny the motion.

"As to your apology for the extra work you might feel badly about having put this court to, let me say this. It seems I write a lot for practice, Mr. McHenry. This is not the first case to be dismissed after the court has put considerable effort and time into it. The court appreciates your apology, but it's not necessary. As to my written reasons, since I hear no objection they will remain sealed in the record." He slipped the sixteen-page document into the folder on his bench top, showing no dismay the matter of *McHenry versus The Catholic Church* would never become public.

"So, if there's nothing else …" the judge began, looking up, hiding any thought on the dramatic denouement yet waiting for the last word lawyers habitually like to get in. "Very well, since there's nothing else, plaintiff is to submit an approved motion and order of dismissal within ten days. Is that all right with you, Mr. Lieber?" At Sol's nod, Judge Daigre concluded, "Fine, ten days it is. At his request, costs to the plaintiff. The reporter will close the record. Court is in recess."

On cue, the bailiff delivered his lines again. "All rise. Court is in recess." Without another word the judge and his entourage left the courtroom, followed by the Phillips, Dawson crew. Mac smiled at Sol. "I'll explain later. Give me a day or two, okay, before you head out for wherever it is you go when you leave these parts."

The older man returned the smile, and promised to stick around long enough to hear the explanation. He shook Mac's hand, patted his shoulder, and headed for the door, about the same time as Rich Quisenberry was saying good-bye to Katherine Carson. They met at the swivel gate of the bar, the rail that separates the rest of the courtroom from the bench and counsel tables, the area reserved for those who do the law.

"Nice tie there, Rich," Sol began. "Where might a fellow like me who's headed into retirement find something so genuinely stylish as that?"

They were still talking as they cleared the courtroom's oversized oak doors, Rich Quisenberry oblivious to the sarcastic wit of one Sol Lieber, newly-retired lawyer. Mac and Katherine Carson were the only ones left.

"Well, Sister, was it a good day for the Church? Did we do right by my daughter? By the Holy Father? By you?"

"You're a man of surprises, Mr. McHenry. I have a feeling you take a certain element of pride in that quality, though. And, yes, I think we did accomplish a lot today,

✝

but I think mostly for you. Will I ever know what's happened to bring this about? Or am I to just wonder?"

"Oh, I suppose we can talk about it, but it will have to be later. Right now I need to go. I have a hard drive ahead of me. We'll talk, and soon. I promise.

"You understood what I meant when I advised the court there were no strings? That was clear to you, wasn't it?"

"I think so."

"It means I expect nothing, Sister. Not for me, not for my daughter. It means that all is over, forgotten. I free you from the task I had no business putting you to. A task I regret ever making you responsible for. I should ask your forgiveness for ever burdening you with it."

"There is no need, you know that." She studied him, realizing there was something else in the air, something far afield from the reason they were standing in the courtroom. "Is everything all right, Mr. McHenry? I don't mean to pry, but I sense there is something very dark in your life right now. Call it intuitive, or being nosey, but I know something's not right. Not a boating accident, I hope?"

He smiled at her, quizzically. "Of all things, why would you ask if there was a boating accident?"

"I have been trying to reach you for days, ever since I returned from Rome, and all I've been able to learn is you went sailing, but had not returned. That was a week ago. No one's heard from you. It isn't such a far-fetched notion."

He detected the concern in her voice. "We did go out. Made it as far as Point Clear, Alabama. Might've kept on going, too, but we had to put into port. We can talk about that later, though. And, I suppose, about Rome too." It was the first he'd heard of her being in Rome. A chill ran its course through his body. He was filled with curiosity, but there wasn't time. "Good bye, Katherine. For now." He leaned in close, and gave her a soft embrace, just before he headed to the elevator.

She watched him leave the courtroom. When he was gone, and she stood alone, before the bar, looking up at the imposing bench at which moments earlier a strange and surely very wise man had sat. She knew this was her swan song. There would be no more courtrooms for Sister Katherine Carson. All the loose ends had been tied this day. The new one, to be sure, but curiously, an old one too. Trying hard not to seem sanctimonious or vindictive as to the latter, she calmed herself into thinking one last lawyerly thought: man's justice had been done. Old wounds that could have been reopened weren't, and justice delayed had not been justice denied.

He'd called her Katherine. Now wasn't that just something?

Packing her briefcase for the last time, she left the courtroom, and made her way down to the street, where the passersby saw her but saw nothing more than an attractive, matronly woman, wearing no makeup, carrying a briefcase, walking briskly. If they'd looked closely, they would have noticed the spring in her step was bouncier than it had been earlier. If they could have seen inside the woman, they'd have seen her spirits were divinely buoyant. It was because she had some good news to deliver to the archbishop. Some wonderful news in fact.

A soul had been saved.

✝

56

Elizabeth was sitting up in the bed when he returned, sipping weak tea through a straw. She made an icky face at the taste. It was a good sign for the worried husband to see. They hugged warmly as he sat precipitously on the edge of the bed.

"So how's my girl?"

"She's better. How's my guy?"

"He couldn't be better, unless his girl was up and out of here."

"Here" was Point Clear General Hospital, where Elizabeth had been admitted five days earlier as an emergency patient. Where Mac had learned from a concerned young doctor while his wife was sedated that she was on the sort of pain medication normally prescribed for cancer patients. Terminal cancer patients. A quick call to Patti Moreau confirmed the doctor's suspicions, and brought Mac face to face with more grim reality than he was prepared to handle. Besides his mother, there had only been two women with a place in his heart, ever, and he was faced now with the loss of the last of those three. Priorities quickly reshuffled, and everything first and foremost became last and least. He left her only long enough to take care of business no longer important. Courthouse business. Now he could concentrate on caring for his wife. His cancer-stricken wife.

The shock had sent him reeling. He had cause to be angry. Where was the truth from Elizabeth? How could she have been angered at him for not being entirely truthful when the secret she harbored was, by degree, unimaginably greater? But it wasn't anger alone Mac felt. Emptiness and shame coursed through him at the thought of his lovely Elizabeth withering, dying. The thought of her in pain broke him down. The thought she would rather die without fighting, keeping her suffering from him, ripped him apart inside. Had he done this to her? How had he become so misguided? Decisions had to be made by Mac McHenry the first night at Point Clear General.

Throughout the night, between prayers that sought forgiveness and help, he had searched the recesses of his heart and mind for what to do. When the prayers and the thinking drove him to the brink of exhaustion, he slept at her bedside, on a cold metal chair with a tattered gray vinyl seat. His head rested on the bed, inches from his wife, who would not wake until noon the following day.

"Am I going to live?" she'd asked him.

"Only if I tell them to let you, which I'm still contemplating." He walked over to her, bent and kissed her. "You have something to tell me, Elizabeth?"

"What do you mean?" she answered defensively.

"Please, Elizabeth, now isn't the time. I had to rummage your purse when we got here—you do remember being on the boat, don't you? Collapsing in the head while you were throwing up?"

"Vaguely. Where are we? I know I'm in a hospital bed, but where?"

"We motored into port at Point Clear. I radioed for an ambulance. It brought you here. I followed in a taxi after I took care of the boat. The doctor saw your prescription bottle. He told me the prescription was one normally for cancer patients … terminally ill cancer patients. Not exclusively, he was quick to add, but usually. I gave him permission to call your physician, your oncologist friend Patti Moreau. So, let's try it again. Do you have something to tell me?"

"Oh, Bradley, why did it have to happen like this? I'm so sorry. I didn't mean for you to learn this way." She was crying, unable to talk further.

He comforted her, a whole new set of issues before them. Where to begin? "Elizabeth, I really don't want to ask this … it's maybe the last thing in the world I truly want to know, but why didn't you tell me?"

"I'm not really sure. It was more than one thing. Not wanting to worry you. The timing was bad. The other business of yours … but I did mean to tell you."

Mac leaned to kiss her forehead. He smiled at her. "What am I supposed to say? I should be angry, but after what I've put you through, it wouldn't be fair. I'm more interested in getting you into treatment. First our young doctor needs to run some tests."

"No tests, please. I've already been through this." She wouldn't betray Barrett Dupuis, but knew the protocol well enough to recite it. Mac could only hang his head in disbelief.

"I can't accept this, Elizabeth. Your information comes from only one doctor. Patti, right? She's an oncologist, she helps people die. What about finding a doctor to help you fight to live?"

There was no convincing him otherwise, so she agreed to the tests. The lab results were due the day after Mac's return from New Orleans and his date with a federal judge.

Mac wasted no time after returning from his appearance before Judge Daigre. The test results were presented to them by the fellow they'd taken to calling "the young doctor," actually one Doctor Michael Adams. Mac couldn't accept his wife was dying of cancer, that she could be so vibrant one minute and so doomed the next. He demanded Dr. Adams recheck his lab test results, run the tests again.

Dr. Adams stood his ground. A recheck or a retest, he assured Mac, would produce no different result.

Mac grudgingly relented. The only question left unanswered was the most obvious: how long? How long until he had to bury his wife? There was no way to tell, he was told. Even a minimal treatment would add perhaps a month or two to whatever time she had left.

Elizabeth would have no part of treatment. She would—defiantly, as her husband would say—face death with dignity. It was Elizabeth Anne Rogers McHenry's choice of a holistic, dignified way out, and nothing Mac could say would change her mind. There would be no medication other than to help relieve the pain.

They checked out of Point Clear General the day after Mac's return from New Orleans, armed with a new prescription that would be gentler on her system, and headed for the *Nepenthe* and the continuation of their sail. Dr. Michael Adams, their new friend, drove them on his lunch hour to the dock. On the drive, taken slowly through the scenic road that split the rows of the majestic live oaks and grand homes the coastal resort town was famous for, Dr. Adams surprised them with a personal touch.

"You know, I shouldn't say anything, but for the life of me I can't stop myself. I feel like if I don't, I'll regret it for the rest of my life."

"Speak up, young fellow," Mac said. "You have nothing to fear from us two old folks." Elizabeth smiled at her husband's touch.

"I don't mean to intrude, but I know who you are. I was pretty sure the first night. It took me a while to jog my memory."

"And who are we?" Mac asked, fairly certain of the answer he'd get.

"This is the hard part for me. You're the parents of the nun who was—who was—"

"It's all right, Doctor Adams," Mac said, "you can say it—*the nun who was killed.*" He reached into the back seat and took Elizabeth's hand. It didn't feel so bad now. It still hurt, but it was becoming manageable.

"I don't know why it's difficult for me. After all, I deal with death every day even at our small hospital. Your daughter's death, it wasn't the kind of death I deal with. But that's not my point. I saw it all on the news, and the stories that came out afterward, then everything sort of went away. To nothing. I had thought there would be some element of closure to it all. Some epilogue, some final comment on the life of such a wonderful person, and I watched for it every day, but it never came. Do I dare ask you now whatever happened? Is there an ending yet?"

Mac was deep in thought. It was Elizabeth who spoke, sparing their new friend any embarrassment from the prolonged silence. "The ending is still in progress, Dr. Adams. A work in progress. You are so kind to share this with us."

"Elizabeth is right, Doctor, the ending isn't finished yet. But I think it just took a big step in the right direction. Someday we'll let you know, how would that be?"

"I'd like that." He pulled into the parking area of the Point Clear Marina, and helped Mac with his immobile wife. The two men got her onto the deck of the *Nepenthe*, before she got fussy. "I'm not an invalid yet," she barked, moving below deck under her own power. Mac made sure she was comfortable.

Elizabeth safely below, Mac went topside to say good-bye. "Thank you for everything, Doctor. For helping with Elizabeth, for caring enough to ask about our daughter. As much as anything, for the loan of your car so I could make that trip to New Orleans."

"You'd have done the same thing for me, Mr. McHenry." He reached out his hand.

"Mac. It's Mac, okay?"

"Okay. And I'm Mike."

"Then God bless you, Mike." Mac bypassed the handshake and gave the younger fellow a manly embrace.

In another hour, while Dr. Michael Adams was making rounds as he did routinely, brightening others' lives with a friendlier healing touch than most other young physicians, Mac and Elizabeth were back on the Gulf waters. They were headed east, though, toward waters that lapped on the shores of south Florida, not west toward home. Their lives had forever changed. Old concerns and agendas needed revisiting. Long-term mattered little, as their horizon no longer had the certainty of being as far out as the eye could see. A shorter, faux horizon lay deceptively close. While there were calm seas and fair winds, there was sailing to be done, and closeness too long missing to be clumsily and wonderfully rediscovered, and long talks, and searches and plans into future courses for them to decide upon.

Home could wait just a little longer.

§

In another part of the world attention focused on things more dangerous than the possible end of fair winds and calm seas. The business of war and death was still on the minds of those in power, and those who would seize the power. There had been only minor outbreaks since the Refugio rebellion was crushed. There had been truce talks, and leanings by the government toward social reform, with promises to establish commissions to study abuses—yet no lasting peace had been forged. The government, always before quick to engage in reprisals, resisted retaliatory measures. Far from an attack of conscience, the forbearance came about by the threat of economic sanctions, the true big stick to wield while America walked softly.

The Deputy Minister had this on his mind as he reviewed the file on his desktop once again. The political prisoner had caused no trouble, had asked for no quarter. Without knowing of the bullying tactics of the neighbors to the far north, he had offered his life more than once if the government would take no action against his people, his village. Such an ignorantly noble gesture, the official sneered. They could snuff out the prisoner's life with little more than a snap of the finger, and take whatever action they pleased with his or any other village. Who did the impudent man think he was anyway? What chance did he or his band of stragglers ever have? This prisoner's foolish act of bravery offended the official to the core.

The order to execute the man still had not come, and it was this omission causing concern to the official. Normally a routine matter, the execution of rebels, especially one who had taken the life of a government soldier, was swift in coming. Examples were made quickly and publicly, to discourage similar acts. Why not this one? What made this man special, if indeed he was special? The official was bothered by the unanswered questions. He closed the folder, and slipped it back into his desk. He would review it again next month. With luck, the prisoner would die of some natural cause in the meantime.

Yes, and save the state the cost of a bullet in his brain.

§

"May I speak with Sister Katherine Carson please?" Elizabeth was nervous at the prospect of speaking to a total stranger, someone she knew so little about, yet who knew so much about her, and her daughter. It was not like her privacy had been invaded, but close to it. That is, if a nun could be thought of as invading anyone's privacy.

"Speaking," was the reply.

"Sister, this is Elizabeth McHenry. I'm—"

"Mrs. McHenry, you've caught me by such surprise." Her voice was warm, soft, like Nicole's. Part of the nervousness ebbed. Elizabeth was about to say something else when the woman spoke again. "I had hoped we would speak to each other one day. This is such a wonderful surprise."

"You make this too easy for me. I was ready for you to be standoffish, and brusque. Hoping otherwise, but prepared for the worst, you know."

Katherine replied, "I hope your husband hasn't poisoned the well where I'm concerned. I would shudder to think I impressed him as standoffish."

"Quite the contrary. I believe my husband holds you in high esteem. I'm just nervous because I have you pictured as this larger-than-life figure who has calmed the savage beast in him, when I wasn't able to."

"Not to seem rude, but is there any way we could continue this discussion in person? I have wanted to meet you for so long. Meeting over the telephone is awkward for me."

The ice was broken. In two days they would sit down for lunch together, the way women do, and talk about things, the way women do, only this meeting would be different than the ones drawing most women together.

Before they hung up, Elizabeth had a request. Just one small but important favor ...

§

The traveler was weary. The long, overnight flight, then the trip over the rugged terrain had taken a toll. He was hungry, and needed a shower. Food, he learned, would not come until later, and a shower not at all. He was welcome to bathe in the tub, but water was going to be a problem. Maybe by morning. Father Luigi thanked Father Art for the hospitality, and decided the stale bread he'd brought from Rome would be better than nothing. The loaf cracked as he broke off the jagged pieces. This was certainly a far cry from life in the Vatican, where the kitchen was open twenty-four hours, every day. This was desolation. He'd missed this in his training. He wondered whether to hold this village priest in the highest esteem or to question his sanity when he remembered his purpose for being there. Personal reflections weren't on the agenda. Building a case for the beatification of Sister Nicole was. Reflections on Father Art would keep.

He'd endured a brief conversation with the archbishop in Guatemala City, feeling afterward the man was a bit detached from the matter of Sister Nicole … and preferred to keep it that way. He'd been no help to her cause, other than by his ambivalence. Sometimes saying nothing good at all could help, for the Church recognized pettiness. Father Luigi chalked the unwillingness to treat his visit as a serious matter as the product of an aloof, uncaring man who'd fallen victim to prejudice, for he constantly referred to Sister Nicole as that American nun.

Tomorrow he would rise early, find a way to draw water for his bath, and eat a nourishing meal. And set about on his mission. For now, he would make himself as comfortable as he could, in the room where she had lived her short life in this tiny hamlet.

§

Mac sat across from Father Robichaux. It had been months since the two men talked as friends. Robichaux was in deep thought over what he'd just heard. Truthfully, he wanted to yell out quickly what a splendid idea it was, but he felt it deserved more discussion.

"A 'Celebration of Life' for Nicole? To make amends for the secluded family service? Open to the public, her friends, anyone who'd want to pay respects, is that the general theme? What's not to like about it? It's a fitting remembrance for your daughter."

"You know it leaves out the Church, don't you? This is a purely secular thing. No Mass, not much more than an opening prayer if even that."

Robichaux nodded. A secular service for a Catholic nun. The idea of a Celebration sounded good to him. Something very light, very cheery. Trite as it sounded, it's what Nicole would have liked, insisted on even. He shared his thoughts. "We've had a Mass. We don't need another one. I've heard of these Celebration things before. They are great releases for grief. Our young people seem to handle their grief differently these days. I think it's healthier than our old way. I'm all for this, Mac. And Elizabeth agrees?"

"Yes, Father, Elizabeth and I are in total agreement. It's something that grew from a chance meeting with a young man over in Point Clear week before last. More importantly, this must happen quickly—within the next three weeks. There isn't time to waste. Can you help us organize it? We'll give you names of her closest friends to help get you started. What do you think—can we do it?"

"Mac, I'll make it work."

With that it had started. While Mac tended to his wife, Father Paul tore into the Celebration planning with a vengeance. Even on short notice, the response was overwhelming.

§

The recording stated its message so clearly the caller wasn't sure at first if it was Memorex or the real thing. "Hello, this is Tom Dillon with the State Department. At the tone please leave your name, number and a brief message. Thank you for calling."

Mac disliked leaving messages, but he had no choice. He made it brief and to the point. "Mr. Dillon, Mac McHenry here. You've got my number. Please call me back as soon as possible. It's important. Thank you and good bye."

He would wait, and hope the return call would come sooner than later.

425

†

57

KATHERINE SAT ACROSS THE small table from the attractive woman who had insisted *Elizabeth* sounded better than *Mrs. McHenry*. Likewise, *Sister* gave way to *Katherine*. One plate of fresh fruit and another with a Cobb Salad sat before them. Two glasses of Chardonnay stood invitingly beside the plates. The restaurant was quiet, exquisite; their table was in a semi-private room. Amenities had reached the point of exhaustion, a cue it was a good time, as her husband might have put it, to fish or cut bait. Elizabeth smiled at the thought.

"What? You've thought of something amusing? Tell me, please." Katherine wanted her guest to feel relaxed. This was a time for sharing … setting convention aside.

"I was just thinking of something Bradley would probably say at a time like this. It's not important enough to repeat, really, just one of those old trite sayings of his. You were right, it did seem humorous to me."

"You can tell me later if you like. I want you to know, you're not the only one who's nervous, Elizabeth. I'm trembling with apprehension. I think what we're doing, getting together like this, is long overdue, and much better than talking over the phone. I hope you agree."

"I do. My nerves aren't the steeliest right now either. And I have no appetite, even though this looks heavenly."

"Me either. Maybe we'll get hungry as we talk.

"Speaking of talking, I want to bring up the main reason I wanted us to meet face to face. It's about the lawsuit. Do you feel comfortable talking about it?"

Elizabeth frowned. "It's over, isn't it? Please don't tell me it's not over."

"Yes, completely. The way it came to be over, it's left me mystified. Your husband simply walked into court, and, *presto!* it ended. Came as a total surprise. I had so much to talk to him about, but he wasn't interested. I'd hoped he would call. There are things I thought he'd want to know."

"Well, let's just say he's been busy this past week. He may yet get around to calling you. But I have a feeling I'm about to get a preview of what he would hear."

"Not if you don't want. I won't force anything on you."

"I think I'd very much like to hear what you have to say. But first, did you remember to bring the letters? I'd so much like to see them before anything else."

Katherine reached into her purse. "These are copies. I am very sorry, but the originals are in the hands of a very special priest right now. I may never see them again, frankly. But I did make these first. I hope you aren't terribly disappointed."

Elizabeth took the copies in hand. "It's probably much better for me. There is a sterile, antiseptic side to holding these, instead of the real things. I cry a lot, Katherine, when it comes to my daughter. It's better you see me composed. So, yes, copies are better."

Katherine didn't say anything. She wanted to tell this woman that shedding tears over Nicole was the last thing she would discourage. She'd shed her share of them, too. She held her silence. Sharing could come later.

Elizabeth read them quickly once, then slowly a second time, savoring every word. Katherine saw the tears form, then brushed away her own. She reached out a hand to Elizabeth until she was finished reading.

Elizabeth handed the copies back. A bond had been forged. They could talk about anything now. And they did, and there were more tears, and there were fingertip embraces, and there was laughter too, as the mother came to know what her husband had discovered. Katherine learned from Elizabeth, beginning with the turmoil of her husband on Nicole's floor to the caring man he had become all over again, when she needed him most of all. At the mention of the cancer Katherine shuddered, but Elizabeth waved her off. It wasn't worth the bother, she told her, when there was no fear of dying involved.

Elizabeth held the letters up. "These are wonderful. You know, I'm surprised. As close as you and she were, I wonder why she never wrote to you. Have you ever wondered why?"

Katherine grew quiet at the observation that somehow had evaded Elizabeth's husband. She averted eye contact with Elizabeth for an instant before sitting erect again, before taking on her visitor's inquisitive gaze. "I received three letters from Nicole." She pulled three more envelopes from her purse, and handed them over. "I wanted to show them to your husband, but the opportunity never seemed right. Not before my trip to Rome, anyway. In Rome, as I told you, my mission basically failed, so I kept them for myself. Today, I wasn't sure ...." She delicately stepped around the subject of Elizabeth's cancer.

"But I offer them to you now, if you'd like to read them. No one but me has ever seen these. They are about all I have left of her. You can imagine how much they mean to me."

Elizabeth unhesitatingly opened the one with the earliest postmark, and read silently.

> *Dearest Katherine,*
>
> *You cannot imagine how tired I am. The 16-hour days at Convent are nothing compared to life in my little village of Refugio. I've only been here two weeks and already I feel like a native, scratching out a bare existence from nothing. It's more rewarding than I thought possible. And Father Art is wonderful. He's from some tiny town in Michigan, and he needed some place that was warm. If you ever ask the Church to send you someplace warm(er), remember to ask for someplace in particular, unless the thought of a Refugio excites you. So while I would love to see you again, you might keep in mind Father Art's story. On a brighter note, I will be getting a bathtub in a week or so. Bathing from a washbowl isn't all that it's cracked up to be, believe me. What I wouldn't give for a warm bath right now. (It's a higher priority than indoor plumbing.) I'm trying to start my school. So far it's not working out, but my Spanish isn't quite what it needs to be yet, and these people don't warm up to strangers quickly. But I'll show them, I won't quit until every child in this village is in my school. There's one little girl, she lives next door to the church where Father Art and I live, who is absolutely precious. Maria is her name. She's too young for school, but I think I'll adopt her just the same. I'll make her my protégé. Her mother has promised to teach me how to cook the local cuisine. Well, it's very late, and I don't have much candle left. That's right. I write at night, by candlelight. How quaint, huh? Enjoy your electricity, and your hot water and your daily luxuries, and think of me down here, the happiest I have ever been in my life. It's more than I ever dreamed it would be. Serving God is rewarding, my dearest friend, but serving my fellow man, that's not far behind.*
>
> *I love you always,*
> *Nicole*

She opened the second one. Katherine watched her touch the words on the paper, desperately searching for anything familiar. She blinked back more tears as Elizabeth shamelessly raised the page to her nose, silently inhaling, desperation in her face for a trace of her daughter's scent, though it was only a copy. The second letter read as quickly as the first.

> Hi there,
>
> I can't remember what I wrote last, so forgive me if I repeat myself. I have a tub now, and my school is overflowing with children who come every day to learn. I teach them English, and grammar and spelling and math. You know, the basics. Then we sing for a while (I've been practicing my guitar, and actually am getting pretty good—not Dan Fogelberg good, but good enough to lead my children in song), and end the day by playing soccer. My parents visited not long ago. We toured several of the ruins not far from here. They still haven't accepted this life I've chosen, but they will, in time. My dad especially is holding back. Katherine, I have this wonderful place I've found. It's like a paradise, with a small waterfall, and a pond, and solitude you couldn't picture in your wildest imaginings. I wait 'til I've finished all my daily tasks before I go down there. It's where I commune with God. I've met a famous journalist. He lives here in the village sometimes. He's British. Other than Father Art, he's my only source of intellectual stimulation. He's older, like you (ha! ha!), and charming. He cares for me like a daughter. He's very special. I am firmly entrenched in this place. I thank God every day for this fulfillment in my life. It is what I was put here on earth to do. I marvel at a certain irony as I consider where I am, and what I am doing. All my life I looked up to my father, and saw such a good man, doing good things, and everything I did was in the pursuit of the law. And here I am today, a teacher, like my mother. I know it sounds corny, but I ended up being more like my mother than my father when I opened my heart to God. I don't know the full significance to that, but the irony is inescapable.
>
> I miss you and love you dearly,
> Nicole

"Katherine, I feel strangely uncomfortable, like I imagine a parent should feel when snooping in a child's diary. Do you suppose Nicole would ever have confided these feelings in me had she lived?" Katherine did not answer. Elizabeth reached for the third letter. Almost as she touched it a chill came over Katherine, who knew the words by heart.

> My dearest Katherine,
>
> So much has happened, I don't know where to begin. The calm and peace of this village has been shattered. The military has been here for months, and there is now talk of an uprising. My children are scared. They hear talk, and they ask me questions. I don't have answers. Chris was here not long ago. Remember Chris? My baby brother. He came to see me after the stories got out about "the miracle". (If you don't know about it, I'll spare you the details. I just wish it would leave me alone, all the fuss over it. Whatever happened is a complete mystery to me. I am just thankful my little Maria is alive and well.) (I wrote about her in my last letter, or maybe it was the first one, I don't recall.) There is something I must tell you. For the first time today, I thought about the possibility that the danger I find myself in might hold me too tightly in its arms, and not let go, and that I might suffer harm, even death. I suppose it is the thought of death that makes me confront everything in my life right now. Am I where I should be? Am I doing what I should be doing? In spite of the danger signals, and the chills I feel at times when I think I am being followed and that there is someone here who would harm me, I know that I cannot leave this place. My job is far from being done. If death comes to me, I pray only that I do not die in a cowardly way, an embarrassment to my God and the Church, that my faith remains strong. I do fear it, you know, the thought of dying. But I won't let that keep me from staying, and showing I stand firmly in my beliefs. Does it make sense that I have never feared more, yet less, in my life than now? If I should die, dear Katherine, and have lived the life that will open Heaven's doors to me, I shall enter as soon as He will have me, and I shall search out John and Kyle for you, and I shall be with them waiting for the day their wife and mother arrives. I must go now, for there is much to be done. I think of you always. Never forget me as your dearest friend.
>
> All my love,
> Nicole

As Elizabeth lowered the third and final letter, Katherine spoke to her in a hushed monotone. "That letter came three days after she died. If it had come beforehand, I swear to you I would have gone after her myself. I had no idea she was ever in danger. I would never have left her in harm's way. I knew too well where your husband was coming from in his lawsuit. For that reason I could not bear to talk to him about this … not to mention because it would also have been the ultimate betrayal of my faith. You know what I am saying: I might just as well have been taking the same position your husband was. My heart was never in the struggle as a defender of the Church. I knew he felt an immense sense of failure, and guilt, over Nicole's death. Me, all I could feel was the frustration of being three days too late to save my friend. Not guilt, not shame, but utter helplessness. Have I done the right thing? Please tell me this is something you can handle. I shall not forgive myself otherwise."

"Katherine, you did what you felt was right in your heart. What else matters?"

Katherine scooped up the letters, and put them back in their envelopes. She looked admiringly at her friend's mother. "What will happen next, Elizabeth? Will you and Mr. McHenry stay close by? Maybe we could see each other." It was more than a hint; it was a plea.

"Since you ask, Katherine, I suppose it's my turn to share a bit of a secret with you. Why don't we enjoy these salads and fruit—I'll have to pass on the wine, though, tempting as it looks—but you go ahead, while I fill you in on what's in store for my husband and me."

"What a grand idea," Katherine replied, admiring Elizabeth for a poor attempt to sound upbeat.

They ate their salads, and made small talk. Elizabeth took another pill for the pain, and when she felt up to it shared the plans that had been made on the *Nepenthe's* return trip. Interesting, exciting, and very short term plans.

§

There seemed so little more to be accomplished here. He had interviewed the village priest, the wife Teresa, the daughter Maria—*what a dear, sweet child, wouldn't she one day make a fine nun?*—the grandfather Miguel, the schoolchildren, and a goodly number of their parents. From a composite of the many recorded accounts they had all given him he'd put together a sketch of Sister Nicole's life in Refugio, from the first days until the last. There seemed to be no disagreement on any part of it: she led an exemplary life, having worked hard at her duties at the little church, harder yet with the schoolchildren, and never exhibiting lapses in her spirituality or her faith. They all revered her, and grieved at her loss no less than they would have a close family member.

The little old man, Miguel, had seemed particularly attached to her, and had gone out of his way to take Father Luigi on a tour of the village and the valley below. Father Luigi was quite interested in the story surrounding the timber, and the deceit of the Palomar family. Miguel had turned uncharacteristically bitter at the mention of the robbery of the timber money. He actually called it a robbery.

Miguel. So helpful, so worried for his son. He practically begged Father Luigi to consult Carlos for more on Sister Nicole. Father Luigi reluctantly explained he would not be allowed to visit with Carlos. The government had forbidden it. But there was some good news from his stay in the capitol. He met with the surgeon, who gave him a fine statement and medical report on what he unhesitatingly called the miracle. The visit with the surgeon gave Father Luigi all the corroboration he needed.

Father Luigi's interest went beyond beatification. He harbored the notion a case might be made for martyrdom. All with whom he'd spoken claimed she had died fearlessly, hands clasped under her chin in prayer even as the blade cut into her. No one, however, could help him with the events surrounding her death, certainly with whether it could be inferred she died rather than renounce her faith, or because of her faith. No one had been close enough to hear what had been said, no one except Juan, Hector, and Carlos. Only Carlos was still alive, and his fate was uncertain.

This was his last night in Refugio. Someone had to know something, but who? The master sleuth in him refused to believe there weren't answers to his questions. If they were answered in the negative, then so be it; she was as good as beatified. If she met the test of martyrdom, now that would be something. It was left up to the vigilant Luigi to make her case. He had adopted her cause as his own. That was his job. That was his calling.

He would not fail her.

He walked to Father Art's room, and asked if they might go over things one more time. As they talked Father Luigi scratched off one name after another as the bits and pieces of the story were rehashed. When it was over, there were only four names left on the list: Monty's, Carlos's, and the two murderers who had also perished. He struck through the first two. The two remaining names, the permanently inaccessible witnesses, he left unstricken. For moments he just sat and thought, quietly, unmoving. At last he raised his head.

"Father, did either of these men have a family? A wife, perhaps, or parents who also lived in the village?"

"Hector, no, he lived alone. The parents are long ago dead. He had two brothers, but one was killed the night of the uprising. He does have another brother who lives here in the village. Yes, a younger brother. They were estranged, I believe, and rarely spoke."

"Could we talk to the brother tonight?"

"We can try. We can go right now if you like."

"What about our other fellow, this Juan, the one who actually struck her? Did he leave any family here?"

"He had a wife and two small children, but they feared for their safety, and we took them into the capital city. That was right after Sister Nicole was killed. I do not know where they might be today. Perhaps the archdiocese might know."

"Be sure to give me their names before I leave. I am going back to Guatemala City in the morning, where I'll catch a plane the following day for America. Ah, my first trip to America. I am most anxious, Father. Tell me, it is a wonderful land, yes?"

"Father Luigi, I think you will find it interesting. Let's leave it at that, shall we?"

An hour later the trail was still cold. Hector, who was older, indeed had been estranged from his brother for quite some time. The younger brother said he knew nothing about the execution of Sister Nicole. Father Luigi had asked of the choice of the word *execution*. Hector's brother had explained that the villagers had all likened it to an execution, for lack of any other way to describe it. Father Luigi scribbled a note and said good night to the man.

It was only another blind path in the maze, not an end to his effort. He would make one more try tomorrow, while he was in the capital, to see the prisoner Carlos. Beyond that, his next view of this investigation would be on American soil. He was going to New Orleans, Louisiana.

Doggedly determined, Father Luigi, investigator of sainthood candidates, had only begun. There were still many tracks and trails left to follow, crevices and caves left to explore.

§

Mac walked into the sunlight, making his way down the steps to the street. It was a busy day in downtown New Orleans. He thought for a moment of dropping in on Katherine Carson, but decided against it. Maybe later, after the events at weeks' end were over, and life had settled back to normal. Whatever normal was.

His meeting with Tom Dillon had been short and pleasant. Mac had been assured he had the full support of his country's State Department.

There was still much to do before Saturday. In five days—not much more than the blink of an eye the way time had moved for him the past two weeks—one of the few remaining loose ends would be tied off, and only the formalities would remain. It was well underway, this healing business. He brimmed with anticipation at the thought of Saturday. Stopping as the steps met the sidewalk to inhale deeply, Mac closed his eyes and savored a sense of accomplishment.

There was no time to waste. He had packing to do, and a plane to catch.

§

How curious it is, the investigator thought, that his life was largely about miracles. He, Father Luigi, knew and appreciated them. There were small ones, grand ones, taken for granted ones, overlooked and seemingly insignificant ones. They were sometimes predictable, but for the most part random and entirely unpredictable.

Like the one he had just experienced.

Absorbed in the self-satisfaction of accomplishment he took pains to remind himself his task was still unfinished. There were details to be attended to; not many, but the ones that were left were important. There was time for celebration later. For now, he opened his notebook to review his findings, to once again make sure that what he'd just experienced had been captured in the proper form. Facts only, personal reflections omitted.

The flight attendant came by to refill his wine glass. Yes, a second glass was called for. It would be a long flight, and sleep would be difficult, so why not a second glass?

Aren't miracles just divinely and supremely wonderful? Most certainly they are.

§

There was only the hush of wooded solitude surrounding Elizabeth as she sat ritually beside her daughter's grave. Early spring blooms now dotted the area, hiding the place further from view. She still liked the privacy. As she did most days when it was dry, she stretched out on the ground, to be whisper near to her daughter. Today her head was propped on the palm of her hand, supported by an elbow resting on a small mound of earth. Her free hand smoothed the soft, cool blades of grass that covered the warm earth. The warmth had always been Elizabeth's way of knowing her daughter was still there.

"You've been busy, haven't you?" she asked. "While I was away, you spent some time with your father, didn't you?

"I'm glad. He needed some time with his daughter.

"Whatever it is you did, it worked. I have him back now, and so do you. And none too soon, either."

She rolled over, and lay on her stomach. "I suppose you know these moments to-gether are numbered now to so very few. Isn't that wonderful? I hope you are as anxious to see me as I am to see you again."

She spread her arm outward, hugging desperately at the earth, closing her eyes hard as the silence protectively cloaked mother and daughter once again.

§

Another woman stood at a different gravesite, only a few dozen miles away, and said prayers over another soul. Katherine Carson crossed herself a last time as she looked down at the freshly dug earth and casket. She smiled in remembrance at the joy this departed soul had brought to her, and to another one she would be joining soon.

"Godspeed, Sister Veronica. I envy you your place beside our Father, with our friend Nicole. May you find another large tree to rest under with her again. Bless you, my Sis-ter." She bent to run her hand over the plain wooden casket, adorned with just a simple cross. She lamented that only a few would notice, fewer yet would mourn, the passing of one who had lived such a flawless, principled life. The irony of it was, Sister Ve-ronica would not have expected or wanted any recognition. She gave up such thoughts a half century earlier when she took her vows. They all gave up such thoughts.

She glanced around while walking back to the convent, absorbed in a new thought. She would meet with Father Luigi tomorrow, after his arrival from Guatemala. His call came as a surprise. She'd thought the investigation would take months, even years. The investigator's call told her otherwise, but it had also given her another piece of news: he had something very important to share with her, something wonderful. But he was hurried, so it must keep until he arrived. A quick *Ciao!* and he'd hung up, leav-ing her emotionally frozen. The service for Sister Veronica had been the only thing to keep her calm. Now her pulse quickened again.

He would arrive at the convent in barely three hours. There was little to be readied for his visit, but there were some old friends at the convent for her to visit with first. And some news to share with them.

She hadn't seen Sister Agnes Ann in weeks. It would be good to visit with the woman who had served so long and well, who was best known for her remarkable wisdom and patience.

Never moreso than once, nearly three years ago, when in the darkest of night she had gone to the Mother Superior's bedside and pleaded the cause of her friend, who surely deserved one more chance. She had drawn from her every experience as a lawyer and well-meaning friend, but most of all, as a Sister in God as she pled the cause for Nicole. The pranks were to hide insecurity, not an indication of her purity or spirituality. Would Mother Superior please reconsider?

And when she'd said she would reconsider, just this one time, it was a jubilant Sister Katherine who'd made her a promise that wasn't called for. "Mother Superior," she'd said, "I swear to you, in the name of Jesus and Mary, you will not live to regret your decision."

Words Katherine wished at times she'd never uttered, their brutal irony so painful.

§

One plane was headed north, the other in the opposite direction. Each had the mirror image origin and destination. Their paths crossed at altitudes between thirty-three and thirty-five thousand feet. While Father Luigi Giuseppe Vincenzo was setting his second empty glass onto the traytop, picturing what America would be like, J. Bradley McHenry was busily pondering his third trip to Guatemala, and every implication connected to it. His emotions were centered somewhere between the excitement of the first and the weight of the second. Thankfully there was no attention centered on him this trip, no garrulous redneck or efficacious passengers or crew, no dolorous public at every turn. He was thankfully inconspicuous.

This was to be a very quick trip. The itinerary Mac had requested had been prearranged by Tom Dillon, down to the last detail. There would be no long waits this time, no surprises.

None for Mac, anyway. But there would be for several of those he would be seeing. Mac derived a sense of incipient satisfaction as he went over the details, making certain one more time he hadn't left anything to chance. He planned on being back at home in less than forty-eight hours, and couldn't risk a delay—or the heavy blame he would place on himself if his planning were inadequate.

§

"I wish I had better news for you, Elizabeth. I really do." Doctor Patti Moreau sat next to her friend, across the desk from the empty high-backed leather chair from which she normally doled out the usual array of prognoses. Friendship transcended the oncologist-patient relationship.

The news was not unexpected. The cancer was still there, grown from its infancy well into maturity. Whatever natural habitat Elizabeth's body had traitorously provided was doing the job. The involuntary watering and weeding and fertilization were, regrettably, right on schedule. There was some good news, Patti had added:

"Strangely, the cancer hasn't metastasized. Your tumor's holding firm right where it formed. It's growing, and likely will spread, eventually, but it hasn't yet. This adds weeks, perhaps even months, Elizabeth. Good, coherent time. Time you and Mac ought to treasure." Elizabeth didn't really hear much after the part about her tumor growing past infancy. The personalization of the growth—"your" tumor—created an eerie feeling. *It's a part of me*, she rued. Always she'd treated her body as a temple, religiously nurturing it. A force beyond her control now made part of her body undeserving of belonging. Not like a few extra pounds she might exercise or diet away, this was a lethal weight gain. But it wasn't, as she'd just learned, an all bad tumor, as tumors evidently go. This one would just keep getting bigger; slowly, inexorably, bigger, but it was not—not yet, anyway—sprouting seedlings, more body parts for her to nurture involuntarily. The bonus, the lagniappe from this dreaded happenstance, is she gets to live a little bit longer, and without a noticeable increase in pain, or loss of faculty. Somehow this good news part of the bad news-good news report (*Bad news always first*, Elizabeth had insisted from the start) offered her no comfort. One killer was enough for her body; multiple assassins, as she joked with her doctor and friend, were nothing more than overkill.

Even at a time like this, a little gallows humor was not beyond Elizabeth.

There wasn't much else for the friends to discuss. The regimen was clear: no stress, continue exercising, cut out the fatty foods and the alcohol, light on the red meat and heavy on the fresh fish intake, don't overdo the pain medication, *et cetera*. Elizabeth knew the drill well. She embraced Patti and headed to the local Delchamps for the groceries she would need for supper. Her husband was returning from Guatemala early this evening. He called to say everything had gone as hoped, and he would be home on schedule. Once the formalities were out of the way, he stayed focused on how she was, insisting she share every feeling and medical nuance with him. Once again the caring, doting husband she'd missed this past year. She'd told him she was just fine, simply tired, that she hadn't rested well without him at her side.

It's not easy to fool a mate of twenty-seven years. She knew he saw through her deception. Maybe a quiet, candlelight dinner at home would distract him from wondering what was really bothering her. She could share with him the good news their sons would be in the next day, a full two days before Saturday's occasion. She'd come to calling it the occasion, *Celebration* too much the malapropism to suit her taste.

Despite the news from Patti, and the better news her husband and sons were due home soon, she felt poorly. Perhaps it was dread of the onset of fatigue. The next few days would be frenetic and tiring; tonight might be the last peace she would know for a while. She was lying to herself. It was more than that, much more. In the rush to reaffirm her life with her husband, to break down their barriers of truthlessness, she'd kept one thing from him. One teeny, tiny thing.

And it was tearing at her insides, even faster than the cancer was.

§

Katherine Carson sat at her desk, as she did most nights, reflecting. Usually she would be working on her latest assignment from the archbishop, but tonight was different. Tonight, a mix of exhilaration, apprehension, reticence and sadness filled her. Father Luigi had arrived, and shared a most extraordinary tale. It was as if, he theorized, he'd been led to the woman, that it was preordained. She'd kept her silence as he meandered along, wondering, first, what had happened, and secondly, what he'd meant by being led to "the woman." She didn't have long to wait. He began his story.

"When there was nothing further to be learned in Refugio, I went to the capital to try once more to see Carlos. And find the family of Juan Pedro de la Zea, Nicole's killer. The same official soundly refused me access to Carlos. No one at the archdiocese had even heard of the de la Zea family. I was prepared to leave the following morning for America empty-handed. Then, the most incredible, miraculous thing happened.

"Father Eduardo, the priest who picked me up at the government office was different from the one who dropped me off earlier. My first driver had a Mass to say. And Father Eduardo had to make a stop at a nearby hospital, where he tended to the sickly and soulless. I told Father Eduardo I was in no hurry—I would go with him to the hospital. When we got there, I even offered to help him with his rounds. Work I had not done since I was a very young priest, near Salerno. Richly rewarding work. Once inside the pitiable excuse of a haven I began to enjoy spreading cheer. Most patients were quite elderly, and bedridden, but I could tell they liked my warm bedside manner."

Katherine smiled at the simple expression of vanity.

"Soon I found myself on a strange floor, dark, not bright or cheery as the others. I asked Father Eduardo why the difference. He told me it was the ward where those of simple or deranged mind were kept, for their own safety as well as the other patients. To me it made no difference. Simple or deranged or whatever, if they sought refuge in the Lord I was there to provide.

"After visiting with two patients, I found myself standing beside the last bed in the first row, the one closest to the corner. The woman in the bed lay perfectly still, eyes frozen open widely, not fixed on me, but I could tell I was in her line of sight. The woman's fingers clutched the white sheet to her chin. They were white-knuckled, the blood drained by the force with which she gripped the sheet. It seemed she was terrified. I moved in her direction.

"'Not that one', Father Eduardo quietly shouted. 'We leave her alone.'"

"'Why?' I asked. 'Is she dangerous?'"

"'No, not dangerous,' he said, 'but she is prone to screaming fits when one of us gets near.'"

"'One of us?' I asked him.'"

"He was quite agitated. He told me, 'Yes, even the nuns who work here are forbidden to approach her. She is cared for by one of the civilian caretakers.'"

"I asked him to explain. He told me she'd been admitted six months earlier, after the police found her wandering the streets, with two small children. They were digging in garbage, begging in the streets. The police thought she was loco, and brought her here. They took her children to Father Eduardo's parish church.

"What he said next sent a chill through me. She told the police she was from a village to the north—Refugio. She also spoke incoherently about her husband, wondering where he was, why he wasn't with her.

"When I heard Refugio, I began to quiver with anticipation. I asked if she had said her husband's name.

"Father Eduardo told me to look on her medical chart, at the foot of her bed. Then he asked me if I knew this woman, or perhaps her husband.

"I told him I might. I walked over to the foot of her bed, careful not to arouse her. Her eyes had not moved, but like the cornered animal, the fear shone in them nonetheless. They widened slightly as I reached for the papers at the foot of her bed. Her fingers tightened even more; the sheet was pulled up higher, from chin to lips. Her body was rigid enough to use as a walkway. Then I saw it, right before my eyes: PATIENT'S NAME: de la Zea, Corinne. NEXT OF KIN: de la Zea, Juan Pedro (Husband).

"Sister, I set the chart back down, and looked straight into the woman's eyes. They looked back, but only in my direction, afraid and unable to connect with mine. So I raised my hands, in a peaceful gesture. Still her grip did not slacken. An idea came to me. I spoke in a hushed voice, and told her I meant no harm. I told her I must speak with her … about her husband, Juan. She flinched at her husband's name, and looked even more terrified, if it was possible. Father Eduardo had come over, and wanted to know what was going on. I said I didn't have time to tell him, but I must speak to the woman. I asked him to bring me someone she would trust.

"He returned quickly. As the specialist approached the woman's bed, one hand released its death grip on the sheet and reached for her. The patient began to whisper, and the woman bent to listen. 'The specialist said, 'She wants to know of her husband. Then she wants you to leave.'"

"Then I said, 'Tell her I will tell her about her husband, and I will leave, but first she must tell me some things. She tells me what I want to know first, then I tell her of Juan.'"

"The two women exchanged more whispers. The specialist then said she would tell me things if she knows them … she cannot tell me what she does not know.

"I had to make a decision. Maybe I would get only one answer to one question. I thought about what I had learned in Refugio. Then it came to me. I said, 'Then ask why he screams out in the night sometimes. He frightens the villagers sometimes when he does this.

"They whispered some more. The specialist told me, 'She says he sees demons in his dreams. Black and white ones, with flashes of red.'

"'Then ask her if it had anything to do with the young nun who came to the village, Sister Nicole,' I said next."

"Father Eduardo was confused, but he took a seat on the nearby chair. I did not know what else I could say to him. But I had to get what I could from the de la Zea woman."

"The specialist said, 'She says the nightmares had stopped years ago, when they were first married and moved to Refugio, but came back when the nun came to the village.'

"Sister, I was trembling. I wasn't sure what to ask next. The woman looked to be drifting away. I did not know how much longer she would be coherent. I was tempted to ask her why she thought the nightmares returned because of Sister Nicole, but I went in another direction. I asked her: 'How does she console him, when his screams awaken her and frighten their children? What does she do to make the demons leave?'

'She soothes the scars. She comforts him by running her fingers over the scars.'

'Please tell her I don't understand. What scars?'

"They whispered some more. 'The scars the other nun put on him, and those his own father added, when he was a boy.'

"I was covered with chills. 'Scars caused how, and for what reason?' I asked.

"The bedridden woman became agitated again. I told the specialist, 'Tell her Juan is fine, and waits for her. He wants to see his children too. He misses his family. He

440

✝

waits for them back in Refugio.' I was careful not to lie outright. Nothing I said was utterly false, only terribly misleading. I would set things straight later, when the opportunity was there.

"'She says the scars were for his laziness, from when the nun burned him with her cigarette on his back and shoulders because he would not read his assignments ... when they were attending the Catholic Church school in Huehuetenango, before they ran off to Refugio.'

"I asked, 'He did not like to read?'

'She says he tried very hard ... he wanted to learn to read like the other children, but he had trouble. The nun whipped him at first, then began to burn him with her cigarettes. Then his father would whip him on his back until he bled. He was punished for his laziness. He lived in shame, even after they were married and left their home for Refugio, and when she would comfort him from his nightmares, they would hold each other in their arms, and he would cry onto her shoulder. It took years for the bad dreams to go away. They returned when the nun came to Refugio. Out of fear for their children he would not allow them to attend school. His bad memories would not allow it to happen.'

"The specialist said, 'Father, let me show you something.' She gently sat the woman upright, and undid the top two snaps of her gown, carefully pulling it down to where it modestly exposed her shoulders and back. Father Eduardo and I gasped simultaneously. Her back was covered with small, hideous, purplish crater-like indentions into the skin. There were easily a dozen of them. The specialist snapped the gown back together. She laid the woman down. She looked catatonic. My questioning was at an end.

"I asked when she might come out of it. She told me there was no way of knowing.

"She asked, 'What of her husband, Father? Can we bring him to see her? They are obviously very much in love. It would do her good, I should think.'

"I explained why that was not possible ... why I'd been deceitful earlier. She seemed to understand. Then she said the most amazing thing. 'I've determined she is dyslexic, if that helps you. She, too, was punished by her own parents for what they thought was her laziness. As we have learned, dyslexic people are often misdiagnosed as lazy, when in truth they only have varying degrees of difficulty with their ability to recognize written symbols. It's a guess on my part, but perhaps her husband had the same condition. I suppose we shall never know.'

"She was right, of course, but by then I already had reached the only logical conclusion I could draw from the encounter. It was clear to me Sister Nicole's death at the hand of Juan Pedro de la Zea was faith-based. She was not the victim of a lunatic without purpose. Hers was a persecuted death. She had been persecuted for her faith by a demented man, tragically made so by the very hand of his own Catholic Church. It was a case of revenge, dementia a contributing factor, yet clearly the result of the cloth Sister Nicole wore.

"She died because of her faith, a faith she did not renounce even in the face of death."

"I have verified that, years earlier, there indeed had been a nun at the Church's school in Huehuetenango who'd been abusive to the children. She came from a small village in Spain, in the Pyrenees, where she returned, it was said, after the Church could no longer turn a blind eye to the reported abuses. Not before she caused her students untold physical and emotional damage. Such a bittersweet realization. The very thing Sister Nicole's father claimed in his lawsuit was unquestionably a cause of his daughter's death.

"Sadness grips me, Sister Katherine." He'd reached into his satchel, pulling out the notebook in which he carried the fruits of his journey. He opened it, slowly. Nicole's photograph, her radiant smile he'd heard so many speak so fondly of. Her innocent, unknowing, betrayed smile.

"Perhaps I am not truly cut out for this line of work after all. I believe there will be some heavy moments tomorrow when I face her parents."

58

THE REALM OF POSSIBILITIES was confounding to her. Tomorrow would find Father Luigi speaking with Mac and Elizabeth McHeanry. What would he share with them? Would all the good come unraveled if they learned everything? What of Elizabeth's health? Would such news throw her off a delicate balance?

She wrestled with the seemingly endless parade of permutations. She tried prayer; her mind too cluttered, she could only get as far as *Heavenly Father*.

Without thought, she rose from her desk and walked to the small chapel. Entering, she was surprised to see someone else in the darkness. A postulate, one of the few, like Nicole before her, honored for their accomplishments while at convent.

Katherine took the kneeler next to the postulate, whose young and pretty face at once jolted her. There was no resemblance, of course, but a certain vivacity leaped from the smile right at her, just as another's had at their first meeting.

"I come here late at night, when everything is quiet, to collect my thoughts," said the young nun. "Hello, I'm Sister Kelli." Katherine introduced herself in return.

"I haven't seen you in here before," the postulate added.

"I'm embarrassed to say I've forgotten prayer can be said as easily in this room as my own upstairs. I shall not be so long in returning. You are from the Sister Theresa of Avila Convent?"

"Yes. I shall be leaving soon, and was offered the chance to spend my last few months in training here at the archdiocese. I am entering foreign mission work. I hope to go to Asia, or perhaps Africa."

The hairs on Katherine Carson's arm bristled. "A noble ambition. And the danger?"

"There is danger everywhere, Sister. It's a question of where I am most needed, not where there is the least danger, or the most comfort. I am prepared."

Recent, sad memories surfaced. "Such a strong response for one so young. Tell me, has your faith been so tested you can accept the unknown you face without hesitation or reservation? Be truthful with me."

"Yes, I am young—in my twenties. What does my age matter? My faith has been tested daily since I came into the Order, and I know it will be tomorrow, and the next day, and the next, wherever I am. In ways I cannot even imagine today. I am prepared to meet these tests, as much, I believe, as I can at this point in my life, and as I continue to grow in God I will be better prepared than I am. Surely it is no different for you, Sister."

"No, of course it isn't." *It's just that I get so wrapped up in myself from time to time, and need a refresher course in faith, you see. You do see that, young Sister, don't you?* "How wisely spoken."

The postulate's warm smile reminded her again of Nicole, of the wisdom beyond her years.

The postulate left first, leaving Katherine alone in the small chapel. Her uncluttered mind recalled a setting not so unlike this one a few weeks earlier, when she had unhesitatingly accepted Cardinal Bertolucci's invitation to attend the evening Mass in the Holy Father's private Vatican chapel, a privilege reserved for only the fortunate few. She had entered the chapel a few minutes early, and had found the small, frail man at the altar, kneeling in prayer. An aura had unmistakably outlined the kneeling figure, the force of which had overpowered her. Reverence permeated the entire room. She'd never felt closer to God, never before been so sure of her faith. Cardinal Bertolucci had arrived soon after, to find her standing petrified beside the few pews, unsure of herself. He had been amused at her display of awe, and had thankfully taken charge. The Holy Father, hearing the familiar voice of the Cardinal, had risen from his quiet reflections, and had walked over to greet his visitors. As she had taken his ring hand in formal greeting, Sister Katherine Carson had known, if ever she had doubted before, this man was truly one with God. Whatever she had come to Rome for would, she knew at that instant, be done as God's will.

Katherine had allowed herself to worry at how Father Luigi's news would be received by Mac and Elizabeth, and had momentarily lost sight that the whole was greater than the parts. A chance meeting with a young postulate had restored her sight. In two days she would take her place beside the family of her friend, and join in their Celebration of her life, content in knowing whatever happened, it had already been divinely blessed.

The labor is done, he thought to himself while entering the last few notes into the binder that had thickened so much in the last few days. All that remained was to prepare the formal report, the *positio*, which he would personally deliver to Cardinal Bertolucci. For over a dozen years he had served the Cardinal as his chief investigator. The earliest years had been a time of trial and error for him, but Father Luigi had learned what was needed and expected. The knowledge gained of experience told him the cause for the sainthood of Sister Nicole was met. Above all else towered her courage. With the *positio*, and Cardinal Bertolucci's endorsement, it would be a perfunctory pronouncement from His Holiness.

So why was he so distraught?

It was the parents.

Their reaction had been so different than he'd expected. He'd left there bewildered. He had two days before he returned to Rome, and his meeting with Cardinal Bertolucci. Two days in which to make his decision.

In the meantime, he had a Celebration to attend.

———————

The sunlight blinded him. Standing alone, in tattered and soiled clothes, his eyes slammed shut to the stabbing pain caused by the brightness, he could not have been more euphoric.

Freedom. Not the kind he'd fought for, that men had died for, but better. He was alive.

Carlos Mendez, revolutionary, prisoner of the state, walked out a free man. Without a word of explanation, his cell door had been opened, and he'd been pulled into the darkened hallway. He'd begun his prayer then, certain his time had come. The guards dragged him down the corridor, at their brisk pace. He'd been too weak to keep up.

Were executions always so hurried? he'd wondered.

They'd escorted him from corridor to corridor, past silent, dark places. Were the others from Refugio there? Was their fate to be as his? He'd wanted to shout words of defiance, words of hope, to those in the darkness, but had lacked the strength.

He'd nearly lost consciousness. He'd wished as much, to avoid the final indignity he would face before his death. He had remained lucid enough to see a rim of light ahead, eking through a doorway. It had to be sunlight. He'd not seen sunlight in so long. Only the light of the dim bulbs hanging on either side of his small cell. He'd not forgotten the brilliance of the sun, and watched as he was dragged closer and closer to the brightness, until he was placed before the door, and left standing there.

Someone shouted an indecipherable command, and the sunlight poured in. Forcefully he was thrust out the door. The only words he'd heard were the ones harshly telling him to return to his home, and never take up arms against his country again.

Return to your home. The words rang magically. His wife and children, his father, his village, and his life before he'd fallen victim to the misguided teachings of a man who died by the knife in those beliefs, waiting out there for him.

Tears streamed down his face as he made his way to the belltower he could make out on the skyline. The cross at its top was beacon enough for him.

Yes, he was free.

It was time he headed home.

†

§

Creases furrowed his forehead, blending with those that exploded outwardly from the corners of his eyes, worry lines earned of constant toil over seventy years. Her report had been uplifting, yes, complete to the last detail of the unconditional dismissal of the lawsuit, the salvation of the father's soul. *He should be pleased*, thought Archbishop Thomas Ryan. There should be rejoicing instead of niggling concern.

It wasn't what had gone right, he reminded himself. Good always takes care of itself. It was the other part—what he called the nasty part—holding him at bay from the joy Sister Katherine radiated as she'd summarized the last chapter of the McHenry story.

He recalled the unfortunate business with the parish priest over in Lafayette. That had been costly, in every sense of the word. The toll on the Church, and on this particular archbishop, had at the time seemed too great to overcome. But time had passed, and calmer waters seemed ahead.

Until this McHenry business came along.

Now, the archbishop worried, there were storm clouds on the horizon. He shuddered at the thought of the litany of abuses McHenry exposed in his lawsuit. While things had been cleaned up in this archdiocese, it might not be so in others. Was it systemic, as McHenry had pleaded in his lawsuit? Were the abuses truly the product of unwatchful eyes, worse yet shrugged shoulders? *Dear God*, he thought, *don't let it be so. Please don't let it be so.*

His prayer for the soul of Mac McHenry had been answered. This new one, the one he'd just uttered, he wasn't so sure about. There was trouble ahead, he felt certain.

The lines at the corners of his eyes and in his forehead only deepened.

§

"Bradley, can we sit outside and talk for a moment? On the patio, out back."

He'd been thinking about addressing the group of mostly strangers, wondering if the last-minute nature of the event would end up some awkward mistake. Father Paul, always the optimist, had assured him everything would work out smoothly … all Mac had to do was show up, basically, and the rest was would take care of itself. His thoughts were interrupted by Elizabeth's invitation. He welcomed the interruption.

She had the sun tea ready. Something was up, he was certain.

He was barely seated when Elizabeth dropped the shoe. "I'm having second thoughts. I just wanted you to know."

Mac stayed calm, on the outside. He sorted out what he'd heard. There was more than one meaning, maybe more than one message. "You mean about everything, or just tomorrow?"

"Tomorrow for sure. The rest? I haven't decided yet."

"You can't do this, Elizabeth. I thought we had everything in order. How can you just change your mind at the last minute like this?"

"I'm not sure I ever made up my mind, Bradley. I remember a wonderfully romantic sail with you not long ago, where you swept me off my feet, and not wanting to say anything you might take as argument. I couldn't bear to do that to you, you were back to your old self, and I didn't want to see that part of you gone again. I know I shouldn't have, but I just bit my tongue, thinking it was something I could grow into. The problem is, I've grown even colder to the idea. It's just not something I care to do."

The door chime rang. Mac wasn't sure whether to be annoyed or grateful. "I'll get it. We can finish this when I get back."

Father Paul stood anxiously at the door. "I hope you don't mind. I literally was in the neighborhood, visiting with Arthur and Effie Hebert—they're former clients of yours, I believe—and thought I'd stop by on my way back to St. Joseph. I hope I'm not interrupting anything."

Mac stepped outside. The signal wasn't lost on Robichaux, who quickly asked if anything was wrong.

"Elizabeth and I were just discussing tomorrow. She isn't feeling well, and I have an idea will want to call it a day earlier than usual. Otherwise, you know I would grab your arm and haul you through the door."

"It's probably just nerves. A good night's rest will do her more good than my being here. I just wanted to see if you had any last-minute details we needed to work out."

Boy do we. "I think we're all squared away, Father. You'll see us tomorrow, as planned. Thanks so much for dropping by. You were kind to go out of your way, and you know you're always welcome."

"It was no bother, Mac," Robichaux said. "Well, please give Elizabeth my regards, and I'll be on my way."

"I'll do that. And thanks again for stopping by."

Elizabeth hadn't moved. "Who was that?"

"Father Paul. Said to give you his best."

"What, 'in the neighborhood' and just stopping by?" There was a touch of sarcasm Mac wasn't sure he understood.

"Well, as a matter of fact, that's exactly why he was here. Just wanted to make sure everything was set for tomorrow, the Cele—" He caught himself. "I mean, the occasion."

"Well, so much for my bad timing. Listen, I've been thinking, while you were inside making excuses for me or whatever," the ongoing hint of sarcasm sliding off her tongue, "and all I can come up with is 'What's the use?' I can't fight it, Bradley. We'll go ahead and do it your way."

"Now Elizabeth," he began, the interruption already a distant memory, "you know I can't accept that from you. Either this is both of us, or it doesn't work. I'm not going to spend the rest of our days together feeling like I forced this on you. So this has to be mutual, understand?"

"I understand very well, and I'm telling you it is. I'm not as gung ho as you are, but I'll not say no."

"Not saying no isn't the same thing as saying yes, Elizabeth."

"All right, Mr. Lawyer, then let me put it this way: I'm saying yes. Is that good enough for you?"

He realized she wasn't angry. Maybe tired, a little frustrated, but not angry. He could accept anything but anger. He took the *yes*, and was pleased with it.

"Okay, then. I'm okay with your *yes*."

"Fine. So, it's way too early for dinner, but I'm hungry. I think I'll have a pear. Would you like a pear, Bradley? They are fresh, from the produce market, and as juicy and sweet as you please." He gave her a look.

ALL THE ANGELS AND SAINTS

"Oh, come on, Bradley, have a pear with me. It might sweeten you up a little. And Lord knows you could use a little sweetening up." She was already heading for the back door.

He shouted after her. "Sure, bring one of those juicy, ripe pears out here to me."

And for the second time in their extended conversation one of them said to the other, "What's the use?"

§

Mac's gaze settled on the crowd that had grown over the past hour from a few dozen to what easily could be more than two hundred ... far more than he'd expected. The rows of chairs were swallowed by the standing mass who'd gathered in the aisles and behind the makeshift stage.

He recognized a number of his children's friends, some Nicole's, some the boys'. They were grown, poised to take the mantle from the older generation and forage on their own. He wondered, as they moved along in their lives, if the memory of this day would hold anything special.

Mac took his seat on the aisle, next to Danny. Chris was somewhere else in the crowd, but it would have been useless to search for him. He caught Father Paul mouthing to him, "It's time. Are you ready?" Mac nodded *Yes*.

Father Paul stepped onto the stage. He fiddled momentarily with the microphone, did the "Testing ... Testing ..." thing, then quieted the crowd with his first words.

"Welcome to everyone. Good friends, I'm the one who gets to start this off. To those of you who knew Nicole, or Sister Nicole as she came to be, I welcome you to this Celebration of her life. It's something her family decided to do, and I think you'll all agree with me it wasn't an easy decision, but it's one—judging by the sheer number of you here—you're glad they made. I know I am.

"The family asked me to say only a few words, to set the only ground rule for what we're doing today. They want this to be upbeat, not an occasion for us all to mourn Nicole. I don't know another way except to just say it—she wouldn't want us to gather in the spirit of mourning.

"The Nicole I knew was a happy child, and a happy young adult. It should not surprise you that nothing changed when she took her vows. It is in this spirit we should remember her.

"I am new to this sort of thing, frankly. But I like the idea. I understand the way it works is, those of you who want to share with the rest of us some special moment you shared with Nicole will take turns up here. I'd go first, but am a little unsure of what I might say, so I think I'll wait 'til later, after I've got the hang of it. Don't be shy … we're all friends here.

"Okay, the monologue is officially over. I am stepping down. It's someone else's turn." He left the stage empty except for the stand in the center.

A few people started up at the same time, like two people trying to squeeze into a revolving door compartment meant for only one. Mac smiled as they awkwardly mediated the congestion, and a pretty young girl stepped up first. She looked barely in her teens.

She was six when she met Nicole for the first time, when Nicole babysat for her one night. Sixteen-year-old Nicole was the prettiest girl she'd ever seen, and the girl had idolized her from then on. She appreciated the kindness Nicole showed her, the special attention. She'd read to her for hours, long past her bedtime. No other babysitter had ever been so attentive, or caring. She concluded by saying that Nicole would forever have a special place in her heart.

It was a nice start, Mac thought. Courageously sweet, for one so young to stand before such a crowd of strangers and speak from within her heart. A touch of the maudlin, but not overdone. It could have been worse.

A young man stepped up next, a friend from school, someone Nicole helped in their seventh grade math class when he couldn't seem to conquer complex division. Later, when trigonometry had stymied him, she'd been there to help again. She was always there to help, he said. He wished he could've done something to help her, when she needed it.

That one was a little tougher for Mac to handle. He hoped the next one would tug a little less on the heartstrings.

Her sophomore English teacher went next. He paid a fine tribute to a student who'd embodied all of what education was meant to accomplish.

A few friends shared some embarrassingly humorous moments. At the earliest age she had a streak in her, they'd all agreed. One prank after another, building to a crescendo with one especially outrageous one. It was the time Nicole had tricked Shelby into thinking she was going skinny-dipping in the Tchefuncte one night. Shelby told the story on herself.

"I was a little full of myself, and our group figured—rightly so—I needed to be taken down a notch. Since none of the other girls were speaking to me, I was pretty pleased when Nicole asked me to go for a swim one Friday night.

"Once we were both in the water, Nicole tossed her one-piece onto the bank, and told me how fun it was, why didn't I do the same? No sooner than I did, Nicole swam to the bank and climbed out of the water. You guessed it; she had on a hidden two-piece suit, and stood on the bank silhouetted by the lights from a dozen headlights shining on the water. I shrieked.

"Nicole said the headlights belonged to the cars of every boy I knew. I shrieked again, begged for Nicole to throw my suit into the water. Nicole just motioned to me with her curling finger to climb out. Even when I started crying, begging, she wouldn't budge. So, out of options, I climbed out. Every horn started honking at the sight of me trying to modestly hide my bareness. When I reached for my suit on the bank, Nicole grabbed it first, and ran back to the lights, which went off as she reached them.

"I just stood there, naked, in the brightest moonlight St. Tammany Parish had seen in some time as, one by one, Nicole and the other girls—no boys, thank goodness—paraded out from behind the cars.

"The message was loud and clear: get too full of yourself, you're ours." Shelby wiped something from the corner of an eye.

"We were all friends again. It made me a better friend. I think it made all of us better friends. A little prank was all we needed to show us we could still be friends. Nicole knew that. It's what made her so special."

Shelby left the stage saying *Thank you, Nicole,* too softly for anyone but Mac to hear.

It was a story Mac hadn't heard before, and he thought he'd heard them all. He wondered how much more there was about Nicole he'd never know. It made him wish the day wouldn't end.

A goodly number of tributes later a lull set in. Not much of a lull, but enough to notice. Mac decided to use the hiatus to look for Chris. He didn't have to look long.

Chris stepped out of the group to the side, the shoes glaringly unshined and the unpressed shirt holding its own, but handsome as ever. He had a different expression on his face than Mac could recall seeing before. It left him wondering, as his younger son took the platform and spoke into the microphone.

"Most of you know me," he began. "For those who don't, I'm Nicole's brother Chris. She has two of us; there's Danny down there, sitting next to our dad, in the front row. Danny's the one in a Marine uniform. He doesn't like it when I say 'moron', so pay attention to the fact that I said 'Marine', okay?" There was a titter of laughter. "I know we're supposed to keep this upbeat, and I'm glad you have, and I'll try too, but hearing all of these things reminds me how much I really miss my sister. I hope every brother out there feels the way about his sister the way I do about mine: she's the best sister in the world. No brother ever had a better sister. Ever. What's really neat, you know, is that I always told her that I loved her. The whole time she was alive, I never held back telling her. So I won't stand up here today and tell you how much I regret not telling her I loved her while she was alive. I just miss being able to still tell her now, that's all.

"Growing up, having her as a big sister, I felt like I was a king. Do you know what it's like to have people accept you just because you're your sister's little brother? I had my own friends, sure, but I had her friends who were mine too. And it was the same with Danny. I'm talking real friends here. Look around you, and ask yourselves who you see. You see your friends, don't you? Sure you do. How many of you got an invitation to this thing? Raise your hands. Yeah, maybe twenty or thirty of you got one in the mail. The rest of you are here because you found out from another friend. That was my sister, your best friend. You know what I'm talking about.

"I was her friend too, as much as I was her brother. She really was my best friend, next to my brother. For all the times I hugged her, and told her I love you Nic, I don't remember telling her what a great friend she was. I do regret that.

"I'm starting to ramble now, and I promised myself I wouldn't. You guys are wonderful to come and share everything about her with everyone, so you deserve better than me standing up here and getting all sappy. But I want to tell you one story about my sister. I could tell you dozens more of them, but this is the only one I need to … to … get off my chest." Anyone who knew Chris already knew this was a different person speaking.

"Anyway, about a month before … before she died—" He was struggling now, trying hard to hold it together. "—I went to see Nicole, in her little village down in Guatemala. Listen, you people don't know poverty, you don't have a clue about primitive, not until you experience something like where she lived. No showers, no indoor plumbing, and until a few weeks before I got there, no electricity. But it was home to her, and she loved it, every muddy, barren, ravaged square inch of it. I went to see her after the news came out about the miracle. You guys heard all about it, right? It was hot stuff, reading about your sister performing a miracle. Think what you'd do if it was your sister: you'd catch the first plane, no matter who told you not to.

"Sorry, Dad," he said, stopping long enough to glance down at Mac, who one-eyed him with a mock scowl for all to see, but who wondered inwardly where this was headed. It was the first he knew about Chris going to Guatemala.

"So I caught a ride with the church delivery truck and quietly slipped into little Refugio, and am walking around in this Stone Age village, no clue where she might be, when I spotted her. She was walking down the street, kind of skipping along, and I'm sure she didn't have a care in the world. Anyway, I ran over to this little alley kind of space between these two huts, and I rolled the new soccer ball I'd brought right in front of her feet. It was a perfect toss, at a perfect angle, the ball rolling directly in her path. Without breaking stride, not slowing down or anything, she kind of instinctively lifted up her skirt, or whatever it is they call a nun's dress, habit, I think … yeah, her habit … right up to about knee-high, stops the ball with the heel of her front foot and locks the ball in with her back foot, and in the smoothest motion you could imagine does this perfect rainbow.

"You soccer players out there, you know what a rainbow is, when the ball just kind of flips over your shoulder from behind. It's the first really advanced trick we soccer junkies try to learn. Me, no matter how many times I've practiced it, I still can't do it more than once in twenty tries. But that day, my sister, dressed in full nun gear, wearing these really ragged Adidas, she just-as-you-please does this perfect rainbow, first try.

"It was awesome. She played a lot when she was younger, but I never saw her do that before. Anyway, while I stayed down there, we spent a lot of time together, got really close again. It was a tough time for me, trying to find my own direction, and who else but my sister brought me back around. Best time I ever had in my life, let me tell you."

He was looking in every eye simultaneously. "You don't need to take baths every day, or watch television, or get in your car and drive, or talk on the phone to experience life. I couldn't take a steady diet of that like my sister did, but she showed me sometimes the goal before you isn't what you might think it is.

"So I hung around for a while, and saw what I thought was a way to maybe do something, something I'd make myself feel proud about. And she pitched in and helped me. It almost turned out really great, for that little village, for me. Then something went wrong … and I think it might've got her killed. I don't know for sure, and I haven't told anyone about this before today, but I really might have put my sister's life in danger. I have lived with that thought pretty much every day since it happened.

"I tried to pray, to tell her I was sorry … but it would have meant I was responsible. So I said nothing, and lived with my cowardice. One morning, when I was feeling really sorry for myself, I gave in. It was an unbelievable release for me. I can't begin to tell you how hard I was crying. I was down on my knees. Can you imagine that? Me, Chris McHenry, on my knees?

"I begged my sister not to hate me, to forgive me. All I could think of was, 'Nicole, please let me know something, just don't let me go through my life like this, please.'

"I was up in the mountains … Colorado … Durango. Great place, great people. It was this really pretty day, just a few clouds in the sky … you could see forever. When the tears and the self-pity dried up, I stood back on my feet where I could look around me. And that's when I saw it, just as clear as the day, right above me, stretching across the sky, the biggest, prettiest rainbow I'd ever seen. Quick as that I knew, no doubt in my mind, it was all right again.

"I'd like to tell you it wasn't up there earlier, that it was some new miracle she was working, but I can't. The shape I was in before I said the prayer, man, I just don't know. I can't swear to anything about anything, much less when that rainbow appeared.

"I will tell you this. Since that day, I see a lot of rainbows in my life. I'm okay now. I still miss my sister, my best friend, and I'd give anything to throw her in the river over there with all her clothes on just one more time, or make her eat grass and tell her there's dog poo on it like I used to, but I can't, and I know it, and even though I can finally live with it, it still hurts. But it's better, and it will keep getting better. That's a promise.

"I'm sorry if I ruined this for any of you, but I really needed to do this. I love you all for coming. She's worth it you know … your time, your laughter, your love. Thank you guys."

He wiped the wetness from under his eyes as he stepped down, where Mac and Danny met him at the steps, where the three of them held each other tightly. Most everyone's eyes were on the three McHenry men huddled together, but for those whose gazes ventured elsewhere, the lucky few managed to catch a glimpse through the tree cover of a rather large, curved, ribbon stretching across the sky, just barely visible, its seven distinct colors brilliant against the blue backdrop.

§

She backed the Saab convertible out of the garage. Checking her watch again, she figured there was still time. It had taken awhile to pull herself together, but it was time to put aside the selfish, self-absorbed feelings and do her part today too. She hoped there was still something to see when she got there.

It was her boys who'd done it for her. *Her boys.* They had stepped forward today, first Danny, who'd quietly, timorously entered Nicole's room just after Bradley left. Sitting beside his mother on Nicole's bed, he'd held her, and told her how much he loved her, and wished she would go through the day with him and his dad and brother. He didn't tack on anything like being able to understand if she chose not to, not like her husband had. Danny hadn't left her a choice. He'd gone on to tell his mother how it would be very hard for him that day, too, how he'd not found forgiveness in his heart for her killers, and doubted he ever would, but how he knew it was important for him to attend the Celebration as a family.

She'd tried to explain why she chose not to, but the words caught in her throat. There were a few more tears shed, and her gallant soldier had dutifully dried them with his handkerchief. For all his military presence, there was still a tender side to her oldest. Someday, perhaps soon, he would marry and have a child, and when that child and all the others he would have were old enough he would tell them about their grandmother, the one who died before they were born, but who loved them from heaven anyway, and watched over them every day of their lives. Yes, Danny would do well as a husband and father.

He'd said good-bye to her, fearful of his father's impatience. She told him to go, to hurry on, that she would come later, really she would. He'd said good-bye again as he'd closed the door, smiling so lovingly at his mother, leaving her alone again with her thoughts. Listening to his clomping footsteps as he bounded down the steps two at a time she got her second surprise of the morning, when her daughter's door opened again, and a smiling Chris had walked in.

He'd come up looking for Danny, and had overheard their conversation. He'd waited down the hall for his brother to leave, waiting to share his own private moment with his mother. Chris, too, implored her to come with the rest of the family. They needed her there, to make it complete. She'd ignored the pain as he held her so tightly.

How truly fortunate she was to have two such wonderful sons. She was still heartbroken over her daughter's death, but the time she spent with her boys in California and Colorado, and the fleeting moments this morning, gave her life new purpose. She hugged her younger son, and felt his tears drop on her neck. She'd not seen him cry since he was a baby, and was startled he would do so now. She asked what the tears were for.

It wasn't something he could explain later, he'd told her. Would she just hold him, like she did when he was young and frightened. Just one more time.

She pulled him close, smoothing the collar length hair again and again as she spoke comforting words to this boy who had been so devoted to his sister. It was she who broke the silence, reminding him he'd better go, or risk upsetting his father, you know, the impatient one waiting in the car.

The mention of his father brought Chris around. He used his brother's dampened handkerchief to dry his own eyes, and told his mother again how much he loved her. He asked her again to join the rest of the family. He had something really important ahead of him this day, he explained, and he wanted his entire family there. He would not explain further. This made it much tougher for her to handle than Danny's simple wish. She'd told Chris to run on, that she would soon follow, and he could trust her on this.

He'd left her, full of expectation, a smile again back to his face. She'd known the day could not pass by without her being there.

†

Minutes after freshening up, she was headed to where a throng of well-wishers were, she was sure, heaping adoration on her daughter. She would join them, and her husband and her boys, but first there was this one last detail to take care of, before things would change forever...

59

"I'M MAC MCHENRY, IF you didn't already know," he began, loosening the tie he'd struggled with what seemed so long ago. He reached inside his coat pocket and pulled out the folded paper, spreading it on the small stand before him, smiling down at the neatly-colored figures. "I speak for Miss Elizabeth, too, when I say thank you. You have all done the most wonderful thing by coming here today, honoring our daughter."

He spoke without notes, authoritatively, able to make each pair of eyes in the sea of faces believe he was engaging only them. He caught Paulette's smile. She was next to his young protégé of sorts, Matthew Courvillon, who nodded his way in return. Young Matthew's mother sat proudly on her son's other side. She also smiled warmly toward the stage, where an old friend was speaking. There was another friend not far away, a restaurateur whose establishment now prominently displayed this most amazing likeness of a former employee in its entry.

"It wasn't easy doing this, at first. I don't want to dwell on it, but a year or so ago, when we brought Nicole back here, the family held a private service. I alone made the decision. I apologize to each and every one of you today for that decision. It was wrong. A lot of things might have been different this past year if a different choice had been made then.

"Like I said, I don't want to dwell on this apology, for there is too much to not be apologetic about. I have sat here and been touched, and joyous, at your expressions of friendship and love for Nicole.

"I've heard so much about my daughter today I'd never known before. Really wonderful things, stories I will treasure always. I see she was something unique to each of you. Perhaps the one thing about Nicole that stood out more than anything else today is how we all saw her in such different lights. The same person, just seen differently through different eyes. Believe me, you are not alone in this.

"We parents, we create our children, and we cradle and nurture you and raise you the best we know how. We sometimes think we know you, who you are, what goes on inside you. Sometimes we're right, and sometimes we're not.

"I wasn't right about Nicole. I've learned that lately. I thought I knew my daughter, along with what was best for her. I was wrong. Bless her heart, she loved me so much she spared me what she felt was some deep hurt by keeping so much inside.

"Nicole always knew who she was. She was confused for a while about what she wanted. She carried within her another spirit. Some of you here today shared with us how you never understood why she one day became a nun, just walked away from you and her family and took off for a place you vaguely remembered from Mr. Carter's eighth grade geography class as being down by the equator or something. You're to be forgiven, first for not knowing where Guatemala is—sorry, but it's too late to change your geography grade—and second for not knowing what drove Nicole to do what she did." He heard a light ripple of laughter at his weak attempt at humor.

"You should know Nicole wasn't running from anything. She was running to it. I made the mistake of assuming the former, and didn't learn until it was too late to say something to her about it being the latter. But I say here in front of you today, knowing she can hear me, that I understand everything now.

"The Nicole I've gotten to know this past year is a much stronger, much better person than the one I thought I knew. I have always been proud of her, and of course still am, but it's a different kind of fatherly pride now. You see, she became the person she'd always wanted to be, not the person she thought I wanted her to be. If there are those of you out there who are struggling with that sort of dilemma, if you don't listen to anything else I say today, please listen to this: be who you know you are, above all else.

"I've learned something else about my daughter this past year too. An even harder lesson than the one I just shared with you. I realize that my daughter had taken on a new life, and a new family. It was one thing to surprise us all with her decision to step from our lives as she did, entirely another to step into others' lives. I was bothered by that because I didn't know her new family.

"Her family was a couple dozen children, and a village of adults who spoke a new language, and had different customs. Even though I know her mother and I were still in her heart, I also know that Nicole had moved on. She'd chosen a new life.

"That's been the hardest part for me, accepting we took on more of a secondary role than we'd prepared ourselves to. Please don't misunderstand me. We know we were always in Nicole's heart. She never forgot her parents, her family. Even though she left from those thoughts more than I'd been prepared for, *the paradise valley, Nicole. Why?* As I have learned this, I glow before you today in the acceptance of the choice she made. The daughter my wife and I raised to be fiercely independent didn't disappoint us. We should be, and are, so very proud she made the choices she did. Her decision to leave what we take for granted in exchange for what her brother Chris described to you as abject poverty was, strangely enough, one of her easier choices. I can't explain it to you, but I do understand it."

He spared them the enigmatic side of his daughter, the part of her that wanted no part of marriage and children, the other that wed herself to God and was mother to two dozen children—one in particular. Motherhood of a different kind was her calling, something she found agreeable and natural, something she excelled at. He and Elizabeth were still struggling to understand the depth of this mystery. It was something he would keep private today. His audience could have everything else … but not this.

"It's just the way she was. Her choice cost her life, and I wish to God it hadn't, and this day had never happened, but I can stand before you and tell you, quite honestly, that I understand my daughter's decision. It is out of the greatest love for Nicole that her mother and I accept her decision."

There was a slight movement down in front, a quiet commotion a few rows back from where Danny sat. He saw her then, walking slowly forward through the silent crowd. She moved with the same grace she always had, the same distinguishing command of style. She eased through the throng, seemingly not so much as touching a shoulder or hip as she elegantly made her way to the front and took the open seat beside Danny. Her smile cracked the last remnants of the armor that still encased his heart. Elizabeth was with him in this, no longer a holdout. The day was complete. The last of the yellow tape was down. He reached his hand to her, an invitation to join him. Still smiling, she mouthed the few words in silent reply, and he understood perfectly. *You're doing fine. We're doing fine. Go for it, Bradley, just go for it.* He mouthed, *Are you sure?* And she mouthed back, *Very sure.*

He'd been ready to sit down, to end it. Now port was a bit further away.

"Which brings me to an announcement. It's not been an easy decision, but it's the only right one. Miss Elizabeth and I have decided Nicole should be with her new family."

A last glance into his wife's glimmering eyes, making sure, seeing, *feeling*, she was with him in this. "This means we will be taking her back to Guatemala in a few days, where she will rest forever in her little village. They wanted it that way, and we realize now, like I said, it's the right thing to do.

"As right as Chris is about it being primitive, it's also a pretty little place, Refugio—which is Spanish for 'refuge', or place of safe haven. And it is safe again. I also suspect it will be going through some changes because of Nicole's homecoming. Hopefully they'll be good changes. Time will tell, I suppose.

"Speaking of changes, Miss Elizabeth and I will be having one of our own too. We'll be saying some good-byes, for a while at least. There's an empty home in Refugio that needs fixing up. We don't know how long we'll be gone ... time will tell.

"So this is good-bye, from Nicole and Miss Elizabeth and me. I hope you'll also forgive me for not drawing it out. It's a short, but very loving good-bye to all you friends. Thank you all again for coming today." Wasting no time, Mac took his first steps toward Elizabeth.

It started with one person, a handsome lad standing off to the side, a blue-eyed fellow with unshined shoes and a rumpled shirt, who put one hand against the other, slowly at first, then a little faster, a little louder, and then there was another handsome young man who joined in, a man in uniform who was standing up next to the pretty woman in the taupe linen dress, then a young black man standing between two women, one white and the other black, who also joined in, and in no time at all there were more hands being put together, until the crescendo echoed through the trees and as far downriver as Madisonville and a good ways upriver as well, where the skittish wildlife could but wonder at the new, strange sound.

§

Then it was time for Mac to step down, to join his family and his friends. He made a last turn to the small stand at front and center stage, and took the paper he'd laid there moments earlier. He looked at it, the page torn from a child's catechism coloring book, the side opposite the one of David the Shepherd, the side with the drawings of the Virgin Mary, arms spread with palms outward, with the cherubic, winged figure seemingly hovering over her head, with the name "NICOLE" neatly printed in a child's hand between the figures, where at the bottom of the page the inscription was printed.

All the angels and saints, it read.

Dusk had set in, and most of the crowd had left.

Elizabeth had grown tired and hungry, so Danny had taken her home in the Saab. Chris would be the last to leave, after he and the remaining faithful took a final, commemorative swing over the river. Mac would ride with Father Paul, as soon as the details for Nicole's move were complete. As Mac gathered his thoughts he looked up to see Tommy standing beside him.

"Mr. Mac," he began, "I—I just wanted—well I just wanted to say I—"

"Tommy, it's good you came today." Mac interrupted, freeing the lad from the embarrassment of his uncertainty. "We hear you're doing well at LSU, almost finished, right?"

"Yes, sir. It's my last semester. I'll be looking around soon for a physical therapist's job." He seemed tentative. "Mr. Mac, there's something I want to tell you. I don't know how to, but I—"

"Tommy, listen to me. Today was meant to put everything to rest." Mac gave it a few seconds to settle in. "Understood?" He put his hand on Tommy's shoulder.

Mac felt the young man's tension release. "Yes, sir." Tommy lowered his head, then quickly raised it.

"You know, Mr. Mac, maybe when you get down there to Guatemala, if you see they need someone like me, I could come down and maybe help out, something, anything, you know ... "

"I can't help you there, son. You need to follow your heart, not some course you think Miss Elizabeth and I, or even Nicole, might wish for you. If I were you I'd start thinking about settling down with that young lady we've heard about, paying off college and making your folks some proud grandparents. Just some friendly advice. You get what I'm saying?"

"Things didn't work out for me and her. Maybe someday, someone else. I've thought about it. Not right now ... you know. I'm still not over her." Tommy's sadness pained Mac.

"It'll happen for you too, son. Nobody's saying you have to forget her. It's okay to move on. That's what today was all about, moving on."

"I suppose. In my time, I will. Just not now. It's not my time."

Mac watched as the young man walked away, his path crossing with a taller fellow, who stopped him, spoke a few words, then grabbed the young man in a huge embrace. Mac could see the surprise in Tommy's face as the man released him from the bearhug, shook his hand and slapped his shoulder in a smiling farewell. A still confused Tommy had stood there, watching the taller man walk away, toward a waiting Mac. The last Mac saw of Tommy, he was walking toward the driveway by the live oak under which Mac had parked hours earlier, slowly shaking his head from side to side.

"Do you think I shook up my young rival?" A wide grin on Evan Montgomery's face spoke of mischief.

"What did you say to him?" Mac asked.

"Oh, just some nonsense about him being a better man than I am, and a much wiser choice for her to have made."

"Did you introduce yourself before you scared him witless?"

"Of course not. I doubt he would've known who I am in any event." Montgomery was in total deadpan.

"Is this confession time for you, too, Evan? The rival thing you just spoke of?"

"I shared it with your wife the day I came to your home, when she took me to the gravesite. The former gravesite, I suppose it'll be in a couple of days."

"Well, she kept your secret crush, if that's what it was, a secret from me. I'm not surprised, and certainly can't imagine you were less than a perfect British gentleman where my daughter was concerned."

"You need to have no doubt on that, Mac. Ever. I seriously doubt she even knew I had feelings for her, frankly. She would've thought of me as a friend, at best, more likely as an amusing distraction."

"Don't be so hard on yourself, old man. My daughter wasn't so shallow."

Montgomery nodded slowly. "You did a good thing today, Mac. A really good thing. If I weren't retired, I think I could write a nice piece on it. I stood back there and listened, and watched, and saw the most generous outpouring of love for anyone I've ever witnessed in my life. Got a little misty-eyed a few times myself. Saw a fine lad you have for a son stand very tall up there, too."

"Yes. He's like his brother; totally devoted to Nicole. I didn't know about the business he was worried about, though. He told me a little bit about it, said we'd finish up later, at the house. I don't suppose you know anything?"

"A bit, but he's mistaken if he thinks he caused Nicole's death. What happened that night was the product of pure fury borne of something I doubt any of us would be able to understand. I can't imagine any plausible explanation he would've brought on what happened to his sister." Montgomery reached a hand out to Mac's arm, grasping firmly. "You should know. So should he."

"I can tell him, but you ought to come by the house and tell him yourself."

"No, thanks, I'll pass. I'm headed out tonight, a late flight to Atlanta, then on to London. Like I said, I've retired. Got myself a little used bookstore in a fashionable neighborhood, where I can while away the days just spreading my charm to the customers, mostly matronly types needing some attention, you know the lot. Anyway, thanks for the offer. I'll be saying good-bye, Mac."

"Good-bye, Evan." The two men shook hands, knowing it would be for the last time. Their bond had been a tenuous one at best, and it was time to move on.

"I meant what I said, my best to the missus, please. You won't forget? Be sure to thank her, too, for the invitation."

"I'll do it. And she would want me to thank you for helping to make your former home available to us. It'll quite an adjustment, about three thousand five hundred less square feet of living area, but, as Elizabeth points out, much easier to keep clean."

Mac smiled at Montgomery, who nodded silently before he turned and headed off in the direction Tommy had just minutes earlier. Mac's gaze followed him for a few paces, then turned in the direction of an old friend. He was standing beside two other familiar faces, one belonging to a new friend, another to a fellow he'd just met but felt, somehow, would be a part of his life as time wore on. Mac walked over to join Father Paul, Sister Katherine Carson and the curious Italian priest who jovially called himself Father Luigi. *Such a collection …*

A soft breeze, the kind that doesn't usually blow in St. Tammany Parish in the early spring, rustled from nowhere, swathing him with a light freshness. He wanted to reach out and grab for the hand fanning it, but thought better. Like the rainbows he'd heard about earlier in the day that brightened his son's life, he had a feeling his face would be brushed by a few more of these subtle breezes in times ahead, so, his heart both empty and full at the same time, he was content to just close his eyes and whisper the breeze's name: *Nicole …*

60

T HE THREE ONLOOKERS stood on a familiar ridge. A blue sky littered by only a few wisps of cottony-white cirri favored them. They watched as the young man worked with a group of youngsters on the soccer pitch below. Light brown hair made almost blond from the sun, bright blue eyes and a wide smile distinguished him clearly from the gaggle of awkward, brown-skinned children who eagerly followed his every movement and instruction. It was clear he was enjoying them as much as they were him, their laughter carrying the full distance from valley floor to the ridge. No music is as sweet as the laughter of happy children. The young man paused only once, just long enough to wave to his audience.

Far across the expanse of valley a ribbon of water threaded its way down a mountainside into a secluded area where a woman eyed her handiwork: the tall gladioli, the shorter irises seemingly clinging to their taller companions, as Elizabeth would say, as maidens-in-waiting worshipfully at their soldiers' sides. The three sets of watchful eyes brimmed in adoration as the slender woman fretted over the flowers, mindlessly brushing back the stray gray hairs falling from under the brim of the straw gardener's hat. Feeling their eyes on her, she too glanced in their direction, taking in the small brown man on one side and the pretty child on the other of the man in the middle, the one she jestfully called *Señor* Bradley these days.

She smiled at them while she straightened some blooms near her feet, at the base of the grotto. She surveyed the entire scene. It was a magnificent wooden structure, expertly carved by the man standing beside her husband. It was seen as a shrine by those who came here to visit, to pray, to seek the blessings of the daughter buried at her feet. They all called her *Santa Nicole*, which was all right with her mother. It was no burden to bear, this attention her daughter received on an everyday basis. She was pleased, in fact, at the joy and comfort her daughter provided them, and the reverence which they showed her. It was a fair exchange.

Her days were better now than when they'd first come. She felt her strength returning, and less pain each succeeding day. After the first month she stopped taking the medication altogether. Her husband hadn't seemed surprised, and after a while the trips to the large hospital in the capital city weren't necessary. The menacing tenant ravaging her insides had seemed to vanish, skipping out on the rent, thankfully leaving with no forwarding address. It became an unspoken awareness to the man and woman who each day and night held tighter to one another. An air of a different inevitability had spread itself over them. They no longer discussed the past, mostly the present, every now and then guardedly venturing into the future.

They drove the short distance to the Belizean coast, to sail, to walk the beach, when Elizabeth took a break from the school. In the mornings she worked with the children; two afternoons a week Miguel taught her and Mac Spanish. Another fair exchange, all agreed.

The other afternoons usually found Mac supervising the installation of the water well and plumbing in the village, with Chris's and Father Art's capable help, and a large sum of money—the portion left over after Chris's two friends took their two-thirds share. Mac's visit to the government official had seen to this end. The official, properly chagrined that any of his countrymen would have participated in such deceit, vowed to take swift, stern action. In a short time, the offending Palomar family made good on the misunderstanding. Ironically, a short time later the Palomar family business inexplicably had dried up, and the entire lot left the country in shame and disgrace, practically penniless. There was no sadness or pity from up Refugio way.

The timber business called for expertise, and a labor force. Thus it came to no one's surprise the young American lad worked closely with Carlos, news of whose freedom had congealed an uneasy truce into months of peace, to carefully cut and plant. It was a worthy enterprise for Chris to pursue. His father had reminded him of something his sister had once said: give them a fish, they eat for a day; taught to fish, the people of this village could feed for a lifetime. Maybe, Chris thought more and more often these days, the Fourteeners back in Colorado could spare him a while longer.

There would be a large ceremony in Refugio in little over a month, as all would gather for the first exhibitions of running water and their first flushing toilet, to go along with the restored electricity. Appropriately the ceremony would take place at the new clinic. The garrison had been restored with a part of the timber profits, and it made a fine clinic. It would be staffed by a waiting list of volunteer physicians from

465

scattered places worldwide. The first visiting doctor was a particularly impressive young fellow from the Point Clear, Alabama area. It would be the first of many visits to come for Doctor Michael Adams. Answering a calling of his own, fulfillment for him would not be of the financial kind.

He would be amazed, but not in disbelief, at the curious turnaround in the health of a former patient.

The village was improving in other ways as well. To the south, more trees had been felled, and new structures dotted the other side of the valley. They would house the visitors, the legions of faithful who would come to Refugio, few at first but their number growing steadily. They came to visit the grotto below, where Elizabeth now stooped in her labor of love, to pay their respects. Already there had been healings— miraculous healings, some said—and none doubted there would be others.

Soon Danny would arrive with his new wife, their firstborn on the way. He was stationed in Florida, which would enable him to visit occasionally. The small house next to Mac's and Elizabeth's, acquired from the woman who was making a slow recovery in the capital, would serve as a guest home for the Danny McHenry family.

Change had taken place in the archdiocese as well. The arrival of a successor to Archbishop Santiago had been announced. Archbishop Luigi Giuseppe Vincenzo, the announcement read, had been previously on the personal staff of the Pope. As for the former Guatemalan archbishop, it seems the Church had an opening for an assistant curator to watch over its renown and very private art collection in the Vatican, a position limiting his contact with the public.

The first official act of the new archbishop had been to designate the continuing donations in Sister Nicole's memory to the Children's Education Fund. It also had the official support of the government, which had adopted a new policy of tolerance toward the Indian minority. More, and better, changes would come in the years to follow. For now, the fund was a good start.

As his second official act, the new archbishop had made a special request for transfer of a certain American nun to assume the new role of liaison between the Church and the new peacetime factions in Guatemala, a nun who enjoyed special training in the field of law, who was becoming especially devoted to the humanitarian cause of the Guatemalan Indians. He had not yet heard the response of the Archdiocese of New Orleans, which had needs of its own for her services, but the new man in the Guatemalan archdiocese felt confident enough things would eventually turn his way.

It seems he had the ear of a friend who sat as close as one can get to the top of the organization.

§

All was good, Mac was thinking as he watched his son and wife below, and felt the familiar tug at his heart as he admired the handiwork of the carpenter who stood to his left. It had been a long voyage, but they had come to a port where he and Elizabeth could feel safe in any storm, a place where their landlegs could give way to sealegs when they chose, a place where fair winds blew every day, and clear skies were abundant.

The small hand that worked its way into his, that gave his a little squeeze, and the shimmering black eyes looking up into his with the fragile trust of the very young and innocent, reminded him just how good it was.

467

✝

EPILOGUE

THE DOOR CLOSED behind him. It was morning, the need for quiet giving way to the day's usual order of Vatican business. He briskly moved down the hallway, the lightness in his step missing far too long. And his back felt much better.

The Pontiff again showed great wisdom during the hours they'd spent on his *positio*. Yet there was one portion at the end for which His Holiness asked the saint-maker for an additional explanation.

Holy Father, when I went to America and met with the parents, I eagerly shared with them what I learned from the hospitalized woman. I felt certain, even though he had dropped his lawsuit, and released the Church from his wish to bestow sainthood on his daughter, the father would nevertheless be pleased to learn Your Holiness would most certainly recognize her martyrdom, and Sister Nicole would be canonized very quickly.

I was mistaken. When I finished my story, and told the parents sainthood for their daughter was virtually assured, they looked at each other for only an instant, before the father spoke.

'Father Luigi,' he said to me, 'my wife and I appreciate what you have done for our daughter, for her memory. There was a time when I would have been overjoyed to hear this, and anxious to learn of her canonization. But no longer. We are content her memory will live on, regardless of any official recognition the Church does or does not bestow. We will not ask the Church not to honor her, but we would ask, if the Church does intend to honor her memory as you suggest, that it be delayed … long enough for our family to have gone on. What happens after we are gone …' *And that was all he had to say.*

It was not a difficult choice for His Holiness to make. Another Pope one day would see a predecessor's decree, and would merely dust off an old pronunciation of saint-

hood for the faithful to rejoice in. Pen to parchment, and it was done. Saint Nicole. It had a good sound.

It was a glorious moment for the saint-maker, who would be leaving the Vatican soon, for life in another hemisphere.

First, it was time for another confession. Ah, vanity …

✝

ACKNOWLEDGMENTS

THIS BOOK TOOK TEN YEARS TO COMPLETE. The story came to mind during a Saturday Mass at St. Anselm Catholic Church in Madisonville, Louisiana, while I viewed a presentation made by a priest who had just returned from his Guatemalan mission. I looked down at my then ten-year old daughter and thought, What if ... The rest filled in over time. I have been fortunate to have so many people contribute their time and creativity. In no way being less thankful to those I cannot name here because of space limitation, I acknowledge the following family and friends for their support.

First, and foremost, to my wife Kelli, who never wavered in her belief this would happen, and to Jeremy, Jacob, Matt, and Emerald, who didn't get as much of their father as they should have, but turned out great anyway.

To those who labored over drafts twice the length of the finished product: Rita and Mathew Dallas, my wonderful in-laws; dear friends Tim Gehl, a good oil and gas lawyer, Caryl Parker-Stough, my law school classmate and a splendid judge, Gary Pittenger, a fellow writer whose support has meant as much as anyone's, and Debby Richardson, a colleague at "my day job" whose smile as she broke the news to me one morning that she'd (finally!) finished the first draft gave me the encouragement to go on. To Ruthie Dodge, my sister, who read excerpts and wanted more, but wasn't allowed because I knew I'd sell at least one copy if I kept the rest from her. To my writer's group, Writers of the Purple Page, for moral and editorial support. And to Greg McKenzie, who unselfishly extends a guiding hand every time he sees me about to stumble.

Thanks to Claudia Ivanova Molina Cifuentes and Kenny Booth for their invaluable insight on life, custom and cuisine in Guatemala. I relied on personal experience for the story portions dealing with the law and legal procedure. Although I am a

Catholic, I knew nothing about the Congregation for the Causes for Saints before conducting research at the nearest public library. There is a world of material in the shelves of any good-sized library if you are interested in such.

As with just about any work of fiction certain liberties have been taken. I assume all responsibility for any errors in the story, and apologize if the end does not justify the means.

An unpublished writer without name recognition faces a tough haul in today's publishing world. I thank six gifted people with proven track records in the writing, editing and publishing world who made it possible for this book to become a reality: Jerry Gross, the Editor's Editor, who is so much more than a book doctor, and who still works with me on my bad (but getting better) case of overwriting; Joan Rhine, who patiently read the penultimate draft and still found much to improve on; Jodie Nida with HAWK Publishing, who caringly has made *All the Angels and Saints* a finished product; Doug Miller of Müllerhaus Publishing Arts, whose stunning cover and interior design captured the essence of the book more beautifully than I ever imagined possible; Kirsten Bernhardt, who read the first draft and saw hope through the horror of the overwriting, and Bill Bernhardt, who listened, and gave me the chance.

Lastly, if it can be fairly said every writer has an inspiration, then I am no exception. As a ninth- and tenth-grader I discovered real fiction in the works of Steinbeck, Hemingway, Buck, and others whose works my English Lit teacher put in front of me as "required reading." Then, to make it worse, he made me write book reports. Indignity upon indignity, I even had to compose themes, poetry and short stories. My first writing was done in your classes, sir, and the feeling and, yes, the inspiration, have lasted forty years, and for that I truly thank you, Frank Rector.